A Surgeon's Heart: The Calling

by
R.W. Sewell, M.D.

Copyright © 2014 R.W. Sewell, M.D.

All rights reserved.

ISBN-10: 0615956254
ISBN-13: 978-0615956251 (Robert Sewell, M.D.)

DEDICATION

To Donna, the love of my life. Thank you for all the times you willingly shared me with my other wife, medicine. Your undying support has been what has sustained me these thirty-plus years. All my love.

INTRODUCTION

The practice of medicine, like all other human efforts, has steadily evolved over the centuries, but at no time in history have the changes been more dramatic than in the last fifty years. The advances in technology have made it possible to successfully treat, and in many instances cure, illnesses and conditions once thought universally fatal. In no area of medicine has this trend been more pronounced than in the surgical management of congenital heart defects. The hearts of babies born with conditions like patent ductus arteriosus, coarctation of the aorta, Tetralogy of Fallot, and many others, can now be repaired, allowing those children, and their parents, to enjoy a normal life.

A Surgeon's Heart: The Calling is a fictional account of one man's struggle in pursuit of his lifelong dream of becoming a pediatric heart surgeon. With two notable exceptions, all the characters and situations described are the product of the author's imagination, and any resemblance to actual persons, either living or deceased, is purely coincidental. The exceptions are Drs. Alfred Blalock of the Johns Hopkins University Hospital and C. Walt Lillehei of the University of Minnesota Hospital, both of whom were among the early pioneers in the development of modern heart surgery. Their inclusion in this story, and all references to those facilities, is solely to provide a historical perspective. All other health care facilities and hospitals described in these pages are fictional and are not intended to represent any actual hospitals, their medical staffs, administrations, or any specific policies and practices.

Although some might suggest otherwise, much of the care delivered in America's hospitals continues to be exemplary, and our health care system remains the envy of the world. I would specifically like to point out the extraordinary care my own son received at Cook Children's Hospital in Fort Worth, Texas, in the summer of 2007. The incredible dedication and expertise of every physician, nurse and staff member were directly responsible for saving my sixteen-year-old's life from the clutches of the rare, but deadly, hantavirus pulmonary syndrome. There are no words to express the gratitude my entire family feels toward those incredible people, and their efforts, and it is in that spirit that I have pledged a percentage of any profits that might arise from the sale of this work to that facility.

The story of American health care does not end with this volume. It goes on, with the only constant being change. While these characters are indeed fictional, they reflect the realities of the changing environment where the physician's role is being challenged by a system that is increasingly centered on the payers, both private insurance companies and government agencies. Every physician, nurse, technician and administrator is influenced by that environment, and as this story unfolds, you will see the myriad forces that are molding the way health care is delivered today as well as the impact they will have in the years to come.

The Calling is also an example of the commitment and dedication required to become a surgeon. Without men and women of compassion and integrity who are willing to meet the challenge, it is the patient who is most at risk. We will all be patients one day, reliant on the caring hearts of those who answer the call to the greatest profession in the world.

Please enjoy.

R.W. Sewell, M.D.

ACKNOWLEDGMENTS

A Surgeon's Heart: The Calling would not have been possible without the encouragement of my office staff. Nadine Collard, Angie Gates, Stacie Bussey, RN, and especially my office manager, Suzanne Jones, helped keep me moving throughout the process. They each provided invaluable recommendations as they willingly proofed every chapter as it was produced.

I would also like to thank my good friend, Hayden Knox, for helping inspire this work after listening to me complain for years about the declining state of health care in America. He suggested a screenplay, but I was more comfortable with this format.

This book would not have been readable without the extraordinary talents and efforts of my editor, Janna Franzwa Canard, of Full Proof. She corrected more errors than I care to admit and was a constant source of encouragement.

The inspiration for the cover of this book, and the photograph that appears there, are the work of my close friend and incredible artist, Gregory Arth. His eye for composition and detail are unmatched. The two children pictured on the cover are Nathan Jones, age five, the grandson of my office manager, Suzanne, and Tanner Gates, age nine, the son of my longtime employee Angie.

Although the situations in this book are fictional, they are in large measure based on my own experiences, first as a surgical intern and resident surgeon from 1974 through 1979, and then the subsequent thirty-four years of private practice as a general surgeon in North Texas. I owe most of what I know to the patients who have entrusted me with their care and provided me the privilege to serve. There is truly no way to thank them enough.

I want to thank my family for their love and inspiration. My children, Julie S., Julie L., Ashley, Tyler, Ryan and Chase, have each contributed to this work in ways they could scarcely imagine. And finally, my wife, Donna, has been, as the lyricist said, "The Wind Beneath My Wings" for nearly thirty-two years. Her faith and devotion have been unwavering, and her love amazes me still.

CHAPTER 1

For Jack, this day started like every other. He was up well before dawn and thirty minutes before his alarm was set to go off. Lately he'd wondered why he even bothered to set one. He told himself he needed to make certain he never overslept, but that's something he hadn't done since residency.

Despite being fifty-six years old, Jack was still in great shape and could pass for a man in his mid-forties. He had an athletic physique, at six foot three and two hundred pounds, but he had clearly lost some of the muscular build of his youth. He had played basketball in high school for the LD Bell Blue Raiders, in Hurst, Texas. However, most of his physical development was the result of hard labor during the summers of his teenage years. He'd worked for his dad doing rough-in plumbing on various construction sites in the growing communities of North Texas. Occasionally he missed the vitality and sense of accomplishment of such manual labor. The closest he came to that type of effort these days was working in the backyard garden on his free weekends. While he managed to get in a round of golf every now and then, it was not nearly as often as he'd like.

Jack's morning routine included some brief stretching in the bathroom before jumping in the shower and allowing his mind to drift to his plans for the day ahead. While the warm water gently massaged his shoulders, he began mentally preparing for what promised to be a difficult day in the operating room. This morning, Dr. Jack Roberts, a seasoned cardiac surgeon, faced what he knew would be an especially challenging case. He had repaired numerous major blood vessels over the last twenty-five years, but the one he faced today promised to be, in his words, "a real bear." For even the most skilled and experienced surgeons, operations to revise a prior procedure presented unknown difficulties, especially if the first operation was performed by someone else.

While in the shower, he quickly shaved the bristly stubble from his face. If there was one characteristic that gave away his age, it was the gradual change in his beard. It had once been almost jet black, but after he turned forty-five, it began to gray. The hair on his head had remained full and dark brown, except for a hint of silver at his temples. His beard was a different story. For that reason he almost never went a day without "clearing the deck" as he put it. The routine revealed his angular face with a prominent square chin. While Jack was certainly a handsome man, he wasn't one that automatically turned heads. His dark brown eyes were his most striking feature, and they narrowed just slightly whenever he flashed his signature, crooked smile.

Shaved and showered, Jack dressed quickly. He typically didn't wear a coat and tie to work the way he once did, but today he had to attend a noon committee meeting at the general hospital, so he made an exception. He expertly tied a half Windsor in his favorite red tie, and slipped on the black gabardine sports jacket Elaina had given him last Christmas. He flipped off the light in the bathroom before opening the door, and quietly heading back into the bedroom. He approached her side of the bed as he did every morning, finding his lovely wife of fifteen years still sleeping. He kissed her softly on the cheek and turned to leave.

"Have a good day, sweetie," she whispered.

He wasn't totally surprised that she was awake as he replied, "I love you," before turning for the door. Then he remembered it was Tuesday, the couple's weekly date night. "See you this evening," he added, knowing there was a lot of work to be done before then.

Jack pulled his silver-blue Chevy Silverado pickup into the doctors' lot behind the massive general hospital and parked in his usual space, near the rear entrance to the building. Over the years he'd had many different cars, but in recent years he'd found it increasingly difficult to get in and out of those sporty, more expensive models. He actually preferred the comfort and utility of what most people in Fort Worth called a "Texas Cadillac."

The eastern sky had just begun to show the first signs of light blue replacing the blackness of a moonless night, and most of the parking lot was empty. The only cars he recognized belonged to Radha Patel, his favorite anesthesiologist, and George Ferguson, his new associate. Fresh out of training, George was going to assist him today and he suspected his young colleague was just as anxious as he was about the first operation of the day. Most surgeons referred to a difficult revision case like this one as a "redo" and Jack was fond of saying, "Redo is a four-letter word."

As he approached the door, Jack spotted the latest security device and swore briefly under his breath. Realizing he couldn't get in without his badge, he quickly returned to his truck to retrieve it. He was a traditionalist, and had trouble remembering to wear that stupid piece of plastic which contained the magnetic strip that would get him through each of the new secured access points in the hospital. He held the badge over the detector, turning the tiny red light green, followed by an audible click as the lock was temporarily disabled. He shook his head wondering why the hospital needed to be locked down like some kind of prison? He knew the answer and was angered by the recent series of hospital break-ins across North Texas. People were seemingly willing to do anything in search of drugs.

Jack made his way through the back hallway toward the doctors' lounge where he ran into Radha. "Well, are you ready for this?" Jack asked with a smile.

"Absolutely, are you?" Radha replied with her typical air of confidence. She had worked with Jack since first arriving in Fort Worth in 1989, just a year after Jack started his private practice. She was a warm-hearted, caring woman who had moved to Texas from upstate New York, along with her husband, Harrish, an interventional radiologist. They had both trained at Johns Hopkins in Baltimore following medical school in New Delhi. Prior to relocating she had been on the anesthesia faculty at Syracuse Medical Center for five years.

Jack was fond of telling the story of how Radha had sought him out on her first day at the children's hospital. She had boldly introduced herself and expressed her desire to work closely with him, especially with his newborn patients. He was immediately taken by her self-confident attitude, so the following morning he enlisted her help with the repair of a congenital heart defect on a two month old. She had proven up to the task and more, afterward offering to rewrite some of the neonatal pre-anesthesia protocols for Jack's budding pediatric heart program. On this morning she was once more displaying that same quiet confidence he had come to expect over the last sixteen years. Through their countless shared experiences at both the children's hospital and the general hospital, Jack had learned he could trust her completely when it came to his pediatric patients. Neither one of them spoke openly of such things, but it was obvious to everyone, including Jack, that the trust was mutual.

"Have you talked to the family yet?" Jack asked.

"Yes, they're waiting for you in the holding room," Radha replied as she headed off to the operating room to prepare for their first case of the day.

After changing into his scrubs he made his way toward the holding room, where patients were made ready for surgery. As he passed the nurses' station, he spotted Susan, the circulating nurse that he worked with routinely.

"Is everything ready?" he asked in his familiar military style.

"Yes, sir!" Susan replied. "We're ready when you are."

"Great," he offered with a bit more appreciation in his voice than usual. He knew he was going to need everyone's help today, and she made it clear the team was prepared.

"Give me just a minute with the family and then we can go."

He pulled back the curtain and entered the small alcove where his eight-year-old patient, Lupe Alvarez, was waiting anxiously along with her parents.

"Hi, guys!" Jack said in his usual cheerful manner. "Anybody seen a young lady with a broken heart?"

Despite his attempt to lighten the mood with his cheesy greeting, clearly the air was filled with tension. He also recognized that coming from Mexico, Lupe likely didn't understand anything he was saying.

Lupe's father quickly rose to his feet as Jack pulled the curtain closed behind him. The confident surgeon extended his hand to this loving father whom he had met only a few days before.

"Good morning," the man offered. His English was laced with a very distinctive Mexican accent.

As Jack accepted the calloused hand of Pablo Alvarez, he replied, *"Buenos días."* He always tried to put Spanish speaking families at ease by comfortably transitioning to his second language. He then reached to shake the hand of the young girl's mother who forced a smile but remained seated.

He turned to Lupe and said, *"Te ves muy bonita este mañana."* He spoke softly as he bent over the edge of the stretcher, gently taking the child's frail hand in his. This compliment had been a key to comforting countless young Latinas over the years, and it seemed to be having the desired effect as Lupe managed a timid smile.

"¿Está lista?" Jack inquired, but everyone in the room recognized that the time for this procedure had come, whether she felt ready or not. Lupe nodded somewhat reluctantly toward the tall doctor, then looked quickly into the stoic face of her father.

Jack also turned back toward Pablo and in his most sincere and confident voice told him simply, "Everything is going to be fine."

Having delivered his final reassurance, Jack pulled back the curtain and asked the transport orderly to show the Alvarez family to the waiting area.

"This will likely take about two to three hours," he added. "Just as soon as I'm finished I'll be out to talk with you."

As they rose to leave, the mother and father each kissed their daughter tenderly on the forehead. Jack turned to head back toward the OR, and for the first time that day he heard Lupe's mother speak softly in his direction.

"Vaya con Dios, doctor."

He turned back and saw her slowly crossing herself, prompting him to acknowledge her words with a smile and a single nod of his head. Like most seasoned surgeons, Jack had developed a sixth sense and on this day it was telling him that to get through this case he was going to need all the help he could get.

◆◆◆◆◆◆◆◆

 Lupe Alvarez was born in Matamoros, Mexico, across the Rio Grande River from Brownsville, Texas. Shortly after birth, the doctors at the government hospital noticed a visible pulsation in her neck, and the lower half of her body appeared to have a bluish discoloration. They correctly diagnosed her as having a congenital defect involving the major artery coming out of her heart, a condition called pre-ductal coarctation of the aorta. Within just a few hours after what was otherwise a routine birth, the baby had become listless and seemed to be struggling to breathe. The doctors explained that her tiny heart was failing, due to high blood pressure in the upper half of her body. They had told her father that without a complicated operation she would almost certainly die within a week or two. They offered him little hope for her survival, since there was no one in Matamoros who could perform such an operation.
 The desperate father could not accept this death sentence, so he picked his newborn daughter up from the tiny crib and bolted from the hospital, followed closely by his wife and four-year-old son. He knew people who, for a price, could sneak them across the border into the United States, where he would do whatever it took to get the treatment needed to save his daughter's life. Despite having little more than the clothes on their backs, the family managed to find their way to Corpus Christi, and two days after leaving Mexico the baby was being evaluated in the emergency room of the largest hospital in Corpus.
 A few months before, a young pediatric surgeon had moved to this coastal town to establish his practice. Dr. Charles Hwang had trained in Southern California and had moved to Texas, seeking what he thought would be a great opportunity. There were no pediatric surgeons along the Gulf Coast south of Houston, and he had grown fond of living near the ocean in Southern California. He wanted to someday own one of those beautiful sailboats out in Corpus Christi Bay, but on this day he had been called by the emergency room doctor to evaluate this three-day-old from Matamoros.
 When Dr. Hwang saw Lupe he could see she was experiencing rapidly progressing heart failure. The diagnosis of coarctation was obvious, but her condition would not allow transfer to a referral center in either San Antonio or Houston. He had never actually performed the procedure this child required, but the young surgeon felt confident in his ability to handle the problem. After all, he had trained at UCLA Medical Center, and he'd scrubbed in on a couple of operations to correct underdeveloped aortas like this one. He had ligated several PDAs in newborns, and this was kind of the same thing, he rationalized, but he knew full well that correcting a critically narrowed section of the largest artery

in the body was far more complicated than just tying off a patent ductus arteriosus. He was convinced that he simply had to try or the child would die.

Hwang explained to the father what he planned to do to repair the baby's underdeveloped aorta, and he was up front about his experience. With no other option, the desperate father reluctantly agreed.

Immediately a team of hospital personnel descended on the struggling infant, drawing blood, starting intravenous fluids, obtaining a chest x-ray, giving antibiotics, and preparing the OR. As soon as everything was ready, the pediatric anesthesiologist, Dr. Pedro Gonzalez, came down to the ER to accompany the baby up to the surgical floor. Gonzalez spoke to the family in their native language, but what he had to say did little to comfort them. He told them that he had called for a priest, and he anticipated Father Jacobs would find them as soon as he arrived.

Dr. Hwang was back in the operating room making sure they had all the instruments he would need. He then met the small entourage, led by Dr. Gonzalez pushing the stainless steel crib, as they came through the double doors and into the sterile corridor. The procession stopped long enough for Gonzalez to point the family in the direction of the chapel down the hall.

Despite his limited experience working with this OR staff, Hwang had done an excellent job getting everyone organized. No one in the entire hospital other than himself had ever seen this procedure performed. Even so, he felt they were ready.

Once the baby was asleep, Hwang made an incision between the ribs of her left chest and expertly moved the lung out of the way, exposing the area of concern. Frank Gardner, an experienced general surgeon, was the only doctor available to assist him and he was clearly out of his area of expertise. Hwang began by identifying the abnormal vascular structures, more as a review for himself than any attempt to educate his assistant.

The young nurse who was scrubbed in to pass instruments innocently asked, "So what happened to this baby?"

"She has an area in her aorta that never developed properly," Hwang explained, pointing with an instrument to the short section of the main artery coming out of the heart. It was obviously much smaller than the vessels just above and below that segment. It was at that point that the flow of oxygen-rich blood was essentially blocked.

"This is a congenital anomaly called coarctation of the aorta," he said emphasizing each syllable of this foreign-sounding word. He went on to explain to them how the other vessels had partially compensated and how the ductus arteriosus was supplying non-oxygenated blood to the lower half of the infant's body.

"The biggest problem is the abnormal pressure this blocked area creates, which is causing her heart to fail."

Once he'd satisfied himself that he had all the landmarks identified, he outlined what he planned to do to fix it.

"So, what we are going to do is take this big artery here," he announced, as he pointed to the rapidly pulsating subclavian artery, "and we're going to attach it directly into the aorta below the underdeveloped area." There was obvious trepidation in his voice as he added, "And we are going to tie off the ductus arteriosus."

There were several more major steps, all of which were extremely risky in this tiny three-day-old child, but as he continued to talk his way through them he became increasingly convinced he could do this. Hwang looked up and once more assessed the readiness of the assembled team. What he saw in their faces hardly instilled confidence, but he was already committed.

"Let's get started," he said, more to himself than to them.

With the nerves of a gladiator, Dr. Charles Hwang systematically did exactly what he had just described with unexpected dexterity. The bleeding was well controlled, but in tiny infants like this, even a small amount of blood loss would be significant. Dr. Gonzalez infused a partial unit of red blood cells and some fresh frozen plasma during the procedure, more as a precaution than as a necessity.

When the skin incision was finally closed, two hours and twenty minutes after Hwang had made the first cut, the small bevy of nurses in the room burst into applause. He was embarrassed by their praise and humbly thanked each one for their help. As he left the OR, there were a half dozen doctors gathered outside the door, each offering their congratulations and patting him on the back. He simply smiled and nodded, obviously more exhausted than satisfied by the effort. He made his way toward the waiting room to talk with the family, passing the scheduling desk where he saw Al Thompson, the hospital administrator, standing alongside Dr. John Morgan, the chief of staff.

"May we have a word with you, Dr. Hwang?" the administrator asked.

"Sure," Hwang replied. "Just as soon as I finish talking with this family."

The administrator was not pleased with what he perceived to be an arrogant snub, but he silently nodded as the exhausted surgeon walked slowly past him. Hwang knew that he was likely to catch some grief for performing a procedure he technically didn't have privileges to do in this hospital, but, what else could he have done? He couldn't just let the baby die. Besides, everything had gone very well, hadn't it?

Mr. Alvarez had remained just outside the entrance to the sterile corridor, pacing back and forth nonstop since he last saw his precious daughter disappear into that inner sanctum. As the young doctor approached, Pablo turned to him with a terrified expression. Father Jacobs quickly took a position alongside the baby's anxious father and Lupe's four-year-old brother, Miguel, timidly joined the small group of men. His mother remained prayerfully seated in a nearby corner.

"We have finished with the operation," Hwang declared, causing Pablo to look expectantly to Father Jacobs who realized he needed to be the interpreter. After the surgeon's initial statement had been repeated in Spanish, he and Pablo both turned back toward Hwang with renewed expectation.

"We were able to successfully repair the problem with the arteries in her chest, and your daughter survived the operation," he offered slowly, both to ensure the priest was able to interpret and from his own fatigue. As the Spanish words flowed from Father Jacobs, Alvarez began to cry. His tears came with a huge sigh and an anxious smile. He then moved too quickly for Hwang to resist as he threw his muscular arms around the young doctor, hugging him a little tighter than was comfortable.

"*Gracias Señor! Muchas gracias para Señor!*" Pablo cried softly into Hwang's chest.

Hwang didn't know what to say. He thought Alvarez was referring to him as *señor*, but when he looked to Father Jacobs for direction the priest explained that *Señor* is the common Spanish word for the Lord. At that realization he understood and gently broke away from the grateful father's embrace.

Before leaving them Hwang was compelled to add, "The danger to your daughter is far from over." Pablo was now embracing his young son. "She could still suffer any number of complications."

After Hwang's words had been repeated in Spanish, he went on to tell Pablo that his daughter would need to remain in the intensive care unit for a few days and that she had several tubes in her body, but none of them were permanent.

"The next twenty-four hours will tell us a lot about whether she will recover or not," Hwang concluded cautiously.

With the interpretation of those final words, Pablo bowed his head slightly and replied, "*Gracias, doctor, muchas gracias.*" He then turned and walked slowly to his wife, falling on his knees in front of her, visibly sobbing with his head in her lap as her hand caressed him tenderly. She did not look up.

Hwang returned to the area outside the operating room and was preparing to write his postoperative orders and dictate a detailed account of the operation, but before he could sit down, the administrator called him into a small, private conference room.

"Just what the hell do you think you're doing, Hwang?" Al Thompson barked once the door was closed. "You don't have privileges to do heart surgery in this hospital!"

"Well," Hwang began, "that baby was going to die if I didn't do something. I knew what to do, and so I did what had to be done." There was just a hint of pride in Hwang's voice.

"You did what had to be done, did you?" the administrator scoffed. "Well, you have jeopardized this hospital and everyone who works here," he added angrily. "If that baby dies we will be subject to the biggest lawsuit ever, to say nothing of what the press will do with this." He turned his back on Hwang and took a few steps before turning to face him again. With flailing gestures he proclaimed, "I can see the headline now. Local hospital allows unqualified surgeon to perform murderous operations on helpless alien children."

"Wait a minute!" Hwang interrupted. "First of all, I am fully qualified to perform that procedure. It was part of my training. I didn't apply for those privileges when I came on staff here because I was told this hospital had no plans to provide support for neonatal vascular surgery." He paused but only briefly. "And, second, that baby is likely to survive and go on to live a normal life." Hwang's words were spoken with far more confidence than he was actually feeling.

Dr. Morgan, the chief of staff and a general internist, decided he'd better speak up. "Look, Hwang, we aren't saying you don't have the training and skills to do that kind of procedure, it's just that you have put the hospital in a very tough spot." He tried to put a different perspective on the situation, "If what Al is saying were to happen, it could cost the hospital big time." He then added, "Hell, as chief of staff, I might even be on the hook for allowing something like this to happen."

Hwang thought Morgan was sounding more like an indignant politician than a physician colleague.

After a brief moment, Thompson added, "You realize that child is an illegal, right?"

Hwang looked up with a questioning expression. "Yes," he said, wondering about the relevance of that remark.

"So," Thompson continued, "this is obviously a total charity case. We aren't going to see one dime of compensation for all the supplies and personnel you used today. This is the ultimate ..." he said disgustedly. "We spend our valuable resources for the opportunity to get sued *and* have our reputation destroyed in the media."

The tension in the air was palpable as Hwang considered what more he could say in his defense. Before he could respond, Thompson added with an air of finality, "I have recommended to Dr. Morgan that your privileges be suspended immediately based on your clear violation of the medical staff bylaws." With that he hurriedly left the room, closing the door noisily behind him. There was a momentary silence as Hwang sat stunned, staring at the door.

"I don't have a lot of options here, Hwang," explained Morgan, breaking the pregnant silence. Hwang began shaking his head slowly, not believing what he was hearing. "I have arranged for Frank Gardner to take over the care of this kid, along with our neonatologist, Lucy Burns."

Hwang turned to face his accuser with a look of protest, but he remained silent.

"Effective immediately your privileges to practice in this hospital are suspended indefinitely."

This isn't happening, Hwang thought, shaking his head yet again but this time in an effort to awaken himself from a nightmare.

"According to our bylaws, you are entitled to a hearing of your peers, which must occur within the next thirty days," Morgan continued, speaking almost as if reading Miranda rights to a criminal. "You are entitled to have legal representation at that hearing, and I would strongly recommend you take advantage of that opportunity."

The stunned surgeon sat motionless, both from fatigue and anger, as Morgan swiftly left the room. After a few minutes he composed himself and made his way back toward the scheduling desk. The only person he saw there was Frank Gardner, who was standing sheepishly with the baby's chart in his hand.

"I don't know what to say, Hwang," Gardner said, with an obvious sadness in his voice. "You did an unbelievable job in there. This is bullshit," he added with disgust. "They're just trying to cover their own asses."

The younger doctor could not find any words to say. He was simply numb from the events of the last few minutes. Gardner put his arm around his shoulder in consolation and asked, "What kind of orders do you want me to write? I don't really have a clue how to take care of a post-op kid like this," he admitted, with obvious anxiety in his voice.

Hwang started to dictate some orders, but thought better of it. "Just tell Lucy to treat this baby like she would any infant with neonatal respiratory distress, and watch her closely for metabolic acidosis." He looked into Gardner's eyes and tried to smile without success. "The chest tube should probably come out in a couple of days." His voice now sounding almost robotic.

"I can do that," Gardner assured. "Where are you going to be if I need you?"

"You don't need me," Hwang said, with obvious resignation. "If you need anything, just call administration or the chief of staff."

With that, he turned slowly away from Gardner and walked aimlessly toward the staff elevators with his head hanging down in utter exhaustion and defeat.

CHAPTER 2

Everyone in the huge operating room was dressed in the same light blue scrubs with heads and faces covered with matching caps and masks. Even their shoes were not visible under the baggy blue coverings designed to be removed after each operation. While the members of the team all seemed to be busy doing something important, the focus was clearly on the tall man standing next to the table in the middle of the room. He had a light on his head, reminiscent of a miner's helmet, but much smaller and much brighter. His head was bowed as he worked intently on the small body hidden beneath a shroud of blue sterile drapes. Only a small opening in the paper cloth exposed the left side of Lupe's chest.

In other operating rooms you might expect to hear music playing, usually a bit louder than necessary, but not in room four. Dr. Roberts didn't allow any extraneous noise in his room during surgery. He was fond of saying, "If I want to listen to rock and roll, I'll go to a bar." Lupe was undergoing a revision of the procedure Dr. Hwang had performed eight years before. As she'd grown, the spot where Hwang had sewn the subclavian artery to the aorta had not expanded along with the rest of her arteries. As a result, the pressure in the upper half of her body had gradually risen, and over the last two years her heart had begun to fail once more. The left side of her heart strained against the obstruction, and the narrow area needed to be fixed again or she would die as an innocent adolescent.

"Kittner," Dr. Roberts commanded. Without a word, Mark Stanton, the scrub tech responsible for managing the instruments, handed Jack a clamp with a small roll of gauze held tightly in the tip of the jaws.

"This thing is really stuck, George," Jack explained, not so much to his assistant as to himself. As he tried to gently tease the heavily scarred tissue away, he shifted his weight slightly just to change his perspective.

The previous operation had been done expertly; that was not the problem.

"This little girl makes scar tissue that would make Conan the Barbarian proud," Jack offered. "I think we can make better progress if we approach this from above."

He turned to Radha and asked, "Is she doing okay?"

"She's doing great, Jack," the anesthesiologist replied. "I have one unit ready to go, but I haven't seen much in the way of blood loss so far."

"Terrific," Jack replied. "I'm hoping we'll be able to get this thing freed up here in a minute so we can get on with revising the anastomosis."

The anastomosis was the point where the two arteries had been sewn together, and beneath it was the point where the ductus arteriosus had been tied off. The surrounding scar tissue made it difficult to know exactly where the connection was, and Jack knew all too well that dissecting out the area of the anastomosis was the most treacherous part of the procedure. The constant pounding of the aorta above this narrowed area made its general location clear, but with everything scarred down, and the pulsations of the aorta rhythmically thumping against every instrument, the process of freeing this part of the vital blood vessel was beyond tedious.

"We've got control above and below," Jack proclaimed with some satisfaction, "but this damned thing just doesn't want to budge." Somewhat frustrated he said, "Let me have those fine Metzenbaums."

Jack looked up at George and said almost playfully, "Now this is the tricky part." He took the precise dissecting scissors, which appeared almost too small for his large hands, and began to sharply dissect the area of the anastomosis. He expertly cut through this danger zone with precision. Finally, he managed to separate the scarred aorta from everything around it except for some attachments on the back side, precisely where he knew the ductus had been tied.

As he teased the tissues ever so gently he felt the unmistakable sense of foreboding in his gut. He felt his adrenaline beginning to flow in anticipation just as it happened — a sudden gush of dark red blood. Instinctively he put the index finger of his left hand over the site of bleeding to stem the flow.

"Suction!" he demanded, and George reached for a long, thin wand connected to the plastic suction tubing. He expertly cleared the pool of blood that had accumulated in the chest more quickly than he could have imagined.

"We've got a hole in the main pulmonary artery," Jack announced to everyone in the room, clearly signaling his entire team like a bugler calling the troops into battle.

Radha immediately reached for the phone to call the front desk, "I need an anesthesia tech in OR 4 right now," she said, as she opened the red cooler beside her anesthesia cart, which contained two small bags of blood from the blood bank. Radha knew she couldn't afford to get behind, or she'd be chasing this baby's blood volume to maintain her pressure for the rest of the case. She was fully prepared for this situation, having already placed a large IV catheter in Lupe's left internal jugular vein. Through it she could run three separate fluid lines at the same time if need be, but right now the child's vital signs remained stable.

"Do you want me to hang the first unit?" she asked, already knowing the answer. She just wanted to make sure Jack knew she was on top of the situation.

"Yes, and make sure you have a couple more available as backup, in case we need it," Jack answered while he worked out the details of the next steps in his head.

"I think the hole is pretty small, but with the aorta overlying it, I don't think I'm gonna be able to get to it to sew it up," Jack said with a hint of frustration. "I had planned to just do a patch angioplasty to widen this anastomosis, but it looks to me as though the guy sewed it with a running suture so we'll have to redo the whole thing anyway." Jack was thinking out loud, not really asking for George's opinion.

"The best approach here is to go ahead and completely divide the artery above and below and remove the old anastomosis. That way we can have full access to the pulmonary artery and repair it before reconnecting the aorta." Jack knew his logic was sound. The only concern would be how long it would take to do all that. Once he clamped off the aorta there would be no blood flow below that point. This included the kidneys, which could be very sensitive to even a few minutes with no circulation. Plus, there was another potential problem. If the blood supply to the spinal cord is cut off, even for just a few minutes, it could result in paralysis from the waist down. A close friend of his had presented a similar case at the Association of Thoracic Surgeons last year that resulted in the child being left paraplegic. While Jack was acutely aware of this potential disaster, he also knew that there was little he could do to prevent it, except work quickly.

"I think we have plenty of aorta and subclavian freed up," Jack confirmed. "What I'd like to do is free my left hand so I can put the clamps on the vessels and do the resection." Jack again looked up at George and asked, "Are you ready to play little Dutch boy?" George nodded and moved his right hand into position, awaiting Jack's call.

"One, two, three," Jack counted, then removed his finger from the vessel. Even though George was fairly quick to make the switch, they still lost about one hundred milliliters of blood almost instantly. In adults that would be easily tolerated, but in this fifty-five pound girl, it was very significant. Radha reported a transient drop in the child's pressure, but since she had anticipated just such an event, she'd already transfused almost that same amount of blood.

"She still doing okay?" Jack asked as he suctioned the blood from the chest cavity.

"Yes," Radha replied. "But I'd just as soon you not do that again. She had a transient dip down to about sixty, but it's back up above eighty now."

Jack realized that the hole was likely bigger than he'd thought and sometimes a small tear in a fragile vessel like the pulmonary artery will get bigger just from applying pressure. While George had control, there was no guarantee that the vessel might not rip open further. If it did they could lose control of it at any time.

Working quickly with no wasted movements, Jack placed angled vascular clamps across the subclavian artery leading into the anastomosis and the aorta, below the area he planned to remove. As he did he asked Susan to start the clock to keep track of how long the flow of blood was completely stopped.

Once the vessels were clamped, Radha noticed a spike in Lupe's blood pressure. The young girl's entire blood flow was now going to less than half her body. To compensate, she gave a short-acting drug that would slow the heart rate and reduce the force of its contraction. This was a bit risky since she would need exactly the opposite effect once the circulation was reestablished to the lower part of the child's body. She was ready with drugs that would counter that as well, but precise timing was critical.

Jack quickly cut the subclavian artery all the way across above the old anastomosis, then did the same with the aorta. Even in this little eight-year-old girl, each of these vessels was nearly the same size as Jack's little finger, so if either of the clamps were to come off, she could bleed out in a matter of seconds.

"Have a Statinski clamp ready," Jack instructed. He planned to place the U-shaped vascular clamp on the side of the pulmonary artery. Mark prepared to hand him the clamp, but Jack realized he really needed to have his own finger over the hole in the vessel instead of George's. Otherwise he wouldn't be able to feel the placement of the clamp.

"Let's switch out one more time," Jack said, as he moved his left hand into position. "One, two, three," he counted. George removed his finger and Jack replaced it with his own, almost instantaneously. This time the blood loss was less than twenty milliliters.

"Still okay, Radha?" Jack asked without looking up.

"Yes, she didn't even flinch that time," Radha reported.

With everything appearing stable, Jack carefully slid the open clamp down along either side of his finger, feeling as the tiny metal jaws obtained a good purchase on the thin-walled pulmonary artery. Jack then uttered one of the often repeated classic lines among heart surgeons.

"George, you know where the soul lives, don't you?"

George quickly responded, "Yes, sir, I've heard you say several times, the soul lives inside the pulmonary artery."

"Well, it's true," Jack said, trying to ease the tension with a vivid metaphor. "If you make a hole in the pulmonary artery the patient's soul is likely to fly out before you know it." The implication was obvious. Injuries of this nature have a high mortality because that vessel is not easy to repair. It often seems to tear further the more you try to sew it. Jack knew he was going to have one good shot at this, assuming the clamp held. Fortunately the pulmonary circulation is a low-pressure system, so a side clamp wasn't likely to be pushed off the vessel by pressure from inside, the way it would if the same kind of clamp were to be placed on a high-pressure vessel like the aorta. Even so, the Achilles' heel of this repair was the paper-thin nature of the pulmonary artery wall.

"Get me a couple of double armed 4-0 Prolene sutures, and preload one side of each with a small Teflon pledget," Jack instructed.

"Already got it, boss," Mark said with pride. Jack had always liked working with Mark as his scrub tech because he was so good at anticipating. Perhaps it came from his military background, but regardless of the origin of his skills and instincts, Mark was simply the best at what he did.

With the clamp in place, Jack carefully removed his finger from the artery and there was no bleeding seen. It only took a couple of seconds for Jack to see the problem. On the back side of the ligated ductus was a metal clip that had been used in addition to the suture that was tied around the vessel to occlude it. As he was manipulating the scar tissue the sharp edge of the clip had torn the main pulmonary artery. While it was hard to find fault with the first surgeon's work, the use of a clip suggested a lack of experience. Then again, Jack thought, he hadn't been there eight years ago, and that clip might well have been necessary at the time.

Jack quickly cut away the old anastomosis and the remnant of the ductus to just below the clip, removing it with the rest of the tissue. The hole in the pulmonary artery was now about four millimeters long and the vessel looked healthy on both sides of the hole. Using his personal needle holder which Jack had designed and fabricated for him nearly twenty years ago by a friend in Tokyo, he made quick work of closing the hole. The sutures were passed through a thin piece of Teflon material that had the consistency of a thin felt. The suture was then passed through both sides of the opening in the vessel then through another piece of Teflon. As the sutures were tied, the hole was sandwiched tightly between the two pieces of Teflon felt. This technique ensured the sutures wouldn't cut through the thin vessel wall, because if they did the soul just might escape. He carefully removed the Statinski clamp and saw that there was no bleeding.

"Suture," Jack commanded, and Mark had it ready. As he began to reconnect the two big vessels to reestablish the flow of blood to Lupe's lower body, he asked, "How long have we been clamped, Susan?"

The circulating nurse looked at the stopwatch-style clock on the OR wall and replied, "Ninety seconds, sir."

"The reason this anastomosis hadn't grown along with her as she got bigger is the fact that they elected to use one continuous running suture," Jack announced to no one in particular. "It is certainly faster to do it that way, but the suture doesn't stretch, so the size of the connection has remained roughly the same size while the vessels gradually grew over time." It was obvious that at age eight, Lupe's aorta was effectively the size of a newborn's, and that's why she had been struggling over the last few years. Instead of performing another running anastomosis, Jack placed multiple individual sutures with Teflon pledgets all the way around the new connection. He tied each one individually, and there was no space between the stitches, since blood under pressure would leak out.

Jack had done this type of anastomosis hundreds of times and it showed. His movements were fluid with no wasted motion. He did not appear to be rushing, but the reconnection was complete in less than five minutes. As he released the clamps he took the upper one off first to make sure there was no obvious bleeding. Then he slowly removed the lower clamp a little at a time. If he were to remove the clamp too quickly, Lupe's blood pressure would drop precipitously before her heart and vascular reflexes could counter the sudden rush of blood into her lower body. It took a full minute to fully remove the aortic clamp, and as he was doing so, Radha was delivering the drugs to keep Lupe's blood pressure in the normal range. Taking the last clamp out of the chest, he held it motionless, ready to reapply if Radha told him the pressure was dropping.

"How long were we cross-clamped, Susan?" he asked.

"Eight minutes and fifteen seconds," she replied.

Jack handed the last clamp back to Mark and said, "Great job, man."

"Thank you, sir," Mark replied with confidence. "You didn't do too bad yourself, sir." The younger man's hidden smile was obvious in his eyes.

"Let's get out of here, George," Jack suggested. They irrigated the area with saline and inspected everything one more time for any sign of bleeding before inserting two chest tubes through the chest wall between her tiny ribs. They would provide drainage of any bleeding and keep the child's lung fully expanded. Jack placed several large sutures around the adjacent ribs to pull them back together, reestablishing the closed chest cavity. The two surgeons then worked simultaneously to sew the multiple layers of muscle together. Finally, Jack closed the skin with dissolvable sutures so there would be no need to remove them later on. The chest tubes were connected to a special suction apparatus and Mark applied a long dressing over the incision as well as small gauze dressings around the tubes.

One last time Jack asked Radha if everything was okay, and she gave him a thumbs-up.

"What did you figure for our blood loss?" Jack asked, knowing she had a better idea of the total than he did since she was watching the volume of blood in the suction as well as how much was present on the sponges used inside the chest.

"About three hundred fifty cc's," She reported after doing the quick addition in her head.

"Wow, that much?" Jack said with surprise. Radha just nodded affirmatively. "How's her urine output?" he inquired.

"Good," Radha offered. "She's put out about seventy-five cc's in the two hours since we came in the room."

As he headed for the door with chart in hand, Jack told Radha, "Once you get her awake, be sure to let me know about her lower extremity movement, would you?"

"I'm planning to keep her on the vent overnight, so we likely won't know anything about her spinal cord function until tomorrow," she replied, understanding his concern.

"Okay," he agreed. "I doubt it will be a problem. Not a lot we could do about it anyway," he added, with some resignation in his voice. If the temporary lack of blood flow had caused an infarction of the spinal cord, the effect would likely be irreversible and any paralysis would almost certainly be permanent.

Leaving the OR, his first stop was the head. Now that all the excitement was over he realized the Diet Dr Pepper he'd had on his way to work was letting him know he had to go. Jack had never been much of a coffee drinker. He just didn't care for the taste, but he still liked a little caffeine jolt every morning. Diet Dr Pepper had been part of his morning routine for a couple of years now. He used to drink Diet Coke, but after about ten years he grew tired of it and switched to DP. Elaina was always on him about how unhealthy diet sodas were, but Jack told her he had to have one vice. If she made him stop drinking Diet DP, he might have to start chasing women. Needless to say, she didn't think he was all that funny.

Jack made his way to the waiting room and spotted the Alvarez family. Pablo jumped to his feet when he saw Jack, and along with Lupe's twelve-year-old brother, Miguel, they met the surgeon in the middle of the room. As they approached, Jack nodded slightly and offered his outstretched hand to the anxious father who quickly accepted it with both of his own.

"Everything went just fine," Jack said calmly. Unlike eight years ago, Pablo understood everything the surgeon was saying in English. "We removed the narrowed area in the artery and reconnected everything. I think she will do fine." His explanation conveniently left out the part about the soul nearly escaping, but Jack figured this family didn't need any more stress at this point in their lives. "She will be going into the ICU for a few days, and I'll have the nurse come and get you when you can see her."

Pablo's reaction to this report was far more controlled than it had been eight years earlier. Perhaps because he knew what to expect having experienced it before, but the circumstances were totally different this time. Dr. Hwang had provided a nearly miraculous solution when his baby was dying in front of his eyes. Jack had merely reversed a steadily worsening problem in a more controlled environment. Nevertheless, the father expressed his gratitude to the surgeon, thanking him repeatedly before returning to his wife. Jack looked over at the stoic woman seated near the wall and she gave him a mother's knowing smile like he hadn't seen in awhile.

♦♦♦♦♦♦♦♦♦

Jack quickly changed back into his street clothes after his second case, a routine four-vessel coronary bypass. He was supposed to be at the committee meeting in five minutes, but he decided to run by the ICU and check on the Alvarez girl before going downstairs to the administrative conference room. On his way to the ICU he flipped open his cell phone and called his office.

"Hi, Mary Anne, it's me," he began. "Yeah, everything went fine with both cases. I was just checking to see what my afternoon looks like," he said with an implied question. "Okay, sounds like we'll be there until five for sure. Have Shelly lay out the stuff I'll need to take out the Williams kid's sutures. I just hope he and his mom are both in a better mood than they were when they left the hospital."

Jack recalled the frustration of dealing with eleven-year-old Dwight and his angry mother. The boy had been accidentally hit in the chest during a drive-by shooting, and Jack had performed an emergency thoracotomy to stop the bleeding. The boy recovered without complication, but his mom continued to blame everybody for her son's injury, and when Jack discharged him to go home, she had a nuclear meltdown, claiming she couldn't take care of her son. She screamed, "Don't you realize that I have to work? You people just need to keep him in the hospital until he's completely well." She caused such a scene that eventually the hospital's security personnel were called and she was escorted from the nursing unit.

Mrs. Williams was only part of Jack's concern. Although Dwight was only eleven, he had all the makings of an angry teenager. The entire time he was in the hospital, the boy rarely made eye contact with Jack or any of the staff. The only conversation he had with him was about the scar on his chest. When Jack told him he didn't think the scar would look too bad once it healed completely, Dwight objected. He said wanted a big thick scar so he could show his buddies just how tough he was. He was to be Jack's first patient in the office that afternoon, and all he could do was hope for the best.

"I should be there by two unless this meeting drags on," Jack said. "If I'm gonna be late, I'll call you."

Jack hung up as he walked through the automatic door leading into the Surgical Intensive Care Unit. Twenty beds were arranged in an array around the central nurses' station. Lisa Blanton, the slender thirty-year-old charge nurse, stood near the bank of cardiac monitors, talking with one of the other nurses. The young RN, BSN had quickly risen up the ranks in the ICU because she was not only smart, she also possessed great instincts. Jack had suggested to her many times that she should have gone to medical school, but she always responded with the same comment, "Somebody has to keep you guys in line."

Out of the corner of her eye, Lisa saw Jack coming and she immediately dismissed the other nurse and turned to meet him as he entered the nurses' station. "Hello, Dr. Roberts," she offered, in her typical professional style.

"Hey, Lisa," he responded, casually. "Where is the Alvarez girl?"

"Bed five. She just got here. They kept her in recovery a little longer to get her blood pressure stabilized."

Jack turned and walked purposefully toward Lupe's assigned cubicle with Lisa alongside. Before they reached the room, she added, "I understand things got a little exciting in there this morning."

"Not really," Jack offered. "It was pretty routine."

Lisa knew he was downplaying the drama that she'd heard about through the hospital grapevine. Within an hour of the actual event, word had spread about how Dr. Roberts had saved the young girl's life, and, as was always the case, by the time the story had been retold a few times, it sounded as though Jack had literally raised her out of the grave. Legends like Jack Roberts were usually based on at least a sliver of truth, but they were always compounded by the imaginations of the mass of hero worshipers.

"Hi," Jack said, greeting Lupe's parents as they stood next to their daughter's bed. "I understand they had to keep Lupe in the recovery room a little longer than expected to get her blood pressure under control."

Pablo nodded before asking, "Is everything okay now?"

"Yes," Jack stated reassuringly. "I kind of expected she might have a little trouble with her pressure for a while since so much more blood is now flowing into the lower half of her body." Jack wasn't sure if he understood, but Pablo smiled and nodded as he took a step back to allow the doctor to move in next to the bed.

Lupe was lying peacefully on her back, still sedated. The clear breathing tube coming out of her mouth was taped to the side of her face, creating a slight distortion of her upper lip. The ventilator was cycling rhythmically, generating the corresponding rise and fall of her chest. Electronic monitors over the bed showed her heart rate was steady at one hundred beats per minute and the central venous pressure wave was vacillating between eight and twelve millimeters of mercury. An arterial line had been placed by Dr. Patel in the child's right wrist to monitor her blood pressure continuously. Jack saw that it was currently ninety-five over fifty-eight and he seemed satisfied given the situation.

"Do we have a post-op H and H?" he asked in Lisa's general direction.

"Yes, sir," replied another nurse who was assigned to Lupe for the day shift. Jack hadn't noticed her entering the room behind him. "It's thirteen point three and forty-one."

"Oh, hi, Joan," he replied, acknowledging the older woman. "How's her urine output?"

"It's been running between fifteen and twenty cc's an hour since surgery, and it's clear."

"Sounds like we could bump up her fluids a little," he reasoned. "Let's increase the crystalloid from forty-five to fifty-five an hour, and keep a close eye on that central pressure."

Lupe's pressure was a bit lower than he liked and her urine output was slightly below what he'd hoped, but overall, he was pleased with how the young girl's body handled the trauma of such a major operation. He took a quick look at the plastic drainage bottles on the floor and saw just a little pink colored fluid in one and virtually no drainage in the other. He nodded in approval, recognizing that neither the anastomosis nor the repaired pulmonary artery had shown any signs of bleeding.

Jack turned back to the parents with a smile smiled, and said, "She's doing great. Couldn't be better." He then added, "I'll be back around later this evening to check on her, but Dr. Goodman, our intensivist, will be here if anything changes. He is very attentive and can deal with virtually any problem that might arise."

Like most hospitals across the country, this facility had hired a group of intensive care specialists who remained on the unit twenty-four hours a day. Each intensivist worked a twelve-hour shift and then was off for twenty-four to thirty-six hours. Dr. Matt Goodman was one of Jack's most trusted colleagues, and he would be on duty until midnight.

♦♦♦♦♦♦♦♦♦

Jack entered the familiar conference room where the meeting of the Quality Assurance and Utilization Review Committee was already under way.

"Sorry I'm late," he offered, then quickly grabbed one of the plastic containers of prepared salad before taking the last open seat at the large conference table. The glass of tea in front of him had been sitting untouched for some time. The ice was mostly melted and the condensation had collected beneath the glass, saturating the cocktail napkin. Everyone else had finished eating and their attention was focused on the screen at the far end of the room. Herb Nichols, the hospital's chief administrator, was going over some financial data as Jack applied the packet of Thousand Island dressing to his mixed greens.

"I'm glad you could join us, Dr. Roberts," Herb said with just a hint of sarcasm. Herb had been with the hospital for nearly thirty years in various capacities, but he'd only been the head man for the last three. As he stood near the screen, wearing a tailored gray business suit and heavily starched white shirt, Jack thought the pink tie was a bit too flashy for the workplace. Jack smiled to himself as he realized he had become hypercritical of virtually everything Herb said or did, solely because he didn't like the direction Herb was taking the hospital. No single policy or action had been all that big a deal; it was more subtle than that. Under Herb's guidance everyone was focused more on the bottom line than patient care. This change in philosophy had actually coincided with their inclusion in a mammoth regional health care conglomerate more than a decade earlier.

"We were just talking about our rising costs in the operating room and what options we have to get a handle on some of the more obvious excesses," Herb added, more as a question than a statement. Jack was acutely aware of the fact that one of the major costs of complex open heart procedures involved disposable supplies for the heart-lung bypass machine. Several companies produced pump tubing and filters, but as far as Jack was concerned, there was one brand he insisted on using, and naturally it was the most expensive.

"I received a bid from a new manufacturer that could save us approximately two hundred thousand dollars a year on bypass disposables alone. That's not chicken feed." Herb's message was a direct challenge to Jack, but was clearly his way of demonstrating his authority to each of the committee members.

"I know about their bid," Jack responded quickly. "They have been all over me for the last six months to allow them to bring their products into my OR. In my opinion they are just not up to the standards to which we have always held our hospital."

"What's the big difference?" Herb questioned, baiting Jack yet again. "They are FDA approved just like the stuff you are using now. I can't imagine that there could be two hundred thousand dollars' difference."

Jack was becoming perturbed with the assumptions Herb was making, and his response betrayed his growing contempt for the man. "Well, for one thing, their tubing is made of much stiffer material. It is cheaper, yes, but far more difficult to work with, and is simply unusable in infants."

Herb interrupted before Jack had finished. "But, Jack, that's not what I'm being told by Dr. Fanning down in Houston. They've been using it for a couple of years now." He spoke as if the other physician was the true expert and his opinion should hold sway over his own staff member.

"Fanning has a consulting contract with that manufacturer," Jack retorted. "Of course he's going to say that. I suspect he's also got stock in the company," he added accusingly. He paused brief before continuing with his original answer. "Also, I understand they've had some major supply issues due to labor problems at their manufacturing plant in Mexico."

Jack was well prepared for these questions since he was sure they'd be brought up eventually. Herb shifted his weight, trying not to interrupt again for fear of appearing too confrontational. He'd get his turn again, and he, too, had prepared his own arguments.

"And," Jack continued his defense, "there have been off-the-record reports of several life-threatening systemic inflammatory responses in patients who have been on the pump more than two hours using their products."

Herb prepared to responded as the rest of the committee members followed the debate as if watching two boxers sparring in the ring.

"I have been assured by Jason Fletcher, our materials manager, that the supply issue is no longer relevant," Herb said more calmly and with a slight arrogance to his tone. "The company has moved their operation to Guatemala, away from the political unrest in Mexico," he announced with certainty, although the move was only hearsay.

"From what I understand," Herb continued without apparent resistance, "there were only a couple of cases of inflammatory response, and neither of those patients died. The company attributed those incidents to a bad sterilization batch, and I've been assured personally by their CEO that it was an isolated event. With their new quality assurance standards there is no way something like that could happen again," Herb added with finality.

Jack had heard about enough. He rose to his feet and stared directly at Herb. "You know," he started slowly, "as I understand it, this committee has two functions. The first one, and the one I am most concerned about, is the quality assurance part." Jack was getting ready to land the haymaker that he'd wanted to deliver for months but had never had the opening until now. "I don't really care what some CEO said about their quality assurance standards or whether they've moved their plant to Timbuktu." Jack was now spouting a little louder than was necessary. "I will not jeopardize the safety of my patients, even if it saves this hospital two million dollars a year."

He stepped calmly to the serving table along the wall behind him and picked up a Diet Dr Pepper. The room was silent as he popped the top and sat back down, sipping the warm, tangy liquid straight from the can.

Herb knew this last big blow had to be returned. His anger at being openly challenged in this way by a physician was obvious to everyone, as his face had gradually begun to match the color of his tie.

"No one is asking you to jeopardize your patients, Dr. Roberts," Herb said, speaking more slowly and softer for effect, trying to hide his frustration with this prima donna surgeon. "I understand you feel strongly about this, so perhaps we should move on with our agenda and revisit this in private."

It was obvious to everyone in the room that this round had ended, but Herb simply couldn't leave it at that, electing to throw one final jab, well after the bell had sounded.

"You know, we likely wouldn't have to consider these kinds of cost-saving measures if we didn't have so many total charity cases coming into our hospital from all over the place."

Jack knew immediately he was referring to the Lupe Alvarez case. The two men had already engaged in a rather heated conversation just a few days before, when Herb had reluctantly agreed to allow Jack to admit the eight-year-old Mexican national for the procedure he'd just performed a few hours earlier.

◆◆◆◆◆◆◆◆◆

Lupe and her family had returned to Matamoros from Corpus Christi following her operation eight years earlier. Pablo had gone back to his job as a laborer at a local cement manufacturing company where he worked overtime for nearly a year to pay back the fifty dollars he'd borrowed from his boss to buy passage across the border. After their experience in Corpus, he realized that if he ever wanted to return to the US he would need to learn to speak English, at least enough to get by. He sought out an American missionary who was working at the local Red Cross clinic who agreed to teach him. For nearly two years, each day he would walk from his job to the clinic, then spend thirty minutes to an hour learning this strange new language he hoped would help him provide a better life for his wife and children. After seeing what life was like on the other side of the Rio Grande, he wanted desperately to return, but legally.

The idea of obtaining an American visa, that oh-so-desirable "green card," became impossible. Pablo had no skills beyond shoveling gravel. He considered the option of sneaking his family back into the US, but with the increase in drug traffic at every border crossing, the American authorities had cracked down hard on the human smugglers. He reluctantly gave up trying to return to the land of opportunity after several years. However, necessity came calling once more when Lupe began having trouble breathing.

Although she had been growing more or less like other children her age, shortly after her sixth birthday her mother noticed her daughter seemed to tire more easily than the other children. By the time she was seven, Lupe couldn't run more than a few strides without stopping to catch her breath, and by the following summer she rarely left the house. She said she just didn't have any energy.

Finally, Lupe's father took her to a local clinic, and the doctor was shocked when he heard the story of the miraculous heart surgery. He'd heard rumors of a baby from Matamoros with a heart problem who had managed to get across the border into Texas, but he wasn't sure they were true until now. He examined her and told Pablo he could hear a loud swishing sound in her back, indicating the problem with her aorta had returned.

Pablo was devastated by this news, even though he had suspected something was wrong with Lupe's heart for some time. While the situation was not as urgent at before, he still felt he had to find a way back across the border to the doctor who had saved his baby's life. He wasn't sure whether he could find the young Asian doctor or not. The man had simply disappeared after he had spoken to him through Father Jacobs. Pablo couldn't even remember the doctor's name, but his wife, Juanita, had always believed that he was actually an angel sent down from heaven, who returned to God's side after he worked his miracle. Now, all Pablo could think about was getting his child back across that border.

A few weeks went by, as Pablo quietly searched for any possible passage into the US. The contacts he'd used years before were long gone. The men he knew were now on the other side, in Pharr, Texas, receiving drug shipments that were crossing the border through Reynosa. A friend at work whose brother-in-law was connected to that illegal operation gave him the name of another man in Reynosa, Miguel Hernandez-Luna, as a possible contact. Perhaps, for the right price, he could arrange to get them across.

Inside the entrance to the small cinderblock building that was the Alvarez home stood a beautiful hand-carved Madonna. It was nearly four feet tall and had been carved by Pablo's grandfather from a huge cypress knee he bought from a peddler for five pesos. The unique work of art had been the pride of the Alvarez family for three generations, and Pablo believed it was the sacred guardian of his family. Over the years many friends had remarked how valuable it must be, but Pablo had never considered it that way. It was simply part of their family, so he'd never thought of it as something that was worth money. Now, in his hour of need, he was forced to consider all his options. He'd seen similar carvings, selling in the market for as much as five hundred pesos, but they were all much smaller and not nearly the quality of the one he possessed.

THE CALLING

Desperate to restore his daughter's health, he concluded he had no choice but to sell the family's only treasure. He decided he would offer it to one of the traders down in the public market, and was sure it would bring at least a thousand pesos. That might be enough to buy their way across the border.

The next Sunday the entire family attended mass in the nearby church. Pablo had insisted they all go, including Lupe. He carried the child most of the way, but with his help she was able to walk into the church and kneel on the hard wooden *prie dieu*. After the service the family returned home with Pablo carrying Lupe the entire way. He laid her gently on her bed, which was little more than a straw mat covered with a thick woolen blanket. He explained that he wouldn't be gone long and walked swiftly out the door carrying the Madonna wrapped in another old tattered blanket.

When he arrived in the market, the crowd was very large, typical of a Sunday afternoon. Many Americans came across the border on weekends to shop for bargains. They bought liquor and cigarettes, and many came for prescription drugs because they were cheap and didn't require a written prescription.

Pablo quickly found a shop that sold premium-quality leather goods, as well as a number of locally hand-carved wooden items. He made his way past several customers as they browsed through the racks of leather jackets and purses. Behind the counter was a middle-aged Mexican merchant who angrily asked him what he wanted. The man knew this local wasn't here to buy anything. More likely he was looking for a hand out. Pablo explained he had something he would like to sell, and as he spoke he carefully unwrapped the Madonna then placed it on the counter with pride. The shop owner peered over his reading glasses, and it was all he could do to hide his interest in this marvelous piece of art. The man protested that the piece was not the kind of thing he usually dealt in, but then offered him a hundred pesos.

Pablo laughed, and under his breath declared the merchant to be *loco*. He quickly began wrapping the blanket around the Madonna prompting the shrewd business man to ask what he wanted for it. Pablo responded by requesting two thousand pesos, about three hundred dollars. It was the merchant's turn to laugh, as Pablo wrapped up his prize to find another, more reasonable buyer.

The unusual negotiation had taken place in Spanish, so most of the Americans in the shop hadn't known exactly what had transpired. None-the-less they were all standing by watching the entertaining exchange. As Pablo stepped through the door onto the wooden sidewalk he sensed he was being followed. He turned to see an American woman in her mid-forties standing behind him smiling.

"*Con permisso, señor,*" she said, with an accent that was distinctly Texan. She had been one of the shoppers who had watched him offer the Madonna to the merchant. "*Puedo verla otravez,*" she said, hoping her Spanish was passable.

Pablo was reluctant to unwrap his treasure out there on the street for fear some young thief would grab it and run through the alley between the buildings, never to be seen again.

"I don't want to show it here," Pablo explained confidently in his new language.

"Oh," she exclaimed with relief, "you speak English."

"Yes, a little," he said shyly. "There are too many men who steal things here. I am afraid to let everyone see."

"I understand," she said, nodding her head much too obviously. "Why don't we go over there, across the street?"

She pointed to a small café that was largely empty now that the lunch crowd was gone. Pablo nodded once in agreement, and led the way across the street crowded with old rusted cars. They were forced to wait briefly as an old school bus rattled past, then hurriedly crossed the street. They bumped their way through the mass of pedestrians on the sidewalk, as some moved briskly while others stopped suddenly in front of them for no apparent reason.

Once inside the little taco shop, they sat down at a table away from the door. A waitress approached them, but Pablo explained that they didn't want to order anything. The young woman protested for just a moment, then walked away, disappointed they weren't customers.

As Pablo unwrapped the Madonna on the floor in front of him, the American woman exclaimed, "That is beautiful." She stretched out her words in a classic Texan twang. "Where on earth did you get that? Did you make it yourself?" she asked with awe in her voice.

"*No, señora,*" Pablo explained shyly. "I could no make something like this," his broken English showing through.

As he was talking, the blond haired woman reached out to touch the Madonna, but stopped short asking, "May I?"

"*Si,*" he said, forgetting his English for a second. "It's okay."

"This is incredible," she said softly as she stroked the fine lines of Mary's delicate face.

"It was carved by my grandfather many years ago," he explained in an almost reverent tone. "I brought it to the market to sell."

"Oh my God!" the woman said with a painful drawl. "You can't be serious. Why would you want to sell something this beautiful?"

Before Pablo could begin to answer, the woman interrupted. "You aren't selling it to buy drugs are you?" Immediately she then realized her accusation and added, "I'm sorry, I didn't mean to ..." and her speech trailed off.

"*No, señora,*" Pablo protested. "Nothing like that." After a momentary pause, for some unknown reason he decided to confide in this stranger. "My daughter is very sick. She needs another operation to fix her heart," Pablo explained as honestly as he could.

The woman wasn't quite sure what to think. Was this guy conning her with this story about a daughter needing an operation or was this for real? She decided to test him.

"Where is your daughter now?" she asked, suggesting perhaps his daughter didn't really exist.

"At our home a few blocks from here," he replied not yet sensing her distrust.

"I really love this carving, and I might be willing to buy it from you," she said cautiously, "but only if I know you are going to use the money for what you say." She realized she had challenged this man, but she needed to know if he was telling the truth or merely playing on her sympathy.

"How much would you be willing to pay?" he asked, eager to see if this woman was serious or just another bargain hunter like the merchant across the street.

"I don't know," she admitted. After a brief pause she added, "I think it's probably worth about five hundred dollars."

"Dollars, *señora*?" Pablo asked slowly.

"*Si*, five hundred dollars," she said, not realizing he might have thought she had meant pesos.

Pablo had never seen five hundred dollars in his life. Could it be true that this woman would give him so much money? "I would be willing to sell it to you, yes," he said, trying not to let his excitement show.

"Well," she said, "before I give you the money I need to see your daughter so I'll know that she's the one who the money is really for." She thought she had him trapped, and fully expected him to argue that his house was too far away, or offer some other excuse why her conditions couldn't be met.

"Certainly, *señora*," he said boldly. "I will be happy to take you to see my Lupe for yourself." He quickly wrapped the blanket around the Madonna. "Come with me."

The woman rose from her chair, and like Pablo she was not believing what was happening.

"How far are we going?" Elizabeth asked.

Elizabeth Burke was a frequent visitor to this market. She had been coming here almost every Sunday afternoon for a couple of years. She was always looking for unique pieces that she could sell in her small boutique on the southern end of Padre Island. Many visitors to South Texas were afraid to cross the border into Mexico, despite the lure of much cheaper prices. Elizabeth had built a nice little retail business by buying and selling quality Mexican-made specialty items in Matamoros. Sometimes she drove up to Nuevo Progreso, and occasionally, she'd ventured as far as Reynosa in search of just the right merchandise.

What she was doing wasn't exactly legal, but she was a small-time operator and the authorities paid no attention. As long as she didn't bring back more than two thousand dollars worth of stuff at any one time, she didn't have to pay duty on the items she brought across the border. Technically, she should have an import license, but so far no one had raised any questions. Perhaps it was because most of the things she sold in her little shop located just off the beach in South Padre were American made products.

"It's not too far, about ten minutes walk," Pablo said as he held the Madonna close to his chest and turned to the right as he stepped out onto the sidewalk.

"Wait a minute," Elizabeth said a little louder than was necessary, but she needed to be heard over the noise in the street. "I have a car just around the corner. Why don't we drive there?"

Pablo paused for a second, watching as she motioned for them to go to the left. He nodded and followed her as she walked briskly up the street toward a small parking area. In her boots, the American woman stood nearly a head taller than the five-feet three-inch tall Pablo. Together with the blanket wrapped Madonna, they made quite an unusual trio walking down the streets of Matamoros.

As she approached her dark blue suburban, Elizabeth reached in her purse and pushed the button on her key ring to unlock the vehicle. Immediately it responded with flashing taillights and a familiar chirp.

"We can put the carving in the back," Elizabeth said as she approached the rear doors of the suburban.

"Please, *señora*," Pablo interrupted. "I will hold on to her."

Elizabeth shrugged and said, "Okay. It'll be a little crowded in the front seat." She made her way around to the passenger side and was preparing to open the front door when Pablo protested,

"*No, señora*. I sit in back."

With another shrug, Elizabeth opened the back door on the passenger side allowing Pablo to step up on the running board and carefully place the Madonna on the seat in front of him. He held it securely with one hand as he climbed over and sat in the seat behind the driver. Elizabeth closed the door, then walked around to her side.

As she took her seat behind the wheel, she looked in the rearview mirror but was unable to see her diminutive passenger. "Which way are we going?" she asked as Pablo leaned forward between the two front seats, still holding the Madonna firmly with his right hand.

"Down this street past the café, and I will tell you when to turn to the right," he instructed.

THE CALLING

She drove slowly down the main street that housed the market until he told her to turn onto a side street. She followed his directions and soon found herself driving through a part of the town that few tourists ever experience. The streets were in disrepair, with many large broken pieces of concrete, creating sizable dips and bumps, causing the suburban to bounce noticeably despite traveling less than ten miles per hour.

"There is my home," Pablo declared, pointing to the small cinderblock structure with a corrugated metal roof. Elizabeth pulled up in front, trying to get as far off the street as possible, but the huge suburban seemed to take up half the width of the remaining street.

She turned the engine off and as she was getting out of the suburban, she noticed a small group of young children who had been playing in the street. They stopped to stare at the sight of a giant truck and a gringo woman in their neighborhood.

Pablo quickly climbed out of the passenger side of the suburban carrying the Madonna in his left arm as he closed the door. "Please come in, *señora*," Pablo requested in a very humble manner.

She followed him through a small gate in the low wooden fence that enclosed a tiny patch of dirt which served as a front yard. Part of the fence was composed of three old white enameled washing machines and one refrigerator with no door. They had been each been laid on their sides as a protective barrier from the street.

It took a moment for Elizabeth's eyes to adjust as she entered the darkened structure. She saw Pablo's wife sitting near a small wood-burning stove located on one wall of the single room dwelling. A large pot of steaming liquid sat on the blackened service, and she could see the flickering flames through the partially open iron door.

Miguel had immediately jumped to his feet when he saw his father step through the door. He halted in surprise at the sight of this tall slender Caucasian woman entering his house. He quickly determined that she was not a threat before cautiously making his way past her to stand next to his father.

Pablo quickly introduced Elizabeth to Juanita and Miguel and explained that the American woman had agreed to buy their Madonna. With that, he sat the carving down near the door exactly where it had been for many years.

In the far corner of the room, beyond the stove, was a small table with two chairs which did not match. On the opposite side of the room, Elizabeth spotted a young girl lying silently on a makeshift bed. Pablo made his way across the room and pointed to Lupe saying, "Here is our daughter."

In a series of rapid communications in Spanish, Pablo told his wife how he'd met this American woman in the market, and how she'd offered to pay five hundred dollars for the Madonna. He explained that the woman had insisted on knowing what he would use the money for, so he brought her here to see for herself.

Juanita seemed visibly upset, and Pablo wasn't sure whether it was because he'd brought a stranger into their home unannounced, or because he was selling their precious family treasure. He never considered the real reason for his wife's reaction. She was angered by the idea that anyone would think her husband was not trustworthy.

Elizabeth slowly walked across the creaking floor and knelt down next to Lupe. It was obvious the young girl was breathing a bit faster and with more effort than seemed normal. Lacking the strength to even generate a smile for the yellow-haired American, she acknowledged her presence only with a warm, but still uncertain gaze. All the questions Elizabeth had about Pablo's story were forgotten. It was apparent that this child was truly ill and needed medical attention. She reached out and touched Lupe's exposed right hand and found her skin to be warm, but the hand was very weak. As she gently squeezed her fingers, Lupe responded with an almost imperceptible returned gesture.

After a few moments, Elizabeth rose to face Pablo who had joined his wife near the stove. "What can I do to help you?" she asked earnestly, with a tiny tear beginning to well up in her eyes.

For the next ten minutes Elizabeth sat quietly at the table listening to Pablo tell the story of how they had been smuggled into America eight years before. He explained all about the miraculous operation in Corpus Christi, and how Lupe had been a normal healthy child until about two years ago. After the first few minutes of hearing this incredible tale, Elizabeth was unable to control her weeping. It was difficult for Pablo to explain any of the specifics of Lupe's illness, but Elizabeth understood clearly that this precious child was in desperate need of another operation.

"Okay," Elizabeth began after composing herself, "here's what we're going to do."

Something had come over her, and she was now uncharacteristically assuming control of a situation for which she had no experience, zero.

◆◆◆◆◆◆◆◆

As she approached the border control station at Progreso, there were about twenty-five cars ahead of her. She had chosen to drive an hour to the West along the southern banks of the Rio Grande because she'd heard the border agents there were somewhat less likely to question her as she returned to the US.

She wasn't really sure exactly why she'd taken the backseat out of the suburban before coming across the border that morning, but it proved to be very providential. Just prior to reaching Nuevo Progreso, she had stopped the car and used a couple of their heavy woolen blankets to cover the small family that was now lying silently where the back bench seat normally rested. It had been Pablo's idea to use a large piece of plywood to cover them, then lay the blankets on top of the flat surface. He told Elizabeth that to anyone just looking in through the window it would look like a stack of blankets rather than the irregular shapes created by human figures. This was similar to the process his previous smugglers had employed to get them across the Rio Grande.

Elizabeth's heart was racing as she slowly advanced the suburban closer to the huge white barrier. There were five openings where vehicles were inspected and the words UNITED STATES OF AMERICA were proudly printed across the top in bold blue letters. Her mind was racing. What if the agent wants to look in the back? What if he senses my fear? How long is the jail time for human trafficking? Would my father understand? Would he even post my bail? What would happen to Lupe and her family? The questions running through her mind were endless. Why was she doing this crazy thing?

Suddenly, Elizabeth spotted the brown uniform of a border patrol agent walking slowly between the lines of cars. He was looking intently down at the ground at a long metal pole with a mirror attached to the end near the pavement. The mirror was mounted at an angle which allowed him to see under each vehicle, searching for secret compartments that might be used to smuggle drugs or other contraband. She knew she didn't have to worry about that, her suburban didn't have any secret compartments. She was smuggling four people across the border using only a piece of plywood and some blankets for cover. This was the stupidest thing she'd ever done, and she began to resign herself to getting caught.

As the officer approached the front of her truck on the driver's side, she hadn't noticed the second agent coming up on the passenger side. He was leading a big German Shepherd on a leash. The dog was systematically inspecting each vehicle with his sensitive nose, searching for even a hint of illegal drugs.

Marijuana was the main export crop of Mexico, and the United States was the chief market. The drug traffickers were always finding new ways to sneak their wares across the border, but these dogs were extremely hard to fool. They had been trained to detect even the slightest scent of the illegal weed, even when placed inside gasoline tanks or tires.

The agents moved on past Elizabeth, without even looking up from their efforts. She continued to inch slowly forward and was now only three cars from the checkpoint. Another agent stood in in front of the building directing traffic and making sure that each car remained behind the yellow line on the pavement, about twenty feet from the gate.

The evening was fast approaching and the huge array of fluorescent lights illuminating the complex seemed to be getting brighter with each passing second. As Elizabeth moved into position on the yellow line, she watched as the young agent she would soon face leaned out of the white stucco and glass enclosure. He accepted the documents of the gentleman in the old brown pickup truck she had been following for nearly half an hour. His license plate was clearly mark with Tamaulipas across the top and Mexico across the bottom. The agent stepped out of his station and walked along the side of the pickup looking intently into the bed. He reached in, attempting to move a large crate, but it was too heavy for his half-hearted effort. He returned to his desk and retrieve a small white sheet of paper. He handed the documents back to the man in the truck along with the white paper and pointed to an area just ahead and to the left, clearly indicating that the man should pull his vehicle around into a holding area for further inspection.

As the pickup slowly pulled away, Elizabeth saw the open space where she was about to be exposed for the idiot she was. The agent was looking down writing something, and she took this last moment to close her eyes as she prayed softly to herself. "God, be with me," she begged.

She opened her eyes and looked up just as the agent motioned for her to come forward. As she approached the checkpoint, she pushed a button on the armrest and the window silently retracted into the door.

"Good evening, ma'am," the officer stated robotically, leaning in and looking quickly around the inside of the passenger compartment for any other occupants. "May I see your passport?"

"Certainly, officer," she said, trying to sound calm and as natural as possible. She handed over the small blue booklet, hoping he wouldn't notice the slight tremble in her hand or the hint of unnatural tension in her voice. He stepped back inside the small cubicle and typed a few keys on his computer. She placed both hands firmly on the steering wheel, trying her best to breathe slowly while not being conspicuous doing so. She looked down and noticed the white skin over her knuckles and realized the extreme tension in her arms. She took a deep breath in an effort to let the tension flow out of her body the way they'd taught her in those Lamaze classes twenty-five years ago. She didn't think it worked then, and it sure wasn't working now.

When the agent returned, he spoke with a little more personality. "What was the purpose of your visit in Mexico, Mrs. Burke?" he asked as he looked alternately from her face to the passport photo and back again.

"I went over to Matamoros looking for a few things for an event I'm planning at my home in Brownsville," she said, carefully repeating the phrase she'd been rehearsing in her mind for the last hour and a half.

Before she could finish her lines he interrupted. "If you went over at Matamoros, why are you coming back through Progreso?"

"Well, I found this Madonna in the market in Matamoros," she said, as she gestured toward the carving that was strapped into the passenger's seat by the seatbelt and shoulder harness. The tattered blanket partially covered the carving where the straps were draped across it, but the head and shoulders were clearly exposed. "I couldn't find the things I was really looking for in that market, so I drove up here to Nuevo Progreso and found the blankets I needed," she stated perhaps a bit too quickly, but remembering to motion with her head toward the back of the suburban. She wanted to make sure he got the impression she wasn't trying to hide anything.

He took a couple of steps back toward the rear of the suburban and looked intently through the window. He returned saying, "That's quite a stack of blankets you got there. What did you say they were for?"

"We're having a big group of kids from our church over for a sleepover next weekend," she lied. "I needed to get a blanket for each of the twenty-five children to sleep on, plus a few extras, you know?" she was actually beginning to relax just a bit as her story seemed to make sense, and just maybe he was buying it.

"You didn't spend more than two thousand dollars did you?" he said with a hint of a smile.

"Heavens no!" she replied with a laugh that sounded just a little fake.

The agent transferred her passport from his left hand to his right and offered it back to her through the window. "Have a nice evening, ma'am." With those few words he motioned for her to go on.

Elizabeth's heart was pounding so hard she was certain he could hear it through the open window. She put the suburban back in gear and pulled away slowly, being extra careful not to accelerate too quickly and squeal the tires. She turned to the right, and followed a late model Nissan, as it too had been cleared to enter the US. She glanced in the rearview mirror and saw the man in the pickup that had been in front of her. He was standing beside his vehicle which was being thoroughly searched.

Once around the first turn, the suburban bounced softly over a pair of tire spikes that would prevent any return by this route. To her left she saw another line of cars heading back approaching the bridge over the Rio Grande heading into Mexico. She'd made it! "Elizabeth Burke," she whispered under her breath, "you are now officially a criminal."

She followed the main road north into the sleepy town of Progreso, Texas. The name just didn't seem to fit the surroundings. As she approached Highway 281, she pulled off onto a side street and then around another corner onto a dark street, well out of sight of the main thoroughfare. Night had come on rather quickly she thought, but given what she'd just been through, she'd completely lost track of time. All she wanted to do now was get that poor family out from under that shroud of blankets and plywood.

She pulled over and jumped out of the truck, nearly losing her balance as her weak knees revealed themselves. She moved purposefully to the back of the suburban then cautiously opened the double doors whispering, "Pablo?" As she began peeling the blankets off exposing the plywood, she realized there was no longer any need to whisper. There was no one around to hear. There were no search lights or sirens to fear.

Pablo and Miguel had been supporting the weight of the plywood and blankets for nearly an hour. They carefully lifted it higher allowing Juanita to crawl out from the den that had seen them safely into America. Miguel came out next as Pablo tilted the heavy plywood to one side. Once free, Miguel slid the board out through the back doors and cast it noisily to the pavement behind the suburban. The blankets were loosely piled behind the backseat as Pablo tenderly lifted his precious cargo off the floor of the truck, cradling her frame in his strong arms. He turned to Elizabeth, who looked both relieved and exhausted, and said simply, "Thank you," using his best English.

With the Madonna wrapped securely in the blankets and laid carefully in the back, the Alvarez family and their new guardian were headed down US Highway 281 toward Brownsville. In the back she could hear Juanita quietly reciting something in Spanish, but she couldn't make out exactly what she was saying. She turned to Pablo who had agreed to sit in the front this time, "What is she saying?"

"It is a traditional prayer of thanks," he explained. "She is praising God for having delivered his children. It is a prayer that includes parts of the 'Cry of Dolores' offered by Miguel Hidalgo y Costilla, the priest who started the Mexican Revolution. He is the man our son is named for," he said proudly.

Elizabeth just shook her head in amazement and drove on through the dark toward home. When she pulled into the driveway of her three bedroom casita on the East side of Brownsville, she reached up and pushed the button on the small electronic box hooked over the visor. The garage door responded allowing her to slowly maneuvered the big suburban into its usual place.

"Please come in," she said with a gesture of her hand as she opened the back door leading into the kitchen. "*Mi casa es su casa.*" For this family her words were clearly more than just a traditional welcoming. Within a few minutes she had made them some sandwiches and poured everyone a glass of iced tea.

"Ham sandwiches and sweet tea is all I've got," she said almost as an apology, but to these refugees from another world it was a banquet.

They marveled at the size and furnishings of her home, having little to compare it to. They ate the dinner eagerly, everyone except Lupe. She was far more exhausted than usual from the whirlwind events of the day.

Lupe hadn't eaten any of the thin beef stew served over rice that her mother had prepared for lunch, and now she was too weak and short of breath to eat anything. Pablo insisted she drink some of the tea, but after just a few sips, Lupe slipped down onto the sofa and fell fast asleep.

"We will be on our way now," Pablo said, after finishing his sandwich.

"Absolutely not," Elizabeth commanded. "You are going to stay right here until we come up with a plan. You have nowhere to go, nowhere to sleep. And besides, this girl is in no condition to be going anywhere right now," she said pointing to Lupe resting comfortably for the first time all day.

Pablo turned to Juanita who shrugged slightly in response to his silent inquiry. "Okay, Miss Burke," Pablo conceded. "But in the morning, we must be on our way to Corpus Christi." He countered her insistence with his own, making sure she understood the temporary nature of their relationship.

Miguel had disappeared only to return from the garage carrying the Madonna with the blanket still covering it like a poorly wrapped Christmas gift. He carefully removed the blanket and stood the carving next to the small artificial fireplace in the family room. Before he turned back toward the kitchen, the young boy paused and crossed himself, offering a silent prayer. Elizabeth stood in stunned silence as she watched this boy, who had yet to utter a word in her presence. As she reflected on the events of the day she had a hard time digesting all that had happened. She marveled at the simplicity of this family's existence yet the incredible depth of their faith. For the second time that day she was reduced to tears, but this time they were tears of joy. She had confidence that somehow everything was going to be okay.

CHAPTER 3

Morning came far too early for Elizabeth. She had been on the phone until well after midnight, first with her father and then with Jennifer Morgan, her business partner. Afterward she spent another hour packing some essentials in a small red duffel bag.

Just after sunrise she dressed quickly and walked into the kitchen. The room was still dark but she could see a small human form kneeling on the floor in front of the Madonna. It was Miguel, and he hadn't yet noticed her. She stood quietly, hoping not to frighten the young man while at the same time marveling at his reverent pose.

Soon Pablo came into the family room from the spare bedroom and approached his son. The boy stood obediently and followed his father back into the bedroom.

Elizabeth now felt safe going on into the kitchen where she put on a pot of coffee, something she rarely did. Most mornings she just grabbed a single cup at the 7-Eleven on her way into the shop. Today she was going to need more than one cup, and she was sure Pablo and Juanita would want some as well.

As the coffee pot began to make its characteristic gurgling sound, the familiar aroma quickly filled the kitchen and family room. Elizabeth looked over to the sofa and saw Lupe still lying in the same position she'd assumed nearly ten hours earlier. A momentary panic raced through her mind. She looked more closely and saw the unmistakable rise and fall of her small chest under the blanket, allaying her fear. The child's breathing seemed easier than the night before, but it was still more rapid and labored than seemed normal for a sleeping child.

While the coffee was brewing, Elizabeth tossed a couple of pieces of bread into the toaster and found the butter and grape jelly in the refrigerator. She didn't have anything in the house to make a proper breakfast. She just wasn't much of a breakfast person, and since her divorce five years before, she ate most of her meals outside the house or brought something home already prepared. The vast majority of her meals consisted of a sandwich from the deli next door to her shop for lunch, and a pizza, Chick-fil-A, or something at the local diner for supper. She couldn't remember the last time she had actually cooked a meal for herself at home.

Pablo entered the main room, breaking her wandering thoughts. He was followed by Juanita and Miguel. All were dressed in the same clothes they'd worn the night before.

"We will be leaving as soon as Juanita gets Lupe up to brush her hair and teeth," Pablo announced.

"No," Elizabeth declared boldly. "I am going to take y'all to Corpus myself."

Pablo started to protest but she held up her hand using an international stop sign gesture.

"I told you yesterday that I was going to take care of this, and I have already worked it out," she insisted. "We are going to leave here in about an hour, once we've eaten a little toast and had some coffee and packed the car."

Pablo looked helplessly toward his wife, but she offered no response.

"On our way out of town, we'll stop by the Walmart and get these children some new clothes and some decent shoes." She had been appalled at the torn sneakers Miguel was wearing and Lupe's bare feet were just another testament to the family's extreme poverty.

"Then we'll head on up Highway 77 to Corpus Christi." She sounded like a drill sergeant laying out a set of plans for a group of fresh recruits.

"We cannot ask you to do this," Pablo explained.

"You didn't ask me," she said. "I'm just telling you what we're gonna do." Elizabeth suddenly realized her voice had a bit more Texan drawl than normal. She'd often used that tactic on her ex-husband when he argued about almost anything. She sometimes wondered if that had anything to do with the fact he was now her ex-husband.

The group shared four pieces of toast and each one had a cup of coffee, even Miguel. Lupe was able to drink a small glass of orange juice, even though Elizabeth wasn't sure how long it had been in the refrigerator. After loading her things in the suburban, Elizabeth asked if they were ready to go.

"We are ready," proclaimed Pablo, and he began leading his young family toward the garage.

"Wait a minute," Elizabeth said. "Aren't you forgetting something?"

As Pablo turned to look back, she was pointing at the Madonna. *"No, señora,*" he protested. "We want you to have her."

"Absolutely not," she said. "That carving is part of your family and I would not accept it even if you gave it to me," she stated emphatically. "Besides," she reasoned, "I never paid you for it."

"But, *Señora Burke,* you got us across the border. That was payment enough."

"I'm not going to discuss it any more. Miguel, come pick it up and put it in the truck so we can go."

Pablo reluctantly instructed his son to retrieve the carving and put it in the car. As the gangly young boy passed Elizabeth, she saw him smile for the first time since she'd met him. It wasn't merely a smile, it was a huge grin.

◆◆◆◆◆◆◆◆◆

After a quick stop for gas and another at the Walmart on the North side of town, Elizabeth cautiously began the drive up Highway 77 toward Corpus Christi. When she told her father, Jeb Murray, what she had done, and what she was planning to do, he told her she wasn't exactly out of the woods just yet. He explained that the border patrol usually operated another checkpoint along the main roads north from the valley where she would almost certainly be stopped. These secondary checkpoints were designed to catch illegals after they had gotten across border, but before they could get further into the heart of Texas. He told her they would usually set up about thirty miles inside the border so there would likely be one on Highway 77 somewhere south of Lyford. They might also be further north, up around Raymondville, but that was less likely.

Elizabeth had studied her map and decided to get off the highway onto County Road 835, then swing west over to Farm to Market Road 508. Then she'd go north on FM 2845 up to County Road 186 where she'd turn back to the East into Raymondville where she would get on 77 again. They should be home free assuming her dad's information was correct, but there was no guarantee that the border patrol might not set up a checkpoint on one of the farm-to-market roads. Her dad had suggested that was unlikely. The more worrisome prospect was a checkpoint north of Raymondville, because there simply wasn't an alternate route around 77 once she passed through that little town.

She followed the route according to plan, passing through several small towns, each one with a four-way stop or a traffic light. She imagined that a border patrol agent would be hanging out at every intersection, so after she got off the main highway she had insisted her passengers remain down on the floor of the suburban. She was certain a caucasian woman driving a big suburban with a Mexican family sitting in the passenger seats would be pretty much a dead giveaway.

Lupe and her mother were lying in the area behind the second set of seats where the entire family had hidden when they were crossing the border. Unlike the night before, there was plenty of room for them to stretch out, no longer sandwiched between the floor and a piece of plywood.

Pablo was lying on the floor in the space between the two sets of seats, while the more youthful and flexible Miguel curled up on the floor in front of the front passenger seat.

The plan seemed to be working perfectly as Elizabeth turned back onto the main highway north of Raymondville and sped away toward the coastal city of Corpus Christi. She hadn't seen any sign of the border patrol along the boring hour-long trek through parts of the King Ranch. As they reached the sleepy town of Kingsville, she decided they all needed some lunch. It had been several hours since they'd eaten those few pieces of toast, so she pulled into a McDonald's for some burgers and a clean restroom. Although she hadn't had anything to drink since her morning coffee, she needed to use the facilities and assumed the rest of her charges did as well. She parked well away from the building in the far corner of the lot and turned off the engine. She told Pablo that it was safe to get up off the floor, and immediately she saw Juanita stick her head up over the backseat. Miguel also started to uncoil from his hiding place. Everyone had risen off the floor except Lupe.

"Let's go get something to eat and use the restroom," Elizabeth suggested. As she opened her door to get out, she could hear Pablo explaining the plan to his family.

"Get back down!" she half shouted and half whispered. Just beyond the far corner of the restaurant she spotted a drab green pickup, the unmistakable vehicle of the US Border Patrol.

"We can't get out here!" she demanded as she started the engine again.

Obviously shaken, Elizabeth quickly backed out of the parking space even before she was sure all heads were down. Exiting the lot through the rear driveway, she turned her big truck onto the side street and headed back toward the highway. While waiting for the light to change, she could see two uniformed agents standing at the counter inside the restaurant. As soon as the light changed, she turned onto the highway and rapidly accelerated away from the danger.

"I'm sorry," she said, trying to calm her own nerves. "There were two border agents back there. I hope everyone can wait a little longer."

She drove on to the outskirts of Corpus, having totally forgotten about the urging of her bladder until she saw the large Valero truck stop just ahead. Now, she really needed to go. She didn't need gas, but decided to use the opportunity to fill up as well as get some much needed relief. She pulled up to one of the pumps at the far end of the row.

"Would you mind filling up the gas tank for me?" she asked Pablo as she quickly exited the suburban and headed into the convenience store.

Pablo pulled himself off the floor and saw the gasoline pump just outside the window. He sat in the seat behind the driver for a moment, scanning the scene, then opened the door and stepped out. He found the small door on the side of the truck where he had seen Elizabeth put gas in earlier that day, but when he tried to open it, it would not yield. He tried pulling from every edge without any success. Finally, in frustration, he hit it with his fist and the back edge popped open.

He removed the bright yellow cap from the fill line and turned to the pump. Confronted with six different grades of gasoline, he had no idea which one he should choose. He decided that an expensive truck like this one must require the gasoline with the largest number, but when he pressed it nothing happened. He looked at the small electronic screen and saw words moving rapidly across the bottom from right to left. Although he could speak English reasonably well, he had yet to master reading the words. He had no way of knowing that a credit or debit card had to be swiped before the fuel could be dispensed. He removed the nozzle from the pump and placed it in the opening, but still nothing happened.

"I'm sorry," Elizabeth said as she returned a few minutes later. "I didn't leave you my credit card."

She reached in her purse and produced a well worn Visa card and quickly swiped it through the reader. After declining offers of a car wash and receipt, she selected the lowest grade of regular gas then prompted Pablo to squeeze the handle which started the flow.

"I think it's safe for everyone to get out here," she announced. "You should all go to the bathroom, and there's a Subway inside where we can get some sandwiches." Pablo opened the door next to where he was fueling the truck and instructed his family as she had requested.

Lupe tried her best to smile when she saw Elizabeth open the back door, but it was difficult given her worsening shortness of breath. Juanita climbed down first, then both women helped the young girl get to her feet. Miguel had also gotten out of the car and was standing next to his father as he finished pumping the gas. As Pablo returned the nozzle to its holder, his son ambitiously stepped in to screw the cap back and close the door. He had to push it three times before the "One Push Latch" decided to hold. Elizabeth sent the four of them on ahead while she pulled the suburban into a parking space near the entrance.

The sandwich ordering went much more smoothly than Elizabeth had expected, largely because the young man behind the counter was also a Latino and spoke to the Alvarez family in their native tongue. Elizabeth thought it would be best for them to sit down and eat so they could talk about what to do next. As she was paying for the five six-inch sandwiches, again using her trusty

Visa card, she wondered how these people would eat if they were here on their own? The bill for just this one meal was over thirty dollars. She shook her head slowly with a questioning expression as she signed the receipt. How had they managed to get all the way up here eight years ago with a deathly ill newborn?

While Elizabeth had worked out what she thought were most of the details for getting these people to Corpus Christi, she hadn't really thought much beyond that. Now that they had reached the destination, where was the hospital Should they just go to the emergency room? She didn't even know the doctor's name. What would she do if he wasn't there?

Her thoughts were interrupted. "We go to the hospital now?" Pablo asked with an almost childlike anticipation.

"I guess so," she replied without much conviction.

"What is the problem?" he inquired, sensing her discomfort.

Hesitantly she offered, "In a city the size of Corpus I'm sure there are several hospitals. I'm not sure where to even start looking."

"It is a big white building with many floors," Pablo offered with certainty.

An older couple occupied the table next to their booth. They had been silently observing the activities of this odd group since they first sat down. The gentleman interrupted, "Excuse me, ma'am?"

The sound of a strange voice caused Elizabeth to turn abruptly, fearing the presence of a brown uniform.

"Based on his description, I suspect you're looking for Corpus General," he offered with a reassuring Texas twang.

Elizabeth just nodded silently, having been caught totally off guard.

"If you just stay on this road about two miles, you'll see it on your right," the man explained. "It's the only multistory white hospital I know of, and I've lived here most of my life."

"Thank you, sir," she said, not sure what else to say as she began to slide out of the booth.

Elizabeth caught the eye of the elderly woman as she watched the small entourage. She looked into her aging blue eyes.

"God be with you, dear," the woman offered softly with a knowing smile.

On the side of the eight story white building were the words EMERGENCY ENTRANCE in bold red letters. As they entered through the automatic doors, she saw a glass window in the wall in front of them. A middle-aged woman was busily typing something on a computer and acted as though she hadn't noticed them at first. As Elizabeth approached, the clerk looked up and slowly slid the glass window to one side.

"May I help you?" she offered in a tired sounding monotone.

"Yes," Elizabeth replied. "This little girl had surgery here about eight years ago and she's having problems again." Somehow, as her words were being formed, she realized how unusual they must sound.

"What kind of trouble is she having?" the clerk asked in a manner that suggested this was not the appropriate place for a surgical follow-up.

"She is having trouble breathing and she's tired all the time."

The clerk robotically turned to her left and picked up a clip board. She handed it to Elizabeth and said, "You'll need to fill this out."

She returned to the group as they sat in a row of chairs near the entrance. Everyone except Miguel. He was wandering down the wide hallway toward the main lobby beyond the attention of his parents. Juanita was speaking softly to Lupe, and Pablo was answering the clinical questions Elizabeth was asking as she did her best to fill out the three page form. It didn't take long since the entire section having to do with insurance or government assistance was left blank.

She didn't know what to put down for an address so she just left that area blank as well, but when she tried to return the form to the clerk the woman said she had to have an address or she couldn't register the patient. Elizabeth quickly wrote in her own address, since she was not going to come right out and tell her the family was in the country illegally, even though she was sure the clerk suspected as much.

When she returned the clipboard a second time, the clerk scanned it quickly, then she wrote with a red highlighter across the insurance section – NONE.

The hospital personnel were used to all kinds of people showing up without insurance. They came to the ER for treatment for everything from kids with fevers and runny noses to the gunshot wounds of victims of the local drug wars. Some were illegal aliens, but the majority were simply poor or unemployed. Many of those who were citizens were actually eligible for either Medicaid or the State Children's Health Insurance Program, known simply by its acronym SCHIP.

Medicaid is the government-funded program designed to provide basic insurance benefits to anyone whose family income falls below the poverty level. This included a sizable part of the local population, so this hospital was very familiar with, and reliant upon, payments from the Medicaid program. The biggest problem they faced was getting people enrolled. A sizable percentage of the uninsured who came here for treatment were eligible for Medicaid, but they had either never heard of the program or had not known they needed to sign up for it. Then there were those proud few who refused to be labeled with the social stamp, "Medicaid Patient." They were simply too proud to accept the government's charity.

SCHIP is a slightly different program. It was designed to help working families and single parents who made too much money to qualify for Medicaid but not enough to afford private insurance. Often these were people who were self-employed or worked for small companies that didn't offer group health insurance as a benefit.

This hospital, like many others, employed several full-time people whose job was to get uninsured patients and families signed up for Medicaid, and to a lesser extent SCHIP. Administrators in hospitals across the country had initiated similar efforts, considering them to be vital to their economic survival. The need to actively get people enrolled in these programs was especially important here in South Texas, where the number of uninsured was measured in the millions.

At Corpus General they had developed an aggressive community outreach program, organized and run by the hospital's social workers, and in recent years they had been successful in getting hundreds of eligible families signed up for a variety of government health care programs. Even so, the hospital's social workers were often tasked with enrolling patients in Medicaid as they arrived in the emergency department.

This part of the hospital used to be known simply as the Emergency Room, largely based on tradition. Forty or fifty years before, most hospitals had only a small receiving area where the rare ambulance would arrive with a critically ill or injured victim. Today, ambulances were coming and going constantly, during all hours of the day and night. In addition, the so-called walk-in patients accounted for thousands of emergency visits each year in this hospital and millions of ER visits across America. As a result, hospitals nationwide were forced to major expand emergency facilities, and this hospital was no exception.

There were already twenty-four beds in nearly constant use, and a temporary wall had been constructed just to the right of the registration desk with a sign that read, "Please Excuse Our Mess As We Expand To Serve You Better." They were doubling the capacity of what was now known as the "Emergency Department" because it had become the main portal of entry into the hospital.

Elizabeth had been sitting anxiously awaiting further word from the clerk who had told her to have a seat more than an hour ago. Pablo sat silently holding Lupe firmly in his lap, and she had drifted off to sleep shortly after they arrived. Juanita sat silently next to her husband, but periodically she reached across and spoke softly to Miguel after he returned from his wanderings.

Across the sizable waiting room sat a uniformed police officer, reading a magazine containing the latest updates on *Guns and Ammo*. She could see the holster on the right side of his belt along with one of those new, bright yellow tasers on the other side. His torso seemed a bit out of proportion to his head and arms due to the standard issue body armor worn by most police officers these days. Violence against police had been on the rise everywhere, but nowhere more than in the southern half of Texas where drug raids usually ended badly for the perpetrators, but all too often the police radios crackled with the frantic plea, "Shots fired, officer down! Send backup immediately."

The middle-aged officer occasionally looked up to investigate a new patient as he or she entered through the sliding glass doors, but he hadn't spoken to anyone. The lone interruption of his routine had been when a nurse came through the controlled access door and motioned for him to assist her. He was gone for only a minute before returning to his post and to his magazine.

What was he there for, Elizabeth wondered silently. Did they anticipate some sort of violence? Maybe he was guarding the place to protect against drug addicts breaking in to steal prescription meds. While these thoughts were part of what was running around in her head, she was mostly concerned about having her recent criminal action discovered by any law enforcement officer.

"Lupe Alvarez?" the nurse called out loudly in no particular direction. The double sliding doors leading back to the heart of the emergency department open noisily just before the young Latin American nurse appeared. She was wearing dark blue scrubs and was holding a clipboard containing the forms Elizabeth had filled out nearly two hours earlier.

Elizabeth, Pablo, and Miguel all rose at the same time. Lupe was awake but continued to rest in her father's arms as they moved toward the open doorway.

"Are you family?" The nurse asked, looking quizzically at Elizabeth.

"No, I'm just a friend," she replied, again not having thought through the process.

"You'll have to wait out here until we get her evaluated," the nurse said without a hint of apology in her tone.

"But ..." Elizabeth protested.

Pablo turned to her and said, "It will be okay, *señora*."

The Alvarez trio followed the nurse, and the double doors closed behind them just as quickly as they had opened. Elizabeth returned to her seat next to Juanita. She wondered why the child's mother had not accompanied her daughter, but then she realized that Mexican culture was far different from her own in these situations. As the head of the family, it was expected the father would assume total control of virtually all interactions with outsiders involving any family member, including her. To have gone with him without specific invitation would have been an insult, a challenge to his authority. The thought of rising to her feet when her daughter's name was called never even entered her mind.

The two women remained silent, mostly because each feared sharing their anxieties. Elizabeth wondered to herself whether they might have come all this way for nothing. Would the hospital ultimately turn this young girl away because her family couldn't pay?

Looking around the huge waiting room, more times now than she could count, it was clear that most of the people waiting were of Latin descent. They all appeared to be poor, and in every respect not unlike the family she had brought here. By all accounts, she was the true alien in the crowd, and the longer she sat there the more she felt that way.

Elizabeth decided to make a call to her father back in Brownsville, just to let him know they had arrived in Corpus safely. She probably should have called an hour ago, but for some reason she hadn't even thought of it until just now. She pulled her well-worn Nokia phone from her purse and flipped it open. She rapidly dialed his number, but when she hit the call button the phone remained silent. There was no cell service inside the building. She turned to Juanita and pointed to her phone, then to the ED entrance as she explained, "*Necesito usarlo telefono. Regresarlo momentito.*"

Juanita acknowledged her statement with a polite nod and a brief smile. Once outside, Elizabeth touched the send button again, and this time she confirmed it was ringing.

"We're not home right now. Leave us a message and we'll call you back ... maybe." Her father's attempt at humor always seemed inappropriate, but her stepmother seemed to like it.

"Pop, this is Lizzy," she announced with no hope of a response. "We made it to Corpus okay using the route you suggested. We are in the emergency room right now." She found herself talking louder than necessary, believing that somehow there would be a loss of volume in the recording process. "I'll give you a call when I know something more. Love you." She started to close the phone when she realized she had forgotten something. "Oh wait," she said, this time assuming the machine was going to hang up on her. "I may need the name of that doctor you said you knew here in Corpus, if we can't get anywhere here in the ER. I'll talk to you soon, bye."

In the examining room Lupe had been made to take off the new white ruffled top and denim skirt Elizabeth had bought for her earlier that morning. Pablo and Miguel waited just outside the door while an aide helped her change, When they were allowed back in they found the bashful young girl wrapped in a hospital gown many sizes too large for her tiny frame. Another nurse came in to take her vital signs and after she'd written them on the clipboard she quickly stepped back out into the hall, closing the door casually behind her.

The nervous father paced slowly back and forth between the narrow stretcher and the wall, while Miguel sat on the small stool on the opposite side of Lupe's bed. He began turning around on the rotating seat until Pablo finally made him stop. After about fifteen minutes there was a sharp knock on the door followed by the almost simultaneous appearance of a rather large woman. She was also carrying a clipboard which she appeared to be studying as she introduced herself.

"I'm Frieda Johnson, and I'm from the business office here at the hospital," she repeated for the umpteenth time that day, and no telling how many times in the twelve years she'd worked there. "I understand you don't have any insurance, so I came by to see how you would be settling your bill." Her voice was cold and matched only by her intimidating stare directly into the face of this small Mexican man. She already knew the hopelessness of the situation, but on more than a few occasions she'd had illegals pack up and leave the ER when she mentioned a financial obligation. She quickly recognized that would not be the case this time.

"I don't know what you mean," Pablo said cautiously.

"Well, the standard charge for the emergency department evaluation is five hundred dollars. If lab tests and x-rays are needed there will be an additional charge," she explained, her voice having reverted to an almost robotic tone. "Depending on the extent of the work-up our doctor orders, it is likely your bill will exceed two or three thousand dollars." As she spoke she was looking back down at the clipboard. Then as she finished she raised her large head, made even bigger by a modified '70s hairstyle, once more employing her icy stare. She was hoping against hope it would have the desired effect.

"Since you don't have any insurance," she added accusingly, "I am authorized to offer you a fifty percent discount for cash." She paused briefly before concluding with, "We accept cash, all major credit cards, or a local bank check."

Pablo stood silently for a moment, processing what he had just heard. He then spoke to this woman who was easily twice his size, employing his best English. "*Señora*, we do not have any money to pay you. We have come here looking for the doctor who fixed my daughter's heart eight years ago in this hospital."

In all her years of seeking payments from people in the emergency department, this was the first time she'd heard this particular excuse. "Well, I don't know anything about that," she offered. "I just know that there will be a charge for the care your daughter receives here in our emergency department."

"Please, *señora*, I just want to talk to the doctor."

"All right, sir, I'll see what I can do."

With that she left the room mumbling something about a "deadbeat" just under her breath. Pablo had no idea what she was saying. She made her way to the nurses' station and waited a few seconds for the nurse to hang up the phone.

"He isn't gonna leave, and you know I can't make him," she offered in resignation.

"It's okay, Frieda," the nurse replied. "Dr. Franks is gonna see her next."

"Wish we could just transfer these illegals to the county hospital. They're the ones who get all the government support money," the angry woman offered as she turned away.

Everyone in the hospital was acutely aware that such transfers had been made illegal under the Emergency Medical Treatment and Active Labor Act passed by Congress in 1986. The so-called "Anti-Dumping Act" had been designed to keep private hospitals from transferring, or "dumping" patients on other hospitals based solely on their inability to pay.

Before EMTALA, patients who were in active labor or who had other non-life-threatening conditions could be denied cared in private emergency rooms if they couldn't produce proof of insurance. There had been reports of babies being born in the backseats of cars in hospital parking lots, as well as patients having undiagnosed appendicitis that progressed to rupture before they could be transported to a public hospital. Stories of patients who were simply told where the tax-supported county hospital was, perhaps aided by a hand-drawn map, then left to their own devices to get there had spread rapidly. While many of these accounts were exaggerated, there was no doubt that some, if not most, facilities were guilty of dumping unwanted patients for economic reasons.

With the passage of EMTALA it became a crime to arbitrarily deny any patient care in any emergency department unless the patient agreed. Even if the hospital didn't offer the particular service the patient required, they were compelled by law to arrange to have them transported as a hospital-to-hospital transfer, but only after their condition had been stabilized and the receiving hospital had agreed to accept the transfer. Violations of the law resulted in significant fines, starting at fifty thousand dollars per occurrence.

The new law had the effect that legislators had intended. Patient "dumping" stopped almost immediately. However, like most government attempts to regulate activities in the private sector, EMTALA had several unintended consequences. Over the next few years, visits to the emergency departments of hospitals across the country skyrocketed. People who had never sought medical care quickly learned they couldn't be turned away. All they had to do was show up at any hospital's door. EDs had effectively become free walk-in clinics for the poor and others who simply chose not to carry health insurance because they considered it too expensive. Most hospitals were forced to expand their ED, both in numbers of beds and personnel to handle the increase in volume. Typical emergency departments went from eight to ten beds with one physician on duty, to giant thirty to fifty bed units with five or six emergency medicine specialists available around the clock.

Once hospitals understood the new paradigm, they were able to make the most of the situation by taking advantage of the huge potential revenue available through Medicaid, thus the need to sign up every eligible patient for this government benefit. Unfortunately, there were still many uninsured patients who didn't qualify for any government support, specifically the illegals whose numbers were also growing rapidly, especially here in South Texas. It was unclear whether denying illegals would fall under the federal EMTALA law, and so far no hospital had been willing to challenge it in the courts. However, since illegals tended to be more naïve about the system, if the hospital staff could intimidate them into leaving the emergency department voluntarily, they'd be able to avoid providing free care. This practice was a little risky, but it sometimes worked because most of the illegals were reluctant to report anyone to the authorities for fear of exposing themselves to possible deportation. Clearly, this is what Frieda had unsuccessfully attempted to accomplish with her not-so-subtle conversation with Pablo.

Elizabeth sat with Juanita, patiently awaiting word from anyone who could tell her what was going on beyond the opaque sliding doors with the words AUTHORIZED PERSONNEL ONLY written boldly across them. She found herself mindlessly watching portions of the afternoon television programming that was displayed on the large screen mounted high in the corner of the waiting room. Most of the people sitting around her were also waiting quietly, so the television volume was considerably louder than necessary. The shouting of the crazies on *The Jerry Springer Show* accounted for most of the noise in the room, but there was a two-year-old child who had been crying continuously for the last ten minutes. He was apparently suffering from a painful ear infection or something similar.

The nurse returned to Lupe's room after about forty-five minutes accompanied by a short, stockily built doctor wearing green scrubs and a short white jacket that looked as though it hadn't been pressed for some time. His name tag was clipped to the breast pocket containing a couple of pens, a small flashlight and some white index cards. Dr. John Franks had been part of the large group of docs contracted to cover this emergency department for the last eighteen months. Before that he'd worked in other ERs beginning in Houston, where he'd completed his residency. He had spent some time in Bay City, then moved to Victoria, where he lived and worked for fifteen years. His wife had wanted to live nearer the coast, so once their kids were out of school they moved to Corpus.

"So," Dr. Franks began. "I understand your daughter is having problems breathing."

"*Si*, I mean, yes," Pablo responded, wanting to make sure the doctor knew he could speak English.

After a few minutes of questioning, the doctor thought he had a good understanding of the situation. He began his examination, and while listening to Lupe's back with a stethoscope, his eyebrows raised almost by themselves. The loud rushing sound over the middle of her back might have been audible even without the amplification of the instrument. Her breathing was also accompanied by the distinct sounds of fluid accumulation, as she was clearly struggling to move air through her congested airways. He moved around to listen to the front of her chest and noticed the rapid, strong heartbeat that was accompanied by a clearly abnormal rubbing sound. He removed the stethoscope from his ears and placed it back in the large pocket near the waist of his white jacket. He placed his right hand softly across the left side of the young girl's chest and felt the rapid thumping of her heart through the rib cage.

"Well," he said as he turned to face Pablo, "it's obvious she's in the early stages of congestive heart failure, and based on what you've told me I suspect her coarctation of the aorta has recurred." Like most doctors, Franks was liberal with his use of terminology that most people, including Pablo, weren't likely to understand. Even so, the anxious father nodded his head in agreement.

"I'm going to get a chest x-ray and give her a breathing treatment," the doctor announced, speaking more to the nurse than to Pablo. "I'll check back again when we have the x-ray report."

The chest x-ray showed the heart was significantly larger than normal, and the fluid that was backing up into her lungs gave a fine white lace-like appearance to what should have been mostly black, air-filled areas. Having confirmed his suspicion, Dr. Franks picked up the phone and dialed the office of the on-call pediatrician. In a few minutes Dr. Alex Gordon, a veteran children's doctor, called back. Franks explained the clinical findings and as much of the history as he knew. Forty-five minutes later Dr. Gordon arrived to examine Lupe for himself.

Pablo and Miguel had remained in Lupe's room the entire time, except for one brief period when Miguel stepped down the hall to use the public facilities. A technician with a small green box mounted on a rolling pole had come into the room to administer a breathing treatment to the young girl about ten minutes after Dr. Franks' visit. Following the treatment, Lupe had drifted off to sleep, but Pablo could not detect any significant improvement in her breathing.

Dr. Gordon stepped into the room and asked Pablo all the same questions he'd been asked several times already.

"They performed heart surgery on her, here in this hospital eight years ago," Pablo began. "The doctor was Chinese I think, but we did not see him again after the surgery."

Something about the story sounded familiar. Alex was trying to remember that Asian surgeon who used to be on the hospital staff. As Pablo continued to explain how his daughter had recovered and was a normal child until about two years ago, the doctor seemed lost in his efforts to recall the details of what he vaguely remembered of a controversial case.

"Do you remember the doctor's name?" he asked.

Pablo responded, *"No, señor,* I'm sorry I don't."

"Dr. Hwang," Miguel stated confidently.

All eyes turned to the young boy who stood on the opposite side of his sister's bed. Pablo had been teaching him some of the English he had learned, but Miguel was quite shy about using it. Now, it was his turn to step forward and share what he recalled of that final encounter with Dr. Hwang. The doctor's name had been clearly visible on his name badge, and along with the vivid image of the larger-than-life hero, it had forever been burned into the young boy's memory.

"Now I remember this case," exclaimed Dr. Gordon with a sudden brightness to his face. "This was the little baby at the center of that huge controversy a few years back," he stated, addressing the nurse who clearly had no idea what he was talking about.

Gordon returned to the nurses' station and immediately called the administrator's office, hoping to catch him before he left for the day.

"Mr. Thompson's office," the secretary said.

"Hi, is Al still there?" he asked.

"I think so. Let me check."

"This is Al Thompson."

"Al, this is Alex Gordon."

"Hello Dr. Gordon, what can I do for you?"

"You remember that infant back in the nineties that Charles Hwang operated on for a heart problem?" Franks asked, knowing that Thompson would recall.

"Of course. Why?" Thompson asked suspiciously.

"Well, you might want to come down here to the emergency department. That baby is now an eight-year-old girl and she's back with congestive heart failure and a recurrence of her aortic coarctation," he explained. "Her father is looking for Hwang."

There was a long uncomfortable silence, then Al finally responded, "I'll be right down."

As the hospital administrator approached the desk where Dr. Gordon was writing his note in Lupe's chart, all the staff members seemed to take notice and made sure they at least appeared to be busy.

Without any additional greeting, Thompson interrupted the doctor's efforts asking in a somewhat demanding tone, "What's the kid's name?"

"Lupe Alvarez, they're in room eleven," Gordon replied while nodding his head toward the closed door immediately across the hallway.

Al Thompson had never met the father of the baby known to him only as "the potential disaster from Mexico." He had labeled her with that designation during a presentation to the medical board of the hospital. On the way down from his office, he had reenacted those challenging four weeks from eight years before. Within twenty-four hours of Hwang's suspension, he was contacted by an attorney from Austin, who demanded that his client have his privileges reinstated immediately. Thompson explained the due process contained within the medical staff bylaws and offered to schedule a hearing with the medical executive committee. The two men had a heated exchange, during which Thompson made it clear that he was not going to yield to the attorney's demands. A date for the hearing was agreed to later that month. Once the hospital's attorneys got involved there were numerous meetings held in Thompson's office prior to the hearing. They met with every physician on the executive committee to make certain they each understood the gravity of the situation, and he wanted to make certain that the hearing was carried out by the book. He knew that these proceedings could be subpoenaed in the event Dr. Hwang decided to file a restraint of trade suit against the hospital and the medical staff. Drs. Gardner and Burns had also been asked to meet with the attorneys on two separate occasions, supposedly to refresh everyone's memory. In truth Thompson simply wanted to make sure they all had the same story at the hearing.

By the time all these meetings occurred, Lupe Alvarez, her parents, and her four-year-old brother were well on their way back to Mexico. The baby had experienced a remarkable recovery and was discharged from the hospital on the seventh day after the epic operation. There were no follow-up appointments scheduled, since the family had headed straight back to Matamoros.

During the four-hour hearing, Dr. Hwang sat completely silent. Occasionally he would turn to his lawyer and whisper something, but he did not offer any open testimony on his own behalf based on his attorney's instructions. Following the formal proceedings, the executive committee unanimously voted to uphold the summary suspension based on Dr. Hwang's obvious disregard for the medical staff bylaws and for placing the hospital and medical staff at risk of professional liability and potential civil prosecution.

Even before the hearing, Al had submitted notification of the summary suspension to the Texas State Board of Medical Examiners and the National Practitioner Data Bank as required by law. Once the hearing was over, the governing body of the state medical licensure received details of the actions taken by the hospital medical staff against Dr. Hwang. It was then up to the state board to decide whether or not his actions constituted sufficient grounds to suspend his license to practice medicine in the state of Texas.

From Hwang's perspective the report to the practitioners' data bank was of nearly equal gravity to the potential loss of his Texas license, but Thompson didn't care about any of that. Those were Hwang's problems, not his.

While he could have appealed the findings of the executive committee to the entire medical board, on advice of his counsel, Hwang elected not to do so. His lawyer told him he'd have his opportunity to appeal but at a different level. So, Hwang left Corpus for parts unknown, and Al never inquired as to where he'd gone. As far as he was concerned he and the hospital had dodged a bullet.

Thompson stepped into the small exam room where the Mexican trio had been waiting for well over three hours now. He introduced himself and shook Pablo's hand briefly without even a hint of compassion. He explained that Dr. Hwang was no longer a member of their medical staff and he had no knowledge of his whereabouts. Pablo wasn't very familiar with this type of formal language but he understood that the doctor who had saved his daughter's life was no longer in Corpus Christi.

"What about the other doctor who cared for my daughter?" he asked.

"As I recall Drs. Gardner and Burns cared for your child after her surgery," Al stated hesitantly, as if he wasn't certain. "Neither of them is a pediatric surgeon, so I don't really think they can help you, I mean help your daughter."

"My Lupe needs to have another operation," he insisted.

"How did you get here?" Al asked with an angry undertone.

"Our friend, *Señora Burke*, brought us here from Brownsville."

"Where is your friend now?" Thompson insisted.

"She is in the waiting room. They would not let her come in here with us."

Thompson turned on his heels and headed straight out the door, angrily closing it behind him. He walked briskly through the sliding double doors out into the waiting room. He scanned the room quickly with his eyes, then half shouted, "Ms. Burke?"

Elizabeth had initially seen a man come through the doors but since he was not wearing scrubs or a white coat she paid little attention. However, when she heard her name called she jumped up and headed rapidly toward the man who she hoped had some news about Lupe.

"That's me!" she said raising her hand and waving toward him.

As she approached, Thompson did not offer his hand but merely said, "Are you Ms. Burke?"

"Yes, I am," she said with a hopeful smile.

"Would you mind coming with me?" Thompson said, as he began walking down the hall toward the main hospital foyer. "I'm Mr. Thompson, the hospital administrator," he added without further explanation or returning her smile.

Thompson escorted Elizabeth into a small conference room which was ordinarily used to deliver bad news to family members of patients who didn't make it out of the emergency room. There was a small sofa and two side chairs in the room, which contained no windows and only a single landscape painting over the seating area.

"Please have a seat," Al recommended sharply.

Elizabeth chose a spot on one end of the sofa and looked expectantly at Mr. Thompson. She had expected to hear that Lupe would be going to surgery soon, but what she heard was far different.

"Why did you bring that girl and her family here?" he questioned angrily. "You had no right to do that."

"It was my understanding from talking with her father that she'd had her original surgery in this hospital," Elizabeth explained, her tone questioning why he was challenging her this way.

"That may well be true," he conceded, "but we are under no obligation to care for a Mexican national in our facility just because she was a patient here eight years ago."

Elizabeth was having trouble understanding exactly what she was hearing. Was this man denying any responsibility for the care this child had received? Was what he was saying legal?

Before she could formulate a response he added, "You have put us in a very difficult situation bringing her here."

As she listened, she wondered if this man had any idea of the situation that Lupe was facing. What about her family? Weren't they the ones who were truly facing the greatest difficulty?

Thompson continued, "It is my understanding in speaking to Dr. Gordon, our pediatrician on call, that this young girl requires a surgical treatment that we do not offer in this hospital. Therefore other arrangements will need to be made for her care. She simply can't stay here."

After all the events of the last twenty-four hours, including the border crossing, Elizabeth was totally unprepared for what she had just heard. "So what are we supposed to do?"

"I really don't know," Thompson said without much sympathy. "The doctor who treated her before is no longer on staff here, and I have no idea where he is."

Elizabeth hesitated then asked, "Is there anyone here who can help us find him?"

Thompson thought carefully. Perhaps this was his opportunity to once again dodge the bullet. "Let me speak to Dr. Gordon and see what he recommends. Why don't you come back into the examining room with me? Let's see what we can work out." His voice had taken on a slightly softer tone.

He led her back through the waiting room where Juanita looked up hopefully, prompting Elizabeth to motion for her to stay seated, indicating that everything was going to be okay. Once through the double doors, Thompson led her to room eleven where she joined Pablo, Miguel, and Lupe for the first time in more than four hours.

"Are you doing okay?" she asked Pablo.

"Yes," he said, "but they tell me the doctor is not here."

"I know, they told me the same thing," she said. "The administrator told me they can't treat her here."

Pablo looked at Elizabeth with a new anxiety and sadness in his face. "What can we do now?"

"I asked him if there is someone who can help us find the doctor, and he said he would, but, I just don't know."

It was another ten minutes before Dr. Gordon reentered the exam room. "I have no way of knowing where Dr. Hwang is, or whether he's even still practicing," he offered apologetically. "But I do know a surgeon from back in my days at Wilford Hall in San Antonio who I can recommend, and I think he can probably help."

"Who is Dr. Hwang?" Elizabeth asked, not knowing that the mystery surgeon's identity had been revealed.

"Hwang was the surgeon who performed this girl's first operation, but he is no longer around," Gordon explained.

Elizabeth was beginning to understand the bigger picture now. "So who is this other doctor that you say may be able to help Lupe?"

"His name is Jack Roberts, and he's one of the foremost heart surgeons in the country," Gordon added for emphasis. "The only problem is, he's up in Fort Worth."

From Corpus to Fort Worth is an eight hour drive, but it was only a one-hour flight to DFW International Airport on American Eagle. Southwest Airlines also offered flights from Corpus, but only into Love Field in Dallas. Either way, Elizabeth knew that the cost of flying this family to North Texas was not something she could easily absorb.

"How do we know that if we go to Fort Worth we won't face the same situation we have here?" she asked, hinting at the disgust she felt with the way Thompson had treated them.

"Let me give Jack a call," Dr. Gordon offered, "and make sure it's okay for me to send you there."

Alex Gordon left the room and flipped through his pocket address book where he quickly found a number for his long time friend.

Back in his days at Wilford Hall Medical Center on Lackland Air Force Base in San Antonio, the young pediatrician had worked closely with the ambitious Dr. Roberts as he established the military's first children's cardiac surgery program. Alex had left the service shortly after Jack, and since then he had referred several difficult cases to his friend in Fort Worth

"Hello, Jack?" he asked, as a male voice answered the phone.

"No, this is the answering service. How may I help you?" The man sounded detached, as if reading a script.

"This is Dr. Alex Gordon in Corpus Christi, Texas. I need to get ahold of Dr. Roberts," he said with a slight urgency in his voice.

"I can page the doctor. Can I tell him the nature of your call?"

"Yes," Alex clearly understood the need for more information. "Tell him this is Dr. Alex Gordon and that I need to speak with him regarding a patient I have here in Corpus."

"I will page the doctor right now. May I have a number where he can return your call?"

Once he'd provided the callback information, Alex hung up and made his way back across the hall and stuck his head in the room to let the Alvarez family know that he was waiting for a return call from his friend.

"But Fort Worth is very far," Pablo objected. "You cannot take us there."

"I most certainly can," she proclaimed, "and I will, as soon as I'm sure they're willing to accept Lupe as a patient."

"But *señora*, I can't let you do that," he protested. "We can get there okay."

"There is no way!" she announced with absolute certainty, even though she wouldn't put it past Pablo to find a way to get his family anywhere he believed he needed to take them. "I'm going to take you, and that's that."

❖❖❖❖❖❖❖❖❖

"Hello, this is Jack Roberts."

"Hi, Jack, long time no see!" Alex said with the casual ease that comes from years of service together.

"Hey, Alex, how are you?" Jack asked.

"I'm fine. Thanks for calling me back."

"Sure, what's up?"

"Well, I've got a bit of a problem," Alex offered, understating the obvious. "I've got this little eight-year-old Mexican girl down here in our ER in congestive heart failure. Seems she was operated on here by Charles Hwang when she was only a few days old."

"Hwang? I'm not sure I know him," Jack questioned.

"He was a pediatric surgeon whose privileges were suspended after he operated on this kid. Seems he didn't have privileges to do the procedure, and from what I've been told he lost his license after a high-profile appeal."

"I vaguely remember hearing something about that, but I didn't really pay any attention."

"Yeah, the last I heard the guy moved to Canada," Alex offered. "Anyway, he fixed her coarctation and apparently she did well until a couple years ago when she started showing signs of recurrence. Now, today she showed up here in our ER with clear signs of a recurrence."

"Are you wanting to transfer her up here?" Jack asked, already knowing the answer.

"Yeah, she's stable enough right now, but according to the dad, she's been getting progressively worse over the last few weeks. He brought her here looking for Hwang, but as you know we don't have anybody in this town who I would trust to fix this."

"Have you considered sending her up to Houston? It would certainly be closer," Jack said.

"Right, right. I already thought of that, but those guys are a royal pain to deal with. Besides I'd really rather you take care of her if you could. Super nice family and it would sure help us out."

"Of course, I'd be happy to help, provided you think she's stable enough to travel."

"Great! I really appreciate it," Alex replied with considerable relief in his voice. "The family has a friend from down in Brownsville who brought them up here. I suspect she will be helping them arrange transportation to Fort Worth."

"Do you think she can drive them up here? I wouldn't feel comfortable transporting a kid in congestive failure in a commercial plane without supplemental oxygen."

"I hadn't thought of that, but you're right. I'll tell her she'll need to drive them. I don't get the impression that she's got the resources to pay for the whole family to fly up there anyway."

"Just give her my office number and have her call Mary Anne to set things up for me to see the child in my office later this week."

"Okay, thanks," Alex offered gratefully.

"Sure. Anytime," Jack replied.

"Say, when are you coming down to do some fishing? The speckled trout have been running pretty good lately."

"I really wish I could, Alex, maybe next year," Jack said, knowing full well that he wasn't likely to be able to take his old friend up on his standing offer anytime soon.

"You know you're always welcome," Alex added.

The two men said their good-byes, then Alex hung up and went to deliver the good news to the family. He explained to Elizabeth that she or someone would need to call Dr. Roberts' office the following morning and speak to Mary Anne, his office manager. He gave her the number and told her that she would be the one to make all the arrangements.

"She will have to go by some form of ground transportation," he added. "Dr. Roberts said that she might not tolerate flying without supplemental oxygen because of the pressure difference, even though the planes are all pressurized. Commercial jets maintain a cabin pressure equal to about ten thousand feet above sea level, and given how short of breath she is, he wasn't sure she could handle it."

"We'll be driving," Elizabeth said, not considering any of the potential problems of air travel.

The nurse returned to provide written instructions before they were allowed to leave. As the nurse was reciting her meaningless discharge instructions Elizabeth was observing Lupe. Despite still breathing faster than normal, she seemed to have a little more energy than she'd had any time since she first saw her, twenty-four hours earlier. Elizabeth stayed with her while Pablo and Miguel stepped out of the room. She was able to dress herself and put on her new sneakers without help.

"What is your relationship to this family?" the nurse asked Elizabeth, suspecting she probably employed one or both of the parents as domestic help.

"I just met this little girl and her family yesterday in Matamoros," she admitted as much to herself as to the nurse.

"So," she said dragging it out as a question, "why are you ..."

"Because they needed help."

That night Elizabeth got a room at the Super 8 with two full-sized beds and a small rollaway. Pablo and Miguel shared one bed while Juanita and Lupe shared the other. The small rollaway was actually more comfortable than she'd expected, but perhaps it had something to do with being totally exhausted. The combination of sitting for hours in an emergency room, the stress of her criminal actions, and the emotional strain watching this family struggle against incredible odds, had led to a numbing fatigue she'd not experienced before. As soon as her head hit the pillow she was asleep.

◆◆◆◆◆◆◆◆◆

The long drive from the central gulf coast to Fort Worth was almost entirely interstate highway so it was pretty boring compared to what the quintet had been through the previous two days. It was punctuated by the occasional stop for gas, sandwiches, and Dairy Queen Blizzards. The latter brought smiles all around, but especially for Lupe and Miguel. Elizabeth couldn't determine if either child had ever tasted ice cream before, but she was certain they'd never had it with chunks of candy mixed in.

Prior to leaving the motel, Elizabeth had called her father again to let him know what had transpired in Corpus and her decision to drive the Alvarez family to Fort Worth. He had always understood what truly motivated his daughter. Even as a child she was the one who stood up to the boys who tried to bully her little brother. In high school she had volunteered on Thanksgiving to serve meals to the people at the homeless shelter. Later in life she had been one of those moms who ferried their kids to every event or activity and she'd been an active participant in the PTA. For her to take on a project like this, out of the blue, was not the least bit out of character for his Lizzy. She wouldn't let anyone get away with calling her that except the guy she called Pop.

"Hey, Lizzy, I tried to call you back yesterday afternoon," her father offered apologetically. "All I got was that guy saying the customer you have called is either out of range or has turned off the phone, try again later."

Elizabeth explained that there was no cellular service inside the hospital and when they finally got away from that place it was after eight o'clock. She had simply forgotten to call him back, what with the stop at McDonald's and then checking in at the motel.

"Listen kiddo, you do what you gotta do," he offered in support of her decision. "I'll keep an eye on your place while you're gone. Anything else you need me to do?"

"There is one thing, Pop," she hesitated. "Don't say anything to Tommy about where I am or what I'm doing."

Tommy was her twenty-five-year-old son who worried about her all the time, especially when she went over into Mexico. He was away on a business trip this week, but if he called to check on her, which he was sure to do, he would call Pop if he was unable to get ahold of her.

"So, what do you want me to tell him if he calls?"

"I don't know," she pleaded. "Just make something up. Tell him I've gone to visit Louise in San Antonio. No wait, he knows her number so he'd call there." She was tired of trying to figure everything out. "Just tell him whatever you can think of so he won't worry."

"Okay, I'll take care of it. By the way, where are you gonna stay?"

"I talked to my friend Andie Lawrence right before I called you. She and her husband live in Arlington, which isn't far from Fort Worth. She said she'd be happy to put us up for a few days."

"Now, which one is Andie?"

"Oh, you remember her. We went to Baylor together. The tall blond who was always calling you Poppy instead of Pop."

"Oh sure, I remember her. Well, listen, kiddo, call me when you get there, and you be careful driving okay?"

"Okay, Pop. Bye," she said with a twinge of nostalgia in her voice. She could never go anywhere without him telling her to be careful. That was part of why she loved him so much.

CHAPTER 4

The afternoon passed quickly. Jack had seen a couple of new patients and six post-ops, including the Williams boy. The mom was certainly more civil than she'd been in the hospital, but she still had an air about her. Taking time off work from her clerical job at the main post office downtown was an inconvenience she didn't appreciate.

"Why doesn't the doctor have after-hours appointments like they do over at the Medicaid clinic?" she complained to Jack's receptionist as she scribbled her name on the sign in sheet. "You should have your doctor see patients in the evenings, or on Saturday."

Phyllis was more than a little perturbed by the implication. She had been with Jack for quite a few years and couldn't understand people like this woman. Even so, she tried to explain as calmly as she could. "Dr. Roberts starts his days before seven in the morning and generally isn't finished until around six in the evening; often much later than that." She was certain that this woman cared nothing of Jack's hours, only her own.

"Well, I can't be taking time off work every time one of my kids needs to go to the doctor," the woman barked angrily, as she sat down in a huff.

When Jack heard about the exchange, he shrugged his shoulders, and told Phyllis not to let it bother her. He started to say something about how Mrs. Williams had abused the hospital nurses with her foul mouth, but decided to hold his own tongue.

It was after five thirty when the last patient left the office, and once again Jack felt bad that his staff had been asked to stay late. In an effort to keep things moving he occasionally asked Shelly, his medical assistant, to interrupt him if he seemed to be spending too much time with any one patient, but she rarely did. She knew he truly enjoyed the casual conversations he had with young children. He often talked with them about school or sports, or what they wanted to be when they grew up. He also liked to get to know his adult patients on a more personal basis. He believed it helped him gain their trust, and it provided a release for his own stress.

Jack had grown to truly enjoy his days in the office, and over the years he had become a far better communicator with non-medical people. Explaining the intricacies of the human heart and great vessels without using words that few could pronounce, had become his forte. He was fond of using visuals, probably because that's the way he learned best himself. While he had a set of professionally drawn illustrations and a plastic model of the heart in every exam room, he preferred drawing his own pictures on scraps of loose paper or sometimes on the back of the office charge ticket. Phyllis had voiced her objection to the later because she needed to hang on to those tickets and his patients invariably wanted to take the drawings with them. She ended up having to make photocopies of the artwork for patients to take home. Jack had paid little attention to her protests about the charge ticket sketches until a few months ago, after Mary Anne attended a workshop for office managers. At the meeting one of the speakers pointed out that any images or drawings used in conjunction with discussions with patients were, by definition, part of that patient's medical record.

Jack had been one of the first practitioners in the area to switch over to electronic medical records from the old paper charts because he thought it would be easier. It hadn't been cheap, and while it made some things easier, others were noticeably harder. Having to add drawings to the record was one of those harder things. He would either have to draw on the computer using a tablet and stylus, something he'd tried to do without much success, or they'd need to scan his paper drawings into the system. As much as he wanted to object to Mary Anne's recommendation, he knew it was probably the safest thing to do from a medico-legal standpoint. This was just one more new thing that his staff would have to do to comply with the world of growing health care regulations.

Jack locked the back door of his small clinic, as he'd done virtually every day for the past seventeen years. The single story, wood-frame building on Eighth Avenue was previously a private home. As the hospital district started to expand, the homeowners grew tired of ambulances coming and going all hours of the night, so in 1988, they sold the building to the young surgeon who remodeled the inside and turned the backyard into a parking lot.

What Jack liked most about his office was the location. He could walk to and from both hospitals if he wanted, it was that close. Despite the proximity he generally he drove the block and a half simply because it was more convenient to have his truck available if he got called to an emergency.

During the three minute drive, he called home. "I'm going to run in and make rounds real quick," he explained to Elaina. She was just getting ready to shower and dress for dinner before he got home.

"No, I don't think it will take long," he said reassuringly through his cell phone. She knew that was not a guarantee he'd be home in time for their seven-thirty dinner reservation at Claude's. She had lost count of the number of times Jack had cancelled their date night because, in his words, something came up. Tonight was going to be a little more special. They had plans to go to their favorite getaway, a country French restaurant on the other side of town. She was going to wear the pale yellow cotton dress he said showed off her still petite figure and for the memories it stirred in both of them.

"I'll call you when I'm headed home, bye."

He pulled his truck back into his usual parking place and jumped out, this time remembering his name badge that doubled as his key to getting in the door. Again he mumbled something under his breath about the prison. It had become a subconscious ritual he went through almost every time he had to swipe the plastic card just to enter the building.

Jack took one of the staff elevators up to the fifth floor and headed toward the nurses' station. He always began his evening rounds on the surgical floor and worked his way down.

"Hello, Dr. Roberts." The familiar voice was coming from off to his right, as he passed one of the small computer alcoves used for charting.

He turned to acknowledge the youthful appearing nurse who was now in her late forties. "Hi, Angela," he said returning her greeting.

Angela Hart was one of the regular evening shift nurses, and Jack had known her since he first moved to Fort Worth. They had dated for a short period back before he met Elaina, but it to him it was never anything serious. She, on the other hand, still had feelings for him, even though they both had long since gone their separate ways romantically.

"Do you have any of my patients tonight?" Jack inquired in his typical professional tone. He made sure not to give Angela even the faintest suggestion of an interest beyond their working relationship.

"Yes," she said. "I have both the Nixon boy and Mr. Stevens."

Angela accompanied Jack into the private room across the hall where his ten-year-old patient was sitting on the side of the bed playing Nintendo. The preteen acted as if he hadn't noticed the doctor and continued tapping away on the electronic controls. Mrs. Nixon rose to her feet showing obvious signs of fatigue from two nights of sleeping in the hospital. She put down the magazine she had been reading and moved toward her son.

"Good afternoon," Jack said brightly to the young boy.

When the ten-year-old failed to respond, his mother spoke deliberately to him. "Put that down for a minute and talk to the doctor." She had to repeat herself with a bit more emphasis before he reluctantly stopped when the familiar musical tones coming from the TV changed to indicate the game had been lost.

"How are you feeling?" Jack inquired with a reassuring smile.

"Okay," was the only verbal response, but it was obvious he was feeling much better even than he had earlier that morning.

Jimmy Nixon had undergone a thoracoscopic partial lobectomy two days before for a collapsed lung. A collection of air sacs in the top of his left lung had become overly expanded, and one of these large blister looking areas had ruptured while he was jumping on their backyard trampoline. This caused him to experience severe shortness of breath and a searing pain in his chest. His mom had immediately brought him to the emergency department, already knowing exactly what the problem was. It wasn't the first time this had happened to Jimmy. Two years before the same thing occurred and that time she had gone into full-blown panic mode. Jack had expanded the boy's lung using a small tube, inserted between the ribs and into the chest cavity. That time the lung was successfully reinflated without the need for surgery, but Jack had warned her it could happen again. So, this time she knew what it was and was prepared when Jack told her he'd needed to remove the area of the lung containing what he called a *bleb*, to resolve the problem permanently.

The thoracoscopy operation had been completely routine and Jimmy was making a rapid recovery. In the old days, as Jack was fond of saying, the procedure would have required a large incision around the chest, and the ribs would be spread apart. That operation was always very painful, and Jack hated putting children through it, so for the last thirteen years, he had been using a much less traumatic technique. A small lighted tube with a video camera attached was inserted through a tiny incision in the chest wall. It wasn't really much different from the small incision used to put in a chest tube. To remove the diseased part of the lung required two additional incisions that were also quite small. Following the surgery, Jimmy had a small drain in his chest, which Jack had removed earlier that morning.

"What do you think about going home tomorrow, Champ?" Jack asked now that he finally had the young boy's attention.

"I guess so," came the abbreviated response from the shy child.

"Do you think he's well enough to go home after just three days?" his mother asked with some obvious anxiety. Jack had anticipated her concerns and was ready with his usual reassurance.

"We'll check another chest x-ray in the morning. If that looks good I think he'll be good to go." This was his standard response, but he had a way of making it sound more personal. "It's been my experience that kids do better in their own environment, so the sooner we can get him there, safely, the better.

Plus, you'll sleep better in your own bed too," he added with a knowing smile.

She nodded in agreement and with a sigh added, "I heard that."

"I'll be back around in the morning, between eight-thirty and nine, and hopefully we can let him go."

"Sounds good," the mom agreed as the young boy returned to his video game.

"I never cease to be amazed how much better these kids do after thoracoscopy than they did when you had to split their chest open," Angela observed as they made their way down the hall toward the next room.

"I wish we could do every operation that way," Jack replied. "But so far, we haven't found a way to do some of the bigger cases without making big incisions." He continued with a hopeful tone, "I have no doubt that one of these days we'll do almost every operation through tiny openings instead of putting kids through those big traumatic incisions."

Jack had been a true pioneer in minimally invasive surgical techniques for more than a decade. He first witnessed a friend perform an operation similar to the one he'd done on the Nixon boy back in 1992. He had marveled at his friend's ability to visualize the inside of the chest so clearly on a video monitor. When he returned from that experience in Atlanta, he was convinced that thoracoscopy was the future of chest surgery. So, despite initial resistance from administration because of the startup costs, and ignoring the warnings offered by most of his local colleagues, Jack had pushed forward with the idea of bringing minimally invasive chest surgery to North Texas. Initially he confined himself to relatively simple procedures on adults, but in recent years he had successfully performed a wide variety of operations using the scope, including repairing several congenital defects of the diaphragm, trachea, and esophagus on tiny infants.

Minimally invasive techniques had certainly revived his interest in non-cardiac surgery, but his first love was still, and always would be, heart surgery. The majority of his patients were adults who required coronary artery bypass or valve replacements, but what he loved the most was doing heart surgery on kids. From newborns to children past puberty, he lived for the opportunity to fix "broken hearts." For now, the vast majority of heart surgery required opening the chest.

"Will I live to see the day?" Jack mumbled to himself.

Mr. Stevens had undergone an aortic valve replacement a week earlier, and although his surgery had gone well, the elderly man had developed some respiratory complications. He had finally been moved out of the ICU earlier that morning.

After the usual greetings, Jack listened carefully to his chest. The rattling sound of a few days ago had been replaced by the clearer rushing of air into all areas of his lungs.

"How are you feeling?" Jack asked.

"Much better, doc" was the reply, as he smiled for the first time in a week.

"How are his SATs?" Jack asked Angela, referring to the level of oxygen saturation in the man's blood.

"They've been running between ninety and ninety-three when he's asleep, but they jump up to around ninety-eight after he does his incentive spirometry."

"Sounds like you're doing great," Jack declared. "Just keep using that little gadget to make yourself take big deep breaths at least once every hour."

"Will do, doc," the man said as he grabbed the clear plastic device and inhaled through the small flexible tube coming out of the side.

"Sometimes things don't go exactly as we plan," Jack offered more as comfort than explanation. "You've had a bit of a bumpy ride, but we're through the worst part, I'm sure."

As he watched his patient working hard to get his inhaled volume over fifteen hundred cc's, he turned to leave and said, "I'll check on you again in the morning."

♦♦♦♦♦♦♦♦♦

As Jack approached the entrance to the second floor ICU, he saw Herb Nichols coming his way along with the hospital's director of nursing, Joan Baxter.

"Dr. Roberts," Herb offered, sounding both pleased and surprised to see him.

"Hi, Herb," Jack said, sensing a renewal of the sparring session they'd had a few hours before.

"Joan," he added with a nod toward the nurse, acknowledging the presence of this woman with whom he'd had countless run-ins over the years. They simply didn't see eye-to-eye when it came to staffing the ICU or the OR. Jack always believed that consistency was the best approach, wanting the same nurses assigned to the same patients day after day, while Ms. Baxter felt it was better for morale if the nurses were rotated around. She insisted "her nurses," as she liked to refer to them, were not to become too fond of any patient. She feared such intimacy would be emotionally traumatizing should their patient happened to die. Jack's response to her position was always to point out that consistent continuity of care had been proven time and again to yield the best outcomes. Besides, in his opinion, all nurses, and particularly intensive care nurses, pursued the profession because they wanted to care for and become attached to the sickest patients. "That's who they are!" he argued, but often to no avail.

When it came to the operating room, Jack had requested the same crew of nurses and technicians for all his cases. He wanted people who knew his routine, people he could trust, people that he didn't have to retrain just because they'd been assisting with orthopedics or tonsillectomies for the last several weeks. This request was also ignored most of the time because, again, it ran completely contrary to Joan's philosophy. She believed that all OR personnel needed to be proficient in all procedures performed in the hospital's operating rooms. She argued that since they all rotated the night and weekend call for emergencies, they all needed to rotate the daily cases as well. Jack was fond of using another of his stock phrases when describing the OR crew: "Jacks and Jills of all trades, but masters of none."

He'd only been successful in demanding a consistent team in the heart room. The OR supervisor, who answered directly to Joan, had agreed with his argument when it came to hearts. She had resisted Joan's policy and allowed Jack to handpick his own crew. Joan's apparent concession might have also had something to do with Jack's veiled threat to take his elective hearts to another hospital a few blocks away. He had already taken most of his pediatric patients to the children's hospital next door, but since most of those cases were either Medicaid or SCHIP, administration had been more than willing to see them go elsewhere. Government payments for care provided for kids was certainly better than nothing, but it typically it didn't cover all the hospital's expenses.

While Jack maintained operating privileges at a couple of the bigger hospitals in town, he rarely, if ever did surgery in any of them. When he first started his practice, he went to all the area hospitals, spending almost as much time driving as he did operating, or at least that's what he told himself. His professional life was much simpler now, confining his hospital practice to just two facilities, the huge general hospital and the children's hospital. They were literally across the street from each other. While there remained the occasional rift with management, he was convinced these were two of the best hospitals in the state, and among the best in the country. He wasn't about to leave either of them over something like a staffing issue. He had always been able to work out any real differences using logic and reason guided by the principle of providing the best care possible. There was also no disputing the fact that he brought in significant revenue to both facilities, especially with his adult patients. This gave considerably more weight to his arguments, and he knew it.

"Sorry about that awkward little episode today," Herb said, sounding truly apologetic.

"That's okay, I understand your position," Jack offered in return. "You've got a job to do, and that includes trying to keep this ship afloat financially."

"Thanks for understanding." Herb sounded more appreciative than he felt. "These are difficult times, you know?"

"I realize times are changing," Jack replied. "I'm just hoping to survive until retirement," he added laughingly. This was something he and many of his colleagues often said in response to all the changes occurring around them in the world of medicine.

"Oh, Jack, come on," Herb smirked. "It's not that bad is it?"

"Not yet, but it's coming," Jack stated as if the outcome were inevitable.

"You can't be thinking about retirement already, you're still a young man. Besides, you can't retire, you're my cash cow," Herb added, trying to sound like he was joking, but both of them knew the truth.

Jack stood motionless, taking an extra moment before offering a response. "Yeah, I know. As long as my patients pay their bills." He just couldn't help himself. He'd let his emotions get the best of him and immediately regretted the implication. It was beneath him to get into an unproductive battle of wits with this man, but there was something about Herb that consistently rubbed him the wrong way.

"That's not nice, Jack," Herb said, feigning indignation. He'd successfully drawn the conversation to precisely the point he wanted to make. "After all, didn't I agree to let you admit that little girl from Matamoros? You knew that was a total charity case when you committed us. I supported you and now you hit me with this? You know we do more charity care here than any other hospital in the city." Herb was on a roll and he wanted this arrogant surgeon to agree with him.

Jack wasn't certain of the accuracy of Herb's claim, but he knew the number of charity cases he had done in the last year had increased slightly over the previous twelve months. It was still less than twenty percent of his practice, and he had always looked at it as his opportunity to return something to the community. He had certainly done well enough with his investments, and he and Elaina had lived modestly compared to many of his colleagues, so his practice income was not as critical as it was for many of them.

The thing that was really eating at Jack, more than the staffing issues or being challenged regarding charity care, was the growing administrative costs in the hospital. Although revenues were steady, the hospital annual reports had been showing dramatic increases in their cost of doing business each year. It was no secret that the administrator was now making more than seven hundred and fifty thousand dollars a year, and his staff had grown from eight full-time employees five years ago to more than twenty-five now. Herb had successfully made the case to the hospital's board of trustees that the increases in his budget were necessary, given all the new state and federal regulations. For the hospital to comply, he needed the extra personnel.

"You know I appreciate you letting me admit that little girl," he said not allowing his emotions to escape his control again. "In fact, that's who I was just coming to see in the ICU. Why don't you come along?" His suggestion was presented in a way that made the invitation sound more like a demand.

"I've got to get back to my office, Mr. Nichols," Joan declared, seizing the opportunity to get away from this growing conflict. She feared it was not going to end amicably.

"Come on," Jack said, motioning toward the automatic doors that were opening as several visitors were coming out. "I want to introduce you to someone."

Herb reluctantly followed along, not sure he wanted to get involved, but Jack had successfully trapped him. They made their way toward the glass enclosure with a large "5" painted in dark blue on what was otherwise a clear sliding door. As they approached, Jack saw Matt Goodman in the room, standing at the bedside.

"Hi, Jack," Matt said as he turned to see his friend. "I was just telling Mr. Alvarez that we've noticed Lupe moving her legs whenever the sedation wears off a little."

"That's great news," Jack said, grateful for the reassurance that apparently his efforts earlier that day hadn't caused any permanent spinal cord injury.

"Who have you got there with you?" Matt asked. He was surprised to see Herb in the unit. The administrator rarely made his way into clinical areas of the facility, and this was the second time he'd seen him in less than twenty minutes. "Weren't you just here?" Matt asked with a bit of a laugh.

"Yes," Herb said. "I can't get enough of this place."

Herb had been fully exposed. He and Joan had just left the unit when they ran into Jack in the hallway. He'd had heard rumblings about what had happened in the OR, and Herb wanted to make sure this wasn't going to turn into one of those month-long marathon stays due to some complication. He'd brought Joan along as cover, and to ask the charge nurse how this patient was doing. Jack had promised him this girl would be out of the ICU within three days. That assurance was part of why he had agreed to let Jack admit this semi-elective "freebie." So, he'd come to check on his bet, not expecting to run into Jack or Matt, yet here they were all together. At least Herb believed he had plausible deniability if asked about the true nature of his visit. He had only spoken to Lisa at the nurses station and had merely waved to Matt in passing when he'd been spotted. What he hadn't counted on was Dr. Goodman quizzing the nurse about this unusual visit. Now that his covert effort had been exposed, he had nowhere to hide.

Jack sensed what had happened, and wanted to take the sparring match to a literal level. His anger was boiling, but he knew he was now in control of the situation, provided he could keep his cool.

As he stepped into the now crowded room, Jack made a space at the foot of the bed for Herb to stand next to him. The shorter man moved slowly at first, then gradually came alongside, looking cautiously at the small frame of the unconscious child lying before him, her chest rising and falling slowly to the rhythmic sound of the ventilator.

"I want you to meet Mr. Alvarez," Jack said, motioning for Pablo to come forward from his position near the head of the bed.

"Mr. Alvarez," Jack continued with far more formality than seemed necessary. "This is Herb Nichols. He is the administrator of our hospital. He is the guy that runs this place." Jack was not going to miss this opportunity to put Herb on the spot.

Pablo bowed slightly but made no offer to shake hands, "It is very nice to meet you, *señor*."

"It's a pleasure to meet you as well," Herb said using his politician voice. He, too, made no outward gesture toward this common man. "You certainly have a lovely daughter."

"*Graci*... I mean thank you, sir."

"It sounds as if she's doing very well thanks to Dr. Roberts here," Herb offered in a vain attempt to turn the tables.

"Yes, sir," Pablo responded with obvious appreciation. "I am very grateful to him and to all the people here who have taken such good care of our Lupe."

At last it was clear, this child had a name. In the future Jack would compel Herb to use it when talking about her, instead of the "freebie" from Mexico. It was important to have him see this girl and her family as people, with faces and names, and he intended to drive that point home.

"Where are Juanita and Miguel?" he asked, but before Pablo could answer, Jack explained, "Juanita is her mother and Miguel is her twelve-year-old brother. Really a great kid."

"They are at *Señora Andie's* home, resting," he said.

As Jack was listening to Pablo, he noticed the figure of another person sitting in the window seat on the far wall. Whoever it was had been obscured from view by the combination of the mechanical ventilating machine and the large metal tower that hung from the ceiling, which housed all the electronic monitoring equipment.

"So, who is that with you?" Jack asked, gesturing toward the darkened figure. He knew exactly who it was, and he was counting on her being here. She was the person Jack really wanted Herb to meet.

"This is *Señora* Burke," Pablo said, somewhat embarrassed for not having mentioned her before.

Elizabeth rose from the window seat, and as she came forward Pablo gestured for her to step in front of him. She appeared a little disheveled from her nap. She quickly straightened her hair and blouse in an attempt to appear presentable before stepping forward.

"Hello, Dr. Roberts," she said.

"Good to see you again, Ms. Burke," Jack said with a familiar tone.

Turning to Herb, Jack explained. "Elizabeth lives in Brownsville. She's been helping the Alvarez family as their guardian and transporter for a little over a week now." Jack conveniently left out the part about smuggling them across the border, but Herb didn't need to know that detail. "She's the one who drove them up here from Corpus when they couldn't find the surgeon who had done Lupe's first operation eight years ago. Without her help I doubt these people would have been able to get here."

Suddenly, everything began to come into focus for Herb. He had wondered how this family of Mexican nationals had managed to get all the way up to Fort Worth from Matamoros.

"Elizabeth," Jack continued, "this is Mr. Nichols, our administrator. He is the man I was telling you about, who agreed to allow Lupe to stay here in this hospital." Jack knew he was laying it on a little thick, but hey, for the first time he had the upper hand, so it only made sense to play it.

Reaching across the bed toward the man standing at the foot, Elizabeth offered her hand to the obviously shaken Herb Nichols. "It is very good to meet you, sir," she said with a tone of sincere gratitude. "I'm not sure what we would have done had it not been for your kindness and generosity toward this dear child."

It was all Jack could do not to grin from ear to ear. He couldn't have written a better script for her to have read.

"It is our pleasure to serve these wonderful people," Herb said, returning her compliment with the only thing he could say. At this point Jack suspected Herb might have softened just a bit, as he heard a hint of sincerity in his voice.

"If there is anything I can do to make your stay here more comfortable," Herb continued, "I hope you won't hesitate to ask."

"Thank you, sir," she replied. "You have already done so much."

There was a momentary silence before Pablo added, "God bless you, *señor*."

Herb smiled meekly and turned to leave, but Jack gently caught his shoulder, stopping his retreat, and compelling him to return his gaze.

"Herb?" he said, "I, too, want to thank you again. This truly is God's work we are doing here."

"I agree," Herb said, with a genuineness Jack hadn't really sensed before. Perhaps Herb was beginning to have a change of heart. He could only hope.

Herb left the room without saying any more, then hurriedly headed back to his office. Jack returned to his review of the data contained in the ICU record Matt had handed him.

"How's she doing, Dr. Roberts?" Elizabeth asked.

Returning to his clinical persona, Jack replied, "Great! Her blood pressure has normalized. She's got good urine output. Nothing much is coming out of her chest tubes, and her labs all look perfect." He rattled off the key things he'd been looking for before continuing. "We're gonna keep her sedated and on the ventilator through the night. She will be more comfortable, and it's generally better to remove the breathing tube in the morning, after another chest x-ray," he explained.

"If everything goes well, how long do you think she will be in the hospital?"

"We'll probably keep her here in the ICU for a couple more days," Jack stated, anticipating no complications. "We'll start her on a liquid diet tomorrow and hopefully we can get the chest tubes out before she goes up to the floor sometime Thursday." Again he was going through the checklist in his mind.

"When do you think she can go home?" she asked.

"If all goes well she should be able to leave the hospital on Saturday or Sunday, assuming she's eating and all bodily functions are working."

"That sounds terrific. I just need to make some arrangements," Elizabeth replied as she began going over her own mental checklist. She'd been here in Fort Worth for a week now and was hoping she wasn't wearing out her welcome at Andie and Jeremy's home. They had been unbelievably hospitable, but she knew that housing three strangers and an old college friend had to be taking its toll.

As Pablo returned to his daughter's bedside, Jack motioned to Elizabeth with a silent head gesture for her to follow him. She acknowledged the invitation and worked her way around Pablo and the nurse to catch up with the doctor.

She cautiously approached this man who had seemed almost larger than life since their first meeting five days before. Suddenly she feared the worst. Had he called her out here away from Pablo to tell her some bad news he didn't want him to hear? She wasn't sure she wanted to hear it either. Her entire world had become wrapped up in these people who now seemed more like family than some of her actual relatives.

◆◆◆◆◆◆◆◆◆

The last week had been a blur. Since leaving Corpus on Tuesday, the drive to Fort Worth had been the easiest part. She spent most of Wednesday getting settled in with Andie, her old college friend, and her husband, Jeremy. He had taken a day off work to take care of their granddaughter, freeing Andie to help their guests get settled. Andie had accompanied her friend on two separate trips to the local Super Target. She'd needed a few things for herself as well as some additional items for both the kids and their parents.

Elizabeth had only planned to be away from home overnight, so she hadn't brought enough clothes. Getting a couple of casual outfits, some underwear, and a new pair of white tennis shoes were her first priorities. She also told herself she needed a new hair dryer anyway, as well as a new suitcase to carry all her stuff back home.

During the first trip to the store, Elizabeth also bought Juanita a simple cotton dress despite her protests. She told her she had to have some new clothes for their visit to the doctor the next day. The lavender and gray print looked perfect with her new black flats. As she stepped out of the dressing room Juanita was literally beaming. She had not had a new dress since before Lupe was born.

Pablo sat quietly watching. He was excited his wife had a new dress, but under his approving smile he felt a twinge of shame because he knew he could never afford such a luxury.

Next it was his turn to get a new pair of blue jeans and a broad-checked shirt with a button-down collar. When Elizabeth told him he had to have a new pair of shoes, he protested. "What's wrong with my boots?" he asked as he pointed to the heavily worn pair of cowhide work boots that looked as if they had never been off his feet. Elizabeth simply shook her head, insisting he remove them.

With Juanita's help he picked out a pair of brown loafers, but he didn't have any socks. Elizabeth picked out a three-pack of white crew socks and he nodded his approval. With the selection of some new underwear they were both all set.

When they got back to the house, Jeremy was entertaining the two children with an old Disney movie on television. When Elizabeth suggested they go with her back to the Target they silently protested, indicating they wanted to watch the end of *Mary Poppins*.

Andie made some sandwiches and poured a bag of chips in a bowl for a quick lunch.

"You are so kind to let us stay with you," Elizabeth said. She hadn't seen Andie or talked to her in more than ten years, but when her friend heard Elizabeth's story over the phone, she opened up her home to them without reservation. *What other woman would do that?* she wondered.

That afternoon the trip back to the Super Target included buying groceries. Elizabeth was not going to allow Andie to feed them, despite her protests. They ended up splitting the eighty-five dollar grocery bill, but there were a couple more items on Elizabeth's list. When she was walking around the store earlier in the day, she had gone down one of the main aisles adjacent to the toy department. She simply had to get these kids something fun. They had been through so much. Each of them needed something special, and she thought she knew exactly what.

Elizabeth had been surprised how well Lupe seemed to be doing since their arrival in Fort Worth. She certainly wasn't able to keep up with her brother as he darted from one side of the aisle to the other, but she was at least able to walk on her own with Elizabeth and Andie on either side.

As they came closer to the toys, Miguel ran ahead, looking first at the huge display of bicycles and skateboards. He looked like the proverbial "kid in a candy store" and both women were smiling almost as much as he was.

"Come over here," Elizabeth suggested leaving Andie holding Lupe's hand. She motioned for Miguel to follow her around a display of soccer balls. They turned down the third aisle and immediately Miguel's eyes seemed to double in size. He stood almost frozen for a moment before reaching out to touch one of the hundred or more baseball gloves hanging on the display. Pablo had told her about Miguel's love of baseball during their drive from Corpus. He had an old glove that was far too small even for his young hand, and it had been repaired with duct tape so many times it was difficult to see any of the imitation leather for all the gray.

Elizabeth allowed him to browse for several minutes then helped him select one that fit him. It was black leather with bright orange trim. When he put it on his hand it was immediately clear that it had become a permanent part of his body. He stood staring at the glove in awe.

"A glove isn't much good without a ball," she said, as she tossed him one of the white spheres wrapped in clear plastic. He caught it reflexively, then pounded it repeatedly into the pocket of the glove. He silently looked up at Elizabeth who was nodding her approval, which generated the most incredible smile she had ever seen.

With one task down, it was time to move on to aisle five. Moving as fast as Lupe could manage, they made their way over to where Elizabeth had seen the stuffed animals. Lupe was mesmerized by the seemingly endless number of dogs and cats and lions as well as several other strange mythical creatures. As the child lingered, petting each of the little stuffed felines, Elizabeth walked further down the row toward the end to make her own selection. As she held out the ultimate prize, Elizabeth crouched down to Lupe's height and called to her softly. When she saw the little brown teddy bear with the red bow tie arranged neatly around his neck, she forgot all about the dogs and cats and literally ran the few steps to accept it. The bear's plush fur was by far the softest thing she had ever felt as she held it to her face. She closed her eyes as her smile broadened, something Elizabeth hadn't been sure Lupe was capable of until now.

◆◆◆◆◆◆◆◆

"I just want you to know what an incredible thing you are doing," Jack said with admiration for this woman's selflessness.

"It's nothing," Elizabeth replied, shaking her head briefly in protest. She was still wondering if this was a prelude to whatever the bad news he was going to deliver next. "It is you and the people here in this hospital who are doing all the work."

It was now Jack's turn to protest. "No, this isn't about our efforts. The love and the kindness you have shown toward these people is truly an inspiration. I just wanted to tell you that."

She paused for a moment and for the first time since arriving in Fort Worth she was overcome with emotion and began crying softly.

CHAPTER 5

The familiar red and white checkered tablecloths on the patio tables out front gave Claude's the look of the French bistro near the Eiffel Tower. The last night of their honeymoon was a scene she would always remember, and she longed to someday return to Paris. These occasional evenings at Claude's were as close as she'd been in the fifteen years she and Jack had been married. When Jack opened the door, the hint of fresh basil mixed with the hearty aromas of the authentic cuisine made her close her eyes and smile briefly.

Claude Duquet welcomed the couple by name and escorted them to a quiet table in the corner. Although they didn't come here more than once a month, at most, Claude always treated them as true VIPs. Jack had cared for Claude's son following a chest injury several years back. The boy had fallen off his bicycle and cracked a couple of ribs. The injuries weren't life threatening and didn't require surgery, but Claude had always claimed that Jack had saved his son's life. Jack found it somewhat amusing to hear this transplanted Frenchman exaggerate the facts with his classic flamboyance. Every time he told the story of the accident, Claude seemed to expand Jack's role in what had been a nearly miraculous recovery.

In less than a minute the waiter arrived at their table inquiring as to their preference of water and to take their drink order. He was dressed in black trousers and a long-sleeve white shirt with a small white towel draped smartly over his left arm. His assistant was an attractive young college coed, not much older than their son. She, too, was dressed in black slacks and a white blouse and was carrying a bulky wooden A-frame stand. She stood the *menu du jour* next to the table so they could both see what had been expertly handwritten on the blackboard. Elaina decided on a chardonnay and Jack elected not to have his usual Macallan on the rocks, preferring a glass of the house cabernet instead.

The waiter then tried to tempt the couple with the chef's featured items for the evening. The first was an Anjou pear salad with fresh arugula and candied pecans, served with a red wine vinaigrette dressing. After waiting just a moment for Elaina to complete her first "yum" of the evening, he also recommended the lobster bisque. It would be served in a puff pastry with sour cream and caviar added tableside. Now it was Jack's turn to express his approval. Although the bisque was a staple on the menu, it was so unique that Claude insisted his waiters always offer it as one of the specials of the day.

"The fish of the day is an eight ounce fillet of John Dory, served lightly breaded and pan fried along with saffron rice, baby carrots, and a homemade tartar sauce with fresh dill from Monsieur Claude's own herb garden," he said, then paused a moment for effect.

"For dessert we are featuring our signature strawberry soufflé, and if you wish to order the soufflé please let me know when you make your dinner selection." Having concluded his presentation he and his silent assistant left to get their wine.

"I always love coming here," she said with a satisfied smile.

"Me too," Jack replied with a loving expression. "Mostly because I know how much you love it."

He reached across the table and took her hand tenderly. "One of these days I'll take you back there," he offered knowing the exact location to where her mind had escaped.

"Oh, I know," she said as she returned to the current time and place.

"Maybe we can get away once David is off to college," he said hopefully.

Their seventeen-year-old son, David, was still in high school, and he had been the center of Elaina's life until Jack came along fifteen years ago. He had actually been the reason they first met.

◆◆◆◆◆◆◆◆◆

Having grown up in Fort Worth, following high school Elaina attended nursing school at the University of Texas – Arlington. It was close to home and had a great reputation for turning out superior nurses. After graduation, Elaina Potter, RN, accepted a position on the surgical floor at the county hospital in Dallas. It was there, in 1985, that she met a senior medical student by the name of Chad Farrell. He was an extremely bright young man with designs on a career in neurosurgery. Elaina fell head over heels for the ambitious young charmer, and she was clearly just the kind of arm decoration he thought he needed to excel.

They soon became an item and when Chad finished school the following summer he was accepted by the University of Kentucky as a surgical intern. Elaina was willing to follow him anywhere, despite not yet having a ring. They moved to Lexington where she took a position in the pediatric ICU of the local children's hospital. As an intern, Chad was rarely home, but when he was, Elaina did whatever she could to please him. Their sex life had been torrid for the first few months they dated, but after the move, and with Chad starting his internship, it became far less satisfying, especially for her. He seemed increasingly less interested, and when he did find the time it seemed more for his enjoyment than hers. Despite her desire to eventually become his wife, she too began to gradually lose interest, and more or less quit trying to please him. What made it worse was that she couldn't really tell whether he even noticed.

Midway through his internship year Chad received word that he'd been accepted into the neurosurgery residency program at Ohio State, his undergrad alma mater. This was the opportunity he had been dreaming of since high school. Columbus was only about a hundred miles from his hometown of Blue Ash, a Cincinnati suburb, so he'd be near his family and able to attend the OSU football games with his college buddies at the horseshoe.

Amid all the anticipation of the move to Columbus, Elaina had some news she knew would not please the man she'd been living with for eighteen months. She waited until she was certain, then reluctantly told him she was pregnant. The news hit Chad like nothing he'd ever experienced. He had his life planned out down to the last detail, and this, well it just didn't fit into his master plan. He was angry and confused, but refused to lose sight of his dream.

Chad knew better than to even mention it, but the day after she dropped the big bombshell on him, he thought he could introduce his idea subtly. "I was just thinking," he began. "With all that's going on in our lives right now, do you think having a baby is a good idea?"

She couldn't believe what he was saying. "Are you suggesting I get an abortion?" she almost shouted.

"I just think we need to weigh all our options."

"Well, that is not one of our options," she said, emphasizing the word *our*. She was going to have this baby whether he wished to be a part of it or not.

"Okay, okay," he said, as he literally backed away from her. The conversation was over until later that evening.

"I guess we need to get married then, don't we?" Chad offered as they shared a delivery pizza. He was trying to sound as sincere as he could.

His tepid proposal created a major dilemma for Elaina. She wasn't sure that he even loved her, and what was more important, she wasn't sure she still loved him. The one thing she was sure of was she didn't want to be one of those single mothers who struggled to provide for a child. That wouldn't be fair to the baby. She felt she owed it to her unborn child to provide a two parent home if possible.

The following weekend the young couple drove up to Cincinnati to meet with Chad's parents and announced their plans to be married right away. Chad's dad, the senior Dr. Farrell, was a family doctor who held firmly to his traditional Midwestern values. He agreed with their plans, but at the same time he suspected Elaina had trapped his son in an effort to ensure her own future. While he didn't come right out and say it, Chad's mom was not as reserved. She made it clear that this Texas floozy was not good enough for her son. Over all, the weekend was a disaster.

Much to Chad's credit, the couple went ahead with their plans. They had a private wedding at the courthouse back in Lexington, with only a few friends, and a Justice of the Peace presiding. It was not exactly what Elaina had hoped her wedding would be, but when Chad suggested it, she agreed, outwardly insisting that it didn't matter. She just didn't want to wait until her pregnancy was showing. To her that would have been the very definition of a "floozy."

The following year in Columbus was nothing short of a nightmare for Elaina. She worked on a pediatric unit at the community hospital while Chad began what promised to be six more long years of training in neurosurgery. Her pregnancy was difficult. She struggled with horrible morning sickness through the first five months, and Chad was rarely around to help. She called in sick more times than she could count, and eventually she was told she was being moved from full-time status to PRN. She hadn't been fired, so she kept her benefits, but this demotion meant they would only call her if and when they needed help. Financially this put an additional strain on the young couple, but it allowed Elaina to make it through the pregnancy.

In the dead of winter of 1988, David Allen Farrell came into the world. Elaina went into labor a couple of weeks early and as a result she was alone for the birth of their child. Chad had said he couldn't get out of his call, but she suspected he hadn't really tried. He seemed unaware of the true importance of the moment. He showed up at the private hospital across town several hours after the delivery, apologizing profusely for not being there for her, but this time she didn't want to hear it and went back to sleep.

That evening the pediatrician came by her room and told them that the baby had a heart murmur, but he explained this was not all that unusual in newborns. He said they would just keep an eye on him for an extra day or so in the newborn nursery. Eventually, he told them that David had what was called an ASD, or atrial septal defect. It was an abnormally large hole between the upper chambers of his heart. He explained that these kind of birth defects typically closed up by themselves with time, and for now their baby's heart seemed to be compensating just fine. The doctor didn't make any other recommendations, he just told her that he wanted to see him again one week after she took him home.

Elaina didn't have a good frame of reference, since this was her first child, but she was a nurse, and as far as she could tell David looked completely normal. She nursed him and he seemed to be feeding okay, and he was sleeping four hours at a stretch. It came as a bit of a surprise to her the following week, when the doctor said he wanted to run some additional tests.

The cardiac ultrasound confirmed the ASD, which appeared to be fairly large. That made it difficult to predict whether the hole would close on its own or not. The doctor warned Elaina that defects like this can sometimes lead to heart failure, which could happen any time. It might not be a problem until his adolescent or even teenage years. The one thing he continued to emphasize was there was still a reasonably good chance it would close on its own, so there was no need to consider surgery at this time. Those two words, *consider surgery*, were all the young mother heard. It was at that moment, sitting alone, holding her precious child, when she realized she could potentially lose him, and she was determined not to let that happen.

The combination of stresses took a toll on their marriage. At times, Chad seemed to be excited to be a young father, but more often he seemed frustrated with the new responsibilities and the impact they were having on the pursuit of his professional objectives. Being a first-year neurosurgery resident was far more than a full-time job. Between the one hundred hours a week at the hospital, and another twenty to thirty hours of reading, studying, and preparing reports for the faculty and senior residents, he stayed exhausted most of the time. With Elaina's reduced income during the pregnancy and now being off on maternity leave they were financially strapped.

Chad's parents, or more precisely his mother, refused to help them. She was not over the shock of not being invited to the wedding, despite how much she had objected to the idea from the start. His dad sent him a few hundred bucks now and then, but he felt if Chad was man enough to be a father, he needed to learn to shoulder that responsibility himself.

Elaina had recognized shortly after the move to Lexington that Chad was already married. His first love would always be medicine. For a while she thought she could deal with it, believing that once they were finished with his training years, their lives would settle down. However, she now had David to care for, and she began to feel incredibly neglected and lonely. She found herself in a strange town where she had no friends except for those who were more Chad's than hers. They were barely a year into their marriage, yet they rarely even spoke to each other except to argue, usually about money.

Shortly after David was born, Elaina's mother had come to Columbus from Texas to help with the baby. She stayed for ten days and during that time she only saw the young father three times. Elaina had insisted that everything was fine between her and Chad, but mothers have a way of seeing through the façade. She told her that if she ever wanted to come back home to Fort Worth, she and David would be welcomed with open arms. Six months later, Elaina had had enough. The one thing she needed more than anything was a pair of open arms.

After living with Chad for a year and a half, followed by fifteen months of a shallow marriage, Elaina was convinced her life and the life of her young son were going nowhere. His father was never going to make either of them his chief priority. When she announced she was leaving him and taking the baby back to Texas, his only response was to say, "I figured as much. I know I haven't been much of a husband, or a father for that matter. I'm sorry. I guess it just wasn't meant to be."

Within two months the couple's uncontested divorce was final and Elaina was back home living with her mom, who was thrilled to have the opportunity to care for her grandson. Elaina got a job working in the ICU of the newly constructed children's hospital, just a couple of miles from her childhood home. She was obviously scarred by the experience and remained reluctant to get involved romantically with anyone, although there were ample opportunities. Old high school friends were always trying to fix her up with somebody new, but she was just not interested in being burned ever again. Besides, she didn't have time in her life for any man other than David.

◆◆◆◆◆◆◆◆◆

As they sipped their wine, the waiter brought their first course. Elaina had decided on the pear salad. The faint yellowish seasonal fruit with its deep burgundy skin mixed with the dark green arugula, all laid over a single pale green leaf of iceberg lettuce, made for a very colorful presentation. The candied pecan pieces were scattered across the plate, and the waiter drizzled the dressing carefully over the entire array.

"This looks too good to eat," she said as she hesitated before picking up her salad fork.

Jack had chosen the lobster bisque, as he always did. When it came from the oven it looked almost like a soufflé. The light brown pastry dome rose an inch or more above the rim of the deep crock bowl. After asking permission, the waiter punctured the center of the dome with a spoon and the distinctive steamy aroma burst out as though it had been bound up in a balloon. He added a generous portion of sour cream through the broken top of the pastry, followed by a spoonful of black caviar. Jack didn't especially care for caviar, except in this one-of-a-kind dish. He thanked the waiter who replied, "*Bon appetite*," before leaving them alone.

"I think I could make an entire meal out of this bisque," he said with obvious anticipation. As he began to use his spoon to crush the remaining top of the puff pastry, he looked up into her soft emerald eyes as she was savoring the first bite of her salad. He remembered the first time he truly looked into those eyes and had been totally captivated.

♦♦♦♦♦♦♦♦♦

Jack had been called to see a two-year-old who had been admitted to the hospital by Dr. Buzz Jackson, a pediatric cardiologist, and his best friend. The boy was showing signs of sudden and progressive heart failure. He had become less active and his mother had noticed he seemed to be having trouble breathing. Buzz performed a heart catheterization to define exactly how big the opening was between the two upper chambers of the heart and precisely where it was located.

The two experts spent several minutes reviewing the video images of x-ray contrast flowing through the young boy's heart. When combined with the pressure measurements Buzz had taken from inside the child's heart, it was clear to them both that this ASD was not going to close on its own. Instead, the pressure in the arteries to his lungs was steadily increasing. Soon it would become irreversible if they didn't intervene surgically.

"This is Elaina Farrell, David's mom," Dr. Jackson said, introducing her to the surgeon whom she had seen a few times in the hospital, but never under these circumstances.

"Don't you work in the ICU?" Jack asked as he thought he recognized Elaina's somewhat familiar face. She had not been one of the nurses who made a point of chasing after the dashing bachelor's attentions, and for whatever reason the two of them had never actually worked together in the year she had worked in the ICU.

"Yes, sir," she answered somewhat indifferently. "What's going on with my son?" Her voice had grown impatient.

"Well, he has a hole between the upper chambers of his heart," Jack began.

"I know all about his ASD," she interrupted. "The cardiologist at Ohio State told me it would probably close on its own."

Buzz felt he needed to take control of the conversation, sensing the friction that was developing between them. "What he told you was correct, but sometimes if the defect is large it leads to the kind of problems your son has been having the last few days."

She turned her full attention to the cardiologist, looking for the answer to her initial question. "So, what did the cath show?" she asked, now more frightened than ever. She was looking for answers, but not from the surgeon.

"Well," Buzz began, "the defect is a mixed-type ASD and the left to right shunt is too great to allow it to close." He wasn't sure she comprehended his words, so he attempted to explain the situation more simply. "The blood is flowing from the high-pressure left side into the low-pressure right side. This puts excessive strain on the right side of his heart, which is beginning to fail." Buzz could see the rising tension in her face, but recognized the need to continue. "There comes a point when the rising pressure in the pulmonary circulation becomes irreversible. Fortunately we aren't there yet," he hurriedly added, but at the same time emphasizing the degree of urgency he'd felt when he called Jack earlier in the day.

"So this means surgery?" she spoke hesitantly. "Is that what you're saying?"

"Yes," Jack agreed, a bit too matter-of-factly. He regretted the finality of his word as soon as it was out of his mouth.

Elaina glanced toward him angrily, acknowledging his statement, but quickly turned back to Buzz hoping his opinion would be different.

"Dr. Roberts is right," he said with a nod of his head. "David's heart is still very healthy right now, but given the pressures we found, it's not likely to stay that way much longer."

Elaina had known Dr. Jackson since shortly after she'd moved back to Fort Worth. He had been seeing David every three months to check on his ASD, and she trusted his judgment. She was a bit less certain about Dr. Roberts.

Jack accurately sensed that the young mother wanted to talk with Buzz alone. "I need to take another look at David's chest x-ray," he lied. "Buzz, I'll check back with you in the recovery room."

Once Jack had left the small conference room outside the cardiac cath lab, Elaina felt free to speak what was on her mind. "I've been worried about David's ASD since the day he was born." She began to tear up just slightly as she continued. "I knew it was going to come to this, I just thought he'd be… bigger."

"I completely understand," Buzz replied with obvious compassion. "I wish we had the luxury of waiting until he was a teenager, but the fact is his heart isn't going to give us that much latitude."

"How much time do you think we have?"

"I don't know for certain, but I think the surgery should be done during this admission," he explained. "There is nothing more I can do, and I feel certain he is not going to improve enough to be able leave the hospital without the operation. Given the size and location of the defect I don't feel comfortable attempting to close it with any of the catheter techniques. He needs open heart surgery."

Elaina's head dropped as she stared at the floor. "I was hoping…" she paused. "Do you think Dr. Roberts is …" again she hesitated.

"Jack Roberts is the finest heart surgeon I have ever known," he said, sensing her extreme apprehension. "All I can tell you is, if that were my son there is no one in the world I would rather have taking care of him than Jack. We are very fortunate to have him here, and I think you will soon come to believe that as well." He spoke with an honesty she could feel.

She raised her head and smiled timidly. "Thanks, I know you're probably right. It's just that he comes across as being a little... well, arrogant," she offered.

"I think you mistake his confidence for arrogance. He is really not like that at all. You just don't know him very well." Buzz continued, "He is a dedicated man of faith, and he gives most of the credit for his incredible talent to God."

With that, Elaina looked into the compassionate face of the handsome black man facing her and said, "Okay... if you trust him that's good enough for me."

◆◆◆◆◆◆◆◆◆

"Hello," Chad said brusquely.

"This is Elaina," she said matching his tone. "I just wanted to let you know that David is having his ASD repaired tomorrow, here in Fort Worth."

"What happened? I thought he was doing fine?" he inquired, trying unsuccessfully to sound sympathetic.

"Well, he started developing signs of heart failure, so they cathed him today and the cardiologist is convinced his ASD is not going to close. So they're going to operate on him tomorrow."

After a momentary pause, Chad said, "Gee, Elaina, this is so sudden." There was another pause as he tried to determine what else to say.

"It's okay, Chad," she offered with an edge to her voice. "Everything is fine. I just wanted to let you know."

"Oh, I'm glad you called, I just wish I could get away to be there for you."

"Look..." she interrupted before he could offer any excuses why he couldn't come there to be with his son. "I will call you when it's over. The surgeon is one of the best in the country and I'm sure he will take excellent care of our," she paused briefly for effect, "I mean *my* son."

The line was silent again. "Wow, you really know how to hit below the belt," he said.

"We both know your situation. That's why I insisted on sole custody of David. I'll take care of everything. I just thought I should let you know."

"Please do let me know how things go and if there's anything you need."

"Okay, bye." She hung up without waiting for a reply, and as she did, the tears began to stream down her cheeks.

◆◆◆◆◆◆◆◆◆

The next morning Jack walked confidently out of the operating room toward the family waiting area. As he approached Elaina he could see the fearful expression on her face. He smiled slightly and nodded his head slowly as he approached her.

He explained that David was doing well in the recovery room, and as he did she looked up at him with the most beautiful green eyes he had ever seen. They were staring back at him with both gratitude and excitement, and immediately he was mesmerized by them. The moments that followed were a blur in his mind and later he could not recall much of what he had said. This wasn't at all what he had expected and was unlike any feeling he'd known before. He didn't understand what was happening, but he couldn't stop staring into her eyes and straight into her soul.

Elaina felt herself relax for the first time in several days and was totally unaware of the hypnotizing effect she'd had on the surgeon. She thought it was a little strange that he seemed to linger longer than was necessary. Didn't he need to get back to the job of caring for her son?

For the next several days Jack remained in what could only be called a daze. His mind was constantly wandering back to those eyes. How could he have missed the five-six beauty with strawberry blond hair and emerald green eyes? She had been right in front of him for more than a year. Had he been so preoccupied with his job that he'd completely missed the most beautiful woman he had ever seen?

David's operation had been a textbook repair, and his recovery was completely unremarkable. One week after his surgery, Jack reluctantly allowed his mother to take the child home. He probably could have discharged the baby a day earlier, but Jack decided to check one more chest x-ray, perhaps more as a reason to keep Elaina nearby than anything clinical.

He had always made a habit of calling the family of each pediatric patient he operated on the day after their child was discharged from the hospital, but in David's case he didn't stop after the first day.

"It's Dr. Roberts again!" Elaina's mom shouted toward the kitchen of her home, holding her hand over the phone. This was the third evening in a row.

"Hello?" she asked, hoping he wasn't calling with some new information that might be bad news.

"Hi, Ms. Farrell," he said, trying his best to sound strictly professional. "This is Jack Roberts." He spoke almost apologetically. "I was just calling to check on David," he lied again.

"He still seems to be doing okay, not much change from yesterday," she responded, totally unaware of the doctor's real intentions.

"Have you changed the dressings where the chest tubes were?"

"Of course," she replied, a little indignant that he would ask an ICU nurse such a silly question.

He didn't know what else to say other than to inquire further about her son. "I was a little concerned about that area before he left the hospital. We've had a couple of kids develop infections that didn't show up for eight to ten days." Now he really was making stuff up. He'd had only one child recently who had developed a very minor abscess in an incision following a chest injury, but there had been no infections in any elective heart procedures over the last two years.

"I didn't notice any redness or swelling when I bathed him this morning," she said her voice now betraying a hint of concern.

"He's not due to come into the office until late next week, and I'd sure hate to see anything get out of hand." What he failed to say was the only thing he was really worried about getting away from him was her.

"I could bring him in sooner if you think it's that important."

"Well, I noticed your address isn't that far from the hospital." He was starting to sound suspicious, even to himself. "I'd be happy to swing by there on my way home and take a quick look."

"A house call?" she questioned. "Doctors don't make house calls anymore."

That was not exactly true. Jack had gone into a number of private homes to check on patients, but always before there had been a good reason. This time his only reason had nothing to do with his patient.

"It's on my way," he lied for the third time in the last two minutes. He actually lived in the opposite direction from the hospital, but to him this trip was definitely on his way.

"Sure, that would be fine," Elaina said, wondering if she had time to change out of her cutoff jeans and tee shirt.

"I'm leaving the office now, so I'll be there in about ten minutes if that's okay."

"Do you need directions?" she asked.

"No, I can find it," he said. The truth was he had already driven by the small frame house more than once, hoping to catch a glimpse of her outside. He thought at the time he might be guilty of stalking, but he didn't really care.

"I'll see you in a bit," he said with a big grin on his face. Had she been able to see through the phone she'd have thought better about allowing him to come over.

"Okay, bye," she said.

He had no sooner hung up the phone than he was out the back door of the clinic. It should have taken ten minutes to drive the two and a half miles, but Jack made it in eight. He parked his BMW out front and walked swiftly up to the house. He rang the bell and soon the door was opened by an attractive woman in her mid-fifties, but she could almost pass as Elaina's older sister. Jack recognized her from the hospital as David's grandmother.

"Hello, Dr. Roberts," she said, "what a pleasant surprise. Please come in. Elaina said you were coming by to check on David."

"Yes, ma'am," he offered, sounding a bit school-boyish.

"Let me let her know you're here."

Jack stood patiently inside the doorway. If he'd had a hat he would have been holding it in front of him with both hands. He scanned the living room, which clearly didn't get used much. An upright spinet piano stood on the far wall, and there was a clean but dated sofa and matching overstuffed chair facing the front window. An oval braided rug partially covered the hardwood floor, under an oval glass top coffee table in front of the sofa. He recognized a feeling of nostalgia coming over him, remembering his own boyhood home, which was not unlike this one.

"Hi, Dr. Roberts," Elaina said as she came into the room. She extended her hand to Jack and he shook it silently, holding on just into that awkward moment.

He had his script all ready, but when he saw her standing there, barefoot and in those shorts and baggy tee shirt, he found it difficult to even speak.

"Hi," he managed, trying not to stutter. "How are you?" This time he stammered just a bit.

"Oh, I'm fine. How are you?"

"I'm great," he offered somewhat reflexively. In reality, he was feeling weaker at that moment than he could ever remember feeling. The awkward silence resumed between them, and for the first time Elaina detected a look in his eye which made her blush slightly.

"Well," she said, breaking the silence, "let me show you to David's room."

She led the way, and as she moved easily down the short hallway he was unable to avoid staring at her shapely bare legs and the seductive gentle sway of her hips. As she turned into David's room she glanced back and caught the hint of a young man's grin. Now she knew he was watching her, and surprisingly she liked it.

David was sleeping quietly, breathing easily, and he had a rich pink color to his cheeks. Jack stood beside the crib, its mattress lowered as far down as it would go and the rails were all the way up.

"I was planning to move him into a regular bed before all this happened, but I'm kinda glad I didn't," she explained. "I feel much safer having him in this crib, at least until he is fully recovered from the surgery."

"Oh, I agree. You can't be too careful," Jack offered. He realized after he'd said it that he might have been talking about her instead of David.

"Do you want to see his incisions?" she asked, finally calling Jack's bluff.

"It seems a shame to wake him. He's sleeping so peacefully."

"He's due to wake up for his supper soon, I don't mind waking him now."

"No... no," Jack whispered. "Let him sleep a little longer. I'll wait." He was staring again, but this time at the small child whose tiny heart he had held in his hands only ten days before. Now he felt the tables had been turned. Someone else was holding his heart in their hands, and they didn't even know it.

"Would you like a glass of tea?" she offered to break another awkward silence.

"Sure," he said slowly, not taking his eyes off the young boy.

"Why don't we go in the kitchen?" she whispered, sensing Jack was in some kind of trance.

He seemed to come back from wherever he had been, and looked directly at Elaina. "You have a precious little guy there."

In that moment Elaina's heart melted. The tenderness in his voice was pure and genuine, something she hadn't heard or felt from any man before about her son. Now it was her turn to stand speechless for a moment. To gain her composure she looked down at her sleeping son and spoke so softly Jack could barely hear her. "Yes, he is..." She was tempted to add, thanks to you, but she decided to hold that thought to herself.

For the next hour they sat at the round oak table in the far end of the kitchen. They talked about how long she had been a nurse and how she'd gotten into pediatric intensive care nursing. The more he watched her smiling, casual manner, the more smitten he became. He couldn't understand how he could have worked in the same hospital and even in the same unit with this woman and not noticed her until that fateful day, less than two weeks ago. Now, he was intent on finding out as much as he could about this extraordinary beauty who had stolen his heart so easily with only her eyes.

When David finally awoke, Elaina went in to check on him with Jack trailing close behind. After all, he needed to at least keep up the appearance of coming here to check on his patient. He took a quick look at the child's incisions and pulled a small stethoscope from his pocket and listened briefly to the child's heart.

"He looks and sounds great," Jack pronounced with satisfaction. Both he and Elaina already knew that, but this house call had revealed something else to both of them.

Their parting handshake was considerably more tender than the one Elaina had offered earlier in the evening. After lingering at the front door a few minutes, Jack walked slowly to his car. He turned to see her standing in the open doorway, watching him walk. Before he got into the car he waved a reluctant goodbye, which was returned with an equally sad effort.

"That was nice of him to drop by," her mother said, sounding more maternal than she had since her daughter was eighteen. She had seen the sparkle in the doctor's eye when he looked at her thirty-year-old daughter, which prompted her to add, "You know, I don't think I'd let that one get away."

"Oh, Mom," she protested. "Don't be ridiculous. He's in his forties," she exclaimed as if the twelve year difference in their ages immediately disqualified him from consideration. "Besides, I'm sure he's not interested in me."

"I saw the way he looked at you," her mother said with a cunning smile, "and I saw the way you looked at him."

She walked over to touch her daughter's shoulder and continued, "You don't think he's called here three evenings in a row just to check on his patient, do you?" she asked without expecting a response. "Then tonight... an hour and twenty minute house call? Well, all I can say is he didn't come over here to see me, and I don't really think he came here to see your son either."

Elaina smiled shyly, admitting that her mother's arguments might have had some merit. "I don't know, Mom," she sighed. "My life is just getting back to normal. David's heart problem is finally on the mend and I'm just now getting comfortable with my job. I don't think I'm ready for another relationship," she said, more as a question than a statement of fact.

"Listen, dear," her mother spoke earnestly as they walked back into the kitchen. "Love doesn't come along every day, and it rarely comes when you're looking for it, or when you think you're ready for it. I don't know if that's what I saw happening between you two or not, but if it wasn't it was a darned good imitation." She took her daughter's shoulders and turned her gently to face her. "Don't shy away from what might be a good thing just because you got burned once before."

"I know you're probably right, Mom, but really, I don't think he's interested in me," she said now hoping she was wrong.

CHAPTER 6

Their conversation drifted to the events of Jack's day as the waiter gathered the dishes from their first course and refilled their wine glasses. Jack's mood darkened as he told Elaina about the committee meeting and the sparring he had engaged in with Herb. It was obvious to him, and to her, that he was becoming quite frustrated with Herb's focus on revenue.

Soon the waiter and his assistant returned with their main courses, allowing them to move on to something more pleasant. Elaina had chosen the fish special and Jack had his usual sirloin, medium rare. It was covered in a red wine and black peppercorn sauce and had been his favorite since the first time they came to this restaurant more than ten years ago.

"How's your fish?" he asked after she had taken her first sampling of the expertly prepared John Dory.

"Wonderful," she replied as she sampled another morsel of the delicate white meat. It was a perfect match to the buttery smooth chardonnay. "I would ask how is your steak, but I already know how much you like that spicy sauce."

Jack smiled slyly as he savored the combination of the crunchy tang of whole black peppercorns in the smooth creamy wine sauce. The beef was prepared perfectly with a slightly cool red center and heavily seared surfaces. As he sipped his full-bodied cabernet he said, "You know? I'm the luckiest guy in the whole world. A good wine, a great steak, and the most wonderful woman in the world."

She shook her head slowly and smiled in mock disgust. "Are you still trying to sweep me off my feet?"

◆◆◆◆◆◆◆◆

Over the weeks that followed his "house call," Elaina saw Jack several times in the hospital. He always smiled and said hello, asking first about David and then about her mother. She didn't sense the same spark from him that she was sure had been there that night in her mother's home. She was convinced the eligible Dr. Roberts had come to his senses and gone back to being the ultimate professional. Sadly she resigned herself to that fact and resolved to go on with her life as she had before all this fantasy romance nonsense started.

Every time Jack saw her his desire grew stronger. Twice she had brought David into the office during the first month after surgery. Once, straight from work, wearing her scrubs, but the second time she had come in wearing a dark gray pencil skirt that was mid-thigh length, along with a pale pink summer sweater, both of which truly showed off her incredible figure. The four inch heels made her the complete package.

She had worn her most provocative outfit on the recommendation of her mother, specifically to see if she could get him to notice her again. After all, that is what she had seen the other nurses do to garner his attention. She felt foolish when Jack appeared to virtually ignore her. The whole time he was in the room with her and David, he stayed busy, reviewing records on the computer screen. When he talked to her he did so without making eye contact. His lack of interest was obvious and it provided her the clear sign that she had simply misread their single encounter six weeks earlier.

So, as she got ready to take David in to see his surgeon for what she assumed would be his final follow-up visit, six weeks after the surgery, she made no effort to impress. She wore a pair of faded blue jeans, a sweatshirt and her cross trainers. She didn't put on her usual makeup, and she didn't even fix her hair, preferring to wear a black baseball cap with a ponytail pulled through the back. This time he seemed more willing to at least look at her, but he remained very professional.

"I think this young man is going to be just fine," he said, standing the two-year-old up on the exam table. "He's gaining his weight back and his heart sounds good as new."

"I can't thank you enough, Dr. Roberts," she replied sincerely. Her remarks had nothing to do with any feelings she might have had for him. She was genuinely grateful to have her precious little boy completely healthy for the first time.

"It's nothing I did," he offered, still sizing up the timid little guy in front of him. "It is God's work, I'm just one of the tools."

"That is the most extraordinary thing I've ever heard any doctor say."

"Well, it's true. I'm sure you've seen many kids get well when by all rights they shouldn't have. That's not us, that's Him," he said pointing to the sky.

Elaina was in awe of the obvious humility of this man. She couldn't help but think back on the conversation she'd had with Buzz before the surgery. How wrong her first impression had been.

"Well, I still think what you did for my son was pretty special, and I wish there was something I could do to repay you."

"Seeing this little guy standing here today is all the thanks I need," he said turning toward her as he placed David's feet back on the floor. "I don't really need to see him again. There isn't anything more I can do for him, but if you have any questions or want to bring him back any time, please just give me a call."

"I will, Dr. Roberts," she said, taking David's hand and leading him out the door toward the front desk. "Say bye-bye." She spoke sweetly to the sandy-headed little boy as she glanced up again at Jack.

"Bye," Jack called out and waved to his little ex-patient.

"Bye," came the soft reply of the two-year-old.

Jack walked back to his private office as Elaina made her way to the front. She stopped briefly at Mary Anne's desk and asked, "Have you heard anything from my insurance company yet?"

"As a matter of fact, we received their payment just yesterday," she replied with a big smile, first toward Elaina and then toward David. "So we're all square."

"That can't be right. I'm sure I haven't met my deductible, besides, I know they didn't pay the whole bill. They never do,"

"No, you're good to go," Mary Anne assured her with a final smile.

"Okay, if you say so. Thanks for all your help," she said to his entire staff of three, all of whom had gathered to see David off.

Later that afternoon Elaina went through her mail and found a letter from Humana. Her health insurance was through work, and the hospital only offered its employees a fairly restricted managed care plan. She opened the envelope and pulled out the explanation of benefits for the surgeon's fee. Jack's office had submitted a charge of three thousand four hundred dollars for David's open heart procedure. The insurance company had only allowed eighteen hundred and fifty dollars. As she suspected she had not met any of her five hundred dollar annual deductible, so the form confirmed that the company had only paid Dr. Roberts thirteen hundred and fifty dollars.

She held the EOB form in her hand wondering if this could be right. Mary Anne told her the bill had been paid in full, but clearly she still owed the five hundred dollar deductible, and doing the math quickly in her head, she actually owed him another fifteen hundred and fifty. She picked up the phone and dialed Jack's office only to hear the answering service operator explain that the office was closed, then ask if this was an emergency. Elaina told the operator her question could wait. She would just call back in the morning. She hung up the phone shaking her head. It had recently cost her more than fifteen hundred dollars to get the transmission in her Nissan Altima overhauled. She figured something was terribly wrong when a surgeon gets paid less than that to fix her child's heart.

After supper, Elaina was giving David a bath and getting him ready for bed when she heard the phone ring. "Can you get that, Mom?"

After a few moments her mother appeared in the doorway of the bathroom. "It's for you, dear."

"I'm busy right now. Just take a number and I'll call them back."

"Let me finish dressing him. You go take the call."

"Who is it?"

"I don't know," she lied, "but it sounded important."

As Elaina rose up off the floor her mom deftly took her place. When her daughter had left the room a broad smile came to her mother's face.

"Hello?" she said impatiently.

"Hi, this is Jack Roberts," he said, once more stumbling slightly with his words. Under his cool, self-confident exterior, he was uncharacteristically nervous. He had been an emotional wreck for the last six weeks. All he could think of was Elaina, but he couldn't tell her as long as he was still David's doctor. It would be considered highly inappropriate and border on being medically unethical for him to have any kind of personal relationship with a patient. Granted, technically she wasn't his patient, but she was his patient's mother, which, as far as Jack was concerned, amounted to the same thing.

"This afternoon you said you wished there was something you could do to repay me."

"Yes, and I want you to know I will. I got the letter from my insurance company today and I saw how little of your fee they paid. I fully intend …"

"No, wait," Jack interrupted. "That's not what I meant at all." He had not been prepared for the conversation to start off this way. "I wasn't calling about that." Now he was really getting flustered.

"Well, I tried to call your office this afternoon, but you were already closed."

"Please." Jack's voice was pleading for her to just listen. "I was calling to see if you would allow me to take you to dinner tomorrow evening."

The phone was silent for several seconds. Finally Jack said, "Hello?"

"Yes, I'm here," she replied. "I don't understand. I thought…" Her voice trailed off.

"I know, you may think it's a bit weird going on a date with your son's doctor, but if you meant what you said earlier today about doing something to repay me, you'll say yes."

After another brief pause she replied. "Yes," she spoke slowly, half expecting him to interrupt her again.

"Great! I'll pick you up at seven?"

"Sure. That'll be fine."

"I'll see you tomorrow then." Jack's confident demeanor had returned.

"Oh wait," she said. "What should I wear?"

"Well, you could wear that gray skirt and pink sweater you wore to my office a couple of weeks ago."

She smiled at the thought that perhaps her mom's suggestion had been right after all. "I'll see you tomorrow evening, Dr. Roberts."

"Please, call me Jack."

"Okay, Jack. I'll see you then. Bye."

As she returned to check on her son, she said, "Just when you think you've got things figured out."

"Who was it, dear?" her mother asked, having known full well who it was from the beginning.

"It was Dr. Roberts, I mean Jack... but you already knew that," she said punching her mother's shoulder playfully.

"I told you so," she said as she turned to go back toward the kitchen. "So when are you going out with him?"

Mothers can really get on your nerves, she thought. Especially when they think they know everything.

"Tomorrow night," she called after her mom as she followed her down the hall. "Oh, and guess what? I asked him what I should wear."

"I'll bet he requested that short skirt, didn't he?"

Elaina didn't reply, she just blushed and nodded slowly.

"Like I said..." her mom continued the lecture with a knowing smile.

The next morning Jack did a couple of minor procedures at the general hospital, followed by an office full of patients in the afternoon. As the day dragged on, all he could think about was Elaina and her gorgeous green eyes. Shelly didn't have to remind him once to keep the flow of patients moving. Today he wasn't interested in idle conversation. He even took a few minutes to sit down between patients, something he rarely did.

"Are you okay?" Mary Anne had asked, when she noticed him just sitting at his desk with his feet up, smiling.

"Sure," he said as he quickly put his feet back on the floor and sat up in his chair. He'd been daydreaming, something she had never seen him do in the two plus years she'd worked for him.

"Just checking," she said with her own smile. She knew something was up. It just wasn't like Jack to drift off to Neverland like that.

At five o'clock he was out the back door even before his staff had locked up the front. He made his way to the hospital and zipped through his afternoon rounds, and in less than twenty minutes he was headed home to change.

Jack drove up about five minutes before seven, despite his efforts to drive slowly. He'd even circled the block a couple of times. He was one of those people who was compulsively early anyway, and the excitement he felt this evening had only compounded that trait.

You can't blow this, he warned himself as he rang the bell. As before, he was greeted by Elaina's mother who immediately invited him into the familiar living room. This time she was accompanied by her grandson who had one arm wrapped tightly around her leg.

"Hi there, David," Jack said playfully, crouching down to get closer to the youngster's eye level. "How are you today?"

The child shied away, hiding himself partially behind his grandmother. "David, you remember Dr. Roberts," she said in a gentle reassuring tone. He had seen Jack just the day before in the office, but the surroundings were much different and like any two-year-old he remained a bit unsure about this man who was still a stranger.

Jack held his hand out toward the boy as he'd done countless times in an effort to gain a child's trust. He was not really anticipating a response, so when the child tentatively reached forward and grasped Jack's finger, his smile grew even brighter.

Elaina walked quietly into the room and watched Jack interacting with her son and thought, *What a gentleman.* He was still crouched down when he saw her out of the corner of his eye. She was indeed wearing the same tight gray skirt and four inch black patent leather heels, only this time his view was accentuated by his position. As he stood he took in the entire image that he had forced himself to look away from when she was in his office. He'd been afraid his mouth would gape open and give away his thoughts, but now he felt free to offer an unfettered opinion.

"Wow," he exclaimed. "You look… stunning."

Her shoulder length hair was arranged in soft curls that framed her gorgeous face. She could easily have pursued a career in Hollywood, had she chosen to go that route. Many friends had encouraged her to do so when she was younger, but she had never seen herself as anything other than a nurse for as long as she could remember. The pale pink cashmere sweater caressed her shoulders with a slight puff to the short sleeves then gathered around her upper arms. It was just snug enough to demonstrate her ample breasts. She always worried that sweaters that were too tight made girls look like they were advertising. This one fit perfectly.

"Thank you," she said with a demure demeanor he hadn't seen before. "I see you and David are getting reacquainted."

Jack couldn't take his eyes off her. "Yes, I was just about to ask him where his mommy was, and there you are." He gestured with both hands toward her as if she'd appeared out of nowhere.

He was wearing a black polished-cotton tee shirt and light gray trousers with a black alligator skin belt and matching loafers. His jacket was a soft gray tweed that matched the gray and black of the rest of his outfit. It also accentuated his dark brown hair, making it appear almost black, except for the wisps of gray at his temples. That was a recent development that was the only feature that hinted as to his age.

"Are you ready to go?" Jack asked, but immediately he realized she wouldn't have come into the room if she wasn't.

"Sure," she said, bending down carefully and turning toward David to avoid having her short skirt show more than she intended.

"Come give mommy a big hug." The young boy scrambled into her outstretched arms and she squeezed him lovingly. "You be good, and mommy will see you in the morning."

"You kids have a good time," her mother said, giving them her implied permission to leave.

"Thanks, Mom." She started to say something stupid like don't wait up, but realized that she would sound like a teenager.

Jack opened the passenger-side door of his jet black 3-series BMW, allowing Elaina to get in very carefully. She was beginning to regret wearing this particular skirt as he watched her maneuver carefully into the low bucket seat.

At six foot three, Jack also required a little effort to fold into the relatively small car with the soft top up, but once seated he loved the sporty way it drove.

"So, where are we going?" she inquired playfully.

"A little Italian place downtown called Francisco's. Have you ever been there?"

"No, but I've heard of it. Sounds yummy!" She smiled with excitement. Looking at this distinguished man sitting next to her, she thought that was exactly how she would describe him.

When they arrived at the upscale restaurant, the valet opened her door and she found getting out a little easier than getting in. Jack held out his arm and she took it instinctively as they approached the entrance.

"Good evening, Dr. Roberts," Francisco said. His heavy Italian accent fit in perfectly with the darkened room and the smell of fresh garlic and homemade bread.

"Hi, Francisco, I'd like you to meet Ms. Farrell. Elaina, this is Francisco. He owns this place."

"I am delighted to meet you, Ms. Farrell. Let me show you to your table." Francisco bowed slightly and motioned for them to follow.

Elaina was overwhelmed as she simply nodded and looked back at Jack not knowing what to say. He took her arm and escorted her as they followed the owner to an especially dark corner table with no other diners nearby. She wondered if the good doctor brought all his conquests here to this ultra-romantic spot. Francisco certainly knew him by name. Perhaps this was his personal table, and she was just another in a long list of unsuspecting women he had lured here?

Sensing her concerns, Jack said, "I've been coming here pretty regularly for the last year or so. Buzz Jackson introduced me to this place. The lasagna is simply the best."

At least he didn't try to hide the fact he was a regular. He just didn't say how many different "guests" he'd brought here.

Jack ordered a bottle of pinot grigio and as they waited for the server to return, they engaged in small talk about David and her mom, and how she was enjoying work. The waiter poured the wine and Jack suggested they weren't quite ready to order yet, so he left them alone.

"To David," Jack said, as he raised his glass a few inches off the table and leaned it slightly toward her.

She raised her glass and softly touched it to his and said, "To my son."

What was this guy doing? He was literally sweeping her off her feet by appealing to her love for her own child. It was as if he was more interested in him than he was in her.

"I have to ask you something," she said after tasting the cool crisp white wine. He looked into her eyes with a new anticipation. "That evening you came over to the house to check on David?" she asked. "You didn't really need to check his incisions, did you?"

He had anticipated her asking that question, but he was still a bit uncomfortable revealing his deceit. He lowered his eyes to his glass and replied, "No, I didn't."

"So why did you come over?" Now she had him on the spot.

"I came over to see you."

"Oh, really?" she said, making him sweat just a bit longer.

"Yes," he admitted. He might as well lay it out now. He looked up to face her again and leaned forward slightly. "I needed to see for myself if your eyes were as beautiful as I remembered them."

Now it was her turn to blush, hearing words no man had ever said to her before. She wanted to hear more. "And ...?"

"Well, they weren't exactly as I'd remembered," he paused. "They are far lovelier than I had even imagined."

She was having trouble breathing as she watched this gorgeous man disarm her with his words. "So... why did it take you more than a month to call me?" she asked. Maybe he had to get out of some other relationship before he felt free to pursue her.

"I really wanted to, but I just didn't think it was right as long as I was David's doctor. It was an ethics thing, and I just didn't feel comfortable."

"So now it's okay?"

"Yes," he said flashing his crooked little smile. "Technically, I'm no longer taking care of him."

"I see," she replied with a sly grin.

"Why? What did you think?"

"I just figured you weren't interested."

"Are you kidding?" Jack stated with amazement.

"Well, I wore this same outfit to your office and you seemed to completely ignore me." She couldn't help pushing her advantage.

"Like I said, at that time I didn't feel comfortable with what I was feeling toward one of my patient's mother." He paused and then scanned up and down the visible portion of her body. "It was all I could do to keep from staring at you then, kind of like I'm doing now."

"I was just confused, because I sensed something that evening at the house, and then it was... well, never mind." She thought it best not to reveal her own interest just yet.

"I'm really sorry," he offered, as honestly as he could. "I should have explained myself, but I just didn't know how to tell you that I wanted to take you out, but because of my medical ethics I'd have to wait until your son was completely over his operation."

He laughed at what now seemed a bit ridiculous and she joined him. It was the first time he had heard her laugh, and her girlish innocence was intoxicating.

"Well, I'm glad we got that cleared up," she said as she sipped her wine.

As they enjoyed the wine and the lasagna, she was becoming increasingly comfortable in the company of this man. However, she had another question she needed to ask. "So, how many other nurses have you brought to this hideaway?" Again she was employing her inquisitive little smile.

"I have been here with a couple of other women over the last year or so," he offered without hesitation. "But, I never enjoyed myself as much as I am this evening."

She thought, *What a smooth talker. I wonder if he's talking about dinner or after.*

"I'm enjoying this evening as well," she offered cautiously, "but, I have to tell you, this is the first real date I've had since my divorce a year and a half ago."

"I understand, and I'm honored that you would come here with me," he said, returning to a gentler tone. He reached across the table to touch her hand, and as their fingers met, Jack felt a warmth and softness that made his eyes close slightly.

Elaina also sensed a new electricity flowing from her hand up toward her heart. Despite all the warnings she had given herself since fleeing Ohio, was she falling for this guy she once thought was an arrogant jerk?

After dinner Jack asked, "Do you want to take a little walk?"

"Yes, I think that would be nice."

He paid the bill and as they walked out into the cool evening air, Francisco wished them "*Buena sera*."

Jack told the valet they would not need the car just yet, and the young man said he would be there until eleven. He faced her and held out his arm. She took it, holding his firm, well-contoured bicep in her left hand. They turned up the street and walked leisurely toward Sundance Square. The downtown Fort Worth area had recently undergone a major renovation, and the streets were filled with people out on the town. They strolled along quietly, watching other couples and groups of singles make their way in and out of the numerous restaurants and night clubs that now populated the area. The city's efforts had been hugely successful in revitalizing downtown. It had the look and feel of a comfortable old hometown, but with the excitement of modern establishments and skyscrapers.

As they approached the Worthington Hotel a line of horse-drawn carriages stood parked in the street in front of the modern hotel.

"Would you like to take a carriage ride?" he asked.

"Yes," she said, almost giddy with excitement.

They walked up to the first open air vehicle where a young woman in jeans, a ranch jacket, and cowboy hat welcomed them aboard. As the broad white animal began to move into the street the carriage lurched forward, startling Elaina enough that she reached again for Jack's arm, this time with both hands for support. As she did she faced toward him slightly and drew herself closer to his side. He looked toward her with approval as she held on perhaps a little tighter than was necessary.

The evening was very pleasant, but the night air had given her a chill. Just as she began to shiver, ever so slightly, the driver called back to Jack, suggesting they could use the blanket on the seat in front of them if they were too cool. Elaina nodded her approval and he pulled his arm away to retrieve the blanket. As she released him, the outside of his hand brushed briefly across the bare skin of the outside of her thigh. The sensation was only momentary, but it was more than obvious to each of them, and they both had a brief second of stuttered breathing.

He carefully placed the blanket across their laps and then put his arm around her soft and welcoming shoulder. She found herself automatically moving even closer to him and soon laid her head gently against his chest. The rhythmic clopping of the horse's hooves seemed to mimic the beating of his heart. It was so strong and so steady. She could not recall ever feeling so safe, or so desirable.

The route took them off the square for a short distance, past the courthouse and down a quiet side street away from the traffic and the crowd, where the lights were dim. Jack turned his head toward her and asked, "Are you having fun?"

She looked up into his dark brown eyes and felt a longing she'd nearly forgotten. "Oh, yes... are you?"

Seeing her radiant smile and glowing eyes Jack could no longer contain himself. He reached across with his right hand and gently raised her chin. As he felt the tender moistness of her lips on his, her response had been just as he had dreamed. In an instant it was as if their two mouths were mirror images, each exploring the other with a sense of vitality and the eagerness of a new, yet familiar relationship. She put her left hand on his chest and felt his breathing quicken. Under the blanket, she moved her legs slightly more toward his, feeling the smooth woolen fabric of his trousers rub gently against her sensitive skin.

As their first kiss lingered, she could feel herself literally melting into this man. The warmth of his mouth on hers and resting securely in his strong arms gave her a sense of their bodies almost merging.

All too quickly the carriage turned back onto the busy street with the bright lights and crowded sidewalks. Jack reluctantly broke away from what was for him the magical kiss he'd been anticipating since that day at the hospital. He pulled back only far enough to allow him to gaze longingly into her eyes. She was still close enough he could feel her breath on his face.

"We are likely to cause quite a scene out here in the open," she said with a grin.

Their embrace lasted only a few more seconds, before Jack turned to the driver. "Would you drop us off in front of Francisco's restaurant?"

The driver agreed, and as they approached their destination, he folded the blanket and placed it back on the seat. Elaina quickly pulled at her hemline, which had crept up a bit too high for comfort.

The valet went to retrieve the car, and as they stood under the canopy, Jack asked, "Are you still cold?"

When she nodded yes, he put his arm around her shoulder yet again in a partial embrace. He was gaining a familiarity with the feel of her body, and she, too, seemed to be growing comfortable with his touch.

On the drive back to Elaina's home, he reached for her hand again and held it gently in her lap. The warmth he'd felt back at the restaurant was now more than doubled as she placed her other hand firmly over his and squeezed his fingers in response to his gentle stroking of her palm. He was tempted in so many ways to take her back to his condo for a nightcap, and whatever else would surely happen, but he had told himself, not this time… not with her. His feelings toward her were so different from any he'd experienced before. He was not about to spoil this evening with what she might perceive as just another meaningless act of physical self-satisfaction.

"Do you want to come in?" Elaina asked as he walked her to the front door. Her mom had conveniently left the porch light off and she could see through the window that the living room was also dark.

"I better not," he said with just a bit of sadness in his voice. "I have a long day tomorrow, and I've got to get an early start."

They stood silently, holding hands and looking into each others' eyes. The crickets were singing softly in the background and neither one seemed to want the night to end.

Her high heels helped negate their height difference, but she still felt herself suddenly straining upward to meet his hungry mouth. She felt his muscular arms holding her, pressing her breasts firmly into his chest. As he held her to him with his right hand behind her neck, his left hand had found the slender curve of her lower back. She allowed herself to be drawn tightly into him as she felt a longing in her lower body that had been absent for more than two years. Instinctively she responded by pressing her pelvis forward into his. There was no mistaking his arousal, and she too was desiring more.

Could it be that she had found the real thing? She couldn't allow her mind to drift off into some unknown future. She still barely knew this man, but she found herself imagining the two of them together, their passions running wild. Each time she tried to bring herself back to the reality of the moment, the feeling of having his tongue possessing her mouth and his obvious excitement sent her mind adrift once more.

The two figures stood as one in the darkness for several minutes, each exploring the other with their mouths and hands and minds. Their embrace was finally broken as he relaxed his hold on her back and touched her cheek softly with the back of his hand. Her lips felt strangely swollen and pleasantly sore as she licked them seductively. He pulled his head back to gaze once more into her hypnotic eyes, savoring the animal instinct he saw reflected in them. Reluctantly he closed his own eyes just long enough to tell himself again… no… not this way… not tonight.

"I really should be going," he whispered.

"I know," she said with a sigh. "You aren't going to ignore me for another six weeks are you?" she asked, teasing him with a pouting smile.

"Not on your life," he said earnestly, staring into her eyes, memorizing every detail. He remained thoroughly entranced.

THE CALLING

"How about tomorrow night?" he asked.

"I'd like that," she answered softly.

He reached for her hands again and held them tighter this time. He kissed her once more, briefly and more tenderly. "Good night, Elaina," he said, savoring the way her name felt coming out of his mouth.

"Good night, Jack," she said as she opened the door and stepped inside. She couldn't force herself to close the door, so she stood watching as he walked slowly down the walkway, just as she had done the only other time he had left her here. It wasn't until he was in his car and began to pull slowly away that she closed the door. Even then she stood motionless for a moment with her back against the frame. She closed her eyes and wondered why he hadn't pressed her for more. The way she was feeling she was certain she would have done whatever he had wanted, but probably she would have regretted it the next day.

She finished her thoughts and headed down the hall to her room. As she passed David's room, she peeked in and saw her child sleeping peacefully in his crib. Perhaps that's why Jack hadn't pressed the issue. Maybe he was afraid of getting involved with a woman who had a child. Well, if that was the case then he was clearly not the one for her.

Jack didn't drive straight home. He drove around aimlessly through her neighborhood, rehashing the events of the evening. He wondered if he'd been too bold, or not bold enough. Had he been able to make her understand why he hadn't called for those agonizing six weeks? Did she understand how crazy he was about her? If he came on too strong would he scare her away? After all she was coming out of a very traumatic time in her life. Newly divorced, and an ex-husband who was nowhere around as their child underwent open heart surgery. He argued with himself as he began to realize how truly vulnerable she was. That was why his ethics told doctors not to get involved with patients who might view them as an authority figure. That was right, she would have no defenses. So why was it that he was the one who felt totally defenseless? He finally headed toward his home a few miles to the east, and he realized how totally possessed he'd become. He would not allow anything to stand in the way of his winning this woman's affection.

"Hello?" She answered her cell phone after the first ring.

"I hope I didn't wake you," he said softly.

"No, I was just getting ready for bed."

"Good... I just wanted to tell you how much I enjoyed being with you this evening and how much I'm looking forward to tomorrow night."

"I had a great time. Thank you for a wonderful evening."

"Is there something in particular you'd like to do tomorrow?" He felt like he was back in high school, running out of reasons to keep her on the phone, but unwilling to allow their evening to end.

"No… not really."

"I thought we might catch a movie before dinner?"

"It's Friday night you know."

"Yeah, you're probably right. The movies might be a bit crowded. How about we just take a drive out in the country? We can come back into town for a casual dinner."

"That sounds like fun."

"I know a great little Mexican place on the west side of town."

"I thought you said you had a long day tomorrow?"

"I know. I start early, but I should be out of the hospital by around four thirty…. Can I pick you up around five thirty?"

"Sure, I'll be ready."

"Great."

"I'm looking forward to it."

"I look forward to it too …"

"Would it be okay if I just wear some jeans?"

"Absolutely, jeans will be fine …"

"Okay, I'll see you tomorrow."

"Okay. Bye."

◆◆◆◆◆◆◆◆◆

"All right, so how did it go?" her mother asked, as they sat drinking their morning coffee. David was not up yet and Elaina still had on her robe and slippers.

"It was okay," she lied.

"Okay?" her mom scoffed playfully. "You can't fool me. I can see that look in your eyes." She smiled broadly and added, "And, I heard your cell phone ring about thirty minutes after you came in. Tell me, is he …"

"Oh, Mom," Elaina blushed as she tried to break the interrogation by taking a sip of her coffee.

"So, are you going to see him again?"

"Yes, we are going for a drive this afternoon and then he wants to take me to his favorite Mexican restaurant."

"He's not wasting any time, is he?"

"You are going to be here to watch David, aren't you?" she asked anxiously. Her mother didn't go out much, but she realized she had just assumed she'd be there.

"I guess you can impose on my good nature to watch over my precious grandson one more night."

"Thanks, I didn't mean to presume, I'm sorry."

"All I ask is that you tell me about your date last night."

Elaina proceeded to share all the details with the woman who had become her best friend and confidant.

"Well, girl, it sounds to me like the real thing."

"I'm scared, Mom," Elaina admitted as she began to accept the accuracy of her mother's assessment. She wasn't sure she was ready for a serious relationship.

"I know, sweetie. Love is both exhilarating and frightening at the same time. The best advice I can give you is something I should have shared with you back when you were dating Chad. If your fear of making a mistake ever outweighs the excitement you feel when he touches your hand, you should get out. But, when that excitement fills your soul such that your biggest fear is the possibility of losing him, you'll know, he's the one."

CHAPTER 7

This evening out with Elaina had been just what Jack needed to get his mind off of work. Even so, he found himself slipping back to those few minutes of tension in the hallway with Herb, followed by the emotion-filled encounter with Elizabeth.

"You know?" he offered casually, "I've decided that Herb Nichols really is a jerk."

"That's not a very nice thing to say," Elaina replied in her maternal tone.

"Well, he is," he responded defensively. "You should have seen how uncomfortable he was just talking to Elizabeth Burke. You remember, she's the woman from Brownsville who brought that little girl and her family across the border from Mexico?"

"Yes, I remember."

"Today, I introduced Herb to her, and you could just tell how angry he was that she'd brought that desperately ill child to his hospital."

"Why do you think that is?"

"Isn't it obvious? Her family has no money and no insurance, and since they are from Mexico she isn't eligible for any government assistance."

"So, you think he was mad because the hospital wasn't going to get paid for her care?"

"Precisely," Jack concluded with disgust.

"Don't they have a contingency fund for charity cases?"

"Of course they do, but Herb doesn't think we should use the money raised at local fundraising events on illegals." The slowly building anger in his voice was now obvious. "He doesn't want to use that money for anything except building on to the hospital so he can get his picture in the paper."

"Jack," she said softly, "can you just let that go for now? This has been such a great evening and I hate to see you spoil it by getting so worked up over Herb Nichols."

"You're right," he said, as the crooked smile returned to his face. "I'm sorry I brought it up."

Claude brought his signature soufflé to their table himself, placing his masterpiece between them. The toasted surface of the egg and sugar mixture was a light golden brown, rising nearly two inches above the rim of the white bowl with straight fluted sides.

"Every French restaurant serves a raspberry soufflé," Claude announced, with his accent adding to the dramatic presentation. "However, none have mastered the strawberry soufflé, except *moi*!"

He very carefully placed a large spoonful of fresh whipped cream gently on the top of the airy dessert, then handed each of the fortunate diners a spoon as if he were handing out dueling pistols.

"Bon appetite!" he added, leaving them to savor the delicate prize.

◆◆◆◆◆◆◆◆

It was a beautiful late spring afternoon and Jack had put the top down on his BMW. He'd told Elaina to bring her baseball cap, and she looked very much like she had when she brought David into his office for his last visit, only a few days earlier.

They drove southwest out of Fort Worth, through the gentle rolling hills dotted with the last remnants of wildflowers. The bluebonnets had peaked a week earlier, but there were a few places where they were still spectacular. The Indian blanket and greenthread flowers were still vivid in many of the pastures and along the roadside. The noise of the wind rushing past made communicating a challenge, so there was not much conversation. They were both simply enjoying the beautiful Texas landscape on the northernmost reaches of the Hill Country.

Jack drove as far as Glen Rose where the hills became noticeably higher, just as the sun was beginning to set. As they crested a hill he spotted the perfect place and pulled off the road and parked under the edge of a large live oak. There were few cars on the country road this time of the evening, so the noise they had been subjected to for the last hour and a half was suddenly replaced by a calming stillness, broken only by the rhythmic drones of the cicadas in the tree above them.

"Let's just sit here and watch the sun go down," he said.

"Okay, but can we move to where we see better?" Elaina suggested. "I don't really want to look through the dead bugs on the windshield," she added with a girlish laugh.

"Why don't we sit back there?" he asked, pointing to the deck behind the small back seat.

She nodded in agreement and they both scrambled into the backseat and sat next to each other on the enclosure where the soft top was housed. The view was already breathtaking, and it was getting better by the minute. The dying sun was slowly sinking toward the row of hills in front of them, while a majestic bank of darkening thunderheads with billowing tops and gilded borders was growing off to the South. Over their heads a collection of wispy cirrus clouds trailed off toward the North. Each was slowly turning into soft yellow and orange brush strokes on the brilliant blue canvas, as they gradually replaced the wildflowers that dotted the darkening hills. A single pickup went speeding by then quickly disappeared.

"This has to be one of the prettiest places I've ever seen," she said, staring into the rapidly approaching evening sky.

Jack placed his arm tenderly around her waist and she willingly allowed herself to be drawn to his side. The colors in the clouds had become more vivid, with the pale yellows gradually replaced by deeper shades of orange and red. The background was also changing as the azure blue merged into the cerulean cream near the horizon, unique to the evening sky. The soft hues provided a breathtaking contrast to the increasingly brilliant colors in the clouds overhead. In the waning light, the hills were turning to deepening shades of gray and purple.

He watched her closely as she marveled at the natural panoramic spectacle, the warm evening colors reflected in the smooth delicate skin of her face. He studied every curve, but found himself focused on the profile of her beautiful lips. He wanted to touch them and taste them again, more than anything.

"I can't think of anyone I'd rather share this moment with," he said, not intending to sound quite so... serious. He was overcome by his desire to hold this woman again, not just for that moment, but beyond.

She turned to face him and smiled softly. "That's such a sweet thing for you to say."

He had watched those pouting lips, allowing them to fill his imagination long enough. He reached around her shoulder and pulled her closer to him. As he brought her mouth to his, her lips parted slightly as she inhaled with expectation. He gently explored the edge of her lower lip with the tip of his tongue, feeling the soft contour he had been studying with his eyes. His heart was beating stronger and faster with the rush of passion generated by the touch of her soft hand on his face. His hot breath mixed with hers as his breathing quickened while he continued to caress each portion of her lower lip. He squeezed it purposefully between his own, then with a gentle tug, he heard her moan softly as her mouth opened wider, providing him full access. He ran his tongue over her teeth and across the inside of her upper lip, exploring every part of her luscious mouth.

His mind was filled with desire for this woman, but was he moving too fast? He gently pulled back and stared into her soul with a burning hunger in his eyes. When he returned to her mouth to repeat his journey of exploration he gently bit on the soft flesh of her upper lip, causing her to groan again, a bit louder than before. She reflexively moved both hands to the back of his head, holding his mouth even more firmly to hers. This was the most erotic moment she'd ever experienced, yet it was only a kiss.

By the time they returned their attention to the sunset, it too had reached a crescendo. The bright colors were gone, replaced by fading shades of magenta, rose and violet. The bank of clouds to the South was growing larger and closer, and the burgundies and deep purple were threatened by flickers of light. While the faint rumble of thunder rolled toward them from beyond the hills, Jack was convinced the sound had originated in his own heart.

The evening sky had rapidly turned to ink, as they reveled in their growing attraction. Finally, in the gathering darkness, he turned to her and said, "I guess we better get going."

"Do we have to?" she said, sounding like a child who'd been told the amusement park was closing.

She moved forward and slid down into the backseat drawing him with her. The area was cramped, but they didn't need much room. They continued to devour each other's mouths, neither wanting to break from the intoxicating feeling they were sharing. The two lovers were soon interrupted as a bolt of lightning streaked across the sky followed closely by a loud clap of thunder.

"We really should go," he reasoned, "and I need to put the top up. It looks like it's going rain."

"Let's leave it down," she pleaded as she looked back to the East where they would be headed. The sky was clear in that direction, filled with a canopy of celestial lights. "I'd like to look at the stars."

"Whatever you want, Angel."

This was the first time he'd called her anything but Ms. Farrell or Elaina, and she liked Angel.

They drove back along the winding country road, well away from the lights of the city. She was mesmerized by the vast array of visible stars as she stared into the night sky. Suddenly, a bright light streaked across the blackness, then disappeared as quickly as it came.

"Oh my God!" she exclaimed.

"What?" Jack asked, as reflexively slowed down, concerned that something had happened.

"I just saw a shooting star!" she answered excitedly. "I've never seen one before."

"Make a wish!" he insisted. "That's what they say you're supposed to do."

As he drove on he glanced over and saw her close her eyes for a moment. When she opened them her huge grin reflected the soft lights from the dash as she resumed her scanning of the night sky.

"So? What did you wish for?"

"I'm not telling you. If I did it wouldn't come true."

♦♦♦♦♦♦♦♦♦

For the next two weeks, Jack spent every evening with Elaina. They went out to dinner a few times, but mostly they spent their time together at her mother's home. They talked some about work, both his and hers, but mostly they just talked about life. Jack shared his childhood and professional background, and Elaina talked mostly about the hopes and dreams she had for her son. They held hands most of the time they were together, punctuated by passionate kisses after her mother had retired to her room. Elaina often remarked how she wished they could go back to their "sunset spot," but the weather had turned unpredictable and afternoon thunderstorms had ruined their plans for another evening drive on two separate occasions.

As they sat in the living room one evening, Jack asked her about the piano and Elaina admitted that she used to play, but not much in recent years.

"Please play something for me," he pleaded.

"Okay, but promise you won't laugh at my mistakes."

From what she implied, he anticipated she would play some elementary piece she'd learned as a child. Instead, she surprised him with a beautiful rendition of Beethoven's *Moonlight Sonata*. While it was clear to her that she was out of practice, to him, her passion and feel for the music were obvious.

When she finished, she turned to find him no longer seated on the sofa. He was standing behind her and gently placed his hands on her shoulders.

"I haven't been practicing much as you can tell," she said, as an apology for what was clearly not up to her standards.

"That was unbelievable. How long have you been playing?" he asked, as he began to tenderly massage the tension from the muscles near the base of her neck.

"My mom had me start taking lessons when I was six, but I didn't really take it seriously until high school. Then when I went to nursing school I didn't have time to play much at all, and when I was living in Kentucky and Ohio, I didn't have access to a piano."

"You play beautifully. It's something you should do regularly. You should always have a piano."

"I started playing again once David and I moved back here, but when he got sick I didn't have any time to spare."

"Well, now that he's well you need to make it a priority... assuming you still want to play," he added trying to avoid sounding paternal.

"Perhaps I'd have more time to practice, if you weren't around here all the time," she replied in an accusingly playful tone.

"I'd be happy to simply sit here and listen to you practice, as long as you let me interrupt every now and then to steal a kiss."

She stood up from the bench and turned slowly toward him. As she did she put her hands on his shoulders and pushed him backward toward the sofa; half stumbling, he fell backward onto it. For the first time, she was being the aggressor. She rapidly advanced, covering him with her body while staring into his surprised eyes.

"It's not exactly stealing, if it's given freely, is it?" she whispered.

She slowly lowered her lips to his, taking him into her mouth as a rush of dominance overcame her. He responded to her passion by wrapping his arms around her waist with the fingers of his right hand touching the pocket of her jeans. She shuddered for a moment but made no objection. He held her tighter than she could ever remember, making it harder to gather her breath. She was unsure whether it was the firmness of the embrace, or the emotion of that moment.

As they lay there together, Jack looked longingly into her incredible eyes, lost once more in the deep green hues with flecks of gold. The color was concentrated more now, as the black centers had grown wider with her growing passion. He broke the trance momentarily with something he'd been meaning to ask.

"I have a conference coming up next weekend in San Antonio. Would you be willing to come with me?"

She had wondered just how long it would take for him to finally move on to the next level of their relationship. She'd been anticipating and hoping for an invitation like this, and she had her response well rehearsed.

"What exactly did you have in mind?" she asked without smiling, trying her best to remain coy.

"I just thought it would be good for us to get away for a couple of days."

"Get away, huh?" she inquired, allowing the hint of a sly smile to break through.

"Yeah, you know, we could spend some time on the River Walk, or maybe go out to Sea World. Just spend some time together," he said, avoiding the obvious.

"Let me think about it," she teased. "When would we leave, and when would we be back?"

"The conference is on Saturday morning, so I thought we might leave Friday around noon and drive down. We could come back Sunday evening."

"I'm supposed to work on Friday," she said, leaving him hanging for an extra moment. "But, I guess I could trade days off with one of the other girls."

"Great! Does that mean you'll go?"

She answered with a simple nod of her head, still trying not to smile.

"I already have a reservation at the La Mansion del Rio," he added, then paused for effect. "Are you okay with that?" He was finally getting to the issue of accommodations, and all that it implied.

"Sure," she said slowly. "As long as you agree to behave." Her tone was playfully stern, and was accompanied by a furrowed brow he'd not seen before.

Jack took a long deep breath and closed his eyes momentarily. When he opened them, she was grinning at him with a new twinkle in her eyes.

"I promise, I won't cross any lines you draw," he said far more seriously than she'd expected.

She kissed him again, this time less passionately, then whispered, "Good answer."

♦♦♦♦♦♦♦♦♦

The Friday afternoon drive down Interstate 35 took five and a half hours, with more traffic congestion than he'd remembered, especially around Austin. The wildflowers that had decorated the roadside in April were long gone by mid-May, and the highway crews had been out mowing the first growth of the season. The smell of fresh cut grass occasionally filled the car as Jack held Elaina's hand much of the way, playfully twirling her fingers with his own.

"I'm really glad you agreed to come with me," he said, once they were well under way.

She removed her seatbelt, kicked off her shoes and turned slowly toward him. As she did she bent her knees and drew her feet up under her.

"What are you doing?" he asked.

Silently she took his right hand and raised it slowly to her lips then began placing tender kisses on the tips of each one.

"As much as I like what you're doing, I wish you'd put your seatbelt back on," he said scolding her a little.

"Aw, you're no fun," she protested.

"It's kinda hard to have that kind of fun when you're driving down the road at seventy miles an hour."

"I don't know about that," she replied with the smile of a temptress.

She leaned across and kissed his cheek then trailed her kisses back to his ear where she half whispered, "I'm not the one who's driving."

He looked down at the speedometer and realized they were now doing eighty-five. "I think you'd better sit back down and put your seatbelt on before I run off the road."

She giggled like a school girl, then reluctantly did as she was told.

They arrived at the La Mansion del Rio in downtown San Antonio at six-thirty. The old Spanish-style architecture of the seven story building was a sharp contrast to the ultramodern amenities of this luxury hotel. The floor of the hotel lobby was covered with glazed Mexican tile, and the walls and ceiling were hand-troweled plaster with heavy wooden beams. Rows of arches separated the many public areas and all the exterior windows were arched as well. The couple could just as easily have been walking into a resort in Vera Cruz or Puerto Vallarta.

The bellman showed them to their room on the fifth floor. The large junior suite had a king-size bed and a balcony that looked out over the San Antonio River just below. Jack tipped the bellman as he placed their two suitcases on the stands near the door that led into the large marble bathroom. Once he closed the door behind him, Jack and Elaina were finally alone.

She walked over to the door to the narrow balcony and opened it, taking in the warm evening breeze that was stirring the tops of the ancient oaks and scattered palm trees lining the river below. As she stood holding the wrought iron railing, Jack silently came up behind her and wrapped his arms softly around her waist. He rested his chin on the top of her head as they both absorbed the unique view of the city. From this spot they were treated to the serene river meandering through the giant trees, combined with the huge modern hotels and office buildings of this multicultural metropolis.

"Let's take a walk," he suggested. "We can grab some dinner on the river."

"That sounds like a great idea," she agreed as she turned in his arms to face him. "Give me five minutes to change," she said before he released her. As she stepped back into the hotel room, he watched her as she walked toward the bathroom, grabbed her small suitcase, then closed the door behind her.

He felt so completely relaxed with this woman. They'd spent nearly every nonworking, non-sleeping hour together for the last three weeks. Now he was finally here in this romantic setting with the woman he had been pursuing in his mind for many years, but had only met two months ago.

While she was changing, Jack called down to the front desk and spoke for a minute with the evening manager. He had just hung up the phone as she emerged wearing a pale yellow cotton dress with a knee-length flared skirt. It had a modest scoop neckline trimmed with a narrow white border, and the same white trim ran all along the hemline and along the edge of the sleeveless bodice. A plain white belt rested just above the top of her hips and a pair of white sandals with two-inch heels completed the summer ensemble. Jack stood motionless, staring at her.

"What's the matter?" she asked.

"You are so beautiful," he said, half mumbling.

"Thank you," she replied shyly. "You really know how to flatter a girl."

He shook his head slowly from side to side, not fully believing the image before him. In that moment a realization hit him. Escape from the charms of this woman had become impossible, but why would he ever consider such a foolish effort.

Jack was still wearing his traveling clothes: a pair of tan linen trousers, a white cotton long-sleeve shirt and a light brown sports coat.

She moved forward quickly and grabbed his hand. "Let's go," she said, pulling him toward the door. "I'm getting hungry and you promised to feed me," she added playfully. Her call to action finally broke the trance and he silently followed her into the hallway.

As they stepped out of the back door of the hotel onto the River Walk, the serene atmosphere they had viewed from above had changed. Hundreds of people were making their way along the broad concrete sidewalks that flanked the meandering river. There were other couples and numerous small groups, all headed in different directions. Many were stopping to take pictures of this unique setting. Others were riding in small flatbed river boats as they noisily passed by. The pilots were charged with pointing out the landmarks along the route, employing a microphone in one hand and the outboard motor tiller in the other. The bright yellow railings of the boat were trimmed with orange and red, and festive Mexican music played through the speakers.

"I think it would be fun to take a boat ride before we leave, don't you?" she asked excitedly, as she looked up into Jack's face.

"Whatever you want, Angel. Your wish is my command," he replied matching her whimsical mood.

That's the second time he's called me that, she thought, then wondered, *Does he really think that, or was he just being silly?*

They walked along near the edge of the dark water where the walkway ended in a two-foot drop off. There were no protective railings, so Jack kept himself between her and the edge. They passed several restaurants with tables placed strategically next to the water's edge, forcing the pedestrians and potential customers to use a narrow path between the groups of diners. They stopped to look at several of the menus, but Jack had something specific planned. He had been here many times during his years in San Antonio, and he was not about to settle for one of the tourist-trap, sidewalk cafés.

As the late afternoon moved toward evening, they walked past a raucous Irish bar near the Hilton Palacio del Rio, one of the older hotels on the river. It had been built for the 1968 HemisFair, and back then it was the place to stay in the city. In recent years it had been dwarfed by several huge new hotels surrounding a major shopping area and the new convention center, all built around the river. Just beyond the Hilton the crowd thinned out considerably and the atmosphere was more serene.

He soon spotted the place he'd been looking for and gestured for Elaina to lead the way. Together they climbed a long set of winding rocky steps up to The Fig Tree, a restaurant where he had dined once before, several years before. He had called ahead to reserve a specific table overlooking one of the river's many bends.

The maître d' seated them on the patio, exactly where Jack had requested. Soon they were enjoying a bottle of Jack's favorite Cakebread chardonnay under the cloudless cobalt sky. They both decided on a light dinner of salad and soup, preferring conversation to food.

"How long have you been planning this?" she asked with a knowing smile.

"Oh, not long," he lied. "About a week or so I guess." He had actually made this reservation two weeks earlier when he first considered asking her to come with him for this weekend meeting.

"This is a very picturesque spot," she said, panning off to her left to an outdoor stage on the opposite side of the river where a group of Mexican dancers were rehearsing.

"They say that all true Texans have two hometowns," he offered, as he watched her taking in the rich Spanish heritage of his favorite city in Texas.

"Oh yeah?" she asked. "And how's that?"

"Wherever they were born, and San Antonio."

She had to admit this city had a distinctly Texas look to it, and she could feel the warmth and hospitality of the spirit of fiesta. With the coming darkness of evening, the lights above the River Walk began to appear, and a few stars were just becoming visible overhead.

"This is such a beautiful evening," she said, looking up into the sky secretly searching for another shooting star.

"Yes, it is," he responded, and as he did, he noticed she had crossed her arms in front of her. Without asking, he stood and removed his jacket, placing it over her shoulders before returning to his seat.

"Thank you," she said, pulling it more tightly around her. "I was feeling a little chill."

"I could tell. Is that better?"

"Yes… much!"

After their meal they walked back down the rocky steps toward the river, where they heard a mariachi band playing on the patio behind the Hilton. An entire wedding party had gathered there for drinks and celebration after their ceremony. All the men were dressed in traditional attire, white short-sleeve Mexican shirts with elaborate embroidery, worn outside their black trousers. The women wore festive long dresses of yellow, red, orange and green, except for the bride. She wore an elaborate white gown with pearls covering the top of the bodice, and a lace tiara.

Jack and Elaina watched them as some of them danced rhythmically to the singing of the small band. Jack held his arm firmly around his own treasure as they made their way back to the hotel. At least he hoped she was his.

"I hope you enjoyed the walk and the dinner," he said as they entered the elevator.

"Oh, Jack it was wonderful, as everything has been these last three weeks."

When the door closed he swept her into his arms and kissed her passionately. She returned his advance by raising up on her tip toes to meet his mouth. The elevator door opened on the fifth floor, but they remained wrapped in each other's embrace. When a younger couple stepped into the elevator, Jack realized they had reached their destination. He muttered a polite apology as he help Elaina from the car. Behind them he heard the other couple chuckling, amused at the sight of an older man and his younger conquest.

As they entered the room, Jack closed the door purposefully and locked it securely. The table lamp beside the bed had been turned on, giving the room a soft yellow glow. As he had requested, a beautiful bouquet of spring flowers had been delivered and was sitting on the small coffee table in the sitting area. Accompanying the flowers was a silver bucket containing a chilled bottle of Moët & Chandon White Star Champagne, and a silver tray of fresh strawberries and a small bowl of powdered sugar.

"What's all this?" Elaina asked with a childlike excitement in the voice he had come to adore.

"We didn't have any dessert after dinner, so I thought we should have a little something."

"I love strawberries. How did you know that?"

"Your mother is a veritable wealth of information." Jack smiled as she looked up at him, one of the large strawberries already in her hand and moving quickly to her lips.

As she sat down on the brocade-covered love seat to taste the delicious fruit, Jack lifted the champagne out of the ice, and expertly removed the foil and the wire covering the cork. He worked carefully to pop the cork into the towel he had wrapped around the cold slippery glass, but despite his best efforts, when the cork popped, some of the bubbly wine spilled out into the towel and dripped onto the carpet. Elaina laughed as he tried unsuccessfully to catch the falling liquid with the towel.

"That was not your smoothest move there, big guy," she said with a chuckle, making fun of him for the first time that he could recall.

He smiled and shrugged, but made no effort to clean up the small areas where the foamy liquid had collected on the floor. Instead he poured the champagne and proposed a toast.

"To the most beautiful woman in this room." His playful laugh let her know this was his way of getting back at her for the smooth move comment.

If she thought he was funny she didn't show it. Instead she resorted to her pouting lip pose that she knew would quickly bring him to heel.

"In all seriousness," he began again. "To the most beautiful... most charming... most intoxicating... and most desirable woman in the entire world..." He held up his glass and waited for a moment for her to match his gesture. When she finally did, the touching of the fine crystal produced a harmonic musical tone.

Not to be outdone, Elaina countered, "To the most handsome, most tender hearted, most dashing, yet most presumptuous man in the entire world." She raised her glass and it was his turn to hesitate.

"Presumptuous?" he asked, as he touched his glass to hers.

"Yes, presumptuous seems like a pretty good description... don't you think?"

"Why do you say that?"

"Well, you said you've been planning this for over a week, but I only agreed to come with you five days ago." She cocked her head to one side asking him to deny the truth of her assessment.

"I have been planning this for more than a week, that's true, but I never presumed you would come. I merely hoped you would."

"I think you had a fairly good idea that I would say yes when you asked me, didn't you?"

"Like I said, I was hoping," he said with a sheepish grin.

She moved closer to him and kissed him softly. Her lips now had the unmistakable taste of strawberries mixed with champagne. He wanted more, but she pulled away, teasing him yet again.

"You knew there was really never any doubt," she stated emphatically.

Jack picked up the tray of strawberries and acted as if he were taking them away from her as a punishment. As he did, the large red envelope he had given to the front desk to be delivered with the refreshments was revealed. The name Elaina was expertly printed on the front in gold embossed lettering. As soon as she saw the envelope, she immediately stopped reaching for the tray.

"I assume this is for me, since it has my name on it," she said as she inspected the envelope.

Jack nodded silently and watched as she carefully tore the gold foil seal. She stood up, with Jack's jacket still draped across her shoulders, and moved slowly across the room to be nearer to the light. Another smaller white linen envelope was inside, and on the front, in hand printed calligraphy, the name Angel had been elaborately written. She stood with her back to him not allowing him to watch her reaction.

She remained motionless as she began to read the words he had written the day after she had agreed to come away with him.

To my Angel

I've been searching for you my entire life,
I was sure God had not heard my request.
Then my angel appeared one day amid strife,
On that day my search finally gained rest.

All my love,
Jack

Silent tears of joy streamed down her cheeks as she read his simple poem again several more times. No one had ever written anything so beautiful, just for her. What had she done to deserve this tender loving man's affection? She turned quickly and saw him standing there, frozen in time, his boyish face yielding with an anxious yet hopeful expression.

She stepped toward him and her smiling eyes were magnified by the tears she was unable to hide. The joy she was feeling spilled out of her uncontrollably like the liquid from the recently opened Champagne. She reached up and held his face, saying, "Oh, Jack, you are the most thoughtful, kind, and loving man I have ever known."

"I can't imagine my life without you." His trembling voice was almost pleading. "I know this is very sudden, but I know that I love you. I've loved you from the moment I looked into your emerald eyes in the hospital, after David's surgery." As he gazed into her beautiful face he found himself lost once more in those eyes. They seemed to beg him to close them with a kiss, but he wasn't finished with the plan he had played out over and over in his mind.

He slowly reached into the pocket of his sport coat as he pulled it off her shoulders and laid it on the chair. When he turned back around he saw her smile had been replaced by a questioning expression. He stared intently into her eyes then slowly dropped to one knee. He opened the tiny box in his left hand and held it up in front of him in the most dramatic gesture of his life. She placed her hands around his as her eyes were widened by the sight of the dazzling three-carat solitaire diamond.

"You are my Angel," he said trying not to fumble over the most important request he'd ever made. "Will you please marry me, and make my life complete?"

His words came so unexpectedly. She suddenly found it hard to breathe. Looking down into this precious man's adoring face, she was shaking so much she didn't think she could speak. The delay in her answer tore at the edges of his heart. He was always so sure of everything in his life, but he realized in this situation he had no control.

Finally, she gathered herself. "Of course I'll marry you," she said as a joyful smile gradually replaced the anxious surprise from a moment earlier.

Suddenly Jack was grinning like she had not seen before. "You have made me happier than I ever imagined I could be," he said, as he slipped the ring carefully on her trembling finger. He looked up into her face and his tone regained its serious nature. "I promise to love you, and care for you, for the rest of my life."

He stood up directly in front of her, still holding her trembling hands. She anxiously looked up from the sparkling ring into his tearful eyes, searching for a confirmation of what had just happened. He put his arms around her and pulled her tightly to him and with a look of satisfaction and relief, he whispered, "I love you more than anything, my Angel."

Experiencing the reality of his body holding hers, and the sincerity of his face, she finally allowed herself to express what she feared was only a dream. "I love you too my sweet man. I love you so very much."

They kissed passionately for a moment before she felt the need to speak again.

"Jack, you have no idea how happy you've made me." She paused for a moment to collect herself. "You know, this is what I wished for that night I saw the shooting star."

"I didn't see it," he said, "but I wished on it too. My wish was that you'd say yes."

They stood in the middle of the room, holding each other in a lovers' embrace. The passion of their kiss had evolved from the probing exploration into what felt more like a ballet, danced by two expert performers. Their mouths were now intimately familiar as each seemed to anticipate the other's movements and desires.

Enraptured by the moment, Jack finally gave himself permission to begin to explore his lover even more intimately. With his right hand caressing the back of her neck his left followed the curve of her lower back, then down to tenderly stroke the smooth roundness of her bottom through the thin cotton fabric. She responded with a faint moan and pressed her lower body forward to meet his. In that moment he felt that she too had given him permission.

His left hand reluctantly released her and moved to the back of her neck to join its partner. Carefully he searched for the clasp at the top of her dress and smoothly unhooked it. As he released it, he felt her breath catch just slightly and she pulled her chest toward him with both arms around his back. That was the signal he needed as he slid the long zipper slowly down to her waist. She released her grip on him only long enough to reach in front of her, quickly undoing the buckle of her white belt, allowing it to fall to the floor.

Their mouths remained a constant point of contact, as neither seemed willing to break the comfortable bond of passion. He finally released the slight suction he'd used to secure her lower lip and leaned back slowly, bringing his hands up to her shoulders. He gently pulled the soft yellow material forward, exposing the smooth white skin on either side of the straps of her bra. She relaxed and placed the heels of her sandals back on the floor then stared up intently into his widening eyes.

Elaina longed for his touch in a way she had read about, but never experienced. How was it possible that her life could have changed so dramatically in such a short time? She had all but convinced herself that it would be okay to live her life with only the love of her mother and her child, but now, looking at this magnificent man in front of her, she couldn't bear the thought of being without him.

He bent over slightly and gently kissed the cool skin on the tip of her left shoulder, sending a shiver from that point through to her spine. As his gentle kisses moved to the nape of her neck she held her breath until she was unable to do so any longer. "Oh ..." she sighed, then inhaled again swiftly.

The loose fabric fell slowly off her shoulders and slid down over her arms and her breasts. Jack felt as though he was opening a precious gift and wanted to do so as deliberately and carefully as possible, savoring every detail of the body he had been aching to see, and to touch. As the dress slid softly over her hips it gathered in a small yellow puddle around her feet.

He took a step back to take in the vision, and as he did, she too took a step back out of her dress. He surveyed her gorgeous form and to his eyes she was perfect. She had taken excellent care of her body, especially after David was born, working out nearly every day. Despite the absence of any scars, stretch marks or blemishes, she remained a bit self-conscious. There was a soft fullness to her lower abdomen, just above her bikini panty line, which betrayed her maternal status. In reality she was the only one who could have even noticed this minimal imperfection.

They stood silently facing each other, and she could feel Jack's eyes caressing her nearly naked body. Her bare arms were draped casually beside her gracefully sculpted torso, clad only in her lacy white bra and bikini panties. His gaze made its way back to her face and she smiled in a devilish way he had not seen before. He remained almost motionless, barely able to draw his breath, staring intently at his seductress. Watching his face, she noticed his lips had parted slightly but he remained otherwise frozen, his eyes incapable of blinking.

Something inside him finally triggered his movement and he stepped boldly forward and reached behind her knees with his right arm and behind her back with his left, tenderly lifting his precious Angel who held firmly to him. She stared into his eyes with an anticipation that was making her heart race as though she'd been running for her life. Effortlessly he carried her to the bed, which had been partially turned down by the housekeeper. As he laid her gently on the fine cotton sheet, he brushed the covers off onto the floor, allowing her to lay there, fully exposed in front of him.

He stepped toward the end of the bed and took her left ankle in his hands, raising it up off the bed. He carefully unbuckled the new white sandal and slowly removed it, gently caressing and massaging her foot with his fingers. He watched as she laid her head back and heard her moan softly under his touch. He repeated this act of ultimate foreplay to free her right foot, and again she made it clear she approved. Then holding her foot firmly, he bent over and raised it to his lips, gently kissing the tips of each of her neatly pedicured toes. She suddenly drew a deep breath through her open mouth and momentarily closed her eyes.

Jack backed away from the bed and calmly unbuttoned his shirt and pulled it off his broad muscular shoulders. His exposed chest was covered with a thin layer of dark hair with only a few gray ones interspersed. He slipped out of his loafers and socks, and pushed them aside before loosening his belt and unzipped his trousers, allowing them to fall to the floor. Standing next to the bed he was wearing only his dark blue silk boxers, only an arm's length from fulfilling his ultimate desire.

"I told you I wouldn't cross any line you draw," he said, again sounding more serious than he'd intended.

Elaina looked up at him impatiently and pointed to the fresh white sheet in front of her. Her voice was deeper and more seductive than she thought she possessed. "I don't see any line here, do you?"

He laid down next to her, but before touching her again, he needed to make his feelings clear. Choosing his words carefully, he said, "You know, I've spent my life fixing broken and injured hearts. God has given me the privilege of literally holding the hearts of little children in my hands. Now, it is my heart that you are holding in your hands. Please be gentle." He was trying to hold back the rising tide of emotion, but she could see the moisture growing in the corners of his eyes.

"I will always shelter your heart with my own. I will guard it with my life," she whispered, struggling to believe this man was now hers.

♦♦♦♦♦♦♦♦♦

The first rays of the morning sun peeked between the drapes, creating two bright lines on the wall. Elaina raised up sleepily on her elbows and looked around the room, but did not see her lover. She heard the water running in the shower and then it stopped. In another minute she heard the door open and saw Jack walk into the dimly lit room wearing only a large white bath towel wrapped tightly around his waist.

"Good morning, Angel," he said as he pulled the draperies open to welcome the new day. "Breakfast is on its way." He'd no sooner spoken the words than a knock came at their door.

Her first impulse was to run to the bathroom, but Jack motioned for her to remain in bed. "Just stay where you are. I'll take care of everything."

He threw on one of the plush terrycloth robes and discarded his towel before opening the door for room service. "Thank you," he said as he tipped the waiter and rolled the cart into the room himself, allowing the door to close noisily behind him.

She lay quietly watching as Jack opened the folding leaves of the portable table and rearranged the place settings. He opened the metal box under the white tablecloth and retrieved the warm plates, covered with gray metal tops. He placed them carefully between the silverware, leaving them covered as he poured them each a cup of coffee before removing the white paper covers from the glasses of fresh orange juice.

He disappeared into the bathroom and promptly returned to the bedside carrying the other robe. He bent down and kissed her swollen lips, still aching from their amazing night. He whispered softly, "Would you like some breakfast?"

"Yes, I'm starving!"

She pushed the covers aside and stood facing him, naked, but without the slightest sense of embarrassment. She turned around as he held open the robe, slipping it onto her arms and shoulders. As she pulled it closed and tied the sash, he reached around her and held her tight against him. "I love you so much it almost hurts," he spoke softly in her ear.

She whirled around and threw her arms around his neck, looking into his freshly shaved face with her brilliant emerald green eyes and said, "Was I dreaming, or did you really ask me to marry you?"

He smiled softly and replied, "Well, I believe it was me who was doing the dreaming, and in my dream my precious Angel said yes."

He kissed her lips again, then held her out at arm's length, taking in the remarkable woman who would soon be his wife. She looked down at her left hand and shook her head as she sighed deeply.

"Let's eat," he said, walking her over to the table. "I ordered you a Belgian waffle with strawberries," he offered as he uncovered the plate, "and warm Vermont maple syrup, with a side of the applewood smoked bacon."

"How did you know I love waffles?"

He looked at her with a sly smile and she nodded. "Mom, right?"

"Like I said, your mother is a wealth of information when it comes to you."

"What are you having?" she asked as he helped her move the heavy arm chair closer to the table.

"I'm having the huevos rancheros."

He watched curiously as she dove into the crispy waffle.

"What?" she asked when she noticed he hadn't started eating but was simply staring at her with his innocent crooked smile.

"I am so much going to enjoy spoiling you for the rest of your life," he said, as she put down her fork and stared back at him.

"Well, you have already spoiled me way more than I deserve."

As they looked dreamily into each other's eyes, it was clear to both of them they had found their perfect match.

"I thought you had a meeting to go to?" she asked, as she placed the linen napkin across her lap.

"It doesn't start until nine o'clock, and the panel discussion I'm part of isn't until eleven." Not really caring for the coffee, he sipped slowly at the orange juice. "I should be back here by around four, so if you want to go shopping, the mall area is just a couple of blocks away, over by the Marriott," he said. "If you want to work out, there is a great spa downstairs. Maybe you would like to get a massage or a manicure or facial."

"I think I'd prefer you give me my massages… if that's all right with you," she said looking up at him with a devilish smile.

"I'd prefer that as well… later."

He finished his orange juice and set the empty glass back on the table, then folded his napkin and laid it casually next to his empty plate. He looked up with a more serious expression, waiting for her to return his gaze. When she sensed he was watching her again, she put her elbows on the table, put her hands together, and rested her chin on her crossed fingers.

"So… what else is on your mind?" she asked, looking a bit impatient.

"There is one more thing I've been meaning to talk to you about," Jack said with a more resolute tone. "I want to adopt David."

"Really?" She hadn't thought about her how all this would impact her son given the excitement of the last twenty-four hours.

"Yes, I think it's very important that a boy have a father to help him grow up to be a man, and I don't want to be his step-dad. I want him to see me as his father."

"Jack," she said, shaking her head. "You never cease to amaze me."

"I knew from the beginning that you two were a package deal. I have always wanted to have my own family, so if it's okay with you I'm going to ask Chad if he will relinquish all paternal rights and allow me to be David's legal father."

"I can't imagine why he would object," she said with indifference. "That would be one less thing to get in his way."

"Oh… there's one more thing," he continued, feeling his stride. "I want you to have whatever kind of wedding you'd like, within reason," he smiled. "The only thing I ask is that it take place soon. I'm not interested in waiting around. You might decide to change your mind."

"I have always wanted a real church wedding," she said, remembering the sterile, secular proceedings at the courthouse in Lexington, nearly three years before.

"You find the church and send out however many invitations you want, and I'll make it happen." He paused, then added, "Just don't make me wait too long, okay?"

◆◆◆◆◆◆◆◆◆

Six weeks later Jack and Elaina were married in a small Methodist church near her mother's home. It was an intimate private ceremony with only about fifty friends and relatives. Buzz stood up with Jack as his best man, and Jack had insisted that David stand beside him as well.

Elaina asked one of her good friends from work to be her maid-of-honor. While she wasn't technically her "best friend," she couldn't very well ask her mother. Most of the other nurses she worked with were so jealous she didn't even bother inviting them to the wedding.

A few of Jack's colleagues came to the wedding, along with several people from the hospital. Among the non-physicians was an aspiring young assistant administrator in charge of finance, Herb Nichols.

The next day Dr. and Mrs. Jack Roberts flew off to Paris for a two-week honeymoon.

◆◆◆◆◆◆◆◆

The dinner conversation at Claude's drifted to their upcoming trip back to Nicaragua to see their friend and colleague, Dr. Domingo Ramirez. They had been going down to Domingo's clinic on the outskirts of Managua every year since 1997.

"I'm really looking forward to seeing Domingo again," Elaina said.

"Me too," Jack replied. "What I'm looking forward to the most is having

David with us this time. I think he will learn a lot about real life, don't you?"

"It's all he's talked about for weeks," she said. "I think he's more excited about this than he is about the end of the school year."

"This trip couldn't come at a better time for me either. The politics around the hospital is driving me crazy."

"Every time we take one of these trips I can see how it relaxes you," she said. "As for me, what I like most is just being able to work together again."

Jack reached past the empty soufflé bowl and picked up his wine glass. He raised it a few inches off the table and leaned it slightly toward Elaina. "To Nicaragua…"

"To Nicaragua…" she replied, touching her glass gently to his.

CHAPTER 8

It was a beautiful late spring morning as Jack headed into the hospital to begin his day. An overnight thunderstorm had passed, leaving a brilliant blue, cloudless sky, and small puddles of water scattered on the pavement of the parking lot. He had a more relaxed manner as he was looking forward to a lighter schedule than he'd had any day in recent weeks. In preparation for taking some time off, whether for vacation or business, he always tried to avoid doing any major elective surgery. He hated to burden his young associate with the post-op care of his patients, and if something unforeseen happened, he might even have to cancel his trip. It was easier, all the way around, to just reduce his schedule for a few days before leaving town.

He was leaving for Managua in two days, and he'd be gone for a week, so he only had one minor case to do this morning, followed by a few patients in the office. His biggest job today also promised to be the most pleasant. He planned to discharge Lupe Alvarez from the hospital after a weeklong stay.

As he made his way on to the fifth floor nursing unit, Jack spotted Buzz Jackson sitting at one of the dedicated computer terminals, poring over one of his many patients' charts.

"How's it going, Buzz?" he asked as he walked up behind him and patted his longtime friend on the shoulder. "We still on for racket ball at twelve thirty?"

"Oh, hi, Jack," Buzz answered, a bit startled by the interruption. "I was just about to call you. I'm not going to be able to make it today. I had a kid admitted to me last night through the ER that I suspect has acute bacterial endocarditis, so I need to get him worked up and stabilized."

"This isn't one of the kids we've operated on is it?" Jack asked, concerned that a postoperative infection might have developed in one of the numerous children whose birth defects he'd repaired.

"No, this child hasn't had any prior surgery," Buzz explained. "He's a local kid with a new onset fever and a loud murmur. It sounds like a mitral valve, but I haven't done the echo yet. Are you gonna be around?" he asked, suggesting the child might require surgery if antibiotics failed to resolve the infection involving one of the valves in the young boy's heart.

"I'm here today and tomorrow, then Elaina and I are headed to Nicaragua for a week."

"Oh yeah, I forgot this is your mission week coming up."

"I stopped calling what we do mission work a few years ago," Jack said with a smile. "I don't think we are saving any souls down there. Most of the people are far more committed to their church than we are. We just go there to help out the local physicians and to get away from this rat race for a while." He chuckled at the thought of escaping to one of the most poverty stricken countries in the world.

"Well, if this kid needs emergent surgery I'll let you know before the day is out," Buzz said.

"George is going to be covering for me, and he is perfectly capable of doing an emergent mitral, or even an aortic valve for that matter," he said, trying to make his friend feel more at ease.

"I know he is. I would just feel more comfortable having you do it."

"If the kid needs to be done today or tomorrow, I will assist George, if that would make you feel better."

"This child is from a high profile family," Buzz added. "They have been major contributors to this hospital, so I think they deserve the best."

Jack spent a moment digesting what he had just heard before responding. "You know, Buzz, I'm surprised to hear you say that." He paused until his friend looked up from his work with a puzzled expression. "You know we make every effort to treat all patients the same, whether they have cadillac insurance or don't have two nickels to rub together."

"I know that, but I guess I've been programmed by administration to make that, quote, extra effort, to please our, quote, paying customers," Buzz admitted, making quotation marks in the air with his fingers. "The philosophy of this so called, not for profit facility," he said, again making the quotation marks gesture, "is rubbing off on me. You're right, I just wish you were going to be around next week if I need you."

"If he doesn't need surgery immediately then it's likely I'll be back by the time you finish his course of antibiotics," Jack said in a calmer tone. "If he still needs a valve when I get back, I'll be happy to help, but I'm not canceling my trip," he added, providing an end to that part of their conversation.

"I'll let you know," Buzz said, "and if I don't see you before you leave, I hope you and that pretty wife of yours have a great time."

"Thanks. I'm sure we will."

Jack walked past the nurses' station toward Lupe Alvarez's room rehashing the conversation just concluded. He wondered to himself how the system got so screwed up that it was expected that a child of a wealthy family should be treated differently than the child of a poor one. On more than one occasion he had made his thoughts on this idea clear to anyone who would listen. He contended that by definition if any group or individual was treated better, that meant they weren't giving their best effort for the others.

He knocked softly on the door of Lupe's room and Pablo said, "Come in."

As he pushed the door open he saw a room filled with people, all eager to see him that morning, anticipating the young girl's discharge. Pablo and Juanita stood behind their daughter's bed, both were wearing the same new outfits they'd had on the day they brought Lupe into his office and every day since. Miguel was sitting on the foot of her bed, tossing the baseball into the glove that had seldom left his hand over the past ten days. Elizabeth Burke stood by the window with her two friends Andie and Jeremy. They all smiled when Jack entered the room, all except for Miguel. He didn't seem to notice as he continued to try to throw the ball through the glove.

Lupe was lying quietly, already fully dressed in another new outfit Andie had bought for her at Target. It was a bright red dress with white puffy sleeves and scalloped collar. She had on a new pair of white sneakers and red anklets and she was still holding her teddy bear firmly in the crook of her arm.

"Good morning," Jack said to everyone, before turning his attention to Lupe. "*Buenos dias, niña,*" he said sweetly.

"Good morning, doctor," Lupe replied. Her voice was strong and clear, and this was the first time he had heard her attempt to speak any English.

"You look like you are ready to get out of here," he said with a smile.

"I think we are all ready to go home, Dr. Roberts," Pablo said with a relieved sigh.

"Well, as far as I can tell she is doing great," Jack offered reassuringly. "She is off all medications and she seems to be eating well enough, so, I guess we can let her go."

He turned to Elizabeth and asked, "Are you planning to leave for Brownsville today?"

"No sir," she said timidly. "We thought we would leave early tomorrow morning. We will be staying one more night with my friends Andie and Jeremy Lawrence," she said, motioning toward her friends.

Jack stepped quickly over to where the middle-aged couple was standing and extended his hand to both of them. "It is nice to finally meet you. Elizabeth has told me about how you opened your home to these people, and I just want to say how much I admire you for that."

"It is our pleasure," Andie said. "It is the least we could do."

Jeremy added, "Watching this whole ordeal has greatly enriched our lives, and we want to thank you for making it possible for Lupe to get the treatment she needed."

"It was this lady right here who made it happen," Jack offered, as he placed his hand on Elizabeth's shoulder.

She blushed slightly and dropped her chin a little but didn't break eye contact with Jack. "I can't tell you how much I appreciate everything you, and everyone here at this wonderful hospital, have done. You have been incredible."

"Like I said," Jack spoke with a familiar calmness to his voice. "This is God's work. We are merely His instruments."

There was no response to his words other than the knowing nods from Elizabeth, Pablo and the Lawrence pair. "I will need to take care of some paperwork, but I suspect we can have you out of here in the next few minutes."

"The family asked if they could get a picture with you and some of the nursing staff out in front of the hospital," Jeremy said. "I brought my camera and was hoping you could accompany us outside."

"Sure," he said, "I'll be around, just have the nurses page me and I'll meet you out front." Jack turned to see the charge nurse standing near the door, and she smiled and nodded her head, indicating she'd heard and understood his instructions.

As he walked toward the door he added, "I'll see everyone downstairs in a bit."

"Dr. Roberts?" Elizabeth called as she followed him out into the hallway.

Jack turned and replied, "Yes?"

She quickly caught up and walked with him back to the nurses' station. "I just wanted you to know how sorry I am to have placed such a financial burden on you and this hospital by bringing Lupe here."

"Nonsense," he said emphatically as he stopped to face her. "Don't be ridiculous. What ever gave you that idea?"

"Mr. Nichols told me how much the hospital was having to write off, and I'm sure your bill is also considerable, and I just wanted you to know how much I appreciate it."

"Herb Nichols talked to you about Lupe's hospital bill?" he questioned, not believing what he had just heard.

She nodded prompting him to ask, "When was that?"

"A couple of days ago I ran into him as we were coming into the hospital."

"You just ran into Herb Nichols?"

"Yeah, Pablo and I were coming in through the front entrance and he was standing in the lobby talking to one of the volunteers. When he saw us he came over and said hello and asked if he could speak to me privately," she explained.

"Really?" Jack was beginning to get the picture.

"Pablo went on up to the room and I followed Mr. Nichols into his office. He showed me a copy of the Alvarez account. I had no idea that the bill was nearly ninety thousand dollars."

Jack shook his head then closed his eyes for a moment. "What else did he say?"

"Well, he told me that he understood that the Alvarez's had no way of paying their bill. He also explained that since they were here illegally, they were not eligible for any kind of government assistance, so the hospital would, in his words, eat the bill. I really felt bad, ya know?"

Jack could feel the warmth building in his ears as his anger level increased with every word she spoke. "What did you say?"

"I told him how grateful I was and how appreciative the Alvarez family was for the charity he had offered them, but I don't think he was very happy with me," she added, dropping her gaze toward the floor. "He said he hoped I wouldn't make a habit of smuggling children across the Rio Grande. He tried to sound like he was kidding, but I think he was really being somewhat serious."

"Listen," Jack said, trying to keep his cool, despite being on the verge of losing control. "I want you to do me a favor."

As he was speaking he pulled out his wallet and began searching. "I want you to take this, and while they are getting Lupe ready for discharge, I want you to go down to Nichols' office and give it to him," he said as he handed her what he had just retrieved.

"I can't do that," she said, trying to avoid taking the paper.

"Please, do this for me," he pleaded.

"May I ask why?"

"What he said to you was completely inappropriate. I need for him to know that, and this is the best way I can think of to convey that message." Jack spoke in as calm a voice as he could muster. "It would be even better if you could tell him how his words made you feel, but I'll leave that up to you."

"I have to admit, he did make me feel like I had stolen from the hospital, but I guess I deserved to feel a little guilty."

"No, no, no ..." Jack interrupted. "You have absolutely nothing to feel guilty about. You are only guilty of committing one of the bravest, most humanitarian acts of kindness I've ever witnessed. For him to suggest otherwise is... is, just wrong." He wanted to say selfish, but thought better of it, not wanting to personalize his criticism more than he already had.

"Okay," she conceded. "I'll go down there right now, but promise me you'll come looking for me if I'm not back in ten minutes." One corner of her mouth raised slightly at this attempt at levity.

"Oh, don't worry," Jack replied. "If you aren't back soon, I'll come find you."

Elizabeth walked directly to the elevators and soon was on her way down to the first floor. When she stepped out of the elevator she walked straight to the office where she had been belittled two days earlier.

"Is Mr. Nichols in his office?" she asked when the secretary looked up from her work.

"Yes, and you are?" the middle-aged woman inquired, obviously perturbed by the interruption.

"My name is Elizabeth Burke, and I have something for him."

The woman hesitated a moment before picking up the phone and pressed the intercom button. "There's an Elizabeth Burke here to see you. She says she has something for you." There was a momentary pause before she hung up the phone then said, "Mr. Nichols can see you for just a few minutes." She pointed toward the partially opened door.

"Oh, this won't take that long."

Elizabeth had been thinking about what Jack had said, and the more she thought about it, the more she realized he was right. She was not guilty of doing anything she wouldn't expect anyone else to do given the same circumstances. Perhaps some of the anger she had seen in Jack's face had somehow been transferred to her, but in the two minutes it had taken to reach this office, she had gone from being sorry for burdening the hospital to being angry at being denigrated for her actions. She quickly stepped through the doorway into the office and didn't bother to close the door behind her.

"Yes, Ms. Burke?" Herb asked without looking up from his work. When his eyes finally pulled away from the papers on his desk, she was standing directly in front of him. His initial demeanor hinted of both contempt and indifference, but that quickly changed. Before him stood a woman who was on a mission. She did not appear at all like the meek person he had easily intimidated two days earlier. He leaned back slightly in his chair, assuming a more defensive posture.

"You know, Mr. Nichols," she said with a sharp edge to her voice. "I've been thinking a lot about what you said the other day, about having to eat Lupe Alvarez's bill." She paused in the hope of gathering momentum. "I figured that it probably didn't taste too good, and it certainly wasn't very nutritious, so... I want to make sure you don't starve." She casually tossed the one hundred dollar bill on his desk and turned immediately, making her way out through the door before he could offer a response.

◆◆◆◆◆◆◆◆◆

Three of the nurses from the floor brought Lupe down to the front lobby in a wheelchair, as the rest of her entourage trailed close behind. Elizabeth had already pulled her suburban around to the covered circular drive and was waiting for them to make their way out into the bright sunny morning. She saw Jack hurrying across the lobby, and he soon joined them. In the distance she could see the figure of another man standing near the vestibule outside his office, watching the proceedings through the large glass façade of this modern facility.

Jeremy lined everyone up for a group photo. Lupe stood in the center with one parent on either side and Jack standing behind the smiling child. Elizabeth stood next to Pablo with Andie outside her as Miguel took his place next to his mother. The three nurses gathered alongside and behind him. After taking several shots, Jeremy asked to take one more of just Lupe flanked by Jack and Elizabeth. They both crouched down to match the young girl's height.

While the final photos were being taken, Pablo and Miguel went around to the back of the truck and loaded Lupe's few personal items. Miguel left his baseball glove and retrieved another bundle. As Jack gave Lupe a final goodbye hug, Miguel came through the small group of people carrying the offering. He carefully removed the old worn blanket and placed the treasure carefully on the ground behind his sister. As Jack released her, she stepped aside revealing the magnificent carving.

"What is this?" Jack inquired at the sight of the Madonna sitting in the hospital driveway.

Miguel's hand remained on top of the precious piece of art as he spoke slowly. "This was carved by my great grandfather," he explained, reciting the English words Elizabeth had taught him over the past week. "It has been the protector of my family for more than sixty years and we want you to have it for saving our Lupe."

Miguel maintained a very serious expression as he lifted his hand slowly off the carving and stepped back toward his parents. Pablo was beaming with paternal pride and Juanita smiled sweetly as she placed her hands on her young son's strong shoulders.

Jack was truly moved by this gesture of incredible sacrifice by this family. His initial reaction was to decline their gift as being far too generous, but he had spent enough time in the Latin community to know better. To refuse their gift would be the ultimate insult.

"I don't know what to say," he stammered as he released Lupe's hand, allowing her to stand in front of her father. After a few moments he looked up at the small family and said, "This is the most precious gift I have ever received, and I thank you more than you will ever know."

Juanita handed Lupe a small envelope. The child then stepped back toward

Jack, handing it to him as he remained crouched in front of her. He took it and quickly opened it, removing the plain white card then read it silently.

"*Vaya con Dios — Doctor*" was handwritten in the center. At the bottom she had printed her name "Lupe Alvarez."

Jack could feel the moisture building in the corners of his eyes, but he was not concerned. He drew her tiny body back into his arms and half whispered, "*Muchas gracias, mija.*"

The nurses were openly crying at the sight playing out in front of them. Elizabeth and Andie were also moved to tears of joy, watching this man holding the little miracle God had delivered through him.

Jack released Lupe and picked up the Madonna, holding it as if it were another child. Pablo extended his hand to the surgeon, thanking him once more for his daughter's renewed health. Juanita also hugged him briefly around his neck and offered a traditional blessing, "*Dios te bendiga, señor.*"

They all scrambled into the suburban as Jack and the hospital staff continued to offer their best wishes. Elizabeth approached Jack with a satisfied grin and said, "Thank you again, Dr. Roberts." As she hugged him she whispered, "You're a saint."

"No, dear," he replied earnestly. "I am but an instrument. You are the saint."

He walked with her around the front of her vehicle then opened the door for her. As she got in he said, "Drive safely, and please let me know when you arrive home."

"I will," she replied. "I feel sure we'll meet again."

Jack nodded as he closed her door and joined the nurses who were waving to them as the suburban slowly pulled away.

◆◆◆◆◆◆◆◆◆

"Come on, David, it's time to go!" Elaina called up the stairs to her seventeen-year-old son. In a few seconds he came bounding down the steps carrying a large duffel bag in one hand and his backpack in the other.

"I'm ready," he said, slightly out of breath from the effort. "Where's Dad?"

"He's bringing the car around so we don't have to carry all our bags through that mess out there in the garage."

When David turned sixteen Jack bought him a used Honda Civic. The teenager thought it was okay, but it wasn't really cool like some of the cars his friends drove. Jack refused to buy him that new, fully loaded Chevy pickup he really wanted as his first car, so they compromised. The Honda would be his day-to-day transportation for now, and Jack offered to help him buy what he wanted for his college years once he finished his project. In addition to the car his father also bought him a 1968 Chevrolet pickup with a short, step-side bed.

It cost two hundred fifty dollars and had to literally be towed to the house. To say that it was in rough shape was being kind, but David had insisted that he could fix it up. Upon completion, Jack said he could either drive it, sell the Honda, and pocket the money, or he could sell both vehicles and buy a new truck, and his dad would cover the difference. The stipulation was he had to at least get the old truck running.

Jack thought this was a good idea, figuring it would teach him some responsibility and allow him to make his own decision about the value of his labor. David's plan was to not only get the old truck running, he was going to take the body apart, a little at a time, then refinish or replace every part. He envisioned a show truck that would be worth at least ten thousand dollars when he was finished with it. That was nearly a year and a half ago, and so far no one had heard that engine running. The garage floor was covered with various tools and engine parts, making it a challenge to get around, even without luggage.

As Jack pulled Elaina's brilliant white, five series BMW sedan up to the front door of the house, he remotely popped open the trunk, just as David came out carrying his mom's suitcase and his own duffel bag.

"Hey, Buddy, you all set?"

"You bet," the young man replied. He set the bags down behind the car and came around to give his dad a solid man hug. David was already six feet tall and his physique was just beginning to fill out. His shaggy blond hair was a little longer than Jack thought was appropriate, but his mom loved the surfer boy look. His eyes were a piercing shade of steel blue which gave him the look of a man in his early twenties. He was a ridiculously handsome young man, with strong facial features and a brilliant smile that rivaled any of the rising young stars on television. Elaina, with the help of the orthodontist, had seen to it that his teeth were perfectly straight, despite his begging to have the braces removed early.

David brought out the rest of the bags as Jack loaded them in the trunk. Elaina made one last pass through the house to make sure the appliances were all turned off and the back doors were locked. As she came out, she turned to the two men in her life and asked, "Everybody have their passport?"

"Got it," confirmed David.

"Yes, Angel... Do you have yours?" Jack asked.

"I think so, let me check," she said, questioning herself.

As she rummaged through her purse Jack could sense the growing panic as she was unable to locate the small blue book. "I can't find it!" she said frantically. When she finally looked up she saw Jack had a sly grin on his face. He was holding her passport at eye level, waving it slowly. He was always doing some little prank to keep the mood light, but she didn't think they were nearly as comical as he did.

"Let's go," he said walking around the car to open her door. Despite the fact they'd been married fifteen years, he still treated her like his Angel.

◆◆◆◆◆◆◆◆◆

When traveling almost anywhere else, Jack preferred to fly on American Airlines. DFW was their major hub, and he could fly nonstop to almost anywhere. Anywhere, that is, except Latin America. For some reason almost all the international flights into Central and South America on American went through Miami. While no airline offered nonstop service from DFW to Managua, the most direct flight was on United Airlines, with a single stop in Houston.

The check-in process at the airport had changed dramatically since the terrorist attacks four years earlier. Just getting from the ticket counter to the gate now took nearly an hour for most international flights. Jack also liked to take surgical instruments with him in a carry-on bag, despite the fact he rarely had a chance to use them in the primitive conditions of Domingo's clinic. With the heightened security, he either had to pack them in a checked bag or just leave them at home. On this trip he opted for the latter, assuming Dr. Ramirez had finally stocked his clinic with at least the basics, like needle holders and forceps for suturing the occasional laceration they encountered.

This was to be David's first international flight and, in his own words, he was "fired up." Once they passed through security he pulled out his cell phone and called Amy.

"Hi, baby," he said to the bubbly seventeen-year-old, the only real girlfriend he had ever had. They'd actually been dating for nearly two years, but even before that they were nearly inseparable both at school and at the church where they first met.

"Are you in Nicaragua already?" she asked, excited to hear his voice. The fact that he had told her he wouldn't have cell service where they were going seemed to have been temporarily forgotten.

"No, we are at the airport, just waiting to board our flight."

"I wish I were going with you," she said with the distinctive whine of a teenage girl.

"Me too," he said. "Maybe your folks will let you come next time."

"I'm really gonna miss you."

"I'm gonna miss you too. I can't remember the last time we were apart for an entire week," David added, but as he was speaking he remembered that her family had taken a vacation to Florida last summer for ten days. That wasn't quite the same since he had talked to her on the phone several times each day.

"I can't believe I won't even be able to talk to you for a whole week," she complained, suddenly remembering the absence of cell service. She sounded on the verge of tears, but that wasn't unusual given her age and hormonal status.

"I know," he agreed. "If I find any place that has service I'll call you, okay?"

"Okay," was her pensive reply.

There was a long pause, then David heard his dad say their flight number had been called. "Well, listen, we're getting ready to board, so I gotta go."

"You take care of yourself and don't get sick or anything while you're down there, okay?"

"I won't," he said. Then he turned his back to where his parents stood and spoke more softly. "I love you, Baby."

"I love you too, David."

"Bye."

"Bye," she said drawing out the word as long as she could.

"Bye," he said softly, then reluctantly he pushed end on his cell phone.

❖❖❖❖❖❖❖❖❖

The flight to Houston was only forty-five minutes, but they had a four hour layover before boarding a different plane. They decided to grab a final American-style meal, choosing the Chili's restaurant in the terminal. Jack and Elaina talked about several of their previous trips, trying to remember if this was their twelfth or thirteenth visit. As they reminisced, David was already missing Amy and wondering if he had made the right choice coming with his parents. Could they possibly know what it was like to be in love the way he was? Probably not, they were too old. He thought about calling Amy again, and almost did, but thought better of it. It would be just as hard to hang up the phone again, maybe harder. It was probably best to leave it like it was.

"Do you think we'll have cell service in Managua?" he asked.

"We didn't the last time we were there," Jack said. "It's possible they've put up some towers since then, but even if they have, your phone won't work because I didn't activate the international service on either your phone or your mom's," he explained. "If we make any calls they will need to be on my phone, and even then it is very expensive."

"I know you would like to talk to her, son," his mom said with a knowing smile, "but she'll just have to miss you for the next seven days."

"Oh, Mom," he said, brushing off the fact that she was reading his mind.

"Besides, absence makes the heart grow fonder," Jack added.

How would he know anything about that? David thought to himself.

❖❖❖❖❖❖❖❖❖

The second leg, from Houston to Managua, was a little more than three hours, plus they gained an hour since Nicaragua did not use daylight savings time. Elaina loved to sit by the window, so with Jack on the aisle, David got the middle seat. The flight was uncharacteristically full with only a few scattered single seats, meaning he was stuck sitting with his parents. He figured he would just listen to the music on his iPod and sleep most of the way, but for now all electronic devices had to be turned off.

"So, how is Amy?" Jack asked, hoping to get his son to talk about his relationship.

"She's okay," David replied, hoping that single answer would be enough to get his old man to drop the subject. Instead, Jack wouldn't be denied.

"What is she planning to do over the summer?"

"Oh, you know, the usual stuff."

"Do the Callahans have a family vacation planned?"

"Actually, they are planning to go to the beach again this year for a week, and they've asked me if I want to go with them."

"Really?" Jack sounded surprised, but Elaina had already told him all about it. Joanne Callahan had asked her if it would be all right if David went with them long before she'd even mentioned the possibility to her daughter.

"Yeah, they rented a house in Seaside, near the beach."

"So, did you ask your mom?"

"Yes," David said emphatically. The question had him concerned that his dad might overrule the tentative permission he had already received. "She said I could go."

"Okay. Were you going to tell me about it?"

"Sure, I just..." he said, sensing that his dad didn't like to be bypassed. Like most young boys, David had always been more comfortable talking to his mom, especially about things like this. In part because she was less likely to say no, but more because he was a bit intimidated by his dad. As a result he didn't talk to him as much as he knew he should.

"It sounds like fun," Jack offered, sounding far more encouraging than David had expected.

"Yeah, they say it's really a cool place. The beach is supposed to be one of the best in Florida." Unknown to David, the brilliant white, sugar sand beaches along the emerald coast of the Florida panhandle were widely acknowledged to be among the most beautiful in the world.

"Is anybody else going?"

"I don't think so," David responded. "Her older brother is still deployed in Iraq and her sister is taking some summer school classes at TCU. So I guess it will just be Amy and her mom and dad."

"And you," Jack reminded.

"Well, yeah, and me."

Jack just nodded his head, recognizing the young man's reluctance to include himself in the initial head count. He really wanted to offer his young son some advice on how to conduct himself given such an opportune situation, but thought better of it. He could try to explain the long-term value of keeping his hormones in check, but he knew that David was a very level-headed kid. Besides, if he and Amy were interested in having sex, they likely already had, given their ample opportunities.

"Don't worry, Dad," David said, sensing Jack's unasked question. "Amy and I already agreed to wait."

"That's very smart of both of you. I'm glad to hear that."

"It was something we decided more than a year ago when we first started going out. One of her friends got pregnant, and she had to drop out of school at sixteen, and neither of us wants to run that risk."

David sounded so much more mature than he had been at that age, Jack thought. He wanted to tell him so, but decided the subject would be best ended right where it was.

"So have you decided where you think you want to go to college and what you want to study?"

"Yeah," he answered quickly, seizing the opportunity to move on to a new subject. "If I can get in I'd like to go to UT in Austin."

"Texas, huh?" Jack was pleased to hear that he had finally made a decision. It had been between Texas Christian University, which was less than five miles from their home in Westover Hills, or UT – Austin, about three hours away. "I've heard they only accept applicants who are in the top ten percent of their class," Jack said, despite the fact he was not the least bit concerned about David's academic qualifications.

"Yeah, I know. My counselor said that currently I'm one of the top five students in my class, so she thinks I can get in as long as I keep my GPA above three point eight."

"What is it now?"

"I don't have my final grades from the end of this year, but I'm pretty sure I made all A's, so it will be three point nine five going into my senior year."

"Are you still thinking about pre-med?"

"Of course. That's all I've ever really considered."

"I know, I was just wondering if perhaps you might have changed your mind," Jack questioned.

"No, I'm still planning to be a heart surgeon, like you," David replied, as if the choice had been part of an inheritance. As he finished speaking the announcement came over the intercom, first in Spanish, then in English, indicating to the passengers that it was okay to use approved electronic devices.

David quickly placed the tiny earbuds into his ears and turned on his iPod, effectively ending their conversation.

Jack had taken David on rounds with him on weekends since shortly after he and Elaina were married. It was a great way for him to develop a bond with his newly adopted son, and the young boy seemed to enjoy the attention he always received from the nurses. It wasn't surprising that David had started saying he was going to be a doctor as far back as eight or nine years old. Jack was proud that his son wanted to follow in his footsteps, but in recent years he felt a growing anxiety about the future of the medical profession. With all the outside influences, health care was becoming more an industry and less a service. He feared his might be the last generation of doctors to be motivated by the true spirit of the traditional healing arts.

CHAPTER 9

Elaina stared out the window on the left side of the airplane as they made their descent into the largest city in Nicaragua. She could see the lush rain forest vegetation that covered the hillsides west of Lake Managua. In the distance the huge lake formed the northern border of the city, and beyond it she could make out the rising peaks of the Amerrisque Mountains. From the air this land appeared to be a tropical paradise, without a hint of the extreme poverty which gripped the vast majority of its people.

As the plane drew closer to the ground, she could pick out several of the vast barrios where a large number of the more than two million residents lived. Most of the damage done by the 1972 earthquake had long since been repaired, but there were still large vacant lots where buildings once stood. In many respects, the city had never fully recovered from that devastating event.

As the trio made their way through the airport, David was impressed by how clean and modern the building appeared. He thought it looked very much like some American airports he'd been in, except for the armed military presence.

Both Jack and Elaina spoke more than adequate Spanish, so they were able to move easily through customs. Once they gathered their luggage they began looking for Domingo. Typically he waited for them outside, and as they stepped out of the air-conditioned terminal they were immediately struck by the oppressive heat.

Coming from Texas they were all accustomed to hot weather. It had been in the mid-nineties in Fort Worth the day before they left, but the sudden blast of the early June ninety-eight degree air, accompanied by ninety-five percent humidity, was far different from what they had left behind. As they searched the area outside the terminal for their friend, Elaina could feel her white cotton blouse beginning to stick to her moistening skin. Within a matter of minutes Jack's light blue shirt was stained with growing areas of darker blue in his lower back and under his arms.

Dr. Domingo Ramirez was standing next to his twelve-year-old Toyota Land Cruiser across the street from the baggage claim area. When he saw them, he immediately began waving and shouted, "Jack!"

Jack waved back, indicating he had spotted his friend. Domingo was dressed in his usual open collar white shirt worn loosely outside his black trousers. Jack wasn't sure he'd ever seen his friend wearing anything else in the dozen years he had known him.

"There he is," Jack said as he looked back and motioned for David and Elaina to follow him across the street. As he reached Domingo, he dropped his duffel bag next to the car and embraced his longtime colleague.

"It is so good to see you again my friend," Domingo exclaimed.

"It is good to see you too, Domingo," Jack replied.

As his family approached, Elaina gave the shorter man a big hug. "Hi, Domingo!" she said with a huge smile.

"*Señora* Elaina, you are more beautiful every time I see you," he said earnestly. "Welcome back to my country."

"Thank you," she replied as she kissed him on the cheek.

"Domingo, this is our son, David," Jack said with pride, gesturing toward the blond headed teenager who was still holding two large bags.

Domingo turned to face the young man who, like Jack, was nearly a full head taller than himself. "It is so very nice to finally meet you. I have heard so much about you."

David set the luggage on the pavement and reached forward to shake hands with their host. "It's very good to meet you, Dr. Ramirez," David said. "My mother and father have told me a lot about you as well, and the work you do here in Nicaragua."

Domingo opened the back of the large vehicle, and helped then load their luggage. Jack told David to sit up front with Domingo, while he and Elaina would sit in the back.

"It's about a forty-five minute drive to my home," Domingo said. "I know it has been a long trip and you're probably hungry, so my wife has prepared supper for you, if you can wait that long?"

"We ate right before we left Houston, and we had another snack on the plane," Jack explained. "So I think we're fine."

"I apologize for the air-conditioning being less effective than it should be," Domingo said. "Freon is a very precious commodity in this part of the world, and the local dealer told me they wouldn't be able to recharge my unit for another three weeks."

Despite the unit not working at peak performance, the eighty degree temperature inside the car was far better than what they'd been dealing with outside.

He left the airport and headed for the Pan American Highway. The route took them west through the northern part of Managua near the southern shore of the lake. The sky was a brilliant blue with only a few scattered white puffy clouds over the sprawling city. The building in Managua ranged from old world Spanish architecture to a few more modern structures. The cars they passed all seemed to be older, most in need of repairs or at least a new paint job. There were many old buses and a few large trucks on the highway, some of which were barely making twenty miles per hour.

As they passed the American Embassy, Domingo pointed out the large white stucco building with the flag of the United States flying proudly over the three-story structure. He told David how the city had been devastated by an earthquake thirty-three years before.

"That is why there were very few tall buildings in the city. Everything built since the earthquake is less than five stories," he said.

There was a high probability of more quakes in the years to come since this was geologically one of the most active regions in Central America. There was more evidence of this fact to the South. The volcanic peaks of Masaya and Mombacho rose like giant cones in the distance, and they were only two of the more than a dozen volcanic mountains in Nicaragua. Some were still active along the Cordillera Los Maribios range, running from southern Guatemala, through Nicaragua and into Costa Rica.

As they reached the outskirts of Managua the landscape began to change. The paved side streets were replaced by dirt roads, and the houses were simpler cinder block structures, many with chickens and goats in small enclosures.

Domingo turned north off the Pan American Highway on the road toward Ciudad Sandino. The countryside was now more rural, with small farms extending from the highway to the mountains to the west.

"What are they growing here?" David asked.

"The number one crop around here is cotton," Domingo said, motioning to the fields to his left. "Off in the distance, on the sides of the mountains they are growing coffee." He then pointed to his right to a broad expanse nearer the waters of Lake Managua. "Over there is a banana plantation."

Soon he turned the big Toyota into a more affluent-appearing neighborhood with paved streets. Each home was surrounded by large trees and mowed lawns. While it was nothing like their neighborhood in Fort Worth, it was far nicer than David had pictured in his mind.

"Please come in," Domingo said as he parked the car. "Leave the luggage, Guillermo will bring it in." He motioned to an older gentleman who was trimming one of the huge magenta-colored bougainvillea vines over the carport, and the man immediately stopped what he was doing to unload their bags from the car.

"Felicia?" he called, as he opened the front door.

Around the corner appeared another familiar face, as the petite, dark haired Mrs. Ramirez came hurriedly into the foyer to greet her guests.

"I am so glad to see you again," she exclaimed at the sight of Jack and Elaina. She quickly moved to hug Elaina. When it was Jack's turn he had to bend far over to embrace the barely five-feet tall Felicia.

"This is our son, David," Elaina said, as she took his arm and brought him forward.

"I'm very glad to meet you, Mrs. Ramirez," David said.

"Oh, my goodness, Elaina!" she exclaimed. "I had no idea your son was such a handsome young man." David stepped forward to receive his hug but instead Felicia placed her hands on either side of the young man's face and held him in front of her for a moment before kissing each of his cheeks.

"We are so happy to have you here in our home," she said to David before motioning to all her guests to follow her. "Please come sit down and have some supper. You must be starving."

They made their way into the dining room where a large rectangular table had been set in preparation for their arrival. Rosa, a middle-aged woman, wearing a white apron, was standing in the doorway which separated this dining room from the kitchen. Once they were all seated Rosa began serving them a traditional home cooked meal. The first course was a leaf lettuce salad with kernels of corn and a tangy dressing. The main course was a grilled chicken breast served on a large corn tortilla with slices of mild peppers, papaya and bananas. On the side was a large patty of rice and beans mixed together then pan fried. It was called gallo pinto and would become a staple in their diet for the next week. For dessert they had a sweet, corn-based fritter with honey and powdered sugar.

"This has been a wonderful meal," Jack offered Felicia with a look of satisfaction. "You are always so good to us. I wish you would find time to come visit us in Texas."

"We will, someday, soon," Domingo said. "It is just very difficult for me to leave. Between my practice in the city, and the clinic in Ciudad Sandino, I don't have time to get away and I have no one else to take care of my patients."

David sat quietly, savoring the new flavors, but even more he was enjoying listening to the conversation between his dad and his physician friend. Domingo's dedication to his patients was obvious and he couldn't help but draw a comparison to his father.

More times than he could count their family plans had been changed or cancelled at the last minute because of something coming up with a patient. If a kid came in needing emergency heart surgery, caring for that patient always took precedence. He remembered a few years ago they had cancelled a family vacation to Colorado because of a baby born with some kind of heart problem that kept his dad at the hospital for three days. As a kid growing up, he had just come to expect his dad would not be able to attend his soccer games or school activities.

It wasn't until just last year that Jack finally found an associate, George Ferguson, who could take care of all of his patients in his absence. Before George, he'd had to rely on a couple of the other cardiothoracic surgeons in town to cover his practice, but neither of them had much experience with pediatric heart surgery. Now he finally had the freedom to schedule time off on a more regular basis.

Hearing Dr. Ramirez talking about his commitment to his practice, David was also reminded what his dad said it meant to be a physician. He silently wondered if he had what it took to be one as well.

"So, what time do we get started in the morning?" Jack asked, as they were finishing their dessert.

"We should leave here around seven-thirty to get to the clinic by eight," Domingo replied. "The patients start lining up around six-thirty, but our volunteers don't get there to start checking them in until just before eight."

"How many patients do you expect?" David asked.

"I have no way of knowing for sure," he said. "It varies depending on who is in the clinic on any particular day. Usually I see between forty and fifty kids, while one of the general internists may only see twenty or thirty adults on his days. But, since the word is out that your parents are here this week, there is no telling. We will just see as many as we can until the clinic closes at five, that's when the volunteers go home," he added.

"What's the most patients you have ever seen in one day?"

"I think last year toward the end of the rainy season we saw just over one hundred children in one day," he explained.

"Wow!" Elaina exclaimed.

"Even then, there were at least fifty more who had to come back the next week," he added.

"Well," Jack interrupted, "if we're going to get an early start, I think I'm going to turn in."

As he stood he offered his appreciation again to Felicia and to Rosa, the cook and housekeeper. Elaina also thanked their hosts profusely for the wonderful hospitality.

Felicia felt she needed to show Jack and Elaina to the small guesthouse, located just behind the main house, even though the couple had stayed there a number of times before. As they entered the quaint little cottage with its own small living room and kitchenette, it was exactly as it had been the year before. Perhaps others had stayed here since, but it didn't appear so to Elaina.

"Your things are in the bedroom," Felicia said, indicating that Guillermo had placed the luggage in their private quarters. "If you need anything just let me know. There are some cold drinks and fruit in the refrigerator and more towels in the cabinet in the bathroom."

"Thank you so much," Elaina stated as she turned and embraced her hostess again.

Felicia turned to face David, who had followed his parents out to inspect the guesthouse. "Come with me young man," she said, with a huge smile. "We have a special place for you."

As she left the guesthouse she called back to Jack and Elaina, "Breakfast will be at six forty-five."

"Thank you again," Jack said as he closed the door.

"You will be staying in our son's room," Felicia announced with pride. "Raphael has gone off to medical school in the US. I hope you will be comfortable here."

She opened the door to a large bedroom with its own bathroom. David's backpack and duffel bag were sitting on the foot of the king-sized bed, which Rosa had already turned down.

"Wow!" David exclaimed. "This is bigger than my room back home." As he looked around Rafael's room he noticed a large computer desk in one corner. Over it hung posters of the young man's favorite sports team. David immediately felt right at home with pictures of Dallas Cowboys' Emmitt Smith and Troy Aikman from their respective Super Bowl MVP performances more than a decade before. On the opposite wall he saw a pennant from Rice University and a large gray and blue poster featuring the Rice Owl mascot.

"Rafael graduated with highest honors from Rice University in Houston," Felicia said, beaming with pride. "He has just finished his second year of medical school at Johns Hopkins University in Baltimore, Maryland."

"Rice and Johns Hopkins? He must be really smart!"

"He is," she said, as her smile grew even brighter. "He received an academic scholarship from the university, which is offered to the top ten foreign students from Central and South America. We are very proud of him. He is planning to be a neurosurgeon."

"Wow!" David said again, raising his eyebrows, not sure what else to say about her son's accomplishments.

"Please, make yourself at home," she said as she started to leave the room.

"This is just great, Mrs. Ramirez. Thank you so much."

"You are welcome," she said, "and please call me Felicia."

"Okay," he said, but he knew he wouldn't feel comfortable doing so.

◆◆◆◆◆◆◆◆◆

Long before the sky revealed the first signs of dawn, Jack was wide awake. His biological clock would not let him sleep past a certain preprogrammed hour. He had been reading in the guest house living room until it was light, then he softly awakened Elaina with a morning kiss.

"Good morning, Angel," he said, arousing her gently.

"Good morning," she returned with a sleepy grin. "How long have you been up?"

"About an hour or so," he replied. "Breakfast is in thirty minutes. Do you want to shower first or should I?"

"You go ahead. I need just a minute to wake up."

"We could save water and shower together," Jack said with a sly crooked grin.

"I don't think we have time for that," she responded playfully.

After a much quicker than usual shower, Jack dried his hair with a towel and dressed as Elaina showered and dressed quickly.

They had brought scrubs from home to wear to the clinic, finding them to be the most appropriate clothing for these trips. They were comfortable, lightweight, and easy to wash. Jack had brought home several pair of the light blue pants and shirts from the OR for himself and for David, while Elaina had on the purple ones she wore as a regular uniform in the ICU of the children's hospital.

Everyone gathered near the kitchen shortly after the first bright rays of the morning sun came streaming through the large window over the breakfast table. After a hearty breakfast of tortilla-wrapped eggs and sliced mangos, the trio headed off with Domingo to his clinic, about twenty minutes to the North, in the town of Ciudad Sandino. As the area's only pediatrician, Domingo was only in the free clinic on Tuesdays. The remainder of the week other physicians and dentists volunteered their time to provide care for the people of this especially impoverished community on the edge of town. This week, with Jack and Elaina visiting, Domingo planned to take them to the clinic Monday through Thursday, but he would only be with them on Tuesday. The other days they would be helping other doctors.

Many of the people of this region had come to depend on the clinic for virtually all their care, including medications and monitoring of a variety of acute and chronic ailments. On this day, the doctor who would be at the clinic was Francisco Hidalgo, an obstetrician/gynecologist who worked in the hospital in Managua with Domingo.

Domingo guided the Land Cruiser through the town where David saw many men standing aimlessly in small groups, appearing to have nothing else to do. Dozens of children were running around in the streets, the younger ones playing games while the teenagers were harassing anyone passing by. They stopped only long enough to allow the giant vehicle to pass then resumed their pursuits. The clinic building was located on one of the narrow dirt roads on the northern side of town. The white stucco structure was also in desperate need of a new coat of paint. On the side facing the street was a large, hand-painted red cross, indicating the general purpose of the building. The front door was guarded by a simple iron gate that now stood open. There was a line of women extending outside the building and halfway down its length. Most of them were quite young, and in various stages of pregnancy. There were several older women, and a few who were well past their childbearing years. Some of the young women were carrying infants in their arms while others gathered younger children around them like baby chicks.

Domingo parked the truck in a driveway between the clinic and the small cinder block house which was occupied by a young Canadian couple who'd come to Nicaragua on a six-month missionary assignment. Once they were finished, another pair would come to serve as caretakers of this medical mission. It had been started more than twenty years ago by an Episcopal church in Calgary, Alberta. One of the many roles of the missionaries was to keep track of the stock of donated medications, and notify the suppliers when they were running low. Unfortunately, they ran low most of the time, especially when it came to prenatal vitamins and diabetes supplies. Occasionally, the local doctors, like Domingo, would help out by bringing supplies from their own clinics, but this was often not enough.

Across the dirt street, David saw something he hadn't expected. There was an open air concrete structure housing the area's potable water pump, the source of this community drinking water. A small crowd was gathered there to draw from the filtered well.

Walking behind Domingo, the three Americans made their way past the line of women patiently waiting for them. Some of the patients recognized Jack and Elaina from prior visits and greeted them briefly as they passed. They did not stop, but quickly made their way into the crowded main room of the clinic.

A middle-aged woman, who was one of the regular local volunteers, was checking the patients in at a small wooden table. After taking some information from each woman, she assigned them a number. Most of them were regulars at the clinic so they had an established chart, such as it was. A second, younger volunteer was responsible for finding each patient's chart in the records room located immediately behind the check-in desk. As she brought them out of the small storage room she stacked the folders neatly in a wire rack, along with the corresponding number assigned to that patient. Another woman was calling out the numbers and putting the patients in one of the three examination rooms where they would be seen first by a nurse who would take their blood pressure and other vital signs before they were seen by the doctor.

"I'm going to leave you here," Domingo said. "I need to get to the hospital in Managua, but I'll be back around five, okay?"

"That'll be great," Jack replied, and Elaina embraced Domingo briefly before he left them.

Jack made his way through the sea of patients to one of the exam rooms where he found Dr. Hidalgo who preparing to see his first patient of the day.

"Good morning, Francisco," Jack said, renewing his acquaintance with the older gentleman whom he'd met on two previous trips.

"Welcome, my friend," Francisco replied in his best English. "I am so happy to see you and your lovely wife again," he said, as he saw Elaina had followed close behind along with David.

She extended her hand to the doctor before introducing David to the seasoned professional. "This is our son, David."

"It's a pleasure to meet you, Dr. Hidalgo," David said as he shook the older man's hand.

"I am glad to meet you, too, young man," he said, then turned back to Jack. "Are you ready to go to work?"

"Absolutely," Jack responded. "Just tell me what you need for us to do."

"It would help me greatly if you could see the second and third trimester pregnancies. Most of them only need a quick check of their blood pressure and their fetal heart tones, and make sure they are taking their prenatal vitamins," he instructed. "If they need more, there is a box of vitamins in the pharmacy," he said pointing to another small room, scarcely larger than a closet next to the chart room. All their medications were kept there and were locked up securely after hours. Even when the clinic was open there was always a volunteer inside the small room to both guard and dispense the valuable supplies.

"I can certainly handle that," Jack said with an air of anticipation. He really enjoyed getting back to his comfort zone of delivering hands-on care, even if it had been decades since he had treated any pregnant women other than those he'd seen here in Nicaragua.

"Just let me know if you have any questions, or if you discover something significant."

"Will do," Jack assured his colleague as if he were an intern responding to the senior resident.

Francisco moved on to the first of what promised to be twenty to thirty patients he would see that day with everything from a missed period and early pregnancy, to severe pelvic pain and anemia, due to heavy menstrual bleeding.

His office nurse accompanied him to the clinic and would assist him as he alternated between two exam rooms. Jack would use the third room which had only a plain exam table without stirrups, so he would not be performing any pelvic exams.

Elaina brought their first patient into the exam room and took her blood pressure with a very old device, She wasn't sure how accurate it was, but Jack assured her that the column of mercury in the glass tube was still very accurate so long as the tube that contained it remained unbroken. She also took the young girl's temperature along with her pulse and respiratory rates before turning the exam over to Jack.

He was excited to see that a small portable Doppler had been added to the equipment since the last time he was here. It made listening to the heartbeat of the tiny life within the mother's womb much easier than the old head-mounted fetal stethoscope he had used previously. With the electronic device it was only necessary to have the young mother lie down on the table, and with the aid of a generous amount of ultrasonic lubricant, the rapid swishing tones of the baby's heart could be found much more easily.

David was instructed to simply follow his dad for the day, and Jack promised he would find something for him to do. The first young girl was no older than he, and was obviously nearing the term of her pregnancy. Jack easily found the point on her swollen abdomen where the sound of her baby's heart was the strongest. The girl's eyes sparkled and her face was beaming as she heard the sound of the life developing within her.

"Count the number of beats over a fifteen-second time span," Jack instructed his son, "then multiply it times four and record the number after the letters FHT on the page where your mom recorded her other vital signs."

David did as he was told and recorded his first chart entry as the minute rate of fetal heart tones. "One hundred forty," he said with confidence.

Jack asked the seventeen-year-old girl about her prenatal vitamins and found that she was not taking any because she had run out. He told David to get her a one-month supply from the pharmacy. Based on the due date written in the chart, she would likely deliver in the next three or four weeks. When David returned he started to hand the bottle of pills to his dad, but Jack motioned for him to give them directly to the young girl. She took them and looked directly at him with a grateful smile, then said, *"Muchas gracias, doctor."*

David was fumbling for a response while the patient quickly jumped up off the table and headed out the door. He turned to his dad with a look of protest, but before he could speak, Jack said, "Well, doctor," he paused for effect. "It seems you have established your first physician-patient relationship."

Like virtually every physician of his era, Jack considered the relationship between a patient and their doctor to be the heart of the medical profession. He defined it as, the trust that each patient has in their physician, which is matched by the physician's responsibility to the patient. Over the last two decades Jack had been witness to a gradual erosion of that sacred bond for a variety of reasons, but he had just seen it again, in its purest form, reflected in the eyes of those two teenagers.

"She thought I was a doctor?" David said incredulously.

"As far as she was concerned," Jack responded, "you were the one offering her the help she needed. It didn't matter to her whether you were a high school student or a graduate of the finest medical college in the world. You were helping her, so you were worthy of that title."

"I don't ..." David was having trouble finishing his own thought.

"I know, son," the veteran physician offered to complete the idea that David was struggling with. "You haven't done what it takes to gain the degree. We both know that, but she doesn't have any idea what that means. She just knows that you are here, helping her, and that's all that matters." He let that thought linger for just a moment before saying, "Now, before your new honorary degree goes to your head, change the paper on the exam table and tell your mom we're ready for the next patient while I finish writing a note in the chart."

David flashed his million dollar grin and quickly did as he was told.

◆◆◆◆◆◆◆◆◆

By noon the trio had seen fourteen young pregnant girls and so far Jack had not had to ask Francisco for any help. They took a break for lunch, which had been brought to the clinic by some of the local women. Behind the building there was an old, but very large picnic-style table the women had covered with a plastic red and white checkered tablecloth. When they saw it, Jack and Elaina looked at each other with broad smiles, both obviously recalling the outdoor tables both at Claude's and in Paris. The meal would be far different from what they'd experienced two weeks before at the fine French restaurant, but it had been prepared with the same great care and presented with no less pride. These women had made this meal by hand from the most basic ingredients of cornmeal, rice, pinto beans, chicken and local fruits. They had first gathered the provisions from their neighbors, since they couldn't just run down to the supermarket. The most talented cooks were selected to prepare the local dishes using generations-old recipes.

As the two doctors, the two nurses and the young teenager sat down, the meal was served by the same women who had spent the entire morning preparing it. The portions were three or four times what they would serve their own families, but they insisted each of the diners have their fill. Only when this group was satisfied did they feed the volunteers who also ate generous portions of the stewed chicken and rice served with corn tortillas and the patties of gallo pinto.

Three large pitchers of red Kool-Aid were used to constantly fill each of small Dixie cups. Jack couldn't help commenting to Elaina, making a comparison with his favorite cabernet sauvignon. On this occasion he truly preferred the cooling and hydrating effects of the sugary sweet drink.

The noontime sun had warmed the air to ninety degrees, but the table was positioned under a large spreading tropical tree, and there was a pleasant breeze, which made it very tolerable.

"It feels better out here than inside the clinic," Elaina said.

Once all the workers had eaten their fill the women packed up their large pots, never considering the idea of eating with their guests. After a few minutes, Jack and Francisco knew it was time to get back to their tasks, so they thanked the women profusely for the noontime feast, and returned to the muggy interior of the clinic building

The building had only two small window units which provided some relief from the rising heat in the main waiting area, but did little to cool the exam rooms. A small oscillating fan at least kept the air moving in Jack's room. It had been moved there from the larger room where Francisco was working, because he knew the Americans were not acclimated to the tropics.

By four thirty the clinic waiting room was empty and the last patient was being seen by Dr. Hidalgo. As he came out of the exam room he approached Jack and Elaina who had gone to the makeshift pharmacy to evaluate what supplies they would have to choose from for the rest of the week.

"Thank you so much for all your help today," Francisco said, the exhaustion clearly perceptible in his voice. "We could not have finished if it hadn't been for you."

"You are very welcome," Jack said. "We appreciate the chance to come and help you with this effort."

"These common people are very grateful to have anyone come to offer them medical care," he replied, "but to have a famous American doctor, like you, come to this tiny community and offer your services is truly an honor."

Jack was obviously a bit embarrassed by such high praise and immediately deflected it by saying, "It was my wife and son who did all the hard work." As he looked at Elaina she was vigorously nodding her head in agreement, teasing him in a way only she could.

"They are an extension of you, *señor*," his colleague responded. "And, I know that you are very proud of them."

"Thank you, my friend," Jack replied, shaking the other doctor's hand. "Perhaps we will see you again next time," Jack said hopefully, as Francisco prepared to leave.

"I certainly hope so," he replied. "You and your family are always welcome here. *Adios, mi amigos.*"

"*Adios,*" replied all three Americans in unison, trying their best to mimic the local's accent without much success.

After helping clean up the waiting room, the trio followed the local volunteers out to the front of the clinic and waited for their ride. The four women they'd been working with had each said very little over the course of the day, but once out of the building the oldest of the group came up to Elaina and gave her a tearful hug. She normally spoke no English, but she managed a phrase she'd heard from the missionary couple who cared for the clinic. "God bless you, señora."

Elaina returned her embrace and responded in Spanish, "*Muchas gracias, señora. Vaya con Dios.*"

Just as the volunteers departed, Domingo pulled up in front of the clinic.

"So, how was it?" he asked David as he got into the car.

"Amazing," he answered in classic teenage style. "I had the best time just watching my parents working together."

Elaina wasn't even aware that David had been paying attention to the team approach she and Jack used to see thirty pregnant women. "You were a huge help, David," she said reaching forward to touch her son's shoulder.

"I thought everybody did a great job," Jack added, "considering we don't usually see babies before they're born." He tried to laugh at his own wit, but was too tired to make much of an effort.

"Well, tomorrow you'll have plenty of opportunities to see many children, from newborns to some kids about your age, David," Domingo promised, as he turned the Land Cruiser back onto the main road and headed back south.

◆◆◆◆◆◆◆◆◆

When they arrived at the clinic the next morning Domingo's earlier prediction seemed rather modest. The line outside the front door extended well past the missionaries' house, as mothers from miles around brought their children in for all manner of medical problems. Some were just there for routine checkups, but it was clear from the way some were being carried that significant pathology would be the order of the day.

"Do you want us to work like we did yesterday with Francisco, just seeing the routine patients while you handle the sicker ones?" Jack asked.

"No, I think what you and I did last year worked pretty well," Domingo replied. "Let's have the volunteers and David move the kids in and out of the rooms, then Elaina can take a quick history and get their vitals. As she moves on to the next room, you can follow her by checking their heart and lungs and abdomens. When you've finished your part of the exam, jot down in your notes if you find anything we need to treat. You can move on to the next child, and I'll follow you with the head and neck and extremities exam. I'll write the final note, give them the meds they need, and schedule any follow-up visits." Domingo was describing his assembly line plan.

"That sounds like a great idea," Jack said, "but we will obviously have to move quickly if we're going to get through this huge group of kids."

"The key will be speeding up the charting," Domingo said.

"I could help with that," David offered. "Yesterday, I felt like I was just standing around watching most of the time. The volunteers didn't really need my help moving patients in and out. What if I just follow my dad and write down what he tells me in the chart? That was the part that took the longest yesterday, wasn't it Dad?"

"Without a doubt," Jack agreed. "I hate charting, and I'm not very good at it. What do you think, Domingo?"

"If it will keep us moving, great," he replied.

Once the team got started things moved along smoothly. Jack had to spell a few words for David, but his son quickly picked up on the systematic examinations being performed by his dad. Elaina loved the idea of getting to see every child, and she found herself jotting down suspected diagnoses based on the history alone. What she hadn't counted on was needing one of the volunteers to serve as an interpreter as often as she did. She was quite fluent in Spanish, following her many years of classes in high school and college, and dealing with the high percentage of families at the hospital in Fort Worth who did not speak English. However, she had always struggled with the accent of the people of Nicaragua. Much of what they said sounded muffled and garbled, like they were speaking with marbles in their mouths, so she sometimes needed help.

The majority of the children were relatively healthy apart from the occasional ear infection or tonsillitis. Domingo was passing out bottles of ampicillin and Sudafed to nearly a third of the mothers and telling them to bring their children back the following week if they were not better.

Early in the day Jack was examining a young girl who was complaining of itching all over. Her mother brought her in because the child had scratched herself until several areas on her arms and legs started to bleed. Jack immediately recognized the problem as scabies, and put on a pair of latex gloves before examining the child. He explained to his son how this highly contagious condition was the result of microscopic mites burrowing into the skin where they laid their eggs. The body reacts to the implanted foreign material with a massive histamine release, causing redness and extreme itching.

"She is going to need some Lyclear," Jack said, spelling the name of the anti-parasitic cream used to treat this condition.

David asked the volunteer if they had the medication in the pharmacy, and the young volunteer quickly returned with a six-ounce bottle, which David handed to the mother. Jack explained the importance of boiling the child's clothing and all of her bed linens to kill the mites and prevent reinfection. He also gave her an oral antihistamine to reduce the itching and recommended the mother trim the child's nails to prevent her from scratching.

Over the course of the day Jack saw eight more children with exactly the same condition and three others with head lice. Parasitic infestations were all too common in communities like this, but Jack had to admit they were also more common in the poorer communities of North Texas than most people realized.

By the middle of the afternoon Jack was moving rapidly through the long line of children until he encountered a two-year-old little boy. Elaina had written a note on the top of this child's chart, "Premature birth — tachypneic and tachycardic — possible cardiac problem." The child was described by his mother as sleeping more than normal and not eating well. When Jack saw the little boy he immediately recognized the signs of early congestive heart failure. The child's breathing was rapid and slightly labored and he appeared somewhat anxious in his mother's arms. Jack asked her to have the child stand, and as she placed the child's feet on the floor he immediately crouched down with his bottom resting on his heels.

Jack lifted the young boy on to the exam table where he sat quietly with his legs crossed without any protest. Listening to his chest the experienced doctor heard exactly what he expected. A fine, raspy sound, indicative of chronic fluid buildup within the air sacs confirmed the young boy's failing heart, and as he moved his stethoscope to his heart the cause was obvious. The continuous machinelike murmur could be heard over the entire precordial area and was the signature finding of a large patent ductus arteriosus.

"This child has a large PDA," Jack announced to David who then dutifully wrote down the three capital letters in the boy's chart.

"What does that mean?" David asked, having heard the term many times in conversations between his mom and dad, but never knowing exactly what they were talking about.

"There are two sides to the heart. The right side pumps blood to the lungs where it receives oxygen. That's what we refer to as the pulmonary circulation. The left side of the heart pumps blood to the rest of the body through the systemic circulation. Before babies are born there's a large blood vessel connecting the pulmonary circulation and the systemic circulation which shunts blood away from the lungs, because they aren't working yet. That vessel is called the ductus arteriosus," he explained. "Normally, at birth, when the lungs fill up with air, the ductus closes by itself, and the two circulations are separated. If the ductus remains open, or patent," he said, pausing to emphasize the meaning of the word, "it results in higher than normal pressures in the pulmonary circulation and eventually that side of the heart begins to fail."

"So what can we do about it?" David asked, hoping to be a part of a solution to what sounded like an ominous situation.

"The only thing that will fix the problem is surgery to ligate, or tie off, the ductus," Jack stated, knowing that such a procedure was not likely available here in Nicaragua. "I need to talk to Domingo."

He walked out of the exam room, leaving his son with the child and young mother. David watched as the girl, who was not much older than himself, picked up the child and carefully sat him on her lap. She held him close to her chest and whispered softly to the child, but David had no idea what she said.

In less than a minute Jack returned with Domingo. "Like I said," Jack said to his colleague, "I'm certain this baby has a PDA, and from the looks of things I think he isn't likely to survive more than another six months."

His statement brought an entirely new perspective to what David was watching. Suddenly the serious and even desperate nature of what his father had described had a whole new meaning.

"As you know," Domingo responded, "we don't have anyone here in Managua who could perform that procedure."

"I could do the ligation easily enough provided you had an operating room and an anesthesiologist," Jack announced without a second thought.

"There is a new young anesthesiologist at our hospital who trained in Florida," he said, thinking aloud. "He has some experience with children, but I don't know about pedi hearts."

"This procedure doesn't require cardiopulmonary bypass, so I suspect it could be done at your hospital, assuming that guy is comfortable with putting this kid to sleep."

"I don't know, Jack," Domingo said hesitantly. "The government runs the hospital, and they may or may not allow you to perform surgery there. The politics could get pretty ugly," he added as he looked at the mother and child and shook his head.

"So, who do we need to talk to?" Jack asked with a bit of contempt behind his otherwise casual manner.

"We can start with the hospital director. He is appointed by the Minister of Health."

"Do you think you could set up an appointment for us to see him tomorrow? If we can get an okay we could fix this kid's PDA on Thursday or Friday. What do you think?" Jack spoke as if this were a concluded plan rather than a question.

"I will try, if that's what you really want to do."

"Absolutely, this is the kind of thing I do every day," he said with an air of excitement. "The only other option would be to take the baby back to the States, and the logistics of that would likely make it impossible."

Domingo began explaining exactly what Jack had discovered, and what he was recommending to the terrified mother. As she heard the doctor speaking she seemed to shrink into the chair, holding her young son tighter with every word.

CHAPTER 10

"Hello, Radha?" Jack said in response to the familiar voice on the other end of the international call. "This is Jack."

"Hi, Jack," she replied. "I thought you were in Nicaragua."

"I am, and that's why I'm calling," he said, a little louder than normal, subconsciously trying to make up for the considerable distance between them. "I need to ask you a big favor."

"Anything," she responded without hesitating.

"Do you think you could come to Managua on Thursday and sleep a two-year-old for me? He's got a big PDA, and I need to ligate it on Friday."

The phone was silent for a few seconds, and Jack was just about to ask if she was still there when her response came. "Sure," she said with a bit more enthusiasm than Jack had expected.

"There is a young anesthesiologist here who trained at one of the private hospitals in Miami. He seems like a nice enough kid, but he hasn't done any pedi hearts," Jack explained. "He's more than happy to help out, but he's not really comfortable doing something like this solo."

"I will need to get someone to cover for me, but things have been pretty slow here this week with you out of town, so there is no reason I couldn't come," she said, then suddenly realized there were bound to be some logistics to be overcome for her to practice in a foreign country.

"Great!" Jack exclaimed.

"What about licensure and privileges?" she asked.

"I've spoken to the director of the hospital and he has approved everything," Jack explained, having anticipated her question. "All you'll need are copies of your medical school diploma and your Texas license."

"What about malpractice insurance?"

"Not an issue here," Jack stated as a matter of fact. "The family will sign a no-fault waiver that eliminates the whole liability issue. It's the way they handle everything here."

"I will need to check on flight availability. How can I get back in touch with you?"

"This is my regular cell phone, so you can call me direct. I'll arrange to have you picked up at the airport."

"What about returning home?"

"We are scheduled to fly out on Sunday morning on United. It connects in Houston. There's only one flight, so you would be coming back with us."

"I'll see you tomorrow then," Radha said.

"Thanks for doing this," Jack offered in a quieter and very sincere tone.

"Like I said," she replied, "anything for you, my friend."

♦♦♦♦♦♦♦♦

The phone conversation with the director of the hospital had gone much smoother than Domingo had expected. The government appointee had been aware of Jack's regular visits to the region, and he was quick to recognize the political points that could be gained for his state-run hospital if this famous American surgeon operated on a local resident in his facility. He offered the two doctors a tentative go ahead over the phone, but said he would need to get final approval from the Minister of Health. After explaining the situation to the minister, the director had no trouble convincing him of the public relations benefits that would come out of this, assuming the child did well.

"You have received approval from the very top to proceed with your plan," the director announced to Jack and Domingo as they entered his large office. "The minister was more than happy to know that you, and your American colleague, are willing to provide your considerable experience and expertise to one of our youngest citizens." The overly dignified tone and formal language, made it clear to Jack there was more behind the man's words.

"Thank you very much, sir," Jack replied, as he and Domingo shook the soft hand of the overweight man.

"Please let me know if you need anything," he said as the two doctors left the surprisingly plush office and headed for the operating room.

"I don't know," Domingo said once they were out into the hallway. His voice was almost a whisper.

"What do you mean?" Jack asked, already suspecting Domingo's concerns.

"I think he is going to try to use this situation to gain publicity for the hospital."

"So, what if he does?" Jack asked in response. "That little boy needs this operation and if the politicians get a few votes out of it, I say that's a small price to pay. Besides, he and the Minister are letting us do it, so they deserve some credit, don't you think?"

"Perhaps you are right," Domingo conceded. "I just fear they will make it look like you are doing this on behalf of the government."

"No matter how it may look to others," Jack replied, "we know why we are doing it, and that's all that really matters."

Domingo was not at all familiar with the operating room, but he still felt it was his place to introduce Jack to the OR staff, all of whom were excited to have an American heart surgeon visiting their humble facility. It was indeed primitive by American standards, but he'd seen worse during his travels. After the initial greetings he explained what he planned to do, then asked to see their pediatric instruments and their vascular set. They brought out the instruments they had, and he immediately became concerned he might have promised more than he could deliver. The majority of the clamps and retractors were far too large to use on a two-year-old, but eventually he found some things he thought would work as he systematically went through the steps of the familiar procedure in his mind. He thought to himself that he could really use a pair of ductus clamps, since he didn't see anything that remotely resembled what he really needed.

As Jack dialed his cell phone again, he thought of something his father had told him repeatedly many years before. *It's a poor workman who blames his tools.* In general he always agreed with that statement, but he also recalled how on one occasion he'd challenged his old man, generating a quote of his own. *Any workman would be hard pressed to use a hammer when the task called for a screwdriver.*

"Hi Radha, it's me again," he said.

"You haven't changed your plans have you?" she asked.

"No, no, nothing like that," he said with a brief chuckle. "Could I get you to run by the OR at the children's hospital and ask Ellen if I could borrow a couple of ductus clamps?"

"Sure, anything else?"

"Yes," he said as he realized she could also bring him a couple of other instruments that would make life easier. "Ask her to wrap up my personal vascular needle holder and my long fine forceps. She'll know the ones I need if you just tell her I'm doing a PDA ligation."

"I can do that," Radha agreed. "I've already made my flight arrangements. I'll be there on the United flight that arrives around six o'clock."

"Terrific!" he said. "Domingo and I will be there to pick you up tomorrow afternoon."

◆◆◆◆◆◆◆◆◆

Dr. Ramirez admitted Juan Carlos Ochoa to the hospital the day after they'd seen the child in the clinic. The boy's father brought him in on Wednesday afternoon so they could perform the necessary blood tests, including a type and crossmatch for two units of blood. Domingo also ordered a chest x-ray and an electrocardiogram to be done before the scheduled surgery on Friday morning. Such standard preoperative tests would require only an hour or two at the most in virtually any American hospital, but here the pace was considerably slower.

After his meeting with the hospital director, Jack and his family spent the rest of Wednesday at the free clinic helping one of the local general internists. They saw mostly older patients with high blood pressure, diabetes, emphysema, and gout. Based on symptoms of chest pain, Jack thought at least two of the older gentlemen he saw might well have benefited from a cardiac catheterization and stenting of partially blocked coronary arteries, but that treatment was only available in Nicaragua at the one private hospital in Managua, and only for those few people with money. He was certain these men had high cholesterol, but the pharmacy at the clinic didn't have any of the high-priced statin drugs so commonly prescribed back home. For now he could only offer them a beta-blocker and some nitroglycerine to control their pain. He urged them to quit smoking, increase their exercise, and avoid eating the fried foods which comprised the bulk of their diet. He was certain his instructions would be ignored, but at least he felt better knowing he had made the effort.

David could sense his father's frustration as the day wore on. At one point he heard him curse under his breath when he was told the pharmacy was out of allopurinol. He needed the common drug to treat a fifty-year-old man with disabling gout in his left foot. The only thing he could offer the man was a bottle of generic ibuprofen, and he was certain it would do little to relieve his suffering. His father's demeanor changed dramatically when the gentleman produced a small silver cross, and offered it as a token of his appreciation.

"*Gracias, señor,*" Jack said, as he was truly touched by this poor man's generous gift. The man put his old work boot back on and limped slowly out of the room, joining his wife who was waiting near the front door of the clinic. He handed her the bottle of cheap anti-inflammatories and she clutched it to her breast as if some miracle were contained in that small white plastic container.

"That was really something, Dad," David said in an almost reverent tone.

"I never cease to be amazed," Jack said with a humility David hadn't heard before. "These people are so poor they are barely surviving, yet they are willing to give anything they have of value to anyone who cares for them." He turned and handed the cross and chain to his son. "I want you to keep this as a reminder of that fact."

"I know this is my first time to come here," David said in a subdued tone as he accepted the trinket from his father, "but from what I've seen, these people are genuine, unlike a lot of people I know back home. They don't want something for nothing, and when they sense that you truly care, they will do anything for you. That's why they offer you gifts and food or sometimes just the smile on their face."

For the second time in less than a minute Jack was truly moved. In just those few words his son had spoken the wisdom it had taken him most of a lifetime to acquire. He knew in that moment that one day his son would be a great physician.

♦♦♦♦♦♦♦♦♦

David had watched his dad perform several operations over the years, including some complex procedures, but he was looking forward to this one more than any before. What he noticed first about this operating room was that it was not nearly as well illuminated as the ones he'd been in before. He and his mom stood quietly a couple of steps away from Radha, as she squeezed the tiny rubber bag, rhythmically forcing oxygen into the young boy's lungs. Her local protégé was busily monitoring the child's blood pressure and writing down his measurements every few minutes.

The child was lying on his right side covered with heavy green cloth drapes, rather than the typical light-weight paper kind David had seen used before. As he watched his dad make the initial incision, the room was completely silent except for the rapid beeping of the heart monitor and his father's voice requesting the next instrument. It was clear that some of the instruments were not exactly what he wanted, but he made do with what was available.

"Can you drop the left lung?" Jack asked Radha.

She had placed a special double lumen endotracheal tube that would allow her to ventilate one lung while allowing the other to collapse. Jack hadn't asked her to bring it, but she had correctly anticipated they might not have one available, so she brought a couple of different sizes with her on the plane. She quickly made an adjustment to the tube and began breathing for the child using only his right lung. As the left lung slowly collapsed, the heart and great vessels were revealed, allowing Jack access to the patent ductus.

David was spellbound as he watched his father's hands moving expertly within the young boy's chest. Within a few minutes Jack was asking for the ductus clamps that Radha had brought through security after considerable questioning from the TSA personnel at the airport.

"Watch his pressure, Radha," he announced. "I'm getting ready to clamp the ductus."

As he applied the vascular clamps the young boy's blood pressure increased significantly for a few minutes before settling back down to normal.

"He is tolerating it just fine, Jack," Radha said, giving him the go-ahead to divide the large vessel.

Within another five minutes the ductus arteriosus had been divided and each side carefully sutured closed. When the clamps were removed there was no sign of any bleeding.

"That should do it," Jack said calmly. "You can bring the left lung up."

With another adjustment to the tube, Radha began inflating both lungs again as everyone watched the bright pink surface of the lung rise up to fill the entire chest cavity once more. He placed a small chest tube through a separate incision to insure the lung wound remain inflated then said, "Let's get this kid out of here."

David had always known his dad was a very accomplished surgeon. He made enough money to provide him and his mom with a very good life, but today, working in these third world conditions, he witnessed for himself the true character of the man he called Dad. As he watched him close the tiny chest his only hope was that one day his father would be as proud of him as he was of his father at that moment.

◆◆◆◆◆◆◆◆

On Saturday morning Jack and Domingo planned to leave early for the hospital, but when they met in the kitchen at six-thirty, David was already sitting at the table waiting for them.

"Good morning," he said to the two older men.

"What's up with you?" Jack said with a grin.

"I didn't want to miss going in with you guys to see our patient."

"Okay," Domingo offered, "that's the spirit."

Jack smiled at Domingo's choice of words, but he couldn't help but agree. "Well, did you get some coffee?"

"You know I don't like coffee," David said, as he sipped from the bright red can of Coca-Cola.

Jack laughed to himself as he considered the facts and concluded that genetics were overrated. "Has your mom started giving you grief yet?"

"Of course," he said. "She says it's gonna make me fat like you." They all laughed as they headed out the door.

Just as Domingo opened the front door he heard another voice from the direction of the spare bedroom. "You aren't leaving without me, are you?" Radha said, as she moved quickly to join the boys.

"Good morning," Jack said. "We thought you were going to sleep in."

"After that big dinner last night I almost did," she admitted. Rosa had prepared a huge turkey with all the Nicaraguan trimmings.

As they drove into town the conversation moved to their plans for their return to Texas the following day. "Our flight leaves at eleven, so we'll need to be at the airport by nine to get through international security," Jack suggested, based on his experience at the airport in Managua. "How long do you think it will it take us to get from the hospital to the airport?" he asked Domingo.

"It shouldn't take more than twenty minutes."

"I would like to go by and check on this kid again before we leave, so we should probably plan to leave your house no later than seven," Jack concluded. David had become accustomed to his dad always planning the family's time management the same way he did his professional schedule.

Domingo found a parking space in the doctor's lot and the quartet entered the hospital through the back entrance. They took the slow moving elevator up to the third floor where their young patient was in the intensive care unit. It was hardly what Jack would consider a full fledged ICU, but at least the nurses seemed to be very attentive and eager to do whatever they could to impress the American physicians.

They walked into the open ward with ten beds arranged around the perimeter and a nurses' station in the middle. When they saw the doctors come in, all the nurses immediately stood up. Jack had witnessed this kind of respectful behavior when he was in the military, but the tradition had long since been abandoned in private American hospitals.

"Good morning, Dr. Roberts," the head nurse said as the group approached. While she was Nicaraguan, she had received her nursing degree in California, and spoke fluent English. "Your patient is doing very well this morning," she said, handing him the child's chart. "He has been breathing easily since he was extubated yesterday afternoon. He has not had any fever and his blood pressure has been very stable. The only time his pulse rate has been elevated has been when he's experienced some incisional pain. We have medicated him a total of three times through the night, and he slept very well."

Jack had come in prepared to ask all the questions this nurse was answering without his asking. He nodded his head approvingly as she continued. "His urine output has been excellent and there has been very little drainage from the chest tube."

"Has there been any sign of an air leak?" Jack asked, mostly to show her that he was paying attention to her report.

"No, sir," she answered. "His morning chest x-ray is on the view box around the corner," she added, pointing to the opposite side of the nurses' station. "This morning, his blood work is unchanged from what you saw last evening."

Wow! Jack thought. He hadn't heard this kind of thorough report since he was a senior resident. Back in those days it was the intern who had been up all night taking care of a sick patient who was expected to provide a systematic review on morning rounds.

"Very nice," he said with a genuine appreciation for the job this nurse and her staff were doing.

"Thank you, sir," she said as she pointed Jack toward the old white enameled crib that had replaced one of the adult beds in the space nearest the nurses' station.

The child's sleeping mother sat slumped over in the straight back chair next to her son's crib. As Jack and the rest of the entourage approached she stirred slightly then raised her head. When she saw the approaching surgeon she jumped to her feet as if startled by an approaching threat. Jack motioned for her to sit down and calmed her fears with his crooked smile. "*Buenos dias, señora.*"

"*Buenos dias, doctor,*" she responded, offering a timid smile in return.

Jack moved quickly to the bedside and found the young boy lying on his right side, sleeping peacefully. He produced a stethoscope from his jacket pocket and deftly listened to his chest without waking him. The machinelike murmur was gone and the child's lungs already sounded much clearer than they had four days earlier. He inspected the boy's neck and the prominent veins he had seen before were no longer visible. His face was now a richer brown, not the washed out sallow beige color he had seen in the clinic.

"I couldn't be more pleased," he said, looking first at the head nurse and then to the rest of her staff who had gathered behind her. "The care you are providing this boy is as good or better than I have seen anywhere. Thank you very much," he offered earnestly, then repeated his words in Spanish.

"We all want to thank you and Dr. Patel for coming here to save this young boy's life," she replied, gesturing first to her staff and then to their patient. "It is our honor just to be a part of this historic event in our country."

David was sure he had never seen his dad speechless, but on this occasion he clearly was.

◆◆◆◆◆◆◆◆◆

As the group left the ICU, the director of the hospital stood waiting for them, just outside the door. He had made sure one of the nurses called him as soon as the American doctors arrived.

"Good morning, Dr. Roberts," he said with a bright, yet disingenuous smile.

"Good morning," Jack responded. "This is Dr. Radha Patel, my colleague from the US, and this is my son, David," he said as he gestured casually to the two people the director had not yet met. "This is the director of the hospital," he announced as Radha stepped forward to shake the large man's hand. David did the same, but the director seemed completely disinterested in the young man.

"How is our patient doing this morning?" the director asked in a way that seemed mildly inappropriate.

Jack paused for just a moment and tilted his head, making it clear he thought the pronoun used in the question was inappropriate. "He's doing very well."

"Great! I had no doubt," he replied with enthusiasm. "I was told everything went very well in the operating room yesterday?"

"Your staff did a terrific job given the conditions and their relative inexperience. And the nurses here in the ICU have been terrific," Jack replied, making it clear that it was the people who were to be credited.

"I am so glad to hear that you have found our hospital to be up to your standards," the director said proudly.

Jack thought that either this man was not paying attention, or perhaps he'd been too subtle with his remark about the conditions. At this point it didn't matter, so he decided to let him assume whatever he wanted.

"This is a truly extraordinary event for us," the director added. "The entire community is talking about the surgery you performed on the Ochoa child, and there are several members of the local media downstairs in our conference room who are waiting to hear from the American doctors."

Jack had a feeling this was coming and he didn't think there was any way to avoid talking to the press. "I will be glad to issue a brief statement if that is what you would like," he said, emphasizing the word brief.

"That would be wonderful," the politician said as he beamed from ear to ear.

As the small group entered the starkly furnished conference room, they saw twenty-five or thirty reporters and cameramen arranged around a small lectern with the hospital's name and logo prominently displayed beneath the array of five or six microphones. Each was labeled with the name or call letters of local and national television stations. There was also a large Nicaraguan flag draped as a backdrop on the wall behind the podium.

"I knew it!" exclaimed Domingo under his breath. "He has arranged this press conference for his own political gain."

"It'll be all right," Jack said calmly, as the group made their way to the front of the room. David and Domingo remained out of the camera shot as the director stepped up onto the low platform, followed by Jack and Radha. The director stepped in front of the microphones, and tapped on the largest one in the center to make certain it was working before making his introduction in Spanish.

"Ladies and gentlemen," he began, "I want to thank you for coming here today to the National Hospital of Nicaragua in Managua. We are honored to have with us today a distinguished pair of physicians from the United States of

America, Drs. Jack Roberts and Rhonda Patrel."

How embarrassing… He doesn't even know her name, Jack thought.

"Yesterday they performed an extremely complex open heart operation on a two-year-old boy from Ciudad Sandino."

He's exaggerating to get the maximum emotional impact, Jack thought, unable to keep from shaking his head. *This was not an open heart operation and it wasn't really all that complex.*

"I have asked Dr. Roberts to give all the people of Nicaragua an update on the status of this young boy," he said, then invited Jack to the podium. "Dr. Roberts?"

As he approached the microphone Jack considered his options and decided not to challenge the director. He would allow him to have his way, at least today. He also decided to give his report in Spanish in part to diminish the fact that he was a foreigner, and to ensure that he wouldn't be misinterpreted.

"Thank you, director," he said, choosing to avoid giving him any personal credit. "A few days ago I was assisting my colleague, Dr. Domingo Ramirez, with a large group of children in his free clinic in Ciudad Sandino. Mrs. Ochoa brought her two-year-old son into the clinic because he was not eating and had no energy," Jack explained methodically. "It was apparent that the child had been born with a condition which was causing excessive strain on his heart, causing it to fail. These types of birth defects are relatively common, occurring once or twice in every ten thousand births, and they are most common in children who are born prematurely, as was the case here," he continued, trying to make his audience recognize that this was not a single isolated event, but was something that occurred far more often than they might suspect.

After a brief pause he continued. "Juan Carlos's condition was what we call a patent ductus arteriosus, or PDA, and if this abnormality does not correct itself during the first few weeks of life, surgery is required to ensure normal growth and development. In this boy's case it was necessary to save his life."

There was a collective groan issued from the reporters and a few started to ask questions. Jack held up his hand in protest before continuing. "Thanks to the courtesy of the director, allowing us to utilize this hospital, we were able to successfully correct the problem. Dr. Radha Patel…" he said with added emphasis, deciding he just could not let the previous mistake go uncorrected, "my anesthesiologist colleague, flew here from Texas, as a personal favor to me, specifically to assist with this procedure. It would not have been possible to perform this type of operation without her experience and expertise, and I want to thank her again for her extraordinary efforts." Jack gestured toward Radha, but she declined to come to the microphone.

"Today, I am happy to report that our young patient is doing extremely well, and barring any unforeseen complications, he should be able to return home with his mother and father within the next week or so."

Jack took a step back from the microphones amid a barrage of questions from the reporters. He nodded toward the director who quickly seized the opportunity to offer some additional remarks. Jack moved back next to Radha who placed her hand partially over her mouth and whispered, "You handled that extremely well."

"Thank you, Dr. Roberts. We are all indebted to you and your colleague for the fine work you have done here." The director wasn't going to risk making the same mistake with Radha's name twice.

"As you all know, the Nicaraguan Ministry of Health provides all the resources needed to run this hospital and to make it possible for such miracles to occur. Despite not having any insurance or personal resources, the Ochoa family was able to obtain the finest health care in the world, right here in this facility," he said with a completely straight face. "This is just one more example of how the people of Nicaragua can rely on the generosity of their government."

At this point Jack tuned out the ramblings of the government functionary. He turned to Radha and whispered, "Sorry I got you into this." The two of them stood silently for the next few minutes while the director mentioned the names of every government official he could think of, recognizing that each of them would want to be part of what had become the biggest news event in recent memory. He then took a few prearranged questions from what was obviously a puppet press corp.

"How much would such an operation cost in a private hospital?" inquired one of the planted reporters.

"I do not know for certain," the director replied, "but, I would estimate at least fifty to seventy-five thousand American dollars." His was a guess based on charges he had heard discussed for coronary artery bypass in the US.

"Was the Minister of Health made aware of this procedure beforehand?" The question had been shouted by one of his designees in the back of the room.

"Yes," he responded, ignoring several other questioners directly in front of him. "The minister was made aware of this child's dire needs and he insisted that we do whatever was required to save the young boy's life."

He paused as he scanned the room. "One last question."

The person he had been looking for stepped forward as the director pointed his way. "What steps is our government taking to ensure that other children will be afforded the same kind of care Juan Carlos Ochoa received?"

"I have been informed by the office of Representative Miguel Federico Calderone-Garza that he will be introducing a bill in the national legislature next week, calling for the creation of a national task force on birth defects," the director boldly announced. In reality the politically motivated program would end up being another superficial and ultimately meaningless government effort.

"We must do everything we can to ensure that every child has the opportunity to live and prosper in our great country," he concluded.

Despite additional questions being shouted toward him the director said, "Thank you all again. If there are any further updates my office will let you know." He proudly stepped away from the podium, joining Jack and Radha. He shook Jack's hand again as still cameras flashed and the television cameras continued to capture the circus event.

Jack and Radha escaped as quickly as they could, collecting Domingo and David as they all headed for the exit, but before they could get away, one of the older reporters stopped their progress and asked for just a moment with Jack. He was obviously not one of the partisan members of the press who had dutifully gathered around the director.

"Tell me something, Dr. Roberts," the veteran reporter requested in English. "If you hadn't been here, what would have happened to that boy?"

"I'm not sure I understand the nature of your question," Jack responded as he tried to think of a diplomatic way to avoid the obvious.

"Well," the reporter continued. "Are there any surgeons in Nicaragua who could have done the operation you performed?"

"I'm not sure I know the answer to that …"

"No," Domingo interrupted. "I know of no Nicaraguan surgeon who can perform such a procedure. Furthermore, had it not been for Dr. Roberts' ability to train the operating room staff, they would not have known what to do for this very fortunate young boy," he stated with conviction. "The director can say what he wants about this hospital, but without highly skilled people like Dr. Roberts and Dr. Patel, this kind of advanced health care is simply not possible. So, to answer your question, if he had not been here that child would have died within a few months," Domingo added with finality.

◆◆◆◆◆◆◆◆◆

"We saw you on television," Elaina said as the weary group came through the front door.

"We were railroaded into that dog and pony show," Jack exclaimed. "It was the political price we had to pay in order to fix that kid."

"I thought you handled it very well," she said, giving her husband a big hug.

"I'm glad they didn't let Domingo up there. We likely would have been forced to leave the country."

"Oh really?" she said, smiling inquisitively at Domingo.

"You should have been there, Mom," David said excitedly. "After the press conference was over, Dr. Ramirez told one of the reporters that if Dad hadn't been here that little boy would have died."

"Okay, okay," Jack said in an effort to end the discussion. "I think we've beaten this issue to death. I'm hungry. What's for lunch?"

The group took their seats around the table as Rosa served them a huge casserole that Jack said tasted like chicken enchiladas. When the conversation turned to their planned departure the following day, Felicia asked, "When will you be coming back?"

"I suspect we will be back about this time next summer," Jack said. "Provided your government will allow us back into the country."

"I'm quite sure," injected Domingo, "based on what happened today, that you will be allowed into Nicaragua any time and for as long as you like."

"That might depend on whether that last reporter puts anything you said in the paper," Jack replied with a smile, as he took another bite of the deliciously cheesy dish.

The Ramirez's telephone rang in the living room and soon Rosa approached Domingo interrupting the banter between the two men. She indicated the call was for him, so he quickly excused himself and left the room. In a few minutes he returned with a look of concern on his face.

"Is everything okay?" Jack asked, anticipating there might have been a change in the Ochoa boy's status.

"That was the nursery at the private hospital," he said as he reviewed the message again. "They have a newborn that isn't doing well, and they've asked me to come take a look at her."

"What do you mean, she isn't doing well?" Elaina asked before Jack could.

"Her APGAR score was initially seven, but it dropped to five in the first five minutes, and at one hour it is still only a six. She just isn't oxygenating very well." Domingo was referring to the universal method used to evaluate the relative health of a baby at the time of birth. The acronym APGAR stands for Appearance, Pulse, Grimace, Activity and Respirations, five different things that can be easily assessed by the nurse. Each is given a score of zero, one or two, and the total score is the sum of the five individual assessments. Most baby's score between seven and the maximum of ten within the first minute of birth, and even those who don't will typically improve to nine or ten within five minutes.

"That's not good," Jack said. "Let's go take a look at her."

"I can't ask you to get involved in this," Domingo said cautiously. "The baby is the daughter of Franco Gutierrez, one of the wealthiest men in Nicaragua," he explained. "He owns the largest construction company in Central America and has very close ties to this government."

"So, what difference does that make?" Jack asked.

"You don't understand. This is not like the Ochoa boy. These people are not likely to react well to bad news. Apparently, they have been having trouble having children and this baby was the product of a very long and expensive process of in vitro fertilization."

"All the more reason we should go down there and see if we can help."

"Can I come too?" David asked, not wanting to miss out on any adventure that involved his dad.

"What do you think, Domingo?" Jack asked.

"If you are determined to go, I don't see any reason he can't come along."

In less than two minutes the two doctors and Jack's shadow were out the door and back in the Land Cruiser again.

The private hospital was located on the more affluent side of town and was one of the more prominent buildings built after the big earthquake. Domingo had admitting privileges there, but rarely used them. The vast majority of his patients could not afford the luxury of private insurance, and the Nicaraguan National Health Plan did not come close to covering the cost of care in this facility. As a result, he was only called to see the occasional child who needed a pediatrician and was already in the hospital for something else, like surgery or an injury. This was only the third or fourth time he could remember being called to this neonatal unit to see a newborn.

As he drove his Land Cruiser into the physicians parking lot he noticed something new had been added. Instead of the mechanical arm that could be raised by simply inserting a plastic card into a slot, there was now a small structure next to the gate. As he pulled up he saw the uniformed guard who appeared to be heavily armed step out to stop him. Domingo showed him his name badge and the officer inspected it carefully, both front and back. He took a long look at the two Americans and asked, "Who are these men?"

"These are my assistants," Domingo lied, hoping this wasn't going to turn into an ordeal.

The guard returned his badge and raised the barrier allowing them access. Jack thought to himself how this was another full step beyond the security system that angered him so frequently back home.

Once inside Domingo led his two friends up to the newborn nursery on the second floor. He pushed the intercom button next to the massive metal doors that guarded the youngest of patients from being abducted by those whose interests included human trafficking. The video camera above the door allowed the nursing staff to see, as well as hear, anyone seeking access.

A loud buzz was followed immediately by the doors opening, and Domingo led the way through to the change area. They each put on one-piece paper suits which zipped up the front, covering their street clothes. As they entered the nursing unit, Domingo introduced Dr. Roberts and his son to the charge nurse.

"It is very nice to meet you in person, Dr. Roberts," the nurse said with a distinctly German accent. "I saw you on television earlier today."

Jack wondered if there was anyone in this country who hadn't seen that press conference. "I hope you know that was not my idea."

"Oh, everyone knew what that was about," she replied with a smile. He could only hope that was true.

Domingo spoke up saying, "Where is the Gutierrez baby?"

"She is in the incubator back here in our ICU," she said, then led them to a corner of the unit where there were three incubators along the wall. Two nurses were attending babies as the group approached. One of the nurses had her arms through the round holes in the side of the first tiny enclosure. When she saw Dr. Ramirez, she pulled her gloved hands out of the unit and stepped aside.

"There has been no change since I called you earlier," said, speaking to him in Spanish.

Domingo stepped forward as he put on a pair of latex gloves and placed his hands through the openings. He quickly removed the small cotton shirt from the infant's torso, and as he did Jack moved up behind him to look over his shoulder. Through the clear plastic covering he saw exactly what he had expected. The child was a pale grayish blue color and seemed listless with little visible movement other than her rapid breathing. Domingo retrieved the small stethoscope that was hanging on the side of the incubator and listened intently to the baby's chest.

"Take a listen," he said, motioning for Jack to assume his position.

Jack put on a pair of gloves and began to examine the newborn. She was fully developed and appeared to weigh about seven pounds. Her limbs were normal aside from their color, and her neck showed slightly distended veins. Her eyes were open but didn't seem to be focused on anything. All signs pointed to a developmental problem with the baby's heart, but it wasn't until he listened to her chest that he was certain of his diagnosis. There was a distinctive "whooshing" sound with each contraction of the heart muscle, and it was most obvious over the area of the right ventricle outflow tract.

"She's got it," Jack said as he turned to Domingo. "There is no doubt in my mind."

"I agree," was his response.

"Got what?" David asked with a puzzled look on his face.

"Tetralogy of Fallot," replied his dad. "The classic blue baby condition, and this one is pretty severe. Without surgery she will not survive more than a couple of weeks."

David looked through the top of the incubator and saw the dusky blue child who was clearly struggling just to survive. "So, what are you going to do now?" he asked.

"This is not like the Ochoa baby. It's not something we can take care of here," Jack admitted. "It requires cardiopulmonary bypass, far more sophisticated instruments, and trained support staff, none of which is available anywhere in Central America as far as I know."

"So, why not take her back to Texas and fix her there?" David asked.

"That's not as easy as you might think," Jack replied as he was thinking of ways it might be accomplished.

"Dr. Ramirez said the baby's father was a very wealthy guy, and I've heard you say a million times how money always seems to get things done," David said.

"Perhaps we should go speak to Mr. Gutierrez," Domingo suggested.

"This is your show, Domingo. I'm happy to back you up, and I'll do whatever I can, but they consulted you, not me," Jack said, making certain to maintain their professional relationship.

"Okay," Domingo replied casually, "and since you insisted on coming down here with me, now I'm consulting you." The two doctors shared a moment of what those in the profession called classic one-upmanship.

"Let's go talk to the father together," Jack suggested as a way of ending the game.

In the family waiting area they found the distinguished Franco Gutierrez. They approached a man in his mid-forties who, at just over six feet, was taller than most Nicaraguan men. He was dressed in his customary gray slacks, open collared shirt and black blazer. The nurse had alerted him to the fact the two doctors had been examining his newborn daughter, so he was standing near the window, ready to greet them.

"Mr. Gutierrez?" Domingo began, prompting the businessman to nod his head. "I am Dr. Ramirez and this is Dr. Roberts."

"Dr. Roberts," Gutierrez said in his well-schooled English. "I saw you this morning on the television. Seems you've made quite an impression here in Managua."

Jack shook the man's firm hand and after introducing David, he asked if there was somewhere they could sit down and talk about his daughter. Domingo pointed to a small alcove around the corner which would offer a more private place for their discussion.

"Mr. Gutierrez, I'm sorry to have to tell you that your daughter has a serious congenital heart defect," Jack offered as compassionately as he knew how. "The condition is called Tetralogy of Fallot. It is named after a French doctor who first described the four separate elements of the defect. I won't go into all the specifics unless you want me to, but I will say that if it is left untreated your daughter is not likely to survive more than a couple of weeks."

The previously composed Franco was visibly shaken by the news, but he remained silent, waiting for the rest of the explanation.

"I understand this comes as a shock to you and your wife, but there was nothing either of you could have done to prevent this from happening," Jack explained in an effort to thwart the feeling of guilt that he knew all parents felt when informed that something was wrong with their child. "I assume your wife is still in the hospital?"

The anxious father nodded again, then stared down at the floor.

"We will speak to her as well in a bit, but right now I would like to discuss what our options are for getting your child the care she needs."

Franco raised his head and his eyes seemed to brighten as he heard a ray of hope in Jack's voice. He'd been married to his thirty-five-year-old wife for fifteen years and they'd been trying desperately to have another child for nearly a decade. Their first baby boy had died of sudden infant death syndrome one year to the day after their wedding, and Gabriella had been emotionally devastated by the tragedy. It took her nearly five years to agree to try again, despite Franco's pleadings.

Over the last nine years the couple had tried everything, including three separate trips to a specialty clinic in Houston for in vitro fertilization. They had both decided they would make one final attempt nine months ago, and were beside themselves with excitement when they learned that she was finally pregnant. The news of their daughter's heart problem was difficult for Franco to absorb, but he knew it would likely destroy his wife.

"So are you saying there is something that can be done to save my daughter?" he asked, obviously afraid of the feeling of hope that was growing inside him.

"Yes," Jack said cautiously. "There is an operation that can be done to correct her problem and if successful your daughter could potentially go on to live a normal life."

Hearing this, Franco stood up straighter and asked, "What do I need to do?"

"The operation requires equipment and personnel that are not available here in Managua, or anywhere in Central America for that matter," Jack said, making clear the complex nature of the procedure. "She will need to be transported to a children's hospital in the United States, and ..."

"Is this an operation that you can do?" he asked without allowing Jack to continue.

"Yes, I have performed this procedure many times at our hospital in Fort Worth," Jack answered him, again being cautious not to get too far ahead of his explanation.

"Then we will take her to your hospital immediately!" Franco stated, emphatically.

"It may not be that simple," Jack continued. "She would need to be transported in an oxygen filled incubator, like the one she is in now, and commercial aircraft are not able to handle that kind of equipment."

"I have my own plane," Franco announced, suggesting that transportation would not be a problem.

"That's great, but I'm sure it's not equipped to function as an air ambulance."

"Just tell me what modifications are needed and I will have them done immediately."

"Okay," Jack decided to concede the transportation issue for the moment, "but there is the problem of getting her through immigration."

"I will speak to my friend, John Langdon, at the American embassy," Franco responded, "I am certain that will not be a problem. You just take care of the operation, I'll take care of getting my daughter to Fort Worth."

Jack looked over at Domingo who simply shrugged his shoulders and raised his eyebrows, indicating he could see no reason not to proceed.

"Okay, I'll make a few phone calls and get everything arranged," Jack said as he shook the determined father's hand once more. "I think it would be best to transport her on Monday rather than tomorrow, since it may take some time to get your plane ready and for me to get everything arranged back home. Besides, I'm sure your wife will want to accompany you and your daughter."

"Whatever you say, Dr. Roberts," Franco stated, "I have every confidence in you."

"Perhaps we should go speak to your wife, just to let her know what is going on," Jack suggested.

"I will tell her myself," Franco insisted. "She is quite upset right now, so I will take care of breaking this news to her."

"Okay," Jack replied reluctantly. It suddenly occurred to him that he was scheduled to return home tomorrow. "My family and I were planning to leave tomorrow, but I would feel much better if I could accompany your child."

"My Challenger 300 seats eight passengers, so there is more than enough room for you and your family if you would like."

Jack turned to face David who had been listening intently to the conversation, observing how his dad was systematically handling this situation the same way he had worked his way through the operation on the Ochoa boy. "I think it would be best for you and your mom to go on home tomorrow as planned."

"I was kinda hoping I could come with you?" David said with obvious disappointment.

"No, I need for you to stay with your mom," he said, understanding his son's enthusiasm, but also not wanting Elaina to fly back by herself.

"Dr. Patel would be with her," David pointed out, trying to find a way to change his father's mind.

Jack had completely forgotten about Radha until David brought her up. He turned back to Franco and said, "My anesthesiologist colleague is here with us, and she will be the one providing the anesthesia to your daughter during her surgery. I think it would be a good idea for her to accompany us on your plane. She could prove very useful in the event we encounter any problems en route."

"Whatever you say," Franco replied. "I will let my pilot know that there will be four adults and one incubator with oxygen for the flight to Fort Worth on Monday morning."

David was disappointed, but knew that his dad was right about his flying back with his mom.

◆◆◆◆◆◆◆◆

"Hello, Buzz," Jack said, speaking loudly into his cell phone.

"Hey, Jack, are you back already?" the pediatric cardiologist asked, excited to hear his friend's voice.

"No, I'm still here in Managua," he replied. "Listen, I've got a newborn down here that I'm certain has tetralogy and I'm going to bring her up there on Monday," he explained slowly and again louder than was necessary. "I'd like to get you to cath her as soon as we arrive to confirm the anatomy so I can get her to the OR first thing Tuesday morning."

"Sure," Buzz responded. "How do you plan to get this one past administration?"

"Well, first of all, I'm going to do her at the children's hospital, and secondly, I don't expect that payment will be a problem, if you catch my drift."

"Okay, when do you think you'll be here?"

"Mid-afternoon on Monday, so if you could reserve the cath lab for around four we should be there by then."

"Will do. By the way, what's the kid's name?"

"Baby Gutierrez is all I have."

"Okay, I'll see you on Monday," Buzz said.

"Thanks, buddy. I owe you one," Jack said as he pushed the end button on his phone.

◆◆◆◆◆◆◆◆

"Hi, Bob," Jack said when Robert Anderson, the children's hospital administrator answered his cell phone.

"Hey, Jack," he responded with surprise, immediately recognizing the surgeon's voice. "I thought you were out of the country?"

"I am. We're still here in Nicaragua, and that's why I'm calling," he said, and when he heard no immediate response he continued. "There's a newborn here in Managua that has Tetralogy of Fallot and I need to bring her up to our hospital for surgery."

"You are going to bring a newborn here from Nicaragua?" he asked, not sure exactly how he could accomplish the feat.

"Yes, we will be arriving by private plane on Monday, and I've scheduled the surgery for Tuesday morning. I just wanted to give you a heads up."

"Okay ..." Bob wasn't sure what else to say. "Do you need me to do anything to assist you?" he asked, not really wanting to bring up the question of payment.

"If you would ask the hospital's ambulance service to meet us at DFW around one on Monday afternoon, that would be great."

"No problem. I'll contact Louise as soon as we get off the phone."

"Oh, by the way, these people are more than capable of paying for this, so don't worry about it."

"I wasn't worried," Bob said, somewhat relieved that for once they were going to see a patient from outside the country that wouldn't strain their charity budget.

"I'll see you in a couple of days," Jack said, knowing that his friend would never tell him no when it came to providing care for kids, no matter what their financial status.

◆◆◆◆◆◆◆◆◆

That evening, Jack and Elaina sat out on the small patio behind the guesthouse, sipping on some Argentinian merlot as they watched the sun go down over the low mountains to the west. In recent years they hadn't had many opportunities to relax like this, and this evening they were both feeling a little nostalgic.

"Remember our first sunset together?" Elaina sighed, as she moved over closer to him on the old metal glider.

"How could I ever forget?" he replied as he looked lovingly into her gorgeous green eyes. "That black BMW was one of the best cars I've ever owned. I wish I still had it."

"That back seat wasn't really all that comfortable," she admitted.

"I thought it was," he protested. "Of course I was considerably more limber back in those days."

"So was I," she laughed, but Jack knew better than to agree with her. Instead he took another sip of his wine and returned his attention to the orange glow over the mountain ridge.

"You know," she said, as she snuggled closer, wrapped in his strong left arm, "when we get back home we should take a drive back down to Glen Rose one evening, just to see if we can find our spot."

"You're on, Angel," he said, then he kissed her deeply.

CHAPTER 11

The streets of Managua were quiet at five o'clock on Monday morning, as Domingo drove the big Toyota toward the government hospital. Jack had insisted on swinging by there to check on the Ochoa boy one final time. From there they would continue on to the private hospital where they were to meet Franco and Gabriella Gutierrez and their baby daughter, Christina.

Gabriella had been discharged from the hospital the previous afternoon at her husband's insistence, but her doctor was not at all happy about her plans to fly to the United States the following day. Jack spoke to the young physician and assured him that should the need arise, she would have immediate access to an obstetrician in Fort Worth.

The concerned parents were waiting just outside the newborn nursery when Jack, Radha, and Domingo, arrived just after six. "Good morning," Franco said. "This is my wife, Gabriella." It had been barely forty-eight hours since she gave birth, and it was clear the new mother was fatigued. It was also clear she was a stunningly beautiful woman, with black hair, dark eyes, and a smooth olive complexion.

Jack stepped forward and extended his hand and as she took it he could feel both her fear and her frailty. She was visibly trembling and her grip was weak. "I am very glad to meet you," he offered in his most articulate Spanish.

"Thank you so much for helping us," she replied in English. "We feel that God has brought you here to Managua because we needed you."

Jack smiled timidly and said, "Thank you, *señora*. I would like you to meet Dr. Radha Patel. She is the anesthesiologist who will be helping me take care of your baby."

Radha stepped forward and calmly accepted the young woman's hand and held it between both of her own. "It is nice to meet you, and I want you to know, we will take very good care of Christina."

The mere mention of the baby's name caused a tear to appear once more in the corner of Gabriella's eye. "Thank you," she said, as she recognized the obvious confidence of the older woman, both through her hands and her face.

Domingo stood silently behind the American doctors, anticipating he would soon see them off to the airport. "Mrs. Gutierrez?" Jack said. "I'd also like you to meet Dr. Domingo Ramirez," he gestured toward his colleague to step forward. "When you bring your daughter home in a week or two, I want you to have her examined by Dr. Ramirez, okay?"

With those few well-chosen words Jack had done more to raise her expectations than anything she might have imagined. She smiled at Domingo and then back toward Jack and nodded in agreement, the tears now streaming down her cheeks.

The nurses had connected the incubator to a portable oxygen tank as well as a battery powered heater to maintain a constant temperature during their trip. There were two extra tanks of oxygen and a spare battery on a separate metal cart, pushed along behind by an older gentleman who had put the traveling incubator system together.

The group made their way to the elevator, and down to the emergency entrance of the hospital where an ambulance was waiting to take the baby and her mother to the airport. Radha elected to ride with the baby while Jack would go with Franco in his limousine. He had sent his large duffel bag home with David and Elaina the day before, leaving him with only a small satchel that contained one change of clothes and his shaving kit. He quickly transferred it from Domingo's truck into the trunk of the limo then embraced his friend one final time.

"Than you for everything, my friend," Jack said, as he joined Franco in the back of the long black Lincoln. Domingo silently nodded, unable to express his own gratitude.

The traffic had increased significantly, but they were still able to reach the airport in less than twenty minutes. The government personnel waived both vehicles through a security gate that led out onto the tarmac. As they neared the private hangars, they pulled up in front of a gleaming white jet with the tail emblazoned with the corporate emblem of Gutierrez Enterprises, Ltd. — an eagle soaring over a volcanic peak.

The pilot came out to the car to greet Franco, and accompanied him aboard the plane to inspect the modifications they had made to accommodate the incubator, spare oxygen tanks, and batteries. They returned almost immediately and motioned for Radha and Gabriella to get on board. The limo driver unloaded the luggage, and along with one of the ground crew, placed the bags into the cargo hold in the tail of the plane.

The ambulance driver and Jack carried the small incubator assembly up the steps and into the plane. Both men were forced to bend over as they entered the aircraft, and due to his height, Jack was forced to remain hunched over as they placed the container holding the precious cargo on the left side of the passenger compartment in a spot previously occupied by a large leather chair. They secured it using a pair of straps mounted to the floor, ensuring it would not move during the flight.

The ambulance driver moved past Jack and back down the steps as the young flight attendant climbed the stairs and entered the cabin. She went forward to the galley and began making preparations for an immediate departure. She suggested Jack take the back seat on the left side of the compartment and when Franco finally boarded, he took his customary seat across the aisle from him. Gabriella was seated behind the incubator and Radha sat across from her.

The pilot and copilot quickly ran through their preflight checklist and soon the twin jet engines were whining, and the luxury aircraft taxied slowly to the end of the runway. They were third in line for takeoff behind a Mexicana 727 and an Avianca MD-80. When it was finally their turn to depart, the engines roared to life, accelerating the multimillion dollar aircraft down the concrete strip and propelling it into the air in a matter of seconds. Franco had asked the pilot not to climb out as steeply as he usually did because he feared the unrestrained infant would slide to the end of the incubator and could potentially be injured.

As they climbed steadily over the mountains to the East, the plane banked gently to the left toward Guatemala, Mexico, and the United States.

"Would you like some breakfast?" the attendant asked Jack.

"No, thank you," he replied, "but I would like a Diet Coke if you have one." He was pretty sure she wouldn't have Diet Dr Pepper, so he decided not to even ask.

"Certainly, sir, and what can I get for you, Mr. Gutierrez?"

"I'll have my usual, Tina," he said.

"Yes, sir," she said before moving forward to take the ladies' order. In a few minutes she returned with the drinks. She set Jack's Diet Coke along with a glass of ice in the holders in the small table beside his spacious leather chair. She did the same for Franco, only his soda was a Diet Dr Pepper.

"I can't believe it," Jack said.

"What?" Franco asked, looking at Jack with surprise.

"That is what I drink every morning, but I was certain you wouldn't have Diet Dr Pepper on board so I didn't ask for it."

Franco laughed briefly then said, "I hope that you are not wrong about other things that you claim to be certain of." He was obviously referring to his daughter's diagnosis. He pushed a small button on the console to his right and Tina was quick to respond.

"Yes, sir?" she asked.

"Please bring Dr. Roberts one of these," he said as he lifted the can of soda.

"Certainly, sir," she replied, then turned to Jack. "Was there something wrong with your Coke, sir?"

"No, it was fine, I would just prefer a Diet DP."

"No problem, sir, I'll bring it right away."

"So, tell me, Dr. Roberts," Franco said, "how did you come to be a children's heart surgeon?"

"Well, it's kind of a long story," Jack replied.

"This is a three-and-a-half-hour flight, and I would like to know a bit more about the man to whom I have entrusted my child's life."

Jack's mind drifted back to December 1953. He was a precocious five-year-old, the son of a plumbing contractor and an elementary school teacher in the small North Texas town of Hurst. His father, Harold, whom everyone knew as Harry, and his mother, Faye, had lived in the sleepy little community between Dallas and Fort Worth since Harry's return from the war. That was where Jack was born and where he grew up.

◆◆◆◆◆◆◆◆◆

Jack stood in his mother's room in the small local hospital. She was lying in the hospital bed, obviously very anxious. Next to her bed was a small crib with an oxygen tent draped over it, and inside was a bundled up infant. The bewildered five-year-old looked on as his dad tried to explain to him that his new baby brother was sick. He didn't understand anything except that his two-day-old brother looked blue.

His eight-year-old sister, Janet, was curled up in a chair on the other side of the bed, crying. Her baby brother had been diagnosed by the family doctor with "Blue Baby Syndrome," and he told them the most likely cause was a birth defect in his heart. The doctor had recommended the baby be transferred to the big hospital in downtown Fort Worth where he could be evaluated by a specialist.

This news also had his father visibly upset. "How are we going to pay for a specialist?" he asked his wife.

Faye seemed more hopeful. "I'm pretty sure the Blue Cross insurance policy we have through the school district will pay for it. If not, we'll find a way."

The Texas Teachers Retirement Fund had been responsible for creating the first employer-based health insurance. The major medical policy was offered as an employee benefit in lieu of higher wages during the tough economic times following World War II. The Roberts family had not had an occasion to need it until now, so they were unsure what it would, or wouldn't, pay for. Faye was also uncertain whether the baby would be included on the policy, since she had only listed Harry, Janet, and Jack as her dependents when she signed up.

They heard a knock on the door and Harry took the few steps to open it. He saw the familiar face of Andrew Stroud, the pastor of the Baptist church where they had been members for several years. Andy had come to visit this family he knew very well, expecting to share in their excitement over their new child.

"So, how's the new addition?" he asked with a big smile. When he didn't hear a response he said, "What's wrong?"

Andy looked at Harry and could see the emotional strain on his friend's face.

"The doctor has recommended our baby be transferred to Fort Worth to see a specialist," Faye said. "He says there is something wrong with his heart."

The pastor now recognized why Harry was so quiet and continued to stare alternately between his wife and the floor. After a brief prayer at the bedside, Andy asked Harry to join him out in the hallway.

"I know why you are so upset."

"This isn't about me," Harry said, trying to deny his anxiety.

"Look, Harry, it's me you're talking to." Andy had been one of Harry's closest friends since before the war.

"I don't want to lose this baby," Harry admitted, "but if he needs some kind of expensive treatment there is no way I can afford it."

Andy put his hand on Harry's shoulder and spoke with a strong but compassionate voice. "I understand, but I would suggest you wait until you know more about the situation before you worry about all that. Maybe it's nothing more than a short-term problem that will resolve itself." He was trying to encourage his friend by pointing out the positive possibilities. "I suspect Doc Harrison is just being extra cautious."

"I don't think so," Harry responded. "He seemed very concerned when he spoke to Faye and me. He wasn't his usual smiling self. I hope you're right, but I can't help but worry about the cost."

"God has a way of providing for our needs," Andy offered in his usual pastoral manner. "It is times like these He tests our faith in Him to do just that, trust Him."

"Faye seems to think this new medical insurance she got through her work will pay for stuff like this, but I don't know. We've never had to use it before. Sounds a little fishy to me."

"It doesn't do you any good to worry about that now, just try not to think about all that money stuff. Your wife and family need you to be strong for them, and I know you, you're a strong and faithful man."

Harry smiled slightly before replying, "It's really Faye who is the rock in this family."

Andy nodded and told Harry that he and his family would be in his prayers, and to let him know if there was anything he or the church could do.

The next morning the ambulance ride to Fort Worth only took twenty minutes. Harry and Jack followed in his pickup which Jack thought was great. He'd never gone this fast before, so he got up on his knees to watch the flashing lights of the speeding ambulance just ahead. With the windows down the sound of the air rushing by accentuated the sense of sheer speed, but it was loud. Harry told Jack to sit down, but the young boy didn't hear him, mesmerized by the combined sounds of the rushing wind and the rise and fall of the blaring siren.

Faye remained behind in the hospital for at least one more day. Dr. Harrison told her he needed to make sure she was sufficiently recovered from the trauma of childbirth. It hadn't been a particularly difficult labor, but a minimum of three days in the hospital was considered mandatory. Before leaving, Harry told her he'd call once they got settled and heard what the specialist had to say.

Shortly after they arrived at the emergency entrance of the huge hospital the baby was placed in a small rolling crib with an oxygen tent. The complex looking assembly was rolled noisily off to the pediatric floor as Harry and Jack followed along. The nurse was moving so fast that Jack was having trouble keeping up. When they reached the doors to the newborn nursery the nurse told them they would have to wait outside.

"You can look in through the windows around the corner," she said.

Jack ran around the corner and jumped up on the steps placed there specifically so siblings could get a glimpse of their new playmates. Harry soon stood next to his son and told him to keep his hands off the glass, but Jack seemed completely caught up in the sights and sounds of this new world.

"Look at all the little babies!" he exclaimed pointing to the bassinets lined up in front of him. In the back of the room he saw the nurse place his brother on a bed that seemed a little larger than the others. Like the transport crib, it had an oxygen tent over it. As he watched, he noticed the clear plastic sides of the tent began to fog until he could no longer see his baby brother.

Harry just stood there, silently staring at this strange sight, wondering what would come next. A few minutes later, he and Jack watched as a young man rolled a machine into the nursery that Jack said looked like a large bird with a long neck. The nurse showed the man where the new arrival could be found, and the young radiology technician pushed the portable x-ray machine into place. When he was ready the nurse quickly pulled the oxygen tent back and Jack excitedly pointed out to his dad that he could see his brother again.

The baby appeared to be asleep as the nurse lifted the tiny body off the mattress to allow the radiology technician to slip an x-ray plate under him. As the nurse laid the baby down on the hard surface, she positioned him to ensure his entire torso was on the film. Other than the child's persistent rapid breathing, Harry couldn't detect any other movement from his son. The technician paused a couple of seconds to time the picture as best he could with the infant's rapid respirations. Once the picture was taken the nurse lifted the infant again and the hard case containing the x-ray film was removed. She quickly placed the baby back on the bed and reestablished the oxygen-rich environment.

A few minutes later the technician returned with a small x-ray that he adeptly flipped up on the unlighted view box on the wall next to the nurses' station. He left the way he came in, pushing the bird-like machine in front of him.

Nothing more appeared to be happening and Harry wondered if he should use the pay phone in the nearby waiting room to call Faye. He decided to just wait until the pediatric cardiologist came, so he took a seat in one of the hard wooden chairs that lined the wall opposite the nursery window. Jack continued to stand mesmerized by the newborn nursery scene. He watched silently as a couple of other families came by with the proud dads pointing out to their children which of the little bundles belonged to them.

After about an hour, a tall gray-haired gentleman in a long white coat made his way past the dozen or so infants arranged in neat rows over to the one containing Jack's baby brother. It was the one closest to the nurses' desk. He spoke to the nurse for a moment then turned and unzipped one side of the foggy oxygen tent.

"They are doing something to him." Jack called out to his dad.

Harry rose quickly and stood alongside his son as the doctor pulled a stethoscope from his pocket and placed it around his neck. They watched intently as his head and shoulders disappeared back inside the tent to examine the new arrival.

"What's he doing?" Jack asked.

"I suppose that's the doctor we brought your brother here to see," Harry said. "I guess he's examining him."

"He's not gonna hurt him is he, Dad?"

"No, he's gonna try to help him," Harry stated hopefully.

After a couple of minutes the stoic doctor emerged from the tent and zipped it closed. He turned to the nurse and she handed him the infant's chart, which included records sent from the other hospital as well as the baby's current vital signs. The doctor appeared to ask the nurse some questions. They couldn't hear what was being said, but she initially pointed to the chart, then to the x-ray view box. After another question from the doctor, the nurse pointed toward Harry and Jack through the window. He glanced briefly in their direction before heading over to the x-ray view box. He flipped a switch on the side of the box, and after a couple of brief flickers the bright white light came on, illuminating the x-ray of the infant's tiny body. He studied the film carefully for a minute or so, then sat down and wrote something on the chart. When he was finished he handed the chart back to the nurse and offered some parting remarks before exiting through a back door.

In a few seconds, Jack saw the doctor coming around the corner heading right toward his dad. "Are you Mr. Roberts?" he asked.

"Yes," Harry said solemnly.

"I'm Dr. Reichmann. I'm a pediatric cardiologist — a heart specialist." Harry acknowledged only with a nod of his head. "I have just finished examining your son, and I'm afraid I have some rather bad news."

Harry stood motionless holding Jack's hand. Without realizing it he was squeezing a bit too hard, and Jack winced as he tried to pull his hand away. Harry looked down apologetically as he softened his grip. As he looked back up at the doctor he heard the words he had been fearing. "Your son has a birth defect involving his heart. The technical name is Tetralogy of Fallot, but the more common term is Blue Baby Syndrome," he said as calmly as he could. "What that means is that during development the two main pumping chambers of the heart muscle didn't form properly. There is a large hole between them, and the blood that should be going through the lungs to gather oxygen is being blocked and shunted out to the rest of his body."

Harry was a plumber. He had no idea what Dr. Reichmann was saying. "What does all that mean, doc?" he asked.

"Well, it means his body isn't getting enough oxygen. That's why he's not moving around. He's breathing rapidly in an effort to get more air, but that doesn't really help because not much of the blood is flowing through his lungs. It's also the reason he wasn't nursing well when your wife tried to feed him," the doctor explained in a very matter-of-fact way.

"Okay," said Harry, "but, what's going to happen?" Before the doctor could answer he asked the most important question, "Is he gonna make it?"

Reichmann hesitated and looked down at young Jack before speaking. "The outlook for survival for infants with Tetralogy of Fallot is not very good." He paused, then added, "Especially when they are having this much trouble so early in life. This condition is rare. It only occurs once in a million births, and it is variable. Some children seem to compensate pretty well, but others, like your son, have trouble right from birth and struggle to survive beyond a few weeks."

The doctor's words hit Harry like a blow to his gut. Through clinched teeth and a growing tear in his eye he said, "Well I guess that's it then?" He looked down into Jack's questioning face. He was obviously unable to understand any of what was going on. He just saw his dad's face and couldn't help being afraid.

"There is a surgeon in Baltimore, Maryland, by the name of Alfred Blalock," Reichmann said almost as an afterthought. "He has reportedly performed surgery on several babies with tetralogy, but there isn't anyone around here who has ever performed such a procedure." He was trying unsuccessfully to sound hopeful. "I'm not really sure whether he is even still doing that operation, but if you'd like I can try to contact him. I think he's at the Johns Hopkins University Hospital," Reichmann added almost to himself. "I don't know how we'd transfer your son to Maryland, or whether that is even possible."

Harry interrupted the doctor and said, "I'd appreciate it if you'd try to call that doctor and see if he would be willing to help us. If he is, we'll find a way to get our son to Baltimore." As soon as the words were out of his mouth he realized how insane they sounded.

As Reichmann turned to leave he added, "I'll try, and I'll let you know just as soon as I know something." He turned back and spoke seemingly more to Jack than to Harry, "I'm truly sorry."

Once the doctor was around the corner, Jack pulled on his dad's hand and asked, "Is my brother going to be okay?"

Harry turned to the young boy, holding back his emotions, saying, "I don't know, Buddy, I hope so."

Harry wandered down the hall to the pay phone to call Faye, not really knowing what he was going to say. Jack jumped back up on the steps in front of the window, and peered intently into the nursery for any signs of change in the all too familiar static scene.

"Yes, I spoke to the heart doctor," Harry said, trying his best to hold his emotions in check, but he was sure Faye could tell he was discouraged.

"So what did he say?" she asked impatiently.

"Well, he said, the baby has some kind of tetro something in his heart. It didn't form right."

"I knew it," she said, "This is all my fault ..."

"No honey, he didn't say anything about it being your fault. He said these things just happen to one kid in a million," Harry said trying to calm her down. "I guess he is just one of the unlucky ones."

There was no response for several seconds, then she spoke again. "Is there anything that can be done?"

"The doc said there is some surgeon named Blanton, or Black, or something like that, in Baltimore, Maryland, who's about the only guy anywhere who has had any luck fixing this kind of thing," Harry continued, trying to sound positive, but his heart just wasn't in it. "I asked him to see if he could contact the surgeon and see what he..."

"Do you have any idea how we'd get the baby to Baltimore?" she interrupted.

"No, I don't, but …"

Again she interrupted. "Oh, Harry," she said as she began to cry, "it sounds like we're going to lose him."

"Don't talk like that," he shouted just a little too loud. "This doc is gonna get back to me once he talks to the surgeon in Baltimore, and I'll call you back just as soon as I hear from him, okay?"

"Okay," she said, somewhat calmer.

Harry seemed ready to hang up the phone but realized he hadn't asked his wife how she was doing. "How are you feeling?"

"I feel fine."

"Did the doctor say when you could get out of there?"

"He said maybe tomorrow. How's Jack doing?"

"He's fine. He has his nose plastered to the nursery window. He's just staring in there like he's trying to will his little brother well," he answered, his voice a little lighter now.

"When did you guys last eat something?" she inquired in a classic maternal fashion.

"I don't know. We'll eat something. I'm sure they have a cafeteria or something here," he shrugged.

"Do you have any cash?"

"Yes, I have some money. Jack and I will be fine." After another brief pause he added, "Tell Janet we'll be by there to take her home, but I don't know exactly when. It just depends on when the heart doctor comes back out to talk to us, and what he says."

"Okay," she said, "I love you."

Harry was beginning to feel the exhaustion that comes with prolonged emotional strain, but he summoned the energy to add, "I love you, too. I'll call you back when I know more. Bye." When he heard her say goodbye he hung up the phone and walked dejectedly back to Jack's side and put his arm around the young boy's shoulder.

It was about two in the afternoon, and Harry had fallen asleep sitting in the hard wooden chair. Jack came away from the window for the first time since the doctor left them nearly four hours before. He shook his dad's arm and Harry awoke with a start.

"I need to go to the bathroom," Jack said.

"I'm sorry, Buddy, I must have dozed off," Harry said as he got up and walked down the long hallway with Jack alongside. He found the door marked "MEN" and started to go inside with his young son.

"I'm okay to go by myself, Dad," Jack said somewhat indignantly.

"I know you are, but I need to go too."

Harry had to lift the young boy to the sink to wash his hands, and as he did he asked, "Are you hungry?"

"A little," Jack replied.

"Let's go down to that cafeteria we saw on our way in and see if we can find something to eat."

"Okay, but what if that doctor comes back while we're gone?"

Harry thought to himself, *This kid is way smarter than I was at his age.* "I'll let the nurse know where we are. Besides we won't be gone long."

Back at the nursery Harry managed to catch the nurse's attention and in response she came over to the glass and asked very curtly, "Yes?"

"We are going down to the cafeteria to get a bite. We'll be back in half an hour or less." Harry half shouted through the glass.

The nurse simply nodded, acknowledging that she'd heard him and then rather indifferently turned away to get back to changing a newborn's diaper.

Harry and Jack were sitting at a table along one wall of the nearly deserted cafeteria. Harry was trying to generate some interest in the cold and boring turkey sandwich on the tray in front of him while Jack made short work of the fried chicken leg. He was not as keen toward the potato salad, but his dad told him he could just eat the chicken if that's all he wanted. The small bottle of cold milk was already half empty and Harry smiled to see his healthy son eating well. His mom would be glad to hear that.

Harry turned suddenly as he felt someone's hand on his shoulder. "Mr. Roberts?" Dr. Reichmann said as Harry started to stand. "Please keep your seat," Reichmann insisted as Harry sank back into his chair with a look of fear and expectation.

"You didn't need to come all the way down here," he said with a forced smile.

"I have some good news for you," Reichmann replied. His mannerisms and his voice seemed much more optimistic than just a few hours before. "It took a while, but I was able to talk to Dr. Blalock a few minutes ago."

Harry repeated the doctor's name silently to himself: Blalock, right.

Reichmann continued, "I explained the situation to him and he said based on the information I gave him he thought we have about a week to get your son to Johns Hopkins. In his experience these kind of kids with Tetralogy of Fallot remain relatively stable for the first ten to fourteen days before the right side of the heart begins to fail."

For the first time Harry felt a sense of hope, but it was now mixed with one of urgency. The doctor then added, "He said we should keep him here in the nursery on oxygen until an air ambulance can be arranged."

"Air ambulance?" Harry said, "What's that?"

"Your baby will need to travel to Maryland by airplane and he will need to be on oxygen continuously. It is too far to drive in a regular ambulance so you will need to go by plane," Reichmann explained.

Harry had a questioning look on his face, and the doctor could see that the confused father had no way of knowing what to do next. "There is a fairly new company based out of Meacham Field on the north edge of Fort Worth that offers this kind of flight service."

After a moment Harry asked, "Do you have any idea what that costs?"

"No, I don't, but I have their number here. You can call them and I'm sure they'll be able to tell you," the doctor replied.

"Okay," Harry said, taking the card with the handwritten number scrawled on the back. "I'll call them right now," he added. "Thanks a lot, doc, I really appreciate your help."

Dr. Reichmann smiled more genuinely than Harry had seen since meeting him earlier that day. "You're welcome, and I wish you all the best." With that he stood and walked briskly out of the cafeteria toward the elevators.

"They're gonna take my baby brother in an airplane?" Jack asked excitedly.

"We'll see," Harry responded. "We'll see." He was still trying to digest what he had just heard from Dr. Reichmann. Yes, Dr. Blalock was willing to see his baby, and that was indeed the first good news he'd heard since the child was born. However, they would need to fly him to Baltimore in an air ambulance, and that couldn't possibly be cheap.

The father and son made their way back up to the nursery where most of the babies were gone. His brother's crib was still there, looking just as it had since Dr. Reichmann finished his exam. Jack wondered out loud, "Where are all the other babies, Dad?"

"They are probably with their moms in their rooms," he said reassuringly. "Will you be okay here while I make a couple of phone calls?" he asked.

"Sure, Dad," Jack responded trying to sound grown up beyond his years. "I'll come get you if they start doing anything to my brother."

His father smiled and walked back toward the pay phone.

"Hi, my name is Harry Roberts, and I was given your company's number by the doctor here at the hospital." He wasn't sure exactly what to say or how to say it.

❖❖❖❖❖❖❖❖❖

"Hey, sweetie," he began, not knowing which direction this conversation might take.

"Do you have any news?" Faye asked.

"Yes, I spoke to the heart doctor again, and he was able to get in touch with Dr. Blalock in Maryland." Harry went on to tell Faye exactly what Reichmann had said. She sounded so relieved over the phone, almost as if this whole ordeal was finally over instead of what Harry knew was just the beginning.

"The doctor said he will have to go to Baltimore by plane." Then he quickly added, "I've already checked into it, and there is a company out of Meacham that can fly us up there for five hundred dollars."

"Harry, we don't have five hundred dollars!" she exclaimed telling him what he already knew.

"I know that's a lot of money, but we'll find a way."

"Where would we stay? We don't have any family in Baltimore and we sure can't afford a hotel." She sounded even more stressed, as her initial excitement had clearly disappeared.

"I don't know where we'll stay when we get there, but this is the only option we have." Harry was trying to process the entire situation as he was talking to Faye, and until now he hadn't even thought about what he would do with the kids. "We can talk about that when I see you this evening."

As he was talking he realized he was sounding a bit too harsh. "It's gonna be okay," he offered reassuringly. "Andy told me just yesterday that these kinds of situations are God's way of testing our faith." Today, he thought, that had been a gross understatement. "Jack and I be there within an hour or so," he said.

"Okay," Faye responded through her fear and fatigue.

He pushed the small chrome lever down, disconnecting the call, but immediately put in another dime to call the church, hoping to find Andy still at work.

"Hi, is Andy Stroud in the office?"

"Yes," came the response he had hoped for.

"Great, can I speak to him?"

"May I say who is calling?"

"Yeah, this is Harry Roberts."

"Can you hold, Mr. Roberts?" The woman's voice was not one Harry recognized.

"Sure, I'll hold." After about a minute Harry heard Andy's voice on the phone,

"Hi, Andy," he said. "Listen, I'm at the hospital here in Fort Worth right now, but I'm getting ready to come back out to Hurst to pick up Janet and take her and Jack home. I was wondering if you would be willing to meet me up there. I need to ask your advice about something and I'm not comfortable talking about it over the phone."

"Sure, what time?" came Andy's response.

"I should be there around six o'clock, so any time after that."

"I'll be there around six-thirty," the pastor said with certainty.

"I appreciate it," Harry said. "I'll see you then. Thanks. Bye."

Harry hung up the phone and headed back to collect Jack. As he approached the nursery window he saw Jack explaining his brother's situation to a couple of other kids, both of whom were a few years older. His son spoke very authoritatively.

"Yeah, my baby brother is in that big tent over there. He's in there because he was born with a busted heart, and my dad is going to take him up in an airplane so that the angels can fix his heart."

Harry turned and took a couple of steps around the corner away from his son, and for the first time he broke down and wept.

♦♦♦♦♦♦♦♦♦

Jack broke away from his father's grasp two doors before reaching Faye's room. He bolted through the door and rushed in to tell his mom all about the gigantic hospital and all the babies in the nursery, and how Dr. Reichmann had on a white overcoat that went almost down to the floor. Faye wanted to hear all the details but she was more excited just to see her vibrant five year old. When Harry walked through the door her expression quickly matched his. He was exhausted and frightened, still searching for answers. After hugging his daughter and kissing her on the top of her head, he asked her to take Jack down to the gift shop. He gave her a dime so she could buy them each a candy bar.

Once the kids were gone, Harry embraced his wife, holding her closer than he had in years. When they finally separated, Harry looked into her face with a renewed conviction. He had come up with a plan he thought might work during the drive back from Fort Worth.

"We've got about two hundred dollars in our savings account and I'm pretty sure I can borrow a couple hundred from my dad," he stated hesitantly. "I'm meeting with Andy in about thirty minutes and I'm gonna ask him if he would talk to Frank Gorman down at the bank."

Harry had an account at First National, but he had never established any credit there, or anywhere else for that matter. They had bought their home using a VA loan when Harry came home from the war. Now, following the conflict in Korea, their home value had dropped to about what they owed against it, so he really didn't have anything they could offer as collateral.

"Hopefully we can borrow a hundred bucks from the bank, and that should be enough to get us to Baltimore," Harry said almost wishfully.

"But, what about the kids?" Faye asked.

"I figured Janet could stay with the Johnsons, so she won't miss any school. I guess Jack will have to come with us."

"I don't know, Harry," Faye said, shaking her head slightly. "Don't you think Jack is a little young to be exposed to all this?"

"I think he'll be fine. You should have seen him today down at the hospital.

You'd have thought he owned the place," Harry said with more than just a little paternal pride.

"Well, what if we can't get the money together?" Faye asked. Before Harry could respond there was a knock on the door.

"Come in!" Faye called out, and Andy pushed the door open far enough to stick his head in. "Come on in, Andy," she said.

"Thanks for coming," Harry offered.

"Sure," Andy replied as he sat down carefully in the small chair near the end of the bed. He feared it might collapse under his considerable weight. Andy was a very large man in his late thirties. He had played football at Baylor before going to the seminary and then served as a Navy chaplain during the war. Over the years Andy had put on quite a few pounds from the combination of minimal exercise and being fed on a regular basis by every woman in the church. It seemed that they all felt obligated to feed the preacher as part of their offering. As a lifelong bachelor, Andy was never one to turn down a good home-cooked meal. Once seated, he turned his full attention to Harry and asked, "What's up?"

"Well, like I explained on the phone, we took the baby to Fort Worth and the specialist said he has a birth defect in his heart. I still can't pronounce it," Harry said. "It's something like tetra-link, or tetra-flow, or something like that." He was fumbling with his words and trying not to sound too ignorant, but he had always been uncomfortable discussing anything medical.

"Anyway, the doc said he will likely only live a few weeks unless he gets this new operation that was developed by a surgeon in Baltimore, Maryland." Harry was visibly shaking as he spoke the words he had rehearsed over and over in his mind during the drive from Fort Worth.

"He said he would have to be transferred from here to Baltimore by air ambulance because he couldn't handle the two-day drive." He paused briefly before relating what he knew would be the toughest part. "There is a new company that flies an air ambulance out of Meacham Field but it's gonna cost five hundred dollars."

"Wow!" Andy exclaimed. "You could almost buy your own plane for that much money."

"Don't I know it," Harry replied shaking his head. "That's the problem… I've got a little over two hundred in savings and I think I can borrow a couple hundred from my dad, but he's not made of money for sure." Andy sat forward, listening intently as his friend continued. "You said that I could call on you to help, and I was hoping I could get you to speak to Mr. Gorman down at First National to see if he would float me a loan for the other hundred bucks. It would have to be unsecured, because I don't really have anything to offer in the way of collateral,"

Harry felt himself shrink a little, because in his mind what he was doing was almost like begging. "I would ask myself, but I don't really know the guy, and I know you do. I thought it might be better coming from you. I don't know, what do you think?" Harry concluded, a bit less sure of himself than he had been during his rehearsals.

Andy stood up slowly and thought for just a moment, then he said, "Listen, you've got a lot on your mind right now, so why don't you let me go to work on this? I'll take care of getting you what you need."

"No, wait a minute, Andy, I'm not asking you to do that. I just need an introduction to Gorman, that's all I asked," Harry pleaded.

"I know what you asked for, but I'm asking you to let me do this for you," Andy said with a finality in his voice. "I'll make sure you get the extra money you need, you just get the transportation arranged."

Andy placed his hand on his friend's shoulder then asked, "When are you planning to go?"

"Well, I figured we'd try to leave on Monday. That will give Faye a few more days to recuperate and allow me time to get Hank, my foreman, organized to keep my business running while we're gone. Faye already has substitute teachers arranged since she's out on maternity leave anyway," Harry said, having also worked out this part in his head over the last hour.

"Sounds like a plan," Andy assured him. "I will be at your house around two on Sunday afternoon," Andy added as he turned to leave. "Oh, and by the way, the women from the church office have already set up meals to be brought to your house for the next few days." Andy was quickly out the door before Harry had a chance to thank him.

When the kids returned from the gift shop, Jack was still holding the last part of a Baby Ruth, some of which he had eaten, but by all appearances most of it was on his face, fingers and shirt sleeves. Harry made him wash his face and hands in the bathroom of his mom's private room. It was one of only two in this wing of the hospital with a private bathroom.

"Amazing the perks you get when you're the fourth grade teacher of the hospital administrator's daughter," Faye had said the day she checked in.

The following morning Harry and Jack were at the hospital to see Faye bright and early. Janet was off to school and she'd already made arrangements to stay with her best friend, Lisa Johnson, who lived just across the street. The Johnsons were also close friends with the Roberts family, having daughters the same age, and a son just a year older than Jack. They also had an older daughter, Betty, who often babysat Jack when Harry and Faye needed an evening to themselves. Unfortunately, those times had been far too infrequent, and now there was no telling when their lives would ever get back to normal again.

"Hi, Mom!" Jack exclaimed as he bounded through the door.

"Hi, baby," Faye replied with a smile.

"I'm not a baby," he protested.

"How was your night?" Harry inquired, his voice sounding much more rested.

"It was okay," Faye said without much conviction. "I'm tired of being here. They come in every four hours and wake me up to take my blood pressure then ask me if I want a sleeping pill to go back to sleep."

"Dad and I are gonna go check on Ben this morning," Jack declared.

"Who's Ben?" his mother asked.

"My brother!" Jack reported. "I decided he needed a name so I thought we'd call him Big Ben after the clock at Grampy's house. Dad and I are going over there right after we check on Ben." The youngster was on a roll.

"Well, we'll need to talk about that name since Dad and I had been leaning more toward Matthew, after my father."

"Matthew can be his middle name. Like my middle name is Wayne, after Grampy."

Faye just rolled her eyes and shrugged as she looked at Harry with a smile and a shake of her head.

"Do you think Dr. Harrison is going to let you go home today or will it be tomorrow?" Harry asked.

"He talked like it might be today depending on how well my stitches are healing," she said. "I sure hope so, I'm sick of sitting in that stupid bucket of warm water five times a day."

"Okay," Harry sighed. "We'll come back here after we see my dad."

As he leaned over to kiss her goodbye, Faye fought back the urge to burst into tears.

"I miss my baby," she whispered almost to herself. "I want to hold my baby."

Harry cupped her cheek with his hands. "I know, sweetie. It won't be long before you get to hold him again."

"Promise?" she asked through her tears.

"I promise," he said with a reassuring smile. Then two of the three men in her life were off to check on the third.

❖❖❖❖❖❖❖❖

Harry's encounter with his father went well, with Grampy dipping into an old metal lock box he kept hidden behind boxes of shotgun shells in the back of his closet. He handed his son ten twenty-dollar bills, which amounted to most of what he had been able to save over the previous three years. Harry knew he had better leave before he became too emotional over his father's generosity, so he hugged his dad and then his mom, before he headed for the door, leading

Jack by the hand.

As the screen door closed noisily he heard his mom say, "God be with you, son."

On Sunday afternoon Andy came over to deliver the love offering that had been collected that morning at the church. He handed Jack four hundred fifty dollars in cash along with a separate, personal check from Mr. Gorman for one hundred dollars.

◆◆◆◆◆◆◆◆◆

The Roberts family — Harry, Faye, Jack and Benjamin — arrived at the Baltimore airport on Monday afternoon. The name Benjamin had stuck, and his birth certificate listed his full name as Benjamin Matthew Roberts. An ambulance marked with a large blue and yellow logo, and the name Johns Hopkins University Hospital, was waiting as they wheeled the small stretcher off the plane. One half of the thin mattress was covered with an infant oxygen tent, while two small green tanks of oxygen were lying on the uncovered portion of the stretcher.

The hospital personnel quickly assumed control and expertly transferred the infant to their own oxygen-rich incubator, then into the back of their vehicle. Faye rode in the back with the baby, while Harry and Jack sat up front with the driver.

This was the second time in three days Jack was traveling rapidly to the sound of a loud siren. He was still very excited from the plane ride, although he had slept for most of the six hours it had taken for the DC-3 to cover the fifteen hundred miles.

The driver backed the ambulance up to the emergency entrance of the giant hospital building where their precious cargo was unloaded. A nurse approached Harry and Faye and instructed them to follow her. Harry was carrying their two large suitcases as they trailed behind the matronly woman. She was wearing a starched white dress with a floor length skirt and white cap with a black stripe around the upper edge of the vertical brim. Faye insisted that Jack hold on to her hand so he wouldn't get lost in the maze of hallways that were filled with young doctors and nurses hurrying in every direction. The young boy seemed hypnotized by all the activity around him. As they stood waiting for the elevator, she looked down at her son and saw his mouth agape and his eyes wider than she had ever seen them.

"Welcome to the Johns Hopkins University Hospital," said a tall young physician. He was wearing a short white jacket with the same logo on the pocket that had adorned the side of the ambulance, and the name Roy Bertram, MD, was embroidered above it. "I am Dr. Bertram, the chief resident on Dr.

Blalock's service," he added, extending his hand to Harry and then to Faye. He didn't acknowledge Jack, but instead asked the parents to be seated in a small family waiting area outside the newborn nursery.

The young doctor pulled out a notepad and began interviewing Harry and Faye. He had them go over every detail of her pregnancy and delivery as well as their own medical histories and those of their other children. He wanted to know about any medications Faye might have taken before or during her pregnancy and whether she had ever been exposed to any toxic chemicals.

"If you will wait here, Dr. Blalock will come and find you once he has had a chance to examine your baby," Bertram said as he rose from the chair and prepared to leave.

"When is my brother going to get his operation?" Jack said rather insistently.

The resident looked startled as he was finally forced to acknowledge the young boy's presence. "I don't know the answer to that," he said addressing his parents. "Probably tomorrow, but that will be up to Dr. Blalock." He turned away again and left them to wait.

After about thirty minutes, a middle-aged couple walked into the waiting area and appeared to be looking for someone. They made their way over to where the anxious family was sitting.

"Are you the Roberts family?" the dark-haired woman asked.

"Yes," Harry responded, uncomfortable with the idea that some stranger would know their name.

"I am Jenny Nance and this is my husband, Fred," she said with a timid smile. "We are from the Bethel Baptist Church here in Baltimore. We understand you folks are going to be here for a few days while your child is being treated at this hospital, and we would like to have you come and stay with us while you are here. Our house is only a few blocks away."

Harry stood motionless for a moment not believing what he had just heard. "What?" was the only response he could manage as Faye also slowly rose to her feet.

"Our pastor, Jerry Thorp, is a friend of your pastor, and he shared your situation with our congregation yesterday during our service. Our kids are all grown now, so we have a couple of extra rooms that aren't being used, and we thought you folks could use a place to stay." The woman's smile was tempered by the questioning look in her eyes.

"That is so very kind of you folks to offer," Faye said, "but we couldn't possibly trouble you ..."

"Nonsense!" Fred interrupted. "It would be our honor to have you stay with us. Besides, I'm sure they won't let you sleep here in the hospital."

"I don't know what to say," Harry mumbled as his eyes began to moisten again. He was not one to shed tears, but these last few days he seemed to be doing so on a regular basis.

The Nances waited with their newfound friends, talking about their families and various past illnesses and injuries that had required trips to the doctor, but none of them could share any experience like this one. An hour passed, and the group was joined by Pastor Thorp who explained to Harry how Andy had called him on Saturday to make sure the young family from Texas had some support while they were so far away from home.

Harry was overcome by the love of these strangers and of his good friend Andy, and for the first time Jack saw his father openly weeping. The young boy was worried that something had happened to Ben and he had missed it.

"It's gonna be okay, Dad," he offered as he wrapped his arms around Harry's muscular arm and squeezed it tightly. "Ben is going to be okay, I just know he is."

◆◆◆◆◆◆◆◆◆

Dr. Alfred Blalock was a very distinguished looking man, who wore a long white coat with the same Hopkins logo that they had seen on the resident's jacket. He was about Harry's height but had a much slighter and more delicate build. His wavy brown hair was sprinkled with gray, especially around his temples.

"Hello, Mr. Roberts?" he said as he approached the small gathering in the waiting room.

Harry was already standing when he saw the older doctor heading his way. He stepped forward and extended his hand. "That's me," he stated with a timid smile.

"I'm Dr. Blalock," the man said with a distinctly southern accent. As Harry accepted the famous surgeon's hand, he was struck by the fact it seemed somehow both fragile and firm. There were no calluses like those on his own, but his grip was steady and confident. "This is my wife, Faye, and our son Jack."

Blalock smiled at them and said, "I have just finished examining your baby, and I agree with the diagnosis made by Dr. Reichmann back in Texas. Your son has Tetralogy of Fallot, a birth defect that is going to require surgery to correct."

The doctor's eyes were full of confidence as he said, "We have successfully performed more than five hundred of these procedures over the last few years, but you must be aware there is considerable risk." His eyes narrowed slightly as he continued. "The majority of children who have undergone this procedure have been at least two or three years old, and many were considerably older. We have performed the surgery on only about fifty newborns, but I feel confident in doing so, it's just that the risk of complications is higher the smaller the child."

Jack was watching breathlessly as the doctor explained how he intended to fix his brother's heart the following morning. He couldn't understand any of the details of what was going to be done to Ben, but he thought he heard the doctor say that he expected the operation would be successful, and that's all he needed to hear.

Jack stepped forward and boldly asked the doctor, "Is this operation going to let my brother grow up big like me?"

"Well," Blalock said slowly, taking in the sight of the fearless five-year-old, "I certainly hope so." His confident smile made Jack believe the man had the power to fix anything.

"Then, what are you waiting for?" Jack exclaimed.

◆◆◆◆◆◆◆◆◆

It had been nearly three hours since they'd last seen Dr. Blalock and his assistant, Mr. Thomas. They'd told them it might be as long as four hours, but Harry had begun pacing after only two. Faye was trying to keep her mind occupied reading the same *Look* magazine again. She had brought some yarn and her knitting needles along on the trip, but she was afraid to resume the process of making the little blue booties she had started before Ben was born. The idea of putting anything blue on his tiny feet seemed almost cruel, but her biggest fear was that she might never be able to put them on him at all.

The door to the waiting room opened without warning and she saw Dr. Blalock standing in the open doorway. Harry spotted him as well from the other side of the room where he had been wearing out the already thin carpeting. Both parents went quickly to where the surgeon stood, and Jack was right behind his mom.

"Why don't we step in here?" the veteran surgeon said as he pointed to a small family conference room off the hallway.

Faye was visibly trembling as Harry put his arm around her. They sat down on the sofa with Jack standing next to his father's knee.

"Well," the doctor began, "we are finished with the operation, and your baby is doing fine." His voice was both reassuring and cautious. "He will be in the recovery room for a few hours before we transfer him to our pediatric heart unit. I expect him to be there for several days, assuming everything continues to go well."

The sudden release of tension within Faye caused her to nearly collapse into her husband's chest as he held onto her. Her muffled crying was mixed with what could only be described as a nervous giggle. While holding his wife, Harry clumsily extended his hand to the doctor and offered, "Thank you, Dr. Blalock."

"So, he's gonna be okay?" Jack said excitedly.

"Yes, I think so," Blalock said, smiling at the innocence of the young boy. "He's got a ways to go, and he could have more trouble down the road. So he's gonna need his big brother to watch out for him, but with God's help he'll soon be good as new."

"I hope he's better than new," Jack said with a concerned look, "because when he was brand new, he was blue."

CHAPTER 12

"Would you care for anything, Dr. Roberts?" Tina asked, after she'd cleared the breakfast dishes off of Mr. Gutierrez's tray.

"I could use another Diet Dr Pepper, if you don't mind," he said. It was only nine thirty in the morning, but he typically had a couple of the caffeine-loaded drinks by this time nearly every day.

"Yes, sir," she said as she headed back up to the galley.

"So you've been committed to being a pediatric heart surgeon since you were five?" Franco asked, shaking his head in amazement.

"More or less," Jack responded, "but there were a few challenges along the way."

"It had to have been tough, considering your family didn't have the money to send you to school."

"That was certainly a problem," he agreed, "but we managed."

♦♦♦♦♦♦♦♦

The Nances had been extraordinarily hospitable, allowing Harry, Faye, and Jack to stay with them for two weeks. For the first ten days they rarely saw them except late at night and early in the mornings because they were always at the hospital, but for the last three days things were much different. The doctors had allowed baby Ben to leave the hospital, but insisted on checking him again before allowing them to return to Texas.

After Benjamin moved into their home their lives had become incredibly busy. Suddenly Faye needed everything she had left back home, including routine things like diapers, diaper pins, baby powder, baby lotion, shampoo, baby clothes, blankets and, of course, formula.

Faye had tried pumping her breasts to keep her milk flowing, but she simply couldn't maintain a schedule in the hospital, so she was not able to nurse her baby. The doctors told her that would be fine, she could just use one of the recently developed commercial formulas. While that may have been okay for Ben, it was not okay for her. Again she felt she was at fault, and struggled with guilt and depression.

Aside from the phenomenal recovery that the infant had made, there was another bit of very good news. She and Harry had learned that her Blue Cross policy was going to cover all but two hundred dollars of the hospital and doctors' bills. They didn't pay for any of the cost of the air ambulance, but Harry knew he'd gotten a major bargain. It had only cost him seven hundred dollars total to restore the health of his youngest son, and the love offering from the church had been almost enough to cover the cost.

He had not planned for the return trip, figuring they would either take the train or a bus. Once again, Andy came through. He had been keeping up with Benjamin's progress through his counterpart in Baltimore, and when he learned that the baby was going to be discharged he made the two-and-a-half-day drive from Hurst to Baltimore in Jack and Faye's 1951 Chevrolet station wagon. Andy hadn't counted on the doctors making them stay in Maryland four additional days, so he was forced to impose on his old friend Jerry Thorp for a place to stay.

Jack was awake and had dressed himself even before the sun came up on the designated day. Taking his brother home after all this time was even more exciting than Christmas. He was waiting in the kitchen when Jenny Nance came in to start the coffee percolator.

"My goodness," she said, "you certainly are up early."

"We're gonna take Ben home today," he said, assuming she didn't know their plan.

"I know. I'll bet you'll be glad to get home too, won't you?"

"Yes, ma'am," Jack responded using the manners his father had been drumming into him since the day they arrived. "It's gonna take two whole days, but my dad and Pastor Stroud are gonna take turns driving so we can get home quicker." Jack had heard the two men discussing how they might be able to drive straight through if one drove while the other slept.

"So, what are you planning to do when you get home?" she asked.

"I have to go to school. Mom said so. But mostly I'm gonna take care of Ben," he said without hesitation. "The doctor told me that was my job."

"I'm sure you'll do a fine job, too," she said with a big smile.

"I'm gonna be a heart surgeon when I grow up," Jack volunteered. "That way kids in Texas won't have to come all the way to Baltimore to get their hearts fixed."

"I suspect you probably will," she said as she took the milk out of the refrigerator.

♦♦♦♦♦♦♦♦♦

The entire ordeal had been exhausting for Faye. She had not slept well the entire time they were in Baltimore, and now that they were home, she was still unable to sleep because Ben was up every four hours. Harry's mom had come to stay with them for a few days, but she was not in good health and simply wasn't able to do much other than assist with meal preparation. Several of the ladies from the church brought food over the first few days, but now that they'd been home for a week, and her mother-in-law had gone home, she was on her own.

Harry had also gone back to work and fortunately his contracting business was doing very well, but that meant he wasn't home much to help with the baby. Janet was some help. She could fold clothes and change wet diapers, but she was not about to change the dirty ones. Plus she had homework every night.

Jack was far more helpful than Faye ever dreamed a five-year-old boy could be. He helped her in the kitchen every evening, pulling a chair up to the sink to stand on, so he could dry the dishes. He also volunteered to mop the floor, take out the trash and help her with the laundry. He wasn't able to change Ben's diaper by himself, but he was happy to take the diaper pail to the laundry room, and he kept the clean one stacked neatly beside Ben's crib.

When he went back to school after two weeks in Baltimore, Jack's first grade teacher asked him to stand up in front of the class and tell everyone what had happened.

"My baby brother was born with a heart that wasn't made right. The doctors called it tetra-flow, and without an operation he was not going to make it to the first grade." Jack was completely certain of his facts, and was willing to share them with anyone who would listen.

"The only doctor in the world who could fix his heart is in Baltimore, Maryland, which is a long ways away from Texas. So, my mom and dad took him there in a huge airplane, and I got to go too. The surgeon fixed him up better than new, but we had to stay there for about two weeks before we could bring him home. We drove for two days to get home, and we didn't stop except for gas and to get something to eat, at what dad said were greasy spoons. We stopped once at the Dairy Queen and I had a chocolate-covered ice cream cone."

Ben seemed like a pretty normal kid, but he was always a little frail, especially compared to Jack. Perhaps because he was the youngest, or maybe because of his close brush with death, Faye had clearly been more protective of Ben than either of her other children. Jack was okay with that, mostly because he tended to be favored by his dad. He would often go out to job sites with him, and as he got older, he'd help by carrying tools or fetching plumbing fixtures out of the truck.

While Harry enjoyed taking Jack with him, he was determined that no son of his would "live by the sweat of his brow," as he often said. They were going to make something of themselves, and to ensure that happened he had begun pushing Jack to excel in school. He was a well above average student, and seemed to enjoy school, especially math and science. He also truly loved his little brother, and played school with him nearly every afternoon. He taught him to read what he called his "baby books," and by the age of three Ben was able to read some of Jack's second grade school books.

By the time he was seven, the younger boy was showing exceptional scholastic aptitude. Based on a standardized test, his teachers had recommended to Harry and Faye that he skip the third grade. He already knew everything they were going to teach him, and there was some discussion of moving him to a private school for especially gifted children. Harry thought it was a great opportunity, especially when they told him that Ben would qualify for a scholarship. Faye was initially in favor of it, but when she was told her baby would be placed in a boarding school in Dallas, she refused. There was no way she could allow him to live in a dormitory and only come home on the weekends.

The elementary school principal had never encountered a student with as much potential as he had seen in Benjamin Roberts, and he desperately wanted to see what the young prodigy could become. He had been the one to arrange the scholarship, and when the family turned it down he decided to explore other options. He found a private foundation that was dedicated to nurturing gifted children, and after telling them of the remarkable scores Ben had achieved, they offered to have a private tutor work with him three days a week.

Jack had become an excellent student, and perhaps some of Ben's precocious development was due to his exposure to the early schooling he received from his brother. He loved teaching him everything he knew, but once Ben started with his advanced tutoring, Jack turned his attention to playing sports. He played Little League baseball and Pop Warner football until he got to junior high school. He'd begun to grow rapidly beginning around age ten and by the time he was twelve he was already a gangly five foot eleven, so he played on the eighth grade basketball team.

Ben continued to focus all his energies on school, and with the aid of a series of tutors on a daily basis, he moved through the entire elementary school curriculum by his eighth birthday. He wasn't really interested in physical activities other than playing catch or shooting baskets in the driveway with his brother from time to time. As a result he remained thin and looked almost feeble. His family didn't recognize that he was having problems again until he was nine.

One early summer afternoon, Jack came home from playing baseball with the neighborhood kids and found his brother sound asleep in his room. He started to go on down the hall to his own room, but noticed something was different. Ben seemed to be breathing more rapidly than normal and when he walked into his room and called his brother's name there was no response. He reached down and touched his hand and noticed it was cool and his fingernails had a slightly bluish color.

"Hey, Ben? Are you okay?" he asked, arousing his brother.

"I'm just really tired," was the response as Ben closed his eyes again.

"I was gonna go outside and shoot some baskets, you wanna come?"

"No," Ben answered, his voice weaker than Jack had ever heard.

Jack turned away without further attempts at conversation. He walked into the kitchen where he saw his mom putting something in the oven, and said, "Mom, there's something wrong with Ben. He's in his room sleeping and he seemed too weak to get up."

"Oh, he's probably just tired from all the extra studying he's been doing. That Spanish tutor has been working him pretty hard," she said.

"I don't think that's it," he offered. "His hands are cold and his fingernails look kinda blue. You don't think he could be having trouble with his heart again, do you?"

Faye tried desperately to avoid thinking about the last thing Dr. Blalock had said before they left the hospital. She was so excited that her baby wasn't going to die, she didn't pay much attention to the doctor's warning. He had explained that the operation he had done did not completely fix the problem. There was a chance that as he grew the shunt that had been created to take away the strain on his heart might not grow with him. There was a possibility he could need more surgery at some point.

She rushed into the young boy's room and saw him sitting up on the side of his bed, still breathing a bit more rapidly than normal. "Ben? Are you all right?" She was relieved to see that it wasn't as bad as Jack had made it sound, but she remained concerned.

"I'm okay, Mom," Ben replied. "I'm just tired."

That night at dinner, Ben didn't eat much, renewing her fears. The roast and potatoes she had prepared was one of his favorites, but he seemed uninterested and was clearly not himself.

After dinner, Janet and Jack were doing the dishes when his sister asked, "What's the matter with Ben?"

"I don't know for sure, but I'm worried it's his heart."

"Oh, don't be silly," she half giggled in a way only sixteen-year-old girls can.

"I remember the doctor in Baltimore saying something about his possibly having problems down the road."

Faye came back in the kitchen to check on whether the kids had finished cleaning up, and Jack said, "Mom, I think you should take Ben to the doctor just to make sure he's all right."

"I'm sure he's fine," she said without much conviction.

When Harry came to bed she said, "I think I'm gonna take Ben in to see Dr. Harrison tomorrow."

"How come?" Harry asked casually.

"I'm just a little worried. He hasn't been himself," she offered, letting her voice trail off.

"The last time you took him in the doc said he was fine, didn't he?" he stated more than questioned.

"Yes, but that was almost a year ago, and today he slept most of the afternoon."

"Okay, but he looks fine to me."

◆◆◆◆◆◆◆◆◆

"So, how's our little miracle boy?" Dr. Harrison asked as he came into the exam room with his usual friendly demeanor.

"I'm okay," Ben stated in protest. He had objected to missing his algebra tutoring session, and had seen no reason to come to the doctor's office.

"He's been sleeping more than usual doctor, and yesterday his brother thought his fingernails looked a little blue," Faye said, trumping her young son's protests.

"Well, let's take a look at you," Harrison said, motioning for Ben to get up on the exam table. He noticed that the boy seemed to be having trouble gathering the strength to pull himself up, something the typical nine-year-old could do without any problem. He helped him onto the table and asked him to take off his shirt, exposing the large scar that marked the sentinel event of this family's collective life.

As Ben sat quietly on the table the doctor took his hands and examined them carefully. There was no question the nail beds had a faint bluish hue. He checked his pulse and it was elevated at one hundred ten, while his respiratory rate was twenty-two breaths per minute. As he placed his stethoscope on Ben's chest he heard the unmistakable swishing sound of a new heart murmur.

"I think we need to have him seen by Dr. Reichmann again," the doctor said, trying not to sound overly concerned.

"What's the matter?" Faye asked as a bolt of fear struck her own heart.

"He has developed a new murmur," Harrison said with a slight hint of concern in his voice.

"What does that mean?" she asked.

"I'm not sure," he responded truthfully, "but given his symptoms, I think the cardiologist should check him out."

♦♦♦♦♦♦♦♦♦

The next day, Faye, Ben, and Jack sat in the office of Dr. Reichmann in downtown Fort Worth. Jack had insisted that he was going with his brother, still feeling the responsibility of Dr. Blalock's charge. Faye knew it was no use arguing with her stubborn fourteen-year-old.

The three of them followed the nurse back into the examination room where Ben was told to remove his shirt and put on a hospital type gown, but with the opening in the front. He sat quietly on the exam table while his mom sat in the only chair in the room. Jack stood between them, looking intently at the color diagrams of the heart that hung on the wall behind the doctor's writing desk.

After about fifteen minutes the doctor entered the room. He appeared much older than Jack had remembered, and his hair was now white. He was still wearing the same long white coat and his smile was the same one Jack had seen when he had wished them luck in the cafeteria.

Dr. Reichmann had seen Ben two weeks after he had come home from Baltimore, and then again a couple of months after that. On each occasion he had declared his heart healthy, and following that last visit he'd told Faye he didn't need to see the young child again unless he started having problems.

"So, what seems to be the trouble?" the older doctor asked in his usual paternal way.

"Dr. Harrison said we should bring Ben back to see you," Faye offered nervously. "He said he heard a new murmur."

"Ben has been more tired than usual and his fingernails and his lips have been a little blue," Jack added on his own. He hadn't said anything to his mom, but he had definitely noticed the slight change in the color of his brother's lips over the last few days.

Dr. Reichmann stared intently at the older boy who was now nearly as tall as he was. "Are you the young man who came to the hospital with your dad, when they brought your brother in? What was it, nine years ago?"

"Yes, sir," Jack said taking a small step forward and extending his hand.

"You have certainly grown," Reichmann said with a smile as he took the youthful but strong hand in his own.

"Yes, sir," Jack said repeating himself. "Ben and I have both grown a lot since the last time you saw us."

The doctor glanced back and forth between the two boys, then spoke to Faye. "A couple of fine young boys you have here."

"I hope you have better news for us this time than you did the last time," Jack said, speaking a bit out of turn.

"Well, let's see," the doctor replied with smile and a slightly furrowed brow.

He repeated the same exam that Dr. Harrison had performed, but also listened to the back of Ben's chest. He had him lie down on his right side and then on his back, listening carefully with his stethoscope. He raised the head of the table a few inches several different times, each time examining him to see how upright he needed to be before the dilated veins in his neck went down.

"I'm afraid Ben is showing signs of early right-sided heart failure," he announced without hesitation.

As she heard the words, Faye felt that her own heart was about to fail. "I thought the operation fixed that," she said with disbelief and fear.

"The procedure that Dr. Blalock performed was actually just a temporary bandaid," he replied. "We have seen some kids compensate very well, but others have had to undergo additional surgery, sometimes within just a couple of years."

"Are you saying Ben is gonna need another operation?" Jack demanded.

"I'm afraid so," Reichmann said as compassionately as he could.

Jack stood motionless, fearing that the doctor was going to tell them they would have to take Ben back to Baltimore.

"The good news is there is a new technique that has been developed by a Dr. Lillehei in Minnesota, that can completely repair all the anatomic problems of Tetralogy of Fallot," he said, trying his best to sound encouraging.

"Minnesota?" was the simultaneous response from both Jack and his mom.

"The operation involves the use of a heart-lung bypass machine, and Lillehei is the only one that I know of who has done this procedure so far."

"Do you know Dr. Lillehei?" Jack asked.

"Not personally," he responded, "but the surgery program at the University of Minnesota is one of the best in the country."

"So what do we need to do?" Faye asked, resigned to going through the hellish ordeal once more.

"I will contact Dr. Lillehei's office in Minneapolis and give them all the information and ask them to contact you. The situation is not nearly as emergent as last time," he added. "We have some time, but I would recommend this be addressed within the next month or so, because it will only get worse."

Ben had been sitting silent throughout the entire conversation, but once he sensed the doctor had concluded his assessment, he asked, "So, you think I'm tired because my heart is wearing out?"

"It's not really wearing out," the doctor answered, "it's just having trouble working against a gradually rising pressure in your lungs."

He gave Faye a prescription for a medication to improve the function of Ben's heart and told her he should start taking it right away. "If you haven't heard from Dr. Lillehei's office in the next couple of days give me a call and I'll follow up for you."

◆◆◆◆◆◆◆◆

Faye had made the bed and was getting ready to do laundry when the phone rang. "Hello," she said picking up the new pink princess phone sitting on the bedside table. They had added it as an extension just a few weeks earlier.

"I have a person to person, long distance call for Mrs. Harry Roberts," said the operator's voice.

"I am Mrs. Roberts," she said rather formally, hoping this was the call she had been expecting, but at the same time fearing what she might hear.

"Go ahead, ma'am. Your party is on the line."

"Hello, Mrs. Roberts? This is Dr. Lillehei's office at the University of Minnesota, Department of Surgery," the woman's unfamiliar voice on the other end of the line was faint and somewhat difficult to hear over the static.

"Hello," she responded.

"Could you hold just a moment for the doctor?"

"Of course."

After a brief pause she heard the high-pitched voice of a man say, "Good morning, Mrs. Roberts, this is Walt Lillehei in Minneapolis. Can you hear me?"

He spoke with a very distinctive accent, similar to one of her favorite television stars, Lawrence Welk. "Yes, I can hear you just fine, doctor," she replied louder than she probably needed to, but she wanted to make sure he could hear her.

"I understand that you have a nine-year-old son who was operated on as an infant by my good friend, Al Blalock."

"Yes, that is correct," she said, relieved to know that he had gotten some information from Dr. Reichmann, and eager to hear what more he had to say.

"How is he doing now?" the doctor asked.

"He seemed to be doing okay until a few days ago when he started complaining of being tired all the time," she replied.

"From the sound of things, I would say he is following the pattern we've seen in many children who underwent the Blalock-Taussig procedure for Tetralogy of Fallot," he said.

Faye was a bit confused by the addition of the new name he had used to describe her son's lifesaving operation. "Yes, sir?" she said slowly as she waited for further instructions.

"We have operated on several children like your son, using our new open heart method to completely correct the anatomy of the heart," he said confidently. "It sounds as if that is what your son needs."

"That's what Dr. Reichmann said," she offered, more to confirm his words in her own mind than as a reply to the surgeon.

"If you can bring your son here to the U of M hospital, we would be happy to take a look at him and see if we can help."

"That would be great," she said with genuine relief in her voice as her shoulders visibly relaxed. "When should we bring him?"

"Anytime," he said, "but, I would recommend you plan to bring him to my clinic on a Monday morning. That way I can evaluate him and possibly do the surgery either Tuesday or Wednesday. He will likely need to stay in the hospital for seven to ten days afterward, before you can take him home."

"That would be fine," she said, mentally going over the tentative plans she and Harry had made the night before. "I will speak to my husband tonight when he gets home from work and I'll call your office tomorrow."

"That will be fine," he said, "I look forward to meeting you and your son. Let me put my secretary back on the line and she will take some more information and give you our number."

"Okay," Faye said, suddenly struck by the reality of the situation.

◆◆◆◆◆◆◆◆◆

Their 1959 Pontiac Bonneville Safari station wagon was loaded up with everything Harry could think of that the family might need for a two-week stay in Minneapolis. Janet was staying with the Johnsons again, because she said she didn't want to lose her summer job at the music store. Faye thought it probably had more to do with not wanting to be away from Charles Pearson, her boyfriend of the last two years.

As they headed north on Saturday morning the general mood was light, almost as if they were embarking on a family vacation. As the afternoon sun began to set on Sunday they were all weary from the trip as they crossed the Mississippi River and pulled into the Holiday Inn near the campus of the University of Minnesota. The secretary had made their reservation, getting them a discounted rate of only twelve dollars per night for a room with two full size beds. Jack helped Harry unload the car and carry everything up the stairs to their second floor room.

The next morning the family ate breakfast at the small diner across the street before proceeding into the maze that was the huge university campus. The instructions they were given seemed totally inadequate, and Harry found himself on a one way street, going the wrong way. Eventually, Faye spotted the name of the street they were looking for and the parking lot the secretary had described. The massive brick buildings all seemed to look alike to these visitors, but they finally found the one marked Outpatient Clinic.

"We are here to see Dr. Lillehei," Harry explained to an older woman sitting behind a modern looking desk just inside the main entrance.

"His office is on the seventh floor," she replied in a sterile voice while pointing to the elevators down the hall.

The quartet made their way up to the surgical clinic and eventually found the crowded waiting room where the receptionist asked them to have a seat. They could only find two seats together, so Faye and Ben sat while Harry and Jack stood next to the wall, near the water cooler. After about fifteen minutes a nurse appeared at the door and called out a name. A middle-aged man and his wife who were sitting next to Faye and Ben stood up and went with the woman through the doorway and into the examination area. Jack and Harry took their seats, and Harry picked up a *Field & Stream* magazine from the small end table next to his chair.

It was nearly an hour before the nurse finally called, "Benjamin Roberts!" They all stood and followed her into a small exam room. There was only one chair next to the exam table and Faye sat down while Harry and Jack stood uncomfortably between the door and the end of the exam table where Ben was sitting. The nurse checked the young boy's blood pressure in both of his arms and recorded it along with his pulse and respiratory rates.

"Dr. Lillehei will be with you in a few minutes," she said as she left the room and placed Ben's chart in a small wooden enclosure mounted on the outside of the door.

Jack noticed a small plastic model of the heart on the desk where the doctor sat to write on the chart. He wanted to reach over and touch it, but knew his mother would get upset, so instead he simply looked at it from every angle he could manage as he moved around her into the far corner of the room. As he was taking in every detail the door opened and Dr. C. Walton Lillehei stepped in carrying the clipboard that held Ben's chart.

"Good morning," he said with his Minnesotan accent even more obvious in person. He noticed Jack was studying the heart model before he raised his head and saw the famous heart surgeon.

"Hello," Harry answered, "I'm Harry Roberts and this is my wife, Faye, and our sons, Jack and Ben." As he spoke he pointed directly toward each of his family members.

"It is nice to meet all of you," the doctor said as he shook hands all around. When he got to Jack he added, "I see you've been checking out my model of the human heart."

"Yes, sir," Jack stated with confidence. "I'm going to be a heart surgeon one day."

"Excellent!" replied the man who had pioneered open heart surgery in the late 1950s. "Your name is Jack, right?"

"Yes, sir," came Jack's immediate reply, accompanied by a big smile.

"We need more bright young heart surgeons," the doctor said earnestly. "When you finish college and medical school, I expect to get a call from Jack Roberts, MD, and when I do I'll see what we can do to get you lined up with a good heart surgery training program."

Jack was already in awe of this man based on the things Dr. Reichmann had said, but to have him call him by name, with the assumption of MD, well that was beyond inspiring. He didn't know what to say, and he just stood there for a moment finally managing, "Thank you, sir."

The great man turned to Ben and said, "Now let's see what's going on with this young man." He put his hand on Ben's shoulder and asked, "How are you feeling, son?"

"Okay, just a little tired is all," Ben said in a voice that was more timid than his family was accustomed to hearing.

"You are one very fortunate young man," he said as he reached into his coat pocket for his stethoscope. "You weren't aware of it at the time, but Dr. Blalock is one of the greatest surgeons in the world, and what he did for you when you were less than a week old, saved your life." It was clear that Lillehei wanted this family to know that nothing that the previous surgeon had done was in any way responsible for this current situation.

"Until just a few years ago we were doing the exact same procedure Al did, for all children with tetralogy, but now, with the perfection of the cardiopulmonary bypass machine we can actually fix the defective areas of the heart."

"I thought that's what they did in Baltimore," Harry said, clearly not understanding fully.

"In order to truly fix the problem it is necessary to stop the heart from beating long enough to enlarge the underdeveloped artery that goes from the right side of the heart muscle to the lungs, and then close the abnormal opening between the two pumping chambers. To do this we use a special pumping machine that also adds oxygen to the blood while the heart is stopped." Harry and Faye both looked terrified by the thought of having their son's heart stopped, for any reason. Jack, however, was fascinated by it.

"How do you get the heart to start beating again after you've fixed the parts that need fixing?" Jack asked, eager to learn more about the process.

"That's a very astute question," the surgeon noted. "That is actually one of the two challenging aspects of doing open heart surgery. The first problem is to get the heart muscle to stop beating once the bypass pump has taken over its function. That is not as easy as it sounds because the human heart muscle is biologically programmed to contract with a regular rhythm about seventy-five times every minute. To stop it from doing what it does naturally, we cool the muscle down by packing ice around it. Then we inject a solution that contains a high concentration of potassium into arteries of the heart. That blocks the cardiac muscle cells from contracting."

Faye was feeling faint and Harry put his hand on her shoulder.

"I see tell that your mother isn't comfortable with this discussion," Lillehei said when he noticed Faye's reaction. "Perhaps we can talk about this privately," he said to Jack who nodded enthusiastically, before looking down at the heart model again.

"I'm sorry if that was a bit too intense," Lillehei apologized as Faye seemed to have recovered from her temporary swoon. "I have scheduled Ben's surgery for Wednesday morning, but I would like to have him admitted to the hospital today," he said, with a tentative smile. "That will allow us to do a couple of tests and get some blood ready for him in the blood bank."

He turned to face Ben and said, "How does that sound to you?"

"That will be okay," he replied. "I just have one question."

"Certainly," said the learned surgeon, expecting a typical question about how much will it hurt, or how long will the operation take.

"While I'm on this heart-lung bypass machine, is there any chance my brain will be affected?"

Lillehei had never had that question asked by a patient, although there had been considerable discussion within the surgical community about the risk of potentially lower than normal profusion pressures causing brain hypoxia. "There is some risk, yes. Why do you ask?" he inquired with a tilt of his head.

"His IQ is just under two hundred," Jack said before his brother could respond. "He is currently taking the same classes I am and he's doing better."

Dr. Lillehei paused and looked at Ben, then back at Jack, then at Ben again before responding. "There have been reports of injuries to the brain with prolonged periods of low pressure during bypass, but they are rare. I can't guarantee that something like that couldn't happen. Anything is possible, but I think the risk is very low."

"I just don't want to wake up stupid," Ben said with a nervous smile.

♦♦♦♦♦♦♦♦♦

All the tests were normal, other than the echocardiogram. It showed that Ben's heart had a sizable hole between the two pumping chambers and a very narrow outflow from the right ventricle to the pulmonary artery. The muscular wall of the right ventricle was thickened from years of pumping against the higher pressure of the aorta. There was no question about the diagnosis, and Lillehei was convinced that the operation he had planned was the appropriate treatment.

On Wednesday, Ben's was the first operation on the schedule. The senior resident had told the family that the procedure would likely take about three hours, but after just over an hour and forty-five minutes Dr. Lillehei came out to the waiting room to speak to them.

"Everything went very smoothly," he said with a reassuring smile. "We were able to fix Ben's heart completely without any problems, and he is currently in the recovery room."

"That is really great news," exclaimed Harry as he held Faye close to him.

"Did you have any trouble getting his heart restarted?" Jack asked, hoping the doctor would finish his explanation as to how they managed to do that.

"No problem at all, Jack," he said remembering the promise he had made to the future heart surgeon. "Say, I have a small group of medical students that are going to be observing our next case. Would you like to join them in the gallery?"

"Really?" Jack exclaimed. "I could watch a real heart operation?"

"We have an observation gallery where the students are able to sit and watch operations, and I'm sure that you could join them if it's okay with your mom and dad."

Harry nodded his approval. He was very excited for Jack to have such an opportunity. Jack hadn't talked about wanting to be anything except a heart surgeon since returning from Baltimore, nine years before. Faye wondered if he might pass out at the sight of blood like she did, but seeing the look on the teenagers's face she couldn't possibly say no.

"Sure," she said, "as long as he won't be in the way."

"I'll assign one of the senior medical students to watch out for him," Lillehei said as he motioned for Jack to come with him. "Ben will be in the recovery room for another couple of hours, but I'll bring Jack back out to you after we finish this next procedure."

Jack had never been so excited in his life. He walked back to the change room with Dr. Lillehei and quickly took off his tee shirt and blue jeans, and for the first time in his life he put on a pair of scrub pants and tied the drawstring around his waist. He put on a medium scrub shirt that initially felt too big.

Walt Lillehei was a born teacher and he was at his best when he could mold an attentive young man like Jack. "Put these covers over your shoes and tie this cap on your head like mine."

Jack could not believe this was happening. He'd dreamed of being in an operating room for as long as he could remember, and while he wouldn't technically be in the room, he would be watching everything that happened just as if he were. Dr. Lillehei spotted the group of five medical students in the hallway outside the change room. They had been assigned to him for the week, and today they were going to watch him replace a heart valve.

"Fellas, this is Jack Roberts," he said, introducing the fourteen-year-old to the twenty-two and twenty-three-year-old men. "His brother underwent a Tetralogy of Fallot repair this morning, and he says he wants to be a heart surgeon. I thought you guys could let him sit with you up in the gallery for this aortic valve replacement."

"Yes, sir," said one of the young men who was dressed exactly like Jack. "He can sit next to me. I'll keep an eye on him."

As Dr. Lillehei made his way toward the scrub sink the five soon-to-be doctors plus the one who was still a decade away, went around to a side door and climbed the stairs to the narrow room with two rows of eight stadium-style seats facing a large plate-glass window. Jack took the first seat on the front row and stared down into the operating room. He was immediately transported back to the hours he had spent, nose plastered to the window of the newborn nursery.

There were two women in the room busily making preparations for the operation to come. One of them was wearing what looked like a long green dress over her scrubs that was tied in the back, and she had on a pair of rubber gloves that extended up over the long sleeves of the dress. Both women were wearing white hats that covered their hair and cloth masks over their faces. The walls of the operating room were covered in six-inch white tiles, except for a single row of dark blue tiles that ran around the entire room about five feet up from the floor, which was slate gray concrete that had been polished to make a smooth, satiny surface. There were several tables and stools in the room, all of which were made of stainless steel, and in the center was a rectangular table about six feet long and two feet wide covered with a white sheet and supported by a central pedestal. Above the table were two large dome-shaped lights, mounted in the ceiling. Near one end of the operating table was a large machine with several metal tanks mounted on the back. Two of them were green and one was blue.

Jack watched intently as a doctor and another nurse carefully rolled a stretcher into the room. They were dressed in the same scrubs, hats, and shoe covers that he and the students were wearing, and their heads and faces were covered with the same white cloth hats and masks worn by everyone else in the room. The doctor had the patient move over onto the operating table, while two of the nurses held the stretcher firmly against it. When the man was in position one of the nurses rolled the stretcher away while the other one put some additional parts on the sides of the table up by the patient's shoulders. She then had the patient place his arms out on the narrow table extensions and she wrapped a green towel around each arm before securing them with straps. As the man was lying there with both arms out, Jack was struck by the fact that the patient was the only person in the room who was not wearing a mask over his face or a cap on his head. He also thought the man looked much like the hundreds of pictures he had seen of Christ on the cross.

The doctor placed a black rubber mask over the patient's face. It was connected to two hoses that were attached to the large machine behind him. He appeared to be talking to the patient, but there was no way to hear what he was saying. He turned several dials on the machine, and in a couple of minutes he removed the mask and placed an angled metal instrument into the patient's mouth. As he did, he lifted the patient's chin and looked in through his mouth. He expertly inserted a brownish-red tube the size of his index finger, down the man's throat, then promptly removed the instrument and connected the tube directly to the hoses coming out of the machine behind him. He used some white adhesive tape to secure the tube to sleeping patient's face, then sat down on a stainless steel stool and began squeezing the rubber bag that was hanging from one of the tubes.

One of the nurses placed a wide black strap across the patient's legs and secured him firmly to the table. She pulled down the sheet that was covering him, exposing nearly his entire body. Then with a safety razor she proceeded to shave all the hair from his chest. She then washed his entire chest and upper abdomen with a soapy solution for about ten minutes. When she was finished she used one of the green towels to blot the area dry, leaving him fully exposed as she turned on the two bright lights that shown down on the middle of his chest.

Three doctors, led by Dr. Lillehei, came into the room holding their arms out in front of them, with their elbows bent so their hands were nearly at shoulder level. Water was dripping off their elbows onto the floor, and the nurse who had been preparing the instruments and sponges on a separate table, handed each of the doctors a towel to dry their hands. She then put one of the operating gowns on each of them, while the other nurse tied the outer garments in the back. They each put on rubber gloves in final preparation for the procedure.

Dr. Lillehei turned to the students and their guest in the gallery and asked the nurse to flip a switch, activating the intercom. Suddenly the silence in the gallery was broken by what sounded like several conversations taking place at the same time inside the busy operating room.

"Can you hear me?" he asked as he looked into the eager young faces through the glass. Everyone nodded, including Jack. "This morning we are going to replace this patient's aortic valve which has been severely damaged by a bout of rheumatic fever. He has both aortic stenosis and insufficiency, meaning the one-way valve that leads from his heart muscle out to the main artery is scarred to the point where it is both restricting normal flow through it and at the same time is allowing blood to abnormally flow backward. We will be replacing his diseased valve with one of the newest Starr valves." The students all nodded their heads indicating they understood what the professor was saying. Jack couldn't help but nod as well, despite having no idea what the surgeon was talking about.

The other two doctors went about the task of placing green towels and sheets over the patient until the only area that remained exposed was the front of his chest. It was almost as if the man had been converted into an inanimate work area. The team of surgeons along with the nurse who was also wearing a gown and gloves, gathered around the operating table and began the two-hour procedure.

Jack sat completely spellbound by the scene. He watched as Dr. Lillehei assisted one of the younger surgeons who made a long incision through the skin and down to the breastbone. He was surprised at how little blood he saw, as the doctors expertly controlled the bleeding through each of the steps. Dr. Lillehei narrated most of the procedure to the students, but most of his conversation was directed toward the other doctors at the table. The resident physician expertly split the breastbone using what Jack thought looked like the power jig saw in his dad's shop out in the garage. Then he placed an instrument into the opening and slowly turned a small crank, spreading the bone, and exposing the heart.

Jack couldn't believe he was actually watching the patient's heart beating in his chest. The movement seemed to be more of a rolling action, far different from what he had expected. As the upper part contracted it was followed immediately by the contraction of the lower part. He thought the organ looked as though it was dancing. The coordinated contractions maintained a constant rhythm which was matched by the steady beeping from the monitor on the anesthesia machine.

Another man came into the room and approached a large piece of equipment that was up against the wall below the gallery window. He pushed it forward toward the operating table and began turning dials and attaching tubing.

"What's that?" Jack whispered to the medical student sitting next to him.

"That's the heart-lung machine," he answered also in a whisper. While the intercom was a one-way speaker system, and their conversation couldn't be heard by the people in the OR, neither of them knew that so they kept their voices down.

The nurse carefully passed the ends of two plastic tubes to the pump technician, while she held on to the rest of the tubing which was resting on the patient. The surgeons worked quickly around the steadily beating heart, passing what looked like strips of white yarn around each of the major veins and the giant artery.

"Are you ready?" the resident surgeon asked as he turned partially toward the pump technician.

"Yes," the other man responded.

"We are about to put the patient on the pump," Dr. Lillehei announced to everyone in the room, and those in the gallery.

Within a couple of minutes Jack could see dark red blood flowing from the patient down through one of the clear plastic tubes and into the machine. It was pumped up through a clear flat chamber where oxygen was bubbled through it, turning the color a brighter, more brilliant red. The oxygenated blood was then pumped back to the patient through the other clear plastic tubing.

"Okay, we are now on pump," the resident said. "Let's have the ice."

The nurse passed him a stainless steel pan full of finely crushed ice, and Jack watched in amazement as he carefully poured it around the beating heart muscle. The heart rate began to slow until after about a minute it was less than half of what it had been.

"We are ready to cross clamp," the resident said as he placed a large metal instrument across the main artery coming out of the heart. As he did, the heart skipped a beat, then resumed, only to skip another. The resident then took a large syringe and injected a solution into the big vessel near where the clamp had been applied. Within a few seconds the heart rate slowed dramatically and after a couple of random beats it became deathly still and there was no longer any beeping sound in the room. The anesthesiologist also stopped the ventilating machine he had connected to provide constant breathing to the body hidden under the drapes. The other machine was now performing all the vital tasks of the heart and the lungs.

Jack thought to himself that his brother had been the one under those drapes only a couple of hours before in this very room. He was in awe of what was going on, but knew these were daily occurrences for the surgeons and nurses in the room below.

Dr. Lillehei assumed the role of the primary surgeon as he expertly cut through the wall of the huge blood vessel to locate and remove the damaged valve. Jack was amazed by the smoothness of his motions. It was the surgeon's hands that now appeared to be performing an intricate dance. Within thirty minutes the old valve had been replaced with an artificial device that looked like a small metal cage with a brilliant white ball inside. All the time the blood continued to flow through the machine and back into the patient.

"We are ready to reverse," Lillehei said, signaling to everyone that it was time to restart the slumbering heart. The icy solution that had surrounded the organ for the last half hour was removed and replaced by a warming bath. After a minute the nurses handed the chief resident a different syringe filled with medicine which injected it into the aorta, the same way he had when his task was to stop the heart.

The team waited patiently for a few seconds as nothing seemed to be happening, then suddenly the heart leaped once before falling still again. Dr. Lillehei reached into the patient's chest and grasped the heart tenderly in his hand. He squeezed the huge muscle a couple of times and it seemed to spring to life. The beating was random at first, but after just a few beats it started gathering momentum as the rhythmic contractions and the beeping sound of the monitor resumed as if they had never ceased. The resident quickly released the clamps across the large vessels and the anesthesiologist restarted the ventilator which provided life-sustaining oxygen into the patient's lungs. The pump technician clamped the tube containing the dark blood that was coming from the patient, but continued to return the bright red blood back into his circulation. When the reservoir of blood was nearly empty he turned off the pump that had kept the patient alive for more than thirty minutes.

Jack thought he could hear a new sound in addition to the beeping. It was a distinct clicking noise that was synchronized with the heartbeat. He then heard Dr. Lillehei say, "I hope you can all hear the sound of the new Starr valve as the ball is forced up into the end of the cage with each contraction."

The resident doctor placed a drainage tube into the sac surrounding the heart then removed the instrument that was holding the breastbone apart. He placed several wire sutures completely around both sides of the bony protection, and as he pulled the bone together the clicking sound was no longer audible.

"You guys close up and stay with this patient until he gets to the recovery room," Lillehei said to the resident surgeons as he stepped away from the operating table and removed his gown and gloves. He looked up to the audience in the gallery and said, "Gentlemen, would you join me out in the hallway?" As he did, his smiling eyes looked straight into Jack's.

CHAPTER 13

The private jet soared over the mountains of central Mexico, carrying the five passengers and three crew members toward the giant airport between Dallas and Fort Worth. Radha and Gabriella were engaged in what Jack suspected was a conversation about anything but surgery.

Suddenly the plane shuddered a couple of times before smoothing out again. In another second the turbulent shaking was repeated, and the pilot's voice was heard over the intercom. "I am sorry, sir, for the bumpy ride here over the mountains. I am climbing to forty-eight thousand feet to find some clear air."

"Never fails," Franco said. "The air over central Mexico is as volatile as their political scene."

"My wife and I took a couple of mission trips into northern Mexico shortly after we were married," Jack said, "but the drug wars near the border made that area unsafe. That's one of the reasons we ended up in Nicaragua."

"We are very glad you decided to come to our country, even if it's only for one week each year."

"Elaina and I love it, and I consider Domingo to be one of my closest friends in the world."

"So, I assume your brother's surgery was successful?"

♦♦♦♦♦♦♦♦

The morning after Ben's operation, his family was waiting patiently to see him. They had been allowed in his room briefly the evening before, but the hospital had a very strict visitation policy, so they had gone back to their hotel room around nine o'clock, when visiting hours were over. They had also been informed that only one person at a time would be allowed to visit him in the new surgical intensive care unit. At exactly 9:00 a.m. the doors to the unit opened, and an angry looking nurse stood guard to ensure that only one visitor per patient entered. Faye went in first and stayed only about five minutes. When she came out she went straight to Harry, and as she reached him she started crying again.

"What's wrong?" he asked wrapping his arms around his wife.

"He's still on the breathing machine. He isn't moving," she said with halting breath.

"The doctors told us he might need to be on the ventilator for a couple of days," Harry replied. "I'm sure everything is fine."

Jack said he was going to go check for himself, and made his way past the nurse who was acting as the guardian of the unit. Technically he wasn't old enough to go in, the sign said no visitors under the age of sixteen, but he figured if Dr. Lillehei thought he was old enough to watch heart surgery, then he was certainly old enough to visit his brother. When asked, he lied about his age, and because of his size, they hadn't questioned him further.

He approached Ben's bedside and saw the large blue box was still standing next to his bed. It was cycling continuously moving air into and out of his lungs through a system of hoses connected to the dark red tube in his windpipe. He had two separate IVs, and there was a tube coming out of his body just below the breastbone. It was connected to a grouping of three large glass bottles that were taped to the floor.

"Hey, Ben?" he said as he stared at his brother, searching for any reaction.

"I don't think he can hear you," the nurse offered, as she checked on one of the glass bottles of fluid hanging over his bed.

Jack ignored her as he reached inside the rails that guarded both sides of the bed. He noticed his brother's arms were tied to them with long gauze ropes.

"Why do you have him tied down?" he asked the nurse impatiently.

"Because if he wakes up he will try to pull out his breathing tube."

"Has he been awake?"

"Oh, yes," she said nodding her head. "We've had to give him medication about once an hour to keep him sedated."

"When are they going to take out the breathing tube?"

"That's up to the doctor," she said not wishing to hazard a guess. "They should be making their rounds any minute."

Right on cue, the chief resident and Dr. Lillehei stepped into the small alcove. "Well, good morning, Jack," Lillehei said to his youngest protégé.

"Hello, Dr. Lillehei," Jack responded more timidly than he had before. He now had even more respect for the man, knowing something of the extent of his talents and skills.

The professor turned to the chief resident for a full report on how Ben had fared through the night. The resident gave him a summary of all the laboratory tests from the morning as well as his current vital signs along with his own assessment of his physical exam. He had been in the unit to see all the patients two hours earlier and received a similar report from the junior resident and the intern. They had taken their report in turn from the senior medical student assigned to the case around 5:00 a.m.

Lillehei removed a stethoscope from his coat pocket and carefully listened to the young boy's chest. The murmur was no longer present and his lungs sounded surprisingly clear.

"Why don't we let him wake up and see how well he can breathe on his own? I think the sooner we can get that tube out the better," he said with a satisfied nod toward the resident. "He looks great!" he said, his remarks now directed toward Jack. Then he looked at Jack quizzically. "I thought you had to be sixteen to get in here," he said with a sly smile.

"Yes, sir," Jack said, wondering if that meant he should leave.

"I suppose we can bend the rules a couple of years," he offered as he turned to join the residents at the next patient's bedside.

"They're gonna let him wake up and see if he is able to breathe on his own," Jack announced to his parents as if giving his own official report. His parents both looked at him with questioning expressions. "Dr. Lillehei said he wants to get the tube out of him as soon as possible."

That afternoon when they came back around, Harry went in first. He only stayed a short while, then told Faye to go in next. She stayed for about ten minutes. Both parents had come out of the unit with concerned looks on their faces. When Jack went in he saw his brother lying in the bed with his head elevated slightly. He appeared to be dozing. The ventilator was gone and so was the tube in his throat.

"Hey, Ben," he said cautiously.

After a couple of seconds his brother slowly opened one eye. As he started to speak his mouth appeared unable to make any words. Finally he spoke with a very slurred voice. "Who are you?"

Jack's mouth fell open and he could scarcely draw a breath. His brother didn't recognize him and he could barely speak. *What had happened? Was he still on medication? Had he suffered some kind of brain injury? Oh, no!* Jack thought. *How could something like this happen? Had his brilliant brother had the one complication he feared the most?*

"It's me, Ben... it's your brother, Jack..."

Ben couldn't hold back any longer. He open his other eye and grinned at his big brother, "Gotcha!" he said as he laughed hard enough that he winced in pain.

The nurse was laughing too. It seemed that everyone, including his mom and dad had been in on the joke. Jack laughed too, once he finished threatening to get even.

♦♦♦♦♦♦♦♦♦

The two boys stayed best friends through the remaining years they were at home together, despite having distinctly different physical characteristics and interests. Ben spent nearly every waking hour studying or reading, while Jack was always doing something in the way of sports or working with his dad.

For the rest of that summer, Jack worked for Harry. He spent long hours on job sites helping the workers dig trenches and lay sewer lines by hand. It was hard labor, but Jack enjoyed the sense of accomplishment it provided as well as the spending money. His dad taught him the value of hard work and he had refused to accept poor quality, even from a teenage boy. His favorite phrase was "Any job worth doing is worth doing right."

As the summer of 1963 progressed, the gangly fourteen-year-old began to fill out, as his muscular development was aided by daily manual labor and the massive amounts of food he consumed at every meal. He would routinely eat two or three times as much as his younger brother, but all the weight he gained was in the muscles of his shoulders, chest and thighs. By the time he started the tenth grade he was six-one and weighed one hundred seventy pounds.

Unlike most of the other boys in his high school, Jack didn't really care that much about playing football. A year earlier the coach persuaded him to play wide receiver because of his height, but the junior varsity team didn't have a quarterback who could throw the ball, so for most of the plays Jack just stood around. He was so bored with it he quit the team, and the coach really couldn't blame him. He decided never to play football again.

On Jack's fifteenth birthday, his dad told the boys that President Jack Kennedy was coming to Texas to visit Fort Worth and Dallas. Harry was not especially political, but he loved the new president from Massachusetts almost as much as he had revered his predecessor, General Dwight Eisenhower. Kennedy was a Navy hero, about his own age, and Harry had also served four years in that branch of the service back during the war.

Faye agreed to let Jack skip school on Friday morning, November 22, and Ben rescheduled his calculus tutor for the afternoon. Around 5:00 a.m. the three of them left the house and headed for the Texas Hotel in downtown Fort Worth. It had started raining sometime during the night, and a soft drizzle continued as they made their way toward town. Harry thought the rain might keep the crowd down, but he feared it might also keep the president from making an open air appearance, as had been announced.

The traffic was more than Harry had expected, and by the time he reached the area around the courthouse he worried they would miss seeing the president if he didn't find a place to park soon. He pulled off onto one of the side streets several blocks away and finally found a place to park his pickup. As the boys piled out of the passenger side he handed Jack a black umbrella.

The two boys walked along the sidewalk as close together as possible to stay under the cover. Harry wore his Sunday fedora because it was the only hat he owned that was not a ball cap. He also held the morning newspaper over his head to provide some additional protection from the steady rain. They reached the parking lot of the hotel where a crowd of two or three hundred people had already gathered. They made their way as close to the wooden barricades as possible, in hopes of getting to see the president and his wife.

Harry knew that Vice President Johnson would also be there, but he didn't much care for him. He had come to see JFK, and he wanted his boys to one day be able to tell their children that they had seen him as well.

The trio stood huddled together under the umbrella, with Ben, who was almost ten, sandwiched between his dad and his older brother. While he remained reasonably dry, he wasn't tall enough to see over the man and woman who were immediately in front of him. After about an hour, a group of men came out of the hotel and climbed the few steps onto the temporary podium. Jack could see them very clearly over the heads of the people around him and announced excitedly, "There he is!" as he saw the president for the first time.

The crowd cheered loudly as Kennedy shunned the umbrella the Secret Service agents continued to offer. Harry took down their umbrella as well to make it possible for everyone around them to see. Congressman Jim Wright of Fort Worth made some brief introductions of both Senator Yarborough and Vice President Johnson, before the vice president introduced President Kennedy. As he moved in front of the microphones Ben could finally see him in the gap between the shoulders of the couple in front of him. Everyone around them cheered loudly despite the inclement weather, but the crowd grew quiet as he began to speak.

The president only spoke for about three minutes, first apologizing that his wife was not there, claiming she was back in their room because she needed more time to get ready, but everyone knew it was the rain that kept her away. In his classic Bostonian accent he then talked about the greatness of America, and of Texas, and finally of Fort Worth. He bragged about how important the city had been to the war effort by building bombers. Then he challenged the community to put forth that same effort in producing the newest fighter jets.

Harry understood that Congressman Wright, Senator Yarborough, and then Senator Johnson had used much of their political capital to land a huge defense contract for General Dynamics and its manufacturing plant in Fort Worth.

The rain had let up slightly just as the president began to speak, and by the time he had finished it was little more than a light mist. As he stepped off the podium he turned in their direction and began shaking hands with the people standing in the front. The enthusiastic crowd had grown to more than two thousand and continued to cheer more loudly than ever. He passed from hand to hand before he found a small breach in the wooden barriers and made his way into the crowd. He was shaking hands with all the people around them, and finally he reached Harry. He shook his hand briefly then turned to Ben who was certainly the youngest person in attendance.

"Thank you for coming out in the rain, young man," the president said, looking directly into Ben's eyes as he took his hand briefly.

"Nice to meet you, Mr. President," Ben said.

As he shook Jack's hand, he failed to make eye contact, but his grip was solid and sincere. Kennedy moved quickly on to the next group of adoring followers, eventually circling back around to the front where the Secret Service agents nervously escorted him back to the safe side of the barriers, then quickly inside the hotel.

"Wow!" Harry said. "I never expected we'd get to shake the president's hand."

"I can't wait to tell Mom," Ben said. "I even got to talk to him."

◆◆◆◆◆◆◆◆

By the time the trio got home the president was on his way from Carswell Air Force base on the North side of Fort Worth, to Love Field in Dallas, on Air Force One. It took about three times as long for his motorcade to travel the seven miles from downtown to Carswell than it did for the huge jet to make the trip of nearly fifty miles.

Harry and the boys decided they would stay home and watch the local television coverage of the president's arrival in Dallas. They were beyond excited as they told Faye all about their encounter with the great man. Their enthusiasm continued as they watched live television coverage of his arrival at Love Field. She was far more excited to see the first lady as they all watched the famous couple get off the plane. They made their way over to a chain link fence where they shook hands with many of the people who had come to the airport to see them.

"That's just the way he came up to us!" Ben said excitedly, as the pictures showed the president and the first lady slowly making their way toward the

THE CALLING

limousine that would take them through the streets of downtown Dallas. As they drove off, the coverage of their arrival was concluded and the announcer said there would be more live television later from the Dallas Trade Mart.

They left the television on while they ate their lunch. Faye had prepared some chicken salad sandwiches earlier in the morning so while there was nothing important on TV she served them to Harry and the boys along with a large bowl of potato chips.

"Dad, come quick," Jack said, as he turned up the volume. The local news had broken in during some kind of noontime fashion show to report the president had been shot.

♦♦♦♦♦♦♦♦♦

Harry was beyond depressed over Kennedy's death. He had just seen the man. He had shaken his hand. His sons had met him and he had even spoken to Ben. How could this be? Nothing Faye could say or do could break the despondent spell he was under, and he seemed no better, even as Christmas approached.

Jack had also been shaken by the personal nature of the tragedy, but he had returned to school after the Thanksgiving break and quickly got caught up in the upcoming basketball season. He had just turned fifteen and was now a sophomore at LD Bell High School, and was a starting forward on the varsity team.

Ben had seemed relatively unaffected by the president's assassination and resumed his aggressive private tutoring. The only thing Faye had heard him say about that day was he knew something bad was going to happen. She passed it off as his way of handling the difficult situations. However, he had told his brother that when he looked into the president's eyes he thought he seemed afraid, almost as though he knew his fate. Ben never shared that with anyone else after Jack told him he'd better keep those thoughts to himself. Otherwise, someone might suspect he had something to do with it.

As the weeks wore on, Harry tried to escape from his anger by working harder. He seemed to be eating more and Faye could tell he had gained about fifteen pounds over the course of two months.

"Maybe you should see the doctor," she suggested one evening.

Harry just stared at her without speaking, but she got his message. He had no intention of going to the doctor. There was nothing wrong with him that hard work wouldn't cure. What he failed to tell her was that for the past year he'd occasionally experienced pain in his middle of his chest.

♦♦♦♦♦♦♦♦♦

By the middle of February, Harry seemed to have recovered from the shock of being so close to the events of November. His business was growing as construction in the area was really beginning to boom. The new Six Flags Over Texas park had opened in nearby Arlington a little more than two years before, and the rest of the area between Dallas and Fort Worth had become prime real estate for residential development.

As his business grew so did the pressures of running it. Harry now had six full-time employees, and if he got the latest contract he had bid, he'd likely need at least four more. He wasn't sleeping more than five hours a night, waking up worrying about meeting payroll or how he was going to make the payments on the new three-quarter-ton pickup he'd bought. He also worried about corporate taxes and the cost of his new accountant he'd hired to prepare them. All the time he was trying to save some money for Jack's college education, and the cost of everything seemed to be rising faster than his income.

One evening Harry came home exhausted and barely ate any dinner. Faye asked him what was wrong and all he said was, "Nothing." He went to bed early and seemed to be sleeping when Faye finally joined him around eleven. When she reached over to kiss him good night his pajamas were soaking wet with perspiration. She flipped on the light and saw that his color was ashen. When she tried to arouse him he simply groaned and offered no response. She ran into Jack's room and found him lying in his bed reading a copy of *Sports Illustrated* magazine. "Come quick," she cried, "there is something wrong with your father."

Jack leaped out of bed and ran down the hallway, passing his mother as she entered their room. He saw his dad laboring to breathe and he was unresponsive. "Call an ambulance!" he said as calmly as he could as he tried to wake his dad by shaking his shoulders.

It took about twenty minutes for the ambulance to arrive, and while they waited Faye got dressed and told the boys to do the same. Jack met the emergency workers at the front door and directed them into the bedroom where Faye and Ben were waiting at the side of the bed. Harry was awake and he was able to speak, but the only thing he said was that his chest was killing him. The ambulance driver and his assistant quickly loaded Harry onto a stretcher and wheeled it out to their vehicle. Faye got in the back with Harry and she told Jack to meet them at the hospital.

While he was still a year away from getting his driver's license, Jack had already been taught by his dad how to drive the pickup. He and Ben jumped in the old truck, but by the time they pulled out of the garage the ambulance was long gone. Jack knew where the hospital was and he made it there in ten minutes. He parked in the emergency room lot, and the two boys quickly found their mom just inside the door.

The ER consisted of two small examination rooms and was used mostly to set broken bones and sew up lacerations. The door into one of the rooms was open and Jack could see that they had just moved his dad off the ambulance stretcher onto a narrow bed. There simply was not enough room for the two ambulance guys, their stretcher, the ER bed and the nurse to be in the room at the same time, so the nurse was forced to wait out in the hallway until the guys made the transfer and rolled their stretcher out.

The nurse was dressed in a white uniform and worked very efficiently. She put a small green tubing with two openings under Harry's nose then took his pulse and blood pressure. She asked Faye to come into the room and started asking her about her husband's heart.

"Harry has never had any trouble with his heart," she responded.

The nurse looked at her with disbelief. "Has he ever had high blood pressure?"

"Not that I know of, but he has been under a lot of stress lately," she added.

"Who is your family doctor?" she asked.

"Dr. Harrison, but I don't think he has ever seen Harry. He's never sick," Faye said, repeating what Harry always said.

A technician showed up to do an EKG, so Faye and the nurse stepped out of the room while she hooked up wires to Harry's wrists and ankles and another one to his chest. When she turned on the machine it began producing a strip of paper with squiggly black lines that represented the electrical activity in Harry's ailing heart. She stopped the machine several times to reposition the wire on his chest before restarting it. Once she was finished she removed the wires and collected the long strip of paper before leaving the room with her machine.

"Can't you give him something for the pain?" Jack asked.

"Not without an order from the doctor," the nurse responded. "I have a call in to Dr. Harrison."

As she was speaking the phone rang, and she quickly answered it at the small desk near the emergency entrance. After a few moments she returned and spoke to Faye and the boys.

"Dr. Harrison is on his way in, and he has instructed me to start an IV and to give your husband some nitroglycerin under his tongue." They all nodded as she left to get the medications and the intravenous setup.

It was straight up midnight when Dr. Harrison came through the door. He went into Harry's room and found him resting a little easier, but he still had a grimace on his face as the doctor stepped up to his bedside.

"How are you feeling, Harry?" he asked as he took his left wrist in his right hand. His pulse was rapid and thready.

"I'm not doing too good, doc," he said still in obvious pain.

The nurse came in and handed him a piece of cardboard with the EKG mounted on it. The doctor looked at it carefully and furrowed his brow. "Well, Harry, it looks like you've had a heart attack."

"It feels like an elephant is sittin' on my chest, doc."

"I know, I'll get you some pain medicine when I'm sure your blood pressure can handle it."

"I just need some relief, doc."

Dr. Harrison asked Faye and the boys to join him down the hallway that led to the main part of the hospital. When they were all seated in the make-shift waiting room he began. "I'm sorry to say he's had a massive heart attack."

"What do you mean massive?" Jack asked.

"Based on his EKG, it involves most of the front half of his heart muscle, and his blood pressure has remained pretty low since he got here. I can't really predict what's gonna happen, but I have to tell you, there is a real chance he may not make it." There was an implied "I'm sorry" in his voice.

"Isn't there anything you can do?" Faye pleaded. "He's all I have." She was on the verge of breaking down as she leaned over and grabbed Jack's shoulder.

"About all we can do is give him supplemental oxygen and keep him at rest. The next twenty-four hours is likely to determine whether or not he survives." The doctor paused to make sure they understood the gravity of what he had just said. "The best thing you can do right now is pray."

Faye went in to see him and thought he looked a little better. He wasn't writhing in pain like before, but his color was still the pasty gray she saw in the dim light of their bedroom. "Hi, sweetie," she uttered softly.

"I'm sorry," he said through the pain.

"You don't have anything to be sorry for," she responded, shaking her head.

"I should have gone to the doctor when you told me to."

"It's okay. You're gonna be all right."

"You keep thinking that way," he instructed her with a forced smile.

She laid her head on his shoulder and tried her best not to cry.

"Have you called Janet?" he asked.

"Not yet, but I will in just a minute." Their daughter was away at school. She was a freshman at Stephen F. Austin University in East Texas. She would be very upset not being here to see her father.

"Would you please send the boys in while you call her? I'd like to talk to them one at a time."

"Sure. They're both right outside." She raised her head and kissed him on the cheek. "I love you."

"I love you too, more than anything," he said. "I'm so sorry."

She couldn't bear to hear him saying those words again with such finality. She squeezed his hand as she rose slowly and walked out of the room. Once she was beyond the door she turned to the side to escape his vision. She started crying openly and didn't want him to see her. Jack came to her side and held his sobbing mother to his chest.

"Ben, why don't you go in and sit with Dad a minute?" he said not wanting his brother to watch their mom coming apart.

"Hey, Dad," the younger son said, as he sat down on the side of the bed.

"Hey, Ben," Harry replied, trying his best to generate another smile without much success. "I want you to know how very proud I am of you. I believe you can be anything and accomplish anything you set your wonderful mind to." He coughed heavily from the effort of speaking.

"It's okay, Dad. You don't need to talk."

"Yes, I do," he said composing himself after the coughing spasm. "Your brother loves you very much, and I need to know that you'll listen to him the way you would listen to me."

"I will, Dad, but you're not going anywhere."

"You need to know that I love you very much. I just wish I'd told you so more often."

"I've always known how much you loved me," Ben said as tears began welling up in his eyes.

"Send your brother in will you?" He had held his son firmly by his arm while they were talking, but released it as Ben stood.

"Dad wants to see you," he said to Jack.

"I'm okay," his mom said. "I need to go call your sister. You go in and talk to your father."

As Jack walked into the room Harry was lying very still with his eyes closed. As Jack approached his bed he said, "Dad?" in a softer voice than he intended.

Harry opened his eyes, but clearly even that action required more effort now. "Hey, Buddy," he said, trying his best to keep them open.

Jack reached down and took his dad's hand in his. It was not only weak, but it felt colder than any he had held before. "I'm right here, Dad."

"I'm sorry to put so much on you, but I know you are up to it."

"Everything I know I learned from you, Dad."

"Listen to me," he said as he tried to raise up to get closer to his son. Instead Jack leaned over to close the distance enough to hear his father's failing voice. "Never let anything stop you from living your dream."

"I won't, Dad," Jack said, feeling his father's final bit of strength flowing through into him.

"Tell your sister I'm sorry I didn't get to say goodbye. I love her so much."

"I will, Dad."

"I love you, son," he said as he seemed too weak to cough out the growing congestion deep in his throat.

"I love you too, Dad," Jack said, unsure whether his father heard him.

Harry had said everything he needed to say before he closed his eyes and drifted off. Jack had never watched anyone die, but as his father breathed his last breath, he felt a sense of peace. He placed the cold hand back on the bed and left to find his mother.

♦♦♦♦♦♦♦♦♦

A few weeks later Faye's brother, Joe Scott, came over to check on her and the boys. Joe was retired Air Force, having spent more than twenty years as a pilot. Many of his buddies from back in the war had taken jobs with the rapidly growing airline industry, but Joe loved flying fighters, and he especially loved teaching the young kids how things were done. He had flown combat missions in Europe and then in Korea, but for the last ten years he had been a teacher. Now he felt a sense of responsibility to help his sister with her two exceptional boys.

Joe felt the first thing he needed to do was help Faye ensure their financial wellbeing. He knew that Harry hadn't had any life insurance, but his business was probably worth a lot more than she was aware. After sitting down with her it was clear that Harry had put aside some money that he had intended to use for Jack's college tuition.

Janet had gotten a music scholarship to SFA, and other than some incidental expenses, her education would not be much of a drain on the family's finances. Ben was still receiving private tutoring in a home school program at no cost to Faye. Amazingly, he would be eligible to take a standardized test that would allow him to enter college within the next two years. He hadn't indicated where he wanted to go, or what he wanted to study, but it was clear he would be receiving numerous scholarship offers.

Jack had initially told his mom that he would quit school and take over running his dad's business. He felt obligated to provide for the family, and that would be the easiest way. At least that was his plan. Faye wouldn't hear of it and was thrilled when Joe said he was sure he could find a buyer for the family business. He sat down with Jack one afternoon to discuss the future, and before long he had made it seem as though selling the plumbing contracting company was really Jack's idea.

While he maintained his excellent grades throughout the remainder of his sophomore and junior years, Jack hoped to qualify for a scholarship in premed, but the issue of whether or not he would go to college was not up for discussion in Faye's mind, whether he got a scholarship or not. She would find a way to pay for it.

There were several colleges within easy commuting distance of the house, but Jack was not too keen on living at home and driving back and forth to school every day. Joe recommended he look into the University of Colorado in Boulder. That is where he had gone to school, and he knew one of the professors in the biology department who might have some connections to some scholarship money. Jack seemed excited about the prospect of living near the mountains of Colorado. He had been there once on a family vacation. They had driven up Pike's Peak, then to the Garden of the Gods, but what he remembered most was how beautiful the scenery was in Rocky Mountain National Park.

The discussion about college choices continued throughout the spring and early summer after Jack's junior year. Joe thought it would be a good idea for Jack to visit the CU campus in Boulder to give him a better idea what it had to offer. They all agreed, so in mid-July they took off for the mountains in Joe's Winnebago. Janet wasn't excited to go on what turned into a family trip, but her mother told her she needed her to come along for support.

Faye had returned to work after the Easter break following Harry's death, but now more than a year later she was still emotionally stressed. Other than going to the grocery store and occasionally to church on Sundays, she had barely left the house for the last fifteen months.

As they crested the hill and started down into the valley, the small city of Boulder lay directly ahead. The university was a large collection of light brown buildings concentrated off to the left, nestled at the base of the appropriately named Flat Iron Mountains. From this first impression, Jack was sold on CU.

The day after they arrived in Boulder, Joe had arranged a personal tour of the campus by his old friend and former classmate, Edward Hamilton. He was now the chairman of the department of biology and had been teaching several of the senior level premed classes since returning from the war. He was immediately taken by the young Jack Roberts, based on his personality and the information Joe had shared about how he was committed to becoming a heart surgeon.

The tour ended in Professor Hamilton's office and Jack was thoroughly impressed and so was Hamilton. He handed Jack an application for an academic scholarship to attend CU, one of only three that were available directly through the department. Jack couldn't believe what he was hearing. He had no idea that his uncle had done all the work behind the scenes to make this happen, but Hamilton had insisted on meeting the young man before completing the favor his friend had requested.

A year later Jack started college as a Colorado Buffalo. The premed major lived in the freshman dorm and quickly made a number of friends. About midway through his first semester he met a cute young co-ed named Erin Freeman. She was a sophomore, majoring in accounting, and had grown up in Denver. They met at a Halloween party at one of the fraternity houses and he was immediately attracted to her.

Erin had long dark hair, and what most people described as mysterious dark eyes. She was only five foot three, but had an athletic body, having grown up skiing the mountains just west of Denver. By Christmas break Jack had already been skiing with her three separate weekends up at Loveland Pass. He was technically not as good as she was, not even close, but he was picking it up much faster than most beginners. By the end of that first season he was taking most of the intermediate trails and even tried a couple of black diamond runs.

She had invited him to spend a week with her family at their condo in Steamboat Springs over Christmas, but he said he couldn't. He hadn't been home since school started in early September. His only contact with his family had been an occasional brief long distance phone call from his mother. He wanted to spend time with his new girlfriend, but he missed his mom and his brother, and his new father figure, Uncle Joe.

Just after turning thirteen, Ben was finishing the last high school courses available to him, so he began the process of applying to several universities for admission into the highly competitive aerospace engineering programs. Ben loved all the sciences, but more than anything he kept up with all that was going on in the international space race. He took President Kennedy's challenge to put a man on the moon before 1970 seriously and wanted to be a part of it. Within a few weeks he had received scholarship offers from MIT, Cal Tech, Cal Poly, Georgia Tech, Michigan and Stanford. He even received letters from several schools where he hadn't even applied. Over the holidays, he discussed his options with his brother and together they decided his best opportunity would be Stanford University in Palo Alto, California. It had a great engineering school, but it also offered a broad range of other studies. Ben was interested in chemistry and biology as well as astrophysics, so he planned to pursue as many different paths as he could.

In the fall of 1967, Benjamin Matthew Roberts entered the freshman class at Stanford. He had yet to reach his fourteenth birthday and was one of the youngest full-time students ever to attend that prestigious university. Jack spent more than a month back at home that next summer, but in the fall he, too, was back in school in Colorado. While their mother was thrilled to see both her sons fulfilling their dreams, she was now all alone.

◆◆◆◆◆◆◆◆

Jack had a singular focus: get into medical school as quickly as possible. He was seventeen when he started college and after only two years he had distinguished himself in the biology department. Professor Hamilton suggested he apply to med school early, since there were several schools that were accepting applicants after their junior year. He decided to take the MCAT test in the fall just to see how well he could do, knowing he could take it again during his senior year if he needed to improve his score. While still awaiting his entrance exam results, Jack submitted applications to several medical schools, including a single application to all five in the state of Texas. When his MCAT score came back it was an outstanding thirty-eight, indicating the breadth and quality of the education he was getting in Colorado.

Jack was also convinced he had found the love of his life, as he and Erin were getting serious. He had been skiing several times with her mom and dad and they were already functioning like his local family. The two of them seemed destined to be together, at least that's what Jack kept telling himself. He told her he thought it would be best for them to wait to get married until after graduation, but they had been living together in her apartment for almost a year.

Erin was nearly two years older than Jack and would be finishing her degree in accounting in the spring, so she had been considering entering graduate school to stay in Boulder while he completed his fourth year. When the news came about his test scores it began to look like she would need to find a job wherever he got accepted.

In January of 1969 Jack received invitations to interview at five different medical schools, including three in Texas, the University of Colorado in Denver and Tulane University in New Orleans. The visit to the school in Denver was easy enough to schedule, and he had already decided against Tulane because Erin said she didn't think she'd be comfortable in Louisiana. He was able to schedule interviews at the three Texas schools in San Antonio, Galveston, and Dallas all in the same week, so he decided to use the interview process as an excuse to finally take Erin home to meet his mom.

Faye had aged considerably in the five years since Harry's death. She tried to act like she approved of Erin, but Jack could tell his mom wasn't pleased with either the fact they were living together, or the slightly older woman who just wasn't up to her expectations. He told himself that all moms feel that way, and with time she would learn to love Erin.

The interviews went well, and based on what he heard from each of the people he talked to, Jack was hopeful that he would get in somewhere. The first week in March was one of the most exciting times in Jack's young life. First he received a letter of acceptance to the University of Colorado School of Medicine to begin in August 1969. "I'm in!" was all he could say for an hour after opening the mail on Monday. The next day he went directly into Professor Hamilton's office to share his news. Erin was very excited and phoned her mom and dad with the news that it looked like they would be staying in Colorado.

On Wednesday two more official looking letters arrived, one from the University of Texas Medical Branch in Galveston and the other from the University of Texas Southwestern Medical School in Dallas. Both were invitations to enter classes in the fall. Suddenly, Jack had more options. Colorado was close to Erin's home and many of the activities they both enjoyed, while UTMB in Galveston was one of the oldest and most respected schools in the Southwest. UT Southwestern was thought of by many of the people he had talked with as perhaps the premier school in the region, and it was close to home. The deadline for accepting one of these three invitations was March 15, so Jack had little time to decide.

Erin tried to be excited that Jack had so many choices, but she had already told everyone they were moving to Denver. Over the next several days Jack talked to Professor Hamilton on two separate occasions about his choices. Hamilton was obviously pushing CU, but understood the benefits of the other two options. When he called his mom and Uncle Joe they were both eager for him to come back to Dallas. His mom didn't even mention Erin during the discussion, secretly hoping she would stay behind in Colorado. Jack even called Ben and asked his advice. His brother wasn't much help except to say he hated that they were both so far away from their mom.

♦♦♦♦♦♦♦♦♦

In June of 1969 Jack and Erin were married in the small Baptist church in Hurst, Texas where Jack had been baptized fourteen years earlier. His mother had gladly accepted Erin into the family in exchange for their decision to move back to North Texas. Jack was due to start classes at UT Southwestern in August, and the young couple had found an apartment off Harry Hines Boulevard near the campus. Erin had also landed a job with an accounting firm in downtown Dallas.

Before starting this new phase in their lives they decided to take a two-week honeymoon and drive up to the Canadian Rockies. They took off the day after the wedding in Erin's brand new, bright red Chevelle Malibu that her parents had given her as a graduation present. Their route took them through Denver where they spent one night at her childhood home before continuing north.

The Best Western hotel in Banff was not exactly the same as the nearby Chateau Lake Louise, but it was what they could afford and Jack had convinced himself that the scenery was the same no matter where they stayed. The mountains east of Calgary were spectacular and they couldn't wait to go exploring the back roads and hiking trails.

They had been in Canada for three days and were feeling adventurous so they decided to take a picnic lunch and head up a steep trail that led to a high mountain lake hidden among the snowcapped peaks. It was not one of the more frequently used trails, and when Jack told the hotel manager of their plan, he insisted they take one of his walkie-talkies along in the event of an emergency. The device had a range of ten miles, and the lake was only about six miles from the hotel. Jack assured him they would be fine, but reluctantly stuck the walkie-talkie in his backpack, just to satisfy the old man.

About three hours into their adventure a rock on the edge of the trail gave way under Erin's weight and she tumbled about six feet down the slope. She screamed in pain when her right foot twisted under her and the force caused an audible crack as the small bone on the outside of her ankle snapped. Jack scrambled down to where she was lying between a small granite boulder and a large pine tree.

"Are you okay?" he asked, already knowing the answer.

"It's my ankle," she screamed through the pain, before her tears began.

He tried to help her up, but every time he moved her she screamed. Eventually, he was able to get her into a sitting position and elevated her injured leg on a nearby fallen tree trunk. He gently removed her hiking boot and saw her foot was turned slightly inward and a bluish swelling had already begun. Jack was no doctor, he hadn't even attended his first day of medical school yet, but he knew her ankle was broken and he was going to need some help. He silently thanked God and the old man at the hotel for the walkie-talkie.

❖❖❖❖❖❖❖❖

From the hotel, Jack took his new wife to the emergency clinic in Banff. The manager had offered to call an ambulance once the two young men of the Canadian Mountain Rescue Service had successfully gotten her down off the mountain in an all-terrain vehicle. It was only a couple of miles up the road, so he decided to take her himself in the car. She seemed to be handling the pain better once they applied the splint and ice pack.

When they arrived, a teenage boy brought a wheelchair out to the car and helped Jack get her into the waiting area where there were eight other patients waiting to be seen. Jack filled out a short form and handed it to a woman sitting behind a sliding glass window. It took more than an hour for the nurse to call Erin's name and Jack rolled her back into a very stark exam room where another younger woman took a quick look at her ankle and recorded her blood pressure and pulse rate on a sheet of paper. She said they were going to get an x-ray and started to leave the room. Before she could get through the door Jack stopped her and asked when his wife was going to get something for the pain. It had been more than five hours since the accident. The woman said she would talk to the doctor once she had the results of the x-ray.

It was another thirty minutes before a technician came into the exam room and wheeled her down the hall to a small room with an x-ray machine that Jack thought must have been installed shortly after World War II. It was another fifteen minutes before a middle-aged doctor entered the room wearing a short white jacket. It reminded Jack of the ones he had seen the interns wearing at the U of M hospital, only this one desperately needed to be washed and pressed. He explained that she had fractured her fibula and would need to be seen by the orthopedic specialist. When Jack asked why he couldn't fix it, he explained that he was just the emergency physician. They would have to wait for the surgeon to come from Calgary.

"Can't you at least give her something for the pain?" Jack pleaded.

"She hasn't had anything?" the doctor asked.

"No!" they both said simultaneously.

"I'm so sorry," he replied. "She should have gotten some morphine immediately when she got here. That is our protocol. I'll have the nurse get her a shot right away."

◆◆◆◆◆◆◆◆◆

It was eleven that night before the young orthopedic surgeon finally arrived at the emergency room having driven the two hours from Calgary where he had already put in a very long day. He seemed competent but clearly detached as he studied the x-ray that was now eight hours old.

"The fracture is not displaced and should heal with just immobilization in a cast," he said, happy it didn't need surgery because that would mean a transfer back to Calgary.

"How long will she need to be in the cast?" Jack asked.

"At least six weeks," he said. "However, this initial cast will need to be changed in one week, because once the swelling goes down it will become loose."

"We live in Texas," Jack announced. "Will she be able to travel home by car?"

"Yeah, sure," he replied, "as long as she can keep her foot elevated. If her ankle swells more after the cast is put on, it could cut off the circulation. If she loses feeling in her toes you'll need to stop somewhere and get the cast split to relieve the pressure."

"How long have you been an orthopedic surgeon?" Jack asked.

"Three years," he replied, and Jack detected a sense of frustration in the young doctor's voice.

"I'm starting medical school in about three weeks," Jack announced, hoping to gain some words of wisdom from his counterpart.

The doctor's response was more revealing than Jack had expected. "That's great, I understand things are different in the States. For your sake I hope so." When he saw the questioning look on Jack's face he continued. "Here in Canada the government took over our system two years ago when they passed the Medical Care Act, and since then many of our physicians have left the country. That's why I typically have to put in more than a hundred hours a week and rarely get to see my wife and my newborn son. I'm one of only three orthopedic surgeons in the Province."

"Really?" Jack asked in disbelief. "Why did so many docs leave?"

"They saw the handwriting on the wall. The government controls everything, including how much money they can make."

"Where did they go?"

"Most of them went to the US, but some went to the Caribbean or Central America. Some even went all the way to South America."

"Why didn't you leave?"

"I went to school on a government grant, so I'm still paying off my obligation. I have another five years. After that I plan to look for an opportunity somewhere south of the border.

"If you are as busy as you say, you're bound to be making a bunch of money."

"Actually I make about half what American ortho docs make, and I can't imagine they are working as many hours as I do."

Jack just looked at him and shook his head.

"Here in Canada, the patients don't have to pay for anything because the government pays the doctors and the hospitals," he explained, "but it isn't really the low government pay that most of us object to. It's the fact that trying to do what is best for our patients is sometimes difficult in the face of ridiculous government regulations. They have implemented broad new practice guidelines, allegedly to ensure quality care for everyone, but in reality they obstruct the delivery of care at nearly every turn," he said with an increasingly angry tone. "I just hope you guys don't fall into that trap or I may not have anywhere to go."

Suddenly, Jack understood why their wait in the emergency clinic had been so long, and why no one seemed all that concerned about his wife. They were all government workers.

♦♦♦♦♦♦♦♦♦

"We are about twenty minutes out," the pilot announced.

Franco touched a button on his console and responded, "Thank you."

He turned to Jack and suggested they continue their conversation later. He stood and moved forward to check on his wife and their baby. When he returned, Tina came back with him, retrieving their cans and glasses in preparation for landing.

CHAPTER 14

The pediatric ambulance service was waiting on the tarmac near the general aviation terminal at DFW International. The customs agent came aboard the plane first, and based on the instructions he had received from the State Department, his search was largely a formality. He quickly gave them the approval they needed to disembark and expedited their passage through immigration.

The ambulance crew boarded the plane with their own infant transport system, complete with state-of-the-art monitoring and the ability to provide portable ventilator support if necessary. Once Christina had been transferred out of the makeshift system, which had served her needs admirably during the flight, they carried her to the waiting ambulance. They pulled away from the plane and headed toward the controlled access gate and waited there for the others to clear immigration. The two pilots unloaded the luggage onto a large cart and wheeled it into the international arrival terminal. The process of passport review was quickly dispensed with and the entire group was allowed to enter the United States in less than five minutes.

Gabriella and Radha made their way to the ambulance for the ride into Fort Worth, and Franco and Jack rode in yet another limousine, this one arranged for by Franco's company. The limo driver loaded their luggage and began the forty minute trip to the children's hospital in Fort Worth.

"That was faster than I've ever cleared customs," Jack remarked as the limo began to move.

"I've found that it is often more important who you know, than what you know," Franco replied.

"Obviously you know some very influential people."

"It never hurts to have friends in high places. Now, you were about to tell me about your medical education."

"In just a few minutes we will be driving right through the community where I grew up, and where my mom still lives."

♦♦♦♦♦♦♦♦♦

Although he was much closer to home, once he started medical school Jack rarely saw his mother. Once a month he and Erin would drive the forty-five minutes from Dallas out to his boyhood home, usually on a Sunday afternoon. Faye was always excited to see her son, and she tried to embrace Erin as her daughter-in-law, but she couldn't help but resent her. She suspected that she was the reason Jack seemed preoccupied. The truth was he was totally absorbed in his studies. The first year was not all that different from college except there were no breaks during the course of the day. He told her that it was more like taking six or seven different courses all at the same time, rather than the four or five per semester he had carried at CU. Many of the courses also had labs in the afternoon, with the most notable being Gross Anatomy.

Three afternoons a week, Jack and his two lab partners spent three hours in the cadaver lab, dissecting a human body. The smell of the formalin preservative was overwhelming at first, but Jack soon learned to equate the obnoxious fumes with a learning opportunity. He knew that anatomy was the foundation of everything he would need to know as a surgeon.

While the first semester went by quickly for Jack, it seemed far slower for Erin. After they returned from Canada she was scheduled to start her new job on July 1, but that didn't happen. She remained on crutches until the middle of the month when she was finally allowed to wear a walking cast. The accounting firm had allowed her to start out working part time until she got her cast off in early August.

Her job was okay, she thought, but starting at the bottom of a group of fifty accountants was pretty boring. She made a decent living putting in about fifty hours a week, mainly preparing spreadsheets for one of the junior partners and filing automated quarterly reports for several of his lesser clients. So far she didn't have any clients of her own and wasn't likely to have any assigned to her until she had been there for at least three months.

The young couple seemed to have little time for anything other than school and work. Jack was rarely home. He usually left for class before she got up in the mornings and he rarely got home before eight in the evening. They both convinced themselves there would be plenty of opportunities for intimacy once their schedules settled down. For six weeks, Erin's broken leg had been a major challenge, and once school was under way it seemed that Jack was either too tired or he was studying for an important exam. On those occasions when they were together, the physical excitement was just not the same as it had been during the year and a half they lived together in Boulder.

In the fall of 1968 the war in Vietnam dominated the news, and as required by law Jack had registered with his local draft board on his eighteenth birthday, November 19, 1966. The military draft had been established back in 1940, and allowed for men, ages eighteen to twenty-five, to be drafted. The system called for the older men to be selected first to fill the needs that were not met by volunteers, but in 1968, Congress changed that policy. They established a new system where all draft-eligible men would be selected based on their date of birth. A national lottery was scheduled to take place on New Year's Day 1969 to determine the order of selection. As a twenty-one-year-old, Jack would be entered into the first draft lottery and there was a real chance that he could get drafted depending on what number his birthdate drew.

When the lottery numbers were posted, November 19 was number two hundred three and Jack felt a tremendous sense of relief. He knew a couple of his friends from high school who were serving in Vietnam, and another classmate whom he hadn't known well had recently been killed in a fire fight with the North Vietnamese army during the Tet Offensive. It wasn't that he didn't want to serve, he just wanted to finish his education first.

While it was now unlikely Jack would be drafted out of medical school, he later learned that he would be subject to another so called "doctor draft" once he finished school.

◆◆◆◆◆◆◆◆◆

As his second year began, Erin was becoming frustrated with the fact that her marriage was not what she had expected. She was convinced that she was not a priority in her husband's life. He was seldom home, and when he was he spent his time reading or studying. She still dreamed of being the wife of a successful doctor, but was wondering if it was worth what she was having to sacrifice. Her entire life up to the point when she met Jack, had been centered on her. She was her father's only daughter and he had spoiled her far more than her two brothers. He gave her almost everything she asked for, but more importantly he showered her with nearly constant attention. She was now starved for attention and there was no one to provide it, so when Daryl, one of the other young accountants at the office, suggested she join him for a drink after work, she figured, why not?

Their first meeting outside the office seemed innocent enough. Just a quick drink at a local bar on lower Greenville Avenue, and Daryl didn't say any more about it the rest of the week. She thought it wasn't a big deal, but the following

Monday he suggested they try another bar he knew a little further up that same popular street. This time they sat in a quiet booth, talking, mostly about work. He asked her what she did for fun and seemed truly sympathetic when she admitted she hadn't done anything fun in over a year. They each had a couple of margaritas, and as she got up to leave she felt a little tipsy, so the thirty-year-old bachelor walked her out to her car. She insisted she was okay to drive since she wasn't going very far, but before he closed her door he reached in and touched her shoulder, asking her if she was sure she was okay. The touch of his hand reminded her of the physical contact she was missing, and was now craving. When she got home Jack wasn't there. He had left a note telling her he'd gone to the library to study.

The next day she decided to wear a new summer dress with an elastic neckline that could be worn either on or off her shoulders. It was okay for work provided she kept her shoulders covered. As she had expected, Daryl stopped by her cubicle early in the day to check on her. He expected she might be suffering from a bit of a hangover, but instead she seemed even brighter and more cheerful than usual. After some casual conversation about a client he was meeting for lunch, he asked if she'd like to grab some dinner after work. Remembering his touch from the night before she agreed to meet him at an upscale restaurant on McKinney Avenue, near downtown.

This time she was the one who wouldn't be home until late. She left work a few minutes early so she could run by the apartment, and as expected, Jack wasn't home. She left him a note telling him she was going over to a friend's house and wasn't sure when she'd be home. As it turned out there was more truth to her statement than she had intended.

On her way to the restaurant she converted her neckline to the off-the-shoulder look, secretly hoping Daryl would touch her again. After a couple of drinks he did just that, putting his arm casually around her as they sat in a private booth, enjoying some live piano music. The sensation of having a man's hand on her bare skin was exhilarating. She knew what she was doing was wrong, but she reasoned that what Jack was doing, or more accurately not doing, was equally wrong. When Daryl suggested they go to his place for a nightcap she hesitated for a moment, then agreed.

◆◆◆◆◆◆◆◆◆

It was after midnight when she opened the door of their apartment. Jack was still up, sitting at the kitchen table reading an embryology textbook and taking notes.

"Hey, baby," he said. He hadn't called her that in weeks, but then she hadn't seen him much over that time.

"Hi," was all she said.

"Did you have a good time?"

"Yeah," she replied, not revealing what kind of time it had been. Seeing her husband sitting there studying she was suddenly filled with guilt, but he didn't sense it. "I'm going to bed," she said. "I've got a long day tomorrow."

"Okay," Jack replied, "I've got to finish preparing for this exam." She was glad he wasn't interested in her, and she quickly prepared for bed, knowing she would have trouble falling asleep.

Between her guilt over what promised to become an ongoing affair with Daryl, and her sense of incredible loneliness, Erin was on the verge of an emotional collapse. A few weeks later one of her closest friends from college called to say she was in town for a job interview. The two young women spent Saturday afternoon talking. Erin felt she had to talk to someone about the conflicts she was feeling in her life, and Stephanie was the perfect sounding board. She was a clinical psychologist, but more than anything she was her friend.

After asking all the usual questions about love, anger, infidelity and guilt, Stephanie helped Erin outline her options. There was no way she was going to tell Jack about her affair unless he asked. Instead, she decided to confront him with the question of whether she was a priority in his life or not. If he couldn't provide her with an answer she could live with, then she would suggest that it would be better for both of them if they went their separate ways.

The following day was the Sunday she and Jack were scheduled to go visit his mom. She woke up early and dressed before he got up. She went into the kitchen and poured herself a cup of coffee, then waited patiently for Jack to join her. As he came into the kitchen she asked him to sit down. She said they needed to talk, and her look was very serious.

Jack wasn't sure what this was about, but he knew whatever it was it wasn't going to be good. He had sensed her dissatisfaction with her life for some time, but he thought it had something to do with her work. Perhaps she was upset over having to support both of them. Her salary more than covered their living expenses, but he was paying for his tuition and books using the money his dad had set aside for college. If she told him she wanted to quit her job he wasn't sure how they'd be able to make it.

Was she going to tell him she was pregnant? That would be okay he thought, even though it would really strain their finances. The idea of starting a family was something they had talked about, but they had decided to wait until after he finished school. However, what she said over the next few minutes came as an even bigger surprise. She explained that she was unhappy with the way things were going. She needed more in her life than just work. She pointed out how she had willingly come with him to Texas, leaving her family and friends who were all back in Colorado, only to find that he was never around. She told him she had never felt more alone in her life. Without saying as much, it was clear that she wanted him to give up the pursuit of his dream to spend more time with her. This wasn't something he had ever even considered.

As he sat listening to her, Jack thought about a couple of his classmates who had confronted similar situations. One had recently dropped out of school and the other had gotten a divorce. He sat silently absorbing the body blows from this woman he had been sure shared his dream. Then he was reminded of what his father had told him on his deathbed.

"I can't give up my dream," he said, finally breaking his silence. "It's part of who I am. I thought you understood that." He paused to make sure she had time to absorb his response to her challenge, then added, "I guess if you can't live with that I understand, but I can't change." His words had a finality that made it clear the choice was up to her.

"Jack, I loved you, but... I just don't love what you love," she spoke with an honesty that he couldn't help but respect.

◆◆◆◆◆◆◆◆◆

That afternoon Jack drove out to visit his mom.

"Where's Erin?" she asked. "Is she sick?"

He dropped his head slightly and began to explain. "Things just aren't working out between us," he said with a sadness in his voice she had rarely ever heard. "She is not happy with all the hours I'm putting in at school and wants me to drop out of med school. I told her I wouldn't do that, so we've decided to call it quits."

"I'm so sorry," Faye said earnestly as she put her arms around him. The emotional stress had been obvious on his face, and like any mother, she felt compassion for him, but at the same time she was glad that she didn't have to continue to act as though she liked the woman he had married. They spent the rest of the afternoon talking about his immediate future. He was going to need a place to live, and with no income he would need the rest of the money his dad had saved. While Faye still had the small nest egg it wouldn't be enough to cover his needs for more than about a year at most.

Uncle Joe stopped by around supper time because Faye had told him Jack was coming home that afternoon. It didn't take long for him to gain a clear picture of the new situation, and he thought he might be able to offer some advice.

"Well," he said, "I'm sure you could get a bank loan to complete your education, but then you'd be saddled with paying it back over several years."

"Dad always warned me about going into debt," Jack replied. "He was convinced that it was better to do without, but I have to finish school."

Joe paused a moment then offered an alternative. "Another option might be the military's Berry Plan," he said hopefully. "As I understand it you can sign up for military service now and get paid more than enough to afford an apartment. Then you'll owe them some time after you finish your training."

That sounded like a great idea to Jack. His father had always spoken fondly of his years in the Navy and Uncle Joe had nothing but great things to say about the Air Force. The more he thought about it the more he liked the idea. It fit nicely into the philosophy his dad had stolen from JFK and drilled into him. "Ask not what your country can do for you. Ask what you can do for your country." In this case it seemed that he would be serving his country and at the same time it would be helping him achieve his dream. He left his mom's that night with a plan. The only question was Navy or Air Force?

◆◆◆◆◆◆◆◆◆

The military option wasn't exactly as Uncle Joe had described it, but according to the Air Force recruiter it was still workable. The Berry Plan was only for doctors after they finished medical school, so Jack wasn't eligible yet. However, he could join the Air Force Reserve while still a student and get paid a monthly stipend. He would need to spend most of his summer vacation on base, going through basic, and he would need to train several weekends during the year. He would also be subject to being called up to active duty if the need arose, but according to the recruiter that was unlikely.

Before making a commitment, Jack felt he needed to talk to someone at the school to make sure he would have the flexibility to meet his obligations. He was relieved to find out the dean of the medical school was very familiar with this option. Jack had been in the top ten percent of his class since the first semester, and the dean didn't want to lose him for financial reasons. In situations like this he was often able to find scholarship money for financially strapped students, but he decided not to offer Jack that option since he had already worked out his own solution. The dean actually encouraged him to take advantage of the military option before the start of his third year. He also informed Jack of still another possibility. Provided he remained in the top third of his class, he might be eligible to actually graduate after his third year, provided he could get accepted into a university hospital-based internship.

The prospect of saving another entire year had Jack excited. When he started high school he told his dad that he'd be finished with school in eighteen years, three years of high school, four of college, four more of medical school and the seven years of residency. He had already trimmed one year off by getting out of college after three years, so if he could graduate from med school in three years he'd be starting his residency before his twenty-fourth birthday.

Jack signed up for the USAF Reserve and was committed to doing his basic training during his time off that summer. He spent six weeks at Randolph Air Force Base on the North side of San Antonio and by mid-July he was back in Dallas, ready to start his clinical rotations. His divorce from Erin was uncontested, and since he didn't really have any assets, he didn't need to enter into any kind of settlement. Texas was a community property state, so he might have had a claim against her, since her car was worth a lot more than his old truck, but Jack didn't want to pursue it. He had merely taken his clothes and other personal effects and left her the meager furniture in their apartment. She decided to stay there since she was already the one paying the rent and it was close to her work.

Jack felt his life was finally transitioning from his boyhood dreams to the reality of a life as a physician. He found a small efficiency apartment that was close enough to the school and Parkland Memorial Hospital that he could walk most days. His first rotation was on the surgical service, and he loved finally being inside the operating room. It didn't matter to him what procedure was being done, he was fascinated by the whole process. The residents were the ones performing most of the operations, and generally they would allow the medical students to scrub in and suture the skin incisions closed. Jack was always first to volunteer, and at the end of every case he would ask the nurses if he could have any extra packets of suture that had been opened but not used during the case. He would take them home and practice tying knots, using all the various techniques the residents had shown him. Eventually, he was as proficient as they were, if not more so.

Every six weeks his schedule required that he move on to another rotation. He didn't care much for internal medicine or psychiatry. He thought they were boring. Obstetrics and gynecology was more interesting because, like surgery, it involved doing something to patients rather than just ordering tests and prescribing medications. Watching babies being born was exciting, especially the occasional cesarean section. He also enjoyed his time on the pediatric rotation. It reminded him of the years he had spent caring for his brother.

There were opportunities to take a few electives, and Jack had signed up early for one of the most sought after rotations, cardiothoracic surgery. It was just after the first of the year when he and one of the fourth-year students showed up for their first day of what turned out to be one of the most demanding periods of their young lives.

The students rarely had a chance to go to the OR to witness any major heart or vascular operations, and when they did there were always three or four residents and interns scrubbed in with the faculty surgeon, so they couldn't really see anything. Their job was to keep up with every detail of every patient's history, physical findings, vital signs, fluid intake and output, all medications that were given, daily laboratory results and x-ray findings, along with any new electrocardiograms and anything else the intern or resident wanted to know on a moment's notice. If any urgent tests were ordered during the course of the day, which happened very frequently on the sicker patients in the ICU, the student was responsible for getting them done. Typically, it involved drawing the blood themselves, then taking it down to the lab to get one of the technicians to run it through the machines while they waited. The interns referred to this as "scut work" and while Jack didn't know the precise origin of the term, he knew it was exhausting. His typical day started at four thirty in the morning and didn't end before eight in the evening, and every third night was spent in the hospital, shadowing the intern.

In addition to caring for patients, the medical students were required to attend regular teaching conferences. The interns and residents presented cases to the faculty, and frequently they were subjected to what could only be described as harassment. Often the criticism was for not knowing some seemingly minor detail, so after each conference the berating usually continued down the ranks, eventually ending with the students.

Two days prior to one of the Surgical Grand Rounds, Jack learned that the chief cardiothoracic resident was going to present a case of a kid with Tetralogy of Fallot. During rounds he told him he was excited to attend his presentation because his brother had tetralogy and he had studied everything he could get his hands on about that specific birth defect. The resident asked him what had happened and Jack explained that his brother had been operated on by both Dr. Blalock and Dr. Lillehei. The resident was amazed by the medical student's story, and insisted that he participate in his presentation.

Standing up in front of the small auditorium, facing twelve faculty surgeons including the chairman of the department, the two cardiothoracic residents, thirty-two other surgery residents and interns and two dozen or more of his fellow students had the potential to be one of the most intimidating experiences of his life, but once he overcame his initial fears, he was able to describe the specific defects of tetralogy in detail, along with the various clinical presentations. This was a subject he was intimately familiar with, a fact that was not lost on anyone in the audience, including the faculty. He described the Blalock-Taussig procedure in detail and contrasted it with the complete correction made possible by the introduction of open heart surgery. When he finished, the chairman of the department of surgery asked him how he knew so much about this particular subject.

"I met Dr. Blalock at Johns Hopkins University Hospital in 1953 when he operated on my one-week-old brother," Jack said confidently. "I also had the opportunity to meet Dr. Lillehei in 1963, when he performed the complete repair of my brother's tetralogy at the University of Minnesota." As he spoke about his personal experience with these pioneers of heart surgery, he realized he had never openly shared that information with anyone other than his family prior to telling the chief resident about it two days before.

Jack Roberts was now officially a superstar among his fellow students, and he had caught the attention of the faculty as well. He had made the chief resident look good too, and the young doctor took him under his wing for the next several months, even after he had moved on to other clinical rotations. Although he was ten years his senior, Jack thought of him almost as a contemporary. Perhaps it was because he wore his long hair in a ponytail. He wanted so badly to be like him that Jack let his hair grow a little longer, but that didn't last. The Air Force frowned on anything other than a short haircut, even for reservists.

As he approached the end of his third year Jack decided to apply for early graduation. He had been watching the senior medical students and realized they were doing some of the same work that the interns did, so he saw no benefit to doing another year of electives as a fourth-year student. He didn't need to check out all his options, he already knew exactly what he wanted to pursue and the sooner he could get under way the better. He would need to do a one-year surgical internship, then four years of general surgery residency, followed by two years of residency in cardiothoracic surgery. He was convinced that another year of medical school would be spent just doing scut work, and he thought it made more sense to get paid as a lowly intern rather than paying for being a student.

Jack thought his interview for an intern position with the chief of surgery at UT Southwestern went okay. His Grand Rounds presentation was something the seasoned surgeon recalled very well. He also interviewed with the department chairmen in Galveston and San Antonio to ensure he would have more than one option. There were other private training opportunities that might be easier to get into, but in order to qualify for early graduation he had to get into a university-based program.

Following his interviews he submitted his preference list to the National Resident Matching Program, and each program director also submitted their list of applicants, ranked according to who they wanted to accept as trainees. In mid-May the results of the matching program were released, and Jack had matched to his first choice. He would be staying in Dallas, at least for one more year. He thought it would be interesting working alongside some of his classmates who would be senior medical students while he would already hold the title M.D.

◆◆◆◆◆◆◆◆◆

The graduation ceremony was a more formal affair than Jack had expected. He hadn't actually attended his college graduation since he left for med school before he completed his degree. CU had mailed him his diploma after giving him credit for his first year of medical school as the equivalent of his last two semesters of undergraduate studies. He wasn't sure how he was going to explain to people how his college diploma was dated 1970 and his medical degree would be dated 1972, but he didn't really care.

Several members of the faculty spoke, droning on about the obligations that came with being a physician, and challenging them to never lose sight of the responsibilities that were inherent to the profession. Near the end of the proceedings, Jack and his fellow graduates stood and recited a somewhat modernized version of the Hippocratic Oath. This was a day he had dreamed of all his life, and when it was finally accomplished he felt somewhat inadequate. His entire life had been dedicated to achieving this singular goal, but how could he be sure he'd be able to meet the needs of the people who would entrust their lives to him in the future?

His internship year passed quickly, and by early spring he had decided to take advantage of the Berry Plan, which offered a couple of options. He could stay in a civilian training program like the one he was already in at Parkland, then fulfill his military obligation after completing his residency, or he could complete his training as a member of the active duty Air Force. If he chose to stay in a civilian program he would owe the Air Force six years, one for every year he deferred while in training. However, if he did his training at Wilford Hall Medical Center, the Air Force's main hospital here in the States, he would only owe them two years when he finished.

Wilford Hall was located on Lackland Air Force Base in San Antonio, and it was the Air Force's equivalent of the Army's Walter Reed and the Navy's Bethesda hospitals. After talking to several of the more senior residents and a couple of faculty members, he decided to take the military training route. In the end his decision was based mostly on something the Canadian orthopedic surgeon had said to him three years earlier. It wasn't so much what he had said about having an eight-year obligation to the government as much as it was the way he said it. He sounded like a slave to his job, and Jack never wanted to feel that way.

There was one other factor that steered Jack's decision. The commander over Wilford Hall had guaranteed him a residency spot in their new cardiothoracic surgery program upon completion of his general surgery training. That was something the chairman of the university program said they couldn't do. Jack would have to apply for that highly competitive position, and he didn't want to risk being shut out of the one thing he wanted now, more than anything else.

Dr. Jack Roberts demonstrated exceptional skills during his years at Wilford Hall, and he quickly gained the respect of his fellow physicians. His personality fit in perfectly with the military-style medicine. He devoted virtually every waking hour to the pursuit of his goal of becoming the best surgeon he could be. His general surgery training and later his cardiothoracic experience were supplemented by several rotations at the nearby University of Texas Health Science Center in San Antonio. It was affiliated with both the huge Bexar County Hospital with its regional trauma center, as well as the Audie Murphy VA Hospital where cardiovascular disease was abundant. His experiences included interaction with his civilian counterparts and with the distinguished university faculty. He found it more than just a little ironic that most of the faculty had trained at the University of Minnesota under the great Owen Wangensteen, and of course C. Walt Lillehei, who had moved on to become the chairman of the department of surgery at Cornell. Jack often wondered if the elder statesman would have remembered him.

Throughout his training, Jack relished any opportunity to take care of kids. It wasn't that he didn't like adult surgery, it was just the idea of caring for kids the way he had watched others care for his brother, gave him a special sense of accomplishment. In the final year of his training he again expressed his intense interest in pediatric heart surgery to the base commandant. The Air Force didn't have a children's heart program, so virtually everything he did at Wilford Hall was adult heart surgery. What experience he received in pediatrics was through the university, and they didn't really do that many kids either. After several months of pleading, along with a promise to help establish a pedi heart program for the Air Force, the base commander allowed him to take a three-month sabbatical to work with a children's heart surgeon in London.

While in England, Jack solidified his love for pediatric cardiac surgery. His new mentor was one of the world's authorities and restricted his practice to only children. He received referrals from throughout what was once the worldwide British Empire, so Jack gained more experience in those three months than most American surgeons could obtain in a year. They were doing three or four major cases a day, with Jack assuming the role of first assistant. However, over the last month of his tour he was doing most of the operations himself, as the primary surgeon.

His experience in England extended beyond the operating room, and much of it was quite disturbing. He discovered that a number of premature infants with complex heart problems never made it to the operating room. Under the British National Health Service, there were constraints placed on the availability of such care. These weren't things that were talked about openly, for obvious reasons, but Jack saw for himself how government regulations impacted many children and their families. The cost of caring for kids, especially the preemies, was extremely high, so the system discouraged their treatment using behind-the-scenes review processes under the guise of quality assurance. The impact of these policies was to reduce the total number of children who were treated for conditions where the outcome was considered doubtful or not worth the cost. The chief mechanism used to accomplish the goal of cost containment was to discourage surgeons from performing any so-called "hero procedures." Complex operations could only be done in highly specialized centers, like the one where he was working, and unfortunately, many of the kids in need weren't able to make it that far.

Jack came away from his experience in London enthused about his chosen life's work, but it was tempered by a profound sadness. His mentor told him that he understood exactly how he felt, but based on his own experience it was fruitless to fight the politicians. They had gained near total control of the once-proud British health care system by assuming responsibility for paying all the bills. Jack thought to himself that such a thing could never happen in the US, could it? He vowed to himself that he would do whatever he could to ensure that every child in need would at least have a fighting chance at life.

◆◆◆◆◆◆◆◆◆

After completing his seven years of residency in June of 1979, the thirty-year-old Captain Jack Roberts was assigned to the US Air Force hospital at Ramstein Air Base in Germany. He was sent there to work with a career military surgeon whose skills were in decline. The veteran doc was experiencing a slowly worsening tremor in his left hand. He was still able get the job done, but he welcomed the steady young hands of a new surgeon. Everyone welcomed Jack except the circulating nurse in the heart room. She saw Jack as overconfident and still wet behind the ears. Perhaps she had a point, but everyone except Jack knew that the real reason she didn't immediately accept this young buck, as she referred to him, was her longstanding relationship with his older colleague. Their love affair dated back nearly fifteen years, and she simply couldn't accept the fact they were both getting older.

Shortly after arriving in Germany Jack made friends with a local civilian named Klaus Bachman. He worked on base as the cardiopulmonary bypass pump technologist, a position critical to open heart surgery. He had been hired because the Air Force didn't have a training program for CP pump techs, so they had none to assign to Ramstein. Klaus was exceptional at what he did, and it was obvious to Jack that he was an invaluable member of the team.

The war in Vietnam had ended six years earlier and the military hospital was no longer as busy as it once had been. Most of what Jack saw were enlisted men with smoking-related tumors of the lung or esophagus and some of the older officers who needed coronary artery bypass. Few kids were ever treated at the base hospital for anything beyond a common cold, so Jack felt his real talents were being wasted.

One great thing about being stationed in Germany was the numerous opportunities to travel around to see the great cities like Munich and Stuttgart. In the six months he was there he had access to Air Force transportation that allowed him to visit other cities in Europe including Vienna, Zurich, Paris, and Rome. Finally he was transferred to what he hoped would be a somewhat less boring post.

In early 1980 Jack was reassigned and reported for duty at Yokota Air Base, in Fussa, Japan, a suburb of Tokyo. He had also been promoted to the rank of major and was being sent there to start the Air Force's first cardiac surgery program serving the Far East. Before he arrived, there were no heart surgeons in any branch of the US military between Germany and Hawaii. One of the first things Jack did was to request that the Air Force hire Klaus Bachman by whatever means necessary and move him to Japan. He had to have an experienced pump tech, and there wasn't anyone he could think of with whom he'd rather work.

Jack was really in his element in Japan. While the local language was a bigger challenge than he had expected, the people he was working with seemed far more enthusiastic than those he'd left behind in Germany. He also didn't have to beg for money to get his program started. The Air Force had given him what amounted to a blank check to establish a state-of-the-art facility dedicated just to heart surgery.

It didn't take long to ramp up once the equipment arrived. He had acquired everything he needed to set up two adult cardiac operating rooms and a cardiac catheterization lab. The only push back he'd experienced came when he requested a set of pediatric vascular instruments along with a modification to one of the pumps that would allow him to do infants and small children. The additional expense required approval from the top, so it wasn't clear whether he would get it or not. In the end he simply couldn't show the top brass that there was a need.

About six months after he arrived in Japan there was an international meeting of heart surgeons in Tokyo. As was usually the case, the meeting was sponsored almost entirely by companies that made products used by surgeons. Jack knew many of the manufacturer's reps back in Texas, but for international meetings like this one, the companies sent their vice presidents of sales or corporate marketing directors to represent their products. Jack took advantage of the occasion to meet many of them, anticipating he might need their help

THE CALLING

keeping his program on the leading edge of the ever-changing technology.

On the second day of the meeting he was introduced to the president of a surgical instrument manufacturer located only a few kilometers west of Tokyo. Shinti Naryama was a thirty-five-year-old entrepreneur who was trying to break into an industry that had been dominated by German companies for more than a hundred years. To do so he decided he would need a very narrow focus, so his goal was to restrict his company to making cardiovascular instruments only. What he hoped would differentiate his brand even further was not just the exceptional quality, but also his company's willingness to custom fit instruments for individual surgeons. To Jack, this idea was nothing short of brilliant.

At six-three, Jack's hands were naturally much larger than those of the five-two female resident he had trained with, and both of their hands were much different than those of one of the stout faculty surgeons who had trained them, yet they were all expected to use basically the same instruments. He had seen many aspiring young residents struggle as they tried to work with the one-size-fits-all tools of the trade. The surgeon's ability to adapt had become another variable critical to the outcome of the procedure. It only made sense to contour the tools to match the user instead of the other way around.

The argument made against individually tailored instruments was that they would be too expensive. Jack thought that sounded like an excuse fabricated by the hospitals who wanted to standardize equipment, like they did everything else, to save money. He accurately pointed out that in the early days of surgery every surgeon owned their own instruments, and most of the pioneers had them custom made to their own specifications. This fact was reflected in the names of nearly every instrument in every hospital set. They all had surgeons' names attached to them, like Mayo, DeBakey, Crile, Oschner, Cooley, Metzenbaum, and many others. While he didn't feel the need to have an instrument named after him, he did see the benefit of making modifications to the more critical hand tools to fit his specific needs.

"What would it take to get a custom made vascular needle holder?" he asked.

"That depends on whether it is a minor modification of an existing design or one where we have to start from nothing," Naryama replied.

"I think your ideas have some real merit, and I'd like to talk with you about some modifications I would like to see to the vascular needle holder and forceps I've been using."

The young businessman smiled knowingly and responded, "I'd be happy to come by your office. I am leaving the country for another meeting in Los Angeles in two weeks, but I am free to meet with you next week."

"Great!" Jack shook his hand and suggested Naryama call his secretary to arrange a time when they could get together.

◆◆◆◆◆◆◆◆◆

"Mr. Naryama is here," Joyce announced over the intercom.

"Send him in," Jack replied.

The diminutive Japanese businessman came into Jack's cluttered office carrying a large briefcase in his left hand. "Hello, Dr. Roberts," he said as he extended his right hand and nodded his head slightly combining the customary greetings of their two cultures.

Jack responded in kind, and after the usual pleasantries he asked Naryama what he had in his briefcase. The businessman needed no further prompting as he quickly put the case on Jack's desk and opened it, revealing an elaborate display of stainless steel instruments, all with gold plated handles. "These are our standard pediatric vascular instruments, any of which can be modified to meet your specific needs."

What Jack had always complained about was the instruments that felt good in his hand, based on weight and balance, were larger and more bulky than what he needed for the extremely delicate tissue manipulation required in pediatric heart operations. The ones he preferred based on their finer, more precise tips had handles that seemed too small and fragile in his large hands. It didn't take long for him to identify a couple of needle holders in the case which fit the two categories he had just described.

Of all the instruments used by surgeons, Naryama knew the most critical one was the needle holder. This was especially true of cardiac and vascular surgeons. The needle holder is used to pass small curved suturing needles through the thin walls of veins, the thicker walls of arteries, and even the tough fabric of artificial vascular grafts. He understood the importance of the surgeon's ability not only to control the needle, but also to feel the variable resistance that each material offered to ensure the smooth passage of the trailing suture. It came as no surprise to him that a custom needle holder was the first priority of Dr. Roberts, as it was for most of the surgeons he encountered.

"What I'd like is a needle holder with these jaws," he said, pointing to a delicate five-inch instrument, "with the weight and feel of this handle." He held up the second instrument, which was more than three inches longer and at least twice as heavy."

"We can definitely do that. It will require a slight modification to the central fulcrum of the larger handle, but it will not change the way the handle feels in your hand. It will allow the delicate jaws to open and close with the precision of the smaller one."

"That sounds perfect," Jack said. After a brief pause he added, "I have the same issue with forceps."

Naryama had anticipated that the forceps would be the next priority. Surgeons typically use vascular forceps in their non-dominant hand, to hold the tissues as they suture with the needle holder in their dominant hand. Together they are the two major tools of the surgeon's trade, and are truly extensions of their fingers. As such, they need to fit better than any glove.

Jack again selected a longer, heavier pair that rested comfortably in his left hand along with a smaller more delicate pair with a fine, non-crushing tip. "Can you merge these two as well?" he asked.

"Absolutely," he replied. "Would you prefer a step-off transition or a more tapered one?"

"Tapered, for sure."

"How far from the tip would you like the transition to begin, and how long would you want the transition zone to be?"

Jack held the long forceps in his hand and simulated its use by grasping the skin on the back of his right hand. He then repeated the process using the shorter instrument. "To maintain the weight and feel I think the transition should start about here," he said, pointing to a spot two inches from the tip, "and it should end about here," he said, moving his finger down to within a half inch of the tip.

♦♦♦♦♦♦♦♦♦

Two months after his facility became operational, Jack was the subject of high praise at a meeting of the Pacific Air Force Command at Hickam Air Force Base near Honolulu, Hawaii. One of their own colonels had been visiting a Japanese facility near Tokyo when he started having severe chest pain. He was rushed to the Yokota Air Base hospital where he underwent emergency heart catheterization followed by a four vessel coronary bypass performed by Major Roberts. The emergency processes Jack had put into place had worked flawlessly, and had saved the senior officer's life. He was on the verge of a massive heart attack due to a near total blockage of the left main coronary artery, the so-called "widow maker" lesion.

Jack received a citation for the exemplary work he had done setting up the facility, and he didn't know it yet, but he was now in line for promotion to lieutenant colonel. The morale of his team was also very high, not just because of the officer they had helped save, but because of Jack's management style. He believed that well trained and highly skilled people should be allowed to function with more autonomy than was typical in a military installation. The nursing staff was allowed to create many of their own nursing protocols, rather than relying on templates produced by some functionary back at the Pentagon. As a result they tended to be even more critical of their efforts and worked even harder to ensure optimal results. Jack had challenged every one of them to adopt the cultural slogan of their buddies in the Marine Corp, "Improvise, Adapt, and Overcome."

Their collective abilities and composure were tested again about a month later when, over a one week period, three critically ill children came in through the receiving department, all in need of cardiac surgery. The first was a local defense contractor's eight-month-old son whose heart was rapidly failing due to a large atrial septal defect. Jack recognized the problem and would have treated it himself had he had the modified heart-lung machine he'd asked for, but instead he was forced to transfer the child to a civilian hospital in Tokyo. He learned the next day that the child had died during surgery.

The second child was the newborn daughter of an American couple living and working near the base. This baby had a different, even more serious birth defect where the main arteries coming out of the two sides of the heart were switched. It was called transposition of the great vessels, or TGV. Again, Jack could have fixed the problem, but due to the lack of pediatric bypass, he was forced to transfer this baby as well, this time to Hawaii. Two days later he was informed that infant had also died, not from the surgery, but from an intestinal condition known as necrotizing enterocolitis.

Jack's entire team was in a state of depression when a third baby was brought in by his father, an enlisted man. The one-week-old boy was the product of his relationship with his Japanese girlfriend. The child had been born at a local hospital, but when he started breathing heavily and became listless, the mother called the airman who brought him to the base hospital. The baby had a large patent ductus arteriosus and was in rapidly developing heart failure when Jack saw him. He estimated the child might not make it through the night, and since the problem could be corrected without the need for cardiopulmonary bypass, he decided to take the baby to the OR himself. He didn't have all the instruments he felt he needed so he called his friend Shinti Naryama to see if he could borrow a pediatric vascular set.

Within an hour the young CEO personally delivered a complete set of pediatric cardiovascular instruments, including the new custom needle holder and forceps Jack had ordered. The surgeon was beyond grateful and asked, "Do you want to come in and watch this procedure?"

"Of course!" Naryama said with the excitement Jack knew all too well.

As Jack performed the ligation of the PDA using the new instruments, the Japanese businessman was mesmerized by what he thought was the truest art form he had ever witnessed. There was something about watching a highly skilled surgeon using precision instruments to correct a problem with a living,

THE CALLING

beating heart, that transcended what most people referred to as health care. Like Naryama, no one else in that hospital had ever seen this procedure and when the baby survived, the legend of Jack Roberts grew.

◆◆◆◆◆◆◆◆◆

After fourteen months in Japan, Jack was transferred back to Wilford Hall Medical Center. He was nearing the end of his two-year commitment, but he was truly enjoying his time in the Air Force and was considering making a longer term commitment if the opportunity was right. The commander of the hospital called him into his office shortly after he arrived.

"Roberts," he said, "I know you are close to getting out, but I'd like for you to consider heading up our cardiac surgery section here at Wilford Hall."

Jack stood silently in front of the colonel's desk, but not at attention. He knew he needed him, and he intended to see what he could get in return.

The old man, as he was often referred to, was only in his early fifties but his hair had grayed and he'd developed more than just a bit of a belly.

"Of course that would mean an additional commitment of at least two years," the colonel stated.

"I'd like to think about it, sir," Jack replied.

"That's fine... Take a few days, but I need to know your decision no later than the end of the month." They both realized that was only three days away so he wasn't giving him much time. "And by the way," he added with a smile, "it comes with a promotion to lieutenant colonel." He let his statement hang in the air, waiting for Jack to respond.

"That is a very enticing offer, sir." Now it was Jack's turn to lay out his terms. "When I was here as a resident I was allowed a three-month sabbatical in London to study pediatric heart surgery, but other than that I have not had formal training in that area. I would like to request the Air Force allow me to spend one year in a pediatric cardiac surgery fellowship. If you can make that happen I would be willing to sign on for an additional four years and establish a pediatric heart program here at Wilford Hall."

The colonel furrowed his brow. He wasn't used to negotiating with anyone over appointments or promotions, but he knew Jack had him over a barrel. "When exactly would you plan to take this year off?"

"I was at a meeting of the Association of Thoracic Surgeons last month and I spoke to Dr. Fleming, the head of the pediatric cardiac surgery section at Johns Hopkins, in Baltimore. They have an opening coming up next summer and he said I could have it, but I would need to let him know fairly soon." In fact, Jack had already committed to the position, he just figured he'd try and get the Air Force to pay him while he got the training. "That would give me a little over a year to groom one of the existing faculty members to take over for me while I'm gone. When I return in the summer of 1983, I would reassume my role as section chief, and go to work setting up the US military's first pediatric heart program."

There it was! He had outlined what it would take for him to stay in the Air Force beyond the next three months, and now it was the colonel's turn to "think about it."

"You drive a hard bargain, Jack, but I like the way you think. Let me run your proposal by a couple of people at the Pentagon and I'll let you know. Fair enough?"

"Fair enough, sir…"

The old man didn't have any doubt that he could get the necessary approval, he just wanted to let Jack stew a bit. What he didn't realize was that Jack had an alternate plan if this didn't go through the way he wanted. Fleming had invited him to join the surgical faculty at Johns Hopkins for a year prior to the fellowship.

♦♦♦♦♦♦♦♦♦

Jack Roberts was a born leader. He seized the position of section chief with the same enthusiasm and dedication he used when performing every operation. He actively sought the opinions of his fellow surgeons, but also interviewed every nurse and most of the surgical technicians, asking each one what they saw as problems and how they would fix them if given the opportunity.

Morale had never been higher as their new boss attempted to implement many of the suggestions they offered. He started a twice monthly Grand Rounds conference and invited not only the physicians but also the staff nurses from the operating room, the recovery room and the intensive care unit. They were held on Saturday when there was no elective surgery and attendance was strictly voluntary. At first the turnout was modest, but within a few months word spread regarding the inclusive nature of the presentations and discussions. Soon the small auditorium was full for what became known as Roberts' Rounds.

When it came time for Jack to leave for Baltimore, he appointed Dr. Robert Franklin, another young cardiothoracic surgeon, to serve as interim section chief. Franklin was a couple of years older than Jack, but he had come to Wilford Hall six months after Jack. He was a very capable heart surgeon, but his real love was peripheral vascular surgery. Together he and Jack made a great team, since Jack did almost all the hearts and Robert did the major blood vessel work, largely outside the chest. Jack knew the section was in capable hands, but he made Franklin promise to continue conducting what would now be called Robert's Rounds. The difference was subtle, but the importance of the name change was not lost on Dr. Franklin.

The year he spent at Hopkins was one of the best of Jack's life. He worked closely with Dr. Fleming and learned so much more than just the techniques, he learned how to communicate with the children and their parents. He tried to mirror the educational approach the older surgeon had mastered many years before. He saw a wide variety of conditions, rivaling his experience in London, but this time he was the primary surgeon for virtually every case. He could not have asked for better training or a more remarkable man under which to study.

While Jack was away, a bright young pediatric cardiologist was recruited into the Air Force through the Berry Plan and was assigned to Wilford Hall. The commandant had rightly assumed that Jack would need a non-surgeon heart specialist to get his program up and running. What he hadn't considered was the naturally competitive relationship that usually existed between cardiologists and their surgeon counterparts.

Dr. Horatio "Buzz" Jackson was born and raised in rural Alabama. He was a brilliant student who had attended the University of South Alabama in Mobile on an academic scholarship. He had gone on to medical school at Emory University in Atlanta, Georgia, where he also completed his internal medicine and cardiology training. He then did an additional fellowship in pediatric cardiology at the Massachusetts General Hospital in Boston. Like Jack he was a "Berry Planner," but unlike Jack, his single mother, who was raising three other children, had no means of helping him financially. The fact that he was a minority student in the South was both a curse and a blessing. There was no way he could get a loan from any of the banks in southern Alabama, despite what everyone claimed about equal opportunity lending, but because of affirmative action he had been highly sought after. He'd been accepted to ten different medical schools, including Harvard, Johns Hopkins, Stanford, and Duke. He chose Emory because they had offered him a full scholarship.

Buzz was acutely aware of the fact that many minority students had been admitted despite having below average test scores, simply because of the color of their skin. His MCAT scores and college GPA were in the top ten percent of all applicants, but he still felt he needed to work harder than anyone in his class, just to prove that he belonged. Financially, he had been totally reliant on scholarships, part-time jobs and ultimately it was the assistance of the Air Force that made it possible for him to get through his final two years of training.

When he arrived at Wilford Hall, Buzz established a pediatric cardiology clinic and started promoting the latest nonsurgical catheter techniques for closing congenital heart defects, something he'd learned at Mass General. Robert Franklin hadn't really paid much attention to what the bright young cardiologist was doing, but when Jack returned from Hopkins things were different.

Upon his return to San Antonio, Jack was ready to make good on his promise to establish the region's first pediatric heart program. He had everything planned out. It would be housed at Wilford Hall, but he would enlist the help and active participation of his civilian friends at the nearby UT Health Science Center, making this program the first of its kind; a joint military/civilian health care delivery system. What he hadn't counted on was running into Horatio "Buzz" Jackson.

As soon as Jack got back to his home turf, he encountered the young cardiologist who had assumed control over the pediatric part of the intensive care unit. He went straight to the old man to inquire what was going on.

"Jackson seems to be doing some good work," the colonel said in response to Jack's question. "He came right in and hit the ground running."

"So, is he going to head up the pediatric heart program, or am I?" Jack asked with more hostility than he had intended.

"You are, of course," he replied, trying to calm Jack's fears. "But I figured that you'd need a cardiologist to help out with the diagnostic testing and that sort of thing. I think he'll be a real asset."

"I don't mind working with him as long as he's willing to abide by the rules I set." Jack realized he was sounding confrontational, and that wasn't his usual style. It was just that he had planned this whole thing out, and now he had a potential rival. His experience with cardiologists had always been confrontational, and in his mind that was because they always wanted to run the show. What he failed to recognize was that the cardiologists said the same thing about the heart surgeons.

Initially the relationship between Jack and Buzz was chilly to say the least. To the staff of the hospital it seemed each one was looking to prove themselves smarter and more dedicated than the other. About six weeks after Jack's return, a one-year-old girl with a known sinusvenosus-type atrial septal defect was brought to the cardiology clinic by her mother. The mother had noticed the child was sleeping more than usual and her breathing was becoming more labored. Buzz did the standard work up and was convinced the defect would close on its own. When the mother asked about surgery to fix the problem he simply reassured her that everything would be fine. Two days later she returned with the baby who was clearly getting worse. He admitted her to the hospital, placed her on oxygen, and scheduled her for an urgent cardiac catheterization.

At Mass General, Buzz had used a new procedure where an artificial patch was inserted through a special catheter threaded into the heart through a major vein of the leg or neck. These new approaches were designed to close some of the more common birth defects, including ASDs like this one. Unfortunately, Buzz had a problem getting the patch to deploy properly and had to abandon the attempt. That's when he decided he had to call the surgeon.

The baby's condition was deteriorating rapidly and Jack carefully reviewed the results of the cardiac cath that Buzz had performed.

"I think we need to get her to the OR right now," he said to Buzz who was obviously shaken by his inability to fix the problem.

They went out together to talk to the mother who was extremely worried and upset. Although Buzz was standing right beside Jack, she said, "I have been asking about surgery to fix my daughter's heart for two days, but he said he could fix it without an operation." The mother motioned toward Buzz but didn't take her eyes off Jack.

Despite the fact the child's condition was critical, Jack calmly explained, "Most of the time these ASDs can be closed with the technique Dr. Jackson used, but not always. It was certainly worth the try, but given the fact that it didn't work, and your daughter's condition is getting worse, I would recommend surgery as soon as possible." He was trying his best to reassure the anxious mother without blaming Buzz for the delay. "I have called in the heart team and we should be ready within the hour."

The procedure took just over an hour and a half to complete. Buzz came into the OR after they were on the pump and watched as Jack expertly sutured a small piece of the child's own tissue, harvested from the sac around the heart, over the dime-sized defect between the two upper chambers. Once they were in the recovery room they went together to talk to the mother. She was extremely relieved and grateful, not just to Jack, but to Buzz as well.

"I really appreciate the way you handled the situation," Buzz said with obvious contrition in his voice.

"I wasn't sure we were gonna make it," Jack responded.

"What do you mean?" Buzz asked in surprise.

"That baby almost didn't make it through induction of anesthesia," he replied. "Her pressure and her O2 sats dropped just as we were putting her to sleep."

Jack knew that his colleague hadn't been aware that the baby had crashed, because by the time he came in the room everything was under control. "If we'd waited any longer I don't think she would have pulled through."

Buzz thought Jack was exaggerating for effect, so his response was a bit more casual than Jack thought appropriate. "Well, I appreciate your help, especially with the mother."

Jack thought his response was a little strange, but he wasn't going to pursue it further. There would be a time and place to discuss the management of this case later.

The next day as Buzz was headed into the ICU he ran into the anesthesiologist who was leaving the unit after checking on the little girl.

"So, how's she doing?" Buzz asked in a rather nonchalant manner.

"Pretty good, considering," he replied.

"What do you mean, 'considering'?"

"Well, considering we came damned close to losing her. If Roberts hadn't gotten her on the pump as fast as he did she would have died. I was giving her everything I had to support her pressure, but she was sinking fast." He paused as Buzz stood motionless. "This morning she actually looks a hell of a lot better than I expected."

Buzz turned quickly from what had become a one-sided conversation and headed into the unit. The one-year-old's color was pink and her lungs sounded much clearer than they had before surgery. The heart murmur was gone. This was the result he had expected from the treatment he had tried.

He went to the nurses' station and started writing a note on the baby's chart as Jack came up from behind. "How's she doing?" he asked.

"She's doing great, thanks to you," Buzz said as he turned to face Jack. "The anesthesiologist told me what happened, and I owe you an apology."

"Don't be silly," he responded with a slight wave of his hand.

"No, seriously, I really owe you. I had no idea how bad things were. You saved my butt."

"Listen," Jack said, "this isn't about saving anybody's butt. The work we do is to save our patients, not each other."

"Well, I still appreciate the fact that you were there when that little girl needed you."

"You know, I just spent a year at Hopkins and I watched a bunch of kids treated successfully with catheter-based techniques, and I saw a few that didn't go so well. I'm not gonna tell you not to try what you did, because I think the less trauma we cause, the better it is for these kids. The only thing I would ask is that you discuss these cases with me in advance."

"You're right, I should have made sure you were available."

"What would be even better would be for us to discuss each case, even if not as formal consult. I think our patients would benefit from our collective knowledge. At Hopkins we didn't operate on any elective cases without involving the cardiologist, and they didn't cath any kid without discussing the case with us."

"I think that sounds like a great approach," Buzz said as he extended his hand.

As Jack took his hand, they began a professional relationship that would last far longer than either of them anticipated.

◆◆◆◆◆◆◆◆◆

"As soon as we get to the hospital Dr. Jackson will be taking your baby to the cath lab to confirm the diagnosis," Jack said, as the limo exited the freeway on the South side of downtown.

"So you've been working with him for how long?" Franco asked.

"Let's see, he came to Wilford Hall in '83, so more than twenty years. After our years in San Antonio we both decided we wanted to go into private practice in '88. The children's hospital here in Fort Worth was brand new, and we thought it would be fun to keep working together. After all these years we're still best friends. It's almost like we're married, you know?" Jack said with a laugh.

CHAPTER 15

Buzz Jackson was standing just inside the emergency entrance to the children's hospital when the ambulance arrived. As the paramedics rolled the baby through the doors the young woman who was in charge of the transport caught his eye and silently shook her head. Buzz understood her meaning, the baby was not doing well. Her oxygen levels had dropped and her respiratory rate had increased from thirty to forty breaths per minute. Perhaps it was the pressure change during the flight or maybe the right side of her heart had chosen that moment to fail. Either way the situation was far more critical than he had expected.

"Let's take this baby straight to the cath lab," he said, as he recognized the need to bypass the usual emergency department staging. "Dr. Patel, would you come with me?"

Radha understood what he needed and responded, "I'll be right behind you," she said before turning to Gabriella who stood wide eyed as she watched the sudden increase in activity around her baby.

"Dr. Jackson is going to take Christina directly up to the cardiac cath lab where he'll have everything he needs to stabilize her condition," she explained to the suddenly frightened mother.

The limo, with Franco and Jack, was still several minutes behind the ambulance, so Radha realized she was about to abandon this terrified woman, leaving her alone in a strange hospital, in a foreign country, surrounded by people she didn't know, while another stranger was taking her baby away. She grabbed one of the ER nurses and said, "Come with us."

The three women hurried to catch up to the small group led by Dr. Jackson. They reached the staff elevator just as it was closing, but Buzz reached out and stopped the sliding stainless steel doors, allowing them to crowd in before the mechanism closed again behind them.

Radha turned to Gabriella again and gestured toward the ER nurse. "This is Amy Price, one of our staff nurses," she said, as calmly as she could manage. "I'm going to need to help Dr. Jackson in the cath lab, so I'm going to leave you with Amy, at least until your husband and Dr. Roberts arrive." The young mother's look had progressed from alarm to panic as she grasped the gravity of what was transpiring.

"I'm Dr. Jackson, the cardiologist," Buzz said, addressing Gabriella across the small stretcher where her baby lay struggling to breathe. "Your daughter's condition appears to have worsened as a result of the flight, and I need to see what we can do to stabilize her before Dr. Roberts can correct her heart defect."

He wasn't sure she understood him as she stood silently crying. Radha had placed one arm around her shoulder both for emotional and physical support. As the elevator door opened on the second floor the group of six adults and the tiny infant moved rapidly down the hallway to the cath lab. As Buzz and the transport staff entered through the automatic sliding doors, he motioned for Radha to accompany him.

"I'll be right there," Radha said as he disappeared into the lab. She continued to hold Gabriella, walking with her to the small waiting area just across the hallway. She sat down next to her and spoke again in her tender yet authoritative voice. "You will need to wait here with Amy," she instructed. "I feel sure Dr. Jackson will be able to help Christina, but he needs me to help him, so I'm going to leave you here with Amy. Your husband should be here very soon, and I'll be back out to let both of you know how she's doing just as soon as I can."

Gabriella looked into Radha's concerned face through her own stream of tears and nodded. As Radha stood to leave, the young mother grabbed her wrist with both her trembling hands, causing the doctor to pause and turn back toward her again. "God be with you," she said, holding on another second before finally releasing her desperate grip.

As Radha disappeared through the doors, Gabriella put her hands over her face and began sobbing. Amy put her arm around her shoulder and the young mother automatically turned her head into this stranger's knowing embrace.

◆◆◆◆◆◆◆◆◆

"Where is the Gutierrez baby?" Jack asked as he and Franco entered the ER.

"Dr. Jackson took her straight to the cath lab," the head nurse replied, revealing the new gravity of the situation.

"Where is the mother?"

"She and Dr. Patel went with them to the second floor."

Jack turned to Franco whose face had lost its controlled calmness. "They are all upstairs," he said, trying not to show his alarm. He led the way as the two men went up the elevator to find Franco's wife and child.

As Franco saw his wife sobbing in the arms of a woman he didn't recognize he assumed the worst. He rushed to her, and embraced her with his familiar arms. They spoke rapidly, but softly to each other in Spanish, as she tried to explain what had happened. Jack stood silently watching them until Amy approached him with her own explanation as to why Dr. Jackson had brought the child directly to the lab.

"I'm going to go check on Christina," he said as he put his hand on Franco's shoulder, before leaving the two of them once more in the care of the young nurse.

◆◆◆◆◆◆◆◆◆

"Dr. Jackson has stabilized her condition somewhat," Jack said, as he sat down next to the couple who were emotionally drained. It had been more than an hour since they had received any word.

"Dr. Patel placed a breathing tube into her windpipe, and she is now on a ventilator." His voice was still very concerned, but he was trying his best not to alarm them as he made the ventilator sound like a routine measure. "I feel pretty sure that the air pressure change during the flight caused her to lose the ability to maintain enough oxygen in her bloodstream," he explained, as they both looked at him anxiously, hoping what he had to say next would be better news.

"The cardiac catheterization showed exactly what we expected," he continued. "She definitely has Tetralogy of Fallot, but she has also developed an abnormal heart rhythm that is reducing the heart's ability to pump efficiently." He paused for a moment to make sure they understood there was a complicating factor. "Originally, I had planned to wait until tomorrow to do the surgery, but given this change in her status, I think it best we proceed with the surgery right away. All we are waiting on is the blood to be available from the blood bank, and then we'll go straight to the OR."

"Does this change make the procedure more dangerous?" Franco asked.

"Unfortunately, yes," Jack replied without hesitation. "There is an increased risk we may not be able to get her off the pump, and the longer we wait the greater that risk becomes."

"Can you give us an idea what her chances are?" he asked. The businessman was used to making decisions based on probabilities. Everything he did had a risk/reward analysis attached.

"I'm sorry to say that the presence of this rhythm problem changes things considerably. I'd say her chances of surviving the operation are at best about fifty percent."

Franco nodded his head knowingly as Gabriella began crying again as she buried her head into his chest.

One of the ICU nurses had come up behind him with the documents he'd requested. She handed them to him on a clipboard with a pen attached.

"I have a couple of permits for you to sign," he said apologetically. He was always uncomfortable with this process because it seemed so insensitive, especially during such an emotional time. "One for the surgery and the other for the cardiac cath, which she's already had."

He handed the documents to Franco and indicated where he needed to sign. As he accepted the pen the trembling in his typically steady hand revealed the fear Franco was trying desperately to conceal. He signed both forms rapidly and handed the clipboard back to the nurse who quickly returned to the cath lab.

"There is a chapel just down the hall," he said, pointing to the sign that marked "Interfaith Chapel."

Gabriella raised her head, pulling slightly away from her husband as she looked at Jack and asked, "Can I see my baby?"

"I'm sorry," he said sadly, she is still being treated in the cath lab, and there just isn't any way for me to make that happen."

Gabriella closed her reddened eyes briefly, and when she opened them again she asked, "Is there a priest in this hospital?"

"Yes, of course," he said. "I will send for Father Stevens and have him meet you in the chapel."

◆◆◆◆◆◆◆◆

"I don't know, Jack," Radha said shaking her head. "I've got a rhythm but I'm not able to get a pressure." She felt she was losing the young life.

"Just give me another thirty-seconds and we'll be on pump."

Jack was working feverishly. He had gotten her tiny chest open in less than three minutes and was now placing the loops around the two large veins leading into the heart. The upper portion of the tiny organ was quivering instead of beating, and Jack knew it wouldn't be long before the thick muscular pumping chambers followed the same pattern. If that happened before he got her on the pump it would be unlikely that anything he did after that would change the ultimate outcome.

As soon as he inserted the last line he said, "Okay, Alex, start the pump." Jack instructed the technician to begin taking over the function of the child's heart and lungs. He clamped the aorta and as he did the heart skipped a beat, then another, then suddenly the lower chambers began to quiver. This ventricular fibrillation was what he had feared, but now that she was on the pump he knew her brain and other vital organs were getting the oxygen they desperately needed, but had not been getting since the moment the umbilical cord had been cut.

Jack quickly filled the area around the heart with ice, and the quivering slowly subsided. His mind drifted back to the first time he saw a human heart lying motionless in the chest, and how Dr. Lillehei had revived it with just a squeeze of his hand. He could only hope that he'd be able to duplicate that feat once the repair was completed.

◆◆◆◆◆◆◆◆◆

"Dr. Roberts wanted me to let you know that your daughter is on the pump now and he expects the operation to take another hour or so." The nurse giving the report had come out of the main OR doors dressed in light blue scrubs. She found the parents in the chapel where they had been joined by Father Stevens. The trio was sitting on one of the padded bench in the front of the chapel with Gabriella flanked by the two men.

"Thank you," Franco replied somewhat dismissively, but Gabriella acknowledging the messenger with a tentative smile.

"Please tell him we are praying for God to guide him," she said, the strength in he voice having returned.

"I will," the nurse replied before leaving them to their prayers.

"I have known Dr. Roberts for many years," the priest said. "He is an excellent surgeon, but more than that he is a man of strong faith. He believes that God does his work through him and the members of his team."

"We spent several hours together on the plane," Franco said. "He told me he grew up near here and returned to be near his mother after his years in the military."

"Yes," the priest said. "He and Dr. Jackson came here at the same time in 1988."

◆◆◆◆◆◆◆◆◆

It turned out Jack and Buzz didn't need the help of the civilian physicians in San Antonio as they created the Air Force's first pediatric heart program. In 1986 they opened the doors of the US military's only facility dedicated exclusively to the care of children with all types of heart problems. It hadn't required any new construction, they were able to remodel an older part of the hospital previously used for rehabilitation of war-related injuries back in the Vietnam era. They created two dedicated operating rooms, a cardiac cath lab, a six-bed ICU and a twenty-bed inpatient unit. An outpatient facility was carved out of an adjacent office building, and that's where both officers set up their personal offices. Buzz had been named the director of cardiology services and based on Jack's recommendation, and he was promoted to the rank of major. Jack became the director of cardiac surgical services for the new unit, but by the end of the year he was also named chairman of the department of surgery. Both men appeared headed for lifelong careers in the Air Force.

The idea of a career in the Air Force wasn't something Buzz had anticipated when he first signed up. He didn't want to have to answer to a superior officer for the rest of his life, but since coming to Wilford Hall he had enjoyed far more autonomy than he'd ever expected. He knew that was in part because of the highly specialized nature of his training, but it was mostly due to the relaxed atmosphere that Jack had created. He knew many of his fellow Air Force physicians who were based in other facilities where the environment was far more regimented.

There was another reason why Buzz was enjoying his time in the military. Shortly after coming to Wilford Hall, he had met a beautiful young Air Force nurse who was working on the medical floor. It wasn't long before he and Charlotte Robinson became romantically involved and after a year Buzz decided it was time to commit to a lifetime with the twenty-five-year-old from Georgia, who he described as "the perfect peach." A few months later they were married in a formal military wedding in the base chapel. Naturally, Jack was his best man.

At the reception, Jack proposed a toast to the young couple.

"I have known Horatio Jackson for about two years now," he said, holding the microphone in one hand and a glass of champagne in the other. "After we got past our initial jousting to determine who would be the alpha male of the local herd, one of the first things I asked him was how he got the name Buzz. He told me he couldn't recall, but I suspected he wasn't being completely honest. So, yesterday I had the chance to meet his mother, and I asked her the same question. It seems that when he was eight years old, young Horatio decided he would attempt to cut his own hair with a pair of his mom's sewing scissors."

The crowd of officers and hospital staff members began to chuckle politely as Jack continued. "When she came home from her job at the beauty parlor, she found him still holding the scissors and sporting a big smile. It seems his thick curly hair had been assaulted and there were several huge holes, randomly scattered over his head." The laughter increased at the visual Jack had created.

"The only option his mom had was to take him down to the beauty shop and have one of her friends take the clippers to his head, just to even things up." Buzz was smiling, but he was obviously a little embarrassed by the story as Jack continued. "The next day when he showed up at school, the other kids started teasing him, led by his older brother. He tagged him with the name Buzz, as he repeatedly rubbed the top of his head." Jack was forced to paused a moment to allow the raucous laughter to subside.

"Obviously the name and the hairdo stuck, right up to today, but what I believe was more important to young Horatio's future than replacing the distinguished name with a more descriptive one, was the lesson he learned. He clearly had no talent with the scissors, so surgery was out of the question." Again the room erupted with laughter as Buzz raised his hands in protest.

"Charlotte," Jack said, directing his attention to the young bride, "be sure to keep all sharp objects out of his reach."

When the hoots and laughter subsided he continued. "In all seriousness, Buzz, whatever it was that prompted you to choose pediatric cardiology, the children of all Air Force families are forever grateful. You are not only my best friend, you made our heart program possible," he said with true admiration in his voice.

He waited another moment allowing the applause to subside then raised his glass, prompting everyone to raise theirs. "To Charlotte and Buzz... May life reward to you both according to all the good you do for others."

A career in the Air Force wasn't something Jack had considered either. However, he had distinguished himself early on, and had done nothing to tarnish his stellar record. He was recently appointed by the Air Force to be their delegate to the American Medical Association. It was a great honor, and it meant he had to attend two separate five-day meetings each year. He always enjoyed the camaraderie with physicians from all over the country representing every specialty during the June meetings in Chicago as well as the interim meetings in November, which were held in a different city every year. What he didn't particularly enjoy was the constant bickering that took place at these meetings. It seemed that every discussion eventually deteriorated into why specialists were paid more than primary care doctors. The arguments reminded him of a group of children arguing over who got the most Halloween candy.

In 1986 Jack was nominated by Dr. Fleming to serve on the board of directors of the Association of Thoracic Surgeons. His election was a foregone conclusion, since the nominating committee simply mailed its recommendations to the membership, and the balloting process was virtually automatic. He enjoyed being part of this prestigious organization and appreciated the fact he was among likeminded physicians.

Unfortunately these extra time commitments were competing with his full time duties. Running both the department of surgery and the pedi heart program, along with his involvement in various civilian organization had Jack spending more time traveling, or behind a desk, than he was in the operating room. One of the requirements of his new job that he despised was the creation of an annual budget. He had enlisted the help of a senior airman, Teresa Perkins, to assist with the process. The bright young woman had an accounting degree, which he thought would help her sort through the myriad costs associated with his department. He hadn't thought about Erin in years, but having a female accountant working on his staff stirred those now distant memories. Teresa was the polar opposite of his ex-wife in many ways, including the fact she was married. She was extremely self-confident, and prepared a comprehensive budget in less than a month. After three months Jack promoted her to staff sergeant and put her in charge of running his office.

As Gorbachev and Reagan ushered in the era of Détente the cold war began to thaw and the top brass at the Pentagon started catching heat from Congress to reduce its budget. Their directive was to cut unnecessary spending, but they failed to define what was meant by unnecessary. President Reagan created a new independent entity called the Base Realignment and Closure Commission for the expressed purpose of cutting the Air Force budget by recommending closure of redundant or obsolete bases. To stay off the list, each base had to convince the nine-member commission that it was vital to the security of the nation.

Jack went to Washington on two separate occasions to testify before the BRAC commission, pointing out the critical importance of Wilford Hall Medical Center, and in turn Lackland Air Force Base. He told the bureaucrats that the base and its medical facilities were vital to maintaining a healthy United States Air Force. He couldn't be sure his arguments would be successful, because the process had become highly politicized. Every military installation had a significant economic impact on the surrounding civilian community, and no politician wanted to see a base in their state of district closed. So far, no bases had been closed, but the cuts were coming for sure by early 1989.

Even though it was unlikely that Wilford Hall would get axed, Jack's boss told him he would need to cut his operations budget by ten percent to show the top brass their facility could be run more economically. With Teresa's help he was able to do his part. Together they found several places where significant savings could be achieved, mostly by eliminating redundant processes and excessive inventories. They found several expensive items in their sterile supply inventory that hadn't been used in more than five years, yet every year when those items on the shelf expired, they were simply reordered, only to gather dust until they expired again. It hadn't been necessary to furlough any personnel, but as members of the hospital staff retired or left upon completion of their tour of duty, he was able to rearrange assignments to increase the efficient use of existing personnel.

Eventually the stresses of running his department started taking their toll on

THE CALLING

Jack. He had put on about fifteen pounds due to the lack of exercise and all the fancy dinners he was attending on a regular basis. Late one afternoon Buzz stopped by his office on his way out the door well after six. Jack's staff had gone home more than an hour earlier.

"What are you doing for dinner?" he asked as he stuck his head through the door, and found his friend poring over a stack of papers.

"Hey, Buzz," Jack said as he looked up from a recent directive from the commandant, which he was rereading for the third time. His boss was requesting an itemized list of all the supplies used in open heart surgery, along with a cost analysis of each item over one hundred dollars. "What are you still doing here?.

"Charlotte took a few days off to visit her mom in Atlanta, so I'm batchin' it this week. You want to go grab a bite?"

"Sure, I was just looking for an excuse to get away from this mess."

"Let's check out that new Mexican place over on Bandera Highway," Buzz suggested.

"Okay, I'll meet you there in about twenty minutes."

It had been several months since Jack and Buzz had done anything together off the base, and he had been meaning to catch up on how married life was treating his friend. This would be a great opportunity, and since Charlotte was out of town he wouldn't feel guilty if they stayed out late.

◆◆◆◆◆◆◆◆

"I'll have a Lone Star," Buzz said, ordering what had become his favorite beer since moving to Texas.

"I'll have the same," Jack said, thinking that for whatever reason he hadn't had a Lone Star beer since he left Dallas, nearly fifteen years ago. "So, how's married life treating you?"

"It's great," Buzz replied. "You should try it," he added with a grin.

"Oh no!" Jack protested. "Been there... done that... I'm officially a confirmed bachelor."

"You just haven't met the right gal."

"Yeah, right," Jack said, with just a hint of disgust. "I'm not sure that woman exists, plus I don't have time to even be looking."

"Oh, she's out there all right, but I know what you mean about not having any time."

"Since I got my last promotion it seems I spend my time everywhere except the operating room."

"I believe they call that the Peter Principle," Buzz offered with a chuckle. "Everyone rises to a position that is at least one level above their competence."

277

"I'm not sure," Jack said, "I believe Teresa is competent to do my administrative job, and she is several pay grades below me."

"I know what you mean. I don't really manage my service. My staff does everything, I just sign orders and show up wherever they tell me."

The waitress sat the longneck brown bottles down in front of the two Air Force officers, whose blue uniforms stood out in the crowd of civilians that filled the restaurant. She also sat a large bowl of tortilla chips in the middle of the table along with two small bowls of homemade salsa. After a quick look at the rather limited menu, they both ordered the special, chicken enchiladas with sour cream sauce.

"You know," Jack said after a long draw on his beer, "I'm afraid the Pentagon is going to force us to shut down our pediatric heart program."

"Really?" Buzz said, never having considered the possibility.

"I believe that once they see how few kids we are seeing, compared to the large number of adults, they are likely to pull the plug."

"Surely not," Buzz objected.

"I received a notice from the commandant asking for an item-by-item list of all the supplies we use doing pedi hearts, and that can only mean one thing. They are looking to measure the costs of doing those procedures in-house, versus farming them out to one of the civilian hospitals." Jack had heard talk about similar cost-cutting measures at Walter Reed and Bethesda, and he figured the Hall would be next.

"Wow!" Buzz exclaimed. "If they pull something like that, I'm gone. I've fulfilled my obligation to the Air Force. I'd take my chances in private practice."

"I thought you might feel that way," Jack said calmly. "I've had some feelers out for several months."

"What do you mean, feelers?"

"Well, I never intended to make the Air Force my career, but as long as things were going okay, I figured I'd see where it led. But, as soon as they started talking budget cuts I started looking for opportunities in the civilian world."

"So, what have you found?" Buzz asked, knowing that his friend never talked about any problem until he had a solution to propose.

"There is a new children's hospital in Fort Worth and they don't have a heart surgeon yet," Jack explained the opportunity he had been introduced to by a pediatrician at the last AMA meeting. "It's a true state-of-the-art hospital, but they need someone, or ones, to help them put together a heart program."

"Fort Worth, huh?"

"Yeah, it's very near my old stomping grounds. My mom still lives in Hurst, which is only about twenty minutes away. Since my Uncle Joe passed away last year, she's pretty much alone now. I'm sure she'd love to have me a little closer."

"Don't you have an older sister?"

"Yeah, Janet," Jack agreed. "She teaches a class on music appreciation at the University of Houston. She and her husband, Leonard, have lived there since they finished college. They've got a couple of kids in high school and they are into all sorts of activities that make it difficult for her to get up to see Mom."

"What about your brother?"

"Ben is still out in California. When he finished his PhD in aerospace engineering at Stanford he went to work for the Jet Propulsion Laboratory at Cal Tech, but after a couple of years he got bored with that. He went to MIT for a year on a grant from the National Institutes of Health and got a second PhD in bioengineering. Now he's working for some big medical device consortium in Southern California."

"He obviously got the brains in the family," Buzz said with a laugh and a shake of his head.

"Yeah, he's beyond smart, but he never developed any real people skills. He's the ultimate lab rat."

"Do you see him much?"

"Not often enough… He usually comes home for Christmas and a week or so during the summers. We try to catch up occasionally by phone, but he's always busy, and so am I." There was obvious sadness in Jack's voice. "Anyway, I figure if I do end up leaving the Air Force, I should probably move a little closer to home."

"You said they are looking for someone, or ones, what did you mean by that?"

"Well, as we both know, to have a comprehensive heart program takes both cardiac surgery and cardiology."

"So you just presumed I would want to go with you to Fort Worth?" he said, cocking his head slightly to the side. Jack remained silent but smiled his crooked smile. "That's rather presumptuous of you, don't you think?"

"I wasn't presuming anything," Jack said, "and I haven't committed to anything yet." Technically that was true. "I told them that I'd consider it, but only if I could name my own chief of cardiology."

"You've got this all figured out, don't you?"

"I'm just planning ahead."

◆◆◆◆◆◆◆◆◆

In the summer of 1988, Jack and Buzz submitted their respective resignations as officers in the United States Air Force on the same day. Their actions came one day after Jack received a notice from the commandant that due to budgetary constraints, Wilford Hall Medical Center would be closing the pediatric heart program. The old man wasn't surprised by the actions of his two star physicians. He had expected it.

"So, what are you gonna do now?" the colonel asked.

"I figured I'd stay on until the unit closes September 1, then I'm moving back to North Texas to be near my mom. I'm going to start the pediatric heart program at the new children's hospital in Fort Worth, sir."

"Sure I can't talk you into another few years?"

"No, sir, I don't think so."

"I could make you a full colonel right now, and that would be a really sweet retirement in a few more years."

Counting his six years of residency, Jack had thirteen years in the Air Force, so he'd be eligible for full retirement in another seven years, and the idea of a retired colonel's income was enticing, but... "I'm not ready to start thinking about retirement just yet, sir."

"We're gonna miss you around here, Jack."

"I will miss you as well, sir, and everyone here. I will always consider this place my home."

"You are welcome to come back to visit anytime."

"Thank you, sir," he said. "I'm sure I will."

◆◆◆◆◆◆◆◆◆

"Okay, let's see if we can get this little lady off the pump," Jack said.

They had been on bypass nearly an hour. The defect between the two pumping chambers was larger than Jack had expected based on the cath pictures, and the right ventricular outflow tract was the tightest he had ever seen. It was no wonder this child was so near death when they arrived at the hospital.

He put the warm saline around the heart and injected a dilute solution of adrenaline directly into the right ventricle through one of the suture lines of the repair. He waited several minutes, but nothing happened. He repeated the process with more warm saline and adrenaline, this time adding some calcium chloride. Again he waited several minutes... nothing. The heart showed no sign of movement or electrical activity.

"How are we doing up there?" he inquired of Radha, but he knew if there was a problem on her side of the drapes he would have heard about it by now. In reality he was just trying to find something to do while he waited. This was always the most difficult time for him. He was naturally not a very patient person, but he had been taught, both by his mentors and by his own experience, that patience was necessary in these situations.

Jack turned to look at the clock, and as he did George said, "There's something."

He returned to inspect the heart again and saw nothing.

"I thought I saw a slight twitch in the left ventricle," George said. "Maybe I was just hoping."

Jack decided to try the Lillehei maneuver. He placed two fingers of his right hand behind the tiny heart and with his thumb gave a gentle squeeze. He waited for a few seconds then repeated the maneuver, but still nothing.

"Let's try injecting into the left ventricle," he said. Blake, the scrub nurse, handed him a small syringe filled with the most potent heart muscle stimulator in existence. He removed the plastic cover from the two-inch-long needle and pierced the center of the main pumping chamber. As he drew back on the syringe a small amount of blood that had filled the ventricle returned, then he rapidly injected the adrenaline into the center of Christina's heart. He waited and again, nothing was happening. Three more minutes passed.

"We've been on the pump for an hour and twenty minutes now, Dr. Roberts," the pump tech announced.

"What the hell difference does that make?" Jack replied angrily. He felt himself losing his composure for the first time in recent memory. "Let's try just the calcium chloride," he said a bit more calmly. Blake handed him another syringe and again he plunged it into the lifeless heart, but still nothing happened.

Jack was growing frustrated as he sensed his efforts might be futile. He began gently massaging the tiny heart again, and after a few compressions he paused for another few seconds before repeating his effort. Another ten minutes went by and the tiny organ that was biologically programmed to contract rhythmically for a hundred years or more remained motionless.

"How long has it been since we started warming?" he asked the circulating nurse.

"Thirty-five minutes, sir..."

Jack had never had a child develop what is known as a "stone heart," but he was certainly familiar with the phenomenon in adults. If the heart muscle remained without circulation for a prolonged period it can contract and remain firmly in spasm. The result is universally fatal, but this heart didn't appear to be contracted, it looked very relaxed, and inexplicably lifeless in this otherwise normal child's chest.

Jack sighed heavily, and everyone in the silent operating room heard him. He closed his eyes and prayed for guidance. What else could he do?

He decided to release the clamp on the aorta slightly to allow some of the back pressure from the pump to fill the coronary arteries. As he did the sudden pressure increase caused the heart to move just a fraction. He let off a little more and the muscle appeared to develop a deeper burgundy color but remained motionless.

"Let's try the adrenaline, calcium mixture again," he said through another sigh.

He injected into the right side again, but still nothing. He placed his fingers around the heart and squeezed two more times, but saw no reaction. He continued to hold the precious pump gently in his fingers and looked up at George. "You got any ideas?" he asked almost pleading with his assistant.

"I think you've done about everything that can be done, Jack."

At that moment he thought he detected a slight quivering with the tip of his index finger on the back side of the organ. He still couldn't see any motion, but he was pretty sure what he felt was a fine ventricular fibrillation.

"Let's have the paddles," he ordered. He knew it was pointless to defibrillate a heart that had no electrical activity, but perhaps what he felt was too faint to be detected. He placed the two electrical wands which looked like flattened iced tea spoons, connected to a machine near the head of the table.

"Charge!" he instructed Susan, and he heard the whine of the machine ramp up to a solid high-pitched tone. "Clear!" he instructed, as everyone stepped back so as not to be shocked themselves. "Now!" The nurse pushed the large red button on the defibrillator and the electric shock was delivered. The current flowed between the paddles, directly through the heart. He put the paddles down and reached into the chest to hold the tiny heart again.

"Yes!" There was definitely a fine quivering of the muscle. He could feel it ever so subtle, but it was there.

"Let me have the lidocaine," he said, sounding more hopeful than he had at any point during the forty-five minutes since they had begun trying to get the miniature heart started. Again he plunged the needle directly into the center of the heart and administered another drug.

"There!" George shouted as he pointed to a definite quiver in the dark red muscle.

"Let's have the paddles again," Jack said more quickly than before. "Charge!... Clear!... Now!"

As he pulled the paddles away the quivering had stopped and there was still no beating. He gently grasped the heart again and gave it a gentle squeeze, then another, and another. Suddenly he felt a rhythmic contraction, then another, but then nothing. "Atropine!" Jack demanded. He injected the heart one more time, this time with another medication to speed up the sluggish rhythm.

He began his massage again, and after two more compressions the tiny heart seemed to leap back to life in his hand. Slowly at first, then the contractions came faster and stronger.

"That's more like it!" he said, totally unaware that his forehead was covered with perspiration and under his gown his scrub shirt was soaked with sweat.

He quickly removed the clamps and tapes, allowing the heart to take over the function it was destined to perform, hopefully for many years to come. As they came off the pump, he asked Susan, "What was our total pump time?"

"Two hours and eight minutes, sir…"

"Is she doing okay, Radha?"

"Great!" she replied. "I had to give her something to slow down her heart, but her pressure is good and her O2 sats look great, much better than before we started."

Jack and George both worked quickly to close the tiny sternum that protected the now vigorously beating heart. "Would you finish closing for me, George?"

"Sure," his assistant said, recognizing the exhaustion in Jack's voice.

"Very well done everyone, thank you all," he said, as he stepped slowly away from the operating table.

CHAPTER 16

Franco stood as he saw the doctor approaching, placing his hand on his wife's shoulder, both to reassure her, and to support himself.

"Well," Jack said smiling through his fatigue, "It took a little longer than I anticipated, but your baby seems to be doing okay. We had a bit of trouble getting her off the pump. Her little heart didn't want to cooperate, but it seems to be beating normally now, and her color has improved dramatically." He just couldn't tell them how close they had come to losing their only child.

"Thank you, Dr. Roberts. I can't express our gratitude enough," Franco said as his eyes glistened with tears of relief.

"You are very welcome," Jack replied as he shook the grateful father's hand, "but I think it is God you should thank. I'm convinced He pulled her through with His own hands."

"That is what we have been praying for," Gabriella said through halting breath and tears of joy. "You are truly His instrument, and we have no other words to say except thank you."

As he stood in front of Franco, he realized just how weary he was. They had all been up since before dawn in another country. They'd flown three and a half hours, then he'd performed an extremely stressful two-and-a-half-hour operation. His fatigue reminded him of the nights on the trauma rotation at the county hospital, during his second year of his residency. He found that in instances like this, the exhaustion never showed until the task was completed, then it literally fell on his shoulders like a heavy yoke.

Franco stepped forward to hug him, wrapping his arms around Jack's shoulders, pressing his still moist scrub shirt against his back. "If there is ever anything I can do for you my friend, you only need to ask. Anything…"

"Thank you, but honestly, I have everything any man could ever want."

◆◆◆◆◆◆◆◆◆

Over the next few days Christina's recovery proceeded uneventfully. It was as if her operation had been totally routine. Franco and Gabriella were staying in a suite at the Worthington Hotel, but like most parents they spent most of waking hours at their child's bedside.

"Good morning," Jack said to the smiling couple as he entered the child's room in the ICU.

"Good morning," Franco replied and Gabriella smiled as broadly as she could manage given her level of physical exhaustion.

"How are we doing this morning?" he asked as he approached the sleeping infant. The breathing tube had been removed the day before, and she seemed to be breathing easily with only a small amount of supplemental oxygen. The heart monitor showed a smooth regular rhythm and her color was a warm pink. The nurse at the bedside was taking down an empty bag of beige-colored formula that had been connected to a small feeding tube placed through the baby's nose and into her stomach.

"She's doing great, Dr. Roberts," the nurse replied. "She's been sleeping for the last couple of hours during this most recent feeding. She's had two wet diapers for me and she had a good-sized stool during the night." Jack knew that her kidney and bowel function was as important to her recovery as her heart rhythm, so he was glad to hear this part of the report.

"How about her labs?"

"They all look great except her albumin. It's better than yesterday, but is still a little low."

"I suspect it will take a few weeks before her nutritional status gets back to normal," he responded. "She wasn't getting many calories for the first few days of her life, and she's been using what little stored energy she had to heal that big incision."

Jack examined the thin line down the center of the baby's chest. The four inch long incision in the skin had been closed without any visible sutures, and the clear plastic dressing allowed Jack to see that it was healing without any signs of infection. He used his stethoscope to listen to her heart and lungs, then as he removed the instrument from his ears he smiled at her parents reassuringly.

"She sounds great. She looks strong enough to start taking some formula, so I think it's time to get the feeding tube out and see if she can fly on her own."

"How much longer do you think she will need to be in the hospital?" Franco asked.

"Assuming she's able to take enough fluids orally, I think we will be able to move her out of the ICU tomorrow. Another three or four days in the nursery and she should be ready to go."

"I know it is early," Franco said, "but I need to begin making plans for our return to Managua. Do you know when that might be possible?"

"My preference would be to have her stay here in the area for at least four or five days after discharge from the hospital, just to be sure she doesn't develop any problems." This was what Jack routinely recommended for all patients and their families from out of town. The hospital had a discount rate at a nearby hotel, but Jack was certain the Gutierrez family wouldn't be staying there.

"That reminds me," he said, "Elaina and I were discussing your situation last night."

Franco looked at him quizzically, and Jack realized they didn't know who he was talking about. "Elaina is my wife. She and my son David, whom you met, were with me in Nicaragua."

Franco nodded, understanding now to whom Jack was referring. Gabriella hadn't met either Elaina or David, but Franco had told her about Jack's enthusiastic teenage son, so she also nodded politely.

"Anyway, we were talking about your circumstance, and she suggested you come stay in our guesthouse until Christina is cleared to travel."

"We couldn't possibly impose on you and your family," Franco said shaking his head in protest.

"It would not be an imposition at all," he argued. "Besides, my wife is a long time pedi ICU nurse, and she would love nothing better than to help take care of Christina for a few days."

Franco looked at Gabriella to gage her response, then said, "I don't know. Let us discuss it and we will let you know."

"Fair enough," Jack agreed. "Oh, I almost forgot. Elaina asked me to ask you to join us for dinner tomorrow evening at the house. You guys have been eating restaurant food long enough. We figured you could use a home cooked meal."

Franco glanced again at Gabriella and she smiled approvingly. "We would be honored to have dinner with you and your wife, but please tell her not to go to any trouble on our account."

"Great! Here is our address." Jack quickly jotted down the number and street on the back of his business card and handed it to Franco. "I assume your driver can find it, but if not my number is on the front of the card. Around seven tomorrow evening?"

"We will be there, thank you for the invitation, Dr. Roberts."

"Please, call me Jack," he said as he moved on to see his next patient.

◆◆◆◆◆◆◆◆◆

The following evening at 7:00 p.m. sharp, the doorbell rang and Elaina answered it. She was dressed in a well-tailored, navy blue skirt and a white cotton pleated blouse. Jack loved this outfit, and he told her he thought it made her looked more like thirty than her actual age of forty-five.

"Hello," she said as she opened the door. "You must be Franco and Gabriella. Please come in."

Elaina was awestruck at the sight of the beautiful couple. Franco was wearing an expertly tailored suit she was certain had to be an Armani. It was charcoal gray with a fine silver pin stripe that matched his glistening tie. He had on a pair of thousand dollar alligator shoes that she suspected were also either Armani or Gucci.

Gabriella looked like anything but a new mother. She was wearing a stunning, pink satin dress that was cut off one shoulder. It had to be a designer original she thought. How in the world could she get into a custom fit dress less than a week after giving birth. Her hair was gathered expertly up on the back of her head exposing the smooth lines of her slender neck. Around it she wore a thin gold rope chain with a dazzling solitary five-carat diamond that rested just above the center of slanting neckline. She thought the couple looked as though they had just come from the red carpet at the Oscars.

"Thank you so much for inviting us to your home," Franco replied as he guided Gabriella by the hand across the threshold.

"Please come in and make yourselves at home," Elaina offered nervously. "I'm sorry Jack isn't home yet, but he should be here any minute. He just called and said he was leaving the hospital. Can I get either of you a drink? I have a bottle of chardonnay open, or I can fix you whatever you'd like."

"A glass of wine would be fine," Gabriella said.

"Nothing for me just now, thank you," Franco replied with more formality than she had expected. "You have a beautiful home," he added.

"Thank you. Please, make yourselves comfortable."

Elaina left them in the foyer as she went into the kitchen to retrieve the wine. The couple looked around the elegantly decorated entry with a large curved staircase leading to the second floor landing. The marble flooring in the foyer opened into a large formal living room with floor-to-ceiling windows at the far end. The landscaped backyard was highlighted by a rectangular pool that appeared to be an extension of the living room. At the far end of the room stood the magnificent white enameled Steinway grand piano. It had been Elaina's wedding gift from Jack fifteen years earlier.

As Franco looked around the foyer, among the various houseplants and antique accessories, he noticed the carving of a Madonna sitting under the open staircase. He was intrigued and left Gabriella's side to take a closer look. When Elaina returned with Gabriella's wine and a glass for herself, Franco asked, "Where did you get this Madonna? It is exquisite."

"The family of a little girl Jack operated on last month gave it to him," she explained. "Apparently her great grandfather carved it from a cypress knee about sixty years ago."

"Was this family from here in Texas?"

"No, they live just across the border in Matamoros, Mexico."

"I have never seen such detail in a wood carving," Franco said. "May I?" he asked as he reached to touch the statue.

"Of course."

He crouched down and stroked the smooth, delicate lines of the wooden image, inspecting it with both his vision and his touch. This was truly a masterpiece he thought.

"Sorry I'm late," Jack said as he came through the kitchen and into the foyer.

Franco stood and extended his hand toward his host, "It is good to see you, Dr. Rob... I mean, Jack."

"Thanks for coming," Jack offered as he shook Franco's hand before turning toward their other guest. "Gabriella, you look incredible," he said as he took her hand and leaned forward to kiss her cheek.

"Thank you," she said shyly.

"Are you all going out on the town later?" Jack just assumed by the way they were dressed they were going somewhere fancy after dinner.

"No," Franco said, wondering why their host would say something like that.

Jack started to inquire why they were so dressed up, but he caught Elaina's stare, and recognized he had better not go there. "I see you spotted our newest addition," he said, gesturing toward the Madonna.

"Yes, it is a magnificent piece," Franco replied. "Your wife was just telling us it was a gift from one of your patients."

"Yes," he began. "We were able to help a little eight-year-old girl from down in Mexico, and her family gave me this piece before they went back home. Apparently they considered it something of a family guardian, and they insisted that I have it."

"Was this a wealthy family?"

"Hardly," Jack replied with a sad smile. "They were extremely poor. They were in this country illegally trying to get medical help for the little girl. It's a long story." Jack paused then asked Franco, 'Can I get you a drink?"

"I'll have whatever you're having," he responded.

"Scotch okay?"

"Of course!"

"Why don't we sit down in the living room?" Elaina suggested, as Jack left to fix the drinks.

"Excuse me just a minute," Jack said. :I'll be right back." Instead of heading toward the bar, he turned down the hall into their bedroom. He felt uncomfortable in the clothes he had worn to work, especially given the way their guests were dressed, so he quickly changed into a pair of linen trousers and a fresh white shirt. He thought about wearing a tie, but figured that would make it obvious he was uncomfortable in his own home. He threw on a navy blue blazer and a pair of black loafers, then headed back to join the others.

He handed Franco a short crystal glass containing a couple of ounces of golden brown liquid. "Cheers!" he said as he raised his glass.

Franco tasted the straight whiskey and smiled. "My favorite! eighteen-year-old Macallan…"

"Wow!" Jack exclaimed. "You have quite a discerning pallet."

"I have been very fortunate in my life and my business," he responded. "I have been able to enjoy many of the finer things, and rare scotch is one of them," he said as he raised his glass to his lips again. He turned to Gabriella and took her hand and looked lovingly into her eyes. "However, this is the rarest of all my treasures, and thanks to your incredible skills, and God's guidance, she is the happiest I have ever seen her."

Gabriella smiled, and the small tear in the corner of her eye sparkled as the last golden rays of the setting sun streamed through the living room window, on to her beautiful face.

Jack didn't know what to say so he just took another sip of his scotch. Franco obviously loved Gabriella with much the same passion he felt toward Elaina, but for this man to credit him with providing her happiness, was beyond any compliment he had ever received.

"We are all so glad that Christina is doing well," Elaina said, feeling the need to break the silence. "I know how stressful times like this can be." She elected not to elaborate on her own experience with her own son.

As if on queue, the young man came into the kitchen from the garage, and half shouted, "Mom?"

"We're in here, David."

He came into the room and saw that his parents had guests. "Oh, excuse me," he said politely. "I didn't know…"

"David, you remember Mr. Gutierrez," his father prompted as the two men stood.

"Of course!" David said, excited to see the man who had flown his dad back from Nicaragua in his private jet. "How do you do, sir?"

"It is good to see you again, young man," Franco said as he shook David's young, but surprisingly strong hand. "This is my wife, Gabriella."

"It is very nice to meet you, ma'am," he said as he shook her delicate hand. He couldn't help but be impressed by this woman. He thought must be a movie star or something.

She remained seated, but spoke softly to him. "I understand you are planning to follow in your father's footsteps?"

"Yes, ma'am," he said with a shy confidence.

"I can only hope and pray that you will have the same impact on the lives of your patients that your father has had on ours."

Jack was feeling even more embarrassed, and was beginning to believe that inviting the parents of a patient into their home wasn't such a good idea afterall. "Are you having dinner with us?" he asked David.

"No, I'm going out with Amy. We're going to the movies."

"What are you planning to see?" Elaina asked.

"I don't know. I want to see the new Batman movie but Amy says she wants to see some chick flick about traveling pants, or something like that."

"Go see the chick flick," Jack said. "If you don't you'll never hear the end of it."

They all laughed as David said goodbye and ran up to his room to change.

"What an incredibly handsome young man," Gabriella said.

"Thank you." Elaina was now the one who was searching for words. "I better go check on dinner."

"Why don't you let me show you our guesthouse while Elaina is finishing up in the kitchen?" Jack said, motioning for them to follow. He opened the patio door and a warm evening breeze blew in, rustling the drapes.

The one bedroom guesthouse was located just off to the side of the pool area. It was separated from the garage by a small breezeway, covered with the new summer growth of English ivy. The front of the small bungalow faced the pool, and there was a private sitting area with an inviting canvas-covered swing.

"It's not terribly large, but it is comfortable," Jack said as he opened the door. The living room was furnished with a bamboo and wicker sofa and lounge chair, with tropical print cushions and a glass top coffee table. A small kitchenette was at the far end of the room, and the two areas were separated by a small breakfast bar, with two bar stools that matched the sofa and chair. The generous-sized bedroom was similarly furnished with a king-sized bed and dresser. The bedspread was a lavender and white floral print that complemented the off-white walls and bleached-oak flooring. A flat screen television was mounted on the wall above the dresser, and along the wall facing the pool was a pair of large French doors, offering a view of the pool and the landscape beyond. Elaina had asked Jack to retrieve David's old baby bed out of the attic, and after she cleaned it up, she'd had him set it up in one corner of the room, near the door leading into the large bathroom.

"This is such a beautiful place," Gabriella said, as she held on to Franco's arm.

"I hope you will accept our invitation to stay here," Jack said, as he looked questioningly at Franco.

"I don't know, Jack. You have already done so much for us."

"Look, this place is just sitting here. My mom comes and stays with us one or two weekends a year. Other than that it never gets used. Besides, I don't want to have to take David's old baby bed apart again, at least not just yet." He paused for a moment then added, "Why don't we go back in the house and have some dinner, and we can talk over the terms of your surrender."

◆◆◆◆◆◆◆◆◆

"Do you only operate on children?" Gabriella asked as she enjoyed the homemade lasagna and crisp garlic bread.

"No," Jack replied, "I still do some adult heart surgery over at the general hospital. When I first came to Fort Worth there weren't enough pediatric heart operations to keep me busy, so I did quite a few adult coronary bypasses and other cardiovascular procedures. Over the last few years several more surgeons have moved to town and they now do most of the bypasses and peripheral vascular procedures, which is fine by me. Most of the adults I do now are heart valve replacements and revision procedures that the other guys don't want to touch."

"What do you mean they don't want to touch?" Franco asked.

"Well, it's a little complicated," he said. "You see Medicare is the payer for most adult heart operations, since obviously most of those patients are older. A few years ago Medicare started a program to track the results of each individual surgeon, and compare them with what they said the results should be. If your results are as good as or better than the national average, you get paid a little more. But if your complication or death rates are higher than the average, your payments are reduced."

"That sounds reasonable," Franco said using his business logic.

"Well, theoretically I guess it is," Jack conceded. "The problem is the program makes many surgeons more concerned about their statistics than they are the patients. The highest risk patients, like the redo operations I mentioned, are much more likely to have a negative impact on the surgeon's numbers, so most of the guys do whatever they can to avoid taking those high-risk patients."

"That's disgusting," he said, staring at Jack with indignation.

"Well, it is just one of the problems with our payment system."

"I think I understand," Franco said. "As you know we have government-run health care in Nicaragua. It is not the same as here in the United States, but anyone who has any money doesn't go to the government hospital or the government clinic."

"Why don't we have our dessert out by the pool?" Elaina said, hoping to shift the conversation away from politics and medicine. She knew that if she let him, Jack would talk about what he called the decline in American medicine for the rest of the evening.

As Jack led their guests out onto the patio, the clear sky had allowed the evening temperature to drop into the mid-seventies. The azure blue pool was illuminated by an underwater light in the end nearest the house, creating a gentle glow to the entire patio area. Elaina brought out a tray of fresh strawberries and powdered sugar, along with four wine flutes and a bottle of chilled Asti Spumante. She sat the tray on the glass top oval table and put out four plates.

Jack poured the sparkling wine and he and Franco each took a glass and wandered slowly out toward the pool. They talked about the politics of Nicaragua and the coming political season in the US while Gabriella and Elaina sat at the table, savoring the sweetness of the fruit, dipped in the powdered sugar and the bubbly wine.

◆◆◆◆◆◆◆◆

The day before Christina was to be discharged Franco asked Jack if he would introduce him to the hospital administrator. Jack arranged the meeting to take place in Bob Anderson's office during the noon hour. Bob's administrative assistant had a light lunch brought in for the three men.

"Robert Anderson," he began his introductions, "this is Mr. Franco Gutierrez."

"It is very nice to finally meet you," Bob said as the two men shook hands briefly.

"I must apologize for not having come by to meet with you sooner," Franco said, "but we have been rather preoccupied, as I'm sure you can appreciate."

"Absolutely," Bob replied. "I trust your daughter is doing well?"

"Yes, very well, thanks to Dr. Roberts and Dr. Jackson and all of your wonderful staff."

"I'm very happy to hear that. I assume then that you found the service here to be satisfactory."

"It has been exceptional," Franco stated. "My wife and I have not encountered a single person who has been anything but kind and compassionate. Including all the doctors and nurses — even your janitors and housekeepers have a smile on their faces."

"I appreciate you saying that more than you know. That is what we strive for, and it is good to know that we are succeeding."

"I can assure you, you are," Franco responded then paused. "The reason I asked Dr. Roberts to arrange this meeting is to discuss our bill. As you know we do not have health insurance, so I will be paying for my daughter's care myself."

"Before you go any further," the administrator interrupted, "I want you to know that we are happy to work out a payment plan that will meet your needs, and for our cash customers we routinely offer a thirty-five percent discount off the billed charges."

"Do you have any idea how much we will owe?" Franco asked sounding concerned.

"Yes, I do. When Jack told me you were coming by, I had my staff pull the account information. Assuming your daughter is discharged tomorrow the total charges amounts to $103,405. With the thirty-five percent discount, that calculates out to $67,213. If you are able to pay that out over twelve months there will be no interest charges, and the monthly payments would be $5,601."

Anderson looked up from the paper that contained his handwritten calculations to see Franco smiling slightly. "I hope that arrangement will be satisfactory," he said, still waiting for a response.

"Actually," he said, "I had a different figure in mind."

The administrators face took on a look of concern as he said, "I'm authorized by the board of trustees of the hospital to offer either two years interest free payments or an additional five percent off, but that's as much as I can do." Bob's eyes hardened as he felt he was being challenged. As the silence persisted he looked at Jack who just shrugged.

Franco reached into the inside pocket of his jacket and produced a large leather wallet. He opened it and drew out a piece of paper and placed it on the table in front of him face down. "That is the amount I am willing to pay."

Bob slowly reached forward and picked up the check. He turned it over and his eyes widened. "But... this is a cashier's check for one million dollars," he uttered in disbelief.

Jack's jaw also dropped. He had no idea what Franco had in mind when he'd requested this meeting. He figured Franco might write the hospital a check to pay the bill in full, but he had not expected this.

"That is correct," Franco said with a sly smile. "I would ask you to use it to pay my bill and apply the remainder to cost of caring for any additional children from my country that my friend, Dr. Roberts, brings to your hospital for heart operations."

❖❖❖❖❖❖❖❖❖

THE CALLING

Word of the foreign businessman's huge payment to the children's hospital spread rapidly through the Fort Worth hospital community. Herb Nichols was among the last to hear. His golf buddy, the director of finance at one of the system's sister hospitals broke the news during their Saturday afternoon round.

"Did you hear about the big donation Anderson landed from a foreign patient?".

"No, what was that about?" Herb said.

"Seems the dad of some kid from Central America wrote him a check for a cool mill, after his daughter had a successful heart operation."

Herb quickly put two and two together and concluded that he had been the one left holding the bag. He'd let Roberts bring an illegal Mexican kid to his hospital, knowing he'd get stiffed. He was sure that the same surgeon had steered this million dollar donor to the children's hospital instead of his facility.

On Monday morning Jack had an elderly man on the schedule for an aortic valve replacement at the general hospital. Herb stormed down to the OR around nine, but Jack was still in surgery. He instructed the nursing supervisor to give Dr. Roberts a message, then handed her a folded piece of paper and returned to his office.

When Jack finished his case and sat down to write his postoperative orders, the nurse gave him the note and said, "It's from Mr. Nichols."

"Thanks... I think."

The note read, "Please come by my office when you finish in surgery. We need to talk."

He had a few minutes before he was supposed to be in surgery at children's, so he stopped by administration on his way to the parking lot.

"Hi, Sylvia, is Herb in his office?" he asked the administrator's assistant.

"Yes, sir," she said, "he's been expecting you."

"Hi, Herb," Jack said, as he walked into the huge office. "What's up?"

"Have a seat, Jack," he said without getting up. "Thanks for coming by."

"Sure."

"I suppose you know why I asked to see you?"

"No, I have no idea."

"Oh come on, Jack, everybody's heard about the million dollar donation to children's."

Jack sat silently for a moment, trying to determine where this conversation was going.

"I understand the donor was the father of one of your patients."

"That's right, but it wasn't exactly a donation."

"A million bucks is a million bucks, no matter what else you want to call it."

"He simply did what is referred to as paying it forward."

"What's that supposed to mean?"

"He paid for his daughter's care, and the rest of the money is payment in advance for future kids from Nicaragua."

"Well, I just have one question. Why didn't you bring that kid here, the way you did that Mexican girl a few weeks back?"

Now Jack understood. He hesitated to even dignify the question with an answer. Instead he just stared into the eyes of this man he was beginning to loath.

"You've been after me for years to bring my pediatric cases here, and you told me you needed me to bring a few charity cases, because that would help this hospital maintain its not for profit status." Jack's anger was beginning to boil to the surface. "I brought Lupe Alvarez here because she was eight years old. The Gutierrez baby was less than a week old."

Herb stared back, not remembering their earlier encounter quite the same way. "What I said was, our ability to raise funds in this community depends on our not for profit status, as well as our ability to demonstrate that we do a few local charity cases. I didn't say anything about illegals."

Jack had known for some time that for Herb the whole health care system was only about the money, but now he was as much as admitting it. For him, charity equaled fundraising opportunities, period. He knew there was no sense arguing, but he couldn't help himself.

"First of all, I had no idea that guy from Nicaragua was going to write a big check, and I don't think he came here with that in mind. He decided to make that, donation, as you call it, because his daughter received service well beyond his expectations. And second, I suspect that if I had brought his daughter here, your money-first philosophy would have pissed him off the same way it has me, and you and your hospital would have been stiffed, and I wouldn't have blamed him."

Jack stormed out of the office without saying goodbye, as Herb stood silently behind his desk where he spoke aloud to no one but himself. "I'm gonna get you, you prima donna son of a bitch."

◆◆◆◆◆◆◆◆◆

After finishing with his afternoon office, Jack was still steaming over "Round Two" with Herb Nichols when Mary Anne stuck her head around the door. "While you were in with your last patient your brother called."

"Really," Jack's mood lightened considerably at the thought of hearing from Ben. "Did he say what he wanted?"

"He just asked that you call him back when you have a minute," she said. "I'm getting ready to leave, do you need anything?"

"No, I'm fine. See ya tomorrow."

THE CALLING

Jack reached for his cell phone to find Ben's number. He thought it was sad the way he couldn't remember anyone's phone number anymore, probably because he didn't have to. They were all stored in his phone. He wasn't sure what he'd do if he ever lost it.

"Hey, Ben," he said, excited to hear his brother answer the phone.

"Hi, Jack, how's it going?"

"It's all good, Buddy. How the heck are you? I haven't heard from you in what's it been, three months?"

"I'm fine, just working."

"So when are you coming home this summer?"

"That's one of the things I called about," Ben spoke just a bit slower. "I have an opportunity with a device manufacturer to head up a new top secret project, but it means I will need to move to Tokyo for at least a year, maybe longer."

"What's the project?"

"Like I said, it's top secret. All I can tell you is it could significantly impact the way you do your job."

"Really? You're gonna just leave me hanging like that?"

"Sorry, but I'm sworn to secrecy. All I can say is I think it is going to be a big deal, and I don't want to miss out on it. Like I said they are offering me the job of heading it up, and I think I'm going to take it."

"Well, if you're asking my opinion, I say go with your gut. If you think it's what you want to do then don't hesitate."

"Thanks, that's what I thought you'd say."

"Have you talked to Mom about it?"

"Not yet," Ben paused a moment before adding, "I was kinda hoping you might talk to her for me."

"No way!" Jack replied. "You're a big boy, you do your own talking."

"I just don't know how she's going to take me being out of the country for what I suspect could be two or three years."

"I'm sure she won't like it, but she would never tell you not to go. Besides, you could still fly home at least once a year. In fact, if I were you I'd make them include that in your contract; a first class ticket from Narita to DFW and back, every Christmas, for as long as you're there."

"I knew there was a reason I called you," Ben said. "You always seem to find a way to solve problems that I never even considered."

"Well, that may be, but I still owe you big-time in the advice department."

"What do you mean?"

"You remember back in October of 1985 when you told me I should look into Apple Computer?"

"Yes?"

"Well, I took your advice. It cost me fifteen thousand dollars to buy a thousand shares in '85, then it split two for one in '87. The stock didn't do much for almost ten years, but when the price went back down to fifteen dollars a share I bought two thousand more in '97. It split two for one again in 2000. So, I bought another two thousand shares in '01 at fifteen dollars a share and two thousand more in '03 for thirteen dollars a share. Well, earlier this year the stock split again, two for one, so now I've got twenty-four thousand shares and at today's price, my one hundred and one thousand dollar investment is worth a little over a million bucks."

"Wow, Jack, that's great," Ben sounded excited but confused. "I'm really happy for you, but I have to admit I didn't know anything about Apple stock. I just thought you should look into getting one of their cool little computers."

Jack laughed out loud. "What was it Dad always used to say? Better to be lucky than good?"

"I'd say a thousand percent profit is better than lucky or good."

"Well, just so you know, I did in fact look into their computers too, and I bought my first one in '85. I'm now on my fifth desktop and my third laptop, and I'm looking into putting an Apple network in my office."

"And you call me a geek!"

The two brothers had a good laugh and promised to stay in touch using their latest communications tool, e-mail. By the time Jack hung up he had nearly forgotten about his run-in with Herb, but in the coming months those issues would resurface, over and over. It was becoming clear that his profession was being compelled to change and to adapt to a whole new set of economic pressures. Guys like Herb seemed committed to running their facilities the way the executives at Apple Computer ran their business, and for the same reasons. Jack worried that the entire health care system was becoming more about the money than the medicine.

CHAPTER 17

Elaina was more nervous than Jack had ever seen her. For nearly six months she'd been preparing for David's high school graduation. She had put on a big luncheon at their home and helped organize a formal ceremony at their church to recognize all the graduates in the congregation. However all those stresses paled compared to this day. As she sat squeezing her hands together, the tips of her fingers were crimson and her knuckles were white.

"I just hope he doesn't mess up," she said as she continued to stare at the podium in the center of the large stage. The auditorium was filled with other parents and grandparents, brothers, sisters, aunts and uncles of the four hundred eighty-seven graduates.

"He's going to do just fine," Jack reassured her. Faye, was sitting on the other side of him, straining to hear what her son was saying.

"Relax, dear," her own mother offered as she patted her arm. "He's going to be great."

The two people who had been closest to Elaina, one for her entire life and the other for the last sixteen years, were sitting on either side of her, in the second row behind the students in their burgundy caps and gowns. They were in the center of the huge auditorium on the campus of Texas Christian University. Her son was going to give a speech to nearly two thousand people. What was more nerve racking than anything, was the fact that David hadn't shared what he planned to say with her, or anyone else.

The ceremony began with an invocation, during which she decided to offer her own prayer. Please don't let him screw up, was all she could think of to ask. The school principal, Sara Grant, and the chairman of the school board, Edward Block, both gave some forgettable remarks, followed by the keynote speaker,

Congressman Herman Sheffield. The five-term, so-called conservative Democrat, spoke for about fifteen minutes. He emphasized the value of a quality education, and the need for America to stay competitive in the growing world economy. He challenged the graduates to make a difference by finding ways to cooperate with the rising cultures of China, India, and South America. He garnered a respectful round of applause and when it quickly wound down, Mr. Block took to the podium again.

"Ladies and gentlemen, it is my distinct honor and privilege to introduce this year's senior class valedictorian, David Allan Roberts."

The audience applauded in anticipation, but a few of David's classmates offered some hoots and hollers, as the six-two, blond-headed student arose from his seat in the front row. He made his way up the steps and across the stage, and stepped to the podium filled with confidence. Unlike the congressman, he didn't use any notes, instead delivering his message entirely from memory.

"Congressman Sheffield... Chairman Block... Principal Grant... faculty members... fellow classmates... ladies and gentlemen... I stand before you today, the product of a very complex set of human interactions. My mother chose to bring me into this world, despite the potential economic hardship my existence created. As an infant I had a heart defect that nearly killed me, but my life was saved by a remarkable surgeon who subsequently became my father. I have been nurtured by my grandmother who sacrificed countless hours as she taught me to read and write by the time I was three years old. My teachers have worked tirelessly to ensure that I learned everything from how to conjugate Latin verbs, to the Periodic Table of Elements. I was made to read Shakespeare and Chaucer, as well as Orwell and Fitzgerald. I have grown physically, mentally, emotionally, and spiritually under the guidance of countless mentors, some of whom taught me by example what not to do."

The audience laughed as David flashed his million dollar smile. His incredible good looks, and the way he carried himself, held everyone's attention.

"But I am not alone on this day of commencement. I share this stage with four hundred eighty-six other equally talented and equally capable young men and women, any one of whom could be addressing you today on our collective behalf. So, to every one of you who has been a part of making each of us the individuals we are, I can only say thank you on behalf of myself and my classmates. Thank you for caring enough to make a difference in our lives."

Applause began slowly but quickly increased and lasted for several seconds before subsiding abruptly as David began speaking again.

"Perhaps the most important lessons that any young person learns are the ones that mold not just our minds, but also our character. It is one of those lessons that I would like to share with you today. A year ago I had the opportunity to accompany my mom and dad to Nicaragua on what they called a medical mission. You might think that going on a mission would involve some form of religious outreach, but that is not what I witnessed. Their mission was a humanitarian one. They went to a place filled with millions of people who were not really part of the world economy that the congressman spoke about. They were not part of the internet community that you and I live in every day. These people had little more than the clothes on their backs and a faith in their hearts. Faith that God would protect them from harm if they worked hard and prayed often. It was in that humble environment that I learned an important lesson about character.

"A two-year-old child was brought to a free clinic where he was found to be in need of an operation to repair his defective heart. If he didn't receive it, he likely would not have lived more than a few months. Such had been the certain fate of every other child in that community with a similar need for untold generations. Without hesitation and without considering the obstacles or the odds, my father took on the task of performing that operation under conditions we would consider primitive at best here in America. He had nothing to gain personally from the effort, other than the satisfaction of helping another human being in their hour of need. To him it was about doing the right thing, and in doing so he taught me the true meaning of the word character. Dad, I just want you to know that the lesson was not lost on what you might have thought was an immature teenager. I thank you for being the example of the kind of man I hope one day to become."

David's smile was more serious as he directed his gaze toward where his dad was sitting. As the audience responded with a more vigorous round of applause, Jack seemed to slump slightly in his seat in an obvious effort to avoid the spot light. The audience grew silent as David continued.

"And to my classmates, I would propose the following challenge. As we go forward to create our own places in this world, I'm reminded of the advertising slogan for a famous sporting equipment company, 'Just Do It.' Unfortunately, they don't tell us what 'It' is. I would suggest that on this day, which symbolizes our transition from childhood to adulthood, each of us should commit to a slightly different version and make it our personal motto — Just do the right thing. In the end it will be our positive example to our children and future generations that will make this world a better place for all mankind. Thank you."

The entire audience erupted in applause as everyone rose to their feet. Jack was on the verge of losing his composure and Elaina already had tears streaming down her cheeks. Her mom reached around her shoulders and hugged her, saying, "I told you he'd be great."

At the reception in the foyer, Jack and Elaina were smothered by other parents and teachers as well as many of David's classmates, all offering their congratulations. Elaina was incredibly proud of her son, but also humbled by the words he had spoken. Jack said very little to those who greeted them other than to offer a simple thanks.

Congressman Sheffield came up to them and said, "That's quite a boy you've got there."

"Thank you," Elaina said modestly as she shook his hand.

"You know, I was an idealist like him once, then I went to Washington. The realities of the world have a way of crashing down on your head when you have the responsibility of taking care of millions, instead of just one at a time." His smug tone reeked with the arrogance that comes with power.

Jack was now truly speechless, as his anger threatened to boil to the surface. He seriously considered flattening the fat little man right there in front of the entire gathering. Instead he simply glared at the obnoxious little weasel.

"Anyway," the politician continued in a more conciliatory tone, "he gave a very nice speech. I know you must be proud." He didn't wait for a response, but simply turned away and walked on toward a waiting group of supporters. He shook as many hands as he could in the remaining few minutes he had available for campaigning. It wasn't long before he'd be heading to his waiting limo that would take him to the airport and back to DC.

♦♦♦♦♦♦♦♦♦

In the fall of 2006, David began his freshman year at the University of Texas in Austin. He'd received a one-year academic scholarship, with subsequent years potentially available based on his academic performance. Jack thought that made a lot more sense than the "full rides" that were common back in his college years. What he didn't realize was that David's entering class had twenty-three valedictorians, thirty-one salutatorians and more than one hundred kids that were in the top ten in their high school graduating classes. The academic competition was going to be stiff.

"I'll be fine, Mom," David said, as Elaina hugged him tightly.

"You will call every Sunday, right?" she said through the tears she had promised not to shed.

"Yes, Mom, of course I will."

She finally released him and allowed his father to embrace him and tell him goodbye. "We love you, son," Jack said. "Be safe, and let us know if you need anything, okay?"

"I will, Dad. Don't worry. I love you guys too," he said, as he kissed his mother on the cheek.

David walked them back to the front door of the dormitory, passing dozens of other young men and their parents, all going through the same move-in process. As they made their way back to Jack's now empty pickup, he held Elaina's hand tighter than usual.

"I'm not the least bit worried about him," Jack said. "He's going to be fine. It's you I'm worried about."

"Don't be silly. I'm just fine," she lied. This was her only child, and the separation anxiety was far greater than what she had been imagining for the last several months. She had become so used to having her son around, it was going to be very difficult for her not hearing him call out "Mom?" every afternoon when he came in the back door.

She'd endured week long previews of his absence each of the last two summers when he'd gone to Florida with Amy and her parents. Joanne Callahan always raved about what a perfect gentleman he had been, and how much she enjoyed having him around. That was good to hear but was little consolation for the void his absence had left in her life when he wasn't home. She feared this move to college was going to be more than she could bear.

"It's only a three hour drive, ya know," Jack said as he pulled out onto Interstate 35, headed north, and back to Fort Worth.

"I know," she replied, "but it wouldn't matter to me if he'd decided to go ten minutes away to TCU. The fact is he's gone."

Jack knew there was nothing he could say at this point to change her mood, so he simply reached across the center console and took her hand gently in his as they rode silently along the crowded highway.

◆◆◆◆◆◆◆◆◆

"Are you moved in yet?" Amy asked excitedly.

"More or less... My mom and dad just left, and I'm organizing this tiny closet." David couldn't believe how small his living quarters were. The entire room was about half the size of his bedroom back home, and he was sharing it with another guy.

"My parents are still here, and they wanted to know if you would like to join us for lunch at TGI Friday's."

"Sure, what time?"

"We are headed there now."

"Okay, I'll meet you there in fifteen minutes."

David decided he'd finish unpacking the last of his stuff later and hurried down to the student parking lot near the dorm. He considered walking the eight blocks to the restaurant, located just off campus, but decided to drive because it looked like it might rain. As he pulled his Honda out of the full lot, another car quickly pulled in and took his spot. It was clear that parking on campus was going to be a major hassle, just as the registrar had said when he gave him the parking sticker.

When they finished their lunch, the Callahans said they needed to get back to Fort Worth. As they walked out of the restaurant, Amy and David were holding hands, the way they had done for most of the time they were together over the last three years.

"You guys don't need to come back to the dorm," Amy said. "David can take me."

Both her parents looked a little surprised and saddened by the realization that they were leaving their daughter on her own for the first time. Joanne looked at David and smiled cautiously, knowing she wouldn't be truly alone. "Okay, I guess we can say our goodbyes in this parking lot as well as we can anywhere."

Amy hugged her dad first and then her mom, giving them both a kiss on the cheek. Her huge grin was in contrast to the half smile that Joanne was forcing through the tears that were welling up in her eyes.

"Bye, sweetie, I love you," she said as Amy's dad coaxed her gently toward the car. "Call us, okay?"

"I will, Mom. I love you too."

The two blond-haired teenagers waved as they watched the Callahans pull out of the parking lot, then they headed for David's car. He opened her door for her, as he always did, then got in behind the wheel. Before he started the car he turned in his seat to face her, and put his arm around her shoulder. She reacted by rising up in her seat and turning her body toward him. Before he could say anything she threw her arms around his neck. Their mouths met in a familiar way, but there was something different about this kiss. For the first time the two eighteen-year-olds were truly alone, without even a hint of parental supervision.

"I'm really glad you decided to come to Austin instead of SMU," David said.

"Me, too," she cooed. Her green eyes twinkled as she gazed into his face. She so easily became lost in his steely blue eyes.

It was still early afternoon so they decided to take a drive around the campus again, just to be sure they knew where they needed to be the following morning when classes started. David knew exactly where the biology building was, and he had a map of the campus, but he thought it best to find the buildings where his other classes in Chemistry, American history, Spanish, and British literature would be held.

He had taken almost all advanced placement classes his senior year of high school, so he already had credit for two semesters of biology, one semester of chemistry, and both semesters of freshman English. Having eighteen hours of college credit on the books was a huge head start, but it meant the classes he would be taking were also more advanced, and he suspected they'd be harder.

"I know you know this already," he said as they drove by the massive history building, "but I've really got to study hard, especially this first semester, to make sure I can maintain my scholarship."

"I know, silly. We both have to study," she said with a question in her response.

"It's just that I know how easy it would be for us to spend all of our free time together, and I don't want you to get upset with me if I can't do that."

She stared at him, not sure she understood. "Are you saying you don't want to spend time with me?"

"Of course not, Baby. I love spending time with you. You know that. I just know that if we start spending all our time together I won't be able to keep my mind on school, and I have to keep up my GPA to get into med school."

"I know," she said with a sadness in her voice. "It's just that this is the first time we've ever been alone together and I want to be with you."

"I want to be with you too," he insisted. "I just think we have the rest of our lives to spend together, and I want to be able to provide for you the way my dad provides for my mom."

The young couple had talked about their future together many times, but this was the first time David brought up the idea of being her provider. Amy wasn't sure how she felt about that. As a finance major, she thought she would be able to provide for herself, and him if she needed to, so she sat silent for several moments pondering what he'd said.

"How about if we do this?" he said, sensing she was not satisfied with his answer. "We both have classes Monday through Friday, but our Wednesday schedules are pretty light, so let's make Wednesday our weekday date night. We can also hang out together on Saturday evening and go to church together on Sunday morning."

"That sounds like an okay idea," she agreed reluctantly. *David always had to have everything so structured*, she thought. *Why couldn't they just take each day as it came?*

"But, I have to reserve Sunday evenings for studying."

"That's fine... by the end of the weekend I'll probably get tired of having you hanging around anyway." She laughed as leaned forward and kissed his ear, whispering, "I love you, David Roberts."

"Sit down and put your seatbelt on before the campus cops stop us and give me a ticket."

◆◆◆◆◆◆◆◆

"What do you mean Mr. Anderson isn't there anymore?" Jack almost shouted into the phone.

"That's all I can tell you, Dr. Roberts," the secretary said. "He notified me yesterday that he was leaving for another opportunity."

"Did he say where?"

"No, sir," she said sadly, "but just between you and me I don't think it was about another job. Two days ago the chairman of the board spent nearly an hour in his office, and I suspect that had something to do with it, but you didn't hear that from me."

"So, who's in charge?"

"Traci Bryan is the acting administrator. Would you like me to transfer you to her office?"

"No, I'm sure she's covered up right now, and what I called about can wait until tomorrow. Thanks a lot, Sylvia."

"You're welcome. And like I said, you didn't hear any of this from me."

"Got it." Jack hung up the phone and wondered what had happened that would cause Bob to resign as administrator, or worse yet, be fired.

The children's hospital relied heavily on payments both from Medicaid and SCHIP. Both government payment programs were run by the state, but received major federal funding. In the face of soaring federal deficits, the US Congress was threatening to reduce that support, which would shift more of the cost to the states. The Texas budget, like most states, was always under pressure, and with a generally conservative electorate, the idea of raising taxes to pay for medical care for the poor would be political suicide.

Jack wondered if the looming cuts in these government programs and their potential impact of the financial viability of the hospital had anything to do with Bob's unexpected departure as administrator. He had always been a very low-key guy when it came to financial issues. He shared Jack's philosophy of treating the patients without regard to how payment would be obtained. Obviously, he was exactly the opposite of guys like Herb Nichols, who believed that health care existed solely for the profit of those who were smart enough to manipulate the system.

The next morning Jack stopped by Traci Bryan's office, which was just around the corner from Bob's old office on the first floor.

"Hey, Traci," Jack said as he stuck his head through the door.

"Good morning, Dr. Roberts, please, come on in." The thin forty-year-old woman stood behind her desk and extended her hand. She was tall, but made taller by the four-inch heels she typically wore. Her dark blue suit created an excellent contrast with her short blond hair, and gave her a distinctly corporate look. Traci was a nurse who had initially distinguished herself as a manager on one of the larger patient units of the hospital. She'd been tagged for leadership training several years before, and after a yearlong course in hospital

THE CALLING

management, she was made an assistant administrator nearly two years ago.

"What can I do for you?" she asked, wanting to sound more authoritative than she felt.

"Well, I just came by to see if there was anything I could do to help you, now that you are the acting administrator," he said as he took a seat in front of her desk.

She smiled reluctantly, then glanced down at her hands that were uncomfortably folded on top of her desk. As her eyes rose again to meet Jack's gaze, she shook her head silently. "I have no idea what I'm doing. Bob Anderson was a stellar administrator, and there is no way that I can possibly fill his shoes."

"Oh, I'm sure you're going to do fine," Jack said, flashing his crooked smile.

"I suppose you want to know what happened?"

"Well, I was wondering, but I figured I'd hear about it at some point."

"Would you mind closing the door?" she asked, nodding toward the door behind him.

Jack stood and closed the door then returned to his chair.

"I'm not really at liberty to discuss the specifics of Bob's departure, but I can tell you it wasn't his idea."

"I didn't think it was," Jack replied. "He loved his job, and as far as I could tell he was really good at it."

"That's certainly what the rest of us thought, too, but apparently the board of trustees wasn't pleased with his efforts at fundraising."

"Well, Bob never really liked asking people for money, and over the last few years it seems that that's all they asked him to do." Jack recalled several conversations he'd had with the former administrator regarding the constant pressure to raise money in the community.

"I think that was part of it, but like I said I can't really discuss the specifics."

"Do you have any idea what he's planning to do?" Jack asked.

"I heard him say something about moving back to Ohio to be near his family, but I really don't know, and I'm not sure he does either."

Jack was saddened that his friend of more than ten years was suddenly out on the street looking for work, but he figured a smart guy like Bob would land on his feet somewhere. "Well, like I said, I just came by to see if there was anything I could do for you."

"Actually, there is one thing." Traci was obviously troubled by something, and she wasn't sure exactly how to even ask Jack.

"Anything, just ask."

"Can you tell fill me in on the specifics of that million dollar payment that guy from Nicaragua made? Were there any written documents or contracts exchanged that you know of, or was that just a verbal agreement?"

As he heard her raise the issue of Franco's gift, he realized that it was somehow connected to Bob's departure. "I don't know of any written contract, or other records of the transaction. I just know that Mr. Gutierrez gave the money to Bob with the specific understanding that it would go to paying his bill, which was under seventy thousand, and the remainder was to be used to cover the cost of future Nicaraguan children in need of heart surgery."

"That's what I understood too, but it seems that the board of trustees, and the VP of finance didn't look at it that way."

Jack was beginning to get the picture. Obviously, the board wanted access to that money and Bob wouldn't release it. There were no records of the funds being designated for anything specific other than the word of Bob Anderson, and now he was gone.

"Are you telling me that the hospital's finance department has seized the money Gutierrez gave?" Jack asked, his eyes narrowing.

"Like I said, I really can't talk about the specifics of any of this. I need to keep my job. You can draw whatever conclusions you want." Traci looked back down at her folded hands, and sighed.

"Don't worry, you didn't say anything," Jack assured her as he stood, preparing to leave her office.

"Thanks, Dr. Roberts," she said, in a voice that was considerably softer than her usual authoritative tone. When he left her office she remained seated, still staring at her hands, helplessly folded on the desk.

◆◆◆◆◆◆◆◆

Normally Jack swept Elaina into his arms the moment he came through the back door, but this evening was different.

"You won't believe what happened today," he said as he stormed into the kitchen where Elaina was preparing a taco salad for their dinner. When she looked up she saw the anger and frustration in her husband's face.

"Whatever it was, it obviously wasn't good," she said.

"I found out why they fired Bob Anderson," he spouted.

She watched him fuming, anticipating that he would eventually finish telling her what had happened.

"They needed him out of the way so they could steal the money Franco donated."

"You've got to be kidding!"

"No, I'm not." He put his hands on the counter and leaned forward as he shook his head in disbelief. "There was no written contract stipulating the use of that money, so they decided to use it to offset the cost of a new CT scanner."

THE CALLING

Jack had found out about the accounting maneuver indirectly, when he asked his friend in the radiology department how they planned to cover the cost of the new Siemens machine that was being installed that very day. "I'm guessing Bob objected to the diversion of the funds that he had set aside the way Franco requested. So, they got rid of what I'm sure they must have figured was their only obstacle."

"That's terrible! Can they do that?" Elaina asked as she walked over and sympathetically touched his arm.

"Without any written document, I'm guessing they can legally do whatever they want," he replied with disgust, "but I don't think they know that Bob wasn't the only witness to the transaction."

"Are you saying you're going to confront the board of trustees over this?"

"I haven't decided yet what I'm going to do, but this is just not right, and I can't sit by and do nothing," he said, feeling a renewed sense of frustration. "I never thought I would see the day when the children's hospital reminded me of Herb Nichols and the general hospital."

✦✦✦✦✦✦✦✦

Their summer trip to Nicaragua had been pushed back to mid-September because of David's graduation and his subsequent move to Austin. As their plane landed in Managua, the air was only slightly cooler than prior years, but the humidity was still oppressive. Domingo greeted them at the airport as he always did, renewing their friendship with a big hug for his American friends.

"I'm sorry to see that David is not with you this year," he said as they climbed into the same old Toyota Land Cruiser.

"He wanted to come, but he's started college and there's no way he could get away for a week," Elaina replied.

"How's the Gutierrez baby?" Jack asked.

"She's doing great! Her mother brought her in just two weeks ago and her heart sounds perfect. She's walking and is even starting to say a couple words. She is a truly beautiful child."

"That's great to hear. How about the Ochoa boy?"

"The last I saw him he was fine, but his father had an opportunity for work in Belize during the tourist season, so the family moved there about nine months ago."

"Have you seen Franco?" Jack asked, almost afraid to bring up the subject. He feared he would have to reveal what had happened to the money he'd donated.

"I haven't, but I spoke to him on the phone last week, and when he learned you were coming, he asked me to invite you and Elaina to their home Tuesday evening for dinner."

"That sounds great," Elaina said. "Unfortunately, Jack and I didn't bring our red carpet outfits." She laughed to herself, but Domingo didn't understand her meaning, and Jack seemed absorbed in his thoughts.

He had been trying to figure out a way to handle the situation with Franco ever since he got wind of what he'd first called theft, but later decided to refer to as the hospital's financial treachery. Traci had discovered that Bob Anderson had actually created a separate category in the hospital's bookkeeping system which he had named the Nicaraguan Surgical Fund. When she innocently asked about the seventeen hundred dollars sitting on the books, no one on the board was willing to admit they knew anything about it. Jack had concluded that there was no way he could explain this to Franco if he asked, and he wasn't even going to try unless forced to do so. He hoped the subject wouldn't come up, and if it did he would just play dumb.

"Oh, Jack," Domingo suddenly remembered, "there's a five-year-old girl I want you to take a look at on Tuesday in my clinic. I'm pretty sure she has tetralogy, but she's been getting along quite well until recently."

"Sure, I'll be glad to take a look at her."

Well, it looked like the subject was going to come up, he reasoned. As he mulled it over in his mind, he decided to just let things unfold. He figured it would be easier to deal with the consequences than try to anticipate what might happen.

Tuesday morning in Domingo's clinic, the five-year-old girl was brought in by her mother. She brought two other children with her, one was seven and the other four. The first thing Jack noticed was the four-year-old boy was about the same size as his five-year-old sister, and the seven-year-old was more than a full head taller than either of them. He asked the mother about her three pregnancies, and determined that she hadn't had any medical care for herself or any of the children. Each of them had been delivered by the village midwife, and as far as she knew everything had been normal. She admitted that her middle child, the one that was now having problems, had come much earlier than she had expected.

As Jack examined the frail child he noticed was her hands, specifically her nail beds had a slight bluish tinge, but the most striking feature was the bulbous appearance of the end of each finger. This clubbing deformity was characteristic of low oxygen levels in the blood over an extended period of time.

He asked the little girl to walk down the hallway then back to the examining room as quickly as she could, a total distance of only twenty-five feet. About halfway back up the narrow hallway she stopped and crouched down, placing her bottom on the back of her heels, out of breath. Jack walked over to the child and lifted her off the ground and carried her back to the exam room. He took out his stethoscope and listened to her chest, already knowing exactly what he was going to hear. Over the center of the sternum he heard a distinct high-pitched swishing sound with each contraction of her heart.

"You're right," he said to Domingo. "She's clearly lagging behind in development, has clubbing and cyanosis, displayed the classic squatting posture with exercise, and her murmur is certainly consistent with right ventricular outflow obstruction."

After a period of discussion with the mother about her daughter's congenital heart defect, Jack's only concern was how to get the child to Fort Worth. She obviously didn't have the connections with the State Department that Franco used to get his own daughter into the US. He decided it would be cruel to suggest the child could have corrective surgery back in Texas until he'd had a chance to talk to Franco.

♦♦♦♦♦♦♦♦♦

As they drove up to the massive iron gate that guarded the Gutierrez estate, a uniformed man, carrying an automatic rifle, stepped out of a small enclosure and moved cautiously toward them. Domingo explained who they were and why they had come to the expressionless sentinel. He walked purposefully around the old Toyota then stepped back into the enclosure. Soon the barrier swung open, allowing them entry to the two-hundred acre grounds.

It took several minutes to negotiate the winding narrow road through a dense forest of giant mahogany trees, and when they finally emerged into a large clearing they saw their destination. Beyond the expanse of manicured lawn stood a magnificent three-story white marble structure that reminded Jack of a castle he'd once seen in central France. The stately house appeared to almost glow as it reflected the golden rays of the late afternoon sun.

Between them and the impressive façade the driveway encircled a large pool of crystal clear water, and in the center stood a statue that Jack immediately recognized. Water was spewing from the mouths of each of the four horses pulling the chariot of Apollo. He was certain it was a smaller version of the original fountain he had seen on the grounds of Versailles outside of Paris.

"It's obvious we are terribly underdressed," Elaina said. She was wearing a simple summer dress she had found at a specialty shop in Managua just the day before.

"Relax, Angel, we're not here to impress them, and by the looks of things I don't think that would be possible anyway."

As Domingo pulled up to the entry a pair of attendants rushed out to meet Domingo's aged Toyota. They quickly opened the doors and directed the four of them toward the main entrance where an older woman stood ready to greet them.

"Are you sure we're at the right place?" Elaina asked Jack as she looked around in awe. "This looks more like the Presidential palace."

"This is indeed the Gutierrez estate," Domingo replied. "I have seen pictures of it, but it is far more impressive in person."

As they stepped into the magnificent mansion, Elaina gasped. "I can't believe this," she muttered. "This foyer is the size of our living room."

The two story entry was flanked by twin curved staircases ending in a suspended walkway which overlooked the huge great room. The soaring white walls were covered with family portraits and works of fine art. The furnishings all looked to be old world antiques, and the marble floor was covered with an ornate Persian rug.

Elaina grabbed Jack's arm, both to gain his attention and for support and she looked up. "Oh, my God!" she exclaimed "That is unbelievable."

She seemed hypnotized staring up at the most striking feature of the home, the magnificent painting far above their heads. The ceiling of the great room had a normal flat appearance around the perimeter, but in the center it rose to the full height of the three-story building as a large oval dome. The inside had been painted to replicate an evening sky with gradient blue background and a few white puffy clouds accented with shades of pink, purple, and orange scattered across the main expanse. The far end was marked by golden rays of a setting sun, emerging from behind a small bank of irregular clouds of purple and dark gray.

"Doesn't that remind you of something?" she whispered.

"Yeah," Jack agreed. "It almost looks as though there is no ceiling,"

"We had it commissioned by an American artist we discovered a few years ago during one of many trips to your country," Franco interrupted. "In fact he lives very near your home in Texas,"

The sound of his friend's voice drew Jack's attention, while the others remained mesmerized by the ceiling.

"Good evening, Franco," Jack said as he stepped toward their host and extended his hand. "This is quite a place you have here."

"Thank you. It is so good of you to come."

"You remember my wife, Elaina," he said, more to her in an attempt to break her away from the hypnotic scene.

"I'm sorry," she offered, apologetically. "I was caught up by your magnificent home. How are you, Franco?"

"It is so good to see you again, my dear," Franco said as he embraced her warmly. "You are even lovelier than I remembered. Welcome to our home."

"Thank you," she said. "It is breathtaking."

Franco quickly greeted Domingo and Felicia, and invited them all to be seated in the large grouping of ornate sofas and chairs covered with rich silk brocade.

"Where is David?" he asked, looking around as though he had missed someone.

"He started college last month, so he wasn't able to come this time," Jack said as he sat down next to his wife. He was relieved to see that Franco was dressed casually, without a jacket or tie.

"I'm sorry to be late," Gabriella said, as she came hurriedly from a side hallway to join the group. "I was getting Christina ready for bed."

Jack stood and turned to see the Latin beauty walking across the room. Her gorgeous face was framed by her long dark hair that flowed in large curls over her shoulders. He stepped forward and held out his hand, but she stepped inside his arm and gave him a warm embrace.

"I am so glad you were able to come," she said as she released Jack and turned to Elaina, repeating her welcoming gesture. "Franco and I have been looking forward to having you in our home."

She approached Domingo, and offered him a similar greeting, but spoke to him in Spanish. Domingo introduced his wife, and the two women greeted each other warmly.

The older woman who had met them at the door came in carrying a silver tray with three delicate flutes filled with Cristal Champagne for the ladies, and three highball glasses containing generous portions of eighteen-year-old Macallan whiskey for the gentlemen.

As they sipped their drinks and engaged in small talk, the nanny came into the room carrying fifteen-month-old Christina to say good night to her parents before putting her to bed. When the adorable toddler saw her mother she wiggled in the nanny's arms and demanded "down."

Once on the floor, she teetered excitedly toward her mother before stumbling into her arms. Gabriella picked her up, kissed her face tenderly, and carried her precious child around to each of her guests to say hello and good night. When she got around to Jack he held out his hands to see if she would come to him, but she shied away into the safety of her mother's arms.

"Christina is the spitting image of her mother," Jack remarked, and Elaina agreed. He always enjoyed getting to see any child he had operated on months or years before, and this little girl was certainly no different. She was so vibrant and full of life.

"I don't have to tell you how grateful we are for what you did to save our daughter's life," Franco said.

Jack smiled meekly and said, "I told you before, I can't take credit for that. The truth is we very nearly lost her." He paused as he recalled the agonizing minutes in the OR, which seemed more like hours. The vivid image of the child's motionless heart filled his mind, as he remembered the feeling of utter helplessness, unable to alter fate.

"I didn't want to tell you at the time just how desperate the situation was, because I knew the stress you were already under. The fact is she nearly died before we could even get her on the pump," he admitted. "Then after the repair, I tried everything I knew, including some things that didn't make any sense, in an effort to get her little heart restarted, but nothing worked. I have to admit I felt completely helpless. It was God who restarted her heart. He pulled her through that ordeal, not me."

Franco sat silently studying his friend's face as he spoke of the divine intervention he had witnessed. "That may be true my friend, but the All Mighty Father used you as His instrument, and I have to believe you were the one who summoned that miracle."

Gabriella smiled broadly as she kissed her daughter's face again, then handed her back to the nanny who quickly took the child off to bed. "I think dinner should be about ready. Shall we move into the dining room?"

Once they were seated at the elaborate dining table the conversation moved from Christina's recent accomplishments of walking and speaking her first words, to Franco's latest construction projects in Costa Rica and Belize.

"The tourist industry is growing rapidly in both of those countries," Franco said. "I only wish we had something to draw tourists here to Nicaragua."

"Do you think your government is really interested in building a tourist-based economy?" Jack asked.

"Of course! They have been talking about it in the General Assembly for many years, and President Ortega made it a priority in his last election campaign. Unfortunately, we lack the infrastructure needed to support the modern seaside and golf resorts that attract foreigners."

"The new airport is certainly a good start."

"Yes, that was a major part of Ortega's strategy, but we don't have a large enough tax base to allow us to build the other elements we need like water treatment facilities, highways, and bridges."

"What about private investment capital?" Jack asked.

"We have had a number of foreign groups look at our country, but they have been lured away to places like Belize, Costa Rica, and even El Salvador where a tourist base already exists."

Jack wondered what it would take to make Nicaragua competitive with the other Central American countries. Currently there wasn't much to attract visitors here, and he was certain the political climate was a strong deterrent to most outside investors. Currently the only thing that set this country apart was the fact it was perhaps the poorest nation in the western hemisphere.

"I understand Dr. Ramirez has another patient with the same heart problem

Christina had," Franco said, changing the subject yet again.

"Yes," Jack said. "We saw the little girl this morning. Her condition is not nearly as severe as Christina's, but it has caused her physical growth to be retarded somewhat, and she really needs surgery."

"Do you plan to operate on her soon?"

"I would, but I'm not sure how we are going to get her to Texas. Her parents are among the extremely poor we were talking about earlier."

"That will not be a problem," Franco offered almost casually.

"What do you mean?"

"After we returned home last year I established a foundation to take care of transporting children to the US for treatment. We have a contract with an international air ambulance company that will handle the transportation needs of children who are unsuitable for commercial flights. And I have received approval from our Ministry of Foreign Affairs, as well as your State Department, to allow any child you designate as being in need of surgery, to enter the US on a medical visa."

"That's incredible!" Jack said excitedly, turning from Franco to Elaina and then to Domingo and back to Franco. "How did you pull that off?"

"Like I said, it is far more important who you know than what you know."

✦✦✦✦✦✦✦✦

Monday morning Jack walked confidently into the administrator's office at the children's hospital and announced, "There is a five-year-old girl in Nicaragua that I am scheduling for a tetralogy repair next week."

Traci looked at him with widened eyes and stated, "You know there's no money available to pay for it, right?"

"Oh... the money will be there. I'll see to it," he declared.

"Look, Jack," she said lowering her voice, "I've been instructed to keep the charity work to a minimum given the recent cuts in our payment rate from Blue Cross and United Healthcare. The board is all over my butt because they are worried the Medicaid cuts are also coming soon."

"I understand the position you are in," he offered with sympathy in his voice, "but I am not going to let those guys steal the money my friend donated. I have an appointment tomorrow afternoon with the chairman of the board, and I intend to set him straight."

"I wish you luck. Just remember you didn't learn about any of this from me."

"Don't worry, I know how to deal with those guys."

✦✦✦✦✦✦✦✦

"Mr. Fitzgerald can see you now," the executive secretary said, as she opened the door into the large corner office on the thirtieth floor of the downtown skyscraper. Jack had never met this man. He'd only seen him at a distance at a hospital gala.

"Come in, Dr. Roberts," the elderly gentleman said. James Prescott Fitzgerald was well past retirement age, but was staying on as CEO of the regional oil company he'd started in the mid sixties. It was part of his agreement when he recently sold the company to a New York-based investment firm for just shy of two billion dollars. Two years ago the oil tycoon had been named chairman of the board of the hospital after making a five million dollar donation. Jack suspected his generosity had more to do with taxes than it did caring for kids, but he wasn't here to judge the man's personal motives.

"Thanks for agreeing to see me," Jack said, as he shook the man's hand, then took a seat in one of the soft leather chairs in front of his desk.

"What can I do for you?" Fitzgerald's voice sounded more youthful than Jack had expected given his appearance. His white hair and beard were more consistent with a man in his early eighties, but his eyes were still sharp, and so was his tongue.

"I wanted to come by and discuss a situation that I suspect you are familiar with." Jack said, then paused a moment, making sure he had the older man's full attention. "I don't have to tell you that since Bob Anderson left, things have been a little unsettled at the hospital."

"Yes, I'm aware of the fact that Bob was well liked by his management team, and I'm sure it will take some time for them to adjust to his absence."

"I think you and the board made a good choice for his successor. Traci will do a great job, I'm sure."

"Thank you. We thought she would be the best person to oversee the transition, but I don't know whether she'll get the job long term. We have a search firm working on finding an experienced administrator. She'll certainly be given an opportunity to compete for the job, assuming she wants it."

That was exactly what he'd expected the old executive to say, and he was prepared to use it to transition into what he'd really come to discuss.

"Yes, I know she's inexperienced, and that brings me to the reason I'm here," he continued. "When I explained to her that I was bringing a little girl up from Nicaragua for open heart surgery next week, she was obviously not familiar with the arrangements that had been made with Bob Anderson."

The old man's eyes narrowed slightly but he sat silently waiting for Jack to finish.

"I'm sure you were aware of the fact that Mr. Franco Gutierrez, a wealthy businessman like yourself, gave Bob a cashier's check for a million dollars a little over a year ago. The first sixty-five thousand dollars was to cover the cost of his daughter's surgery, and the rest was to be set aside to pay for the care of other children from Nicaragua, in the future. Obviously Traci didn't know anything about it, so I wanted to make sure that Bob had shared that agreement with you and the board before he left."

Fitzgerald sat motionless while Jack was speaking, trying to determine exactly how he would respond to this challenge. If he said he knew about the agreement, but the money had been moved into the general fund to offset the cost of a CT scanner, he'd reveal himself a crook. If he denied knowing about the agreement, he'd have a difficult time covering that lie, since the entire board had signed off on Bob being fired over it.

"I think I recall Anderson saying something about a verbal agreement with the gentleman from Nicaragua, but I didn't recall the details quite the way you describe them."

"Oh? What was your understanding of the agreement?" Jack asked, skeptically.

"I thought the guy gave the money to the hospital because he was grateful to us for saving his child's life. Bob did mention something about there potentially being other children down there, but I don't recall anything about the funds being set aside."

Jack could feel the growing heat in his ears as his anger and his blood pressure rose. Anticipating the conversation might go in this direction he'd rehearsed his response, which was the only reason he was able to maintain his cool.

"Well, I'm not sure if you were aware, but I was there when Mr. Gutierrez gave Bob the check, and there was no question what it was for," Jack revealed. "I just wanted to make sure those donated funds were available next week to cover this child's expenses."

Jack knew he had the old man right where he wanted him, and Fitzgerald knew it too.

"Don't worry, Jack," Fitzgerald said, trying to defuse the situation using a common tactic, casual familiarity. "I'm sure it's just an accounting glitch. The money is there to cover your patient's expenses."

"Good... I'm glad to hear you say that. I was afraid it might have found its way into the general fund," Jack responded, knowing the old man was being forced to lie to cover his previous deceit.

"No, no... Don't you worry. That money is secure," Fitzgerald said, knowing he'd been caught by someone who was almost as shrewd as he was.

"But... speaking of the general fund," he said, hoping to regain the advantage, "I'm sure you know, the state is threatening to cut our Medicaid and SCHIP payments by about ten percent next year."

"Yes, I am aware of that possibility."

"If they do, it will put a major strain on our budget and might even keep us from moving forward with those operating room upgrades we had planned."

Fitzgerald knew how to counterpunch. He had been a clever negotiator for many years and was not likely to be outwitted by a lightweight like Jack.

"Yeah, I heard about the hearings next month in Austin," Jack admitted. "Isn't it interesting how politicians always seem to wait until right before an election to discuss issues that are politically charged?"

"Absolutely," Fitzgerald agreed, then he added, "You know, you could do me and the hospital a huge favor if you would go down there and testify about the damaging effects those cuts would have on our ability to provide care to the children of Texas."

Jack recognized this request was the old man's quid pro quo, and he figured it was a relatively small price to pay.

"I'm not sure I'm the best person for the job, but if you don't have anyone else to carry that message, I'd be happy to go."

"Great," the old man said as he stood, signaling the meeting was concluded. "I'll have my secretary make all the arrangements. We'll take care of your expenses, of course," he added, as if he was doing Jack a favor.

"That's not necessary," Jack objected.

"Oh yes it is," Fitzgerald argued. "You're going down there on our behalf, so it will be on our nickel. We'll get the specifics to you some time in the next few days. Just check with Traci Bryan's office," he said as he walked Jack toward the door. "I appreciate your coming by, doctor," he added with a satisfied smile.

"Thank you, sir, for making time for me," Jack said with a hint of his own sarcasm as he shook the old man's hand again.

"Oh, you're welcome, and by the way," Fitzgerald added, "keep me updated on how the child from Nicaragua gets along. Let me know if there is anything I can do." What he wanted to say was, make sure that kid doesn't end up having any costly complications. He'd have a hard time justifying a huge write-off like that to the board.

◆◆◆◆◆◆◆◆

The five-year-old with tetralogy arrived as scheduled, and Buzz completed her work up as planned. The following day the operation went very smoothly, and Jack anticipated she'd be out of the hospital in less than a week.

That afternoon Traci called him into her office under the pretense of discussing his testimony in Austin the following month, but when he arrived, she greeted him and closed the door.

"What in the hell did you say to Fitzgerald to get him so riled up?" she said almost in a whisper, as she dropped heavily into her desk chair.

"I just asked him whether he knew about the strings attached to the Gutierrez donation, he denied it, I called his bluff, and that was about it, other than him asking me to testify at the Medicaid hearing in Austin."

"Well, he is really pissed!" she said, again trying to emphasize her point in a loud whisper.

"I don't really care," Jack said dismissively. "He raided the wrong cookie jar, and he got caught."

"I'm not sure you know who you're dealing with, Jack. He's an extremely powerful man in this town, and he doesn't like being shown up."

"What's he gonna do, fire me? I don't work for him. Besides, he needs the revenue that comes in through the heart program. He knows it. I know it. He'll get over it."

"I don't know. He was steaming during the last board meeting and made a particular point of criticizing me over the cost of proposed upgrades to the ORs."

"That son of a bitch!" Jack mumbled under his breath. Fitzgerald had made a threat just to get him to testify in Austin, something he would have done anyway if the old man had just asked. Now it seemed he was making good on that threat despite what Jack agreed to do.

"Don't let it get to you, Traci. I'll try my best next month to get the state to avoid cutting payments for children's hospital care. If that happens this whole thing will blow over."

"I hope you're right. By the way, how did that case go with the little Nicaraguan girl?"

"Fine. We just did her this morning. If everything goes as planned, she should be out of here in five or six days."

◆◆◆◆◆◆◆◆◆

Unfortunately, everything didn't go exactly as Jack planned. Shortly after he walked into the house following his evening rounds, the pediatric intensivist called him on his cell phone.

"Hello, Jack?"

"Hi, John, what's up?"

"I know you were just here, but something is going on with the little girl you operated on this morning."

"What's the problem?"

"Well, her pressure has dropped and we're seeing a fair bit of blood coming out through the chest tube."

"I'll be right there!"

He turned toward Elaina, who was dressed and ready to go out to dinner. It was Tuesday. "I'm really sorry, Angel, I've gotta go back to the hospital. It looks like our little girl is bleeding."

She didn't say anything as she blew him a goodbye kiss as he headed back out to the garage. On his way he called the OR and told the evening supervisor not to let the crew go home. It was likely he would need to bring the heart case from that morning back. Fortunately, the crew was still there and there wasn't anything going on in the OR at the moment.

He rushed into the ICU and quickly reviewed the situation, confirming what the Intensivist had told him. He turned to the charge nurse and said, "Call Dr. Patel and tell her I need to bring the heart from this morning back for bleeding. Also, call the pump tech and have him come in to stand by, and we should still have a couple of units available in the blood bank. Would you also check on that for me?"

It was unlikely they'd need to go back on the pump, since it was probably just a bleed from the patch over the right ventricular outflow tract, but he knew better than to assume anything. He wanted to be prepared for whatever he might find. The child's pressure was eighty over thirty and her rate was slowing.

"I suspect she's in tamponade," he said to the other doctor. All signs pointed to blood accumulating around the heart, and the chest tube was likely clogged with clotted blood. If that continued, the pressure of the blood gathering around the heart would slowly squeeze it, keeping it from beating and the child would die.

"Get the emergency thoracotomy tray to the bedside, STAT!"

The head nurse ran into the storage closet and came back with a tray of sterile instruments used to open the chest in an emergency. As Jack was watching the monitor, the little girl's heart rate had slowed to seventy-five and her pressure was now seventy over thirty.

"I'm going to see if I can get this chest tube to drain," he said as he put on a pair of sterile gloves. The tube had been placed in the space behind the breastbone in front of the heart, and it should have allowed any blood to drain out, preventing the very problem he was seeing evolving right before his eyes. One nurse opened the tray of instruments while the other poured some brownish-colored disinfectant on the child's exposed chest.

Jack rummaged through the instruments and quickly found a pair of scissors which he used to cut the single suture that was holding the plastic tube to the skin. As he began twisting the tube a small amount of blood rushed out through it, followed by a dark red clot. He pulled the tube out slightly and another rush of blood came flowing out through the clear plastic. He looked up at the monitor and the heart rate had increased to eighty-five, but her pressure remained dangerously low.

"Did you call the blood bank?"

"Yes, sir," the nurse replied. "There are four units available and one is on its way up right now."

"Let's hang it as soon as it gets here and run it wide open."

The flow of blood from the chest tube was still not what he hoped for, so he twisted it again and pulled it out another inch. Very little blood came out and the cardiac monitor showed her rhythm had become irregular. He really didn't want to open this child's chest in the ICU, but if he couldn't evacuate the growing amount of blood that was literally strangling her heart, he would be forced to do just that.

He continued to manipulate the tube without much success so he decided to pull it out, assuming it was clogged with clotted blood. As he did there was a sudden gush of blood from the small hole in the skin under the child's breastbone. It accumulated on the bed on both sides of her chest and abdomen.

"That's more like it," he said, as he checked the monitor again and saw her heart rate was back above one hundred and her pressure was now ninety over forty. The flow of blood had slowed as he covered the opening with a blue sterile towel.

"Call the OR and tell them we are coming right now," he said to the nursing supervisor who had come back to see if she could help. The other nurse hung the unit of blood just as they were wheeling the bed out of the glass-walled room toward the OR across the hallway. For some reason, perhaps as protection or perhaps in a subconscious attempt to stem the bleeding, Jack placed one gloved hand over the sterile towel on the child's chest as he walked quickly alongside the bed.

Realizing he hadn't spoken to the family, he called back to the nursing supervisor. "Let this girl's family know what's going on and tell them I will be out to talk to them once I get this bleeding under control."

The ICU nurse, an aide, and Jack rolled the bed through the double doors with the word SURGERY printed above in large blue lettering. When they reached the wide red line on the floor that indicated the transition to the sterile corridor, the surgical crew took over the transport back into the operating room. Jack was still in his street clothes as he spotted Radha coming out of the heart room.

"I've got it," she said. "You go change."

He bolted back to the doctor's dressing room and hurriedly changed into scrubs. He covered his head with a paper hat and his dress shoes with some paper booties, then headed back to the OR. On his way he grabbed a paper mask and tied it over his face as he burst through the door, just as the ICU bed was being moved out.

"How's she doing?" he asked, as Radha was finishing transferring the electronic monitoring module to her anesthesia machine.

"Her pressure is seventy over thirty and her rate is ninety. I think you better get in there," she said.

Jack rubbed his hands with an alcohol-based disinfectant and quickly donned his gown and gloves as the circulating nurse attempted to prep the child's chest. It seemed she was doing little more than spreading the oozing blood around.

He quickly covered the child's body with a large blue paper sheet with a hole in the center exposing only the area of operation. Using a scalpel he opened the skin incision that had been expertly closed less than ten hours before with no visible sutures. As he reached the breastbone he cut the heavy plastic sutures that had been used to pull it together.

"Her pressure is fifty and so is her heart rate," Radha said, as if to speed him along.

As he spread the sternum he couldn't see the heart as he immediately began evacuating the clotted blood with a suction cannula.

"She's coming up," Radha said, encouraged by the improvement she was seeing. "Her pressure is eighty and her pulse rate is seventy-five."

Most of the blood around the heart was clotted, but as he evacuated it, the source of the bleeding became apparent. One of the sutures he'd used to secure the patch over the narrowed outflow tract had pulled through the muscle, allowing a small amount of dark blood to leak out with every contraction.

"Get me a 3-0 Prolene on a pledget," he ordered as he temporarily placed his left index finger over the tiny hole to stem the bleeding. "It's a suture line bleed," he explained to Radha. "I should be able to control it without the need to go on pump."

He could feel the beating of the small heart increasing in rate and strength as Radha administered the second unit of blood, along with some fresh frozen plasma to aid with the clotting process. Within a minute he had the hole closed and the bleeding controlled.

"That's more excitement than I needed tonight," he said to reassure the team that the crisis was over. He placed another chest tube back into the same location and closed the chest just as he had earlier that day.

"Your daughter started bleeding from her heart, and we had to go back in very quickly to stop the bleeding," he explained in Spanish to the panic-stricken parents. "I'm sorry I didn't have time to speak to you before we went back to the operating room, but it was an emergency."

The parents continued to look at Jack with unbridled fear in their eyes. "She's doing okay now," he offered calmly, "but there is a chance the same thing could happen again. I think that's unlikely, but it is impossible to say for certain. We will need to watch her for an hour or so in the recovery room before taking her back to the ICU."

The young Nicaraguan couple looked slightly relieved by his words, but they would remain anxious as they sat in the waiting area for their daughter to return to the ICU where they finally could be with her.

Jack sat around in the recovery room for an hour and a half until he was sure his young patient was stable. Radha cleared her to return to the ICU and Jack decided it was safe to head back home. It was just after midnight when he walked out of the hospital and headed for his truck.

As he walked through the back door, the house was dark except for a small light in the kitchen. Elaina had left a plate covered with aluminum foil sitting on the stove. He lifted the foil and saw the cold piece of grilled chicken and mashed potatoes, but he was too tired to eat, so he covered the plate and put it in the refrigerator.

The door to their bedroom was slightly open and as he entered he saw Elaina partially propped up in the bed. The lamp on the bedside table was still on and the book she had been reading lay open on her chest. She was still wearing her reading glasses, but was sound asleep. He turned on the light in the bathroom, then quietly approached her side of the bed. He gently pulled the book out from under her limp fingers and marked her place with the cross-shaped bookmark. He knew she would be angry if she lost her place.

For a moment he stood there, watching his incredibly beautiful wife sleep. Over the years he learned that she was just as beautiful on the inside as she was on the outside. He still couldn't believe how fortunate he was to have her.

He carefully removed her glasses and slowly pulled the extra pillow out from under her head, and as he did she rolled on her side without waking up. He turned off the bedside lamp, and went back into the bathroom to get undressed before finally joining her.

As he slipped in beside he kissed her softly on the cheek and whispered, "Good night, Angel."

She stirred slightly and managed a muffled "Good night."

CHAPTER 18

The alarm buzzed softly at 5:45 a.m., and Jack rolled over to turn it off. His first case at the general hospital wasn't scheduled to start until 7:30, but he needed to check on the child he'd taken back to surgery last night. He showered and dressed quickly, then kissed Elaina goodbye. This time she didn't wake up.

As he approached the ICU bed where the five-year-old Nicaraguan girl remained on the ventilator, he saw the intensivist in her room along with two nurses.

"How's she doing?" Jack asked as he approached the bedside.

"She's had a pretty rough night," the intensivist offered. Roger Latham had taken over from John Crockett at midnight, and he'd been managing the child's care through the night. "I've had to treat her for some cardiac arrhythmias, and her pressure has been up and down. She seems to be oxygenating okay, but her chest x-ray looks a little hazy."

"How's her urine output?" Jack asked, with obvious concern.

"It's been a little low, and I've been giving her Lasix about every four hours."

Jack had feared that her kidney function might have suffered as a result of the period of low blood pressure. He'd hoped her urine output would have picked up by now with her pressure back to normal. There was really no way to know for sure whether any significant damage had occurred to her kidneys. They'd just have to wait and see.

"Has she tried to wake up?"

"Not really, but I've kept her sedated through the night to make it easier to ventilate her."

The child's exhausted parents were both asleep on the window seat bed in the back of the small room. They'd obviously been up most of the night, and had finally been able to rest.

"What do you think about placing a feeding tube?" Roger asked.

"That's probably a good idea, but let's keep the protein content of the feedings to a minimum, at least until we see what her kidneys are going to do."

◆◆◆◆◆◆◆◆◆

It was difficult for Jack to devote his full concentration to the mitral valve replacement he was performing on his forty-seven-year-old patient. His mind kept drifting back to the evening before and what he might have done differently to avoid that episode of bleeding and the severe hypotension his younger patient had suffered. As soon as he completed the routine valve replacement and all the required paperwork, he headed directly back to the children's hospital.

"Has there been any change?" he asked the nurse as he entered the ICU.

"Not really," she said. "Her urine output is still only about five milliliters per hour, so we've backed off on her IV fluid rate."

Jack was becoming increasingly concerned about the poor urine output. "Let's consult Dr. Jacobson," he said, figuring it was a good idea to get the pediatric nephrologist involved now, before her kidneys shut down completely. Acute renal failure had the potential to be a major complication, not just because of the toxins that would build up in her blood, but also the resulting fluid overload, which would make it difficult for her lungs to function.

The young girl's father approached the bedside, and Jack tried to explain that his daughter's kidneys had been affected by the episode of low blood pressure the evening before, so he was calling in a kidney specialist. There was a chance that she would need to undergo dialysis if her urine output didn't improve soon. The Nicaraguan man nodded as if he understood, but Jack knew he was unable to grasp the true nature of what he'd been told. The fatigue and anxiety in his face were obvious as he stood helplessly next to his child's bed.

The morning chest x-ray clearly showed signs of fluid accumulating in the lungs. As he stood at the view box, Radha came up behind him and peeked around his shoulder at the films.

"I understand she may have suffered some acute tubular necrosis," Radha said, acknowledging the medical term for the condition Jack had suspected.

"Yes, I'm afraid so," he agreed. "She was only hypotensive for fifteen or twenty minutes, but combined with the stress of being on the pump earlier in the day, I suspect her kidneys just couldn't handle it."

"There wasn't anything you could have done differently, Jack," his longtime friend offered as consolation.

"Isn't that what we always say whenever there's a complication?" he asked through a forced smile.

"I don't know how many times I've heard you say it, Jack, but your quote is very accurate. 'The only surgeons who never have complications are the ones who don't operate.'"

"Well, I just wonder if the problem could have been avoided if I'd used pledgets on every suture from the start?" He was now questioning the technique he'd used successfully for years on countless other children.

"It doesn't do any good for you to beat yourself up over something that can't be changed now. Again, I'd use your own words to deal with this situation. 'Just do the next right thing.'"

He finally looked away from the x-ray view box, and into the brown weathered face of his longtime friend. He smiled at her kind words and said, "Yeah, you're probably right, but it doesn't make it any easier."

Late that morning, Dr. Jacobson came by to see the girl. After reviewing her lab results and her intake and output records, he ordered a scan of her kidneys, but he was pretty sure what it was going to show.

"Jack?" Ernie said through the phone. "This is Ernie Jacobson. I'm looking at your little girl here in the ICU. Looks like she's in ATN. I've ordered a renal scan but right now it doesn't look good."

"That's pretty much what I figured. You thinking about dialyzing her?"

"Not just yet, but I would suspect eventually we'll need to. I've seen some of these kids turn around in the first twenty-four hours, but if her urine output hasn't picked up by tomorrow morning, we'll certainly need to consider that option. By then her potassium levels will likely force our hand."

Acute tubular necrosis was something Jack was very familiar with in adults, but it was unusual in children. In adults it was a short-term problem that required dialysis for only a few days while the kidneys recovered. In children the impact could potentially be much greater and more prolonged. He could only pray that wasn't going to be this child's fate.

◆◆◆◆◆◆◆◆◆

"Hi, Traci, what's up?" Jack said as he picked up his office phone.

"I just got a call from Fitzgerald," she said. "Seems he has his own spies in the hospital, and he's asking me what's going on with that kid in the ICU. What should I tell him?"

"Well, she had a post-op bleed with cardiac tamponade that required us to take her back to surgery last night. Now she's showing signs of renal failure, and she may require dialysis."

"Wow!" she responded. "What's your prognosis?"

"I really can't say right now," he admitted, trying to sound optimistic, "but if she goes on dialysis it might take a while to get her kidneys functioning again."

"What exactly do you mean by a while?"

"Hell, Traci, I don't know." He was beginning to become frustrated with what he knew were questions that weren't coming from her, but from the chairman of the board. "It could be anywhere from an extra week to an extra month in the hospital. Just tell Fitzgerald that I'll try and spend as little of his money as possible."

"Look, Jack, don't take it out on me," she said defensively. "I'm just the messenger here."

"I know, I know. I'm just frustrated with the idea of having that… that… billionaire looking over my shoulder."

"You just do what you have to do, and I'll try my best to run interference for you, but I need you to keep me informed. Okay?"

"Fair enough," he agreed. "I'll give you an update tomorrow morning once a decision has been made regarding dialysis."

"Thanks, I'll talk to you tomorrow."

♦♦♦♦♦♦♦♦♦

"It's Wednesday, and you promised it would be our date night," Amy appealed into her cell phone.

"I know, Baby," David sighed, "but I have a chemistry exam tomorrow morning covering the first chapter of the textbook, and I haven't finished reading it yet."

"Can't we just go grab some dinner somewhere?"

"Yeah, sure," he said with resignation. "I just need to be back to my dorm by eight o'clock."

"Are you going to come by and pick me up then?"

"Sure, give me fifteen minutes and I'll be out front."

As David pulled up in front of the freshman girls' dormitory, Amy came bounding out in a pair of short blue jean cutoffs and a tight-fitting tee shirt gathered and tied under her breasts. His eyes nearly popped out of his head as she jumped in the car before he had a chance to get out and open her door.

"Wow!" was all he could say, as she grinned at him and flashed her wide green eyes. "It's a good thing your mom isn't around, she'd never let you out of the house dressed like that."

"What? You don't like the way I'm dressed?"

"I didn't say that. I think you look… fantastic!" he said staring at her bare legs and abdomen.

"Thank you, I decided to wear this because it's so hot."

"Are you talking about the weather, or the outfit?"

She leaned over and kissed him passionately before sitting down and buckling her seatbelt. David's mind was now totally distracted, overcome by the hormones surging through his veins.

"Where are we going?"

"Why don't we grab something at the Sonic and take a drive out west?"

Soon they were parked on a hill overlooking Lake Travis, where they both quickly consumed their burgers and tater tots. As they sipped on their soft drinks, they watched the evening sun slowly approach the horizon.

"Let's get out and watch the sun go down over there in the grass," she said playfully.

David looked at his watch and it was already seven forty-five. "Okay, but just for little bit. I need to be getting back."

She jumped out of the car and pranced out in front of him down the steep hill. He followed her, and could not keep his eyes off of her shapely bottom and athletic legs. As she reached a grassy area surrounded by a white rocky outcropping, she sat down and looked up at him with a big smile as she patted the ground next to her. He reluctantly sat down as she stretched her arms behind her, leaning back and shaking her hair freely off her shoulders.

"This is a really neat spot," she said, staring off into the rapidly setting sun.

"Yes, it is," he agreed, as he took in the panoramic view of the sunset and the sparkling lake below.

After a couple of minutes, Amy lowered her back onto the grass and put her hands behind her head. David looked over at her and saw her smiling as she stared up into the cloudless sky, her gentle blond curls radiating out from her beautiful young face.

"What are you thinking about?" he asked.

"I was just thinking what it will be like when we're married."

David turned to face her, hovering just a few inches above. "It will be amazing," he said. "At least it will be for me." He smiled and lowered his mouth to hers, finding it more receptive and more tender than any time he could ever recall. He could sense that she was transitioning from the girl he first started loving into a young woman. As he put his weight on her chest she moaned softly and bit his lower lip a little harder than she'd intended.

"Ow! What was that for?" he said as he jerked his head back.

"What's wrong?"

"You bit me!"

"I'm sorry, I didn't mean for it to hurt. It was supposed to be a love bite."

"It felt more like one of those blood-sucking vampire bats!" He realized as soon as he said it, he had hurt her feelings. She hadn't started to cry yet, but he thought she looked on the verge. "I'm sorry, Baby. I know you didn't mean to hurt me."

He bent over to kiss her again, but she turned away. She'd had this all planned out in her mind. She had dressed in the skimpiest, sexiest outfit she owned, and was lying on her back, ready to be caught up in one of those passion-filled moments like she'd seen in the movies. Then, he called her a vampire bat and the mood was shattered. She was not about to allow him to kiss her again, even if he did apologize.

"I think we'd better go," she said as she sat up, no longer paying any attention to the brilliant sunset in front of them. "You said you needed to get some reading done, and I have some stuff to do, too."

He tried to put his arms around her again, but she turned away and stood quickly before heading back toward the car without waiting for him to catch up. She climbed in and slammed the door noisily, making it clear how she felt. David was stunned. *What had just happened?* He had known Amy to be moody at times, but she just went from being the hottest chick on the planet to ice cold. He clearly was not yet familiar with the subtle courting practices of the human female.

Later that evening he called her cell phone and heard, "Hi, this is Amy. I can't get to my phone right now, but if you leave me a message I'll call you back. Bye!" He wasn't used to hearing her voice mail greeting. Usually she picked up as soon as she saw it was him on caller ID.

"Hi, Baby," he began. "I just wanted to call and tell you again how sorry I am about this afternoon. I wasn't thinking. Please call me, I'll be up late,"

As he finished rereading chapter one of the chemistry text, his phone finally rang. It was nearly midnight, and he quickly answered her call.

"Hey, Baby," he offered meekly.

"Oh, David, I'm so sorry," she said. She'd obviously been crying for some time before she called. "I acted like such a witch, only with a capital B."

"No, no... I was the one to blame. I should have thought before I spoke. You had every right to be mad."

"I love you so much," she said through her tears. "I wanted this evening to be so special."

"It was special. I've never seen you look any hotter than you were in those shorts. You really know how to get my attention."

"Do you really mean that, or are you just trying to make me feel better?"

"All I can tell you is you just about had me ready to break our vow."

"I know," she said. "I'm not sure I can wait until we finish college four years from now."

David paused, afraid to really speak what was on his mind. "We can talk about that this weekend. Right now I just want to make sure we're okay." He paused again then said, "I love you, Baby."

"I love you too, more than anything, and nothing will ever change that."

After another pause he said, "I'm really glad you called me back. I was beginning to wonder if you were going to make me try and go to sleep knowing you were still angry."

"I couldn't call until just now, because I was crying too hard."

"You know, my mom told me something when I was in junior high that has always stuck with me," David said. "She said, 'Don't ever go to bed mad. You'll wake up mad, and it's much harder to get glad the next day.' I think we should make a promise to each other to never go to bed mad, what do you think?"

"I don't ever want to be mad at you again, and I couldn't bear for you to be mad at me."

"So, is it a deal?"

"Of course," she said. "I just wish you were here right now so I could kiss that place on your lip where I bit you." Her voice was now more sultry, but it still had the underlying tone of an innocent girl.

"I wish I was there, too," he said sadly. "How 'bout if we try again tomorrow night? I'll pick you up around six o'clock, in front of your dorm."

"That sounds great." Her voice was more cheerful as the tears had finally subsided.

"Okay, listen, I gotta get some sleep. My chemistry test is at eight o'clock in the morning."

"All right. I'll let you go, but only if you promise to dream about me."

"Always… Good night, Baby…"

"Good night…"

Like all young lovers, they had a hard time saying goodbye, neither one wanting to hang up first.

◆◆◆◆◆◆◆◆

"It looks like we are going to need to dialyze her," Ernie said as Jack walked into the ICU room. "Her potassium is up to five point eight and her output has dropped to under five ml per hour despite Mannitol and Lasix."

"Okay, I'll take her over to the OR and put in a temporary vascular access catheter," Jack said, having resigned himself to what he knew would be the best course of action. "Any idea how long she's gonna need it?"

"You know as well as I do that it could be four or five days, or maybe a month before her kidneys start functioning again."

"Yeah, I know. I was just hoping you could give me your best estimate, so I could let administration know how big the bill is likely to be."

"I thought this kid was covered by the Nicaraguan grant I heard about."

"What do you know about that?" Jack asked, surprised that Ernie knew anything about Franco's gift to the hospital.

"Are you kidding? Last year that was all anybody talked about for more than a month after that baby went home."

Perhaps Jack had more ammunition in his gun than he thought. If everyone knew about the stipulations Franco had placed on the million dollars, there's no way Fitzgerald and the board could get by with using it for anything else. He decided not to say any more to Ernie about his conversations with administration, at least not yet.

"Even so, it's important that we keep our costs down to avoid depleting that fund any faster than we otherwise might," Jack said as he left to schedule the procedure.

"She needs to go on dialysis," Jack said as he stepped into Traci's office. He had walked down to administration to deliver the news in person.

"Any idea how long she'll need to be on it?" she asked.

"Like I said yesterday, it could be a few days or it could be a month or even more. Just depends on how quickly her kidneys start working again."

"Okay," Traci said with frustrated resignation. "I'll let the folks up the line know."

That afternoon Jack took the girl back to surgery for the third time, and on this occasion he placed a large catheter in the main vein under her right collarbone. When she arrived back in the ICU, Ernie was there to initiate dialysis. Jack was sure that Franco had expected the huge amount of money he'd given the hospital would help a dozen or more kids, but if this little girl had to stay on dialysis for a month, it was going to eat up a good portion of those resources.

◆◆◆◆◆◆◆◆

As David drove up in front of the dorm he saw Amy walking out toward his car. He was disappointed to see that she hadn't dressed as a temptress again. Instead she wore faded blue jeans and a new white sweatshirt with an orange Texas longhorn across the front and the word TEXAS written in bold orange letters across her chest. She was carrying a big orange and white blanket draped over her arm. She'd gotten both at the campus book store earlier that day.

"Hey, Baby," David said, still sounding apologetic as he jumped out to open her door.

"Do you think my mom would be okay with this outfit?" she asked as she tossed the blanket casually in the backseat.

David just smiled as he kissed her, before getting back in the car and driving away.

"How about some pizza?" he asked.

"That sounds good to me, but only if we can get it to go."

"Okay," he said. "Any place in particular you want to go to eat it?"

"You said we'd try again tonight, so I just figured we'd go back to our place up on the hill."

"Our place?" David asked with a smile.

"Yeah, I think it could be our place, but we need to start over."

David carried the pizza box and two cans of Coke, while Amy carried the blanket and some napkins as they made their way back down the hill out of sight from the road above. She spread the blanket over the grassy area where the crushed vegetation gave witness to their presence the day before. The sun was still fairly high in the sky, and there were no clouds to create a picturesque sunset on this day.

"I'm starving," David said as he opened the pizza box.

"Me, too," Amy said, but she didn't reach immediately for the pizza.

As he took his second bite, he looked at her quizzically and asked, "What's the matter, Baby? I thought you were hungry."

"I am... but not for pizza."

"Well, you should've said something before we went there. We could have had something else."

Amy had decided that David was totally clueless when it came to matters of the heart. She was going to have to be more direct. "I'm hungry for you, silly."

He put his pizza back in the box and closed the lid, then moved the box off the blanket onto one of the rocks next to the two Coke cans. He turned back to Amy who was on her side, facing him, propped up on one elbow. He assumed the same position facing her, and stared into her beautiful green eyes as they picked up the golden reflection of the afternoon sun.

"I think we need to talk about this," he said, knowing exactly what they were each thinking. "I'm hungry for you, too, but I just don't know whether I'm ready."

"I know," she admitted. "I don't know whether I'm ready either. I just know when I'm with you, it's all I think about, and when I'm away from you, it's all I think about." She laughed at herself. She'd never been so transparent with anyone, but she trusted him to understand her, and what she was saying.

"It would be so easy, right here, right now, but I can't imagine what would happen if you were to get pregnant like Sandy did back in high school."

"Before I left to come to Austin, I had a long conversation with my mom. She told me that there would come a time when I might not be able to resist temptation, so she sent me to see Dr. Fielder, and he started me on birth control pills."

David looked into her languid eyes and felt helpless to resist his urges. He quickly moved to kiss her tenderly, and as he did he silently slipped his hand under her bulky sweatshirt.

♦♦♦♦♦♦♦♦♦

"When will you be back?" Elaina asked as she watched Jack prepare his travel shaving kit.

"My testimony is tomorrow morning, and then I was going to have an early dinner with David. So I think I should be home by ten o'clock tomorrow evening, at the latest."

It was mid-October, and Jack was set to testify before the Texas Medicaid advisory panel in Austin. The hospital board of trustees had provided him with a set of talking points, which he thought were a ridiculous way to present information, but he took them and promised Traci he'd make all their points. She offered to come with him, but he declined, telling her he was capable of managing this assignment on his own.

She, too, was convinced of his abilities after the whole ordeal with Fitzgerald had come to a head. The little girl had only required dialysis for six days, so the total charges for three surgeries, seven days in the ICU, and five more days on the nursing floor came to $173,204. Once all the negotiating was over, Fitzgerald had agreed to deduct $110,000 from the $935,000 that had magically shown up back on the hospital books as the Nicaraguan Surgical Fund. The old man hadn't been at all happy being forced to backtrack on the board's prior actions, but once Jack informed him that the entire medical staff was aware of the stipulations attached to the Gutierrez gift, he had little choice.

"Call me when you get there, okay?" Elaina asked as she kissed him goodbye.

"I will, Angel. I love you," he said, then walked out into the garage. He stumbled over the chrome bumper of David's truck project and swore softly under his breath. He knew his son would never finish reassembling the parts that had been scattered on the garage floor for more than two years, and now the whole thing just needed to be hauled off to the junkyard.

The trip down to Austin only took three hours. While he was driving he went over in his mind what he planned to say to the legislators on the advisory committee deciding the fate of the Medicaid and State Children's Health Insurance Program payments for the next year. The final decision would be up to the state legislature, which only met every other year in Texas, and this would be one of the first items on their agenda after the first of the year. He thought it was interesting that they would have this hearing now, less than a month before the statewide elections, since there was a chance some of the representatives on the advisory committee might not get reelected. They might not even be there when the issue came up for a vote. He knew this was more of a campaign forum than anything else, but he figured it was his opportunity to speak to the issues from a physician's perspective.

He checked in to the Embassy Suites hotel near downtown and called Elaina as promised. He then called David to tell him he had arrived. As he answered the phone his son sounded out of breath.

"Are you okay?" he asked.

"Yeah, sure." David replied, before offering an explanation. "I was just doing a little workout."

"We're still on for dinner tomorrow evening, right?"

"Oh yeah, I almost forgot about that. Sure, what time?"

"I expect my hearing will be over by three o'clock so any time you get out of class would work for me."

"My last class is over at four, so how about five o'clock?"

"That would be great. That way I can get back home by around nine-thirty."

"Would it be okay if Amy comes to dinner with us?"

"Sure, I don't see why not. I assume you two have been studying together?"

It was all she could do not to giggle out loud as she overheard Jack's question through the phone. They were lying together in their favorite spot, and they had indeed been studying each other very carefully.

"Yeah, we've been hanging out together some."

"Is there a nice steak restaurant near the campus?"

"There's a Sammy's steak house over on I-35. Do you want to just meet there at five o'clock?"

"Sounds good," Jack said. "I'll see you guys there."

"Okay, bye Dad."

As he heard the phone click off, Jack wondered what kind of workout David had been doing.

◆◆◆◆◆◆◆◆◆

The hearing was not held in the Capitol as Jack had expected. Instead it was in a government office building a couple of blocks away. The conference room was relatively small, and the commission consisted of only seven legislators: four republicans, two democrats, and one independent. There was a videographer to record the proceedings and about a dozen interested spectators. Jack was scheduled to be the third person to testify.

The first to offer an opinion was a representative from an organization called Texans for Responsible Taxation. She was a fiery fifty-year-old from Houston, and she spouted one statistic after another supporting her claim that Medicaid was killing the Texas economy. The idea of increasing the state's role in maintaining the program's federal support was in her words, "A foolish waste of the taxpayers' money."

The second person to speak was the president of the Bexar County Hospital District in San Antonio. Jack had spent plenty of time in those hospitals, and he knew exactly what this guy was going to say. Without adequate Medicaid payments, the county hospital could not remain open, and they were the primary referral hospital for much of South Texas. They were already providing uncompensated care to tens of thousands of illegals, and Medicaid was a major source of revenue that helped offset those losses. He made most of the points that were on Traci's list, and Jack thought the guy must have been reading from the same document.

The commissioners sat silently throughout the first two testimonies. They thanked the second presenter and then the chairman called out, "Dr. Jack Roberts, representing the children's hospital in Fort Worth."

Jack rose from his seat near the back of the room and approached the small table that had been set up in front of the commissioners who were lined up behind a long table across the front of the room. Each member had a paper placard in front of them with their name and nothing more. He didn't have any idea which ones were the Rs and which ones were the Ds or the I. As he prepared to take his seat an aide hurried out to his table with a placard with his name on it, replacing the one used to designate the prior gentleman.

"Well, Dr. Roberts, what have you got for us?" the chairman asked with undo sarcastic emphasis on the word doctor.

Jack took a breath and smiled, determined to remain calm and relaxed.

"First, I'd like to thank the commission for the opportunity to come here today on behalf of my hospital, but also on behalf of all the children of Texas. As I'm sure you know, Medicaid is the primary insurance for nearly two and a half million children in this state, and there are another half million children of working families who depend on the Texas State Children's Health Insurance Program. These are statistics you all know. I only mention them to emphasize the enormity of the problem.

"Mr. Chairman, you asked me what I've got for you, and I will admit, not much that you haven't already heard. What I do have are real life stories about individual boys and girls that I have been privileged to care for over the last eighteen years at the children's hospital in Fort Worth. Kids like Manuel Ortega, who was born with a huge hole in his heart. He was born in a small, run down house on the South side of Fort Worth. The Medicaid program was the only resource available to his parents who are second generation Texans. He underwent a heart operation at our hospital seventeen years ago, and this past year Manny graduated from high school with honors, and last month he joined the same freshman class as my own son, right here at the University of Texas.

"Ten years ago I had occasion to see a beautiful thirteen-year-old girl with a rare type of tumor inside her heart. The SCHIP program was the only health coverage available to her family after her father lost his job at the Tandy Corporation. His daughter's story is remarkable for many reasons, but you might know her if you watched the recent Miss Texas Pageant earlier this year. She didn't win, but she was the first runner up.

"I also cared for a child from Midland five years ago who had a congenital defect involving the major vessels of his heart. Medicaid made it possible for him to have corrective surgery at age ten. Last year the teenager rescued his drowning father during a fishing trip when their boat capsized.

"If you'd like I can site many other examples of how the Medicaid and Texas SCHIP programs have provided funds that have not only saved lives, but provided untold dividends to the people of Texas."

"May I interrupt you for just a moment, Dr. Roberts?" asked one of the members of the commission sitting near one end of the table. Without waiting for a response he simply continued with what would ultimately be a question.

"I understand you have saved tens, if not hundreds of thousands of children during your illustrious career, and for that we are all grateful. But, I dare say, you have likely profited quite nicely at the state's expense. Not that any of us begrudge your ability to make a living," he added as he looked up and broke into a disgustingly toothy grin. "But, I'm certain that you and the fine folks who run your hospital up there in Fort Worth do not understand the magnitude of the problems we face here in Austin. Our job is to take care of all the people of Texas, not just the poor and the sick. We would love to be able to provide the very best health care in the world to every child and every adult within our borders, but the fact is, sir, money doesn't grow on trees, even here in the great state of Texas. I would suggest that you go back to your hospital and tell them that it is very likely they will need to learn to do more with less. I suspect your hospital could function just as well if not better without a few of their high-priced assistant administrators and unnecessary file clerks." He paused again to visually measure Jack's response before continuing.

"Anyway, my question is, what is your opinion of the Pay-for-Performance initiative being discussed in Washington as a means of cutting Medicare costs, and do you think it would work the same here for Medicaid?"

Jack hardly knew where to begin his response to this uninformed, pompous, bloviating politician. Why not start with the last remark and work his way backward? But then he thought, if he answered his question first, he might not be allowed to address the remainder of his exaggerations, fabrications, misconceptions, and outright lies.

"Thank you for your question, Representative Johnson," he began, glancing briefly at his notes. "I would like to address each of the points you raised. First,

I have been a heart surgeon for twenty-seven years, and in an average year I perform three to four hundred heart operations, so all together I've performed between eight and nine thousand procedures, with only about half of them on children. So, your suggestion of tens, or hundreds of thousands of lives saved, is flattering, but inaccurate. As to the profitability of Medicaid, I would like to point out that the average payment doctors receive from Medicaid is less than twenty percent of the charge, and typically is not sufficient to cover the cost of providing that service. My office manager considers Medicaid to be only marginally better than charity when she factors in the time and resources required to collect from the program. Incidentally, payments are typically not received for at least six to eight weeks.

"I would also beg to differ with your assertion that it's your job to take care of all the people in the state of Texas. Last I looked, most of the people in this state are perfectly capable of caring for themselves. In fact, the efforts by you guys here in Austin and everyone in Washington to get yourselves reelected every few years by giving away money and services to people who don't need your help, is the major reason why there aren't enough resources to take care of those who are truly poor or legitimately unable to work.

"I agree with you that money doesn't grow on trees, but neither do children. They are our future, and if you and your colleagues have one absolute duty, it is to exercise fiscal responsibility to secure the blessings of liberty to ourselves and our posterity, as called for in the preamble of the United States Constitution.

"As to the issues of hospital staffing and belt-tightening, I agree. We could all do with some belt-tightening, but perhaps before you start making suggestions about how a hospital might be run more effectively, perhaps you might want to consider ways you could run your own office and this government more efficiently. You might just find a few high-priced staff members or unnecessary campaign trips you could do without." He could see all the committee members squirm noticeably at this accusation.

"And finally, sir, with regard to your question about the Medicare Pay-for-Performance initiative. I would point out that quality of care was never an issue in this country when health care was delivered in a free market, supported by community charity. It wasn't until politicians attempted to control it through highly regulated payment systems that quality began to decline and access became an issue. The idea of Pay-for-Performance is simply another in a long list of misnamed government initiatives that impose inappropriate and overly constraining controls on those of us who are already sworn to provide the best care we can for those in need — our patients. Furthermore, there is no evidence that such a program actually improves care, but it does increase the cost. Did I answer your question, sir?"

The legislator did not respond, but instead sat staring a hole through Jack, who stared back until Johnson finally looked down at the papers in front of him.

The chairman broke the silence and said, "Dr. Roberts, you are obviously passionate about this subject, and we respect your opinion. Unfortunately, you may be speaking to the wrong audience. Yours is the kind of message the guys in Washington need to hear. After all, they're the ones threatening to cut off our funds. Perhaps, if you would give them a piece of your mind like you have my distinguished colleague from East Texas, they might be able to find the money in the federal budget to maintain funding of the Medicaid program."

"I have a suggestion," added another member on the opposite end of the table. "Maybe you should run for Congress, doctor, and see if you can straighten out this health care mess." The sarcasm was very apparent in the voices of all three members who spoke. It was clear that Jack's style of openly confronting an elected official was considered disrespectful, and as politicians, they tended to close ranks even across party lines whenever one of their own was challenged by an outsider.

♦♦♦♦♦♦♦♦♦

Jack was seated in a booth at Sammy's, sipping on his second glass of tea when David and Amy came rushing in at five-twenty.

"Sorry we're late, Dad," David said as Jack stood to greet them. He hugged his son and then the young girl who seemed almost attached to David's hip. They sat next to each other on the opposite side of the booth. Jack thought he detected a difference in his son's demeanor, but he couldn't put his finger on it.

"So, how's school?"

"Great," David responded quickly, "but it's different from what I expected."

"In what way?"

"Well, first of all none of the professors take roll. I don't think they care whether you go to class or not."

"I trust you aren't taking advantage of their lack of discipline," Jack said with a questioning tone.

"No, of course not," David responded. "I haven't missed a class since I've been here." Technically what he said was correct, but he had slept through a couple of British literature classes on mornings after he and Amy had been up late.

"Anyway, I think the biggest surprise to me is how much free time I have. It used to be, back in high school, I would sit in class all day and then have to study every evening, so the only free time I had was on the weekends. Here, my classes are spread out throughout the day, so I can get most of my studying done between classes. That has given me time to do other things I didn't expect to be able to do."

"Like what?" Jack sounded excited for his son to be branching out, but he had some concern that, like so many other freshmen, he might let his studies slide.

"Well, Jarrod, my roommate, and I have played golf a couple of times. And I signed up for a flag football league."

"Terrific, that sounds like fun," he said, smiling at the enthusiasm David was displaying. "How about you, Amy, what have you been up to?"

"Not much, just studying mostly," she said, avoiding the real answer that would have been unacceptable to David's father.

Over the next hour David talked about each of his courses and how he'd aced some of the tests, but struggled a bit with others, especially British literature.

"Your mom was upset that you didn't call her last Sunday," Jack said during a lull in the conversation.

"I'm sorry," David replied. "I got tied up and it just slipped my mind." What he couldn't say was that he and Amy had skipped church on Sunday morning and driven out to Fredericksburg for Oktoberfest. He drank way too much beer, and she'd had to drive home. The thought of calling his mom never even crossed his mind until the next day.

"Well, you know she worries about you all the time, and you owe it to her to call her at least once a week."

"I know, I will."

"When are you coming home?"

"I'll be home for Thanksgiving, and then over Christmas break," he said, as he thought of something else he needed to say. "That reminds me, some of the guys are going to Steamboat Springs, Colorado, between Christmas and New Year's, and they've asked me if I want to go."

"Who are these other guys? Do you know them well?" Jack wanted to ask about possible drugs and alcohol, but he didn't want to seem too controlling.

"It's a bunch of guys from my dorm that I've been hangin' out with. They all seem to be pretty solid, as best I can tell."

"Well, I'll talk to your mom about it. When do you need to let them know?"

"The signup ends on Halloween, so a couple of weeks."

"We will have discussed it by the time you talk to your mom on Sunday, and she can let you know then." Jack remembered how much fun he'd had as a freshman, skiing with Erin. He just hoped David wasn't doing the things with Amy that he did with his girlfriend after their days on the slopes.

◆◆◆◆◆◆◆◆◆

On Monday afternoon Jack strolled into Traci's office and stuck his head around her open door.

"You got a minute?"

"Sure," she said. "Come on in."

"I just wanted to give you an update on the hearing in Austin."

"You're a bit late," she said with a smile. "Seems the Austin American-Statesman beat you to the punch."

"What do you mean?"

"There was a big article in the political section of that paper on Friday. Apparently those legislators weren't too pleased with the way you dressed down that representative from Tyler."

"What did they have to say?"

"The article quoted you a couple of times," she said. "I've got it right here." Traci produced a printed version of the newspaper she had first read online. "The first quote — 'the efforts by you guys here in Austin and everyone in Washington to get yourselves reelected every few years by giving away money and services to people who don't need your help' — kinda made you sound like you were opposed to any government support," she said.

"They obviously took that phrase out of context. What I said was that giving money and services to those who didn't need them was the reason why they were running out of money to take care of the people who need it."

"I know, I know, but there's more." Traci looked back down at the paper and read aloud, "The doctor appeared to take offense to the representative's suggestion that he'd personally profited from children's illnesses with money coming from the state. He said, 'My office manager considers Medicaid to be only marginally better than charity when she factors in the time and resources required to collect from the program. Incidentally, payments are typically not received for at least six to eight weeks.' To confirm this we had a reporter from the Fort Worth Star-Telegram drive out to Dr. Roberts' home in the exclusive Westover Hills area, and he took this photograph of his million-dollar mansion." Traci looked up from the paper and half smiled at Jack, then pointed back down at the page and said, "There is a picture of your house, but at least they had the courtesy of not posting the address."

"Those sons-of-bi..." he growled. "Is there no limit to how low they can stoop?"

"The article concluded with this," she said, again reading from the text. "In response to the chairman's request for information that would help the state avoid the Medicaid and SCHIP-precipitated financial crisis, the good doctor's response was: 'You asked me what I've got for you, and I will admit, not much...' I spoke to Mr. Johnson after the hearing and he said 'Dr. Roberts is well meaning, I'm sure, but he should go back home to his fancy house and fancy cars and thank his lucky stars that we haven't recommended the twenty percent cut in Medicaid physician payments called for by the state's budget office.' It seems that the medical community didn't do itself any favors when it sent Dr. Jack Roberts to plead its case in Austin."

"I have half a mind to sue the pants off that rag," he said with more anger than he'd felt in years.

"I saw the transcript of your remarks on the state's website, and, while those quotes were clearly taken out of context, they were accurate, as best I could tell. I don't think you'd have a case. If I were you, I'd just drop it, and recognize this is what politicians do to anyone that disagrees with them."

That night when Jack got home there was a Channel 3 mobile news truck sitting in front of his house. He pulled his pickup into the garage, and by the time he entered the kitchen the doorbell rang.

"How long have they been here?" he asked Elaina as he gave her a brief hug.

"About two hours…"

"Have they been hassling you?"

"No, they just came to the door once, and asked for you. I told them you weren't home. They asked if I thought you'd be home before six, and I said I didn't know. They've been waiting outside in that truck since then."

Jack walked to the door and opened it to find a young female reporter standing a few feet away with a microphone in her hand. The cameraman was standing in the driveway just off to the side, and Jack could see the blinking red light, indicating he was already rolling. A cable ran from the back of his shoulder-mounted video camera across the yard out to a truck with a small satellite dish extending several feet in the air.

"Dr. Roberts, I'm Rhonda Martinez from Channel 3 News. Would you mind if I ask you a few questions?"

"If this is about that story in the Austin newspaper, I'm not sure there is much I can say, except my remarks were taken completely out of context and were grossly misinterpreted by the reporter."

"Are you saying that you did or did not make those remarks?"

"I'm saying that if anyone cares to read my entire testimony before the commission, they would see that the implications made in that 'so-called newspaper' were completely false."

"So, do you think doctors should or shouldn't profit from the Medicaid program?"

He knew better than to get drawn into this kind of one-sided debate. He was standing in front of his home that he'd bought fifteen years before, and had only last month retired the mortgage. It was now worth three times what he'd paid for it, so if he were looking to buy it again today he couldn't even qualify for a loan based on his practice income. The people who were watching this broadcast didn't know that, and furthermore didn't care. All they saw was a rich doctor, and nothing he could say would change that perception.

"I believe that everyone should be compensated for the work they do, according to the value they provide. The problem with our current system lies in the fact that payments are made by third parties who have no knowledge of the personal services they pay for, and don't care to consider the value to those who actually receive the care. I'm sure there are a few who may be in the medical profession for their own profit, but I know I can speak for myself and many of my colleagues when I say we care for patients according to their needs, not according to what some bureaucrat thinks is consistent with the state or federal budget. I don't apologize to anyone for the successes any physicians have attained, but I can assure you that my personal success hasn't been because of Medicaid payments."

"There you have it, Chip," she said as she turned to face the camera. "Straight from the controversial doctor himself. This is Rhonda Martinez, Channel 3 News."

Jim Fitzgerald sat watching the live feed of the news broadcast from his private office. He was sipping the finest Kentucky bourbon, with his feet propped up on the desk. As the interview proceeded he began sporting a very satisfied smile. The general manager of the station had done exactly as he'd instructed.

When the reporter signed off, the anchor added, "Thank you, Rhonda, for that report. It seems the doctor may be unaware of the details of our next story. For that report we go to Gilbert Swain in Dallas."

"Thanks, Chip. I'm here outside a Medicaid clinic in South Dallas where the FBI has just conducted a raid of the office of Dr. Fernando de Garza. The doctor has been the center of a massive Medicaid fraud investigation. I have not been able to obtain many details, but one of the investigators told me that they were seizing records dating back ten years, to 1996. What we do know is that Dr. Garza was implicated in a Medicaid fraud case in Arizona in 1995 but was never charged. He moved here to Dallas the following year and has run this clinic since then. I suspect we'll have more details as this story unfolds over the next few weeks. Back to you, Chip."

CHAPTER 19

"Did you hear the good news?" Traci asked when she ran into Jack outside the entrance to the OR. "Congress managed to find the money to continue funding Medicaid at current levels."

"So, the state legislators won't have that big decision to make after all," he said. For the last two months Jack had been laying low. He had made no further public statements that might make the news. He had caught enough grief for a lifetime from the hospital administration, his colleagues, and his wife. She made him promise not to make any more appearances on TV unless she approved them.

◆◆◆◆◆◆◆◆◆

Jack drove into the huge parking lot at DFW airport. Terminal D was more crowded than usual with all the holiday travelers, but eventually he was able to find a parking spot and headed into the baggage claim area. After about ten minutes he saw his brother come through the sliding double doors pulling one large suitcase and carrying an oversized briefcase. He had just cleared customs.

"Hey, Ben! Over here!" Jack called out when he saw his brother searching the crowd for a familiar face.

The two brothers embraced briefly, then Jack took Ben's bag, leading the way toward his pickup through the mass of people. As they drove out of the lot and toward the South end of the airport they talked about the unseasonably warm weather and the heavier than usual traffic, before getting down to more meaty matters.

"So, how's Japan?" Jack asked.

"It's good, I guess," Ben replied. "Not that I've had a chance to see much of it. I've been there for four months, and I haven't seen anything except my small apartment and the inside of my lab."

"Well, I'm glad they let you get out long enough to come home for a few days."

"It was part of my contract," Ben said with an uncharacteristic grin.

"How's the work going?"

"Very well, but don't start asking me about it, because I can't talk about it."

Jack was curious by nature, but this secret project his brother was involved with had him particularly intrigued. "You aren't even going to give me a hint?"

"Look, Jack," Ben said, turning slightly in his seat toward his older brother, "I can't talk about it, and I'd appreciate it if you wouldn't quiz me, okay?"

Jack detected a level of defensiveness in his brother he'd never seen before. "Okay, sure," he agreed. "I won't mention it again."

After they passed through the toll booth and headed toward the freeway, Jack said, "Since you were here last summer, mom has been showing some signs of early dementia."

"What do you mean?"

"Well, she forgets things. Like the other day, she told me she had to make three trips to the grocery store. When she got home the first time she had forgotten to get stuff for her breakfast, so she went back and got cereal, but forgot the milk."

"That's not at all like her," Ben said with concern.

"No, it's not, but that wasn't the worst of it. Last weekend we went out to see her on Sunday afternoon, shortly after David got home from Austin. When we walked into the house, she looked at him and said, 'Now, who are you?' That's when I knew something was wrong."

"Hopefully, she will still recognize me," Ben said, with a nervous laugh.

"Oh, she hasn't talked about anything but your coming home for the last three weeks."

✦✦✦✦✦✦✦✦

The Roberts family Christmas gathering at Jack and Elaina's home provided everyone a chance to catch up. David spent hours talking to his uncle, picking his brain about the part he had played in developing the guidance system for the space shuttle. Ben was pleased to see that his mom's dementia didn't seem as bad as Jack had made it sound.

Janet and Leonard had driven up from Houston for the day. Their two girls were spending Christmas with their spouses' families, so they had planned their family get-together the following day at their home north of Houston. It had been two years since Jack had seen his sister, but it seemed they had little to talk about. Faye scarcely acknowledged her daughter's presence. She had never forgiven her for not being there when Harry died. After lunch Janet and Leonard turned around and drove the four hours back home.

The day after Christmas, David left on his first ski trip to Colorado and the day after that Jack and his mom took Ben to the airport for his flight back to Tokyo. Faye cried as she said goodbye to her younger son, and she didn't stop until long after they'd arrived back at her home. Her tears had scarcely dried when Jack announced that he needed to get back home, which started another emotional meltdown.

"I wish you would call me more often," she sobbed. "I know you're busy, but it gets very lonely here in this house all by myself."

"I know, Mom," Jack said. "I'll try and call you at least a couple of times a week." Jack felt bad that he wasn't able to spend more time with her. He had invited her to come live with him and Elaina in their guesthouse six months earlier, but she said, "Oh, no. I'll be fine right where I am. You young people have your own lives to live, and you don't need an old woman hanging around."

As he drove home, he allowed his mind to drift back to those days when life was so much simpler. He remembered how secure he used to feel sitting around the dinner table every night with his mom and dad and his sister and little brother. Now things were so very different. He and Elaina rarely ate at home, and when they did it was usually just a delivered pizza. Life had become far too complicated. He suddenly realized that simplicity was what he enjoyed the most about their trips to Nicaragua.

❖❖❖❖❖❖❖❖❖

Two days before the new year, Elaina went to the grocery store to pick up some chips and some of Jack's favorite salsa. They planned to spend a quiet New Year's Eve at home watching television. While she was in the store she ran into Joanne Callahan and asked about Amy. She tried not to act surprised when Amy's mom told her how excited Amy was to go on a ski trip with her girlfriends from college.

When David came home the day after New Year's, she confronted him, away from his father, asking why he hadn't told her Amy had gone with him. "You know you can talk to me about anything," she said to him as she made him sit down next to her on the sofa.

He looked at her sheepishly and said, "I know, Mom, I'm sorry I didn't tell you Amy was going with me, I just figured you wouldn't approve."

"David," she said as she put both her hands on his arm, "I know you and Amy have been having sex. I've known it since you came home for

Thanksgiving."

"How ..."

"Let's just say, mothers have a way of knowing these things," she said. "I just hope you are being discreet and that she's on the pill."

"She is, and we are, Mom," he responded quickly to her challenge. "I just don't want Dad to know. He'd be very disappointed that I didn't keep my pledge."

"I don't think there is anything you could do that would disappoint your father."

"Amy and I are in love, Mom. This isn't some kind of a fling, ya know?" David spoke earnestly, sharing his true feelings about Amy with her for the first time. "I just don't think Dad would understand."

"You underestimate your father. He is one of the most romantic men I've ever known."

He looked up at her with both surprise and disbelief. "Really? He sure doesn't come across as a romantic."

"Let's just say he swept me off my feet with a combination of charm and tenderness that I had never known existed in a man. The final thing that made me fall in love with him was the way he loved you," she said, squeezing her son's arm. She was near tears as she shared one of the secrets of her heart with him. "Anyway, I think most of what you see in his matter-of-fact style, and his seemingly tough exterior, is his way of protecting himself from getting too emotional."

David just stared at her for a moment then said, "Well, he's done a great job hiding it from me for my entire life."

"I think you should sit down and talk to him some time, man to man."

"You want me to tell him I'm having sex with Amy? I can't do that."

"Sure you can, and you should tell him how you feel about her, and about your dreams and your plans for the future. You might be surprised how he responds, and it will make you feel better, not having to sneak around behind his back."

How could she possibly know that, he wondered? He had felt awful since that afternoon he and Amy had dinner with his dad in Austin. He hated the idea of lying, even if it wasn't actually telling a lie. He wasn't being forthcoming with the truth, and he felt like that was the same thing.

"I know you're right, Mom. I just don't know how I could even start the conversation."

"You're going to be home for a couple more weeks, why don't you ask him if you can go to the OR with him one day and then shadow him in the office? By the end of the day you two will be talking about a lot of things. Just let me know what day you're going to do it, and I'll plan a night out with one of my girlfriends so you guys can go out to dinner together."

"That sounds like a great idea. Thanks, Mom."

"I learned how to plan things like this from your father. That's part of his romantic side."

That evening at dinner David brought up the fact that he missed going into the OR with his dad the way he had when he was younger. Jack quickly invited him to tag along the next day. "I've got a couple of cases tomorrow morning, one at children's and one at the general hospital. I think you'll really like to see the one at children's."

"What is it?" David asked.

"You'll see. Just meet me down here in the kitchen at seven in the morning."

"Okay," he said, satisfied that his mom's idea seemed to be working so far.

♦♦♦♦♦♦♦♦♦

"Who do we have here!" Radha exclaimed, smiling broadly beneath her mask. She hadn't seen David since the trip to Nicaragua a year and a half ago.

"Hello, Dr. Patel," David replied. "It's good to see you again."

"I understand you're in college now," She said. David was Jack's pride and joy, and he talked about him all the time. All the time that is except when he was talking about what he called the organized assault on the medical profession.

"Yes, ma'am, I'm at UT down in Austin," he replied. "I just finished my first semester, so I'm home for a few weeks."

"You stay here while I go scrub my hands, okay?" Jack instructed more than asked, before leaving his son next to the anesthesiologist.

David watched intently as Radha expertly intubated the tiny trachea of the one-week-old boy. "What operation is my dad going to do to this baby?"

"He didn't tell you?"

"No, he said I'd see when I got here."

"Well, in that case I think I'll just let him tell you."

The nurse turned the infant so the left side of his chest was fully exposed with his arm extended up over his head. She washed the area thoroughly and then applied an antiseptic solution as Jack reentered the room.

As he dried his hands and put on his gown and gloves he said, "This baby was born with a tracheoesophageal fistula. It was diagnosed by his pediatrician up in Wichita Falls."

"What's that mean?" David asked, not having heard the term before.

"Well, during fetal development the swallowing tube and breathing tube form parallel to each other in the chest, and every now and then that development goes haywire and an abnormal connection forms between the two tubes. I'm sure you've had times when you've had something go down the wrong pipe, and you felt like you were choking, right?"

"Sure," David replied.

"That's pretty much what this little guy has had going on every time he swallows. Some of the fluid goes into his lungs, so what we are going to do today is separate the two tubes."

"I see."

"What he's not telling you," Radha interrupted, "is he is going to do that without opening the boy's chest."

David turned to look at her, questioning what she meant. Most of the operations he'd seen his dad perform were heart procedures, but he had watched a couple of lung biopsies and that sort of thing done using a scope in adults, but never on a little baby.

"He is going to put several tiny tubes into the baby's chest and operate through them while watching the procedure on that flat screen monitor." She pointed at one of the large video monitors hanging from the ceiling. Currently it was just showing bars of primary colors.

"You know, your dad has been one of the pioneers in pediatric thoracoscopic surgery," she said, in almost a whisper. She knew Jack didn't like to be singled out, but he had been an innovator in the use of this minimally invasive technique since his days in the military. He'd made numerous presentations of procedures like this one at various surgical meetings and had given numerous lectures to colleagues on these revolutionary techniques over the last fifteen years. More than any other aspect of his practice, thoracoscopic surgery in children was where Jack had first gained national recognition. David had always been so caught up in heart surgery he had been totally unaware of this part of his dad's work.

Jack quickly inserted three small tubes into the baby's chest between his tiny ribs as Radha adjusted the breathing tube so that the left lung collapsed out of the way. David stood staring at the high definition image of the inside of the baby's chest. He had no idea what he was looking at, but the rapid rhythmic movements in one part of the screen made the location of the heart obvious. An additional tube was inserted and Jack used it to place an instrument to hold the lung out of the way.

"Radha, could I get you to move the feeding catheter just a bit?" Jack asked. She reached up and manipulated the tiny plastic tube in the infant's nose. As she did, the movement of the tube inside the esophagus revealed the location of the organ of interest on the video monitor. As she continued to gently slide the tube up and down a few millimeters, Jack was able to identify the location of the abnormal connection between the esophagus and the trachea. He carefully divided the paper thin layers of tissue covering the two tubular organs and quickly identified the fistula between them and passed a small rubber tape around it.

The nurse was standing on a wide-based platform behind Jack, holding the small camera, which allowed him to use both hands to expertly dissect the baby's delicate tissues. The tiny instruments and the tissues were greatly magnified on the screen, but his movements were fluid and controlled as he rapidly isolated the esophagus above and below the fistula.

"It looks like he's got more than enough length to allow us connect everything without tension," he announced to the team. David wasn't sure he understood, but figured his dad would explain it eventually. "I'm going to divide the fistula right here," he said as he pointed to an area on the back of the trachea, "then sew the two ends of the esophagus together."

As he carried out the various parts of the procedure, he explained how important it was to have enough length of the swallowing tube so that the two ends could be reconnected without having to stretch them.

"A fundamental principle of surgery is to avoid tension." He briefly looked away from the video screen and toward David, then added, "Same principle as life."

David nodded, but Jack wasn't sure he'd conveyed the bigger message. He returned to performing the delicate procedure with instruments that were about eight inches long, and they remained rock steady in the hands of the experienced surgeon.

"The most tedious part of the procedure is suturing the two ends of the esophagus together," he said and he prepared to sew the two ends of the tiny tube together. "The esophagus is not an especially forgiving organ. It is easy for the sutures to tear through it, especially if there is tension, and a tear can lead to all sorts of trouble."

Jack effortlessly manipulated the small curved needle through the fragile tissues and deftly tied each knot inside the infant's chest. David wondered if he could ever learn to do anything as incredibly tedious as what he was witnessing.

Once the problem had been corrected, Jack used one of the instruments to cut away a small piece of the tissue lining the chest wall and carefully placed it between the newly connected esophagus and the area on the trachea where he had sewn the fistula closed. "We put this little piece of pleura between the two tubes to help keep another fistula from forming. You just can't be too careful." Again, Jack was delivering a message to his son, but he was sure the awestruck college student hadn't fully understood his subtle meaning.

◆◆◆◆◆◆◆◆◆

They arrived at the general hospital just after ten a.m. The new OR supervisor spotted an unfamiliar face as David accompanied his dad as he headed for the pre-op holding area. She quickly approached them and asked, "Who is this with you, Dr. Roberts?"

"Hi, Fran, this is my son, David. David this is Fran, our OR supervisor."

"Is your son authorized to be back here in the OR?" she asked without the hint of a smile.

"What do you mean, authorized? He's with me."

"I'm sorry, Dr. Roberts, but we don't allow visitors in the operating room, unless they are performing a function, or have prior authorization from administration."

"Since when?"

"Since as long as I've been here," she said.

"So, I'm supposed to ask permission from administration to do something physicians have been doing since the beginning of time?" He was referring to the practice of doctors taking their kids on rounds and into the OR, a tradition as old as the profession. It was the reason so many children of physicians grew up to be doctors themselves. They frequently became captivated by the environment and the mysteries of the hospital. But it seemed that, too, had changed.

"I'm sorry, Dr. Roberts, but those are the rules, and I'm afraid I don't have any latitude in enforcing them."

"Let me call Herb," he said to David and added, "Wait for me in the change room. I'll be right back."

Jack went to the scheduling desk and picked up the phone and had the operator connect him with administration. When the secretary answered, she indicated Mr. Nichols was out of the office and would not be back until after lunch. He started to say something but remembered his agreement with Elaina. He wasn't going to make any waves, so he decided to just drop it.

When he returned to the change room he found David sitting on the wooden bench in front of the locker where he'd left his street clothes. Jack was visibly upset and angry, when he told his son he wouldn't be able to come watch the redo, four vessel coronary artery bypass.

"It's okay, Dad. I'll just wait for you in here."

"No, this is going to take at least a couple of hours. Come with me; you'll be a lot more comfortable in the doctors' lounge."

There was no one else in the lounge when they arrived, so Jack showed him where the snacks were kept and pointed to the refrigerator, which contained soft drinks. The television was already on and was showing highlights of the prior weekend's NFL playoff games on ESPN.

"Just sit tight in here and I'll come get you when I'm finished."

"No problem, I'll be fine."

As Jack turned to leave, David surprised him by adding, "Remember, Dad, avoid tension." He grinned at his dad when he turned around and offered a knowing smile and a shake of his head.

It was more than an hour before David saw anyone else. A man from the hospital's cafeteria came in the lounge around eleven o'clock with a cart containing trays of sandwiches, chips, cookies, and brownies. He unloaded them onto the countertop next to the refrigerator and left without saying anything. David decided to try one of the tuna fish sandwiches, and as he was walking back to his seat, a couple of doctors came in, in the midst of a heated conversation.

"I don't know why, but it is what it is," the larger man stated.

"How can they get away with it?" the second man asked. He was slightly younger and shorter but was completely bald.

"They're the friggin' insurance company, they can do whatever they want."

"But, a ten percent cut across the board? Do they think we're just gonna sit here and accept that kinda crap?"

"Unfortunately, that is exactly what they think. And what's worse, they are probably right. I'm sure everyone will just swallow hard and accept it, the way we always do."

"I don't know. That company is one of my main sources of income, and a ten percent cut is going to hurt. Especially since the other insurance companies are almost certain to follow suit."

"At least Congress came through and stopped the scheduled Medicare cuts."

"Right, but all they've done is kick the can down the road another year. Those SGR-mandated cuts are going to get implemented sooner or later. They are up to fifteen percent already, and one of these days Congress is going to let them kick in, and when they do, I'm done."

"Hopefully, it won't be until after I've retired."

"By that time you'll be the one on Medicare and you won't be able to find any docs to take care of you," the younger man said with a laugh.

David turned his attention back to the television and the highlights of college basketball, and soon other physicians began to come into the lounge. A few just grabbed some chips or a brownie and went back to work, while others gathered around one of the half dozen small tables and talked as they ate their lunch. It was about twelve thirty when an older physician came into the room. His neck was severely bent forward from years of bending over an operating table, so as he made his way between the other physicians he peered over his glasses in an awkward sort of gaze. He picked up a sandwich and some chips then came over to the small group of chairs near where David was sitting.

"What's on TV?" he asked as he sat down. His abnormal posture seemed much less pronounced once he was seated.

"I was just watching Sports Center, but you can change it if you want,"

David said.

"Aren't you Jack Roberts' son?" The gray-haired gentleman asked, as he looked quizzically at David and smiled.

"Yes, sir, I'm David Roberts."

"I haven't seen you in probably ten years. I'm Larry Lawson, one of your dad's old golf buddies."

"It's nice to meet you, Dr. Lawson," David said, reaching over and shaking the older man's hand.

"So what are you up to?"

"Today, or in general?"

"Well, let's start with today." The older man smiled again.

"I came to the hospital with my dad to watch him operate on one of his patients, but the nurse told him I wasn't allowed in the OR."

"Yeah, the staff around here kinda has their panties in a wad over all the new privacy regulations," he said, understanding what must have transpired. "So, are you thinking about a career in medicine?"

"Yes, sir, I just finished my first semester at the University of Texas in Austin, as a premed major."

"Well, good for you," the old man said, sounding more enthusiastic than he felt. "We're gonna need some good young doctors."

"What is your specialty, Dr. Lawson?"

"I'm just an old general surgeon," he replied. "Not glamorous like heart surgery, but I like it."

"My dad has told me a lot about his years as a general surgery resident, and the long hours, especially on the trauma rotation at the county hospital."

"Yeah, those were the days. I never worked so hard in my life, but I also learned to love it, and the training I got was invaluable," he said. "It's not like that anymore."

"What do you mean?"

"Well, most of the kids nowadays are getting about half the experience your dad and I got. They passed a damned rule that requires docs in training to put in no more than eighty hours a week. We routinely put in twelve to sixteen hour days, seven days a week, plus two or three all-nighters. That's how I was able to perform more than two thousand operations as a resident. The kids nowadays average about eight hundred in their five years of general surgery training."

"You mean the law limits the number of hours a resident can spend in training?" David asked.

"It's not really a law, but the group that governs postgraduate training made it their national policy. They decided that residents were being worked too hard, and were sleep deprived, you know, that sort of argument. So, they established the eighty-hour workweek, and if a program is caught exceeding that limit they can jerk their certification. Without that certification they can't get paid by Medicare, Medicaid and the insurance companies for the work the residents do."

"My dad always says just follow the money."

"He's absolutely right. But, in this case it's also about politics. This whole thing started up in New York where a group of the residents formed a union and complained about their long hours, and that they couldn't concentrate because they were exhausted, and that's why they made errors. Some legislator got wind of it, and passed a state law limiting the hours those whiny babies could work, and that was picked up by the national governing organization and became their policy. I suspect it's gonna get worse, because currently in parts of Europe the guys in training are limited to just fifty-four hours a week. There is no way to learn anything close to what you need to know, and gain any level of confidence in that little time. Even at eighty hours, most of the young kids coming out can't operate their way out of a paper bag."

"Wow! Couldn't they just extend the number of years of residency to make up for the shorter hours?"

"They've talked about it, but it's hard enough to get some of these young people to commit to the training as it is. They are already having trouble filling the residency programs in surgery, and it's likely there wouldn't be any neurosurgeons if their seven-year program became nine or ten."

Realizing he was being extremely critical of David's generation, the older man turned away from the television and faced David, saying, "I don't mean to imply that all young people are like that."

"Oh, no sir, I didn't take it that way at all," David replied. "I understand exactly what you mean. I'm surrounded by kids my age that feel somehow entitled to a good grade just because they signed up for a course, but they never go to class."

"Exactly! And God help us all when we get an entire generation of entitled physicians. There ain't nothin' easy about this line of work, and when you start cuttin' corners in training, the public is gonna reap the reward of bad medicine."

"So, do you have any kids?"

"Yeah, I've got a daughter who is thirty-five and a son who is thirty. She's a pharmacist and he is an electrical engineer."

"Did either one of them want to become a doctor?"

"Actually, they both did early on, but they came to their senses, after years of watching their old man killing himself. I didn't have to talk either of them out of it, they figured it out on their own." There was a long pause as he recognized what he was implying. "Sorry, I didn't mean to sound so negative about a career in medicine. It's just that the way things are going, I don't think the future is very bright. I'm glad I'm close to retirement."

"So, are you saying you wouldn't become a doctor if you had it to do over again?"

"No, I'm not saying that at all. I think being a physician, and especially a surgeon, is the greatest profession in the world. I've had a wonderful life. There is absolutely nothing more satisfying than using your brain, and your hands, and your ingenuity to help another person in need, and that's what I've been doing for more than forty years. I wouldn't change anything, but I'm afraid the era of the independent physician is coming to an end. The practice of medicine is being regulated by a bunch of morons. I'm sure they mean well, but the only thing that gives them any authority to influence medical decisions is money. Like your dad said, just follow the money."

"How much longer do you plan to work?"

"If I had my choice I'd probably never really retire. I'd prefer to take some young fella, like yourself, under my wing, and spend my final years teaching him some of the things it's taken me a lifetime to learn on my own."

"That sounds like a great idea. Why don't you do that?" David asked with some renewed excitement in his voice.

"I've thought about it, but most young physicians have been brainwashed into thinking everything they need to know is taught by the guys in those ivory towers. As far as they're concerned, old practicing docs like me don't know anything. Besides, the way everything is regulated these days it's damned near impossible to do anything that is outside the box. You found that out today, when they wouldn't allow you in the OR. There's no room for innovation anymore. Everything we do nowadays has to follow some dumb-ass protocol. They've taken the art out of medicine and replaced it with regulations." The old doc realized he was starting to ramble, and caught himself before he went any further.

"My dad always talks about medicine being a calling," David said, wondering if this older man shared that idea.

"Well, I think he's right, or at least it was for me. What I usually say is, it should be a calling." Lawson was nearly fifteen years older than David's dad, but they shared a common philosophy. "I didn't go to medical school and then do five years of residency with the idea of making a lot of money. I did it because it was something I felt drawn to. Hell, my old man was a barber, and his dad was a farmer. They weren't wealthy, and when I was growing up I never thought much about money. I just wanted to help people, and the doctor in our little town in East Texas was a heck of a role model. He encouraged any kid who had an interest to follow him around, just to see what it was like. I helped deliver babies, and sewed up lacerations, and all kinds of stuff when I was in high school. It got into my blood."

David watched and listened in awe as the old sage took a bite out of his sandwich then continued his lecture. "Some of these kids I see going into the profession today..." the old man just shook his head. "Did you know that they did a survey a couple of years ago of students entering medical school, and one of the questions they asked was, 'What's the most important reason you decided to apply to medical school?' You know what the number one answer was? Job security. Can you believe that? If I was a patient I can't imagine going under the knife knowing the surgeon's number one priority is his own job security. What they don't get, and maybe I'm just old fashioned, is that this isn't a job at all. A job belongs to somebody else, and they give it to another person who becomes their employee. But a profession is something you earn, and you provide your services according to a professional code that's established by you and your fellow professionals, not a bunch of bureaucrats or business types who are just looking for something they can control."

The old doc took another bite of his sandwich and looked briefly back toward the television. David watched the expression on his face turn from frustration to what he thought was sadness, as he resumed the one-sided conversation. "I believe that's the fundamental problem, and the reason we are hearing all this crap about health care reform, and it's our fault," he said, pointing to his chest. "When docs started signing contracts with insurance companies and the government, that started the conversion of the practice of medicine from a profession into a job."

David could sense a hint of bitterness in his voice and was about to ask him about it, but Lawson started speaking again. "All these runaway costs that everyone is concerned about are the direct result of docs working for third parties instead of for their patients."

"But," David interrupted, "if we didn't have insurance, how would the average person be able to pay for a major operation?"

"I'm not saying we shouldn't have insurance. I think it's, as you say, a necessary evil. The problem today is that when the insurance companies and the damned government control the money, they control everything. If you really wanted a system that worked, you'd put the money in the hands of the patient. Let them decide how much a heart operation or a night's stay in the hospital is worth. The prices would come down, I guarantee it, and the quality would improve, too, because docs and hospitals would be competing for patients. That's the way every other part of our economy works."

"You sound just like my dad," David said.

"Well, I suspect most docs his age, and even many who are younger, agree with us, but we're powerless to change it. Health care is now thought of by most people as just another utility, like electricity, water and trash pickup. You know, I've got a little ranch out west of Weatherford," he said, seeming to change the subject. "I don't have city water or sewer. I had to drill a well and put in a septic tank. The power co-op made me pay to run the lines to the house, so I could have electricity. Nobody drives by to pick up my trash every Tuesday and Friday, like they do here in the city. If I don't take care of those things myself, they don't get done."

David was pretty sure he understood the connection the old doctor was making, but decided to ask the question that he'd heard discussed on CNN a month or so before. "So, I'm guessing you don't think everyone has a right to health care?"

"Hell no!" he exclaimed. "If you call what I do, and what your dad does, a right, then what does that make us?" He looked at David with a hint of anger, but then softened his expression, realizing who he was addressing. "Any time one person has a right to another person's labors," he paused for effect, "that's the definition of slavery, isn't it?"

The old man let the impact of his question linger another moment before explaining. "Certainly, I think everyone should have access to basic health care, but that implies an element of responsibility on their part."

David had heard his dad talk about individual responsibility more times than he could possibly count. He usually just referred to it as the "R" word. "I heard them talking about this the other day on a news program and they said that millions of people don't have access to health care because they don't have insurance."

"They may not have insurance, but they still have access. All they do is go to the nearest ER and they get treated for everything from a heart attack to a runny nose. Nobody gets turned away. I know! I have no idea how many people I've taken care of over the years that didn't have insurance. Docs have always been willing to care for anybody in need, it's part of our oath. It's the damned hospitals that would turn people away. That's why a few years back they passed that EMTALA law to stop hospitals from denying treatment to people based on their ability to pay."

"My dad said that's why so many people now use the ER as their primary doctor."

"Sure, why not? If you can't be turned away, and you don't have to pay your bill?" Lawson had argued this point for years, but everyone he talked to, other than his colleagues, just countered by saying that those people were too poor to afford health care. "I saw a twenty-five-year-old kid in the ER last week for appendicitis. No insurance, no job, not in school. He was living on unemployment and food stamps, but he had a brand new cellular phone and had probably five hundred dollars' worth of tattoos on his arms and chest. Seems he had money for those things. That's what I'm talkin' about when I say there's a lack of personal responsibility."

As Lawson seemed about to continue, Jack came into the lounge and quickly spotted his son. He said hi to a couple of the other doctors as he made his way across the room to where David was sitting. "Hi, Larry," he said with a smile. "I see you've met my son."

"Yeah, we were just sitting here solving the problems of the world," the old man replied.

"Oh, yeah? You better watch out," Jack said, with a slight chuckle in his voice. "They're likely to put you on the news like they did me."

Lawson laughed and stood as he prepared to leave. "I know you must be proud of this young man," he said gesturing toward David. "I've been trying to talk him out of following in your footsteps, but it appears his mind is set."

"Yeah, I don't think you can convince him otherwise."

"Well, it's been nice talking to you, and I wish you luck in school."

"Thank you, sir," David replied, and as he stood he extended his hand to the smiling doctor. "I enjoyed talking with you as well."

After shaking the young man's hand, he offered his goodbyes and slowly walked out of the lounge, content with his cervical kyphosis.

"So, are you ready to go?" Jack asked.

"Aren't you going to get something to eat?" David inquired.

"No, I'm not that hungry. Let's go change and then I need to run up to the fourth floor to see a couple of patients before we head for the office."

◆◆◆◆◆◆◆◆◆

They walked through the back door of Jack's office just after one-thirty. Mary Anne hadn't seen David in several years, but recognized the handsome young man immediately. She greeted him with a big smile, then handed Jack a handful of messages on small pink pieces of paper.

"Most of those are just requests for prescription refills," she said, "but there's one from Dr. Jackson about changing your racquetball time tomorrow, and there's another from Herb Nichols. His secretary didn't say what it was about."

"Thanks," Jack replied. As he stared momentarily at the administrator's number, he decided he'd wait until after he'd finished seeing patients to return his call... if at all.

"You've got a heavy schedule this afternoon," she added. "Most of them are post-ops, but there are two new hearts referred by John Richardson and a kid from Abilene that supposedly has an ASD. His pediatrician wanted you to evaluate him for possible surgery."

"Why didn't they send the kid to Dr. Jackson first?"

"I don't know for sure, but apparently he was seen by a cardiologist out in Lubbock who recommended they come see you."

"Okay," Jack replied. He always found it difficult knowing what other cardiologists were thinking. He'd become used to working on kids with Buzz, and John Richardson's group on adult patients. "Who's up first?"

"A couple of post-ops."

Jack sat down at his cluttered desk and went quickly through the messages, marking the refill requests for Shelly to call in the approvals. He then called Buzz on his cell phone and agreed to the change in their game time for the next day.

David watched as his father went about his routine, and when he saw him stand up, he asked, "Aren't you gonna call that other guy?"

"Not right now," he said. "I don't want to ruin the entire afternoon. I'm sure he just wants to inform me about the latest privacy regulations, and why you weren't allowed in the OR. I don't need to listen to his BS right now."

David followed his dad into the first exam room where Jack greeted an older man and his wife. "This is my son, David," he said proudly. "He's following me around today, getting a better idea what it's going to be like when he becomes a doctor."

"That's great," the man responded. "Are you in medical school?"

"No sir," David replied, "I just started college, so it's gonna be a few years."

"Well, I can tell you from experience, that time will pass very quickly."

Jack examined the old gentleman who was two months post-op from his aortic valve repair. He had been in severe congestive heart failure before his surgery, and after six weeks of rehab he was now able to climb the stairs to the second floor of their home, and he and his wife of fifty-three years were walking about a half mile every day.

"We can't thank you enough, Dr. Roberts," she said. "George is like a new man because of you."

"I think the major reason he's doing so well is all the hard work he's put in doing his rehab," Jack said, deflecting the accolades the way he always did.

"When do you think it will be safe for me to travel out to California to see our new great-grandbaby?" the old man asked.

"I think you could go anytime you feel up to it. You're not going to hurt anything at this point, but you need to continue your rehab for another month."

"Maybe we should just wait until mid-February, George. I'd hate to get out there and have a problem."

The eighty-year-old started to argue with his wife, but saw the look in her eye and knew it wouldn't do any good, so he just shrugged his shoulders slightly.

"I hope you turn out to be as good a doctor as your dad," he said, looking back at David. "There aren't many like him anymore."

"You guys need to get on out of here," Jack said, "but on your way out I need you to make a final appointment for one month from now."

THE CALLING

"Okay, doc," he agreed. "By the way, has Medicare paid your bill yet?"

"I have no idea," Jack admitted. "I leave all that up to Mary Anne. You can check with her on your way out."

"I want to make sure you get paid for the great job you did."

"I'm certain Medicare will pay soon if they haven't already, and then she'll file your supplemental insurance."

"I'm sure glad we've got that supplemental policy. I know Medicare doesn't pay all that well sometimes, and I want my doctors to get paid."

"Like I said, just check with Mary Anne, and I'll see you guys next month."

When the old couple left the exam room they went to the checkout window, which in Jack's office was staffed by the receptionist, Phyllis Chambers, who also occupied the check-in window. They made their appointment and then went into Mary Anne's office.

"We received payment from Medicare two weeks ago," she said, "and I filed with your supplemental policy the next day. I haven't heard anything from them yet."

"Did Medicare pay most of the bill?" the seventy-eight-year-old woman asked.

Mary Anne knew it would be a waste of time and energy to explain to these people how the system worked, but Jack had instructed her to make every effort to inform all of his Medicare patients exactly how the government program paid him.

"We submitted a bill to Medicare for your operation, which included all the visits you've had, and will have, with Dr. Roberts, through next month," she said, making sure they understood that all the routine follow-up visits were included in the single charge.

"How much was that?" the elderly woman asked.

"The charge was five thousand dollars."

"I think it was worth twice that!" the man responded.

"Well, Medicare only allows eighteen hundred dollars for an aortic valve replacement and they paid eighty percent of that. So, we got a check from them for fourteen hundred forty dollars."

"That's ridiculous!" he responded. "I paid more than that for that plasma TV we bought last fall. I'm sure glad we have that other policy so the doc can get paid."

"Your supplement is only going to pay the three hundred sixty dollars that Medicare approved but didn't pay. We are required to write off the other thirty-two hundred dollars."

"What? That ain't right..." he argued. "There must be some kinda mistake. The guy who sold us that supplement said it would take care of everything Medicare didn't. You guys shouldn't have to write off anything. We ain't no charity case."

This was the point where Mary Anne always struggled, trying to get older patients to understand. "The way Medicare works is they determine the amount the doctor gets paid. It wouldn't matter if we billed them for ten thousand dollars or any other amount we wanted, they are only going to pay the amount they approve, based on the code we send them. That price is fixed."

He looked at his wife and said, "The last time I heard anybody talk about government fixed prices was back during World War II. My mother said they fixed the price of gasoline, but it was always in short supply."

He turned back to Mary Anne and stated, "We aren't wealthy, but I think Dr. Roberts should get paid, so I want to go ahead and pay the difference myself." He motioned for his wife to write Mary Anne a check.

"That is very kind of you, sir, but I can't accept your check."

"What do you mean you can't accept our check? It's good, we've got the money in the bank," he added indignantly.

"I'm sure you do. That's not what I meant," she quickly added. "What I should have said is that the government won't allow us to accept any payments above what they approved. If we did, that would be considered Medicare fraud, which is a federal crime."

"This is the craziest thing I've ever heard of," he continued. "Does the government say how much the hospital gets too?"

"Yes, sir. The payments to the hospital are calculated a little differently, but the amount is determined by the government. Have you gotten a bill from the hospital yet?"

"Yes," the patient's wife responded. "I haven't shared it with my husband, because I didn't want it to upset him and affect his recovery."

"How much was it?" he asked.

"It was just over one hundred thousand dollars."

"What! For eight days in the hospital? That's more than we paid for our house."

"I'm sure they didn't ask you to pay that amount, did they?" Mary Anne asked, knowing the charges were inflated to ensure maximum payment under a laundry list of diagnosis codes filed by the hospital.

"No, they didn't. The statement was clearly marked, 'Do Not Pay. This is Not a Bill.'"

"I feel sure you won't end up owing much if anything, because your supplement will pick up the amount Medicare approves but doesn't pay."

"Do you know how much that is likely to be?" he asked.

"Well, typically Medicare authorizes payments to hospitals somewhere around thirty-five to forty percent of their charges," she explained. "So, they will probably authorize thirty-five to forty thousand, and pay between twenty-seven and thirty-two thousand. That's just a rough guess, based on what I've seen before. So, your supplement will pay seven or eight thousand before it's over."

"This is just not right," the old man said. "It sounds like everybody is getting screwed by the government."

"Everybody except you," Mary Anne added.

The old man's mind was still very sharp. He sat for a few seconds, considering what she had just said, before he responded. She was right. They had gotten excellent care, and it wasn't going to cost them much if anything. "My dad used to tell us kids not to ever depend on the government for anything except to deliver the mail. He said that they would always screw up anything else if you let 'em. I think he was one hundred percent correct. I can understand why our family doctor stopped seeing us in his regular clinic. Now we have to go to a special Medicare clinic, and we usually have to wait for more than two hours to see him. Kinda like the US mail these days."

"I couldn't have said it better myself," Mary Anne added as she stood to help the still-stunned couple find their way out.

After seeing several more patients with his dad, David was impressed by how grateful all the post-op families were. The difference in the looks on their faces and those of the new patients who were still facing surgery was obvious. This was especially true with the young boy from Abilene. His mother held the five-year-old on her lap, protecting him as if he were an infant.

"When did he start acting like he was tired all the time?" Jack asked as part of his assessment.

"It seems like it's been about a year," the young mother said, "but I think he's been having some trouble for longer than that."

"What do you mean 'some trouble?' "

"He had always seemed short of breath, especially when he's trying to keep up with his older brother."

After Jack examined the young boy he turned back to his mother and asked, "What did the heart doctor in Lubbock say?"

"He told us that the hole in his heart wasn't going to close and he would need surgery. That's why he suggested we come see you. He said you were the best, so we came here prepared to stay. Will you be able to do his operation right away?"

Jack didn't really know any of the cardiologists in the West Texas town, but he suspected the guy they saw was likely an older doc, since most of the younger guys would have recommended a catheter-based closure of the ASD.

"Well, based on what you're telling me I suspect he's probably right about the diagnosis. Your son is very likely going to need to have the hole in his heart closed, but nowadays most of these ASDs can be treated successfully without having to open the heart. There's a technique that uses tiny wires passed through the blood vessels and into the heart that allows a patch to be placed over the abnormal opening."

"So, is that something that you can do?"

"No, that's something that an interventional cardiologist does. We've got an excellent guy that I work with every day, and if you'll give me just a minute, I'm going to call Dr. Jackson to see if he can see your son today. I know you've traveled a long way, and I hate to make you come all the way back here to Fort Worth again to see another doctor."

The mother looked confused as Jack excused himself and went back to his office, where he picked up the phone and called Buzz.

"I've got a five-year-old kid here in my office from Abilene, and he's got an ASD. He saw somebody in Lubbock who recommended surgical repair, but I figured you should take a look to see if you think this is one you can patch."

"Sure," Buzz said. "You say they're in your office now?"

"Yeah, I'd like to send them on over if you're going to be there."

"No problem, I'll tell my girls to squeeze 'em in."

"By the way, she said they came prepared to stay for surgery, so if there's any way you can get him on the schedule for tomorrow I'm sure his mom would appreciate it."

Jack returned and explained to the mother that Dr. Jackson would see her son that same afternoon. He gave her directions to the office and told her they might have to wait a little bit since he was going to work them into his schedule. The mother was extremely grateful, and seemed relieved as she left the office.

"That woman brought her son in to see you. Why didn't you just go ahead and fix that kid's heart yourself?" David asked.

"Because, he didn't need it. There's a very good chance Dr. Jackson will be able to fix the problem without the kid having to undergo an open-heart operation," his dad explained.

◆◆◆◆◆◆◆◆◆

Jack and David were greeted by the maître d' at Del Frisco's steak house in downtown Fort Worth. It was still early in the evening, and the restaurant was less than half full. They were seated at a small corner table and given their menus. David had been here once before on his sixteenth birthday, but this was not the kind of place parents brought kids. The waiter took their drink orders and left them to look over the menu.

"I really enjoyed spending the day with you, Dad," David said.

"Yeah, I enjoyed having you along, except for that situation we encountered at the general hospital."

"That was okay, I didn't mind. In fact, I really enjoyed talking to Dr. Lawson. He's a pretty interesting guy."

"Yeah, Larry's quite a piece of work," Jack laughed softly. "What all did he have to say?"

"He told me that the surgery residents nowadays aren't getting the kind of training you guys got because of some eighty-hour workweek restrictions."

"He's right about that. My new associate, George Ferguson, finished his training without having done many of the more complicated procedures that we frequently do in practice. So, for the first year he was here, I spent a lot of my time essentially completing his training." Jack paused as the waiter brought his scotch on the rocks and David's iced tea. "George is a great guy, and he will become an excellent surgeon, I'm convinced of it, but when he first came out a few years ago, he just didn't have much experience."

"Dr. Lawson said that the residents had some kind of union that negotiated the shorter hours because they were exhausted and making too many errors."

Jack took a sip of the fine whiskey, then responded, "Yeah, it seemed they didn't want to put in the same hours we used to, but then I guess it's just part of the new generation."

"I thought that esophageal procedure you did this morning was one of the coolest things I've ever seen. It reminded me of a video game. Those instruments were like joysticks, with the whole thing playing out on the high-definition monitor."

"I never thought of it that way, but I guess you're right. It is kind of like a video game, but the biggest difference is you can't push the restart button if you mess up." Jack laughed again as he took another sip of his drink.

"Why can't you do that kind of operation on the heart?" David asked.

"Well, the biggest problem is the constant motion of the beating muscle. That's why we have to put people on the pump so we can stop the heart. There is a technique that's been used experimentally on animals that uses a computerized robot. It's a very cool concept. The video image and the surgical instruments are made to move by the robot to follow along with the movements of the beating heart. Once the movements are synchronized, the image the surgeon sees on the monitor appears completely still."

"That sounds amazing. Have you done anything like that?" David asked with obvious excitement.

"No. I've seen some videos of it, but like I said, it's still experimental. Besides, the only procedures that it can potentially be used for are the ones on the surface of the heart like coronary artery surgery. To do anything inside the heart still requires bypass because of all the blood moving through the chambers, so there's no way to use minimally invasive techniques inside the heart."

The waiter returned and took their orders, and after he left, Jack asked, "So, how was Colorado?"

David had hoped to save this discussion until later in the evening, but it appeared he wouldn't have that option. "It was great," he said. "I really enjoyed learning to snowboard."

"So, you're now a boarder and not a skier?" Jack smiled, as he realized how much the sport had changed since he first took it up back in late 1965.

"Yeah, it seems easier, and it's what all of my friends do. Nobody skis anymore, unless they are like fifty years old."

"Easy now, don't be making fun of us old guys."

They both laughed a bit, before Jack asked, "How about Amy? Does she snowboard?"

David wasn't sure whether his mom had shared all the facts surrounding the trip with his dad, so he decided to just play it as cool and wait to see what he knew before sharing the whole story. "Yeah, she's actually pretty good."

"Why didn't you tell me she was going with you guys on the trip?" Jack asked without even the hint of emotion in his voice. He figured if David wanted to play it cool, he could as well.

"I don't know. I just figured you knew."

"Did she have a good time?"

"Yeah, I guess so."

"Where did she stay?"

"We rented a big house near the slopes, and the girls stayed in a couple of the rooms and the guys stayed in the others."

"How many girls were there?" Jack was continuing to keep his cool, giving David the opportunity to share the details of what he already knew.

"There were four girls and six of us guys." He didn't want to share all the details of the sleeping arrangements with his dad, but he figured the time was right to at least tell him how he felt about Amy. Before he could get up the nerve to begin, his dad interrupted his thoughts.

"You know, when I was a freshman in college at CU, I went skiing several times with my girlfriend. We were very much in love, and getting away to the mountains gave us the perfect opportunity to be alone together. So, we took advantage of it. One night in the ski lodge was where we both had our first sexual experience."

David couldn't believe what he was hearing. His old man was talking about having sex when he was in college. Something about that whole picture just didn't seem right.

"I was about your age," Jack continued. "We were in love and, like every young man, I was filled with hormones." He chuckled softly at the memory. "Anyway, she and I eventually got married, but it just didn't work out, and we got divorced while I was in med school."

"I didn't know you were married before," David declared, surprised.

"It was a long time ago. We were very young and thought we knew what we were doing."

"Well," David began hesitantly, "Amy and I are in love too. We plan to get married but not until we finish college, but before I start med school."

"Yeah, your mom told me. She also told me you guys have been having sex for several months." Jack paused as he detected a tinge of anger in his son's face at the idea of being betrayed by his own mother. "Before you get upset with her, you need to know, I asked her specifically what she knew about your relationship, because I already suspected as much. She just confirmed it."

"How did you know?" David asked, embarrassed by his father's statement.

"The look on both your faces when I was in Austin last fall was a dead giveaway. I wish you had just told me then." For the first time since their conversation had started down this path, Jack appeared mildly upset.

"I know I should have, Dad, but I knew you wouldn't approve, especially since I told you that we had promised to wait."

"David," Jack said as he looked toward his son who had lowered his eyes toward the plate in front of him. "This isn't about whether your mom and I approve of what you do. The time for us to influence your actions through our approval is over. You're old enough to make your own decisions. Your mother and I are very proud of the man you are becoming. We talk about you, and your virtually unlimited future, all the time. I just hope you know that we are both here for you anytime you need advice or just a sounding board."

"Thanks, Dad, I really appreciate your saying that. It means a lot." David knew that Jack wasn't his biological father, but that had no relevance to the bond that existed between them. "I'm sorry I didn't trust you to understand," he added sadly. "I should have told you about Amy and me."

"One of these days when you have children of your own you'll understand what I'm about to say." Jack had been preparing for this moment for years, but now that it was here he wasn't sure he could get through it without losing control of his emotions. His dad had demonstrated to him throughout his childhood how much he loved him, but it wasn't until his dying breath that he finally spoke the words to him. Jack was determined not to let that happen with his own son.

"A child is an extension of the parent. You love them in a way that's very much like the way you love yourself. The hardest part of parenting is letting your child make their own decisions, and all you can hope for is that you've raised them to know and understand how much they are loved. They will sometimes do things you may not agree with, but to a parent that's no different than tripping over your own feet or accidentally cutting your finger with a knife.

It hurts, but it doesn't change anything."

Jack was starting to feel a tightness in his throat, but believed he'd be able to finish his thought, provided his son didn't look up. "As long as the child knows they are loved, they will remain a part of the parent, and eventually they'll pass that love on to their own children."

David did look up into his father's face and detected the moistness in the corner of his eyes. He knew it was a reflection of what was in his heart, and what he felt gathering inside his own.

CHAPTER 20

After checking on his bypass patient from the day before, Jack was on his way toward the elevators when he ran into Herb Nichols walking briskly toward the ICU.

"What are you doing here so early in the morning, Herb?"

The administrator was starting to show his age a bit. His hair was now almost completely gray and with all the entertaining he did, he was no longer able to comfortably button his suit coat. He always seemed to be in a rush whenever he was out of his office, and today was no exception as he approached Jack.

"Actually, I was looking for you," he said. "Did you not get my message to call me back yesterday?"

"Yeah, I got it, but it was pretty late in the day before I had a chance, so I figured I'd just get back to you today," he lied.

"My secretary told me you called while I was out to lunch. I just wanted to find out what you needed."

Jack was pretty sure Herb knew exactly what his call had been about, but he decided to let him play his game. "I was calling to get approval for my son to come into the OR and watch a case. He's a premed major at UT in Austin, and it's been a few years since he's followed me around. He's in town for the holidays, so I thought I'd rekindle some of his excitement as he pursues a career in surgery."

"You know we can't do that anymore. The compliance lawyers tell us that observation of a procedure performed in the hospital is a violation of the patient's right to privacy."

"That's funny, they didn't say anything about that over at children's. I guess their lawyers either have a different opinion, or they're just not paying attention to the new federal rules." Jack put a little more emphasis on the word rules than was necessary.

"I can't speak for them, I just know what our policy is, and I'd appreciate it if you didn't put my OR supervisor in such a difficult position again." Herb made it sound as though Jack had purposely challenged the hospital's employee.

"I'm not sure what she told you, but I didn't challenge her at all." He paused for a moment then continued, "But I do think that the rule should be challenged, because it's stupid." Jack decided to go ahead and speak his piece on this issue, even though he knew it wouldn't do any good. "If I get my patient to sign a permit for an outside observer, I don't know how anyone could assume that would violate their privacy. Besides, if young people can't get exposed to what goes on inside a hospital, and what doctors and nurses do, how can we expect any of them to choose those careers?"

Herb's face was growing increasingly taut, but he elected not to enter into further debate with this troublesome surgeon. "I will bring up your objections at our next board meeting, but I wouldn't hold my breath if I were you. The legal department at our corporate headquarters has been very clear on this issue."

Jack was also becoming more than just a bit perturbed with this conversation and elected to terminate it in his own way. "You know, Herb, once we start letting the lawyers run the hospital, our whole system is doomed. Maybe the board should consider that the next time they decide to roll over to the demands of some regulator's mandate."

Herb stood silently, but the muscles in his face, and his deep sigh, spoke volumes about his own anger. He watched as Jack walked toward the elevators, trying to think of a way to replace that extremely valuable asset with one that was more controllable.

♦♦♦♦♦♦♦♦♦

"There's a call for you on line one from a Dr. Fleming," Mary Anne announced over the intercom on Jack's office phone.

"Dr. Fleming," Jack said excitedly. "How are you, sir?"

"I'm just fine, Jack," the old gentleman said, in his smooth Virginian accent. "How are you?"

"I'm doing very well, thank you. To what do I owe the pleasure of this call?"

"Well, I wanted to let you know two things. First, I'm stepping down as head of the heart program here at Hopkins. My sight is beginning to fail me, so I've decided to retire."

"I'm sorry to hear you're having trouble with your vision, but I'm glad you finally decided to stop working so hard."

"Thank you. I'm not sure what I'm going to do with myself, but I'm sure Sally will find some kind of project for me to do around the house to keep me busy. The second thing I wanted to tell you is related. I'm also going to be stepping down from my position on the board of the Association of Thoracic Surgeons. I know you were on our board for a while about twenty years ago, but I think it's time we brought you back, this time in a leadership role. I plan to nominate you for the position of secretary-treasurer, but I figured I better ask you first if that's okay?"

Jack was a taken aback by the old man's compliment. Typically, all positions on the executive committee were filled by academic surgeons who tended to only nominate other academics. Jack had been one of three board members back in the eighties who were not in a full-time teaching program, and he figured he was there as a token voice from the military. By the time he finished his three-year term, he was out of the service and in private practice, so he wasn't surprised when he was not renominated for a second term.

"What in the world made you think of me?" he asked.

"I saw a video of you on the internet, taking down that government buffoon in the Texas legislature, and I thought we could use someone with that kind of passion and intestinal fortitude to help guide our organization back to prominence."

Jack wasn't sure exactly where to begin his response. "You saw me on the internet?"

"Yeah, it's a YouTube video. You really gave that guy exactly what he deserved."

"Well, that may be," Jack said with a laugh, "but it sure got me in a lot of hot water with my wife and the hospital, and several of my colleagues."

"I think you did exactly the right thing, and I wish you'd consider bringing that same fire to the ATS. Our profession desperately needs that kind of leadership."

He knew he probably should discuss this with Elaina before agreeing, but then again he figured it wouldn't involve any television appearances. "I'm honored that you would consider me worthy of such a prestigious position, and I'd be glad to serve if elected."

"Terrific, I'll tell the board during our teleconference meeting tonight. Oh, and I wouldn't worry about being elected, that's pretty much a foregone conclusion."

"Thank you again, Dr. Fleming, for your call and for your confidence."

"Somebody from the ATS office will be getting in touch with you within the next couple weeks to let you know about the upcoming board meeting."

The two gentlemen said their goodbyes, and as Jack hung up the phone he realized he'd just committed time that he didn't really have to spare.

◆◆◆◆◆◆◆◆◆

"I knew I never had a chance to get the job," Traci said, when Jack came into her office. He had just heard one of the anesthesiologists in the doctors lounge talking about the new administrator that had been hired to assume the permanent position.

"I'm really sorry," Jack said. "I know how much you wanted it."

"It's okay. I'm sure something even better will come along."

"I think you would have done a great job, and I told Fitzgerald that when I met with him a couple of months back."

"Maybe your endorsement was just what he needed to, as he said, 'go in a different direction.' You know what I mean." She tried unsuccessfully to laugh at her own joke.

Jack suddenly realized what she was saying. "Oh, my God," he gasped. "You're right. He really doesn't like me, and…"

"Don't be silly. He didn't hire Michael Horvath away from that national accounting firm just to get back at you. Trust me."

"Well, I'm sorry if my run-in with Fitzgerald had anything to do with you not getting the job."

"Have you met Horvath?" she asked. Jack just shook his head. "Well, if you had, you'd know exactly why Fitzgerald picked him. They are like two peas in a pod. Both strictly business… You're going to see some significant changes around here, and soon, I'm sure."

"What is your role going to be?" he asked.

"I have a new title, vice president of clinical operations. Horvath told me he was going to rely heavily on me to oversee all aspects of running the hospital on a day-to-day basis."

"I hope they're going to compensate you for that."

"Sort of," she said, sounding less excited than Jack had anticipated. "When I was named interim administrator, they bumped my salary from one hundred fifty thousand a year, to two hundred thousand, which is what Bob was making. With my new position, I'm going to keep the new salary, plus they've included some performance incentives."

"That's great!" Jack smiled, genuinely happy to see Traci was getting the kind of recognition she deserved.

"Not as great as what they're giving Horvath." She paused before continuing what she was certain would remain confidential. "You didn't hear this from me, but they offered him seven hundred fifty thousand a year and the title of president of the hospital. Plus he has performance incentives, a generous expense allowance, and a membership at Ridglea Country Club."

"You're kidding!" Jack knew that hospital administrators were commanding higher salaries these days, but that was nearly triple what he was making as a heart surgeon. "All that for a guy with a bachelor's degree in finance and almost no practical experience in health care?"

"No, I'm not kidding. And, the board authorized two additional vice-president positions to be hired by Horvath. One of them is a position I know you're really going to love. It's called vice-president of provider relations and physician contracting."

"What exactly does that mean?" Jack's voice slowed and his eyes narrowed.

"They have come up with a new strategy to maximize the hospital's revenue. They are going to organize all the pediatricians in the region under a single legal entity, and then the hospital will contract with that group to provide exclusive hospital services for their patients. The hospital will also provide all administrative services to each of the various physician practices, including billing and collections, and the physicians will be allowed to buy all their medical supplies through the hospital's purchasing department at a significant savings."

"Do you think the docs are going to go for that? They will be giving up their autonomy completely."

"Are you kidding? It was their idea. The two biggest groups of pediatricians got together and made the proposal to Fitzgerald a couple of weeks ago. Part of the deal is that they will get to share in some of the profits of the hospital as a means of offsetting the low payments docs are getting under Medicaid and SCHIP. They claim this is being done all over the country."

Jack was stunned by what Traci was saying. "So much for this being a not-for-profit facility, huh?" he said, almost too softly for her to hear. He turned back to face her and asked, "Is that even legal? I thought there was a law against the corporate practice of medicine in Texas."

"That law only prohibits hospitals from putting physicians on their payroll. That's why they are setting up a separate business entity for the docs, so they can contract as a group. It's all strictly legit."

Jack thought for a moment, considering everything he had just heard. "Why are you telling me all this? Don't you stand to benefit from that arrangement?"

"Yeah, sure," she said, "but just because I might profit from it doesn't mean I have to like it, and it doesn't make it right. Oh, and one more thing," she added, "you guys are next. The primary docs are going to try and force all the specialists into a similar contracting arrangement, so they can share in the profits from the procedures you perform."

Jack was finally beginning to understand the full gravity of what she was saying. The hospital was planning to facilitate the feud between primary care and specialty physicians with the hope of further dividing them. They planned to use the pediatricians by creating an organization, which appeared to help them by contracting for services at a discount, but the ultimate goal was to bring down the specialist. If successful, the scheme would put the hospital in a position to control all the docs through one single entity.

"Thanks, Traci, I need to run," he said. "Oh, and don't worry, I didn't learn about any of this from you."

"I don't think it really matters. This will be common knowledge by the end of the day. Dr. Grady and Fitzgerald are having a joint press conference this afternoon to announce the formation of the physician network as part of the new regional health care delivery system."

When Jack got back to his office he called George Ferguson first. "Hey, George, are you busy?"

"No, what's up?" his young associate replied.

"Have you heard anything about the hospital helping the pediatricians organize into a single group practice?"

"I heard some of the guys talking about creating a business entity that would give them more leverage to contract with managed care companies, but that's all I know."

"Apparently, a couple of the more influential docs and this new administrator, Horvath, have come up with a plan that will allow the hospital to control their practices in exchange for some kind of profit-sharing arrangement," Jack said cautiously. "If that's the case, it won't be long before the hospital will try and use them to force all of us into something similar."

"So, what would be wrong with that?" George asked. "I'd like to share in some of the hospital's profits, wouldn't you?"

"This isn't about shared profits, or anything like that. It's about controlling the docs. Once the hospital gains control of all the money, we will be their subordinates. The practice of medicine has always been based on the physician being able to exercise his or her best judgment and act independently on behalf of the patient. They rely on us to be their advocates. That is the gist of the Hippocratic Oath. There is no way we can do that if we become basically employees of the hospital."

"I think you're exaggerating just a little, don't you?"

"No, I don't. They're starting with the primary care guys because they are getting screwed the most by the current payment system. Once they have them, they'll use them to gain control of the specialists. That's what's coming," Jack spoke with authority.

"So, what are you suggesting those guys do? Several of the ones I've spoken to lately have said they are on the verge of bankruptcy. When they get paid twenty-eight dollars by Medicaid to see a kid in their office, they aren't covering their expenses," George argued. "They told me they used to be able to make up for it by charging for lab tests in their office, but they can't do that anymore. It's against the law."

Jack found it difficult to argue against what George was saying. He too knew several of his colleagues who were considering closing their offices because they were having to dip into their personal retirement savings accounts to meet their payrolls. Something needed to change for sure, but he had no doubt that if accountant-types like Horvath and Herb Nichols ever seized control over the docs, it would be the patients who would suffer.

♦♦♦♦♦♦♦♦♦

"Our first board meeting of 2007 will be held by teleconference on Thursday evening at eight, eastern time," Dr. Novak, the current president of the Association of Thoracic Surgeons explained. "I have sent you an e-mail with the most recent financial information, and you will need to give a short summary of our current financial status to the board."

"I will try, but as you know, I haven't been on the board for many years, so I won't be able to provide any context for my report," Jack said in reply to his request.

"Don't worry about that. Our executive director, Carol Reeves, will be on the call to provide answers if anyone cares to question anything in your treasurer's report, but that never happens."

"Okay, Frank, I'll talk with you in a couple days," he said as he hung up the phone and went back to work.

The teleconference began five minutes late, because Dr. Novak was the last one to call in. The discussion included a number of mundane issues, including the unanimous acceptance of several new members. When Jack's turn came to provide his financial report he pointed out that the organization had a little over one hundred thousand dollars in the bank, and appeared to be solvent despite a slight decline in membership dues.

"Thank you, Dr. Roberts," Dr. Novak added. "We are all glad to have you as our new secretary-treasurer."

"I'm happy to be involved again with the ATS, and I look forward to helping in any way I can." With that statement Jack sealed his fate.

"I'm glad to hear you say that," Novak said. "As it turns out we have need for a new delegate from our organization to the AMA, and I think you would do an excellent job. John Trench was our delegate up until last year, but he has retired from practice and no longer wishes to serve in any capacity."

Before Jack could say anything, one of the other board members on the call stated, "I nominate Jack Roberts to be our AMA delegate."

"Second!" came another voice through the line.

"All in favor?" asked Novak.

All ten voices on the phone simultaneously said, "Aye!"

"Any opposed?"

The phone was silent for a moment before Novak declared, "Well, Jack, congratulations. You are our new delegate to the American Medical Association."

The last thing he wanted to do was go to another AMA meeting, but he had told Dr. Fleming he'd do whatever he could, and this was something he could do. Elaina was likely to kill him for agreeing to another meeting, he thought, but then he remembered the annual meetings were in Chicago every June. She always loved going to Chicago because the Magnificent Mile was her favorite shopping area, anywhere.

"Thank you... I think," he said. "I guess I'll need to rejoin the AMA, since like most docs in private practice, I let my membership lapse many years ago."

Novak laughed, "Yes, you have to be a member to be a delegate."

Another voice which Jack didn't recognize was heard through the phone. "No one blames you for opting out of the AMA. They haven't represented mainstream medicine for the last couple of decades. That's why we want you to go set them straight."

♦♦♦♦♦♦♦♦♦

That summer Jack and Elaina's trip to Nicaragua had to be delayed again until August, this time because of the AMA meeting the first part of June and the ATS annual meeting in early July. David didn't go with them despite having come home for part of the summer. He'd gotten a part-time job working in the ER of the children's hospital, and while it mostly involved transporting patients and cleaning up the exam rooms, he took it because he wanted to be in the hospital, and the ER was where the action was.

When Fitzgerald got wind of the fact that Jack was planning another trip to Nicaragua, he called Horvath into his office for one of his famous "strategy sessions." They were more like executive directives, but he liked to make those who did his bidding at least think they had some say in the process.

"I'm sure you are not aware of the Nicaraguan Surgical Fund, are you?" he asked.

"No, sir," Horvath admitted. "What's that?"

"A couple of years ago a billionaire who lives down in Managua made a million dollar donation after his daughter's surgery. He apparently attached a condition to the money, allowing it to only be used to offset the bills of other patients from Nicaragua."

"Really? How many kids do we see from Nicaragua?"

"So far only two, but Jack Roberts goes down there every summer trolling for cases, and he's getting ready to go again in a couple of weeks. He's likely to drag another one or two back up here for free surgery, and I think we need to put a stop to that nonsense."

"I assume these kids don't have any insurance, right?"

"Of course not. Their insurance is that fund that's just sitting there on our books, even though we already used the money. If he brings any more kids up here we'll have to eat the cost, and those heart operations aren't cheap."

"I've got an idea," Horvath said. "Why don't we…"

◆◆◆◆◆◆◆◆

Jack and Elaina arrived in Managua in mid-August, and it was as if they'd never left. Domingo and Felicia were the same, the clinic was the same, and Jack's enthusiasm for the charitable work they did was the same. Domingo told him he had five kids with possible cardiac problems for him to evaluate in the clinic on Tuesday. Apparently word had spread across the entire country of the possibility of corrective heart surgery in the United States. Three of the children were from the cities of Grenada and Chinandega, and one was from the remote Caribbean coastal town of Puerto Cabezas.

When Domingo pulled his big Toyota up in front of the clinic, the line of parents and children extended down the street, well past the missionaries' house. The volunteers had seen to it that the young girl Jack had operated on the summer before was near the front of the line, along with her parents and their other two children. She was now six years old and had grown to be three inches taller than her five-year-old brother, and was rapidly catching up with her eight-year-old sister. They had come back to the clinic to thank the doctor.

The adorable black-haired child gave Jack a big hug, but she didn't speak to him. Instead, she simply smiled timidly as she produced a large paper bag from behind her mother's skirt. She reached in and pulled out a large cloth, with bold blue stripes above and below a broad white stripe through the middle. She took a step back and attempted to stretch the cloth out in front of her, as far as she could, but it wasn't until her mother took one corner that she was able to unfurl it to its full five-foot expanse. The national coat of arms were proudly displayed in the center of the Nicaraguan flag, and on the blue background of the top stripe, in bold letters were the words, "*Muchas Gracias,*" and on the bottom it read, "*Doctor Roberts.*"

Jack stood motionless in amazement as the girl's mother explained that this had been the child's idea, and that she had done all the work, including laying out the letters, then performing the meticulous cross-stitching of each one, using the brightest yellow thread she could find at the local market. The project had taken her more than three months to complete, and she had been so afraid that her doctor might not come back so she could give it to him.

Tears welled up in Jack's eyes as he hugged the precious child again. The volunteers, and many of the other patients who had come to the clinic to see him, began to applaud the scene. Elaina stood next to her husband, who was truly touched by the outpouring of gratitude and affection. She knelt down next to him and carefully gathered the flag, as several other children took the opportunity to hug the neck of their American hero.

By late that afternoon, all the children had been seen, but only one of the five kids that were thought to have heart defects was a candidate for surgery. A twelve-year-old boy had a murmur that was characteristic of the hole between the two upper chambers of the heart. He had been doing pretty well until about six months ago when he passed out suddenly while he was playing soccer. Since then, each time he tried to run more than half the length of the field he felt faint. More recently he'd been having episodes of shortness of breath even with minimal exercise. Jack diagnosed him as having an ASD, but there was no way he could tell whether it was one that Buzz could fix or if it would require open heart surgery. However, he was certain that it needed to be repaired before the adolescent developed irreversible pulmonary hypertension.

Jack called Buzz to discuss the boy's situation, and the cardiologist said he could put the boy on the schedule for the following Tuesday. Jack and Domingo worked out the details for getting him and his father to Fort Worth on Monday. An ambulance was not necessary given his stable condition, so they arranged for two round trip airline tickets to be issued through Franco's foundation. If Buzz was able to patch this kid's heart, he'd be back home by the end of the week. Either way, Jack was sure this one would be far easier and less expensive than either of the previous two cases.

The rest of the week passed largely uneventfully. Jack and Elaina didn't get to visit with Franco and Gabriella this time because their friends were on vacation in Europe. Franco had insisted that they get away for a couple of weeks, just the two of them, so they left Christina totally in the care of their nanny for the first time.

Shortly after they'd arrived in Managua, Jack and Elaina received an invitation from the director of the government hospital, asking them to attend a "dedication ceremony." Jack didn't want to go, and Domingo had said it was likely to be a repeat of the political sideshow of two years before. However, Elaina convinced him he should at least make an appearance to keep up his positive relationship with the hospital, since one day he might need to use it again.

It was indeed a politically motivated event, complete with television coverage. The director had scheduled this ceremony at the last minute, specifically to coincide with Jack and Elaina's visit. As the proceedings began, two young men rolled a rather large, semi-portable unit into the conference room, as the director announced the addition of a new service. According to him it employed the most modern diagnostic equipment available. Jack immediately recognized the older model GE ultrasound machine. It was similar to one the general hospital back home had purchased more than ten years before. The director claimed the machine would allow his hospital to diagnose a wide variety of illnesses and conditions, but what he didn't say was they hadn't yet found an ultrasound technician to perform the studies, a minor detail in the mind of this bureaucrat.

The director made a point of introducing Jack to the reporters, as his hospital's American consultant physician. Jack was not at all happy about being somehow designated as working for the state-run facility, but there wasn't any way he could set the record straight without calling out the director, so he decided once more to just let it slide.

When the event concluded, Jack and Elaina were on their way out with Domingo when the older reporter they'd met two years before came up to him and asked if the American doctor would be available for an interview.

"That depends," Jack answered. "What kind of a story did you have in mind?"

The older gentleman's English was surprisingly good. He replied, "I never finished my story from your last visit. What I'm interested in doing is defining health care from various different points of view. I would like your perspective to go along with those I have already obtained."

"May I ask what other opinions you've gotten?"

"Certainly," he responded. "I have interviewed three different patients and one parent of a young child. Actually it was Mr. Ochoa, the father of the boy you operated on here," he explained. "Then I also interviewed two nurses and the director of the hospital. I've also spoken with two local businessmen and a government employee who wishes to remain anonymous."

"How long will the interview take?"

"I would like to have an hour, but I would accept any amount of time you can give me."

"Well," Jack said as he looked at Elaina and Domingo, "I don't want to make my wife and Dr. Ramirez wait. I would be happy to talk with you, but perhaps another time."

Domingo thought this was a story that needed to be told, so he interjected, "If you want, you could come out to my home this afternoon and conduct your interview there."

"I will gladly follow you, if that's okay with you, Dr. Roberts."

Jack thought for a moment before agreeing. If Domingo was volunteering his home for the interview, somehow he must trust this man.

Jack and the reporter, Gustavo Pasqual, sat for over an hour on Domingo's patio, talking about health care in the United States and elsewhere around the world, including the current system in Nicaragua. When the interview was concluded, Gus stood and shook Jack's hand, and thanked him for his time and his insights.

"Where do you plan to publish your article?" Jack asked.

"I am not certain when I will have it finished, but our leading Spanish language paper *La Pensa* has agreed to publish it, and I am fairly certain I can get *The Nicaragua Dispatch* to publish it in English. I anticipate it will be sometime in the next two to three weeks."

"I look forward to reading it," Jack said as the two men parted.

"How did that go?" Elaina asked.

"It was fine," Jack answered. "He seemed like a very thoughtful guy. Asked a lot of interesting questions."

"And, I'm sure you gave him a lot of interesting answers."

"Nothing you haven't heard me say a hundred times."

"A hundred?" Elaina laughed. Jack's strong opinions about health care were part of their conversation on an almost daily basis.

♦♦♦♦♦♦♦♦♦

Buzz saw the Nicaraguan boy in his clinic on Monday and scheduled him for the cardiac cath lab the following day. He was relatively sure he'd find the ostium secundum defect Jack had predicted, based on the boy's history and his developing symptoms. A transesophageal echocardiogram would be done prior to placing the catheter in the femoral vein, just to make sure there were no surprises once they were under anesthesia.

For local children, Buzz typically had them come to the hospital early on the day of their procedure, but those from out of town were admitted the day before, just to make sure they would be ready early the next morning. In this case he was able to get the pre-op echocardiogram done that same afternoon.

The ultrasound technician called and asked his receptionist if he could speak to Dr. Jackson, and when Buzz picked up the phone the technician sounded concerned. "I think you might want to come look at this echo yourself," he said.

"What are you seeing?" Buzz asked.

"It looks to me as though this kid has an ASD all right, but I think he's got something else going on."

"Just leave the study up on the machine, and I'll come by and take a look at it as soon as I finish here in my office." Buzz knew that ASDs were sometimes accompanied by other heart defects, and he suspected that was what the technician was seeing.

Just after five-thirty that afternoon, he made his way back to the lab to review the video of the ultrasound. Immediately he saw what the technician had suspected. Not only was there a sizable secundum defect, but the boy also had a fairly tight mitral valve stenosis. The valve between the left atrium and the left ventricle, which allowed oxygen-rich blood from the lungs to pass into the main pumping chamber, appeared to be scarred and the deformity was significantly restricting the flow of blood.

It had been a while since Buzz had seen this particular combination, known as Lutembacher Syndrome, and it would change his approach considerably. He called the cath lab to let them know of the change in the procedure, then he called Jack to give him a heads up.

"Yeah, this kid has Lutembacher's, so I plan to go through the ASD to dilate the mitral valve first, then I'll close the defect," he explained.

"That sounds great. How many of these combination-type procedures have you done now?" Jack asked.

"I don't know, five or six probably, but we haven't seen one like this in a few years."

"I'll drop by tomorrow to see how it's going, but if I'm not there and you need me, just give me a call."

"Will do."

◆◆◆◆◆◆◆◆◆

Horvath had learned of the latest patient from Nicaragua from two different sources, almost simultaneously. One was the director of admissions and the other was the scheduling clerk in the cardiac cath lab. He had told both of them, as well as a few other moles, to notify him personally if any kids came through with a Nicaraguan address.

He immediately called Fitzgerald with his report.

"Hey, Jim, this is Michael."

"Hi, Michael... What's up?" the older man asked.

"As you predicted, Roberts brought another kid back with him from Nicaragua, and Buzz Jackson has him on the schedule tomorrow for a cardiac cath."

"Great! Do you have all the documentation from our board meeting last week?"

"Absolutely," Horvath replied excitedly. "I'm going to enjoy this."

"Let me know how it goes."

"I will. Talk to you later."

Horvath hung up with a satisfied smile on his face, knowing he had the backing of the chairman of the board, even if he'd only been able to convince a slim majority of its members to go along with his new policy.

♦♦♦♦♦♦♦♦♦

Jack stuck his head in through the door of the cath lab and saw Buzz manipulating one of the long, thin wires he placed into the boy's heart through a tiny incision in his right groin. The wire entered the femoral vein then passed up through the inferior vena cava and into the right atrium. He had injected x-ray contrast material and watched as it flowed through the chambers of the heart, but since the abnormal blood flow was passing from the left atrium into the right, he couldn't see the hole using the dye. Instead he relied on the ultrasound image to guide the catheter through the opening and into the left side of the heart. When he injected the contrast again the abnormal anatomy was very obvious. A large portion of the blood that should have flowed into the left ventricle to be pumped out into the systemic circulation was instead flowing back through the hole into the right side, causing it to be recirculated back through the lungs again.

The problem wasn't just the hole between the two upper chambers, it was also the tight valve between the left atrium and the pumping ventricle. Buzz accurately surmised that it was the worsening mitral valve stenosis that was actually responsible for this child's passing out episodes whenever he exerted himself. There just wasn't enough blood getting to his brain when his leg muscles demanded more oxygen.

"Looks like you got it under control," Jack said, standing at the doorway without a mask on his face.

"I think so," he said. "As you can see, the right atrium is pretty good sized, and the ASD is a bit larger than most, but I'm sure I'll be able to close it, once I get the mitral valve opened up. His PA pressure is high, but I'm comfortable proceeding."

Jack and Buzz both knew that unless these problems were fixed relatively soon, the boy would progress to irreversible pulmonary artery hypertension. At that point it would be impossible to reverse his course, resulting in gradual heart failure and death within a few years. His PA pressures so far indicated that threshold had not yet been crossed.

"Sounds good. I have a little case to do, so I'll be over in surgery."

"I'll call you if I need you, but right now everything is looking good."

Later that afternoon Jack checked in on the youngster, who was awake and alert in the ICU. The intensivist told him that he was only in the cath lab for an hour and a half and he had gotten to the ICU around eleven. He was breathing on his own and had been asking for something to drink.

THE CALLING

The next day the boy was transferred out of the ICU to a regular room on the nursing unit, and the following day he was walking the hallways and appeared ready to go home. Buzz decided to keep him one more day to make sure he didn't develop any bleeding from the puncture site in his groin. He also repeated the echocardiogram, which showed the ASD was closed and the mitral valve appeared to be functioning normally.

On Friday, the smiling faces of the twelve-year-old and his father greeted Buzz, as he made his way into the hospital room. He told the father he could take his son back to Nicaragua the next morning. When the Spanish interpreter explained what Buzz had said, a huge grin appeared on the child's face. Buzz told them that they would need to follow up with Dr. Ramirez the following week, but he saw no need for any medications or additional testing. The boy would need to take it easy for about two weeks, but after that he could start playing soccer again.

There were handshakes all around before they left the hospital and returned to the Holiday Inn where the father had been staying. Jack had asked one of the social workers to help coordinate their transportation to and from the airport and hotel, and those bills were to be charged to the hospital's Nicaraguan Surgical Fund.

◆◆◆◆◆◆◆◆◆

"Hello, Dr. Jackson," Horvath said, as he welcomed Buzz into his massive office. He'd had Bob Anderson's old office remodeled, and it was now nearly twice as large. "Thanks for coming by," he added.

"It's good to meet you," Buzz said as he shook Horvath's hand before sitting down in one of the large leather chairs across from his desk.

"I'm very glad to be here and to have a chance to work with distinguished physicians like yourself."

Buzz was used to administrator types offering superficial praise to doctors to their faces, then deriding them behind their backs, so he paid little attention to his compliment. "What can I do for you?"

"Well, as you know, I'm still fairly new around here and I'm trying to get to know everyone and get a feel for how things work," Horvath stated in a deliberate tone.

"If I can help, please feel free to ask."

"That's what I had hoped you'd say. In fact that's one of the reasons I asked you to stop by." What he didn't say was it was the only reason he had asked him. "I know that you recently treated a boy from outside the US, isn't that right?"

"Yes, in fact I just discharged him this morning."

"Right, right," Horvath said as he reached for some papers on the far corner of his desk.

"I suspect you're aware of this special fund that was supposedly set aside for kids from Nicaragua, right?"

"Yes, I'm aware of it," Buzz answered cautiously.

"I just wanted to get your understanding of how that fund was supposed to work."

"As I understood it, there was a one million dollar payment made by a wealthy guy from Managua to pay for his daughter's surgery and for other kids in the future from his country."

"Do you know whether any of the money was to be set aside for physician's fees, or was it just for the hospital charges?"

"I don't know anything about that. All I know is that it was to offset the costs for surgery on kids that were identified by Jack Roberts."

"So, as far as you know it was for hospital charges only, since the check was written to the hospital," Horvath stated before pausing briefly. "At least it would appear that way, wouldn't it?" he asked.

"I guess. I never thought about it," Buzz said, questioning where he was going with his line of questioning.

"Let me ask it another way. When you agreed to treat this Nicaraguan boy, did you expect to be paid for your services out of that fund?"

"To tell you the truth, I hadn't thought about it."

"Are you saying you didn't think about getting paid, or didn't consider the hospital's fund to be the potential source of your payment?"

Buzz was becoming increasingly suspicious as the questions made him feel like he was being cross examined by some trial lawyer. "What exactly are you asking me?"

"I just wanted to know whether you were going to submit your bill to the hospital for performing a procedure and providing inpatient care for that boy?"

Buzz thought for a second and realized he truly hadn't considered whether he'd get paid. "I hadn't thought about it at all, until you brought it up."

"What if I told you that Jack Roberts' office submitted a request for payment from that fund for the two other patients he performed surgery on?"

"Well, if Jack thought that was appropriate then I guess I will probably do the same."

"Do you have any idea how much? I'm just looking for a rough approximation."

"I don't know, probably about twenty-five hundred dollars, give or take five hundred or so."

"Would it surprise you to know that is about half the average charge of a surgeon to perform open heart surgery?"

"No," Buzz said, wondering what that had to do with anything.

"So, you think it's fair that a surgeon gets twice as much as you do for performing the same procedure through a large incision as you get for doing it with no incision at all?"

Buzz finally understood what this guy was up to with his interrogation. Horvath was trying his best to bait Buzz into a debate designed to pit him against his longtime friend and colleague.

"Look, I don't get into what other docs charge for the services they provide. I have a hard enough time keeping up with my own practice."

"I just figured you would have an opinion."

"Oh, I have an opinion all right," Buzz said, deciding he'd had about enough of this guy. "I think every doctor is worth way more than they are being paid, especially if you consider the true value of what we offer."

"I'm not surprised to hear you say that. I have yet to meet a physician who doesn't think they are underpaid, but my question was more about the relative levels of payment between various doctors."

"You aren't going to draw me into that mess, because, like I said, I think all docs are under-compensated when you figure in the years of commitment, the hours of work, and especially the level of responsibility."

There was a period of uncomfortable silence between the two men, which was broken by the administrator. "Well, I appreciate your coming by, and I'll be looking for your bill for caring for that foreign child." He spoke with a finality that suggested Buzz Jackson had been dismissed.

The next day Buzz's office manager dropped by the administrator's office with a statement for two thousand three hundred fifty dollars for Dr. Jackson's services in caring for the boy from Nicaragua. Horvath's secretary placed it on his desk, and when he opened it, a sinister smile appeared on his face.

He called his secretary into his office and instructed her to send Dr. Jackson's bill straight down to the accounting office and ask the vice-president of finance to pay it immediately.

CHAPTER 21

Two weeks after his interview, Gus Pasqual sent Jack an e-mail with a rough draft of his article attached for him to review. He indicated this was part one of a two part piece on health care in Nicaragua. This first part was titled "What is Health Care?"

Pasqual began by comparing the vast differences in the number of physicians and hospitals per capita in Nicaragua compared with other Central and South American countries, as well as countries in Europe, Asia, and the United States. He made the point that even if the cost of health care were not an issue, access in Nicaragua would remain a major problem, simply because of the relative scarcity of facilities and trained physicians and nurses.

In the article, Pasqual tried to define health care using the various interviews he'd conducted including the one with Jack, whom he referred to as "the famous American surgeon."

Jack skimmed the lengthy documents for places where he had been quoted, just to make sure they were accurate. The first instance was response to the basic question, "What is Health Care?" Gus quoted him as saying, "Health care is a personal service, provided by highly trained individuals who offer their unique skills in service to humanity, one patient at a time. As a physician, I took an oath to serve my fellow man using the skills and knowledge I obtained through my training, along with my personal experience. It really doesn't matter whether those services are paid for or are provided for free, it is the sworn duty of every physician to provide the best care possible to anyone he or she is privileged to see. In many cases that may involve simply applying a bandage or prescribing an antibiotic, while in others it might require complex surgery. In every case, it is the physician's role to use the available resources to save lives and reduce suffering without regard to personal gain. That is the essence of the Hippocratic Oath." He felt that pretty well summed up his philosophy and that of most of the physicians he knew, at least those of his generation.

"What are you reading?" Elaina asked, as she came up behind him wearing her bath robe.

"Oh, this is that article that Nicaraguan reporter wrote."

"What's he have to say?"

"He's trying to define health care. You know, it's one of those philosophical pieces, like 'what is the meaning of life?' I'm mainly interested in making sure he quoted me accurately."

"Well, did he?"

"So far, but I just got started looking it over."

"Are you going to share with me what you said?"

"It's nothing you haven't heard before. It's late, why don't you go on to bed? I'll be there in a few minutes."

As she turned to leave Jack started reading again, until he caught a hint of the perfumed bath salts she had just finished soaking in, and decided he could finish reading this nonsense later.

◆◆◆◆◆◆◆◆

Jack was still concerned about the pediatricians' alliance with the hospital, despite how they'd tried to soft peddle it at the press conference. He needed some clarification, so he invited his longtime friend and colleague Jerry Grady to have lunch. He had requested the meeting three weeks ago following the announcement, but Grady's secretary had told him that this was the first time he had available, and he'd only have an hour to meet. To maximize their time together Jack offered to just bring some sandwiches to Jerry's office, but the secretary explained that Dr. Grady would be in meetings downtown all day. Actually, he would be begging out of a working luncheon with the hospital executives to meet with Jack as a personal favor. So they arranged to meet at the Chili's restaurant downtown at twelve-fifteen.

It was well past twelve-thirty before Jerry came rushing in and saw Jack raise his hand, catching his attention. He quickly made his way over to the booth, dressed in a dark blue business suit. Jack couldn't remember ever seeing Jerry in anything but his "pediatrician's uniform," which consisted of a plaid or brightly colored shirt, a cartoon theme tie, and khakis. His friend looked incredible. Somehow he wasn't the doctor he'd personally chosen to take care of David shortly after he and Elaina were married.

"Hi, Jack, sorry I'm late," Jerry said, as he sat down quickly and glanced at his watch. "I need to be out of here by one o'clock."

"Wow!" Jack exclaimed, "Looks like they've got you running ninety miles an hour."

"You don't know the half of it. It has been like this for nearly a month now. There hasn't been a day gone by that I haven't had some kind of meeting with lawyers or accountants and the finance guys from the hospital. Plus having meetings with my other partners at least two evenings a week, it's been beyond hectic. I haven't seen a patient in two weeks."

"Sounds like it... I appreciate your taking time to have lunch with me."

"I'm not going to be able to stay for lunch," he said as the waitress came to take his drink order, "I'll just have a glass of iced tea."

"Well, I'll get straight to the reason I wanted to meet with you. I just needed to hear directly from you the specifics of this new practice arrangement, and how you see things playing out."

Jerry looked straight into Jack's eyes with a harshness in his face that Jack had never seen. "I know you don't approve of what we are doing, but things are a lot different for you surgeons."

"Wait a minute, Jerry. I don't know exactly what you are doing," Jack replied. "So, how could I approve or disapprove?"

"Let's not BS each other, Jack. I've known you a long time. You know that we have essentially sold our practices to the hospital, and word is that you don't think that we should give up our autonomy. Well, just so you'll know, that autonomy has been costing me about twenty-five hundred dollars a month for the past year. I've been taking money out of my retirement account just to pay my overhead, and I'm not alone."

"Yeah, I heard several of the older guys were planning to retire."

"None of us wants to retire. Hell, taking care of kids is all I know how to do, but since the vast majority of our patients are Medicaid or SCHIP, we don't have many options."

"Look, Jerry, I understand. I just wonder if there isn't some other way besides getting into bed with the hospital. It was different when Bob was here. He was someone that all of us trusted. This new guy? I don't know. He seems just a little too slick. You know what I mean?"

"You mean he's a businessman."

"Right."

"Well, I have come to the conclusion that is precisely the kind of guy we need. The way our deal is structured, he and his team will do all the business negotiations and all the contracting, and we get a guaranteed paycheck."

"How can you be sure he isn't taking advantage of you?"

"I can't. I'm sure he probably is, but I'm doing a lot better being taken advantage of by the hospital than I was being raped by the government."

"I understand," Jack said sympathetically. "So, you're satisfied with the deal?"

"Yeah, it is very similar to the contracts being used by other primary care groups across the country. It subjects us to quality assurance and utilization review, but that committee consists of four physicians, four admin people and one nurse."

"I just hope they don't try and control your clinical decision making through that utilization review process," Jack warned.

"Look, Jack. This is a new era in health care," the pediatrician said, restating the words his business partners had used to describe the need for change. "The old rules don't apply anymore. We have to be willing to compromise to ensure the greater good is served."

"What exactly does that mean?" Jack asked with a somewhat shocked expression.

"It means we have to consider the bigger picture when caring for patients. The cost of health care is out of control, you know that as well as I do. So, we need to find ways to work together to find more efficiencies in treating our patients. That is why we are working with the hospital to shorten our average length of stay and number of complications. If we can do that the hospital will be more profitable and we will share in those savings."

"My fear is that the hospital's profits will become the driving force behind the practice of medicine. Those guys don't share the same ethics as physicians."

Jerry's look turned hostile at the challenge Jack had raised. "Do you think I'm compromising my ethical principles as a physician? Is that what you're saying?"

"No, I don't think you would do so willingly. All I'm saying is when you get your paycheck from the hospital, it puts them in a position to potentially control your decisions."

"Well, here's the reality," Jerry spoke with a lecturing tone in his voice. "Either we work for the hospital, or we don't work, period. They have control of the money."

"I don't blame you for doing what you have to do," Jack replied. "I just think it's a very slippery slope."

"Instead of fighting this trend, why don't you help us organize the specialists to get them on board? I figured you'd like the idea of sharing in the hospital profits. After all, the concept isn't all that different from the Nicaraguan Surgical Fund."

Jack looked up quickly from his full glass of tea and asked, "What do you mean by that?"

"I mean, it must have been pretty sweet to get paid your big fee out of that pile of hospital money for taking care of those kids, right?"

Jack was puzzled, "I didn't get paid out of that fund. The patient's father paid me directly for the first case, and the second one I considered as charity. I don't know where you got the idea I took money from the hospital."

"Well, that's what I was told," Jerry responded defensively. "I know that Buzz Jackson was paid out of the fund for taking care of that last kid."

"What?" Jack almost shouted.

"Horvath told me Buzz submitted a bill to the hospital and they cut him a check for more than two thousand bucks."

Jack was stunned. He thought Buzz understood that the fund had been established to offset the hospital charges. It never crossed his mind that it would be used to pay for physician fees.

"I don't know why this is such a big deal," Jerry said. "The money is just sitting there."

"No, it isn't just sitting there." Jack offered back slowly. "That money was given to the hospital and was designated specifically to take care of kids from the poorest country in the western hemisphere if they need heart surgery."

"Well, maybe so, but I don't see anything wrong with docs getting paid out of that fund for the work they do."

Jack was having a hard time getting his mind around the concept. Traditionally, physicians and hospitals were completely separate entities. They had always submitted their bills separately, whether directly to patients or to insurance companies. The Medicare program even had completely separate divisions: Part A was for hospital charges, and Part B was for physician services. To have both parties paid from a single fund controlled by the hospital just seemed wrong somehow.

"Global payment systems are the way all care will be paid for in the future," Jerry announced confidently.

The look on Jack's face was one of sad contemplation. "Maybe so, but I just can't see it. If a single payment goes to the hospital, what's to keep them from taking all the money and paying the docs less than what's fair?"

"You are such a skeptic. They wouldn't be able to keep their physician network intact if they consistently shortchanged us."

"Oh, I don't think they'll do it all at once. They'll do exactly the same thing the insurance companies have been doing to us for nearly twenty years. Once they have us under contract, they'll gradually reduce what they pay, and then pit one group against the other to keep us arguing over the crumbs."

"That is the most cynical thing I've ever heard. Sounds like you don't trust anybody."

"I just don't trust guys like Horvath and Fitzgerald. They are no different from the insurance companies. To them, medicine is all about the money. That's why I plan to remain independent."

"You're gonna have a hard time making it as a lone wolf," Jerry warned.

"I don't think I'm alone. Most of the guys I've talked to feel the same."

"Maybe they do now, but I suspect they'll come around. Like you, they all rely on referrals from us primary care docs." Jerry's implied threat was not very subtle.

Jack now had all the information he needed, and correctly assumed there was no point in further discussions with Jerry. He was convinced that his change in clothing was merely an outward reflection of the fact he had become more businessman than physician.

♦♦♦♦♦♦♦♦♦

"How did the conversation with Roberts go?" Horvath asked.

Jerry had entered the large conference room where Horvath and three of his vice-presidents had been enjoying their crab salad while discussing their handpicked members that would make up the physician's governing council.

"He's not going to come along easily," Jerry said.

"That's all right," Horvath replied casually. "We can pick up another heart surgeon to fill that need in our network. He's not as irreplaceable as he thinks."

Jerry nodded slowly, but he began to sense a maliciousness in Horvath's tone as he referred to his longtime friend as if he were just another employee.

♦♦♦♦♦♦♦♦♦

"Come on in, Roberts," Horvath said with his typical artificial smile. "What can I do for you?"

Jack had called two days earlier in an effort to meet with Horvath, and this fifteen-minute slot was the only time available for more than a week. "I just wanted to come by and chat with you for a minute about the Nicaraguan Surgical Fund."

"Sure, have a seat."

"I understand that Buzz Jackson submitted a bill that was paid out of that fund. He told me that you said I had also taken money out of that fund."

"Yes, that was my understanding."

"Well, your understanding was wrong. I haven't taken any money from that fund or from the hospital. What made you think I had?"

"I just assumed you were paid out of that pool of money, since that's what it was designated for."

"No, that's not what it was designated for," Jack quickly responded. "It was set aside to cover the hospital costs for those kids needing heart surgery."

"I think you are splitting hairs, Dr. Roberts. What is the difference?"

"The difference is, that is the hospital's money, and I don't work for the hospital."

"I see," said Horvath with a hidden smile. Jack had unknowingly provided him with precisely what he wanted, total control of the funds. "Then you don't plan to submit any bills to us for your services for any children from Nicaragua?"

"No, I haven't up to now and don't ever intend to," Jack replied.

"Good," Horvath said, "because the fund is nearly depleted."

"How can that be?" Jack asked not sure that he understood. "We've only seen three kids so far."

"Well, based on the direction of the board, the charges have been reviewed for those three cases," he explained. "We went back and found a large number of chargeable items that had slipped through the first time they were submitted. As it turns out the total charges were considerably more than what was originally billed to the fund."

"What? That can't be right."

"Oh, I assure you it is correct. I reviewed the accounts myself."

"Even if that were true, more than half the money should still be available."

"Well, in addition to ordering the review, the board also took action reversing the deep discounts that were originally applied in all three cases. They decided that since the verbal agreement was with a foreign national, the hospital's cash discount policy should not apply. So, once all the corrections have been made, the total payments that have been charged back to the fund amount to nine hundred twenty-five thousand dollars." Horvath was indeed enjoying watching Jack's reaction.

"Are you kidding me?"

"No, I wish I were. I suspect you don't realize how truly expensive those procedures you do are, especially when they are accompanied by complications like renal failure. With only seventy-five thousand dollars left in the account, I'm not sure we can accommodate any more children from Nicaragua."

Jack detected the satisfaction in Horvath's voice, and his distrust of the man had rapidly turned into loathing. "So, I guess you figured a way to get that credit off your books after all, huh?"

"I have no idea what you mean," Horvath said. It took all the self-control he could muster, to avoid breaking into a smile.

"You know exactly what I mean. You've effectively stolen the money from a bunch of unseen children in a foreign country so you could pay for your damned CT scanner," Jack said as he stood to leave. "I hope you're proud of yourself."

"I'm going to let your obvious accusations slide this time," he said, "because I know how personally involved you have been with that Nicaraguan family. However, I would suggest you keep them to yourself from now on. The board would not take kindly to having their actions questioned in such a way."

Jack started to come back with another more personal challenge to this brash young accountant, but thought better of it. He remembered something his father taught him many years before. If you get into a scuffle with a man who's covered in mud, all that will come of it is you'll get dirty. Even so, he just couldn't sit by and say nothing.

"Is this the kind of creative accounting you plan to employ when dealing with the pediatricians?" he asked with dripping sarcasm.

"You know, Jack, you are very well respected in this community. If you would join us in our efforts to make health care more efficient, I'm certain it could be very much worth your while."

"I suspect it would be, but I think I'd prefer to remain well respected."

Jack turned to leave the office without any further exchange, but as he reached the door Horvath spoke up again, refusing to yield the last word. "Let me know when you change your mind."

Jack turned his head slightly as he heard Horvath speak, then proceeded to leave the room without any further response. Horvath leaned back in his chair, gloating in how easily he had defeated the pompous surgeon.

◆◆◆◆◆◆◆◆◆

David was well into the first semester of his second year at UT, and had just received the results of his midterm exams. As usual he was making all A's, all except for organic chemistry. He had gotten a B minus on both the major exams, and he was in danger of making his first B in any class since junior high. He knew that organic was the most difficult class for virtually every premed student, but he was convinced he could still manage to ace the class if he'd just spend more time studying.

He and Amy were still seeing each other nearly every evening, and while their sexual encounters were not as passionate as they had been earlier, they were no less frequent. One evening, Amy was in David's dorm room while his roommate was at a movie with his girlfriend. They had said they would study together, but once she arrived, the idea of studying was quickly replaced by physical contact.

"I have got to spend more time studying the rest of this semester," David said, still slightly out of breath.

"Is that all you can think about?" Amy asked. "Here we are together in your bed, and all you can say is you need to study more?"

"Well, if I don't do better the second half of this semester I'm gonna make a B in organic, and there goes my perfect GPA."

She sat up suddenly in the bed and faced him. "So your perfect GPA is more important than me?"

"What?" he said looking at her as if he hadn't heard what she said.

"I said, you are more worried about your perfect grade point average than you are about me." Her mood was quickly changing from apparent frustration to anger.

David clearly wasn't paying attention to either her body language or the sharp edge in her voice. "I don't think you understand how important this is to me. I'm worried I won't get into med school with anything less than perfection."

"Are you kidding me?"

"No, I'm serious," he said.

"Well, maybe I should just leave so you can study something more interesting than me," she said, as she stood up and started to get dressed.

"Hey, that's not what I meant and you know it."

"No, I don't know it. I come over here to be with you and share my passion for you, and all you want to talk about is your damned perfect GPA. So, I'm going back to my dorm so you can study that benzene ring-thing again." As she finished pulling on her jeans, she slipped on her sandals, grabbed her purse and headed for the door.

David had no idea what had just happened. "Why are you so angry?"

"If you can't figure that out on your own, then you have no chance of making an A in 'organic' chemistry." She made quotation marks in the air, then left the room, slamming the door behind her.

David jumped up and started to go after her, but realized he was still naked.

Later that evening he tried to call her, but didn't even get her voice mail. He figured her battery was dead because she had a bad habit of not charging her phone every day. He never considered the possibility she might have turned it off to avoid his call. He still had a lot to learn about the young woman he loved, especially when it came to how, and when, she needed his undivided attention.

The next day, organic was his late morning class and he came away from the lecture muttering to himself about the differences between thiols, mercaptans and mercaptides. Amy spotted him from a distance, walking with his head down toward the library. She ran across the courtyard to cut him off, when suddenly David turned around and hurriedly headed back toward the chemistry building. She wasn't sure whether he had seen her or not. She stopped and watched him disappear into the building. Was he avoiding her? Why hadn't he called her? She retrieved her phone from her purse and saw that her battery was dead. She decided he had probably just forgotten something, so she sat down on the soft ground under one of the huge oaks and waited for him to reappear.

As she sat staring at the building, a hundred different thoughts were running around in her head. Was his obsession with getting into med school a prelude to their future? Would she always be his second priority? Could she live with that idea? How would he react if he didn't get accepted? Did they really have anything in common other than their physical attraction? He was the only guy she had ever even dated. Was she missing something by focusing all her attention on him?

The longer she waited the more thoughts came to her. Why hadn't he come out? He must have seen her, and he really was avoiding her. After about ten minutes, she realized she was going to be late for her psychology class, which was in the other direction. She decided to head to her class, now wondering whether she even wanted him to come out of that damned chemistry building.

David had gone back to see if he could catch his professor. He wanted to know if there were any study guides or reference materials that he could use in preparation for the next quiz. The old professor was in his office and invited him in for a few minutes. He provided David with encouragement and a three-page study guide one of his former students had developed. When David left the professor's office, he felt more motivated than ever to ace his class. He made his way back toward the library, and tried again to call Amy, but again, she didn't answer her phone.

That afternoon David had planned to go to the driving range with his roommate, Jarrod. They left a little before five and returned around seven-fifteen. As they approached the entrance to their dorm he saw Amy sitting on the steps. Her expression was a combination of anger and frustration.

"Where have you been?" she asked harshly.

"We went to hit some golf balls. I tried to call you but your phone is dead," he replied.

She stood staring at him, not sure whether she believed the part about his trying to call. "Can we talk?"

"Sure, Baby," he agreed.

"I'm gonna go get something to eat," Jarrod offered, artfully excusing himself. "Do you want me to bring you something?"

"No, I'm okay," David replied.

He led Amy back up to his room and she quickly took a seat in his desk chair, leaving him to sit across from her on the bed, alone. She had been rehearsing what she was going to say for the last hour as she sat on the steps waiting for him.

"I understand your concern over your grade in organic chemistry, and your need to study, but I feel as though you are taking me for granted."

"But, Amy..."

"Wait a minute. Let me finish," she said, raising her hand. "I also understand your obsession with getting into med school, but over the last couple of months, you have become increasingly distant. It's like your focus is more on you and your personal aspirations, than it is on me, and on us."

David had always known Amy was insecure, but she hadn't sounded like this since their first aborted sexual episode. "Baby, I don't know what you're talking about. I spend nearly every free minute with you."

"That's the problem, I only get the free minutes. Time when you don't have something else to do. I don't feel like a priority."

"That's not fair!" he said much louder than he intended. "You know I came to Austin to get an education. We both did. I have to go to class, I have to study to keep my grades up, so I can continue to get my scholarship. What do you want me to do? I don't have time for much else."

"You had time to go hit golf balls with Jarrod."

"That was the first time in a month. Besides, I tried to call you and your damned phone is dead." David was growing angry with her implication that he didn't pay enough attention to her, and it was showing on his face.

"Oh, so it's my fault?" she said angrily. "Nothing is ever your fault. You are always in control."

"What? You forget to charge your phone, and then blame me for not calling you?"

"You could have found me if you wanted to," she snarked. "After all, I found you, didn't I?"

"This is crazy," he said, shaking his head. "I don't know what has you so upset, but whatever it is I wish you'd get over it."

Amy stood up quickly and for the second time in two days she bolted for the same door. "Where are you going? I thought you wanted to talk," David said as he stood.

She turned back toward him disgustedly and said, "I don't think I care to talk to you anymore. Maybe it's you I need to get over!" This time she closed the door behind her without slamming it and walked briskly back to her own dorm.

David didn't run after her, like she'd expected. His anger over being challenged about something as trivial as hitting golf balls was still in the front of his mind. He decided to study for his calculus exam to get his mind off her for a while. He'd call her later.

The evening went by much more quickly for him than it had for her. She plugged her phone into the charger as soon as she got back to her room, certain that he would call and apologize any minute. When he hadn't called by midnight she cried herself to sleep.

The next day was Wednesday, their standing date night, but when he still hadn't called by noon, she decided to make him suffer. She'd find an excuse why she couldn't go out, even if he begged.

It wasn't until five o'clock that her phone rang. She let it ring three times before answering, "Yes?"

"Hey, Baby, are you still mad at me?"

"Whatever gave you that idea?" she asked casually.

"The way you just walked out yesterday. What's wrong?"

"Nothing is wrong," she replied. "I just decided to give you some space."

"So are we on for tonight?"

"I've already made plans for tonight. I'm going out with some of my girlfriends."

"But, it's Wednesday!"

"Yes, I know, but since I hadn't heard from you all day, I made other plans."

The phone was silent for a few moments before David responded, "Okay, I guess I'll talk to you tomorrow?"

"Yeah, I guess."

David was confused. He had never heard Amy's voice sound so cold. "I'll call you in the morning, okay?"

"I don't have class until afternoon tomorrow so I'll probably be sleeping in. Just depends on how late we stay out tonight," she lied. "So don't call too early."

"Okay. Whatever you say." David didn't know how to respond to being brushed off like this. He and Amy had always been so completely open with one another, and now she seemed incredibly distant. "I love you, Baby," he said trying to get a sense of where things stood between them.

"Yeah?" she said with just a hint of sarcasm, "me, too." After a brief pause she added, "Listen, I gotta go."

"Okay, have a good time without me."

"I plan to, bye." She hung up the phone without waiting for him to say goodbye.

What the hell is going on, David wondered. He decided it must be that time of the month and her hormones were what was making her act weird.

She sat quietly on the side of her bed trying to decide whether to cry or throw her phone across the room. Why couldn't he just apologize for being distracted the last time they were lying in bed together? Was he incapable of understanding why that was important to her?

"Hi, Mom," David said with a sadness in his voice Elaina hadn't heard before.

"Hi, sweetie… what's wrong?" Elaina asked. Something had to be up for him to call home in the middle of the week.

"Oh, it's nothing. Amy and I just had a fight, that's all."

"What are you guys arguing about?"

"That's just it, I don't have any idea. I told her I needed to study more this semester because organic chemistry is a super hard course, and the next thing I know she doesn't want to go out, and when I talk to her she sounds so cold. I just don't get it."

"Let me let you talk to your father," she said, anticipating that Jack could tell him how to handle an emotional young woman.

"No, wait, please Mom, I called to talk to you." David was still a bit uncomfortable talking to his dad about anything that didn't have to do with school, or medicine, or politics. "I just wanted to know if girls can become irrational if their hormones are screwed up."

Elaina laughed, remembering her own mood swings, especially when she was pregnant. *Oh no!* She thought. *Is that what this is about?* "She's not pregnant is she?"

"I don't think so," he responded with a new fear in his voice. "I never even thought about that possibility."

Immediately she wished she hadn't said anything about the possibility of Amy being pregnant. It sounded so judgmental. She was mad at herself because that had been the first thing that came to her mind. It was only natural though, since she recalled how desperate that time had been in her own life. "I'm sure it will all blow over in a few days."

"I sure hope so."

"When are you coming home?"

I'll be home the week of Thanksgiving," he said. "Hopefully Amy and I will be coming up together the Saturday before."

"Okay, we'll be expecting you in a couple of weeks then."

When he hung up the phone he wondered if he should call Amy right then and ask her about the question of pregnancy. He decided that a question of that nature was better asked in person.

The following morning her phone rang around ten. It was David, so she let it go to voice mail.

"Hi, Baby, it's me. I wanted to see if you could meet me after your class this afternoon. There is something important we need to talk about. Please call me when you get this message. Bye."

There was no, I love you, or I miss you, or anything like that. His voice sounded nervous and even a little worried. What could be so important that he couldn't talk about on the phone? Was he going to apologize? If so, why didn't he sound like he was sorry? Maybe he had gotten some bad news from home. She really had no idea, so despite the vow she had made not to initiate any contact with him until he apologized, she decided to call him back, but not until after her last class later that day.

"I got your message. Where did you want to meet?" she asked coldly.

"How about in the park across from your dorm?"

"What time?"

"I can be there any time. What works for you?"

"Let me go home and change, and I'll meet you there around six."

Her voice remained different from what he was accustomed to hearing. He felt as if he were talking to a stranger. "Okay, I'll see you then."

"Bye," she said as she hung up.

Why had he chosen such a public place? Was he planning to dump her and wanting to humiliate her in front of her friends? A thousand other crazy ideas raced through her head, not one of which made any sense.

The early November evening was coming on quickly, and the temperature had dropped rapidly as the first cold front of the season swept through the area just before six o'clock. It was now in the low fifties after a daytime high of eighty less than two hours earlier. She had put on her old blue jeans, a heavy sweater, and the wool stocking cap that she'd last worn when they went skiing. She crossed the street and found David sitting on one of the wood and iron benches, waiting patiently. He was still wearing his white short-sleeve polo shirt with a small longhorn logo and some lightweight navy slacks. He obviously hadn't known the weather was going to change so abruptly, and he hadn't had time to go by his dorm to pick up a jacket or a sweater.

"You look like you're cold," she said as she approached.

"I'm okay," he lied.

She could see he was shivering just a bit, but she didn't really care. "What was so important that you couldn't talk about it over the phone?"

"Amy," he said, "I don't know what's happening between us, but I don't like it. I need to know what's going on that has made you start acting the way you have toward me."

"I don't know what you're talking about. You said you needed more time to study, so that's what I'm giving you."

"You just seem so... I don't know... angry and cold... I've never seen you like this." David's speech was halting, partly because he wasn't sure exactly what to say, and partly because he was chilled to the bone.

Amy just stood there, staring at him. She wanted to give in to her urge to throw herself into his arms, but she felt she had to hold back until he said he was sorry for not making her his top priority.

"I sense that something is wrong," he said, "something you're afraid to tell me... Are you pregnant?"

Where the hell did that come from, she wondered? "Of course not! Whatever gave you that idea?"

"You've just been acting so... I don't know... weird," he said.

"First you tell me how I'm keeping you from studying, then you say I'm crazy and angry and cold. And now I'm just weird. I wonder why you keep me around at all. I guess it's just for my body."

He was not certain what to say. "Look, I'm sorry I asked you about being pregnant, I just thought..."

"Listen, David," she said. "You don't have to worry that I'm gonna ruin your plans by getting pregnant. I wouldn't want to burden you with that. Not now... not ever!" She shouted, staring into his steel blue eyes that were filled with the same fear she felt but was too proud to admit. Suddenly she turned and ran back across the street and into her dorm. She collapsed on her bed, unable to stop the tears.

◆◆◆◆◆◆◆◆

David came home for the Thanksgiving holiday without Amy. He had tried to call her several times a day for more than a week but she wouldn't answer or return his call. He was having trouble staying focused on his studies. Instead he went to the driving range several times a week, taking out his frustrations by furiously hitting golf balls, not caring where they went.

He moped around the house over the holiday, seemingly lost without her. Elaina was truly worried about him for the first time since his heart surgery more than seventeen years earlier. She decided to talk to Jack about his situation, even though she had promised she wouldn't.

One afternoon after they'd watched a college basketball game together on TV, Jack asked David if he'd join him out on the patio. It was a warm Indian summer evening and the two men sat sipping their sweet teas as the early evening melted rapidly into a dark, moonless night.

"Your mom told me that you and Amy aren't seeing each other any more." Jack spoke with more empathy than David had expected.

"Yeah, I don't know what happened. She got upset about something, and the next thing I knew she wouldn't take my calls, she wouldn't call me back, and I've tried to talk to her at school, but she's always surrounded by her girlfriends."

"You're trying too hard," his dad said. "I know you're gonna say I don't understand, but trust me, I know what I'm talking about. If you try too hard, you'll just push her away."

"But, you really don't understand, Dad. She was upset because I told her I needed time to study. Her response was to tell me I wasn't spending enough time with her."

"I'm not talking about how much time you spend together, I'm talking about the quality of the time you share. Women don't need, or even want, a man around all the time, even though they may say that. What they want is your undivided attention during those times when you are together. It makes them feel safe, and that is what they really want."

"I tried, but there is so much going on. I was freaking out over organic chemistry and she wasn't being supportive."

"Don't you see? She sees organic chemistry, and med school, and eventually your career as her rivals for your affection," he said, speaking from personal experience. "Let me ask you something. If you were dating two girls, when you were out with one would you ever consider talking to her about the other one?"

David shook his head, beginning to understand what his dad was saying.

"It's the same thing with those other rivals. What you have to find is balance in your life, where all of the things that are important to you get the attention they need to keep them safe. I learned a lot about balance in life when I was stationed in Japan. The entire eastern philosophy is based on it. If you go overboard pursuing your education or a career, your personal life will suffer. The same goes for overindulging in your personal life. Your studies or your career will suffer."

David didn't want to admit to his dad, but he knew that was exactly what was happening. Since Amy broke up with him, he had been consumed with trying to develop a strategy to get her back. Now he was assured of no better than a B in organic chemistry and he was teetering on the verge of making something other than an A in calculus and US government. "You're right, Dad, but how do you find that balance?"

"That is the question eastern philosophers have been trying to answer since ancient times. There is no single answer. It's different for everyone, and chances are none of us ever reaches it completely. The most important thing to realize is that some element of balance is required to achieve happiness."

"So, how do you do it?"

"I struggle with it every day. It doesn't get any easier as you get older, but it is easier to define all the rivals. At your age, everything is a potential priority, but by the time you're my age you will have filtered through all the junk, allowing you to focus most of your efforts at balancing those few really important things like your wife, your kids, your faith, and your career. Everything else takes a position of lesser importance. It's not that you neglect them, it's just that other things have to remain subordinate to those top priorities."

As he was speaking to David, Jack realized how often he violated his own rules. He was silently grateful for Elaina being so incredibly independent. She rarely said anything about his other commitments, even though he knew they robbed her of his attentions far too often.

♦♦♦♦♦♦♦♦♦

David returned to school in January 2008, having successfully improved his grades in every subject except organic chemistry. He had accepted the B as gracefully as he could, but was more determined than ever that it would be his last. He had also resigned himself to moving on without Amy. She had joined a sorority and was now into the campus social scene. He rarely saw her, and when he did, she was always polite, but distant. On the surface it seemed that she too had accepted the idea of going forward without him.

Much of the talk on campus was about the upcoming presidential race, and especially the battle over who would be the nominee of the Democratic Party. Hillary Clinton, the senator from New York, and former first lady, was considered the front-runner, but many of the students David talked to seemed excited about a newcomer to the national political scene, the junior senator from Illinois, Barack Obama. Like everyone else, David didn't know much about him. He was focused on finishing his second year of college strong so he could retain his scholarship.

◆◆◆◆◆◆◆◆◆

Jack assumed an active role in the Association of Thoracic Surgeons. He had attended a couple of AMA meetings since accepting the role of ATS delegate, but thank goodness he wasn't involved in any of the major councils or committees. He found the AMA meetings had become even more divisive than they were twenty years ago, when he was there representing the physicians in the Air Force. Now it seemed that every major issue had something to do with money. Whether on the floor of the House of Delegates, in state delegation meetings, or even small group discussions, the topic of physician payment always seemed to dominate, and the government's Medicare payment system was at the top of the list.

Another thing he noticed, which was a significant change from two decades earlier, was the role of the Medical Student Section. He was amazed at the number of resolutions the students brought forward, most of which revolved around some social issue. What astounded him the most was how much power these yet-to-be doctors had in establishing policies of the American Medical Association. Jack found this to be particularly strange and wondered why they had been given the same vote as every other delegate.

It was clear that the AMA was not nearly as influential as it had been, since fewer than twenty percent of practicing physicians belonged to the once-proud organization. The membership had begun to decline as far back as the mid-sixties when the AMA failed to stand up to Lyndon Johnson and the creation of Medicare. While practicing physicians had grown progressively more disillusioned and were abandoning the organization, the AMA was still considered by the press, the Congress, and the majority of Americans, to be the voice of doctors.

At one time the AMA represented the majority of physicians, but it had been awhile since it had taken a meaningful stand. In 1993, one of the first actions of newly elected President Clinton was to develop a national health plan, modeled after the British health system. He put his wife, Hillary, in charge of developing the legislation, which became unaffectionately known as Hillary Care. The AMA actively opposed that attempt to socialize medicine, and as a result of its efforts, the private practice of medicine had been preserved. Now fifteen years later the rising cost of American health care was once more a major political topic that was certain to be a factor in deciding the outcome of the next presidential election. Both Democratic candidates were strong advocates for a government-controlled system. The only question was whether Clinton or Obama would emerge to take on the Republican candidate. Jack was hopeful the AMA's position would remain in clear opposition to any expansion of the government's role in health care, but he wasn't at all encouraged by what he'd witnessed at the meetings.

CHAPTER 22

"No, Mom..." David said. "I won't be coming home over spring break. There's a group of guys from my dorm that is going to South Padre for the week, and I need to get away for awhile."

"Okay," Elaina said. "I miss seeing you."

"Why don't you and Dad come down for a weekend in April?"

"We might just do that. The wildflowers will be in bloom out in the Hill Country, and we've been talking about going to that resort at Barton Creek for several years. I'll talk to your father about it tonight."

"That would be great. It's only about fifteen minutes from the campus. Maybe Dad and I could play some golf?"

"I know he'd like that," she said with a smile. "He has been so uptight about this upcoming election, it would do him good to get away from all the politics on television."

"Yeah, I know what you mean. It's all everybody is talking about down here."

"You are still planning to go to Nicaragua with us this summer, aren't you?"

"You bet! I'm really looking forward to it."

"Okay, sweetie," she said. "We're looking forward to it, too. I'll call you in the next day or two about our coming to Austin."

"Sounds good."

"Oh, I almost forgot. I ran into Amy's mom a couple of days ago and she asked about you."

"What did you tell her?"

"I told her you were doing okay, just studying hard."

David didn't respond, leaving an awkward silence.

"She asked if you were dating anyone, and I told her I didn't know, but I didn't think so."

He wasn't, and she knew it. He didn't tell her, but he was still in love with Amy, and no other girls had interested him since they broke up. "I'm not seeing anybody right now. I don't have time."

She hesitated to say anything else, but she could hear the sadness in his voice. "I think you and Amy make a great couple."

"It's over between us," he replied, with a frustrated sigh. "I haven't talked to her in almost three months. I've tried calling, but she won't take my call."

"I understand, son," she said softly, trying to console him as best she could over the phone. "She'll come to her senses one day and realize what an incredible catch you are."

"Yeah, right," David responded with a laugh. "I'm not going to hold my breath."

"Well, I miss you," she added, "and I'll bet she does too."

"I miss you too, Mom. I gotta go. The weather is so nice, Jarrod and I and a couple of other guys are going for a run this afternoon."

"Okay, I'll talk to you soon. I love you."

"I love you, too, Mom."

After she hung up the phone, she walked into the family room where Jack was sitting in his favorite recliner, watching the Fox News Channel. As usual they were talking about the presidential primaries.

"That was David on the phone," she said. Jack didn't look up or even acknowledge that she had come into the room. "Did you hear me?"

"Yeah," he said. "They're talking about health care, and I want to hear what this guy, Obama, has to say."

She just shook her head. "Well, when they get to a commercial let me know. I'd like a couple of minutes of your time."

Jack was concentrating on the young Illinois Senator being interviewed about his solution to the rising cost of health care and the millions of uninsured. He hadn't heard the subtle anger in Elaina's voice as she went back toward the kitchen. He thought the Senator seemed personable, but he had no experience. There was no way he would ever get the Democratic nomination. However, his rhetoric about expanding health care to forty-seven million Americans currently without insurance was certain to gain him some support from the liberal wing of his party.

The idea of a government-run health care system had always been a high priority for the Democrats. Jack remembered vividly the arguments that occurred in 1993 when President Clinton, with the support of other prominent Democrats, like Senator Edward Kennedy, pushed for a system that would have essentially turned physicians into government employees. Jack had been a

THE CALLING

government employee, and he knew all about the military's complicated and controlling bureaucracy. He could only imagine the red tape that would accompany a system where everyone was essentially on Medicare or Medicaid.

As the program went to commercial, Jack walked into the kitchen to grab a soda from the refrigerator. Elaina watched from the sink where she was rinsing off some dishes and placing them in the dishwasher. He looked to be deep in thought, and when he didn't say anything, she turned and said, "Well?"

He stopped and looked at her with a startled expression. "Well, what?"

"Didn't you hear what I said?"

"Yeah," he responded. "You said you talked to David on the phone."

"No after that... I said, I need a minute of your time."

"Okay, why are you so angry?"

"You're getting so caught up in all this politics on television, I can't even talk to you anymore," she said.

"What did you want to talk about? Is everything okay with David?"

"He's fine, but he's not coming home for spring break. He's going to South Padre with some of his friends in the dorm."

Jack could see that she was upset, and he assumed it was because David wouldn't be coming home as she had hoped. He tried to provide a positive spin. "He is still going with us to Nicaragua, isn't he?" he asked, already knowing the answer.

"Yes, but I want to see him before that. Why don't we go down there for a long weekend?" she suggested. "We've been talking about going to that resort at Barton Creek for several years, and David said it's only about fifteen minutes from the campus. You guys could play a round of golf together." Before Jack could respond she added, "It would do you good to get away from that damned television for awhile."

Now he understood. She was angry at him, not her son. "Okay," he replied with a bit of resignation in his voice. "You pick the weekend and make the reservations, and we'll go."

"How about April tenth through the thirteenth?" she asked, having already looked at the calendar. "We could leave on Thursday afternoon when you get home from the office and come home Sunday afternoon."

"Sounds good," he said, as he quickly returned to his recliner, again seemingly oblivious to her comment about his growing obsession.

In prior years Jack had been interested in politics, but this time he seemed consumed by it. He had generally voted Republican because he believed they were the more conservative party, and he strongly opposed the expansion of the government, which had been the history of Democratic administrations since FDR. The two major candidates for the Democratic nomination both scared him. Hillary was considerably to the left of her husband, but she was bound to garner tremendous support from women, especially considering the way she stood by her husband, a known philanderer. Obama, on the other hand, was still an unknown, but the way he talked about health care, he wasn't all that different from her. If elected, either would be certain to try to pass some type of sweeping health care reform legislation.

Elaina was sick of all the politics. She couldn't see where it made all that much difference who was in office. She frequently said, "They're all the same. They're politicians, and their main job is to get reelected." Jack always countered with the argument that government was too big already, and the Democrats were committed to making it even bigger and more costly, especially when it came to his profession. She refused to yield to that argument, suggesting that President Bush had committed the US to two wars that were costing billions and had expanded Medicare to include prescription drug coverage.

Their arguments were often not so much about which party was better or worse when it came to medicine, they were more about whether it was even possible to do anything about it. She found it difficult to argue against Jack's response when she asked what he thought he could do. "I don't know," he always said in frustration, "but I'm going to do whatever I can to try to save my profession, not just for me, but for our son's future. That means staying informed and staying involved. So that's what I intend to do."

♦♦♦♦♦♦♦♦♦

Pasqual's article had been published in Nicaragua a couple of months earlier to bland reviews. It seemed that in that country the government was expected to provide for the care of its citizens. The director of the government hospital had been quoted as saying, "One of the main responsibilities and duties of the state is to provide health care to all citizens of Nicaragua, without regard to their income or class."

In early March, Pasqual sent Jack a copy of part two of his treatise. This one was titled, "Who Should Pay for Health Care?" He once again quoted from the various people he had interviewed, including the two executives from Managua, both of whom had wished to remain anonymous. They had both stated that providing health care for their employees was not their responsibility. They simply could not afford to offer private health insurance to every employee and remain profitable. They agreed with the director of the hospital, that government should provide for their employees by the government. However, when asked about their own personal care, they were adamant about having the freedom to choose their own physician, and to use the more modern private hospital.

Pasqual went on to describe how the government was attempting to accomplish the goal of universal access, but given the current rate of economic growth, it would take more than one hundred years for Nicaragua to catch up with the more prosperous nations of Central and South America, and he saw no scenario where his country would ever approach the level of health care availability enjoyed in the US.

The two nurses that he interviewed were both employees of the government hospital. One had been a nurse for twenty-five years and the other for only four years, but both conveyed a strong sense of duty to their patients. "Caring for sick patients, especially children, is why I became a nurse," the older woman had said. He also quoted the younger one who'd said, "I love the time I spend at the bedside, but I hate all the paperwork. Unfortunately, if we don't do the paperwork, we don't get paid."

The article went on to outline how every country in the western world, with the notable exception of the United States, provided some form of health care to all their citizens, and in many cases even to visitors, at little or no cost to the individual. He had asked Jack why the US had not yet seen fit to follow the example of other countries and quoted his response.

"First, your basic statement is false. While governments may assume responsibility for paying for health care, they don't provide the care. They frequently talk about the care they provide, but invariably, their statements are made for their own political gain. As you pointed out, without the actual care givers, health care is simply not available. Second, the prevailing belief in the United States is that the private sector works better than the government at providing most things people need, including health care."

Pasqual had also chosen to tackle the question of whether health care is a right or a privilege. The hospital director was quoted as saying, "Every Nicaraguan has the right to have access to the same quality care." When he was asked if that meant the government was obligated to ensure everyone's rights he said, "Absolutely!" Gus pressed him by asking if that meant the government should build facilities, like the one he ran in Managua, in every corner of the country, including the remote and sparsely populated mountainous regions. The director had no answer to that question.

The nurses were split in their response. The older woman said, "I don't think I'd call it a right. I think it's more of an opportunity." The younger nurse said, "All people are entitled to at least a minimum level of care." However, when she was asked what level of care she would consider to be the minimum, she couldn't define it.

One of the businessmen was quoted in the article as saying, "Of course, access to health care is a basic human right, like food and clean water." Gus asked him a follow-up question about whether he thought people should have to pay for something that is a basic right. When he answered, "No, our rights are free," Pasqual pursued the issue with a second follow-up question. "So, by your definition that means no one should have to pay for food?" The executive's response made clear the flaw in his argument. He said, "Of course everyone must pay for food. If it were free, no one would be willing to work in the fields to grow the crops, or herd the cattle, or process the food."

Jack's response to the question of whether people had a right to health care was one he had repeated so often it almost sounded rehearsed. "Access to health care is not a right, any more than we have a right to food, clothing or shelter. Certainly, we all need those things, but it is up to each individual to obtain them for themselves and their family members. Those are fundamental individual responsibilities, not rights. However, one of the advantages of living in a civilized society is that we try to look out for one another, especially for those who are truly unable to obtain life's necessities for themselves. For them we provide assistance. If someone is naked we find a way to clothe them, if they are hungry we make an effort to feed them. If they are injured or sick we help them. That is called charity, and whether it is offered by an individual or a group, the capacity to provide for others in need is a large part of what makes us human beings. Charity is one of the core values of every great civilization."

Gus then asked Jack a follow-up question. "How do you explain the fact that so many people around the world are naked or hungry, and many don't have access to health care? Shouldn't governments provide those basic necessities for everyone?"

He then quoted Jack's response: "Individuals tend to be most charitable toward their neighbors during times of hardship, when the need is greatest. We see this especially during natural disasters. However, if people sense that their government is going to assume control of any and all difficult situations, they become less inclined to participate in charitable activities. Just look at the parts of the world where governments are most actively trying to provide for the people. Those tend to be places where resources are most scarce, and where people are the most dependent. Once people come to rely totally on their government to provide for all their basic necessities, they lose their ability to be self-sufficient, and those who are successful lose capacity for charity. In the end the entire civilization declines, or, in some cases, the people are never allowed to flourish."

The final segment of the article discussed the rising cost of health care and again the opinions varied. The hospital director was convinced the problem was the greed of the pharmaceutical companies and device manufacturers, while the nurses blamed overpaid doctors. The executives both argued that health care needed more regulation, including government price controls.

When Jack was asked about the continuous rise in the cost of health care he was more circumspect. "There are two forces that are driving up costs, but they both stem from the same root cause. The person receiving health services is typically not the one paying for them. Providers and suppliers don't have to justify their charges to the one who is seeking treatment. In most instances the patient doesn't know, or even care what those charges are. The driving motive then is not customer satisfaction, because the patient is not technically the customer. Instead all efforts are made to maximize profits obtained from an otherwise uninvolved payer. The disconnect between patient and payer leads to the second cost driver, and at least in the United States, it is probably more responsible than anything else for the rising cost of care. When a service is essentially free to the consumer, it leads to excessive demand. When that increasing demand is coupled with a profit motive, there are no brakes on the system and costs quickly escalate. This is precisely what we have witnessed in the US, and it is fueled by government programs like Medicare and Medicaid, and other third party payment programs. Our system encourages people to use what they see as their right without considering the cost, which takes us back to your earlier question."

"I have interviewed three different patients and one parent of a young child," Pasqual explained. "The latter was the father of the boy operated on by Dr. Roberts at the government hospital. I asked each of them the same questions, and their responses were all very similar. None of them had the money to obtain care without assistance, but none of them believed they were somehow entitled to the care."

He quoted one patient as being grateful to "the generous charity of God for making doctors and nurses available when he needed them." Mr. Ochoa, whose son had been treated by Dr. Roberts, stated, "The doctors and nurses who cared for him did not ask me for anything, probably because they knew I had no money. If they had, I would gladly have given everything I have to restore my son's health. There is no way to put a price on the care he received."

The article ended without answering the title question. Pasqual stated simply, "There is no simple solution to the health care payment dilemma, but one thing is certain. The cost of care rises whenever it is available and someone other than the patient is paying for it."

◆◆◆◆◆◆◆◆◆

At the Association of Thoracic Surgeons' board meeting, Jack raised the issue of the role of organized medicine in the health care debate and in presidential politics. "I think this is likely to be the deciding issue in this next election, and the ATS should be involved. Otherwise, we risk having a bunch of bureaucrats telling us how to practice medicine," he reasoned.

Another director stated, "The ATS should stay out of it. Our image as a professional organization will be forever tarnished if we get involved in partisan politics." Several other voices were quick to agree.

Jack replied by pointing out that declining Medicare payments was the number one concern of their members. "Isn't it our duty to represent our dues paying members? Don't they deserve to have their voices heard? The average doc out there who is trying to make a living is being systematically squeezed by the system."

"We all understand the problem, Jack," President Novak replied. "The question is whether we can do anything about it? The system is so deeply entrenched, I think the best we can do is find ways to make the most of a bad situation."

"That is precisely what got us into this mess. We should have stood up back in 1987 when the Omnibus Budget Reconciliation Act created a price-controlled payment system under Medicare. We didn't stand up to them then, so ten years later they passed the Sustainable Growth Rate formula that has severely limited our fees and threatens us every year with draconian cuts. What's next?" Jack asked in frustration.

There was silence on the teleconference call for several seconds before Novak spoke again. "So, what are you suggesting we do, Jack?"

"I think the ATS should take the lead on behalf of its members, and all physicians for that matter. The government's latest effort is this so-called Pay-for-Performance initiative. They are going to dangle a one or two percent increase in payment in exchange for making everyone negotiate even more red tape before you get paid. It's obvious they won't increase anyone's pay, but instead use their new, complex data collection system to punish those who refuse to play by their ever-changing rules," Jack was on a roll. "We should actively oppose the whole P4P idea by coming up with our own policy. This is just another layer of government bureaucracy and regulation."

"For us to adopt such a policy, we'd need to poll all our members. Surveys like that cost money, and that is something we don't have," Novak replied.

"What good is a board of directors if we don't provide leadership? I thought that was what we were elected to do… lead," Jack responded.

Again, there was silence on the phone for several seconds until another board member spoke up, saying, "Do you really think anybody gives a damn what we think? The government, the insurance companies, and the public are all convinced we are a group of overpaid country club snobs, who are only interested in protecting our own skins. They have no sympathy for us or anything we say. The only time they care about their surgeon is when they need us to save their lives."

"So, how do we change that image?" Novak responded.

"I'm not sure we can," Jack replied, "but I sure think we should try. That's why I believe we should start by opposing this Pay-for-Performance crap, and expose it for what it is."

Another board member chimed in, "I think we should have our secretary/treasurer draft a resolution that he can present to the AMA House of Delegates, opposing P4P and any other form of discriminatory payments by Medicare."

The board passed that motion unanimously, and Jack became saddled with the responsibility of doing the work. Over the next week he worked on getting the proper phrasing that he hoped would satisfy all physicians in the AMA House, but he knew that was impossible. Considering the last two meetings he had attended it was clear the division was growing wider, with declining physician payments by Medicare and Medicaid being the chief reason. He was convinced that anything he proposed would be shot down by the block of primary care physicians and medical students.

Jack knew some of the leadership of the AMA personally, most of whom were academic physicians with guaranteed university paychecks. He also knew they were not particularly sympathetic to the problems of private physicians. They had maintained control of the organization for decades, and that was the main reason most practicing doctors had simply left the ranks of the AMA. He also thought it was interesting that the decline in membership didn't seem to be a problem for those in charge, as long as the organization maintained their contract with the federal government's Centers for Medicare and Medicaid Services to publish the standardized coding books. The two huge books were used by all doctors and hospitals as the key to getting paid. One contained every known diagnosis, and the other listed all the recognized procedures and services. Every insurance company, as well as all government payment programs, required bills to be submitted using those codes. The coding books cost more than one hundred dollars apiece, and were updated annually, so all physicians' offices were required to buy a new set every year. These publications netted the AMA more than fifty million dollars annually, which was more than the total membership dues collected. Jack was convinced that it was these codes that provided the mechanism for the government and third parties to standardize the payment process and thus the flow of funds. They were using the AMA to force all physicians to play the coding game, and in so doing effectively controlled the practice of medicine.

◆◆◆◆◆◆◆◆◆

"May I speak to Dr. Roberts? Tell him this is Herb Nichols, the administrator at the hospital," Herb added, somewhat annoyed that he would have to go through a receptionist to talk to Jack.

"Let me get him," Phyllis said, as she placed Herb on hold.

Jack was just coming out of an exam room when she caught his attention.

"It's Mr. Nichols on the phone for you," she said.

Jack went back to his office to take the call. "Hello," was all he said.

"Jack! Thanks for taking my call," Herb said with his typical, excessively friendly demeanor.

"Sure, Herb… What's up?"

"I just wanted to get your take on something surgical," Herb said, sounding as though he was actually soliciting an opinion. "What do you think about these new surgical robots?"

"Are you talking about the da Vinci robot?"

"Yeah, the urology group is asking about them for prostate cancer surgery, and a couple of the general surgeons have also shown some interest. Is that something you would have any interest in?"

"I've looked at the robot at several meetings, but in my opinion the technology is not there yet. So, I don't think it would be something I'd have much use for."

"Well, you know, the public loves stuff like that, and if we had one it would help us solidify our market leadership."

Jack rolled his eyes at the suggestion that the hospital might buy a two million dollar piece of equipment, just so they could market it to the public. "It might be useful to the urologists, and maybe even for some complex general surgery cases, but there isn't really a place for it in cardiac or thoracic surgery at this time."

"You know, you could be the region's first robotic heart surgeon, and we would help promote that all across North Texas."

"I don't think so, Herb. I'd rather see you save the two million dollars and spend it on updating our ICU monitors. Those things are ten years out of date."

"Well, we've already ordered the robot. It will be here next month. I was just giving you first shot at being my robotic heart guy."

That comment was more than Jack could stomach. Elaina had warned him repeatedly not to speak in anger, but in this moment he couldn't help himself. "Look, Herb, let me make this clear. I'm not your guy, robotic or otherwise. I don't work for you."

Herb remained very cool despite the rebuke. "That is certainly true, Jack, at least for the time being. I was just trying to help you out. I'm sure there will be other surgeons who will look more favorably on my offer." There was a brief silence before Herb concluded with, "You have a nice day, Jack." Before Jack could respond he heard the phone click off.

That son of a… he thought. It was obvious Herb was going to use the robot as a hook to bind unsuspecting surgeons to the hospital, entangling them in some kind of mutual marketing campaign. The feds were really cracking down on those kind of schemes. He was aware of several colleagues who had gotten into similar arrangements, and eventually found themselves under investigation by the Federal Trade Commission for violations of what were known as the Stark Laws. For more than a decade, Congressman Pete Stark of California had been behind the introduction and passage of three separate laws designed specifically to limit what physicians could do from a business standpoint. Accepting money from hospitals, or equipment manufacturers, including marketing or promotional efforts, were all high on their list of what they referred to as "physician kickbacks." Most hospitals and virtually all device manufacturers employed a bevy of lawyers specifically charged with ensuring compliance with the Stark Laws. Physicians couldn't afford such high-priced counsel so they often just relied on the advice of the hospital's attorneys.

◆◆◆◆◆◆◆◆◆

The cool sand felt great on her bare feet, and the morning air was still quite crisp, as the first truly warm days of spring had yet to come to the beaches of South Padre Island. Amy and four of her sorority sisters had gotten to their hotel room late the night before, and she was the only one who was an early riser. She grabbed a cup of coffee in the hotel lobby and headed for a solo walk on the beach shortly after sunrise.

The beach was nearly deserted, but up toward the boardwalk she could see men busily working, setting up temporary outdoor stages where dozens of bands would start playing outside the local bars later that day. The crowds wouldn't start showing up until afternoon, so for the time being she could enjoy a leisurely stroll along the peaceful water's edge.

It was times like this that she missed David the most. She didn't know what had happened. She had been certain that he would come up to her one day and apologize, but that day never came. Now, five months later, she didn't care about any apology, she just wanted him to hold her hand and tell her he loved her. She'd concluded that it was all her fault. She didn't care about the advice all the other girls were giving, she wanted him back.

As she strolled aimlessly, she watched the sand collect between her toes only to be rinsed away by the gentle surges of foaming water which raced onto the land before slowly retreating. In that moment she vowed to do whatever she had to do once she got back to Austin to restore their lost relationship.

She turned and walked toward the boardwalk, looking for a place to get another cup of coffee. As she walked past the dive shops and swimsuit boutiques, all yet to open for business, she noticed one little specialty store with the door standing open and the florescent lights just flickering on. She stepped inside and saw a middle-aged woman behind the counter, booting up her computer for the start of what she hoped would be a profitable day.

"Hello?" Amy said, more as a question than a greeting. "Are you open?"

"Yes, please come in," the woman replied.

As Amy stepped into what she now recognized to be a novelty shop, she asked, "Do you know where the nearest coffee shop is?"

"Sure, it's about five doors down the boardwalk and tucked just around the corner."

"Thanks," Amy said as she turned to leave. Just then she caught sight of a small wooden carving of a Madonna. It immediately reminded her of the one at David's home. She stopped and walked over to it, then knelt down to touch it, not because she was drawn to the religious carving, but because it represented him. As she lingered there for a moment the woman came up behind her and said, "It's from Mexico."

"I have a friend who has one similar to this but much larger and more realistic. I was just thinking of him." She rose to her feet again and as she turned back toward the door, the shopkeeper saw her sad expression and the glistening tear that had not yet fallen from her eye.

"Have a blessed day, dear," was all the older woman could think to say, recognizing the emotional strain on the face of the beautiful young girl.

Later that morning David, Jarrod, and a couple of the other guys from the dorm made their way down to the beach. "Let's go get some beers," one of the guys suggested. David was not yet twenty-one, but on the beach during spring break no one asked for an ID. If you were there, you were considered of age.

Although he wasn't really much of a beer drinker, David went along, just to be with his friends. They quickly found an outdoor bar facing the beach, and ordered a "Bud Bucket." It consisted of six longneck Budweiser beers in a galvanized metal bucket filled with ice. As they sat on the edge of the newly constructed wooden stage, their bare white legs dangling over the edge, they opened the cold beers and clinked them together ceremoniously.

"To the first of many!" declared Jason, the oldest of the group. They each took a long draw of the golden liquid, after which Jason lifted his bottle in the air again and said, "We are gonna have a great time. Just look at all the chicks on this beach already and it's not even noon. If you can't get laid here, you can't get laid."

David was suddenly shaken by his memories of those nights with Amy. He hadn't thought of any other girls since they broke up. Now, here he was in an environment filled with sun, and beer, and loud music, and sex, and the only person he could think of was her. *What was she doing for spring break? Was she having sex with some other guy?* The thought of that possibility made him more than angry. He was frustrated and sad, to the point of nausea. The beer wasn't what he needed. He needed her, but for now, the beer was the only treatment available for his broken heart.

The guys ordered another bucket and soon, one by one, they had to get up to find the facilities. Around one o'clock, David was still nursing his second beer when the waitress told them they'd have to move off the stage. The first band was about to get started playing. The nearby tables were all occupied so he just grabbed his bottle and started walking toward the water.

"Where are you going?" Jarrod shouted.

"I'm just going to take a walk down the beach. I'll be back in a bit," David replied, indicating he wanted to be alone for a while. His walk lacked any purpose, and he carried the half-full bottle of warm beer more as a substitute for Amy's hand than any form of refreshment. Once he reached the water he turned and walked along the smooth cool sand, watching the small waves of foamy seawater rush up over his feet, then retreat, leaving no trace of his footprints behind.

The number of kids on the beach was growing by the minute. Many were already paired up, sprawled on top of each other on colorful beach towels. Most of the girls he saw were in groups of three to five, apparently seeking the security of numbers. There were a few singles like himself, walking along in search of a friend, or just looking to be noticed.

He passed a group of five guys who were already completely smashed. They were harassing a group of girls, making crude gestures and shouting lewd remarks. The young girls were trying to avoid them, without much success. David saw from the tee shirt that one of the boys was wearing that they were from another well-know Texas university, not UT. He wisely decided not to confront the guys directly. That would undoubtedly turn into a brawl, so he decided to offer the girls a way out. He made his way around behind the group, and came toward them from the boardwalk.

"Okay girls, your table is ready!" he exclaimed, trying to sound as if he were an employee of a nearby restaurant.

The five girls each turned toward him with questioning looks, and he was shocked to see that one of the faces was Amy's. They all got up off their towels and gathered their things.

"Aw, come on. Don't leave us. We were just starting to have some fun," yelled one of the boys. As the girls quickly followed David toward the boardwalk, the boys turned and stumbled on down the beach in search of another group to torment.

"Thank you so much," said one of Amy's friends. "We had no idea how we were going to get away from those creeps."

"Are you okay, Baby?" David said to Amy, ignoring the others.

"Yes, I'm fine now," she said with a huge smile.

"I had no idea you were one of the girls those guys were bothering. If I'd known, I would have punched each one of them in their filthy mouths." David was only just now feeling the return of his anger and the vague nausea he'd experienced earlier in the day.

She looked up into his steely blue eyes and was on the verge of tears.

"Are you sure you're okay?" he asked again, not knowing what else to say.

"I have never been better, now that you're here."

As he looked down into her gorgeous face and the sparkling green eyes he knew so well, he couldn't help taking her into his arms and kissing her passionately. Her response was automatic. They stood there for several minutes, totally unaware of the stares of her friends and dozens of strangers on the beach.

When they finally broke the bond between their lips, he said, "I'm so sorry, Baby. I was such an idiot."

"No," she interrupted, "it was all my fault."

"I love you so much," he said, his voice betraying the rising emotion he was still trying to hold back.

"I love you, too," she replied, reaching up to hold his face in her hands. "Let's get away from here."

They turned away from Amy's group of friends and started toward the beach. "Where are you going?" one of her friends called out.

"I'm running away with the man I love," she said as she turned her head briefly back toward them, clinging to David's hand.

Soon she had her arm around his waist and his was around her bare shoulders. Neither spoke again for several minutes. They passed the restaurant where David's buddies were still hanging out, drinking beer and watching the girls as the first bikini contest was just getting underway. David caught Jarrod's attention and waved goodbye. His friend immediately recognized Amy and smiled as he gave his roommate a thumbs up gesture. He was sure he wouldn't see David again for a while.

"I can't believe I just ran into you," he said. "I didn't know you were coming down here for spring break with your girlfriends."

"I can't believe you just showed up to rescue us from those awful guys."

"Sounds like fate to me."

"I think it's more than that," she said as she kicked playfully at the sand. "I was walking along this stretch of beach earlier this morning, and I was thinking about you."

"Really?" David questioned.

"Yeah, and then when I went into a shop down near the end of the boardwalk and saw something that reminded me of just how much I have missed being with you." She stopped and looked up into David's handsome face and added, "I'd like to show it to you."

"Sure, Baby, I'm completely free to do whatever you want," he said staring down into her adoring eyes.

"The woman in the shop where we are going wished me a blessed day as I was leaving. I think she could tell how bad I was feeling, and how much I missed you. I think her blessing is just what I needed."

As they stood facing each other David reached around her tiny waist and lifted her up to him, and as their passionate mouths met again. She wrapped her legs around him, putting her arms around his neck. The tide had begun to come in, and the gentle surf was now swirling around his ankles, but they were both so caught up in each other, neither cared about the scene they were creating or the hoots and whistles that were being directed their way.

When they walked into the gift shop Amy pulled David by the hand over to the carving of the Madonna. "See? I saw this piece this morning and it reminded me of the one your parents have in their foyer."

"May I help you?" a woman asked from behind Amy.

She turned, expecting the face she had seen earlier, but this woman was at least ten years younger and she had dark hair. "I was in earlier this morning, right after you opened, and I spoke to a woman with blond hair."

"That was my associate," the woman said. "She's gone out to get us some lunch. She'll be back in a few minutes. Perhaps I can assist you?"

"I just wanted to show my boyfriend this carving, and I wanted to thank her personally."

"I see," the woman said with suspicion in her voice. "Well, she'll be back in a few minutes if you want to wait."

"Thank you, we will."

As the woman returned to the counter to assist another customer, David looked at Amy and said, "Wow, she's not especially friendly, is she?"

"The other woman seemed much nicer. You'll see."

They wandered around in the store for another ten minutes, looking at everything, but nothing in particular. Near the front counter was a glass enclosure that contained several unique silver pieces.

"That looks almost exactly like the one my dad gave me when we were in Nicaragua," he said pointing to a simple silver cross.

"I don't think I've ever seen you wear it."

"I don't. I always thought wearing a cross around my neck made me look, well, like a holy roller, or something."

"I disagree," she said. "I think it would make you look like a man with conviction."

"I've got an idea," he said. "What if I get this one for you and then we can both wear them to remind us of the day we got back together?"

"That sounds like a great idea."

"I understand you are waiting for me," the shopkeeper said as she approached the young couple from behind the jewelry case.

As Amy looked up, she smiled and replied, "I was in here this morning."

"Of course, I remember. Is this the young man you were talking about while you were looking at that carving?"

"Yes, ma'am," Amy said, as her smile became a giant grin. "I wasn't sure when I was going to see him again, but you wished me a blessed day, and I just wanted to come back and let you know that is exactly what I'm having."

"I'm glad for you both," she said with a knowing smile.

"I would like to see that silver cross," David said, pointing to the piece he wanted to get for Amy. "I have one like it, and I'd like to get one for her."

She pulled the piece he was pointing to out of the case and laid it on a dark blue leather pad. "This is from New Mexico. Both the cross and the chain are sterling silver."

"How much is it?" he asked.

"Normally it's one hundred dollars, but for you I will take seventy-five."

"I'll take it," he said without hesitation. He picked it up and carefully opened the clasp of the chain and placed it around Amy's neck. The eighteen-inch chain suspended the cross just above her developing youthful cleavage. She reached down and gently rubbed the cool metal between her thumb and finger, then looked up at David and gave him a nod and a smile.

He reached into his wallet and pulled out the MasterCard his mom had given him to use for incidental expenses. The woman quickly ran it through the electronic reader then glanced at the name before handing him the card and the paper ticket. "Interesting you were looking at that Madonna," she said noting the last name.

As he signed it he said, "Yeah, my parents have one sort of like that it."

She watched David sign the charge ticket and asked, "You wouldn't happen to know a doctor by the name of Jack Roberts, would you?"

David looked up in surprise, "Yeah," he said slowly. "He's my dad."

"Oh my God!" she exclaimed.

"What's the matter?" David said, not understanding her excitement.

"I know your father. My name is Elizabeth Burke, and I brought a little girl to Fort Worth for him to do her heart surgery."

"Really?" David inquired as he watched her face light up.

"Your father is the most kind and generous man I have ever known. He took care of that little girl as if she were the daughter of some rich oil tycoon, instead of the child of a poor Mexican laborer."

"Yeah, that's my dad," David said with pride.

"That girl's father gave your dad that Madonna for saving his daughter's life. His grandfather carved it, and it had been in their family for about sixty years."

David remembered his dad talking about the girl from Mexico and her father. "That is amazing," he exclaimed. "My name is David," he said as he reached out to shake Elizabeth's hand. She took it in both of hers, holding it firmly as if trying to keep him from escaping.

"I am so excited to meet you. Where are you two staying?" she asked, looking alternately from David to Amy, but not yet releasing his hand.

"We're down here for spring break with some of our friends from college. We're staying just up the beach. I'm here with three other guys and Amy is with four other girls. It's one of those four or five to a room deals."

"Would you do me the honor of coming to stay with me at my home? It's just about ten minutes from here and I have two extra rooms that aren't being used. I would love to have you." Elizabeth was so excited to have a chance to return some of the kindness that David's father had shown her.

"We couldn't possibly impose," David said.

"Nonsense! It is not an imposition. I would love to have you stay with me. I even have an old jeep you guys can use to come back and forth to the beach during the day to hang out with your friends. Please, I insist."

David looked at Amy and she nodded enthusiastically, hoping to get away from the criticism she knew would be coming her way from the other girls, and desperate for some time alone with her man. He looked back at Elizabeth and asked, "Are you sure we won't be putting you out?"

"Don't be silly," she responded quickly and after a few seconds David nodded with a youthful smile. "Then it's settled. I'll be leaving the shop in a couple of hours. Why don't you guys meet me back here a little before four, and bring your stuff? We'll run by the house and then we can either go out for some dinner, or, if you want, y'all can come back down here to the beach and party."

"That sounds great," David replied. "We'll see you in a couple of hours."

He took Amy's hand walked out of the shop into the brilliant midday sunshine. They no longer seemed interested in the beach, or their friends, or the parties that were now in full swing in the bars along the boardwalk. They were only interested in each other.

Later that afternoon they returned to Elizabeth's shop where she and Jennifer, her associate, were finishing arranging a display of postcards near the front door. David was carrying Amy's small suitcase as well as his own duffel bag, and they both smiled sheepishly as Elizabeth greeted them with a brief embrace. She turned to Jennifer and said, "Well, I'm out of here. It's all yours." The two women alternated opening and closing the shop, so that neither worked more than eight hours, and the store could still remain open from eight a.m. to eight p.m., six days a week.

The trio left through the back door and got into Elizabeth's new suburban for the ten-minute drive back across the causeway, to her home on the outskirts of Brownsville. As she guided the big truck into the garage, the older model black

Jeep Wrangler was parked alongside. It was partially covered with a blue plastic tarp, and looked as though it hadn't been moved for quite a while.

"That's my old Jeep. I'll get you the key and you can use it to come and go as you like," she said as they exited the car and made their way into the house.

"You really don't need to be doing all this," David said. "You don't even know us."

"Oh, but I do," she said. "I know your father, and that's all I need to know. I can't tell you how incredibly kind and compassionate he was to me and to the Alvarez family. So, since I can't really do anything to repay him directly, I welcome the chance to return the kindness to his family."

She showed them around the house and pointed out the two spare bedrooms, neither of which had been used in several months. She could tell these young people were madly in love, so she decided to avoid any awkward moments by saying, "Please feel free to use one or both rooms if you like."

Amy looked up into David's face and gave him a sly grin, as she responded, "Thank you, Ms. Burke."

"Please, call me Elizabeth." The youthful glow of the couple's faces caused her to smile as she reflected on her own young love, many years before. "If you like, we can go grab a bite at a place I know that's well off the beach. During spring break all the places anywhere near the beach are impossible to get into."

"Sounds great," David said.

"I'm going to shower and take a short nap," she said. "It's just now four-thirty, so why don't we plan to leave around six-thirty?"

"I hope this isn't a fancy place," Amy said, "because I didn't bring a dress or even a nice skirt."

"No, no... This is a blue jeans and tee shirt sort of place. In fact, you could probably go just as you are."

Amy looked down at the white shorts she was wearing over her red bikini and flip-flops and said, "I think I'd feel better in jeans and a tee shirt."

"If you need to do any laundry while you're here, you'll find the washer and dryer just around the corner from the kitchen on your left. The towels in the bathroom are fresh, and if you need more they're in the cabinet."

"Thank you so much, Ms. Burke," David said.

She looked back at him with mock displeasure, "David, please, it's Elizabeth."

He smiled uncomfortably and replied, "If you insist. Thanks, Elizabeth."

With the formalities out of the way, Elizabeth started toward her room to freshen up as her two visitors took a quick look at the two spare bedrooms. They carried their things into the one with the queen-sized bed rather than the one with the two twins, and Elizabeth smiled knowingly as they closed the door.

Before they unpacked their things, David swept Amy into his arms and

THE CALLING

kissed her more passionately than she could ever remember. They were finally together again, and they were going to spend the next several days together. Neither of them had any interest in returning to the madness of the beach. All those kids were searching for what the two of them had already found.

After several minutes of intense kissing, Amy looked up into his steely blue eyes and said, "I need to take a shower." He reluctantly released his hold on the bare skin of her lower back. She turned toward the bathroom, and as she walked through the doorway she seductively untied the string of her bikini top. She turned back toward him and without a smile said, "Would you like to join me?"

David watched as she turned on the water and quickly slipped out of her shorts. He could barely contain himself as she slowly turned away from him and untied the strings of her bikini bottom, letting it fall to the floor. While they had only been on the beach for part of one day, her tan lines were already developing, and David couldn't wait to get his hands on her. He quickly stripped out of his tee shirt and swim trunks and joined her in the warm water.

❖❖❖❖❖❖❖❖❖

The interior of the informal restaurant was covered with old Texas license plates, road signs, and photos depicting cattle and oil wells and landmarks from around the Lone Star State. The country music was playing louder than necessary, causing everyone to shout just to be heard, making for a party atmosphere, much like the one they'd left on the beach. The hostess showed the threesome to a corner booth where the noise was at least tolerable. She gave each of them a plastic-covered menu as they were seated. Elizabeth sat across from the young couple who were sitting so close to each other she thought they looked uncomfortable. Again she recalled how it was when she was their age, and realized there was no such thing as too close.

When the waitress came, David and Amy ordered sweet tea, and Elizabeth ordered a beer. She started the conversation by asking each of them the usual questions about where they went to school and what they were studying. She wasn't surprised to hear David talk about his plan to go to medical school and follow in his father's footsteps. Amy told her she was a finance major, but wasn't sure exactly what she wanted to do when she finished school. Even though she would never say it, Elizabeth knew that her real plan was simply to be married to David.

"What about you?" David asked. "What are you planning to do?"

Elizabeth had given considerable thought to her future since her father's death shortly after Christmas, but she hadn't discussed the subject with anyone. "I don't know," she offered reluctantly. "I'm pretty happy with what I'm doing now, running my shop and making buying trips around the region. As long as the economy stays the way it is, the tourist business is very good."

She was making enough to live reasonably well, but she and her business partner didn't always see eye to eye. Jennifer had wanted to expand their shop to include selling food items and drinks, including beer and wine. This idea came up every month when they went over their books, and Jennifer claimed it would double their revenue. Elizabeth wasn't convinced it would be worth the hassle of getting the necessary licenses and installing refrigeration equipment. They had been arguing over this idea for more than a year, and Elizabeth was tired of it.

"I've been considering selling out to my partner and retiring to someplace like Costa Rica."

"Costa Rica?" David exclaimed. "Why would you want to move down there?"

"Well, the cost of living is very low. The weather is terrific. The crime rate is acceptable, and I have some friends who moved down there more than ten years ago and they love it."

"My mom and dad go down to Nicaragua every summer on a medical mission trip. They love that part of the world," David replied. "I went with them a couple of years ago, and I'm going back this summer."

Amy looked at David with surprise. "I didn't know you were going. When?"

"It's toward the end of June."

"Do you think I could go this time?"

"I don't see why not. I think you'd enjoy it," he replied, "but it's pretty hot that time of the year."

"I've been to Costa Rica in the summer," Elizabeth said, "and he's right. It's hot along the coast and in the valleys, but up in the mountains it is very pleasant."

"Have you been to Nicaragua?" David asked.

"No, but the place I've been looking at in Costa Rica is only about a three hour drive south of the Nicaraguan border."

Elizabeth talked about the small community of La Garita, west of San Jose, and the two-bedroom bungalow she'd found near where her friends lived. She hadn't shared her dreams of living there with anyone until now, and she began to wonder if the time wasn't right to retire. Her current home was paid for and was worth at least two hundred fifty thousand dollars. She figured she could sell her half of the business to Jennifer for another two hundred thousand dollars. She had nearly that much in savings, and her father had left her another half million that was still tied up in probate.

"Are you serious? You would actually move to another country?" Amy's question seemed to send the discussion in a whole new direction.

"Absolutely," Elizabeth responded. "Don't get me wrong, I'm Texan through and through, but there are several things about this part of Texas, and this country, that I could do without. The drugs, the taxes, the whole entitlement philosophy..."

"You sound just like my dad," David said. "He is always talking about how our society is crumbling because people have lost their sense of personal responsibility, and I agree."

"I hope you'll give your father my best the next time you see him. He has to be one of my favorite people in the world."

That week was a fantasy come true for both David and Amy. Elizabeth left for work early every morning, leaving them to sleep in together. While they had spent the night together in Austin a couple of times, the majority of their intimate moments ended with each having to go their separate ways, but this week they were truly living together. Elizabeth had left them the keys to the jeep, but they didn't leave the house, except for the evenings they spent with her.

David kept in touch with Jarrod by phone, and when Sunday finally came, he and his friends came by Elizabeth's house to pick them up. With one more passenger, Jarrod's old Ford Bronco was beyond cramped for the nearly six-hour return trip to Austin. David didn't mind that he and Amy had to share a seat, and she would endure anything to avoid riding back with the girls. She knew they would hound her for details of her week with David, and she just couldn't take the pettiness and judgmental innuendos she was certain to hear.

Before they left, David and Amy each gave Elizabeth a big hug and promised to keep in touch. As they drove off, she was once again alone and was unable to hold back her tears. Seeing their youthful enthusiasm for life and their future, she was convinced she needed a change in her own life.

CHAPTER 23

Jack was so caught up in the memories of their first road trip to San Antonio eighteen years before, he almost forgot to exit the interstate in Austin. As they approached the resort west of town, it seemed that every patch of grass along the highway, and every vacant lot was filled with the brilliant colors of Indian paintbrush and bluebonnets scattered under the native live oaks. He was convinced that few places in the world could compete with the beauty of the Texas Hill Country in the spring.

They checked into the huge resort hotel and the bellman showed them to their room on the eighth floor. It had a magnificent view to the north, overlooking Barton Creek canyon. The evening sun cast a golden hue over the greens and fairways of the lush golf course as well as the rolling hills in the distance. As the evening light faded, the lights from numerous mansions where many of Austin's elite lived, dotted the hillsides.

Jack was too tired to get dressed for dinner, having put in a full morning at the office, followed by the three hour drive. "Let's just order room service," he suggested.

Elaina was okay with that, knowing they were planning big dinners with David and Amy the following two evenings. "That's fine by me," she said as she started unpacking the lone suitcase they were sharing.

Jack picked up the leather bound room service menu and started reading off the choices to Elaina. When he had finished she said, "I'm not really all that hungry, I think I'll just have the Caesar salad and a glass of chardonnay."

"I'm going to have the pulled pork sandwich and a cold beer," he replied as he picked up the phone to place the order.

"It will be about thirty minutes," he reported loudly, as Elaina had disappeared into the large marble bathroom.

"There is a huge shower in here," she called back to him. "Just right for two."

Jack never tired of her playful suggestions, but thirty minutes was hardly enough time. "Maybe after dinner," he replied.

"Promise?" Elaina said seductively as she poked her head around the corner.

"I don't know of anything I'd like better," he said, flashing his crooked smile.

She disappeared back around the partition and Jack reached for the TV control. Just as he pressed the on button he heard her say, "I hope you're not turning that television on unless you plan on ordering an in-room movie."

He quickly pushed the off button, "I wouldn't think of it, dear," he replied. She had made it perfectly clear that this weekend was going to be their time to get away from all that political stuff. He knew she was right, but over the last few months he had become addicted to Fox News. While he didn't always agree with everything O'Reilly said, he enjoyed the format of *The Factor*, and *Hannity & Colmes* was always entertaining, mainly because he thought Alan Colmes came across as a left-wing idiot. Unfortunately, Hannity sometimes came across as over the top on the conservative side as well. He guessed he could do without those guys for a few days.

"Do you want something out of the minibar?" he asked, a little louder than was necessary.

"I'll just wait for my wine with dinner."

He pulled a small bottle of Glenlivet from the selection of liquors in the refrigerator inside the cabinet under the television. He twisted off the cap and poured it into one of the short glasses, then added two cubes of ice. As he took the first sip of his scotch, he picked up the card on the dresser that listed all the items in the minibar. He nearly choked on his drink when he saw "Glenlivet — $12."

"Are you okay?" Elaina asked as she came back into the room.

"I was until I saw how much they charge for a shot of whiskey. Two of these cost about what I get from Medicaid to see a new patient."

"You promised," she scolded, "we weren't going to talk about work or politics or anything like that this weekend."

"Sorry, I forgot." He put the card and the glass down on the dresser and turned to her. Sheepishly he asked, "Will you forgive me, Angel?"

She smiled seductively as he took her in his arms and pulled her close to him. She willingly melted into his embrace as their mouths merged in a familiar, yet still passionate union. She knew he was feeling frisky by his use of the pet name Angel, and by the way he reached for her bottom. He had always told her what a great butt she had, especially whenever he wanted her. In recent months, those overtures hadn't been nearly often enough to suit her, but tonight she would make sure that would change.

The waiter brought their dinner, and they ate from the rolling table. Jack sat on the bed while Elaina used the desk chair. The meal was forgettable, but the wine was quite good and the beer was cold.

Jack rolled the table back out into the hallway and placed the DO NOT DISTURB sign on the handle before locking the door. He called the room service extension and told the man who answered the phone that they could come pick up their table. As he hung up the phone he looked toward the bathroom and saw Elaina's reflection in the mirror. She was sliding out of her jeans, revealing her bare bottom. He stood watching as she shed her designer tee shirt and pink lace bra. He remained hypnotized by the woman who had stolen his heart. Although almost fifty years old, to him she looked just the same as she had that first night at the La Mansion del Rio.

♦♦♦♦♦♦♦♦

The next evening David and Amy joined his parents in the Hill Country Dining Room at seven-thirty sharp. Jack was extremely proud of the fact that David was just as punctual as he was. As the young couple approached the table, Elaina and Jack stood to greet them with warm hugs. They all took their seats at the table by a large window, which looked out over the valley, already shrouded in darkness. Elaina was excited to see her son's smiling face again.

"You two certainly look happy. I'm glad to see you've worked things out," she said.

David nodded first toward his mom and then at Amy as he said, "We are, and we have."

"What's up with the crosses?" she asked, having spotted the silver chain and cross hanging around her son's neck and the similar one Amy was wearing.

"Well, like I told you on the phone, we ran into each other on the beach, and we decided we needed something to remind each of us how we got back together. I saw the one Amy's wearing in a small gift shop and it looked like this one Dad gave me in Nicaragua, so I bought it."

"I told David he should start wearing his, and we've both been wearing them since," Amy added.

"I think that is very sweet. Don't you, Jack?" Elaina asked, not really expecting an answer.

"I like it," he said nodding in agreement.

"Dad, you aren't going to believe who we ran into," David said. This was the lead in he needed to talk about their encounter with Elizabeth. He hadn't been quite sure how to tell them he and Amy had lived together for a week, but he hoped it wouldn't come up if he focused the conversation on their hostess. "The owner of the shop where we got Amy's cross knows you. Her name is Elizabeth Burke."

Jack was among the world's worst when it came to remembering names, but he immediately remembered hers. "You're kidding! How is Elizabeth?"

"She's great! She said to tell you how much she still appreciates what you did for that family from Mexico."

"You remember Elizabeth," Jack said to Elaina.

"Of course!" Elaina agreed. "And you just happened to run into her?"

"Yeah, it was the craziest thing. Amy saw a carving of a Madonna that she said reminded her of me. Then we ran into each other on the beach and she said she wanted me to see it. When we went back there we decided to buy the cross, and Elizabeth saw the name on the credit card and together with the conversation about the carving, she put two and two together and asked me if I knew a Dr. Roberts," David explained.

"Talk about a small world," Elaina replied as she looked over at Jack.

The look on his face was a combination of shock and wonder. "That's amazing."

"She treated us as if we were family. She took us out to dinner and invited us to stay at her house," Amy said, not realizing that David didn't really want to get into those specifics.

"I'm not surprised she treated you guys like family, that's just the way she is," Jack added.

"So did you guys stay with her or at the hotel?" Elaina asked.

"She was insistent. She would not take no for an answer. She even offered to let us use her Jeep, but we never did," David hurriedly added.

"So, what is she doing?" Jack asked.

"She and another woman own a gift shop on the boardwalk. She said she was happy doing that, but she also talked about moving to Costa Rica," David explained, gladly moving the conversation further away from their sleeping arrangements.

"Costa Rica? Really?" Elaina asked.

"Yeah, she has some friends who live down there, and she said the cost of living is low and the climate is great," David answered. "I told her about your trips to Nicaragua and she said the place she's looking at is only a few hours south of the Nicaraguan border."

"I can't believe it. What are the chances of you guys running into Elizabeth Burke?" Jack said, shaking his head. "Did she give you a number or an e-mail address, or anything?"

"Oh, sure. I have all her contact information in my phone. I told her we'd stay in touch."

"Great!" Jack exclaimed. "I'd like to get them from you so I can drop her a note."

"Speaking of Nicaragua," Amy interrupted. "Do you think it would be okay if I went with y'all this summer?"

"I don't know why not," Elaina said as she turned toward Jack who nodded a tentative approval. "Have you asked your mom?"

"Yeah, I talked to her about it last week. She thought it sounded like fun, but I think more than anything she was just glad David and I are back together."

"So am I, dear," Elaina said as she glanced from Amy toward her son, who was sporting a shy grin.

"Will we need to let Dr. Ramirez know that she's coming with us?" David asked.

"I'll take care of that," Jack said. "You know the dates, right?"

"Yeah, I think so," David answered. "The twenty-second through the twenty-ninth is what Mom told me."

"Right. We've already gotten our tickets, so I'll look into getting one for you," Elaina said. "I can't guarantee that you and David can sit together," she added with a deadpan expression. When she saw the disappointment in her face, she smiled and added, "But, that flight is usually pretty open. I'll see what I can do." She had made the reservations only two days before and the flight from Houston to Managua was nearly empty. She was only teasing Amy to see her reaction.

The rest of the evening was spent talking about school and golf and dorm life. Jack remained good on his promise not to talk about politics or work. The lone exception was when David started talking about a political rally for Obama that took place on campus. When Jack started to make a comment, Elaina gave him a subtle nudge with her foot under the table. His response was a very timid, "That's nice that students are getting involved in the political process."

As they finished dinner and started to leave, Jack said, "We have a ten twenty tee time tomorrow. I'll meet you in the pro shop around nine thirty, and we can hit a few balls on the range."

"Sounds great! I'll be here."

"And you and I have massages scheduled in the spa at ten o'clock," Elaina announced to Amy.

"Really!" Amy said with surprise. "I've never had a massage before."

"You'll love it. Afterward we'll sit in the jacuzzi and talk about these men," Elaina said, looking at David and Jack with a devilish grin.

"I can hardly wait."

They all hugged each other again before David and Amy headed for David's old Honda, and Jack and Elaina headed to the elevators.

♦♦♦♦♦♦♦♦

The two guys were on the third tee of the Fazio Foothills golf course before Jack got around to asking David about the political sentiment on campus.

"Most of the kids are just crazy about this guy Obama," he said. "I don't get it. To me, he isn't really qualified to run the country."

"I doubt he will get the nomination. I think it's going to be Hillary Clinton against John McCain," Jack said with certainty.

"Do you really think McCain is who the Republicans are going to nominate?"

"I think so. The GOP always seems to go with whoever is next in line. I wish they'd find the courage to pick someone more dynamic, like Mike Huckabee, but that's just too unconventional for the establishment."

"A lot of the kids are saying the same thing. They want someone younger, but most of all they want somebody who will end the wars in Iraq and Afghanistan."

"My biggest fear is that the Democrats will take over like they did in 1992, and try to push socialized medicine on us."

"That has also been a major topic of debate on campus. A bunch of guys I know are saying that it's about time the US caught up with the rest of the world. They think everyone has the right to the same health care and that the government should pay for it."

Jack was preparing to hit his tee shot when he turned to David and said, "I just wonder what they would say if the jobs they were training for were suddenly taken over by the government? None of them ever think of it that way, do they?" With that thought in his mind Jack swung much harder than normal, and the result was a huge slice out of bounds to the right. He swore under his breath, knowing exactly why.

"I guess I let my frustration get the best of me."

David didn't say anything. There really wasn't anything he could say as he hit his drive straight down the middle of the fairway.

"Wow! You've been practicing, haven't you?"

"Just lucky," David said, then he added, "or maybe I did a better job of focusing on achieving better balance."

Jack could only laugh, as his words had come full circle.

♦♦♦♦♦♦♦♦

"That massage was amazing," Amy said as she slipped into the jacuzzi alongside Elaina. "Thank you so much for paying for it."

"You are very welcome, dear. I'm glad you liked it," Elaina replied over the sound of the bubbling water.

Amy sighed deeply as she allowed the warm water to swirl around her shoulders. "This is pretty nice, too."

"Yes, it is. You will likely come to appreciate it even more when you get to be my age."

"You're not old. I think you could pass for a woman in her thirties," Amy said as she faced Elaina.

"Yeah, right."

"No, I'm serious. You've kept yourself in great shape, your hair is still beautiful and you don't have any wrinkles. You look terrific."

"Thank you for saying all that, but I certainly don't feel like I did when I was in my thirties. Time has a way of catching up with you."

"I just hope I look half as good as you do when my kids are in college."

Elaina was hoping to have an opportunity to find out what Amy's plans were for having a family, and she had offered her the opening. "It sounds like you've been giving some thought to raising your own family."

"Absolutely! I want to finish college first, but then I'd like to have two or three kids and just be a mom."

"No career?"

"I guess I could still do something, but I'm really not motivated that way."

Amy was talking with her eyes closed, laying back against the side of the large round pool. She suddenly sat up, bringing her bare shoulders out of the water and turned toward Elaina. "You know that I love your son more than anything in the world, and it's his children I plan on having, right?"

Elaina smiled as she looked into the eyes of this innocent girl. "I know. That is obvious by the way you look at him, and I know that he feels the same about you."

"I can't believe I was so stupid," Amy replied. "I almost lost him because I wanted him all to myself. I will never let that happen again, even when he becomes a doctor. I will be okay with sharing him with his career."

"You know," Elaina said, as she turned to face what she saw as a younger version of herself, "I was married to David's biological father before I married Jack. He was also a surgeon."

"No, I didn't know that."

"I thought I could make do with having a part-time husband, but I couldn't. We divorced when David was less than a year old. I couldn't take the loneliness. He didn't want to be a husband or a father, he just wanted to be a doctor. That's why I left him."

Amy stared in disbelief at Elaina's personal revelation. Why was she telling her all this?

As if on cue, Elaina said, "It wasn't until I met Jack that I realized I didn't have to settle for one or the other. You can have a doctor for a husband, provided he loves you more than he loves his career. I know that Jack has made it clear to David the importance of balance in his life, and as a result, I think he's a lot more like his adopted father than he is the biological father he never knew. Jack is the best thing that ever happened to me and to David, and if he turns out to be half the husband and father Jack is, well, you'll be the happiest woman in the world, next to me of course." Elaina smiled softly and slid back down into the water, soaking the back of her strawberry blond hair.

"While we were in South Padre, we stayed together all week at Elizabeth's house," Amy said, as she returned to her prior position facing the center of the pool. "We never left the house except to go to dinner. It was as if we were truly living together. He was so incredibly attentive. He fixed me breakfast every morning after Elizabeth went to work. He even offered to do my laundry. I can't tell you how that made me feel. I would do anything for him."

"I know. Just let that thought be your guide, and everything will work out."

♦♦♦♦♦♦♦♦♦

Elaina had reserved a table on the patio outside the hotel's 8212 Wine Bar & Grill. As they sipped their drinks and waited for their dinner, they watched the sun slowly glide over the horizon. Jack suggested they take turns sharing their favorite sunset memories. Not surprisingly, Amy and David both talked about the view over Lake Travis from their grassy spot. They conveniently left out the more intimate parts.

Jack was surprised when Elaina spoke about a time when she was a six-year-old child. Her parents had taken her to visit her aunt and uncle in Abilene. She described an evening when she thought the sky was on fire.

"It was the most amazing sight. I was out in their backyard with my cousin, swinging on a rusty old swing set that faced the West. Behind their house was an empty field, so there wasn't a single tree or hill to block the horizon." She sounded as if she were describing an event from just a day or two before. "I remember the sky started out the most brilliant blue I'd ever seen, with just a few puffy white clouds. Then hints of yellow started to show up around their edges. Over the next hour the blue gradually turned to a hazy peach color and the clouds went from cream to bright orange, then red, then a deep burgundy, and finally a gray purple, but throughout, they retained a shimmering golden glow around their edges. Just before the sun disappeared there was one small cloud down near the horizon and when the sun dropped behind it there were these broad rays of light that fanned out across the whole sky. I'll never forget it. I just wish I was an artist. That sunset would be my first painting."

Jack knew it would be tough to top that, so he decided not to try. Instead he turned to David and said, "Well, I've seen beautiful sunsets all around the world, but the most memorable one was the first one I shared with your mom. It was our second date, and we sat on the back of my old BMW convertible and watched the sun go down over the hills west of Glen Rose."

Elaina said, "That was a special view, wasn't it?"

"Yes, it was," Jack nodded.

"You promised me we'd go back there some time, but we never did."

"I know, Angel, but I don't think we're out of sunsets just yet."

Jack flashed her his crooked smile, remembering every detail of that evening in another part of the Texas Hill Country. She had been the missing piece in his life, and having gained her love, his future seemed so secure, so certain from that day forward. Then he recalled how the warmth and beauty of that gorgeous sunset had been followed by a sudden thunderstorm. He worried that storm clouds were building again that could threaten not only the joy of his final years, but more importantly he feared they might prevent the son he had inherited, and loved as his own, from achieving his life's calling.

If you enjoyed *A Surgeon's Heart: The Calling* and want to see what's in store for Jack, Elaina, David and Amy, look for the next volume in this series…

A Surgeon's Heart: The Conflict

Additional titles by R.W. Sewell, M.D. include…

A Surgeon's Heart: The Crisis
A Surgeon's Heart: The Choice
A Surgeon's Heart: The Challenge

to learn more about the entire *A Surgeon's Heart* series by R.W. Sewell, M.D., go to www.asurgeonsheart.com.

ABOUT THE AUTHOR

Robert Walter Sewell was born on November 20, 1950, in Independence, Missouri, and moved to Texas with his parents at the age of twelve. He has lived in Texas since, attending Thomas Jefferson High School in Port Arthur and Lamar University in Beaumont, where he received a bachelor's degree in biology. He went on to the University of Texas Medical Branch at Galveston, where he achieved his medical degree in 1974. He was accepted into the general surgery residency program at the University of Texas Health Science Center in San Antonio and completed his surgical training in 1979.

After finishing his residency, Dr. Sewell immediately began his surgical practice in the Mid-Cities between Dallas and Fort Worth in North Texas. He moved his practice to its current location in Southlake, Texas, in 2003, and remains an active surgeon today, with an emphasis on minimally invasive general surgery at the Texas Health Harris Methodist Hospital Southlake.

As a recognized specialist in the field of laparoscopic surgery, Dr. Sewell has lectured on various minimally invasive procedures throughout the United States and around the world. He is a member of the American Society of General Surgeons (ASGS) and was elected president of that organization in February 2008. He is also a fellow of the American College of Surgeons (FACS) and has served as a governor since 2013. Dr. Sewell maintains memberships in the Association of American Physicians and Surgeons, the Texas Medical Association, the Tarrant County Medical Society, as well as the prestigious Texas Surgical Society.

Along with his wife, Donna, Dr. Sewell resides in Colleyville, Texas, where he enjoys golf, photography, computer graphics, video production, gardening and, of course, writing.

Made in the USA
Columbia, SC
30 July 2017